The Collected Supernatural and Weird Fiction of J. Sheridan le Fanu Volume 1

The Collected Supernatural and Weird Fiction of J. Sheridan le Fanu Volume 1

Including Two Novels 'The Haunted Baronet' and 'The Evil Guest', One Novella 'Carmilla', One Novelette and Ten Short Stories of the Ghostly and Gothic

J. Sheridan le Fanu

LEONAUR

The Collected
Supernatural and Weird
Fiction of J. Sheridan le Fanu
Volume 1
Including Two Novels 'The Haunted Baronet' and 'The Evil Guest',
One Novella 'Carmilla',
One Novelette and Ten Short Stories
of the Ghostly and Gothic
by J. Sheridan le Fanu

FIRST EDITION

Leonaur is an imprint
of Oakpast Ltd

ISBN: 978-0-85706-145-4 (hardcover)
ISBN: 978-0-85706-146-1 (softcover)

http://www.leonaur.com

Contents

Carmilla

PROLOGUE

Upon a paper attached to the Narrative which follows, Doctor Hesselius has written a rather elaborate note, which he accompanies with a reference to his Essay on the strange subject which the MS. illuminates.

This mysterious subject he treats, in that Essay, with his usual learning and acumen, and with remarkable directness and condensation. It will form but one volume of the series of that extraordinary man's collected papers.

As I publish the case, in this volume, simply to interest the "laity," I shall forestall the intelligent lady, who relates it, in nothing; and after due consideration, I have determined, therefore, to abstain from presenting any *precis* of the learned Doctor's reasoning, or extract from his statement on a subject which he describes as "involving, not improbably, some of the profoundest *arcana* of our dual existence, and its intermediates."

I was anxious on discovering this paper, to reopen the correspondence commenced by Doctor Hesselius, so many years before, with a person so clever and careful as his informant seems to have been. Much to my regret, however, I found that she had died in the interval.

She, probably, could have added little to the Narrative which she communicates in the following pages, with, so far as I can pronounce, such conscientious particularity.

CHAPTER 1
AN EARLY FRIGHT

In Styria, we, though by no means magnificent people, inhabit a castle, or *schloss*. A small income, in that part of the world, goes a great way. Eight or nine hundred a year does wonders. Scantily enough ours would have answered among wealthy people at home. My father is English, and I bear an English name, although I never saw England. But here, in this lonely and primitive place, where everything is so marvellously cheap, I really don't see how ever so much more money would at all materially add to our comforts, or even luxuries.

My father was in the Austrian service, and retired upon a pension and his patrimony, and purchased this feudal residence, and the small estate on which it stands, a bargain.

Nothing can be more picturesque or solitary. It stands on a slight eminence in a forest. The road, very old and narrow, passes in front of its drawbridge, never raised in my time, and its moat, stocked with perch, and sailed over by many swans, and floating on its surface white fleets of water lilies.

Over all this the *schloss* shows its many-windowed front; its towers, and its Gothic chapel.

The forest opens in an irregular and very picturesque glade before its gate, and at the right a steep Gothic bridge carries the road over a stream that winds in deep shadow through the wood. I have said that this is a very lonely place. Judge whether I say truth. Looking from the hall door towards the road, the forest in which our castle stands extends fifteen miles to the right, and twelve to the left. The nearest inhabited village is about seven of your English miles to the left. The nearest inhabited *schloss* of any historic associations, is that of old General Spielsdorf, nearly twenty miles away to the right.

I have said "the nearest *inhabited* village," because there is, only three miles westward, that is to say in the direction of General Spielsdorf's *schloss*, a ruined village, with its quaint little church, now roofless, in the aisle of which are the mouldering tombs of the proud family of Karnstein, now extinct, who once owned the equally desolate *château* which, in the thick of the forest, overlooks the silent ruins of the town.

Respecting the cause of the desertion of this striking and melancholy spot, there is a legend which I shall relate to you another time.

I must tell you now, how very small is the party who constitute the inhabitants of our castle. I don't include servants, or those dependents who occupy rooms in the buildings attached to the *schloss*. Listen, and wonder! My father, who is the kindest man on earth, but growing old; and I, at the date of my story, only nineteen. Eight years have passed since then.

I and my father constituted the family at the *schloss*. My mother, a Styrian lady, died in my infancy, but I had a good-natured governess, who had been with me from, I might almost say, my infancy. I could not remember the time when her fat, benignant face was not a familiar picture in my memory.

This was Madame Perrodon, a native of Berne, whose care and good nature now in part supplied to me the loss of my mother, whom I do not even remember, so early I lost her. She made a third at our little dinner party. There was a fourth, Mademoiselle De Lafontaine, a lady such as you term, I believe, a "finishing governess." She spoke French and German, Madame Perrodon French and broken English, to which my father and I added English, which, partly to prevent its becoming a lost language among us, and partly from patriotic motives, we spoke every day. The consequence was a Babel, at which strangers used to laugh, and which I shall make no attempt to reproduce in this narrative. And there were two or three young lady friends besides, pretty nearly of my own age, who were occasional visitors, for longer or shorter terms; and these visits I sometimes returned.

These were our regular social resources; but of course there were chance visits from "neighbours" of only five or six leagues distance. My life was, notwithstanding, rather a solitary one, I can assure you.

My *gouvernantes* had just so much control over me as you

might conjecture such sage persons would have in the case of a rather spoiled girl, whose only parent allowed her pretty nearly her own way in everything.

The first occurrence in my existence, which produced a terrible impression upon my mind, which, in fact, never has been effaced, was one of the very earliest incidents of my life which I can recollect. Some people will think it so trifling that it should not be recorded here. You will see, however, by-and-by, why I mention it. The nursery, as it was called, though I had it all to myself, was a large room in the upper story of the castle, with a steep oak roof. I can't have been more than six years old, when one night I awoke, and looking round the room from my bed, failed to see the nursery maid. Neither was my nurse there; and I thought myself alone. I was not frightened, for I was one of those happy children who are studiously kept in ignorance of ghost stories, of fairy tales, and of all such lore as makes us cover up our heads when the door cracks suddenly, or the flicker of an expiring candle makes the shadow of a bedpost dance upon the wall, nearer to our faces.

I was vexed and insulted at finding myself, as I conceived, neglected, and I began to whimper, preparatory to a hearty bout of roaring; when to my surprise, I saw a solemn, but very pretty face looking at me from the side of the bed. It was that of a young lady who was kneeling, with her hands under the coverlet. I looked at her with a kind of pleased wonder, and ceased whimpering. She caressed me with her hands, and lay down beside me on the bed, and drew me towards her, smiling; I felt immediately delightfully soothed, and fell asleep again. I was wakened by a sensation as if two needles ran into my breast very deep at the same moment, and I cried loudly. The lady started back, with her eyes fixed on me, and then slipped down upon the floor, and, as I thought, hid herself under the bed.

I was now for the first time frightened, and I yelled with all my might and main. Nurse, nursery maid, housekeeper, all came running in, and hearing my story, they made light of it, soothing me all they could meanwhile. But, child as I was, I could perceive that their faces were pale with an unwonted look of anxiety, and I saw them look under the bed, and about the room, and peep under tables and pluck open cupboards; and the housekeeper whispered to the nurse: "Lay your hand along that hollow in the bed; someone *did* lie there, so sure as you did not; the place is still warm."

I remember the nursery maid petting me, and all three examining my chest, where I told them I felt the puncture, and pronouncing that there was no sign visible that any such thing had happened to me.

The housekeeper and the two other servants who were in charge of the nursery, remained sitting up all night; and from that time a servant always sat up in the nursery until I was about fourteen.

I was very nervous for a long time after this. A doctor was called in, he was pallid and elderly. How well I remember his long saturnine face, slightly pitted with smallpox, and his chestnut wig. For a good while, every second day, he came and gave me medicine, which of course I hated.

The morning after I saw this apparition I was in a state of terror, and could not bear to be left alone, daylight though it was, for a moment.

I remember my father coming up and standing at the bedside, and talking cheerfully, and asking the nurse a number of questions, and laughing very heartily at one of the answers; and patting me on the shoulder, and kissing me, and telling me not to be frightened, that it was nothing but a dream and could not hurt me.

But I was not comforted, for I knew the visit of the strange woman was *not* a dream; and I was *awfully* frightened.

I was a little consoled by the nursery maid's assuring me that it was she who had come and looked at me, and lain down beside me in the bed, and that I must have been half-dreaming not to have known her face. But this, though supported by the nurse, did not quite satisfy me.

I remembered, in the course of that day, a venerable old man, in a black cassock, coming into the room with the nurse and housekeeper, and talking a little to them, and very kindly to me; his face was very sweet and gentle, and he told me they were going to pray, and joined my hands together, and desired me to say, softly, while they were praying, "Lord hear all good prayers for us, for Jesus' sake." I think these were the very words, for I often repeated them to myself, and my nurse used for years to make me say them in my prayers.

I remembered so well the thoughtful sweet face of that white-haired old man, in his black cassock, as he stood in that rude, lofty, brown room, with the clumsy furniture of a fashion three hundred years old about him, and the scanty light entering its shadowy atmosphere through the small lattice. He kneeled, and the three women with him, and he prayed aloud with an earnest quavering voice for, what appeared to me, a long time. I forget all my life preceding that event, and for some time after it is all obscure also, but the scenes I have just described stand out vivid as the isolated pictures of the phantasmagoria surrounded by darkness.

CHAPTER 2

A GUEST

I am now going to tell you something so strange that it will require all your faith in my veracity to believe my story. It is not only true, nevertheless, but truth of which I have been an eyewitness.

It was a sweet summer evening, and my father asked me, as he sometimes did, to take a little ramble with him along that beautiful forest vista which I have mentioned as lying in front of the *schloss*.

"General Spielsdorf cannot come to us so soon as I had hoped," said my father, as we pursued our walk.

He was to have paid us a visit of some weeks, and we had expected his arrival next day. He was to have brought with him a young lady, his niece and ward, Mademoiselle Rheinfeldt, whom I had never seen, but whom I had heard described as a very charming girl, and in whose society I had promised myself many happy days. I was more disappointed than a young lady living in a town, or a bustling neighbourhood can possibly imagine. This visit, and the new acquaintance it promised, had furnished my day dream for many weeks.

"And how soon does he come?" I asked.

"Not till autumn. Not for two months, I dare say," he answered. "And I am very glad now, dear, that you never knew Mademoiselle Rheinfeldt."

"And why?" I asked, both mortified and curious.

"Because the poor young lady is dead," he replied. "I quite forgot I had not told you, but you were not in the room when I received the General's letter this evening."

I was very much shocked. General Spielsdorf had mentioned in his first letter, six or seven weeks before, that she was not so well as he would wish her, but there was nothing to suggest the remotest suspicion of danger.

"Here is the General's letter," he said, handing it to me. "I am afraid he is in great affliction; the letter appears to me to have been written very nearly in distraction."

We sat down on a rude bench, under a group of magnificent lime trees. The sun was setting with all its melancholy splendour behind the sylvan horizon, and the stream that flows beside our home, and passes under the steep old bridge I have mentioned, wound through many a group of noble trees, almost at our feet, reflecting in its current the fading crimson of the sky. General Spielsdorf's letter was so extraordinary, so vehement, and in some places so self-contradictory, that I read it twice over—the second time aloud to my father—and was still unable to account for it, except by supposing that grief had unsettled his mind.

It said:

I have lost my darling daughter, for as such I loved her. During the last days of dear Bertha's illness I was not able to write to you.

Before then I had no idea of her danger. I have lost her, and now learn *all*, too late. She died in the peace of innocence, and in the glorious hope of a blessed futurity. The fiend who betrayed our infatuated hospitality has done it all. I thought I was receiving into my house innocence, gaiety, a charming companion for my lost Bertha. Heavens! what a fool have I been!

I thank God my child died without a suspicion of the cause of her sufferings. She is gone without so much as conjecturing the nature of her illness, and the accursed passion of the agent of all this misery. I devote my remaining days to tracking and extinguishing a monster. I am told I may hope to accomplish my righteous and merciful purpose. At present there is scarcely a gleam of light to guide me.

I curse my conceited incredulity, my despicable affectation of superiority, my blindness, my obstinacy—all—too late. I cannot write or talk collectedly now. I am distracted. So soon as I shall have a little recovered, I mean to devote myself for a time to enquiry, which may possibly lead me as far as Vienna. Sometime in the autumn, two months hence, or earlier if I live, I will see you—that is, if you permit me; I will then tell you all that I scarce dare put upon paper now. Farewell. Pray for me, dear friend.

In these terms ended this strange letter. Though I had never seen Bertha Rheinfeldt my eyes filled with tears at the sudden intelligence; I was startled, as well as profoundly disappointed.

The sun had now set, and it was twilight by the time I had returned the General's letter to my father.

It was a soft clear evening, and we loitered, speculating upon the possible meanings of the violent and incoherent sentences which I had just been reading. We had nearly a mile to walk before reaching the road that passes the *schloss* in front, and by that time the moon was shining brilliantly. At the drawbridge we met Madame Perrodon and Mademoiselle De Lafontaine, who had come out, without their bonnets, to enjoy the exquisite moonlight.

We heard their voices gabbling in animated dialogue as we

approached. We joined them at the drawbridge, and turned about to admire with them the beautiful scene.

The glade through which we had just walked lay before us. At our left the narrow road wound away under clumps of lordly trees, and was lost to sight amid the thickening forest. At the right the same road crosses the steep and picturesque bridge, near which stands a ruined tower which once guarded that pass; and beyond the bridge an abrupt eminence rises, covered with trees, and showing in the shadows some grey ivy-clustered rocks.

Over the sward and low grounds a thin film of mist was stealing like smoke, marking the distances with a transparent veil; and here and there we could see the river faintly flashing in the moonlight.

No softer, sweeter scene could be imagined. The news I had just heard made it melancholy; but nothing could disturb its character of profound serenity, and the enchanted glory and vagueness of the prospect.

My father, who enjoyed the picturesque, and I, stood looking in silence over the expanse beneath us. The two good governesses, standing a little way behind us, discoursed upon the scene, and were eloquent upon the moon.

Madame Perrodon was fat, middle-aged, and romantic, and talked and sighed poetically. Mademoiselle De Lafontaine—in right of her father who was a German, assumed to be psychological, metaphysical, and something of a mystic—now declared that when the moon shone with a light so intense it was well known that it indicated a special spiritual activity. The effect of the full moon in such a state of brilliancy was manifold. It acted on dreams, it acted on lunacy, it acted on nervous people, it had marvellous physical influences connected with life. *Mademoiselle* related that her cousin, who was mate of a merchant ship, having taken a nap on deck on such a night, lying on his back, with his face full in the light on the moon, had wakened, after a dream of an old woman clawing him by the cheek, with his features horribly drawn to one side; and his countenance had never quite recovered its equilibrium.

"The moon, this night," she said, "is full of idyllic and magnetic influence—and see, when you look behind you at the front of the *schloss* how all its windows flash and twinkle with that silvery splendour, as if unseen hands had lighted up the rooms to receive fairy guests."

There are indolent styles of the spirits in which, indisposed to talk ourselves, the talk of others is pleasant to our listless ears; and I gazed on, pleased with the tinkle of the ladies' conversation.

"I have got into one of my moping moods tonight," said my father, after a silence, and quoting Shakespeare, whom, by way of keeping up our English, he used to read aloud, he said:

"In truth I know not why I am so sad.
It wearies me: you say it wearies you;
But how I got it—came by it.

"I forget the rest. But I feel as if some great misfortune were hanging over us. I suppose the poor General's afflicted letter has had something to do with it."

At this moment the unwonted sound of carriage wheels and many hoofs upon the road, arrested our attention.

They seemed to be approaching from the high ground overlooking the bridge, and very soon the equipage emerged from that point. Two horsemen first crossed the bridge, then came a carriage drawn by four horses, and two men rode behind.

It seemed to be the travelling carriage of a person of rank; and we were all immediately absorbed in watching that very unusual spectacle. It became, in a few moments, greatly more interesting, for just as the carriage had passed the summit of the steep bridge, one of the leaders, taking fright, communicated his panic to the rest, and after a plunge or two, the whole team broke into a wild gallop together, and dashing between the horsemen who rode in front, came thundering along the road towards us with the speed of a hurricane.

The excitement of the scene was made more painful by the clear, long-drawn screams of a female voice from the carriage

16

window.

We all advanced in curiosity and horror; me rather in silence, the rest with various ejaculations of terror.

Our suspense did not last long. Just before you reach the castle drawbridge, on the route they were coming, there stands by the roadside a magnificent lime tree, on the other stands an ancient stone cross, at sight of which the horses, now going at a pace that was perfectly frightful, swerved so as to bring the wheel over the projecting roots of the tree.

I knew what was coming. I covered my eyes, unable to see it out, and turned my head away; at the same moment I heard a cry from my lady friends, who had gone on a little.

Curiosity opened my eyes, and I saw a scene of utter confusion. Two of the horses were on the ground, the carriage lay upon its side with two wheels in the air; the men were busy removing the traces, and a lady with a commanding air and figure had got out, and stood with clasped hands, raising the handkerchief that was in them every now and then to her eyes.

Through the carriage door was now lifted a young lady, who appeared to be lifeless. My dear old father was already beside the elder lady, with his hat in his hand, evidently tendering his aid and the resources of his *schloss*. The lady did not appear to hear him, or to have eyes for anything but the slender girl who was being placed against the slope of the bank.

I approached; the young lady was apparently stunned, but she was certainly not dead. My father, who piqued himself on being something of a physician, had just had his fingers on her wrist and assured the lady, who declared herself her mother, that her pulse, though faint and irregular, was undoubtedly still distinguishable. The lady clasped her hands and looked upward, as if in a momentary transport of gratitude; but immediately she broke out again in that theatrical way which is, I believe, natural to some people.

She was what is called a fine looking woman for her time of life, and must have been handsome; she was tall, but not thin, and dressed in black velvet, and looked rather pale, but with a proud and commanding countenance, though now agitated strangely.

"Who was ever being so born to calamity?" I heard her say, with clasped hands, as I came up. "Here am I, on a journey of life and death, in prosecuting which to lose an hour is possibly to lose all. My child will not have recovered sufficiently to resume her route for who can say how long. I must leave her: I cannot, dare not, delay. How far on, sir, can you tell, is the nearest village? I must leave her there; and shall not see my darling, or even hear of her till my return, three months hence."

I plucked my father by the coat, and whispered earnestly in his ear: "Oh! papa, pray ask her to let her stay with us—it would be so delightful. Do, pray."

"If *Madame* will entrust her child to the care of my daughter, and of her good *gouvernante*, Madame Perrodon, and permit her to remain as our guest, under my charge, until her return, it will confer a distinction and an obligation upon us, and we shall treat her with all the care and devotion which so sacred a trust deserves."

"I cannot do that, sir, it would be to task your kindness and chivalry too cruelly," said the lady, distractedly.

"It would, on the contrary, be to confer on us a very great kindness at the moment when we most need it. My daughter has just been disappointed by a cruel misfortune, in a visit from which she had long anticipated a great deal of happiness. If you confide this young lady to our care it will be her best consolation. The nearest village on your route is distant, and affords no such inn as you could think of placing your daughter at; you cannot allow her to continue her journey for any considerable distance without danger. If, as you say, you cannot suspend your journey, you must part with her tonight, and nowhere could you do so with more honest assurances of care and tenderness than here."

There was something in this lady's air and appearance so distinguished and even imposing, and in her manner so engaging, as to impress one, quite apart from the dignity of her equipage, with a conviction that she was a person of consequence.

By this time the carriage was replaced in its upright position, and the horses, quite tractable, in the traces again.

The lady threw on her daughter a glance which I fancied was not quite so affectionate as one might have anticipated from the beginning of the scene; then she beckoned slightly to my father, and withdrew two or three steps with him out of hearing; and talked to him with a fixed and stern countenance, not at all like that with which she had hitherto spoken.

I was filled with wonder that my father did not seem to perceive the change, and also unspeakably curious to learn what it could be that she was speaking, almost in his ear, with so much earnestness and rapidity.

Two or three minutes at most I think she remained thus employed, then she turned, and a few steps brought her to where her daughter lay, supported by Madame Perrodon. She kneeled beside her for a moment and whispered, as *Madame* supposed, a little benediction in her ear; then hastily kissing her she stepped into her carriage, the door was closed, the footmen in stately liveries jumped up behind, the outriders spurred on, the postilions cracked their whips, the horses plunged and broke suddenly into a furious canter that threatened soon again to become a gallop, and the carriage whirled away, followed at the same rapid pace by the two horsemen in the rear.

CHAPTER 3
WE COMPARE NOTES

We followed the *cortege* with our eyes until it was swiftly lost to sight in the misty wood; and the very sound of the hoofs and the wheels died away in the silent night air.

Nothing remained to assure us that the adventure had not been an illusion of a moment but the young lady, who just at that moment opened her eyes. I could not see, for her face was turned from me, but she raised her head, evidently looking about her, and I heard a very sweet voice ask complainingly, "Where is mamma?"

Our good Madame Perrodon answered tenderly, and added

some comfortable assurances.

I then heard her ask:

"Where am I? What is this place?" and after that she said, "I don't see the carriage; and Matska, where is she?"

Madame answered all her questions in so far as she understood them; and gradually the young lady remembered how the misadventure came about, and was glad to hear that no one in, or in attendance on, the carriage was hurt; and on learning that her mamma had left her here, till her return in about three months, she wept.

I was going to add my consolations to those of Madame Perrodon when Mademoiselle De Lafontaine placed her hand upon my arm, saying:

"Don't approach, one at a time is as much as she can at present converse with; a very little excitement would possibly overpower her now."

As soon as she is comfortably in bed, I thought, I will run up to her room and see her.

My father in the meantime had sent a servant on horseback for the physician, who lived about two leagues away; and a bedroom was being prepared for the young lady's reception.

The stranger now rose, and leaning on *Madame's* arm, walked slowly over the drawbridge and into the castle gate.

In the hall, servants waited to receive her, and she was conducted forthwith to her room. The room we usually sat in as our drawing room is long, having four windows, that looked over the moat and drawbridge, upon the forest scene I have just described.

It is furnished in old carved oak, with large carved cabinets, and the chairs are cushioned with crimson Utrecht velvet. The walls are covered with tapestry, and surrounded with great gold frames, the figures being as large as life, in ancient and very curious costume, and the subjects represented are hunting, hawking, and generally festive. It is not too stately to be extremely comfortable; and here we had our tea, for with his usual patriotic leanings he insisted that the national beverage should make its appearance regularly with our coffee and chocolate.

We sat here this night, and with candles lighted, were talking over the adventure of the evening.

Madame Perrodon and Mademoiselle De Lafontaine were both of our party. The young stranger had hardly lain down in her bed when she sank into a deep sleep; and those ladies had left her in the care of a servant.

"How do you like our guest?" I asked, as soon as *Madame* entered. "Tell me all about her?"

"I like her extremely," answered *Madame*, "she is, I almost think, the prettiest creature I ever saw; about your age, and so gentle and nice."

"She is absolutely beautiful," threw in *Mademoiselle*, who had peeped for a moment into the stranger's room.

"And such a sweet voice!" added Madame Perrodon.

"Did you remark a woman in the carriage, after it was set up again, who did not get out," inquired *Mademoiselle*, "but only looked from the window?"

"No, we had not seen her."

Then she described a hideous black woman, with a sort of coloured turban on her head, and who was gazing all the time from the carriage window, nodding and grinning derisively towards the ladies, with gleaming eyes and large white eyeballs, and her teeth set as if in fury.

"Did you remark what an ill-looking pack of men the servants were?" asked *Madame*.

"Yes," said my father, who had just come in, "ugly, hang-dog looking fellows as ever I beheld in my life. I hope they mayn't rob the poor lady in the forest. They are clever rogues, however; they got everything to rights in a minute."

"I dare say they are worn out with too long travelling," said *Madame*.

"Besides looking wicked, their faces were so strangely lean, and dark, and sullen. I am very curious, I own; but I dare say the young lady will tell you all about it tomorrow, if she is sufficiently recovered."

"I don't think she will," said my father, with a mysterious smile, and a little nod of his head, as if he knew more about it than he cared to tell us.

This made us all the more inquisitive as to what had passed between him and the lady in the black velvet, in the brief but earnest interview that had immediately preceded her departure.

We were scarcely alone, when I entreated him to tell me. He did not need much pressing.

"There is no particular reason why I should not tell you. She expressed a reluctance to trouble us with the care of her daughter, saying she was in delicate health, and nervous, but not subject to any kind of seizure—she volunteered that—nor to any illusion; being, in fact, perfectly sane."

"How very odd to say all that!" I interpolated. "It was so unnecessary."

"At all events it *was* said," he laughed, "and as you wish to know all that passed, which was indeed very little, I tell you. She then said, 'I am making a long journey of *vital* importance—she emphasized the word—rapid and secret; I shall return for my child in three months; in the meantime, she will be silent as to who we are, whence we come, and whither we are travelling.' That is all she said. She spoke very pure French. When she said the word 'secret,' she paused for a few seconds, looking sternly, her eyes fixed on mine. I fancy she makes a great point of that. You saw how quickly she was gone. I hope I have not done a very foolish thing, in taking charge of the young lady."

For my part, I was delighted. I was longing to see and talk to her; and only waiting till the doctor should give me leave. You, who live in towns, can have no idea how great an event the introduction of a new friend is, in such a solitude as surrounded us.

The doctor did not arrive till nearly one o'clock; but I could no more have gone to my bed and slept, than I could have overtaken, on foot, the carriage in which the princess in black velvet had driven away.

When the physician came down to the drawing room, it was

to report very favourably upon his patient. She was now sitting up, her pulse quite regular, apparently perfectly well. She had sustained no injury, and the little shock to her nerves had passed away quite harmlessly. There could be no harm certainly in my seeing her, if we both wished it; and, with this permission I sent, forthwith, to know whether she would allow me to visit her for a few minutes in her room.

The servant returned immediately to say that she desired nothing more.

You may be sure I was not long in availing myself of this permission.

Our visitor lay in one of the handsomest rooms in the *schloss*. It was, perhaps, a little stately. There was a sombre piece of tapestry opposite the foot of the bed, representing Cleopatra with the asps to her bosom; and other solemn classic scenes were displayed, a little faded, upon the other walls. But there was gold carving, and rich and varied colour enough in the other decorations of the room, to more than redeem the gloom of the old tapestry.

There were candles at the bedside. She was sitting up; her slender pretty figure enveloped in the soft silk dressing gown, embroidered with flowers, and lined with thick quilted silk, which her mother had thrown over her feet as she lay upon the ground.

What was it that, as I reached the bedside and had just begun my little greeting, struck me dumb in a moment, and made me recoil a step or two from before her? I will tell you.

I saw the very face which had visited me in my childhood at night, which remained so fixed in my memory, and on which I had for so many years so often ruminated with horror, when no one suspected of what I was thinking.

It was pretty, even beautiful; and when I first beheld it, wore the same melancholy expression.

But this almost instantly lighted into a strange fixed smile of recognition.

There was a silence of fully a minute, and then at length she spoke; I could not.

"How wonderful!" she exclaimed. "Twelve years ago, I saw your face in a dream, and it has haunted me ever since."

"Wonderful indeed!" I repeated, overcoming with an effort the horror that had for a time suspended my utterances. "Twelve years ago, in vision or reality, I certainly saw you. I could not forget your face. It has remained before my eyes ever since."

Her smile had softened. Whatever I had fancied strange in it, was gone, and it and her dimpling cheeks were now delightfully pretty and intelligent.

I felt reassured, and continued more in the vein which hospitality indicated, to bid her welcome, and to tell her how much pleasure her accidental arrival had given us all, and especially what a happiness it was to me.

I took her hand as I spoke. I was a little shy, as lonely people are, but the situation made me eloquent, and even bold. She pressed my hand, she laid hers upon it, and her eyes glowed, as, looking hastily into mine, she smiled again, and blushed.

She answered my welcome very prettily. I sat down beside her, still wondering; and she said:

"I must tell you my vision about you; it is so very strange that you and I should have had, each of the other so vivid a dream, that each should have seen, I you and you me, looking as we do now, when of course we both were mere children. I was a child, about six years old, and I awoke from a confused and troubled dream, and found myself in a room, unlike my nursery, wainscoted clumsily in some dark wood, and with cupboards and bedsteads, and chairs, and benches placed about it. The beds were, I thought, all empty, and the room itself without anyone but myself in it; and I, after looking about me for some time, and admiring especially an iron candlestick with two branches, which I should certainly know again, crept under one of the beds to reach the window; but as I got from under the bed, I heard someone crying; and looking up, while I was still upon my knees, I saw you—most assuredly you—as I see you now; a beautiful young lady, with golden hair and large blue eyes, and lips—your lips—you as you are here.

"Your looks won me; I climbed on the bed and put my arms about you, and I think we both fell asleep. I was aroused by a scream; you were sitting up screaming. I was frightened, and slipped down upon the ground, and, it seemed to me, lost consciousness for a moment; and when I came to myself, I was again in my nursery at home. Your face I have never forgotten since. I could not be misled by mere resemblance. *You are* the lady whom I saw then."

It was now my turn to relate my corresponding vision, which I did, to the undisguised wonder of my new acquaintance.

"I don't know which should be most afraid of the other," she said, again smiling—"If you were less pretty I think I should be very much afraid of you, but being as you are, and you and I both so young, I feel only that I have made your acquaintance twelve years ago, and have already a right to your intimacy; at all events it does seem as if we were destined, from our earliest childhood, to be friends. I wonder whether you feel as strangely drawn towards me as I do to you; I have never had a friend—shall I find one now?" She sighed, and her fine dark eyes gazed passionately on me.

Now the truth is, I felt rather unaccountably towards the beautiful stranger. I did feel, as she said, "drawn towards her," but there was also something of repulsion. In this ambiguous feeling, however, the sense of attraction immensely prevailed. She interested and won me; she was so beautiful and so indescribably engaging.

I perceived now something of languor and exhaustion stealing over her, and hastened to bid her goodnight.

"The doctor thinks," I added, "that you ought to have a maid to sit up with you tonight; one of ours is waiting, and you will find her a very useful and quiet creature."

"How kind of you, but I could not sleep, I never could with an attendant in the room. I shan't require any assistance—and, shall I confess my weakness, I am haunted with a terror of robbers. Our house was robbed once, and two servants murdered, so I always lock my door. It has become a habit—and you look so kind I know you will forgive me. I see there is a key in the lock."

She held me close in her pretty arms for a moment and whispered in my ear, "Goodnight, darling, it is very hard to part with you, but good night; tomorrow, but not early, I shall see you again."

She sank back on the pillow with a sigh, and her fine eyes followed me with a fond and melancholy gaze, and she murmured again "Goodnight, dear friend."

Young people like, and even love, on impulse. I was flattered by the evident, though as yet undeserved, fondness she showed me. I liked the confidence with which she at once received me. She was determined that we should be very near friends.

Next day came and we met again. I was delighted with my companion; that is to say, in many respects.

Her looks lost nothing in daylight—she was certainly the most beautiful creature I had ever seen, and the unpleasant remembrance of the face presented in my early dream, had lost the effect of the first unexpected recognition.

She confessed that she had experienced a similar shock on seeing me, and precisely the same faint antipathy that had mingled with my admiration of her. We now laughed together over our momentary horrors.

Chapter 4

Her Habits—A Saunter

I told you that I was charmed with her in most particulars.

There were some that did not please me so well.

She was above the middle height of women. I shall begin by describing her.

She was slender, and wonderfully graceful. Except that her movements were languid—very languid—indeed, there was nothing in her appearance to indicate an invalid. Her complexion was rich and brilliant; her features were small and beautifully formed; her eyes large, dark, and lustrous; her hair was quite wonderful, I never saw hair so magnificently thick and long when it was down about her shoulders; I have often placed my hands under it, and laughed with wonder at its weight. It was exquisitely fine and soft, and in colour a rich very dark brown, with something of gold. I loved to let it down, tumbling with its own weight, as, in her room, she lay back in her chair talking in her sweet low voice, I used to fold and braid it, and spread it out and play with it. Heavens! If I had but known all!

I said there were particulars which did not please me. I have told you that her confidence won me the first night I saw her; but I found that she exercised with respect to herself, her mother, her history, everything in fact connected with her life, plans, and people, an ever wakeful reserve. I dare say I was unreasonable, perhaps I was wrong; I dare say I ought to have respected the solemn injunction laid upon my father by the stately lady in black velvet. But curiosity is a restless and unscrupulous passion, and no one girl can endure, with patience, that hers should be baffled by another. What harm could it do anyone to tell me what I so ardently desired to know? Had she no trust in my good sense or honour? Why would she not believe me when I assured her, so solemnly, that I would not divulge one syllable of what she told me to any mortal breathing.

There was a coldness, it seemed to me, beyond her years, in her smiling melancholy persistent refusal to afford me the least ray of light.

I cannot say we quarrelled upon this point, for she would not quarrel upon any. It was, of course, very unfair of me to press her, very ill-bred, but I really could not help it; and I might just as well have let it alone.

What she did tell me amounted, in my unconscionable estimation—to nothing.

It was all summed up in three very vague disclosures:

First—Her name was Carmilla.

Second—Her family was very ancient and noble.

Third—Her home lay in the direction of the west.

She would not tell me the name of her family, nor their armorial bearings, nor the name of their estate, nor even that of the country they lived in.

You are not to suppose that I worried her incessantly on these subjects. I watched opportunity, and rather insinuated than urged my inquiries. Once or twice, indeed, I did attack her more directly. But no matter what my tactics, utter failure was invariably the result. Reproaches and caresses were all lost upon her. But I must add this, that her evasion was conducted with so pretty a melancholy and deprecation, with so many, and even passionate declarations of her liking for me, and trust in my honour, and with so many promises that I should at last know all, that I could not find it in my heart long to be offended with her.

She used to place her pretty arms about my neck, draw me to her, and laying her cheek to mine, murmur with her lips near my ear, "Dearest, your little heart is wounded; think me not cruel because I obey the irresistible law of my strength and weakness; if your dear heart is wounded, my wild heart bleeds with yours. In the rapture of my enormous humiliation I live in your warm life, and you shall die—die, sweetly die—into mine. I cannot help it; as I draw near to you, you, in your turn, will draw near to others, and learn the rapture of that cruelty, which yet is love; so, for a while, seek to know no more of me and mine, but trust me with all your loving spirit."

And when she had spoken such a rhapsody, she would press me more closely in her trembling embrace, and her lips in soft kisses gently glow upon my cheek.

Her agitations and her language were unintelligible to me.

From these foolish embraces, which were not of very frequent occurrence, I must allow, I used to wish to extricate myself; but my energies seemed to fail me. Her murmured words sounded like a lullaby in my ear, and soothed my resistance into a trance, from which I only seemed to recover myself when she withdrew her arms.

In these mysterious moods I did not like her. I experienced

a strange tumultuous excitement that was pleasurable, ever and anon, mingled with a vague sense of fear and disgust. I had no distinct thoughts about her while such scenes lasted, but I was conscious of a love growing into adoration, and also of abhorrence. This I know is paradox, but I can make no other attempt to explain the feeling.

I now write, after an interval of more than ten years, with a trembling hand, with a confused and horrible recollection of certain occurrences and situations, in the ordeal through which I was unconsciously passing; though with a vivid and very sharp remembrance of the main current of my story.

But, I suspect, in all lives there are certain emotional scenes, those in which our passions have been most wildly and terribly roused, that are of all others the most vaguely and dimly remembered.

Sometimes after an hour of apathy, my strange and beautiful companion would take my hand and hold it with a fond pressure, renewed again and again; blushing softly, gazing in my face with languid and burning eyes, and breathing so fast that her dress rose and fell with the tumultuous respiration. It was like the ardour of a lover; it embarrassed me; it was hateful and yet over-powering; and with gloating eyes she drew me to her, and her hot lips travelled along my cheek in kisses; and she would whisper, almost in sobs, "You are mine, you *shall* be mine, you and I are one forever." Then she had thrown herself back in her chair, with her small hands over her eyes, leaving me trembling.

"Are we related," I used to ask; "what can you mean by all this? I remind you perhaps of someone whom you love; but you must not, I hate it; I don't know you—I don't know myself when you look so and talk so."

She used to sigh at my vehemence, then turn away and drop my hand.

Respecting these very extraordinary manifestations I strove in vain to form any satisfactory theory—I could not refer them to affectation or trick. It was unmistakably the momentary breaking out of suppressed instinct and emotion. Was she, notwithstanding her mother's volunteered denial, subject to brief visitations of insanity; or was there here a disguise and a romance? I had read in old storybooks of such things. What if a boyish lover had found his way into the house, and sought to prosecute his suit in masquerade, with the assistance of a clever old adventuress. But there were many things against this hypothesis, highly interesting as it was to my vanity.

I could boast of no little attentions such as masculine gallantry delights to offer. Between these passionate moments there were long intervals of commonplace, of gaiety, of brooding melancholy, during which, except that I detected her eyes so full of melancholy fire, following me, at times I might have been as nothing to her. Except in these brief periods of mysterious excitement her ways were girlish; and there was always a languor about her, quite incompatible with a masculine system in a state of health.

In some respects her habits were odd. Perhaps not so singular in the opinion of a town lady like you, as they appeared to us rustic people. She used to come down very late, generally not till one o'clock, she would then take a cup of chocolate, but eat nothing; we then went out for a walk, which was a mere saunter, and she seemed, almost immediately, exhausted, and either returned to the *schloss* or sat on one of the benches that were placed, here and there, among the trees. This was a bodily languor in which her mind did not sympathize. She was always an animated talker, and very intelligent.

She sometimes alluded for a moment to her own home, or mentioned an adventure or situation, or an early recollection, which indicated a people of strange manners, and described customs of which we knew nothing. I gathered from these chance hints that her native country was much more remote than I had at first fancied.

As we sat thus one afternoon under the trees a funeral passed us by. It was that of a pretty young girl, whom I had often seen, the daughter of one of the rangers of the forest. The poor man was walking behind the coffin of his darling; she was his only child, and he looked quite heartbroken.

Peasants walking two-and-two came behind, they were singing a funeral hymn.

I rose to mark my respect as they passed, and joined in the hymn they were very sweetly singing.

My companion shook me a little roughly, and I turned surprised.

She said brusquely, "Don't you perceive how discordant that is?"

"I think it very sweet, on the contrary," I answered, vexed at the interruption, and very uncomfortable, lest the people who composed the little procession should observe and resent what was passing.

I resumed, therefore, instantly, and was again interrupted. "You pierce my ears," said Carmilla, almost angrily, and stopping her ears with her tiny fingers. "Besides, how can you tell that your religion and mine are the same; your forms wound me, and I hate funerals. What a fuss! Why you must die—*everyone* must die; and all are happier when they do. Come home."

"My father has gone on with the clergyman to the churchyard. I thought you knew she was to be buried today."

"She? I don't trouble my head about peasants. I don't know who she is," answered Carmilla, with a flash from her fine eyes.

"She is the poor girl who fancied she saw a ghost a fortnight ago, and has been dying ever since, till yesterday, when she expired."

"Tell me nothing about ghosts. I shan't sleep tonight if you do."

"I hope there is no plague or fever coming; all this looks very like it," I continued. "The swineherd's young wife died only a week ago, and she thought something seized her by the throat as she lay in her bed, and nearly strangled her. Papa says such horrible fancies do accompany some forms of fever. She was quite well the day before. She sank afterwards, and died before a week."

"Well, *her* funeral is over, I hope, and *her* hymn sung; and our ears shan't be tortured with that discord and jargon. It has made me nervous. Sit down here, beside me; sit close; hold my hand; press it hard–hard–harder."

We had moved a little back, and had come to another seat.

She sat down. Her face underwent a change that alarmed and even terrified me for a moment. It darkened, and became horribly livid; her teeth and hands were clenched, and she frowned and compressed her lips, while she stared down upon the ground at her feet, and trembled all over with a continued shudder as irrepressible as ague. All her energies seemed strained to suppress a fit, with which she was then breathlessly tugging; and at length a low convulsive cry of suffering broke from her, and gradually the hysteria subsided. "There! That comes of strangling people with hymns!" she said at last. "Hold me, hold me still. It is passing away."

And so gradually it did; and perhaps to dissipate the sombre impression which the spectacle had left upon me, she became unusually animated and chatty; and so we got home.

This was the first time I had seen her exhibit any definable symptoms of that delicacy of health which her mother had spoken of. It was the first time, also, I had seen her exhibit anything like temper.

Both passed away like a summer cloud; and never but once afterwards did I witness on her part a momentary sign of anger. I will tell you how it happened.

She and I were looking out of one of the long drawing room windows, when there entered the courtyard, over the drawbridge, a figure of a wanderer whom I knew very well. He used to visit the *schloss* generally twice a year.

It was the figure of a hunchback, with the sharp lean features that generally accompany deformity. He wore a pointed black beard, and he was smiling from ear to ear, showing his white fangs. He was dressed in buff, black, and scarlet, and crossed with more straps and belts than I could count, from which hung all manner of things. Behind, he carried a magic lantern, and two boxes, which I well knew, in one of which was a salamander, and in the other a mandrake. These monsters used to make my father laugh. They were compounded of parts of monkeys, parrots, squirrels, fish, and hedgehogs, dried and stitched together with great neatness and startling effect. He had a fiddle, a box of conjuring apparatus, a pair of foils and masks attached to his belt, several other mysterious cases dangling about him, and a black staff with copper ferrules in his hand. His companion was a rough spare dog, that followed at his heels, but stopped short, suspiciously at the drawbridge, and in a little while began to howl dismally.

In the meantime, the mountebank, standing in the midst of the courtyard, raised his grotesque hat, and made us a very ceremonious bow, paying his compliments very volubly in execrable French, and German not much better.

Then, disengaging his fiddle, he began to scrape a lively air to which he sang with a merry discord, dancing with ludicrous airs and activity, that made me laugh, in spite of the dog's howling.

Then he advanced to the window with many smiles and salutations, and his hat in his left hand, his fiddle under his arm, and with a fluency that never took breath, he gabbled a long advertisement of all his accomplishments, and the resources of the various arts which he placed at our service, and the curiosities and entertainments which it was in his power, at our bidding, to display.

"Will your ladyships be pleased to buy an amulet against the oupire, which is going like the wolf, I hear, through these woods," he said dropping his hat on the pavement. "They are dying of it right and left and here is a charm that never fails; only pinned to the pillow, and you may laugh in his face."

These charms consisted of oblong slips of vellum, with cabalistic ciphers and diagrams upon them.

Carmilla instantly purchased one, and so did I.

He was looking up, and we were smiling down upon him, amused; at least, I can answer for myself. His piercing black eye, as he looked up in our faces, seemed to detect something that fixed for a moment his curiosity. In an instant he unrolled a leather case, full of all manner of odd little steel instruments.

"See here, my lady," he said, displaying it, and addressing me, "I profess, among other things less useful, the art of dentistry. Plague take the dog!" he interpolated. "Silence, beast! He howls so that your ladyships can scarcely hear a word. Your noble friend, the young lady at your right, has the sharpest tooth,- long, thin, pointed, like an awl, like a needle; ha, ha! With my sharp and long sight, as I look up, I have seen it distinctly; now if it happens to hurt the young lady, and I think it must, here am I, here are my file, my punch, my nippers; I will make it round and blunt, if her ladyship pleases; no longer the tooth of a fish, but of a beautiful young lady as she is. Hey? Is the young lady displeased? Have I been too bold? Have I offended her?"

The young lady, indeed, looked very angry as she drew back from the window.

"How dares that mountebank insult us so? Where is your father? I shall demand redress from him. My father would have had the wretch tied up to the pump, and flogged with a cart whip, and burnt to the bones with the cattle brand!"

She retired from the window a step or two, and sat down, and had hardly lost sight of the offender, when her wrath subsided as suddenly as it had risen, and she gradually recovered her usual tone, and seemed to forget the little hunchback and his follies.

My father was out of spirits that evening. On coming in he told us that there had been another case very similar to the two fatal ones which had lately occurred. The sister of a young peasant on his estate, only a mile away, was very ill, had been, as she described it, attacked very nearly in the same way, and was now slowly but steadily sinking.

"All this," said my father, "is strictly referable to natural causes. These poor people infect one another with their superstitions, and so repeat in imagination the images of terror that have infested their neighbours."

"But that very circumstance frightens one horribly," said Carmilla.

"How so?" inquired my father.

"I am so afraid of fancying I see such things; I think it would be as bad as reality."

"We are in God's hands: nothing can happen without his permission, and all will end well for those who love him. He is our faithful creator; He has made us all, and will take care of us."

"Creator! *Nature!*" said the young lady in answer to my gentle father. "And this disease that invades the country is natural. Nature. All things proceed from Nature—don't they? All things in the heaven, in the earth, and under the earth, act and live as Nature ordains? I think so."

"The doctor said he would come here today," said my father, after a silence. "I want to know what he thinks about it, and what he thinks we had better do."

"Doctors never did me any good," said Carmilla.

"Then you have been ill?" I asked.

"More ill than ever you were," she answered.

"Long ago?"

"Yes, a long time. I suffered from this very illness; but I forget all but my pain and weakness, and they were not so bad as are suffered in other diseases."

"You were very young then?"

"I dare say, let us talk no more of it. You would not wound a friend?"

She looked languidly in my eyes, and passed her arm round my waist lovingly, and led me out of the room. My father was busy over some papers near the window.

"Why does your papa like to frighten us?" said the pretty girl with a sigh and a little shudder.

"He doesn't, dear Carmilla, it is the very furthest thing from his mind."

"Are you afraid, dearest?"

"I should be very much if I fancied there was any real danger of my being attacked as those poor people were."

"You are afraid to die?"

"Yes, everyone is."

"But to die as lovers may—to die together, so that they may live together.

"Girls are caterpillars while they live in the world, to be finally butterflies when the summer comes; but in the meantime there are grubs and larvae, don't you see—each with their peculiar propensities, necessities and structure. So says Monsieur Buffon, in his big book, in the next room."

Later in the day the doctor came, and was closeted with papa for some time.

He was a skilful man, of sixty and upwards, he wore powder, and shaved his pale face as smooth as a pumpkin. He and papa emerged from the room together, and I heard papa laugh, and say as they came out:

"Well, I do wonder at a wise man like you. What do you say to hippogriffs and dragons?"

The doctor was smiling, and made answer, shaking his head—

"Nevertheless life and death are mysterious states, and we know little of the resources of either."

And so they walked on, and I heard no more. I did not then know what the doctor had been broaching, but I think I guess it now.

Chapter 5
A Wonderful Likeness

This evening there arrived from Gratz the grave, dark-faced son of the picture cleaner, with a horse and cart laden with two large packing cases, having many pictures in each. It was a journey of ten leagues, and whenever a messenger arrived at the *schloss* from our little capital of Gratz, we used to crowd about him in the hall, to hear the news.

This arrival created in our secluded quarters quite a sensation. The cases remained in the hall, and the messenger was taken charge of by the servants till he had eaten his supper. Then with assistants, and armed with hammer, ripping chisel, and turnscrew, he met us in the hall, where we had assembled to witness the unpacking of the cases.

Carmilla sat looking listlessly on, while one after the other the old pictures, nearly all portraits, which had undergone the process of renovation, were brought to light. My mother was of an old Hungarian family, and most of these pictures, which were about to be restored to their places, had come to us through her.

My father had a list in his hand, from which he read, as the artist rummaged out the corresponding numbers. I don't know that the pictures were very good, but they were, undoubtedly, very old, and some of them very curious also. They had, for the most part, the merit of being now seen by me, I may say, for the first time; for the smoke and dust of time had all but obliterated them.

"There is a picture that I have not seen yet," said my father. "In one corner, at the top of it, is the name, as well as I could read, 'Marcia Karnstein,' and the date '1698'; and I am curious to see how it has turned out."

I remembered it; it was a small picture, about a foot and a half high, and nearly square, without a frame; but it was so blackened by age that I could not make it out.

The artist now produced it, with evident pride. It was quite beautiful; it was startling; it seemed to live. It was the effigy of Carmilla!

"Carmilla, dear, here is an absolute miracle. Here you are, living, smiling, ready to speak, in this picture. Isn't it beautiful, Papa? And see, even the little mole on her throat."

My father laughed, and said "Certainly it is a wonderful likeness," but he looked away, and to my surprise seemed but little struck by it, and went on talking to the picture cleaner, who was also something of an artist, and discoursed with intelligence about the portraits or other works, which his art had just brought into light and colour, while I was more and more lost in wonder the more I looked at the picture.

"Will you let me hang this picture in my room, papa?" I asked.

"Certainly, dear," said he, smiling, "I'm very glad you think it so like. It must be prettier even than I thought it, if it is."

The young lady did not acknowledge this pretty speech, did not seem to hear it. She was leaning back in her seat, her fine eyes under their long lashes gazing on me in contemplation, and she smiled in a kind of rapture.

"And now you can read quite plainly the name that is written in the corner. It is not Marcia; it looks as if it was done in gold. The name is Mircalla, Countess Karnstein, and this is a little coronet over and underneath A.D. 1698. I am descended from the Karnsteins; that is, mamma was."

"Ah!" said the lady, languidly, "so am I, I think, a very long descent, very ancient. Are there any Karnsteins living now?"

"None who bear the name, I believe. The family were ruined, I believe, in some civil wars, long ago, but the ruins of the castle are only about three miles away."

"How interesting!" she said, languidly. "But see what beautiful moonlight!" She glanced through the hall door, which stood a little open. "Suppose you take a little ramble round the court, and look down at the road and river."

"It is so like the night you came to us," I said.

She sighed; smiling.

She rose, and each with her arm about the other's waist, we walked out upon the pavement.

In silence, slowly we walked down to the drawbridge, where the beautiful landscape opened before us.

"And so you were thinking of the night I came here?" she almost whispered.

"Are you glad I came?"

"Delighted, dear Carmilla," I answered.

"And you asked for the picture you think like me, to hang in your room," she murmured with a sigh, as she drew her arm closer about my waist, and let her pretty head sink upon my shoulder. "How romantic you are, Carmilla," I said. "Whenever you tell me your story, it will be made up chiefly of some one great romance."

She kissed me silently.

"I am sure, Carmilla, you have been in love; that there is, at this moment, an affair of the heart going on."

"I have been in love with no one, and never shall," she whispered, "unless it should be with you."

How beautiful she looked in the moonlight!

Shy and strange was the look with which she quickly hid her face in my neck and hair, with tumultuous sighs, that seemed almost to sob, and pressed in mine a hand that trembled.

Her soft cheek was glowing against mine. "Darling, darling," she murmured, "I live in you; and you would die for me, I love you so."

I started from her.

She was gazing on me with eyes from which all fire, all meaning had flown, and a face colourless and apathetic.

"Is there a chill in the air, dear?" she said drowsily. "I almost shiver; have I been dreaming? Let us come in. Come; come; come in."

"You look ill, Carmilla; a little faint. You certainly must take some wine," I said.

"Yes. I will. I'm better now. I shall be quite well in a few minutes. Yes, do give me a little wine," answered Carmilla, as we approached the door.

"Let us look again for a moment; it is the last time, perhaps, I shall see the moonlight with you."

"How do you feel now, dear Carmilla? Are you really better?" I asked.

I was beginning to take alarm, lest she should have been stricken with the strange epidemic that they said had invaded the country about us.

"Papa would be grieved beyond measure," I added, "if he thought you were ever so little ill, without immediately letting us know. We have a very skilful doctor near us, the physician who was with papa today."

"I'm sure he is. I know how kind you all are; but, dear child, I am quite well again. There is nothing ever wrong with me, but a little weakness.

"People say I am languid; I am incapable of exertion; I can scarcely walk as far as a child of three years old: and every now and then the little strength I have falters, and I become as you have just seen me. But after all I am very easily set up again; in a moment I am perfectly myself. See how I have recovered."

So, indeed, she had; and she and I talked a great deal, and very animated she was; and the remainder of that evening passed without any recurrence of what I called her infatuations. I mean her crazy talk and looks, which embarrassed, and even frightened me.

But there occurred that night an event which gave my thoughts quite a new turn, and seemed to startle even Carmilla's languid nature into momentary energy.

Chapter 6
A Very Strange Agony

When we got into the drawing room, and had sat down to our coffee and chocolate, although Carmilla did not take any, she seemed quite herself again, and Madame, and Mademoiselle De Lafontaine, joined us, and made a little card party, in the course of which papa came in for what he called his "dish of tea."

When the game was over he sat down beside Carmilla on the sofa, and asked her, a little anxiously, whether she had heard from her mother since her arrival.

She answered "No."

He then asked whether she knew where a letter would reach her at present.

"I cannot tell," she answered ambiguously, "but I have been thinking of leaving you; you have been already too hospitable and too kind to me. I have given you an infinity of trouble, and I should wish to take a carriage tomorrow, and post in pursuit of her; I know where I shall ultimately find her, although I dare not yet tell you."

"But you must not dream of any such thing," exclaimed my father, to my great relief. "We can't afford to lose you so, and

I won't consent to your leaving us, except under the care of your mother, who was so good as to consent to your remaining with us till she should herself return. I should be quite happy if I knew that you heard from her: but this evening the accounts of the progress of the mysterious disease that has invaded our neighbourhood, grow even more alarming; and my beautiful guest, I do feel the responsibility, unaided by advice from your mother, very much. But I shall do my best; and one thing is certain, that you must not think of leaving us without her distinct direction to that effect. We should suffer too much in parting from you to consent to it easily."

"Thank you, sir, a thousand times for your hospitality," she answered, smiling bashfully. "You have all been too kind to me; I have seldom been so happy in all my life before, as in your beautiful *château*, under your care, and in the society of your dear daughter."

So he gallantly, in his old-fashioned way, kissed her hand, smiling and pleased at her little speech.

I accompanied Carmilla as usual to her room, and sat and chatted with her while she was preparing for bed.

"Do you think," I said at length, "that you will ever confide fully in me?"

She turned round smiling, but made no answer, only continued to smile on me.

"You won't answer that?" I said. "You can't answer pleasantly; I ought not to have asked you."

"You were quite right to ask me that, or anything. You do not know how dear you are to me, or you could not think any confidence too great to look for. But I am under vows, no nun half so awfully, and I dare not tell my story yet, even to you. The time is very near when you shall know everything. You will think me cruel, very selfish, but love is always selfish; the more ardent the more selfish. How jealous I am you cannot know. You must come with me, loving me, to death; or else hate me and still come with me, and *hating* me through death and after. There is no such word as indifference in my apathetic nature."

"Now, Carmilla, you are going to talk your wild nonsense again," I said hastily.

"Not I, silly little fool as I am, and full of whims and fancies; for your sake I'll talk like a sage. Were you ever at a ball?"

"No; how you do run on. What is it like? How charming it must be."

"I almost forget, it is years ago."

I laughed.

"You are not so old. Your first ball can hardly be forgotten yet."

"I remember everything about it—with an effort. I see it all, as divers see what is going on above them, through a medium, dense, rippling, but transparent. There occurred that night what has confused the picture, and made its colours faint. I was all but assassinated in my bed, wounded here," she touched her breast, "and never was the same since."

"Were you near dying?"

"Yes, very—a cruel love—strange love, that would have taken my life. Love will have its sacrifices. No sacrifice without blood. Let us go to sleep now; I feel so lazy. How can I get up just now and lock my door?"

She was lying with her tiny hands buried in her rich wavy hair, under her cheek, her little head upon the pillow, and her glittering eyes followed me wherever I moved, with a kind of shy smile that I could not decipher.

I bid her good night, and crept from the room with an uncomfortable sensation.

I often wondered whether our pretty guest ever said her prayers. I certainly had never seen her upon her knees. In the morning she never came down until long after our family prayers were over, and at night she never left the drawing room to attend our brief evening prayers in the hall.

If it had not been that it had casually come out in one of our careless talks that she had been baptised, I should have doubted her being a Christian. Religion was a subject on which I had never heard her speak a word. If I had known the world better, this particular neglect or antipathy would not have so much surprised me.

The precautions of nervous people are infectious, and persons of a like temperament are pretty sure, after a time, to imitate them. I had adopted Carmilla's habit of locking her bedroom door, having taken into my head all her whimsical alarms about midnight invaders and prowling assassins. I had also adopted her precaution of making a brief search through her room, to satisfy herself that no lurking assassin or robber was "ensconced."

These wise measures taken, I got into my bed and fell asleep. A light was burning in my room. This was an old habit, of very early date, and which nothing could have tempted me to dispense with.

Thus fortified I might take my rest in peace. But dreams come through stone walls, light up dark rooms, or darken light ones, and their persons make their exits and their entrances as they please, and laugh at locksmiths.

I had a dream that night that was the beginning of a very strange agony.

I cannot call it a nightmare, for I was quite conscious of being asleep.

But I was equally conscious of being in my room, and lying in bed, precisely as I actually was. I saw, or fancied I saw, the room and its furniture just as I had seen it last, except that it was very dark, and I saw something moving round the foot of the bed, which at first I could not accurately distinguish. But I soon saw that it was a sooty-black animal that resembled a monstrous cat. It appeared to me about four or five feet long for it measured fully the length of the hearthrug as it passed over it; and it continued to-ing and fro-ing with the lithe, sinister restlessness of a beast in a cage. I could not cry out, although as you may suppose, I was terrified.

Its pace was growing faster, and the room rapidly darker and darker, and at length so dark that I could no longer see anything of it but its eyes. I felt it spring lightly on the bed. The two broad eyes approached my face, and suddenly I felt a stinging pain as if two large needles darted, an inch or two apart, deep into my breast. I waked with a scream. The room was lighted by the candle that burnt there all through the night, and I saw a female figure standing at the foot of the bed, a little at the right side. It was in a dark loose dress, and its hair was down and covered its shoulders. A block of stone could not have been more still. There was not the slightest stir of respiration. As I stared at it, the figure appeared to have changed its place, and was now nearer the door; then, close to it, the door opened, and it passed out.

I was now relieved, and able to breathe and move. My first thought was that Carmilla had been playing me a trick, and that I had forgotten to secure my door. I hastened to it, and found it locked as usual on the inside. I was afraid to open it—I was horrified. I sprang into my bed and covered my head up in the bedclothes, and lay there more dead than alive till morning.

Chapter 7
Descending

It would be vain my attempting to tell you the horror with which, even now, I recall the occurrence of that night. It was no such transitory terror as a dream leaves behind it. It seemed to deepen by time, and communicated itself to the room and the very furniture that had encompassed the apparition.

I could not bear next day to be alone for a moment. I should have told papa, but for two opposite reasons. At one time I thought he would laugh at my story, and I could not bear its being treated as a jest; and at another I thought he might fancy that I had been attacked by the mysterious complaint which had invaded our neighbourhood. I had myself no misgiving of the kind, and as he had been rather an invalid for some time, I was afraid of alarming him.

I was comfortable enough with my good-natured companions, Madame Perrodon, and the vivacious Mademoiselle Lafontaine. They both perceived that I was out of spirits and nervous, and at length I told them what lay so heavy at my heart.

Mademoiselle laughed, but I fancied that Madame Perrodon

looked anxious.

"By-the-by," said *Mademoiselle*, laughing, "the long lime tree walk, behind Carmilla's bedroom window, is haunted!"

"Nonsense!" exclaimed *Madame*, who probably thought the theme rather inopportune, "and who tells that story, my dear?"

"Martin says that he came up twice, when the old yard gate was being repaired, before sunrise, and twice saw the same female figure walking down the lime tree avenue."

"So he well might, as long as there are cows to milk in the river fields," said *Madame*.

"I daresay; but Martin chooses to be frightened, and never did I see fool more frightened."

"You must not say a word about it to Carmilla, because she can see down that walk from her room window," I interposed, "and she is, if possible, a greater coward than I."

Carmilla came down rather later than usual that day.

"I was so frightened last night," she said, so soon as were together, "and I am sure I should have seen something dreadful if it had not been for that charm I bought from the poor little hunchback whom I called such hard names. I had a dream of something black coming round my bed, and I awoke in a perfect horror, and I really thought, for some seconds, I saw a dark figure near the chimney-piece, but I felt under my pillow for my charm, and the moment my fingers touched it, the figure disappeared, and I felt quite certain, only that I had it by me, that something frightful would have made its appearance, and, perhaps, throttled me, as it did those poor people we heard of.

"Well, listen to me," I began, and recounted my adventure, at the recital of which she appeared horrified.

"And had you the charm near you?" she asked, earnestly.

"No, I had dropped it into a china vase in the drawing room, but I shall certainly take it with me tonight, as you have so much faith in it."

At this distance of time I cannot tell you, or even understand, how I overcame my horror so effectually as to lie alone in my room that night. I remember distinctly that I pinned the charm to my pillow. I fell asleep almost immediately, and slept even more soundly than usual all night.

Next night I passed as well. My sleep was delightfully deep and dreamless.

But I wakened with a sense of lassitude and melancholy, which, however, did not exceed a degree that was almost luxurious.

"Well, I told you so," said Carmilla, when I described my quiet sleep, "I had such delightful sleep myself last night; I pinned the charm to the breast of my nightdress. It was too far away the night before. I am quite sure it was all fancy, except the dreams. I used to think that evil spirits made dreams, but our doctor told me it is no such thing. Only a fever passing by, or some other malady, as they often do, he said, knocks at the door, and not being able to get in, passes on, with that alarm."

"And what do you think the charm is?" said I.

"It has been fumigated or immersed in some drug, and is an antidote against the malaria," she answered.

"Then it acts only on the body?"

"Certainly; you don't suppose that evil spirits are frightened by bits of ribbon, or the perfumes of a druggist's shop? No, these complaints, wandering in the air, begin by trying the nerves, and so infect the brain, but before they can seize upon you, the antidote repels them. That I am sure is what the charm has done for us. It is nothing magical, it is simply natural."

I should have been happier if I could have quite agreed with Carmilla, but I did my best, and the impression was a little losing its force.

For some nights I slept profoundly; but still every morning I felt the same lassitude, and a languor weighed upon me all day. I felt myself a changed girl. A strange melancholy was stealing over me, a melancholy that I would not have interrupted. Dim thoughts of death began to open, and an idea that I was slowly sinking took gentle, and, somehow, not unwelcome, possession of me. If it was sad, the tone of mind which this induced was also sweet.

Whatever it might be, my soul acquiesced in it.

I would not admit that I was ill, I would not consent to tell my papa, or to have the doctor sent for.

Carmilla became more devoted to me than ever, and her strange paroxysms of languid adoration more frequent. She used to gloat on me with increasing ardour the more my strength and spirits waned. This always shocked me like a momentary glare of insanity.

Without knowing it, I was now in a pretty advanced stage of the strangest illness under which mortal ever suffered. There was an unaccountable fascination in its earlier symptoms that more than reconciled me to the incapacitating effect of that stage of the malady. This fascination increased for a time, until it reached a certain point, when gradually a sense of the horrible mingled itself with it, deepening, as you shall hear, until it discoloured and perverted the whole state of my life.

The first change I experienced was rather agreeable. It was very near the turning point from which began the descent of Avernus.

Certain vague and strange sensations visited me in my sleep. The prevailing one was of that pleasant, peculiar cold thrill which we feel in bathing, when we move against the current of a river. This was soon accompanied by dreams that seemed interminable, and were so vague that I could never recollect their scenery and persons, or anyone connected portion of their action. But they left an awful impression, and a sense of exhaustion, as if I had passed through a long period of great mental exertion and danger.

After all these dreams there remained on waking a remembrance of having been in a place very nearly dark, and of having spoken to people whom I could not see; and especially of one clear voice, of a female's, very deep, that spoke as if at a distance, slowly, and producing always the same sensation of indescribable solemnity and fear. Sometimes there came a sensation as if a hand was drawn softly along my cheek and neck. Sometimes it was as if warm lips kissed me, and longer and longer and more lovingly as they reached my throat, but there the caress fixed itself. My heart beat faster, my breathing rose and fell rapidly and full drawn; a sobbing, that rose into a sense of strangulation, supervened, and turned into a dreadful convulsion, in which my senses left me and I became unconscious.

It was now three weeks since the commencement of this unaccountable state.

My sufferings had, during the last week, told upon my appearance. I had grown pale, my eyes were dilated and darkened underneath, and the languor which I had long felt began to display itself in my countenance.

My father asked me often whether I was ill; but, with an obstinacy which now seems to me unaccountable, I persisted in assuring him that I was quite well.

In a sense this was true. I had no pain, I could complain of no bodily derangement. My complaint seemed to be one of the imagination, or the nerves, and, horrible as my sufferings were, I kept them, with a morbid reserve, very nearly to myself.

It could not be that terrible complaint which the peasants called the oupire, for I had now been suffering for three weeks, and they were seldom ill for much more than three days, when death put an end to their miseries.

Carmilla complained of dreams and feverish sensations, but by no means of so alarming a kind as mine. I say that mine were extremely alarming. Had I been capable of comprehending my condition, I would have invoked aid and advice on my knees. The narcotic of an unsuspected influence was acting upon me, and my perceptions were benumbed.

I am going to tell you now of a dream that led immediately to an odd discovery.

One night, instead of the voice I was accustomed to hear in the dark, I heard one, sweet and tender, and at the same time terrible, which said, "Your mother warns you to beware of the assassin." At the same time a light unexpectedly sprang up, and I saw Carmilla, standing, near the foot of my bed, in her white nightdress, bathed, from her chin to her feet, in one great stain of blood.

I wakened with a shriek, possessed with the one idea that Carmilla was being murdered. I remember springing from my bed, and my next recollection is that of standing on the lobby, crying for help.

Madame and *Mademoiselle* came scurrying out of their rooms in alarm; a lamp burned always on the lobby, and seeing me, they soon learned the cause of my terror.

I insisted on our knocking at Carmilla's door. Our knocking was unanswered.

It soon became a pounding and an uproar. We shrieked her name, but all was vain.

We all grew frightened, for the door was locked. We hurried back, in panic, to my room. There we rang the bell long and furiously. If my father's room had been at that side of the house, we would have called him up at once to our aid. But, alas! he was quite out of hearing, and to reach him involved an excursion for which we none of us had courage.

Servants, however, soon came running up the stairs; I had got on my dressing gown and slippers meanwhile, and my companions were already similarly furnished. Recognizing the voices of the servants on the lobby, we sallied out together; and having renewed, as fruitlessly, our summons at Carmilla's door, I ordered the men to force the lock. They did so, and we stood, holding our lights aloft, in the doorway, and so stared into the room.

We called her by name; but there was still no reply. We looked round the room. Everything was undisturbed. It was exactly in the state in which I had left it on bidding her good night. But Carmilla was gone.

CHAPTER 8

SEARCH

At sight of the room, perfectly undisturbed except for our violent entrance, we began to cool a little, and soon recovered our senses sufficiently to dismiss the men. It had struck *Mademoiselle* that possibly Carmilla had been wakened by the uproar at her door, and in her first panic had jumped from her bed, and hid herself in a press, or behind a curtain, from which she could not, of course, emerge until the *majordomo* and his myrmidons had withdrawn. We now recommenced our search, and began to call her name again.

It was all to no purpose. Our perplexity and agitation increased. We examined the windows, but they were secured. I implored of Carmilla, if she had concealed herself, to play this cruel trick no longer—to come out and to end our anxieties. It was all useless. I was by this time convinced that she was not in the room, nor in the dressing room, the door of which was still locked on this side. She could not have passed it. I was utterly puzzled. Had Carmilla discovered one of those secret passages which the old housekeeper said were known to exist in the *schloss*, although the tradition of their exact situation had been lost? A little time would, no doubt, explain all—utterly perplexed as, for the present, we were.

It was past four o'clock, and I preferred passing the remaining hours of darkness in *Madame's* room. Daylight brought no solution of the difficulty.

The whole household, with my father at its head, was in a state of agitation next morning. Every part of the *château* was searched. The grounds were explored. No trace of the missing lady could be discovered. The stream was about to be dragged; my father was in distraction; what a tale to have to tell the poor girl's mother on her return. I, too, was almost beside myself, though my grief was quite of a different kind.

The morning was passed in alarm and excitement. It was now one o'clock, and still no tidings. I ran up to Carmilla's room, and found her standing at her dressing table. I was astounded. I could not believe my eyes. She beckoned me to her with her pretty finger, in silence. Her face expressed extreme fear.

I ran to her in an ecstasy of joy; I kissed and embraced her again and again. I ran to the bell and rang it vehemently, to bring others to the spot who might at once relieve my father's anxiety.

"Dear Carmilla, what has become of you all this time? We have been in agonies of anxiety about you," I exclaimed. "Where have you been? How did you come back?"

"Last night has been a night of wonders," she said.

"For mercy's sake, explain all you can."

"It was past two last night," she said, "when I went to sleep as usual in my bed, with my doors locked, that of the dressing room, and that opening upon the gallery. My sleep was uninterrupted, and, so far as I know, dreamless; but I woke just now on the sofa in the dressing room there, and I found the door between the rooms open, and the other door forced. How could all this have happened without my being wakened? It must have been accompanied with a great deal of noise, and I am particularly easily wakened; and how could I have been carried out of my bed without my sleep having been interrupted, I whom the slightest stir startles?"

By this time, *Madame*, *Mademoiselle*, my father, and a number of the servants were in the room. Carmilla was, of course, overwhelmed with inquiries, congratulations, and welcomes. She had but one story to tell, and seemed the least able of all the party to suggest any way of accounting for what had happened.

My father took a turn up and down the room, thinking. I saw Carmilla's eye follow him for a moment with a sly, dark glance.

When my father had sent the servants away, *Mademoiselle* having gone in search of a little bottle of valerian and *salvolatile*, and there being no one now in the room with Carmilla, except my father, *Madame*, and myself, he came to her thoughtfully, took her hand very kindly, led her to the sofa, and sat down beside her.

"Will you forgive me, my dear, if I risk a conjecture, and ask a question?"

"Who can have a better right?" she said. "Ask what you please, and I will tell you everything. But my story is simply one of bewilderment and darkness. I know absolutely nothing. Put any question you please, but you know, of course, the limitations mamma has placed me under."

"Perfectly, my dear child. I need not approach the topics on which she desires our silence. Now, the marvel of last night consists in your having been removed from your bed and your room, without being wakened, and this removal having occurred apparently while the windows were still secured, and the two doors locked upon the inside. I will tell you my theory and ask you a question."

Carmilla was leaning on her hand dejectedly; *Madame* and I were listening breathlessly.

"Now, my question is this. Have you ever been suspected of walking in your sleep?"

"Never, since I was very young indeed."

"But you did walk in your sleep when you were young?"

"Yes; I know I did. I have been told so often by my old nurse."

My father smiled and nodded.

"Well, what has happened is this. You got up in your sleep, unlocked the door, not leaving the key, as usual, in the lock, but taking it out and locking it on the outside; you again took the key out, and carried it away with you to some one of the five-and-twenty rooms on this floor, or perhaps upstairs or downstairs. There are so many rooms and closets, so much heavy furniture, and such accumulations of lumber, that it would require a week to search this old house thoroughly. Do you see, now, what I mean?"

"I do, but not all," she answered.

"And how, papa, do you account for her finding herself on the sofa in the dressing room, which we had searched so carefully?"

"She came there after you had searched it, still in her sleep, and at last awoke spontaneously, and was as much surprised to find herself where she was as anyone else. I wish all mysteries were as easily and innocently explained as yours, Carmilla," he said, laughing. "And so we may congratulate ourselves on the certainty that the most natural explanation of the occurrence is one that involves no drugging, no tampering with locks, no burglars, or poisoners, or witches—nothing that need alarm Carmilla, or anyone else, for our safety."

Carmilla was looking charmingly. Nothing could be more beautiful than her tints. Her beauty was, I think, enhanced by that graceful languor that was peculiar to her. I think my father was silently contrasting her looks with mine, for he said:

"I wish my poor Laura was looking more like herself"; and he sighed.

So our alarms were happily ended, and Carmilla restored to her friends.

Chapter 9
The Doctor

As Carmilla would not hear of an attendant sleeping in her room, my father arranged that a servant should sleep outside her door, so that she would not attempt to make another such excursion without being arrested at her own door.

That night passed quietly; and next morning early, the doctor, whom my father had sent for without telling me a word about it, arrived to see me.

Madame accompanied me to the library; and there the grave little doctor, with white hair and spectacles, whom I mentioned before, was waiting to receive me.

I told him my story, and as I proceeded he grew graver and graver.

We were standing, he and I, in the recess of one of the windows, facing one another. When my statement was over, he leaned with his shoulders against the wall, and with his eyes fixed on me earnestly, with an interest in which was a dash of horror.

After a minute's reflection, he asked *Madame* if he could see my father.

He was sent for accordingly, and as he entered, smiling, he said:

"I dare say, doctor, you are going to tell me that I am an old fool for having brought you here; I hope I am."

But his smile faded into shadow as the doctor, with a very grave face, beckoned him to him.

He and the doctor talked for some time in the same recess where I had just conferred with the physician. It seemed an earnest and argumentative conversation. The room is very large, and I and *Madame* stood together, burning with curiosity, at the farther end. Not a word could we hear, however, for they spoke in a very low tone, and the deep recess of the window quite concealed the doctor from view, and very nearly my father, whose foot, arm, and shoulder only could we see; and the voices were, I suppose, all the less audible for the sort of closet which the thick wall and window formed.

After a time my father's face looked into the room; it was pale, thoughtful, and, I fancied, agitated.

"Laura, dear, come here for a moment. *Madame*, we shan't trouble you, the doctor says, at present."

Accordingly I approached, for the first time a little alarmed; for, although I felt very weak, I did not feel ill; and strength, one always fancies, is a thing that may be picked up when we please.

My father held out his hand to me, as I drew near, but he was looking at the doctor, and he said:

"It certainly is very odd; I don't understand it quite. Laura, come here, dear; now attend to Doctor Spielsberg, and recollect yourself."

"You mentioned a sensation like that of two needles piercing the skin, somewhere about your neck, on the night when you experienced your first horrible dream. Is there still any soreness?"

"None at all," I answered.

"Can you indicate with your finger about the point at which you think this occurred?"

"Very little below my throat—here," I answered.

I wore a morning dress, which covered the place I pointed to.

"Now you can satisfy yourself," said the doctor. "You won't

mind your papa's lowering your dress a very little. It is necessary, to detect a symptom of the complaint under which you have been suffering."

I acquiesced. It was only an inch or two below the edge of my collar.

"God bless me!—so it is," exclaimed my father, growing pale.

"You see it now with your own eyes," said the doctor, with a gloomy triumph.

"What is it?" I exclaimed, beginning to be frightened.

"Nothing, my dear young lady, but a small blue spot, about the size of the tip of your little finger; and now," he continued, turning to papa, "the question is what is best to be done?"

"Is there any danger?" I urged, in great trepidation.

"I trust not, my dear," answered the doctor. "I don't see why you should not recover. I don't see why you should not begin immediately to get better. That is the point at which the sense of strangulation begins?"

"Yes," I answered.

"And—recollect as well as you can—the same point was a kind of centre of that thrill which you described just now, like the current of a cold stream running against you?"

"It may have been; I think it was."

"Ay, you see?" he added, turning to my father. "Shall I say a word to *Madame*?"

"Certainly," said my father.

He called *Madame* to him, and said:

"I find my young friend here far from well. It won't be of any great consequence, I hope; but it will be necessary that some steps be taken, which I will explain by-and-by; but in the meantime, *Madame*, you will be so good as not to let Miss Laura be alone for one moment. That is the only direction I need give for the present. It is indispensable."

"We may rely upon your kindness, *Madame*, I know," added my father.

Madame satisfied him eagerly.

55

"And you, dear Laura, I know you will observe the doctor's direction."

"I shall have to ask your opinion upon another patient, whose symptoms slightly resemble those of my daughter, that have just been detailed to you—very much milder in degree, but I believe quite of the same sort. She is a young lady—our guest; but as you say you will be passing this way again this evening, you can't do better than take your supper here, and you can then see her. She does not come down till the afternoon."

"I thank you," said the doctor. "I shall be with you, then, at about seven this evening."

And then they repeated their directions to me and to *Madame*, and with this parting charge my father left us, and walked out with the doctor; and I saw them pacing together up and down between the road and the moat, on the grassy platform in front of the castle, evidently absorbed in earnest conversation.

The doctor did not return. I saw him mount his horse there, take his leave, and ride away eastward through the forest.

Nearly at the same time I saw the man arrive from Dranfield with the letters, and dismount and hand the bag to my father.

In the meantime, *Madame* and I were both busy, lost in conjecture as to the reasons of the singular and earnest direction which the doctor and my father had concurred in imposing. *Madame*, as she afterwards told me, was afraid the doctor apprehended a sudden seizure, and that, without prompt assistance, I might either lose my life in a fit, or at least be seriously hurt.

The interpretation did not strike me; and I fancied, perhaps luckily for my nerves, that the arrangement was prescribed simply to secure a companion, who would prevent my taking too much exercise, or eating unripe fruit, or doing any of the fifty foolish things to which young people are supposed to be prone.

About half an hour after my father came in—he had a letter in his hand—and said:

"This letter had been delayed; it is from General Spielsdorf. He might have been here yesterday, he may not come till tomorrow or he may be here today."

He put the open letter into my hand; but he did not look pleased, as he used when a guest, especially one so much loved as the General, was coming.

On the contrary, he looked as if he wished him at the bottom of the Red Sea. There was plainly something on his mind which he did not choose to divulge.

"Papa, darling, will you tell me this?" said I, suddenly laying my hand on his arm, and looking, I am sure, imploringly in his face.

"Perhaps," he answered, smoothing my hair caressingly over my eyes.

"Does the doctor think me very ill?"

"No, dear; he thinks, if right steps are taken, you will be quite well again, at least, on the high road to a complete recovery, in a day or two," he answered, a little dryly. "I wish our good friend, the General, had chosen any other time; that is, I wish you had been perfectly well to receive him."

"But do tell me, papa," I insisted, "what does he think is the matter with me?"

"Nothing; you must not plague me with questions," he answered, with more irritation than I ever remember him to have displayed before; and seeing that I looked wounded, I suppose, he kissed me, and added, "You shall know all about it in a day or two; that is, all that I know. In the meantime you are not to trouble your head about it."

He turned and left the room, but came back before I had done wondering and puzzling over the oddity of all this; it was merely to say that he was going to Karnstein, and had ordered the carriage to be ready at twelve, and that I and *Madame* should accompany him; he was going to see the priest who lived near those picturesque grounds, upon business, and as Carmilla had never seen them, she could follow, when she came down, with *Mademoiselle*, who would bring materials for what you call a picnic, which might be laid for us in the ruined castle.

At twelve o'clock, accordingly, I was ready, and not long after, my father, Madame and I set out upon our projected drive.

Passing the drawbridge we turn to the right, and follow the road over the steep Gothic bridge, westward, to reach the deserted village and ruined castle of Karnstein.

No sylvan drive can be fancied prettier. The ground breaks into gentle hills and hollows, all clothed with beautiful wood, totally destitute of the comparative formality which artificial planting and early culture and pruning impart.

The irregularities of the ground often lead the road out of its course, and cause it to wind beautifully round the sides of broken hollows and the steeper sides of the hills, among varieties of ground almost inexhaustible.

Turning one of these points, we suddenly encountered our old friend, the General, riding towards us, attended by a mounted servant. His portmanteaus were following in a hired wagon, such as we term a cart.

The General dismounted as we pulled up, and, after the usual greetings, was easily persuaded to accept the vacant seat in the carriage and send his horse on with his servant to the *schloss*.

CHAPTER 10
BEREAVED

It was about ten months since we had last seen him: but that time had sufficed to make an alteration of years in his appearance. He had grown thinner; something of gloom and anxiety had taken the place of that cordial serenity which used to characterize his features. His dark blue eyes, always penetrating, now gleamed with a sterner light from under his shaggy grey eyebrows. It was not such a change as grief alone usually induces, and angrier passions seemed to have had their share in bringing it about.

We had not long resumed our drive, when the General began to talk, with his usual soldierly directness, of the bereavement, as he termed it, which he had sustained in the death of his beloved niece and ward; and he then broke out in a tone of intense bitterness and fury, inveighing against the "hellish arts" to which she had fallen a victim, and expressing, with more exasperation than piety, his wonder that Heaven should tolerate so monstrous an indulgence of the lusts and malignity of hell.

My father, who saw at once that something very extraordinary had befallen, asked him, if not too painful to him, to detail the circumstances which he thought justified the strong terms in which he expressed himself.

"I should tell you all with pleasure," said the General, "but you would not believe me."

"Why should I not?" he asked.

"Because," he answered testily, "you believe in nothing but what consists with your own prejudices and illusions. I remember when I was like you, but I have learned better."

"Try me," said my father; "I am not such a dogmatist as you suppose. Besides which, I very well know that you generally require proof for what you believe, and am, therefore, very strongly predisposed to respect your conclusions."

"You are right in supposing that I have not been led lightly into a belief in the marvellous—for what I have experienced is marvellous—and I have been forced by extraordinary evidence to credit that which ran counter, diametrically, to all my theories. I have been made the dupe of a preternatural conspiracy."

Notwithstanding his professions of confidence in the General's penetration, I saw my father, at this point, glance at the General, with, as I thought, a marked suspicion of his sanity.

The General did not see it, luckily. He was looking gloomily and curiously into the glades and *vistas* of the woods that were opening before us.

"You are going to the Ruins of Karnstein?" he said. "Yes, it is a lucky coincidence; do you know I was going to ask you to bring me there to inspect them. I have a special object in exploring. There is a ruined chapel, ain't there, with a great many tombs of that extinct family?"

"So there are—highly interesting," said my father. "I hope you are thinking of claiming the title and estates?"

My father said this gaily, but the General did not recollect the laugh, or even the smile, which courtesy exacts for a friend's joke; on the contrary, he looked grave and even fierce, ruminating on a matter that stirred his anger and horror.

"Something very different," he said, gruffly. "I mean to unearth some of those fine people. I hope, by God's blessing, to accomplish a pious sacrilege here, which will relieve our earth of certain monsters, and enable honest people to sleep in their beds without being assailed by murderers. I have strange things to tell you, my dear friend, such as I myself would have scouted as incredible a few months since."

My father looked at him again, but this time not with a glance of suspicion—with an eye, rather, of keen intelligence and alarm.

"The house of Karnstein," he said, "has been long extinct: a hundred years at least. My dear wife was maternally descended from the Karnsteins. But the name and title have long ceased to exist. The castle is a ruin; the very village is deserted; it is fifty years since the smoke of a chimney was seen there; not a roof left."

"Quite true. I have heard a great deal about that since I last saw you; a great deal that will astonish you. But I had better relate everything in the order in which it occurred," said the General. "You saw my dear ward—my child, I may call her. No creature could have been more beautiful, and only three months ago none more blooming."

"Yes, poor thing! when I saw her last she certainly was quite lovely," said my father. "I was grieved and shocked more than I can tell you, my dear friend; I knew what a blow it was to you."

He took the General's hand, and they exchanged a kind pressure. Tears gathered in the old soldier's eyes. He did not seek to conceal them. He said:

"We have been very old friends; I knew you would feel for me, childless as I am. She had become an object of very near interest to me, and repaid my care by an affection that cheered my home and made my life happy. That is all gone. The years that remain to me on earth may not be very long; but by God's mercy I hope to accomplish a service to mankind before I die, and to subserve the vengeance of Heaven upon the fiends who have murdered my poor child in the spring of her hopes and beauty!"

"You said, just now, that you intended relating everything as it occurred," said my father. "Pray do; I assure you that it is not mere curiosity that prompts me."

By this time we had reached the point at which the Drunstall road, by which the General had come, diverges from the road which we were travelling to Karnstein.

"How far is it to the ruins?" inquired the General, looking anxiously forward.

"About half a league," answered my father. "Pray let us hear the story you were so good as to promise."

CHAPTER 11
THE STORY

"With all my heart," said the General, with an effort; and after a short pause in which to arrange his subject, he commenced one of the strangest narratives I ever heard.

"My dear child was looking forward with great pleasure to the visit you had been so good as to arrange for her to your charming daughter." Here he made me a gallant but melancholy bow. "In the meantime we had an invitation to my old friend the Count Carlsfeld, whose *schloss* is about six leagues to the other side of Karnstein. It was to attend the series of fetes which, you remember, were given by him in honour of his illustrious visitor, the Grand Duke Charles."

"Yes; and very splendid, I believe, they were," said my father.

"Princely! But then his hospitalities are quite regal. He has Aladdin's lamp. The night from which my sorrow dates was devoted to a magnificent masquerade. The grounds were thrown open, the trees hung with coloured lamps. There was such a display of fireworks as Paris itself had never witnessed. And such music—music, you know, is my weakness—such ravishing music! The finest instrumental band, perhaps, in the world, and the finest singers who could be collected from all the great operas in Europe. As you wandered through these fantastically illuminated grounds, the moon-lighted *château* throwing a rosy light from its long rows of windows, you would suddenly hear these ravishing voices stealing from the silence of some grove, or rising from boats upon the lake. I felt myself, as I looked and listened, carried back into the romance and poetry of my early youth.

"When the fireworks were ended, and the ball beginning, we returned to the noble suite of rooms that were thrown open to the dancers. A masked ball, you know, is a beautiful sight; but so brilliant a spectacle of the kind I never saw before.

"It was a very aristocratic assembly. I was myself almost the only 'nobody' present.

"My dear child was looking quite beautiful. She wore no mask. Her excitement and delight added an unspeakable charm to her features, always lovely. I remarked a young lady, dressed magnificently, but wearing a mask, who appeared to me to be observing my ward with extraordinary interest. I had seen her, earlier in the evening, in the great hall, and again, for a few minutes, walking near us, on the terrace under the castle windows, similarly employed. A lady, also masked, richly and gravely dressed, and with a stately air, like a person of rank, accompanied her as a chaperon.

"Had the young lady not worn a mask, I could, of course, have been much more certain upon the question whether she was really watching my poor darling.

"I am now well assured that she was.

"We were now in one of the salons. My poor dear child had been dancing, and was resting a little in one of the chairs near the door; I was standing near. The two ladies I have mentioned had approached and the younger took the chair next my ward; while her companion stood beside me, and for a little time addressed herself, in a low tone, to her charge.

"Availing herself of the privilege of her mask, she turned to me, and in the tone of an old friend, and calling me by my name, opened a conversation with me, which piqued my curiosity a good deal. She referred to many scenes where she had met me—at Court, and at distinguished houses. She alluded to little incidents which I had long ceased to think of, but which, I found, had only lain in abeyance in my memory, for they instantly started into life at her touch.

"I became more and more curious to ascertain who she was, every moment. She parried my attempts to discover very adroitly and pleasantly. The knowledge she showed of many passages in my life seemed to me all but unaccountable; and she appeared to take a not unnatural pleasure in foiling my curiosity, and in seeing me flounder in my eager perplexity, from one conjecture to another.

"In the meantime the young lady, whom her mother called by the odd name of Millarca, when she once or twice addressed her, had, with the same ease and grace, got into conversation with my ward.

"She introduced herself by saying that her mother was a very old acquaintance of mine. She spoke of the agreeable audacity which a mask rendered practicable; she talked like a friend; she admired her dress, and insinuated very prettily her admiration of her beauty. She amused her with laughing criticisms upon the people who crowded the ballroom, and laughed at my poor child's fun. She was very witty and lively when she pleased, and after a time they had grown very good friends, and the young stranger lowered her mask, displaying a remarkably beautiful face. I had never seen it before, neither had my dear child. But though it was new to us, the features were so engaging, as well as lovely, that it was impossible not to feel the attraction powerfully. My poor girl did so. I never saw anyone more taken with another at first sight, unless, indeed, it was the stranger herself, who seemed quite to have lost her heart to her.

"In the meantime, availing myself of the license of a masquerade, I put not a few questions to the elder lady.

"'You have puzzled me utterly,' I said, laughing. 'Is that not enough? Won't you, now, consent to stand on equal terms, and do me the kindness to remove your mask?'

"'Can any request be more unreasonable?' she replied. 'Ask a lady to yield an advantage! Beside, how do you know you should recognize me? Years make changes.'

"'As you see,' I said, with a bow, and, I suppose, a rather melancholy little laugh.

"'As philosophers tell us,' she said; 'and how do you know that a sight of my face would help you?'

"'I should take chance for that,' I answered. 'It is vain trying to make yourself out an old woman; your figure betrays you.'

"'Years, nevertheless, have passed since I saw you, rather since you saw me, for that is what I am considering. Millarca, there, is my daughter; I cannot then be young, even in the opinion of people whom time has taught to be indulgent, and I may not like to be compared with what you remember me. You have no mask to remove. You can offer me nothing in exchange.'

"'My petition is to your pity, to remove it.'

"'And mine to yours, to let it stay where it is,' she replied.

"'Well, then, at least you will tell me whether you are French or German; you speak both languages so perfectly.'

"'I don't think I shall tell you that, General; you intend a surprise, and are meditating the particular point of attack.'

"'At all events, you won't deny this,' I said, 'that being honoured by your permission to converse, I ought to know how to address you. Shall I say *Madame la Comtesse*?'

"She laughed, and she would, no doubt, have met me with another evasion—if, indeed, I can treat any occurrence in an interview every circumstance of which was prearranged, as I now believe, with the profoundest cunning, as liable to be modified by accident.

"'As to that,' she began; but she was interrupted, almost as she opened her lips, by a gentleman, dressed in black, who looked particularly elegant and distinguished, with this drawback, that his face was the most deadly pale I ever saw, except in death. He was in no masquerade—in the plain evening dress of a gentleman; and he said, without a smile, but with a courtly and unusually low bow:——

"'Will *Madame la Comtesse* permit me to say a very few words which may interest her?'

"The lady turned quickly to him, and touched her lip in token of silence; she then said to me, 'Keep my place for me, General; I shall return when I have said a few words.'

"And with this injunction, playfully given, she walked a little aside with the gentleman in black, and talked for some minutes, apparently very earnestly. They then walked away slowly together in the crowd, and I lost them for some minutes.

"I spent the interval in cudgelling my brains for a conjecture as to the identity of the lady who seemed to remember me so kindly, and I was thinking of turning about and joining in the conversation between my pretty ward and the Countess's daughter, and trying whether, by the time she returned, I might not have a surprise in store for her, by having her name, title, *château*, and estates at my fingers' ends. But at this moment she returned, accompanied by the pale man in black, who said:

"'I shall return and inform *Madame la Comtesse* when her carriage is at the door.'

"He withdrew with a bow."

Chapter 12
A Petition

"'Then we are to lose *Madame la Comtesse*, but I hope only for a few hours,' I said, with a low bow.

"'It may be that only, or it may be a few weeks. It was very unlucky his speaking to me just now as he did. Do you now know me?'

"I assured her I did not.

"'You shall know me,' she said, 'but not at present. We are older and better friends than, perhaps, you suspect. I cannot yet declare myself. I shall in three weeks pass your beautiful *schloss*, about which I have been making enquiries. I shall then look in upon you for an hour or two, and renew a friendship which I never think of without a thousand pleasant recollections. This moment a piece of news has reached me like a thunderbolt. I must set out now, and travel by a devious route, nearly a hundred miles, with all the dispatch I can possibly make. My perplexities multiply. I am only deterred by the compulsory reserve I practice as to my name from making a very singular request of you. My poor child has not quite recovered her strength.

"Her horse fell with her, at a hunt which she had ridden out to witness, her nerves have not yet recovered the shock, and our physician says that she must on no account exert herself for some time to come. We came here, in consequence, by very easy stages—hardly six leagues a day. I must now travel day and night, on a mission of life and death—a mission the critical and momentous nature of which I shall be able to explain to you when we meet, as I hope we shall, in a few weeks, without the necessity of any concealment.'

"She went on to make her petition, and it was in the tone of a person from whom such a request amounted to conferring, rather than seeking a favour.

"This was only in manner, and, as it seemed, quite unconsciously. Than the terms in which it was expressed, nothing could be more deprecatory. It was simply that I would consent to take charge of her daughter during her absence.

"This was, all things considered, a strange, not to say, an audacious request. She in some sort disarmed me, by stating and admitting everything that could be urged against it, and throwing herself entirely upon my chivalry. At the same moment, by a fatality that seems to have predetermined all that happened, my poor child came to my side, and, in an undertone, besought me to invite her new friend, Millarca, to pay us a visit. She had just been sounding her, and thought, if her mamma would allow her, she would like it extremely.

"At another time I should have told her to wait a little, until, at least, we knew who they were. But I had not a moment to think in. The two ladies assailed me together, and I must confess the refined and beautiful face of the young lady, about which there was something extremely engaging, as well as the elegance and fire of high birth, determined me; and, quite overpowered, I submitted, and undertook, too easily, the care of the young lady, whom her mother called Millarca.

"The Countess beckoned to her daughter, who listened with grave attention while she told her, in general terms, how suddenly and peremptorily she had been summoned, and also of the arrangement she had made for her under my care, adding that I was one of her earliest and most valued friends.

"I made, of course, such speeches as the case seemed to call for, and found myself, on reflection, in a position which I did not half like.

"The gentleman in black returned, and very ceremoniously conducted the lady from the room.

"The demeanour of this gentleman was such as to impress me with the conviction that the Countess was a lady of very much more importance than her modest title alone might have led me to assume.

"Her last charge to me was that no attempt was to be made to learn more about her than I might have already guessed, until her return. Our distinguished host, whose guest she was, knew her reasons.

"'But here,' she said, 'neither I nor my daughter could safely remain for more than a day. I removed my mask imprudently for a moment, about an hour ago, and, too late, I fancied you saw me. So I resolved to seek an opportunity of talking a little to you. Had I found that you had seen me, I would have thrown myself on your high sense of honor to keep my secret some weeks. As it is, I am satisfied that you did not see me; but if you now suspect, or, on reflection, should suspect, who I am, I commit myself, in like manner, entirely to your honor. My daughter will observe the same secrecy, and I well know that you will, from time to time, remind her, lest she should thoughtlessly disclose it.'

"She whispered a few words to her daughter, kissed her hurriedly twice, and went away, accompanied by the pale gentleman in black, and disappeared in the crowd.

"'In the next room,' said Millarca, 'there is a window that

looks upon the hall door. I should like to see the last of mamma, and to kiss my hand to her.'

"We assented, of course, and accompanied her to the window. We looked out, and saw a handsome old-fashioned carriage, with a troop of couriers and footmen. We saw the slim figure of the pale gentleman in black, as he held a thick velvet cloak, and placed it about her shoulders and threw the hood over her head. She nodded to him, and just touched his hand with hers. He bowed low repeatedly as the door closed, and the carriage began to move.

"'She is gone,' said Millarca, with a sigh.

"'She is gone,' I repeated to myself, for the first time—in the hurried moments that had elapsed since my consent—reflecting upon the folly of my act.

"'She did not look up,' said the young lady, plaintively.

"'The Countess had taken off her mask, perhaps, and did not care to show her face,' I said; 'and she could not know that you were in the window.'

"She sighed, and looked in my face. She was so beautiful that I relented. I was sorry I had for a moment repented of my hospitality, and I determined to make her amends for the unavowed churlishness of my reception.

"The young lady, replacing her mask, joined my ward in persuading me to return to the grounds, where the concert was soon to be renewed. We did so, and walked up and down the terrace that lies under the castle windows.

"Millarca became very intimate with us, and amused us with lively descriptions and stories of most of the great people whom we saw upon the terrace. I liked her more and more every minute. Her gossip without being ill-natured, was extremely diverting to me, who had been so long out of the great world. I thought what life she would give to our sometimes lonely evenings at home.

"This ball was not over until the morning sun had almost reached the horizon. It pleased the Grand Duke to dance till then, so loyal people could not go away, or think of bed.

"We had just got through a crowded saloon, when my ward asked me what had become of Millarca. I thought she had been by her side, and she fancied she was by mine. The fact was, we had lost her.

"All my efforts to find her were vain. I feared that she had mistaken, in the confusion of a momentary separation from us, other people for her new friends, and had, possibly, pursued and lost them in the extensive grounds which were thrown open to us.

"Now, in its full force, I recognized a new folly in my having undertaken the charge of a young lady without so much as knowing her name; and fettered as I was by promises, of the reasons for imposing which I knew nothing, I could not even point my inquiries by saying that the missing young lady was the daughter of the Countess who had taken her departure a few hours before.

"Morning broke. It was clear daylight before I gave up my search. It was not till near two o'clock next day that we heard anything of my missing charge.

"At about that time a servant knocked at my niece's door, to say that he had been earnestly requested by a young lady, who appeared to be in great distress, to make out where she could find the General Baron Spielsdorf and the young lady his daughter, in whose charge she had been left by her mother.

"There could be no doubt, notwithstanding the slight inaccuracy, that our young friend had turned up; and so she had. Would to heaven we had lost her!

"She told my poor child a story to account for her having failed to recover us for so long. Very late, she said, she had got to the housekeeper's bedroom in despair of finding us, and had then fallen into a deep sleep which, long as it was, had hardly sufficed to recruit her strength after the fatigues of the ball.

"That day Millarca came home with us. I was only too happy, after all, to have secured so charming a companion for my dear girl."

CHAPTER 13
THE WOODMAN

"There soon, however, appeared some drawbacks. In the first place, Millarca complained of extreme languor—the weakness that remained after her late illness—and she never emerged from her room till the afternoon was pretty far advanced. In the next place, it was accidentally discovered, although she always locked her door on the inside, and never disturbed the key from its place till she admitted the maid to assist at her toilet, that she was undoubtedly sometimes absent from her room in the very early morning, and at various times later in the day, before she wished it to be understood that she was stirring. She was repeatedly seen from the windows of the *schloss*, in the first faint grey of the morning, walking through the trees, in an easterly direction, and looking like a person in a trance. This convinced me that she walked in her sleep. But this hypothesis did not solve the puzzle. How did she pass out from her room, leaving the door locked on the inside? How did she escape from the house without un-barring door or window?

"In the midst of my perplexities, an anxiety of a far more urgent kind presented itself.

"My dear child began to lose her looks and health, and that in a manner so mysterious, and even horrible, that I became thoroughly frightened.

"She was at first visited by appalling dreams; then, as she fancied, by a spectre, sometimes resembling Millarca, sometimes in the shape of a beast, indistinctly seen, walking round the foot of her bed, from side to side.

"Lastly came sensations. One, not unpleasant, but very peculiar, she said, resembled the flow of an icy stream against her breast. At a later time, she felt something like a pair of large needles pierce her, a little below the throat, with a very sharp pain. A few nights after, followed a gradual and convulsive sense of strangulation; then came unconsciousness."

I could hear distinctly every word the kind old General was saying, because by this time we were driving upon the short grass that spreads on either side of the road as you approach the roofless village which had not shown the smoke of a chimney for more than half a century.

You may guess how strangely I felt as I heard my own symptoms so exactly described in those which had been experienced by the poor girl who, but for the catastrophe which followed, would have been at that moment a visitor at my father's *chateau*. You may suppose, also, how I felt as I heard him detail habits and mysterious peculiarities which were, in fact, those of our beautiful guest, Carmilla!

A *vista* opened in the forest; we were on a sudden under the chimneys and gables of the ruined village, and the towers and battlements of the dismantled castle, round which gigantic trees are grouped, overhung us from a slight eminence.

In a frightened dream I got down from the carriage, and in silence, for we had each abundant matter for thinking; we soon mounted the ascent, and were among the spacious chambers, winding stairs, and dark corridors of the castle.

"And this was once the palatial residence of the Karnsteins!" said the old General at length, as from a great window he looked out across the village, and saw the wide, undulating expanse of forest. "It was a bad family, and here its bloodstained annals were written," he continued. "It is hard that they should, after death, continue to plague the human race with their atrocious lusts. That is the chapel of the Karnsteins, down there."

He pointed down to the grey walls of the Gothic building partly visible through the foliage, a little way down the steep. "And I hear the axe of a woodman," he added, "busy among the trees that surround it; he possibly may give us the information of which I am in search, and point out the grave of Mircalla, Countess of Karnstein. These rustics preserve the local traditions of great families, whose stories die out among the rich and titled so soon as the families themselves become extinct."

"We have a portrait, at home, of Mircalla, the Countess Karnstein; should you like to see it?" asked my father.

"Time enough, dear friend," replied the General. "I believe

that I have seen the original; and one motive which has led me to you earlier than I at first intended, was to explore the chapel which we are now approaching."

"What! see the Countess Mircalla," exclaimed my father; "why, she has been dead more than a century!"

"Not so dead as you fancy, I am told," answered the General.

"I confess, General, you puzzle me utterly," replied my father, looking at him, I fancied, for a moment with a return of the suspicion I detected before. But although there was anger and detestation, at times, in the old General's manner, there was nothing flighty.

"There remains to me," he said, as we passed under the heavy arch of the Gothic church—for its dimensions would have justified its being so styled—"but one object which can interest me during the few years that remain to me on earth, and that is to wreak on her the vengeance which, I thank God, may still be accomplished by a mortal arm."

"What vengeance can you mean?" asked my father, in increasing amazement.

"I mean, to decapitate the monster," he answered, with a fierce flush, and a stamp that echoed mournfully through the hollow ruin, and his clenched hand was at the same moment raised, as if it grasped the handle of an axe, while he shook it ferociously in the air.

"What?" exclaimed my father, more than ever bewildered.

"To strike her head off."

"Cut her head off!"

"Aye, with a hatchet, with a spade, or with anything that can cleave through her murderous throat. You shall hear," he answered, trembling with rage. And hurrying forward he said:

"That beam will answer for a seat; your dear child is fatigued; let her be seated, and I will, in a few sentences, close my dreadful story."

The squared block of wood, which lay on the grass-grown pavement of the chapel, formed a bench on which I was very glad to seat myself, and in the meantime the General called to the woodman, who had been removing some boughs which leaned upon the old walls; and, axe in hand, the hardy old fellow stood before us.

He could not tell us anything of these monuments; but there was an old man, he said, a ranger of this forest, at present sojourning in the house of the priest, about two miles away, who could point out every monument of the old Karnstein family; and, for a trifle, he undertook to bring him back with him, if we would lend him one of our horses, in little more than half an hour.

"Have you been long employed about this forest?" asked my father of the old man.

"I have been a woodman here," he answered in his patois, "under the forester, all my days; so has my father before me, and so on, as many generations as I can count up. I could show you the very house in the village here, in which my ancestors lived."

"How came the village to be deserted?" asked the General.

"It was troubled by revenants, sir; several were tracked to their graves, there detected by the usual tests, and extinguished in the usual way, by decapitation, by the stake, and by burning; but not until many of the villagers were killed.

"But after all these proceedings according to law," he continued—"so many graves opened, and so many vampires deprived of their horrible animation—the village was not relieved. But a Moravian nobleman, who happened to be traveling this way, heard how matters were, and being skilled—as many people are in his country—in such affairs, he offered to deliver the village from its tormentor. He did so thus: There being a bright moon that night, he ascended, shortly after sunset, the towers of the chapel here, from whence he could distinctly see the churchyard beneath him; you can see it from that window. From this point he watched until he saw the vampire come out of his grave, and place near it the linen clothes in which he had been folded, and then glide away towards the village to plague its inhabitants.

"The stranger, having seen all this, came down from the steeple, took the linen wrappings of the vampire, and carried them up to the top of the tower, which he again mounted. When the vampire returned from his prowlings and missed his clothes, he cried furiously to the Moravian, whom he saw at the summit of the tower, and who, in reply, beckoned him to ascend and take them. Whereupon the vampire, accepting his invitation, began to climb the steeple, and so soon as he had reached the battlements, the Moravian, with a stroke of his sword, clove his skull in twain, hurling him down to the churchyard, whither, descending by the winding stairs, the stranger followed and cut his head off, and next day delivered it and the body to the villagers, who duly impaled and burnt them.

"This Moravian nobleman had authority from the then head of the family to remove the tomb of Mircalla, Countess Karnstein, which he did effectually, so that in a little while its site was quite forgotten."

"Can you point out where it stood?" asked the General, eagerly.

The forester shook his head, and smiled.

"Not a soul living could tell you that now," he said; "besides, they say her body was removed; but no one is sure of that either."

Having thus spoken, as time pressed, he dropped his axe and departed, leaving us to hear the remainder of the General's strange story.

CHAPTER 14
THE MEETING

"My beloved child," he resumed, "was now growing rapidly worse. The physician who attended her had failed to produce the slightest impression on her disease, for such I then supposed it to be. He saw my alarm, and suggested a consultation. I called in an abler physician, from Gratz.

"Several days elapsed before he arrived. He was a good and pious, as well as a learned man. Having seen my poor ward together, they withdrew to my library to confer and discuss. I, from the adjoining room, where I awaited their summons, heard these two gentlemen's voices raised in something sharper than a strictly philosophical discussion. I knocked at the door and entered. I found the old physician from Gratz maintaining his theory. His rival was combating it with undisguised ridicule, accompanied with bursts of laughter. This unseemly manifestation subsided and the altercation ended on my entrance.

"'Sir,' said my first physician, 'my learned brother seems to think that you want a conjuror, and not a doctor.'

"'Pardon me,' said the old physician from Gratz, looking displeased, 'I shall state my own view of the case in my own way another time. I grieve, *Monsieur le General*, that by my skill and science I can be of no use. Before I go I shall do myself the honour to suggest something to you.'

"He seemed thoughtful, and sat down at a table and began to write.

"Profoundly disappointed, I made my bow, and as I turned to go, the other doctor pointed over his shoulder to his companion who was writing, and then, with a shrug, significantly touched his forehead.

"This consultation, then, left me precisely where I was. I walked out into the grounds, all but distracted. The doctor from Gratz, in ten or fifteen minutes, overtook me. He apologized for having followed me, but said that he could not conscientiously take his leave without a few words more. He told me that he could not be mistaken; no natural disease exhibited the same symptoms; and that death was already very near. There remained, however, a day, or possibly two, of life. If the fatal seizure were at once arrested, with great care and skill her strength might possibly return. But all hung now upon the confines of the irrevocable. One more assault might extinguish the last spark of vitality which is, every moment, ready to die.

"'And what is the nature of the seizure you speak of?' I entreated.

"'I have stated all fully in this note, which I place in your hands upon the distinct condition that you send for the nearest clergyman, and open my letter in his presence, and on no account read it till he is with you; you would despise it else, and it is a matter of life and death. Should the priest fail you, then, indeed, you may read it.'

"He asked me, before taking his leave finally, whether I would wish to see a man curiously learned upon the very subject, which, after I had read his letter, would probably interest me above all others, and he urged me earnestly to invite him to visit him there; and so took his leave.

"The ecclesiastic was absent, and I read the letter by myself. At another time, or in another case, it might have excited my ridicule. But into what quackeries will not people rush for a last chance, where all accustomed means have failed, and the life of a beloved object is at stake?

"Nothing, you will say, could be more absurd than the learned man's letter.

"It was monstrous enough to have consigned him to a madhouse. He said that the patient was suffering from the visits of a vampire! The punctures which she described as having occurred near the throat, were, he insisted, the insertion of those two long, thin, and sharp teeth which, it is well known, are peculiar to vampires; and there could be no doubt, he added, as to the well-defined presence of the small livid mark which all concurred in describing as that induced by the demon's lips, and every symptom described by the sufferer was in exact conformity with those recorded in every case of a similar visitation.

"Being myself wholly sceptical as to the existence of any such portent as the vampire, the supernatural theory of the good doctor furnished, in my opinion, but another instance of learning and intelligence oddly associated with some one hallucination. I was so miserable, however, that, rather than try nothing, I acted upon the instructions of the letter.

"I concealed myself in the dark dressing room, that opened upon the poor patient's room, in which a candle was burning, and watched there till she was fast asleep. I stood at the door,

76

peeping through the small crevice, my sword laid on the table beside me, as my directions prescribed, until, a little after one, I saw a large black object, very ill-defined, crawl, as it seemed to me, over the foot of the bed, and swiftly spread itself up to the poor girl's throat, where it swelled, in a moment, into a great, palpitating mass.

"For a few moments I had stood petrified. I now sprang forward, with my sword in my hand. The black creature suddenly contracted towards the foot of the bed, glided over it, and, standing on the floor about a yard below the foot of the bed, with a glare of skulking ferocity and horror fixed on me, I saw Millarca. Speculating I know not what, I struck at her instantly with my sword; but I saw her standing near the door, unscathed. Horrified, I pursued, and struck again. She was gone; and my sword flew to shivers against the door.

"I can't describe to you all that passed on that horrible night. The whole house was up and stirring. The spectre Millarca was gone. But her victim was sinking fast, and before the morning dawned, she died."

The old General was agitated. We did not speak to him. My father walked to some little distance, and began reading the inscriptions on the tombstones; and thus occupied, he strolled into the door of a side chapel to prosecute his researches. The General leaned against the wall, dried his eyes, and sighed heavily. I was relieved on hearing the voices of Carmilla and *Madame*, who were at that moment approaching. The voices died away.

In this solitude, having just listened to so strange a story, connected, as it was, with the great and titled dead, whose monuments were mouldering among the dust and ivy round us, and every incident of which bore so awfully upon my own mysterious case—in this haunted spot, darkened by the towering foliage that rose on every side, dense and high above its noiseless walls—a horror began to steal over me, and my heart sank as I thought that my friends were, after all, not about to enter and disturb this triste and ominous scene.

The old General's eyes were fixed on the ground, as he leaned with his hand upon the basement of a shattered monument.

Under a narrow, arched doorway, surmounted by one of those demoniacal grotesques in which the cynical and ghastly fancy of old Gothic carving delights, I saw very gladly the beautiful face and figure of Carmilla enter the shadowy chapel.

I was just about to rise and speak, and nodded smiling, in answer to her peculiarly engaging smile; when with a cry, the old man by my side caught up the woodman's hatchet, and started forward. On seeing him a brutalized change came over her features. It was an instantaneous and horrible transformation, as she made a crouching step backwards. Before I could utter a scream, he struck at her with all his force, but she dived under his blow, and unscathed, caught him in her tiny grasp by the wrist. He struggled for a moment to release his arm, but his hand opened, the axe fell to the ground, and the girl was gone.

He staggered against the wall. His grey hair stood upon his head, and a moisture shone over his face, as if he were at the point of death.

The frightful scene had passed in a moment. The first thing I recollect after, is *Madame* standing before me, and impatiently repeating again and again, the question, "Where is Mademoiselle Carmilla?"

I answered at length, "I don't know—I can't tell—she went there," and I pointed to the door through which *Madame* had just entered; "only a minute or two since."

"But I have been standing there, in the passage, ever since Mademoiselle Carmilla entered; and she did not return."

She then began to call "Carmilla," through every door and passage and from the windows, but no answer came.

"She called herself Carmilla?" asked the General, still agitated.

"Carmilla, yes," I answered.

"Aye," he said; "that is Millarca. That is the same person who long ago was called Mircalla, Countess Karnstein. Depart from this accursed ground, my poor child, as quickly as you can. Drive to the clergyman's house, and stay there till we come. Begone!

May you never behold Carmilla more; you will not find her here."

CHAPTER 15
ORDEAL AND EXECUTION

As he spoke one of the strangest looking men I ever beheld entered the chapel at the door through which Carmilla had made her entrance and her exit. He was tall, narrow-chested, stooping, with high shoulders, and dressed in black. His face was brown and dried in with deep furrows; he wore an oddly-shaped hat with a broad leaf. His hair, long and grizzled, hung on his shoulders. He wore a pair of gold spectacles, and walked slowly, with an odd shambling gait, with his face sometimes turned up to the sky, and sometimes bowed down towards the ground, seemed to wear a perpetual smile; his long thin arms were swinging, and his lank hands, in old black gloves ever so much too wide for them, waving and gesticulating in utter abstraction.

"The very man!" exclaimed the General, advancing with manifest delight. "My dear Baron, how happy I am to see you, I had no hope of meeting you so soon." He signed to my father, who had by this time returned, and leading the fantastic old gentleman, whom he called the Baron to meet him. He introduced him formally, and they at once entered into earnest conversation. The stranger took a roll of paper from his pocket, and spread it on the worn surface of a tomb that stood by. He had a pencil case in his fingers, with which he traced imaginary lines from point to point on the paper, which from their often glancing from it, together, at certain points of the building, I concluded to be a plan of the chapel. He accompanied, what I may term, his lecture, with occasional readings from a dirty little book, whose yellow leaves were closely written over.

They sauntered together down the side aisle, opposite to the spot where I was standing, conversing as they went; then they began measuring distances by paces, and finally they all stood together, facing a piece of the sidewall, which they began to examine with great minuteness; pulling off the ivy that clung over it, and rapping the plaster with the ends of their sticks, scraping here, and knocking there. At length they ascertained the existence of a broad marble tablet, with letters carved in relief upon it.

With the assistance of the woodman, who soon returned, a monumental inscription, and carved escutcheon, were disclosed. They proved to be those of the long lost monument of Mircalla, Countess Karnstein.

The old General, though not I fear given to the praying mood, raised his hands and eyes to heaven, in mute thanksgiving for some moments.

"Tomorrow," I heard him say; "the commissioner will be here, and the Inquisition will be held according to law."

Then turning to the old man with the gold spectacles, whom I have described, he shook him warmly by both hands and said:

"Baron, how can I thank you? How can we all thank you? You will have delivered this region from a plague that has scourged its inhabitants for more than a century. The horrible enemy, thank God, is at last tracked."

My father led the stranger aside, and the General followed. I know that he had led them out of hearing, that he might relate my case, and I saw them glance often quickly at me, as the discussion proceeded.

My father came to me, kissed me again and again, and leading me from the chapel, said:

"It is time to return, but before we go home, we must add to our party the good priest, who lives but a little way from this; and persuade him to accompany us to the *schloss*."

In this quest we were successful: and I was glad, being unspeakably fatigued when we reached home. But my satisfaction was changed to dismay, on discovering that there were no tidings of Carmilla. Of the scene that had occurred in the ruined chapel, no explanation was offered to me, and it was clear that it was a secret which my father for the present determined to keep from me.

The sinister absence of Carmilla made the remembrance of

the scene more horrible to me. The arrangements for the night were singular. Two servants, and *Madame* were to sit up in my room that night; and the ecclesiastic with my father kept watch in the adjoining dressing room.

The priest had performed certain solemn rites that night, the purport of which I did not understand any more than I comprehended the reason of this extraordinary precaution taken for my safety during sleep.

I saw all clearly a few days later.

The disappearance of Carmilla was followed by the discontinuance of my nightly sufferings.

You have heard, no doubt, of the appalling superstition that prevails in Upper and Lower Styria, in Moravia, Silesia, in Turkish Serbia, in Poland, even in Russia; the superstition, so we must call it, of the Vampire.

If human testimony, taken with every care and solemnity, judicially, before commissions innumerable, each consisting of many members, all chosen for integrity and intelligence, and constituting reports more voluminous perhaps than exist upon any one other class of cases, is worth anything, it is difficult to deny, or even to doubt the existence of such a phenomenon as the Vampire.

For my part I have heard no theory by which to explain what I myself have witnessed and experienced, other than that supplied by the ancient and well-attested belief of the country.

The next day the formal proceedings took place in the Chapel of Karnstein.

The grave of the Countess Mircalla was opened; and the General and my father recognized each his perfidious and beautiful guest, in the face now disclosed to view. The features, though a hundred and fifty years had passed since her funeral, were tinted with the warmth of life. Her eyes were open; no cadaverous smell exhaled from the coffin. The two medical men, one officially present, the other on the part of the promoter of the inquiry, attested the marvellous fact that there was a faint but appreciable respiration, and a corresponding action of the heart. The limbs were perfectly flexible, the flesh elastic; and the leaden coffin floated with blood, in which to a depth of seven inches, the body lay immersed.

Here then, were all the admitted signs and proofs of vampirism. The body, therefore, in accordance with the ancient practice, was raised, and a sharp stake driven through the heart of the vampire, who uttered a piercing shriek at the moment, in all respects such as might escape from a living person in the last agony. Then the head was struck off, and a torrent of blood flowed from the severed neck. The body and head was next placed on a pile of wood, and reduced to ashes, which were thrown upon the river and borne away, and that territory has never since been plagued by the visits of a vampire.

My father has a copy of the report of the Imperial Commission, with the signatures of all who were present at these proceedings, attached in verification of the statement. It is from this official paper that I have summarized my account of this last shocking scene.

CHAPTER 16
CONCLUSION

I write all this you suppose with composure. But far from it; I cannot think of it without agitation. Nothing but your earnest desire so repeatedly expressed, could have induced me to sit down to a task that has unstrung my nerves for months to come, and reinduced a shadow of the unspeakable horror which years after my deliverance continued to make my days and nights dreadful, and solitude insupportably terrific.

Let me add a word or two about that quaint Baron Vordenburg, to whose curious lore we were indebted for the discovery of the Countess Mircalla's grave.

He had taken up his abode in Gratz, where, living upon a mere pittance, which was all that remained to him of the once princely estates of his family, in Upper Styria, he devoted himself to the minute and laborious investigation of the marvelously authenticated tradition of Vampirism. He had at his fingers' ends all the great and little works upon the subject.

Magia Posthuma, Phlegon de Mirabilibus, Augustinus de cura pro Mortuis, Philosophicae et Christianae Cogitationes de Vampiris, by John Christofer Herenberg; and a thousand others, among which I remember only a few of those which he lent to my father. He had a voluminous digest of all the judicial cases, from which he had extracted a system of principles that appear to govern—some always, and others occasionally only—the condition of the vampire. I may mention, in passing, that the deadly pallor attributed to that sort of revenants, is a mere melodramatic fiction. They present, in the grave, and when they show themselves in human society, the appearance of healthy life. When disclosed to light in their coffins, they exhibit all the symptoms that are enumerated as those which proved the vampire-life of the long-dead Countess Karnstein.

How they escape from their graves and return to them for certain hours every day, without displacing the clay or leaving any trace of disturbance in the state of the coffin or the cerements, has always been admitted to be utterly inexplicable. The amphibious existence of the vampire is sustained by daily renewed slumber in the grave. Its horrible lust for living blood supplies the vigour of its waking existence. The vampire is prone to be fascinated with an engrossing vehemence, resembling the passion of love, by particular persons. In pursuit of these it will exercise inexhaustible patience and stratagem, for access to a particular object may be obstructed in a hundred ways.

It will never desist until it has satiated its passion, and drained the very life of its coveted victim. But it will, in these cases, husband and protract its murderous enjoyment with the refinement of an epicure, and heighten it by the gradual approaches of an artful courtship. In these cases it seems to yearn for something like sympathy and consent. In ordinary ones it goes direct to its object, overpowers with violence, and strangles and exhausts often at a single feast.

The vampire is, apparently, subject, in certain situations, to special conditions. In the particular instance of which I have given you a relation, Mircalla seemed to be limited to a name which, if not her real one, should at least reproduce, without the omission or addition of a single letter, those, as we say, anagram-matically, which compose it.

Carmilla did this; so did Millarca.

My father related to the Baron Vordenburg, who remained with us for two or three weeks after the expulsion of Carmil-la, the story about the Moravian nobleman and the vampire at Karnstein churchyard, and then he asked the Baron how he had discovered the exact position of the long-concealed tomb of the Countess Mircalla? The Baron's grotesque features puckered up into a mysterious smile; he looked down, still smiling on his worn spectacle case and fumbled with it. Then looking up, he said:

"I have many journals, and other papers, written by that remarkable man; the most curious among them is one treat-ing of the visit of which you speak, to Karnstein. The tradition, of course, discolours and distorts a little. He might have been termed a Moravian nobleman, for he had changed his abode to that territory, and was, beside, a noble. But he was, in truth, a na-tive of Upper Styria. It is enough to say that in very early youth he had been a passionate and favoured lover of the beautiful Mircalla, Countess Karnstein. Her early death plunged him into inconsolable grief. It is the nature of vampires to increase and multiply, but according to an ascertained and ghostly law.

"Assume, at starting, a territory perfectly free from that pest. How does it begin, and how does it multiply itself? I will tell you. A person, more or less wicked, puts an end to himself. A suicide, under certain circumstances, becomes a vampire. That spectre visits living people in their slumbers; they die, and almost invariably, in the grave, develop into vampires. This happened in the case of the beautiful Mircalla, who was haunted by one of those demons. My ancestor, Vordenburg, whose title I still bear, soon discovered this, and in the course of the studies to which he devoted himself, learned a great deal more.

"Among other things, he concluded that suspicion of vampirism would probably fall, sooner or later, upon the dead Countess, who in life had been his idol. He conceived a horror, be she what she might, of her remains being profaned by the outrage of a posthumous execution. He has left a curious paper to prove that the vampire, on its expulsion from its amphibious existence, is projected into a far more horrible life; and he resolved to save his once beloved Mircalla from this.

"He adopted the stratagem of a journey here, a pretended removal of her remains, and a real obliteration of her monument. When age had stolen upon him, and from the vale of years, he looked back on the scenes he was leaving, he considered, in a different spirit, what he had done, and a horror took possession of him. He made the tracings and notes which have guided me to the very spot, and drew up a confession of the deception that he had practiced. If he had intended any further action in this matter, death prevented him; and the hand of a remote descendant has, too late for many, directed the pursuit to the lair of the beast."

We talked a little more, and among other things he said was this:

"One sign of the vampire is the power of the hand. The slender hand of Mircalla closed like a vice of steel on the General's wrist when he raised the hatchet to strike. But its power is not confined to its grasp; it leaves a numbness in the limb it seizes, which is slowly, if ever, recovered from."

The following Spring my father took me a tour through Italy. We remained away for more than a year. It was long before the terror of recent events subsided; and to this hour the image of Carmilla returns to memory with ambiguous alternations-sometimes the playful, languid, beautiful girl; sometimes the writhing fiend I saw in the ruined church; and often from a reverie I have started, fancying I heard the light step of Carmilla at the drawing room door.

The Haunted Baronet

(A novella developed from the short story
The Fortunes of Sir Robert Ardagh.)

CHAPTER 1

THE GEORGE AND DRAGON

The pretty little town of Golden Friars—standing by the margin of the lake, hemmed round by an amphitheatre of purple mountain, rich in tint and furrowed by ravines, high in air, when the tall gables and narrow windows of its ancient graystone houses, and the tower of the old church, from which every evening the curfew still rings, show like silver in the moonbeams, and the black elms that stand round throw moveless shadows upon the short level grass—is one of the most singular and beautiful sights I have ever seen.

There it rises, 'as from the stroke of the enchanter's wand,' looking so light and filmy, that you could scarcely believe it more than a picture reflected on the thin mist of night.

On such a still summer night the moon shone splendidly upon the front of the George and Dragon, the comfortable graystone inn of Golden Friars, with the grandest specimen of the old inn-sign, perhaps, left in England. It looks right across the lake; the road that skirts its margin running by the steps of the hall-door, opposite to which, at the other side of the road, between two great posts, and framed in a fanciful wrought-iron border splendid with gilding, swings the famous sign of St. George and the Dragon, gorgeous with colour and gold.

In the great room of the George and Dragon, three or four of the old *habitues* of that cozy lounge were refreshing a little after the fatigues of the day.

This is a comfortable chamber, with an oak wainscot; and whenever in summer months the air is sharp enough, as on the present occasion, a fire helped to light it up; which fire, being chiefly wood, made a pleasant broad flicker on panel and ceiling, and yet did not make the room too hot.

On one side sat Doctor Torvey, the doctor of Golden Friars, who knew the weak point of every man in the town, and what medicine agreed with each inhabitant—a fat gentleman, with a jolly laugh and an appetite for all sorts of news, big and little, and who liked a pipe, and made a tumbler of punch at about this hour, with a bit of lemon-peel in it. Beside him sat William Peers, a thin old gentleman, who had lived for more than thirty years in India, and was quiet and benevolent, and the last man in Golden Friars who wore a pigtail.

Old Jack Amerald, an ex-captain of the navy, with his short stout leg on a chair, and its wooden companion beside it, sipped his grog, and bawled in the old-fashioned navy way, and called his friends his 'hearties.' In the middle, opposite the hearth, sat deaf Tom Hollar, always placid, and smoked his pipe, looking serenely at the fire. And the landlord of the George and Dragon every now and then strutted in, and sat down in the high-backed wooden arm-chair, according to the old-fashioned republican ways of the place, and took his share in the talk gravely, and was heartily welcome.

"And so Sir Bale is coming home at last," said the Doctor. "Tell us any more you heard since."

"Nothing," answered Richard Turnbull, the host of the George. "Nothing to speak of; only 'tis certain sure, and so best; the old house won't look so dowly now."

"Twyne says the estate owes a good capful o' money by this time, hey?" said the Doctor, lowering his voice and winking.

"Weel, they do say he's been nout at dow. I don't mind saying so to *you*, mind, sir, where all's friends together; but he'll get that right in time."

"More like to save here than where he is," said the Doctor with another grave nod.

"He does very wisely," said Mr. Peers, having blown out a thin stream of smoke, "and creditably, to pull up in time. He's coming here to save a little, and perhaps he'll marry; and it is the more creditable, if, as they say, he dislikes the place, and would prefer staying where he is."

And having spoken thus gently, Mr. Peers resumed his pipe cheerfully.

"No, he don't like the place; that is, I'm told he *didn't*," said the innkeeper.

"He *hates* it," said the Doctor with another dark nod.

"And no wonder, if all's true I've heard," cried old Jack Amerald. "Didn't he drown a woman and her child in the lake?"

"Hollo! my dear boy, don't let them hear you say that; you're all in the clouds."

"By Jen!" exclaimed the landlord after an alarmed silence, with his mouth and eyes open, and his pipe in his hand, "why, sir, I pay rent for the house up there. I'm thankful—dear knows, I *am* thankful—we're all to ourselves!"

Jack Amerald put his foot on the floor, leaving his wooden leg in its horizontal position, and looked round a little curiously.

"Well, if it wasn't him, it was someone else. I'm sure it happened up at Mardykes. I took the bearings on the water myself from Glads Scaur to Mardykes Jetty, and from the George and Dragon sign down here—down to the white house under Forrick Fells. I could fix a buoy over the very spot. Some one here told me the bearings, I'd take my oath, where the body was seen; and yet no boat could ever come up with it; and that was queer, you know, so I clapt it down in my log."

"Ay, sir, there *was* some flummery like that, Captain," said Turnbull; "for folk will be gabbin'. But 'twas his grandsire was talked o', not him; and 'twould play the hangment wi' me doun here, if 'twas thought there was stories like that passin' in the George and Dragon.'

"Well, his grandfather; 'twas all one to him, I take it."

"There never was no proof, Captain, no more than smoke; and the family up at Mardykes wouldn't allow the king to talk o' them like that, sir; for though they be lang deod that had most right to be angered in the matter, there's none o' the name but would be half daft to think 'twas still believed, and he full out as mich as any. Not that I need care more than another, though they do say he's a bit frowsy and short-waisted; for he can't shouther me out o' the George while I pay my rent, till nine hundred and ninety-nine year be rin oot; and a man, be he ne'er sa het, has time to cool before then. But there's no good quarrellin' wi' teathy folk; and it may lie in his way to do the George mony an ill turn, and mony a gude one; an' it's only fair to say it happened a long way before he was born, and there's no good in vexin' him; and I lay ye a pound, Captain, the Doctor hods wi' me."

The Doctor, whose business was also sensitive, nodded; and then he said, "But for all that, the story's old, Dick Turnbull—older than you or I, my jolly good friend."

"And best forgotten," interposed the host of the George.

"Ay, best forgotten; but that it's not like to be," said the Doctor, plucking up courage. "Here's our friend the Captain has heard it; and the mistake he has made shows there's one thing worse than its being quite remembered, and that is, its being *half* remembered. We can't stop people talking; and a story like that will see us all off the hooks, and be in folks' mouths, still, as strong as ever."

"Ay; and now I think on it, 'twas Dick Harman that has the boat down there—an old tar like myself—that told me that yarn. I was trying for pike, and he pulled me over the place, and that's how I came to hear it. I say, Tom, my hearty, serve us out another glass of brandy, will you?" shouted the Captain's voice as the waiter crossed the room; and that florid and grizzled naval hero clapped his leg again on the chair by its wooden companion, which he was wont to call his jury-mast.

"Well, I do believe it will be spoke of longer than we are like to hear," said the host, "and I don't much matter the story, if it baint told o' the wrong man." Here he touched his tumbler with the spoon, indicating by that little ring that Tom, who had returned with the Captain's grog, was to replenish it with punch. "And Sir Bale is like to be a friend to this house. I don't see no reason why he shouldn't. The George and Dragon has bin in our family ever since the reign of King Charles the Second. It was William Turnbull in that time, which they called it the Restoration, he taking the lease from Sir Tony Mardykes that was then. They was but knights then. They was made baronets first in the reign of King George the Second; you may see it in the list of baronets and the nobility. The lease was made to William Turnbull, which came from London; and he built the stables, which they was out o' repair, as you may read to this day in the lease; and the house has never had but one sign since—the George and Dragon, it is pretty well known in England—and one name to its master.

"It has been owned by a Turnbull from that day to this, and they have not been counted bad men." A murmur of applause testified the assent of his guests. "They has been steady churchgoin' folk, and brewed good drink, and maintained the best o' characters, hereaways and farther off too, though 'tis I, Richard Turnbull, that says it; and while they pay their rent, no man has power to put them out; for their title's as good to the George and Dragon, and the two fields, and the croft, and the grazing o' their kye on the green, as Sir Bale Mardykes to the Hall up there and estate. So 'tis nout to me, except in the way o' friendliness, what the family may think o' me; only the George and they has always been kind and friendly, and I don't want to break the old custom."

"Well said, Dick!" exclaimed Doctor Torvey; "I own to your conclusion; but there ain't a soul here but ourselves—and we're all friends, and you are your own master—and, hang it, you'll tell us that story about the drowned woman, as you heard it from your father long ago."

"Ay, do, and keep us to our liquor, my hearty!" cried the Captain.

Mr. Peers looked his entreaty; and deaf Mr. Hollar, having no interest in the petition, was at least a safe witness, and, with his pipe in his lips, a cosy piece of furniture.

Richard Turnbull had his punch beside him; he looked over his shoulder. The door was closed, the fire was cheery, and the punch was fragrant, and all friendly faces about him. So said he:

"Gentlemen, as you're pleased to wish it, I don't see no great harm in it; and at any rate, 'twill prevent mistakes. It is more than ninety years since. My father was but a boy then; and many a time I have heard him tell it in this very room."

And looking into his glass he mused, and stirred his punch slowly.

CHAPTER 2

THE DROWNED WOMAN

"It ain't much of a homminy," said the host of the George. "I'll not keep you long over it, gentlemen. There was a handsome young lady, Miss Mary Feltram o' Cloostedd by name. She was the last o' that family; and had gone very poor. There's but the walls o' the house left now; grass growing in the hall, and ivy over the gables; there's no one livin' has ever hard tell o' smoke out o' they chimblies. It stands on t'other side o' the lake, on the level wi' a deal o' a'ad trees behint and aside it at the gap o' the clough, under the pike o' Maiden Fells. Ye may see it wi' a spyin'-glass from the boatbield at Mardykes Hall."

"I've been there fifty times," said the Doctor.

"Well there was dealin's betwixt the two families; and there's good and bad in every family; but the Mardykes, in them days, was a wild lot. And when old Feltram o' Cloostedd died, and the young lady his daughter was left a ward o' Sir Jasper Mardykes-an ill day for her, poor lass!—twenty year older than her he was, an' more; and nothin' about him, they say, to make anyone like or love him, ill-faur'd and little and dow."

"Dow—that's gloomy," Doctor Torvey instructed the Captain aside.

"But they do say, they has an old blud-stean ring in the family that has a charm in't; and happen how it might, the poor lass fell in love wi' him. Some said they was married. Some said it hang'd i' the bell-ropes, and never had the priest's blessing; but anyhow, married or no, there was talk enough amang the folk, and out o' doors she would na budge. And there was two wee barns; and she prayed him hard to confess the marriage, poor thing! But t'was a bootlese bene, and he would not allow they should bear his name, but their mother's; he was a hard man, and hed the bit in his teeth, and went his ain gait. And having tired of her, he took in his head to marry a lady of the Barnets, and it behoved him to be shut o' her and her children; and so she nor them was seen no more at Mardykes Hall. And the eldest, a boy, was left in care of my grandfather's father here in the George."

"That queer Philip Feltram that's travelling with Sir Bale so long is a descendant of his?" said the Doctor.

"Grandson," observed Mr. Peers, removing his pipe for a moment; "and is the last of that stock."

"Well, no one could tell where she had gone to. Some said to distant parts, some said to the madhouse, some one thing, some another; but neither she nor the barn was ever seen or spoke to by the folk at Mardykes in life again. There was one Mr. Wigram that lived in them times down at Moultry, and had sarved, like the Captain here, in the king's navy in his day; and early of a morning down he comes to the town for a boat, sayin' he was looking towards Snakes Island through his spyin'-glass, and he seen a woman about a hundred and fifty yards outside of it; the Captain here has heard the bearings right enough. From her hips upwards she was stark and straight out o' the water, and a baby in her arms. Well, no one else could see it, nor he neither, when they went down to the boat.

"But next morning he saw the same thing, and the boatman saw it too; and they rowed for it, both pulling might and main; but after a mile or so they could see it no more, and gave over. The next that saw it was the vicar, I forget his name now—but he was up the lake to a funeral at Mortlock Church; and coming back with a bit of a sail up, just passin' Snakes Island, what should they hear on a sudden but a wowl like a death-cry, shrill and bleak, as made the very blood hoot in their veins; and looking along the water not a hundred yards away, saw the same grizzled sight in the moonlight; so they turned the tiller, and came near enough to see her face—blea it was, and drenched wi' water-and she was above the lake to her middle, stiff as a post, holdin' the weeny barn out to them, and flyrin' [smiling scornfully] on them as they drew nigh her. They were half-frighted, not knowing what to make of it; but passing as close as the boatman could bring her side, the vicar stretched over the gunwale to catch her, and she bent forward, pushing the dead bab forward; and as she did, on a sudden she gave a yelloch that scared them, and they saw her no more. 'Twas no livin' woman, for she couldn't rise that height above the water, as they well knew when they came to think; and knew it was a dobby they saw; and ye may be sure they didn't spare prayer and blessin', and went on their course straight before the wind; for neither would a-took the worth o' all the Mardykes to look sich a freetin' i' the face again. 'Twas seen another time by market-folk crossin' fra Gyllenstan in the self-same place; and Snakes Island got a bad neam, and none cared to go nar it after nightfall."

"Do you know anything of that Feltram that has been with him abroad?" asked the Doctor.

"They say he's no good at anything—a harmless mafflin; he was a long gaumless gawky when he went awa," said Richard Turnbull. "The Feltrams and the Mardykes was sib, ye know; and that made what passed in the misfortune o' that young lady spoken of all the harder; and this young man ye speak of is a grandson o' the lad that was put here in care o' my grandfather."

"*Great*-grandson. His father was grandson," said Mr. Peers; "he held a commission in the army and died in the West Indies. This Philip Feltram is the last o' that line—illegitimate, you know, it is held—and the little that remained of the Feltram property went nearly fourscore years ago to the Mardykes, and this Philip is maintained by Sir Bale; it is pleasant, notwithstanding all the stories one hears, gentlemen, that the only thing we know of him for certain should be so creditable to his kindness."

"To be sure," acquiesced Mr. Turnbull.

While they talked the horn sounded, and the mail-coach drew up at the door of the George and Dragon to set down a passenger and his luggage.

Dick Turnbull rose and went out to the hall with careful bustle, and Doctor Torvey followed as far as the door, which commanded a view of it, and saw several trunks cased in canvas pitched into the hall, and by careful Tom and a boy lifted one on top of the other, behind the corner of the banister. It would have been below the dignity of his cloth to go out and read the labels on these, or the Doctor would have done otherwise, so great was his curiosity.

CHAPTER 3
PHILIP FELTRAM

The new guest was now in the hall of the George, and Doctor Torvey could hear him talking with Mr. Turnbull. Being himself one of the dignitaries of Golden Friars, the Doctor, having regard to first impressions, did not care to be seen in his post of observation; and closing the door gently, returned to his chair by the fire, and in an under-tone informed his cronies that there was a new arrival in the George, and he could not hear, but would not wonder if he were taking a private room; and he seemed to have trunks enough to build a church with.

"Don't be too sure we haven't Sir Bale on board," said Amerald, who would have followed his crony the Doctor to the door—for never was retired naval hero of a village more curious than he—were it not that his wooden leg made a distinct pounding on the floor that was inimical, as experience had taught him, to mystery.

"That can't be," answered the Doctor; "Charley Twyne knows everything about it, and has a letter every second day; and there's no chance of Sir Bale before the tenth; this is a tourist, you'll find. I don't know what the d——l keeps Turnbull; he knows well enough we are all naturally willing to hear who it is."

"Well, he won't trouble us here, I bet ye;" and catching deaf Mr. Hollar's eye, the Captain nodded, and pointed to the little table beside him, and made a gesture imitative of the rattling of a dice-box; at which that quiet old gentleman also nodded sunnily; and up got the Captain and conveyed the backgammon-box to the table, near Hollar's elbow, and the two worthies were soon sinc-ducing and catre-acing, with the pleasant clatter that accompanies that ancient game. Hollar had thrown sizes and made his double point, and the honest Captain, who could stand many things better than Hollar's throwing such throws so early in the evening, cursed his opponent's luck and sneered at his play, and called the company to witness, with a distinctness which a stranger to smiling Hollar's deafness would have thought hardly civil; and just at this moment the door opened, and Richard Turnbull showed his new guest into the room, and ushered him to a vacant seat near the other corner of the table before the fire.

The stranger advanced slowly and shyly, with something a little deprecatory in his air, to which a lathy figure, a slight stoop, and a very gentle and even heartbroken look in his pale long face, gave a more marked character of shrinking and timidity.

He thanked the landlord aside, as it were, and took his seat with a furtive glance round, as if he had no right to come in and intrude upon the happiness of these honest gentlemen.

He saw the Captain scanning him from under his shaggy grey eyebrows while he was pretending to look only at his game; and the Doctor was able to recount to Mrs. Torvey when he went home every article of the stranger's dress.

It was odd and melancholy as his peaked face.

He had come into the room with a short black cloak on, and a rather tall foreign felt hat, and a pair of shiny leather gaiters or leggings on his thin legs; and altogether presented a general resemblance to the conventional figure of Guy Fawkes.

Not one of the company assembled knew the appearance of the Baronet. The Doctor and old Mr. Peers remembered something of his looks; and certainly they had no likeness, but the reverse, to those presented by the newcomer. The Baronet, as now described by people who had chanced to see him, was a dark man, not above the middle size, and with a certain decision in his air and talk; whereas this person was tall, pale, and in air and manner feeble. So this broken trader in the world's commerce, with whom all seemed to have gone wrong, could not possibly be he.

Presently, in one of his stealthy glances, the Doctor's eye encountered that of the stranger, who was by this time drinking his tea—a thin and feminine liquor little used in that room.

The stranger did not seem put out; and the Doctor, interpreting his look as a permission to converse, cleared his voice, and said urbanely,

"We have had a little frost by night, down here, sir, and a little fire is no great harm—it is rather pleasant, don't you think?"

The stranger bowed acquiescence with a transient wintry smile, and looked gratefully on the fire.

"This place is a good deal admired, sir, and people come a good way to see it; you have been here perhaps before?"

"Many years ago."

Here was another pause.

"Places change imperceptibly—in detail, at least—a good deal," said the Doctor, making an effort to keep up a conversation that plainly would not go on of itself; "and people too; population shifts—there's an old fellow, sir, they call *Death*."

"And an old fellow they call the *Doctor*, that helps him," threw in the Captain humorously, allowing his attention to get entangled in the conversation, and treating them to one of his tempestuous ha-ha-ha's.

"We are expecting the return of a gentleman who would be a very leading member of our little society down here," said the Doctor, not noticing the Captain's joke. "I mean Sir Bale Mardykes. Mardykes Hall is a pretty object from the water, sir, and a very fine old place."

The melancholy stranger bowed slightly, but rather in courtesy to the relater, it seemed, than that the Doctor's lore interested him much.

"And on the opposite side of the lake," continued Doctor Torvey, "there is a building that contrasts very well with it—the old house of the Feltrams—quite a ruin now, at the mouth of the glen—Cloostedd House, a very picturesque object."

"Exactly opposite," said the stranger dreamily, but whether in the tone of acquiescence or interrogatory, the Doctor could not be quite sure.

"That was one of our great families down here that has disappeared. It has dwindled down to nothing."

"Duce ace," remarked Mr. Hollar, who was attending to his game.

"While others have mounted more suddenly and amazingly still," observed gentle Mr. Peers, who was great upon county genealogies.

"Sizes!" thundered the Captain, thumping the table with an oath of disgust.

"And Snakes Island is a very pretty object; they say there used to be snakes there," said the Doctor, enlightening the visitor.

"Ah! that's a mistake," said the dejected guest, making his first original observation. "It should be spelt *Snaiks*. In the old papers it is called Sen-aiks Island from the seven oaks that grew in a clump there."

"Hey? that's very curious, egad! I daresay," said the Doctor, set right thus by the stranger, and eyeing him curiously.

"Very true, sir," observed Mr. Peers; "three of those oaks, though, two of them little better than stumps, are there still; and Clewson of Heckleston has an old document—"

Here, unhappily, the landlord entered the room in a fuss, and walking up to the stranger, said, "The chaise is at the door, Mr. Feltram, and the trunks up, sir."

Mr. Feltram rose quietly and took out his purse, and said,

"I suppose I had better pay at the bar?"

"As you like best, sir," said Richard Turnbull.

Mr. Feltram bowed all round to the gentlemen, who smiled, ducked or waved their hands; and the Doctor fussily followed him to the hall-door, and welcomed him back to Golden Friars—there was real kindness in this welcome—and proffered his broad brown hand, which Mr. Feltram took; and then he plunged into his chaise, and the door being shut, away he glided, chaise, horses, and driver, like shadows, by the margin of the moonlighted lake, towards Mardykes Hall.

And after a few minutes' stand upon the steps, looking along the shadowy track of the chaise, they returned to the glow of the room, in which a pleasant perfume of punch still prevailed; and beside Mr. Philip Feltram's deserted tea-things, the host of the George enlightened his guests by communicating freely the little he had picked up. The principal fact he had to tell was, that Sir Bale adhered strictly to his original plan, and was to arrive on the tenth. A few days would bring them to that, and the nine-days wonder run its course and lose its interest. But in the meantime, all Golden Friars was anxious to see what Sir Bale Mardykes was like.

CHAPTER 4

THE BARONET APPEARS

As the candles burn blue and the air smells of brimstone at the approach of the Evil One, so, in the quiet and healthy air of Golden Friars, a depressing and agitating influence announced the coming of the long-absent Baronet.

From abroad, no good whatever had been at any time heard of him, and a great deal that was, in the ears of simple folk living in that unsophisticated part of the world, vaguely awful.

Stories that travel so far, however, lose something of their authority, as well as definiteness, on the way; there was always room for charity to suggest a mistake or exaggeration; and if good men turned up their hands and eyes after a new story, and ladies of experience, who knew mankind, held their heads high and looked grim and mysterious at mention of his name, nevertheless an interval of silence softened matters a little, and the sulphurous perfume dissipated itself in time.

Now that Sir Bale Mardykes had arrived at the Hall, there

were hurried consultations held in many households. And though he was tried and sentenced by drum-head over some austere hearths, as a rule the law of gravitation prevailed, and the greater house drew the lesser about it, and county people within the visiting radius paid their respects at the Hall.

The Reverend Martin Bedel, the then vicar of Golden Friars, a stout short man, with a mulberry-coloured face and small gray eyes, and taciturn habits, called and entered the drawing-room at Mardykes Hall, with his fat and garrulous wife on his arm.

The drawing-room has a great projecting Tudor window looking out on the lake, with its magnificent background of furrowed and purple mountains.

Sir Bale was not there, and Mrs. Bedel examined the pictures, and ornaments, and the books, making such remarks as she saw fit; and then she looked out of the window, and admired the prospect. She wished to stand well with the Baronet, and was in a mood to praise everything.

You may suppose she was curious to see him, having heard for years such strange tales of his doings.

She expected the hero of a brilliant and wicked romance; and listened for the step of the truant Lovelace who was to fulfil her idea of manly beauty and fascination.

She sustained a slight shock when he did appear.

Sir Bale Mardykes was, as she might easily have remembered, a middle-aged man—and he looked it. He was not even an imposing-looking man for his time of life: he was of about the middle height, slightly made, and dark featured. She had expected something of the gaiety and animation of Versailles, and an evident cultivation of the art of pleasing. What she did see was a remarkable gravity, not to say gloom, of countenance-the only feature of which that struck her being a pair of large dark-gray eyes, that were cold and earnest. His manners had the ease of perfect confidence; and his talk and air were those of a person who might have known how to please, if it were worth the trouble, but who did not care twopence whether he pleased or not.

He made them each a bow, courtly enough, but there was no smile—not even an affectation of cordiality. Sir Bale, however, was chatty, and did not seem to care much what he said, or what people thought of him; and there was a suspicion of sarcasm in what he said that the rustic literality of good Mrs. Bedel did not always detect.

"I believe I have not a clergyman but *you*, sir, within any reasonable distance?"

"Golden Friars *is* the nearest," said Mrs. Bedel, answering, as was her pleasure on all practicable occasions, for her husband. "And southwards, the nearest is Wyllarden—and by a bird's flight that is thirteen miles and a half, and by the road more than nineteen—twenty, I may say, by the road. Ha, ha, ha! it is a long way to look for a clergyman."

"Twenty miles of road to carry you thirteen miles across, hey? The road-makers lead you a pretty dance here; those gentlemen know how to make money, and like to show people the scenery from a variety of points. No one likes a straight road but the man who pays for it, or who, when he travels, is brute enough to wish to get to his journey's end."

"That is so true, Sir Bale; one never cares if one is not in a hurry. That's what Martin thinks—don't we, Martin?—And then, you know, coming home is the time you *are* in a hurry—when you are thinking of your cup of tea and the children; and *then*, you know, you have the fall of the ground all in your favour."

"It's well to have anything in your favour in this place. And so there are children?"

"A good many," said Mrs. Bedel, with a proud and mysterious smile, and a nod; "you wouldn't guess how many."

"Not I; I only wonder you did not bring them all."

"That's very good-natured of you, Sir Bale, but all could not come at *one* bout; there are—tell him, Martin—ha, ha, ha! there are eleven."

"It must be very cheerful down at the vicarage," said Sir Bale graciously; and turning to the vicar he added, "But how unequally blessings are divided! You have eleven, and I not one—that I'm aware of."

"And then, in that direction straight before you, you have the lake, and then the fells; and five miles from the foot of the mountain at the other side, before you reach Fottrell—and that is twenty-five miles by the road—"

"Dear me! how far apart they are set! My gardener told me this morning that asparagus grows very thinly in this part of the world. How thinly clergymen grow also down here—in one sense," he added politely, for the vicar was stout.

"We were looking out of the window—we amused ourselves that way before you came—and your view is certainly the very best anywhere round this side; your view of the lake and the fells—what mountains they are, Sir Bale!"

"'Pon my soul, they are! I wish I could blow them asunder with a charge of duck-shot, and I shouldn't be stifled by them long. But I suppose, as we can't get rid of them, the next best thing is to admire them. We are pretty well married to them, and there is no use in quarrelling."

"I know you don't think so, Sir Bale, ha, ha, ha! You wouldn't take a good deal and spoil Mardykes Hall."

"You can't get a mouthful or air, or see the sun of a morning, for those frightful mountains," he said with a peevish frown at them.

"Well, the lake at all events—that you *must* admire, Sir Bale?"

"No ma'am, I don't admire the lake. I'd drain the lake if I could—I hate the lake. There's nothing so gloomy as a lake pent up among barren mountains. I can't conceive what possessed my people to build our house down here, at the edge of a lake; unless it was the fish, and precious fish it is—pike! I don't know how people digest it—*I* can't. I'd as soon think of eating a watchman's pike."

"I thought that having travelled so much abroad, you would have acquired a great liking for that kind of scenery, Sir Bale; there is a great deal of it on the Continent, ain't there?" said Mrs.

Bedel. "And the boating."

"Boating, my dear Mrs. Bedel, is the dullest of all things; don't you think so? Because a boat looks very pretty from the shore, we fancy the shore must look very pretty from a boat; and when we try it, we find we have only got down into a pit and can see nothing rightly. For my part I hate boating, and I hate the water; and I'd rather have my house, like Haworth, at the edge of a moss, with good wholesome peat to look at, and an open horizon—savage and stupid and bleak as all that is—than be suffocated among impassable mountains, or upset in a black lake and drowned like a kitten. O, there's luncheon in the next room; won't you take some?"

CHAPTER 5
MRS. JULAPER'S ROOM

Sir Bale Mardykes being now established in his ancestral house, people had time to form conclusions respecting him. It must be allowed he was not popular. There was, perhaps, in his conduct something of the caprice of contempt. At all events his temper and conduct were uncertain, and his moods sometimes violent and insulting.

With respect to but one person was his conduct uniform, and that was Philip Feltram. He was a sort of *aide-de-camp* near Sir Bale's person, and chargeable with all the commissions and offices which could not be suitably intrusted to a mere servant. But in many respects he was treated worse than any servant of the Baronet's. Sir Bale swore at him, and cursed him; laid the blame of everything that went wrong in house, stable, or field upon his shoulders; railed at him, and used him, as people said, worse than a dog.

Why did Feltram endure this contumelious life? What could he do but endure it? was the answer. What was the power that induced strong soldiers to put off their jackets and shirts, and present their hands to be tied up, and tortured for hours, it might be, under the scourge, with an air of ready volition? The moral coercion of despair; the result of an unconscious calculation of chances which satisfies them that it is ultimately better to do all that, bad as it is, than try the alternative. These unconscious calculations are going on every day with each of us, and the results embody themselves in our lives; and no one knows that there has been a process and a balance struck, and that what they see, and very likely blame, is by the fiat of an invisible but quite irresistible power.

A man of spirit would rather break stones on the highway than eat that bitter bread, was the burden of every man's song on Feltram's bondage. But he was not so sure that even the stone-breaker's employment was open to him, or that he could break stones well enough to retain it on a fair trial. And he had other ideas of providing for himself, and a different alternative in his mind.

Good-natured Mrs. Julaper, the old housekeeper at Mardykes Hall, was kind to Feltram, as to all others who lay in her way and were in affliction.

She was one of those good women whom Nature provides to receive the burden of other people's secrets, as the reeds did long ago, only that no chance wind could steal them away, and send them singing into strange ears.

You may still see her snuggery in Mardykes Hall, though the housekeeper's room is now in a different part of the house.

Mrs. Julaper's room was in the oldest quarter of that old house. It was wainscoted, in black panels, up to the ceiling, which was stuccoed over in the fanciful diagrams of James the First's time. Several dingy portraits, banished from time to time from other statelier rooms, found a temporary abode in this quiet spot, where they had come finally to settle and drop out of remembrance. There is a lady in white satin and a ruff; a gentleman whose legs have faded out of view, with a peaked beard, and a hawk on his wrist. There is another in a black periwig lost in the dark background, and with a steel *cuirass*, the gleam of which out of the darkness strikes the eye, and a scarf is dimly discoverable across it. This is that foolish Sir Guy Mardykes, who crossed the Border and joined Dundee, and was shot through the temple at

Killiecrankie and whom more prudent and whiggish scions of the Mardykes family removed forthwith from his place in the Hall, and found a retirement here, from which he has not since emerged.

At the far end of this snug room is a second door, on opening which you find yourself looking down upon the great kitchen, with a little balcony before you, from which the housekeeper used to issue her commands to the cook, and exercise a sovereign supervision.

There is a shelf on which Mrs Julaper had her Bible, her *Whole Duty of Man*, and her *Pilgrim's Progress*; and, in a file beside them, her books of housewifery, and among them volumes of MS. recipes, cookery-books, and some too on surgery and medicine, as practised by the Ladies Bountiful of the Elizabethan age, for which an antiquarian would nowadays give an eye or a hand.

Gentle half-foolish Philip Feltram would tell the story of his wrongs, and weep and wish he was dead; and kind Mrs. Julaper, who remembered him a child, would comfort him with cold pie and cherry-brandy, or a cup of coffee, or some little dainty.

"O, ma'am, I'm tired of my life. What's the good of living, if a poor devil is never let alone, and called worse names than a dog? Would not it be better, Mrs. Julaper, to be dead? Wouldn't it be better, ma'am? I think so; I think it night and day. I'm always thinking the same thing. I don't care, I'll just tell him what I think, and have it off my mind. I'll tell him I can't live and bear it longer."

"There now, don't you be frettin'; but just sip this, and remember you're not to judge a friend by a wry word. He does not mean it, not he. They all had a rough side to their tongue now and again; but no one minded that. I don't, nor you needn't, no more than other folk; for the tongue, be it never so bitin', it can't draw blood, mind ye, and hard words break no bones; and I'll make a cup o' tea—ye like a cup o' tea—and we'll take a cup together, and ye'll chirp up a bit, and see how pleasant and ruddy the sun shines on the lake this evening."

She was patting him gently on the shoulder, as she stood slim and stiff in her dark silk by his chair, and her rosy little face smiled down on him. She was, for an old woman, wonderfully pretty still. What a delicate skin she must have had! The wrinkles were etched upon it with so fine a needle, you scarcely could see them a little way off; and as she smiled her cheeks looked fresh and smooth as two ruddy little apples.

"Look out, I say," and she nodded towards the window, deep set in the thick wall. "See how bright and soft everything looks in that pleasant light; *that's* better, child, than the finest picture man's hand ever painted yet, and God gives it us for nothing; and how pretty Snakes Island glows up in that light!"

The dejected man, hardly raising his head, followed with his eyes the glance of the old woman, and looked mournfully through the window.

"That island troubles me, Mrs. Julaper."

"Everything troubles you, my poor goose-cap. I'll pull your lug for ye, child, if ye be so dowly;" and with a mimic pluck the good-natured old housekeeper pinched his ear and laughed.

"I'll go to the still-room now, where the water's boiling, and I'll make a cup of tea; and if I find ye so dow when I come back, I'll throw it all out o' the window, mind."

It was indeed a beautiful picture that Feltram saw in its deep frame of old masonry. The near part of the lake was flushed all over with the low western light; the more distant waters lay dark in the shadow of the mountains; and against this shadow of purple the rocks on Snakes Island, illuminated by the setting sun, started into sharp clear yellow.

But this beautiful view had no charm—at least, none powerful enough to master the latent horror associated with its prettiest feature—for the weak and dismal man who was looking at it; and being now alone, he rose and leant on the window, and looked out, and then with a kind of shudder clutching his hands together, and walking distractedly about the room.

Without his perceiving, while his back was turned, the housekeeper came back; and seeing him walking in this distracted way, she thought to herself, as he leant again upon the window:

"Well, it *is* a burning shame to worrit any poor soul into that state. Sir Bale was always down on someone or something, man or beast; there always was something he hated, and could never let alone. It was not pretty; it was his nature. Happen, poor fellow, he could not help it; but so it was."

A maid came in and set the tea-things down; and Mrs. Julaper drew her sad guest over by the arm, and made him sit down, and she said: "What has a man to do, frettin' in that way? By Jen, I'm ashamed o' ye, Master Philip! Ye like three lumps o' sugar, I think, and—look cheerful, ye must!—a good deal o' cream?"

"You're so kind, Mrs. Julaper, you're so cheery. I feel quite comfortable after awhile when I'm with you; I feel quite happy," and he began to cry.

She understood him very well by this time and took no notice, but went on chatting gaily, and made his tea as he liked it; and he dried his tears hastily, thinking she had not observed.

So the clouds began to clear. This innocent fellow liked nothing better than a cup of tea and a chat with gentle and cheery old Mrs. Julaper, and a talk in which the shadowy old times which he remembered as a child emerged into sunlight and lived again.

When he began to feel better, drawn into the kindly old times by the tinkle of that harmless old woman's tongue, he said:

"I sometimes think I would not so much mind—I should not care so much—if my spirits were not so depressed, and I so agitated. I suppose I am not quite well."

"Well, tell me what's wrong, child, and it's odd but I have a recipe on the shelf there that will do you good."

"It is not a matter of that sort I mean; though I'd rather have you than any doctor, if I needed medicine, to prescribe for me."

Mrs. Julaper smiled in spite of herself, well pleased; for her skill in pharmacy was a point on which the good lady prided herself, and was open to flattery, which, without intending it, the simple fellow administered.

"No, I'm well enough; I can't say I ever was better. It is only, ma'am, that I have such dreams—you have no idea."

"There are dreams and dreams, my dear: there's some signifies no more than the babble of the lake down there on the pebbles, and there's others that has a meaning; there's dreams that is but vanity, and there's dreams that is good, and dreams that is bad. Lady Mardykes—heavens be her bed this day! that's his grandmother I mean—was very sharp for reading dreams. Take another cup of tea. Dear me! what a noise the crows keep aboon our heads, going home! and how high they wing it!—that's a sure sign of fine weather. An' what do you dream about? Tell me your dream, and I may show you it's a good one, after all. For many a dream is ugly to see and ugly to tell, and a good dream, with a happy meaning, for all that."

Chapter 6

The Intruder

"Well, Mrs. Julaper, dreams I've dreamed like other people, old and young; but this, ma'am, has taken a fast hold of me," said Mr. Feltram dejectedly, leaning back in his chair and looking down with his hands in his pockets. "I think, Mrs. Julaper, it is getting into me. I think it's like possession."

"Possession, child! what do you mean?"

"I think there is something trying to influence me. Perhaps it is the way fellows go mad; but it won't let me alone. I've seen it three times, think of that!"

"Well, dear, and what *have* ye seen?" she asked, with an uneasy cheerfulness, smiling, with eyes fixed steadily upon him; for the idea of a madman—even gentle Philip in that state—was not quieting.

"Do you remember the picture, full-length, that had no frame—the lady in the white-satin *saque*—she was beautiful, *funeste*," he added, talking more to himself; and then more distinctly to Mrs. Julaper again—"in the white-satin *saque*; and with the little mob cap and blue ribbons to it, and a bouquet in her fingers; that was—that—you know who she was?"

107

"That was your great-grandmother, my dear," said Mrs. Julaper, lowering her eyes. "It was a dreadful pity it was spoiled. The boys in the pantry had it for a year there on the table for a tray, to wash the glasses on and the like. It was a shame; that was the prettiest picture in the house, with the gentlest, rosiest face."

"It ain't so gentle or rosy now, I can tell you," said Philip. "As fixed as marble; with thin lips, and a curve at the nostril. Do you remember the woman that was found dead in the clough, when I was a boy, that the gipsies murdered, it was thought,—a cruel-looking woman?"

"Agoy! Master Philip, dear! ye would not name that terrible-looking creature with the pretty, fresh, kindly face!"

"Faces change, you see; no matter what she's like; it's her talk that frightens me. She wants to make use of me; and, you see, it is like getting a share in my mind, and a voice in my thoughts, and a command over me gradually; and it is just one idea, as straight as a line of light across the lake—see what she's come to. O Lord, help me!"

"Well, now, don't you be talkin' like that. It is just a little bit dowly and troubled, because the master says a wry word now and then; and so ye let your spirits go down, don't ye see, and all sorts o' fancies comes into your head."

"There's no fancy in my head," he said with a quick look of suspicion; "only you asked me what I dreamed. I don't care if all the world knew. I dreamed I went down a flight of steps under the lake, and got a message. There are no steps near Snakes Island, we all know that," and he laughed chillily. "I'm out of spirits, as you say; and—and—O dear! I wish—Mrs. Julaper—I wish I was in my coffin, and quiet."

"Now that's very wrong of you, Master Philip; you should think of all the blessings you have, and not be makin' mountains o' molehills; and those little bits o' temper Sir Bale shows, why, no one minds 'em—that is, to take 'em to heart like you do, don't ye see?"

"I daresay; I suppose, Mrs. Julaper, you are right. I'm unreasonable often, I know," said gentle Philip Feltram. "I daresay I make too much of it; I'll try. I'm his secretary, and I know I'm not so bright as he is, and it is natural he should sometimes be a little impatient; I ought to be more reasonable, I'm sure. It is all that thing that has been disturbing me—I mean fretting, and, I think, I'm not quite well; and—and letting myself think too much of vexations. It's my own fault, I'm sure, Mrs. Julaper; and I know I'm to blame."

"That's quite right, that's spoken like a wise lad; only I don't say you're to blame, nor no one; for folk can't help frettin' sometimes, no more than they can help a headache—none but a mafflin would say that—and I'll not deny but he has dowly ways when the fit's on him, and he frumps us all round, if such be his humour. But who is there hasn't his faults? We must bear and forbear, and take what we get and be cheerful. So chirp up, my lad; Philip, didn't I often ring the a'd rhyme in your ear long ago?

"Be always as merry as ever you can,
For no one delights in a sorrowful man.

"So don't ye be gettin' up off your chair like that, and tramping about the room wi' your hands in your pockets, looking out o' this window, and staring out o' that, and sighing and crying, and looking so black-ox-trodden, 'twould break a body's heart to see you. Ye must be cheery; and happen you're hungry, and don't know it. I'll tell the cook to grill a hot bit for ye."

"But I'm not hungry, Mrs. Julaper. How kind you are! dear me, Mrs. Julaper, I'm not worthy of it; I don't deserve half your kindness. I'd have been heartbroken long ago, but for you."

"And I'll make a sup of something hot for you; you'll take a rummer-glass of punch—you must."

"But I like the tea better; I do, indeed, Mrs. Julaper."

"Tea is no drink for a man when his heart's down. It should be something with a leg in it, lad; something hot that will warm your courage for ye, and set your blood a-dancing, and make ye talk brave and merry; and will you have a bit of a broil first? No? Well then, you'll have a drop o' punch?—ye sha'n't say no."

And so, all resistance overpowered, the consolation of Philip

Feltram proceeded.

A gentler spirit than poor Feltram, a more good-natured soul than the old housekeeper, were nowhere among the children of earth.

Philip Feltram, who was reserved enough elsewhere, used to come into her room and cry, and take her by both hands piteously, standing before her and looking down in her face, while tears ran deviously down his cheeks.

"Did you ever know such a case? was there ever a fellow like *me*? did you ever *know* such a thing? You know what I am, Mrs. Julaper, and who I am. They call me Feltram; but Sir Bale knows as well as I that my true name is not that. I'm Philip Mardykes; and another fellow would make a row about it, and claim his name and his rights, as she is always croaking in my ear I ought. But you know that is not reasonable. My grandmother was married; she was the true Lady Mardykes; *think* what it was to see a woman like that turned out of doors, and her children robbed of their name. O, ma'am, you *can't* think it; unless you were me, you couldn't—you couldn't—you couldn't!"

"Come, come, Master Philip, don't you be taking on so; and ye mustn't be talking like that, d'ye mind? You know he wouldn't stand that; and it's an old story now, and there's naught can be proved concerning it; and what I think is this—I wouldn't wonder the poor lady was beguiled. But anyhow she surely thought she was his lawful wife; and though the law may hev found a flaw somewhere—and I take it 'twas so—yet sure I am she was an honourable lady. But where's the use of stirring that old sorrow? or how can ye prove aught? and the dead hold their peace, you know; dead mice, they say, feels no cold; and dead folks are past fooling. So don't you talk like that; for stone walls have ears, and ye might say that ye couldn't *un*say; and death's day is doom's day. So leave all in the keeping of God; and, above all, never lift hand when ye can't strike."

"Lift my hand! O, Mrs. Julaper, you couldn't think that; you little know me; I did not mean that; I never dreamed of hurting Sir Bale. Good heavens! Mrs. Julaper, you couldn't think that! It all comes of my poor impatient temper, and complaining as I do, and my misery; but O, Mrs. Julaper, you could not think I ever meant to trouble him by law, or any other annoyance! I'd like to see a stain removed from my family, and my name restored; but to touch his property, O, no!—O, no! that never entered my mind, by heaven! that never entered my mind, Mrs. Julaper. I'm not cruel; I'm not rapacious; I don't care for money; don't you know that, Mrs. Julaper? O, surely you won't think me capable of attacking the man whose bread I have eaten so long! I never dreamed of it; I should hate myself. Tell me you don't believe it; O, Mrs. Julaper, say you don't!"

And the gentle feeble creature burst into tears and good Mrs. Julaper comforted him with kind words; and he said,

"Thank you, ma'am; thank you. God knows I would not hurt Bale, nor give him one uneasy hour. It is only this: that I'm—I'm so miserable; and I'm only casting in my mind where to turn to, and what to do. So little a thing would be enough, and then I shall leave Mardykes. I'll go; not in any anger, Mrs. Julaper—don't think that; but I can't stay, I must be gone."

"Well, now, there's nothing yet, Master Philip, to fret you like that. You should not be talking so wild-like. Master Bale has his sharp word and his short temper now and again; but I'm sure he likes you. If he didn't, he'd a-said so to me long ago. I'm sure he likes you well."

"Hollo! I say, who's there? Where the devil's Mr. Feltram?" called the voice of the baronet, at a fierce pitch, along the passage.

"*La*! Mr. Feltram, it's him! Ye'd better run to him," whispered Mrs. Julaper.

"D—n me! does nobody hear? Mrs. Julaper! Hollo! ho! house, there! ho! D—n me, will nobody answer?"

And Sir Bale began to slap the wainscot fast and furiously with his walking-cane with a clatter like a harlequin's lath in a pantomime.

Mrs. Julaper, a little paler than usual, opened her door, and stood with the handle in her hand, making a little curtsey, enframed in the door-case; and Sir Bale, being in a fume, when he saw her, ceased whacking the panels of the corridor, and stamped on the floor, crying,

"Upon my soul, ma'am, I'm glad to see you! Perhaps you can tell me where Feltram is?"

"He is in my room, Sir Bale. Shall I tell him you want him, please?"

"Never mind; thanks," said the Baronet. "I've a tongue in my head;" marching down the passage to the housekeeper's room, with his cane clutched hard, glaring savagely, and with his teeth fast set, like a fellow advancing to beat a vicious horse that has chafed his temper.

Chapter 7
The Banknote

Sir Bale brushed by the housekeeper as he strode into her sanctuary, and there found Philip Feltram awaiting him dejectedly, but with no signs of agitation.

If one were to judge by the appearance the master of Mardykes presented, very grave surmises as to impending violence would have suggested themselves; but though he clutched his cane so hard that it quivered in his grasp, he had no notion of committing the outrage of a blow. The Baronet was unusually angry notwithstanding, and stopping short about three steps away, addressed Feltram with a pale face and gleaming eyes. It was quite plain that there was something very exciting upon his mind.

"I've been looking for you, Mr. Feltram; I want a word or two, if you have done your—your—whatever it is." He whisked the point of his stick towards the modest teatray. "I should like five minutes in the library."

The Baronet was all this time eyeing Feltram with a hard suspicious gaze, as if he expected to read in his face the shrinkings and trepidations of guilt; and then turning suddenly on his heel he led the way to his library—a good long march, with a good many turnings. He walked very fast, and was not long in getting there. And as Sir Bale reached the hearth, on which was smouldering a great log of wood, and turned about suddenly, facing the door, Philip Feltram entered.

The Baronet looked oddly and stern—so oddly, it seemed to Feltram, that he could not take his eyes off him, and returned his grim and somewhat embarrassed gaze with a stare of alarm and speculation.

And so doing, his step was shortened, and grew slow and slower, and came quite to a stop before he had got far from the door—a wide stretch of that wide floor still intervening between him and Sir Bale, who stood upon the hearthrug, with his heels together and his back to the fire, cane in hand, like a drill-sergeant, facing him.

"Shut that door, please; that will do; come nearer now. I don't want to bawl what I have to say. Now listen."

The Baronet cleared his voice and paused, with his eyes upon Feltram.

"It is only two or three days ago," said he, "that you said you wished you had a hundred pounds. Am I right?"

"Yes; I think so."

"*Think*? you know it, sir, devilish well. You said that you wished to get away. I have nothing particular to say against that, more especially now. Do you understand what I say?"

"Understand, Sir Bale? I do, sir—quite."

"I daresay quite" he repeated with an angry sneer. "Here, sir, is an odd coincidence: you want a hundred pounds, and you can't earn it, and you can't borrow it—there's another way, it seems-but I have got it—a Bank-of-England note of *L*100—locked up in that desk;" and he poked the end of his cane against the brass lock of it viciously. "There it is, and there are the papers you work at; and there are two keys—I've got one and you have the other—and devil another key in or out of the house has anyone living. Well, do you begin to see? Don't mind. I don't want any d——d lying about it."

Feltram was indeed beginning to see that he was suspected of something very bad, but exactly what, he was not yet sure; and being a man of that unhappy temperament which shrinks from

113

suspicion, as others do from detection, he looked very much put out indeed.

"Ha, ha! I think we do begin to see," said Sir Bale savagely. "It's a bore, I know, troubling a fellow with a story that he knows before; but I'll make mine short. When I take my key, intending to send the note to pay the crown and quit-rents that you know—you—you—no matter—you know well enough must be paid, I open it so—and so—and look *there*, where I left it, for my note; and the note's gone—you understand, the note's *gone!*"

Here was a pause, during which, under the Baronet's hard insulting eye, poor Feltram winced, and cleared his voice, and essayed to speak, but said nothing.

"It's gone, and we know where. Now, Mr. Feltram, *I* did not steal that note, and no one but you and I have access to this desk. You wish to go away, and I have no objection to that—but d—n me if you take away that note with you; and you may as well produce it now and here, as hereafter in a worse place."

"O, my good heaven!" exclaimed poor Feltram at last. "I'm very ill."

"So you are, of course. It takes a stiff emetic to get all that money off a fellow's stomach; and it's like parting with a tooth to give up a banknote. Of course you're ill, but that's no sign of innocence, and I'm no fool. You had better give the thing up quietly."

"May my Maker strike me——"

"So He will, you d——d rascal, if there's justice in heaven, unless you produce the money. I don't want to hang you. I'm willing to let you off if you'll let me, but I'm cursed if I let my note off along with you; and unless you give it up forthwith, I'll get a warrant and have you searched, pockets, bag, and baggage."

"Lord! am I awake?" exclaimed Philip Feltram.

"Wide awake, and so am I," replied Sir Bale. "You don't happen to have got it about you?"

"God forbid, sir! O, Sir—O, Sir Bale—why, Bale, *Bale*, it's impossible! You *can't* believe it. When did I ever wrong you? You know me since I was not higher than the table, and—and——"

He burst into tears.

"Stop your snivelling, sir, and give up the note. You know devilish well I can't spare it; and I won't spare you if you put me to it. I've said my say."

Sir Bale signed towards the door; and like a somnambulist, with dilated gaze and pale as death, Philip Feltram, at his wit's end, went out of the room. It was not till he had again reached the housekeeper's door that he recollected in what direction he was going. His shut hand was pressed with all his force to his heart, and the first breath he was conscious of was a deep wild sob or two that quivered from his heart as he looked from the lobby-window upon a landscape which he did not see.

All he had ever suffered before was mild in comparison with this dire paroxysm. Now, for the first time, was he made acquainted with his real capacity for pain, and how near he might be to madness and yet retain intellect enough to weigh every scruple, and calculate every chance and consequence, in his torture.

Sir Bale, in the meantime, had walked out a little more excited than he would have allowed. He was still convinced that Feltram had stolen the note, but not quite so certain as he had been. There were things in his manner that confirmed, and others that perplexed, Sir Bale.

The Baronet stood upon the margin of the lake, almost under the evening shadow of the house, looking towards Snakes Island. There were two things about Mardykes he specially disliked.

One was Philip Feltram, who, right or wrong, he fancied knew more than was pleasant of his past life.

The other was the lake. It was a beautiful piece of water, his eye, educated at least in the excellences of landscape-painting, acknowledged. But although he could pull a good oar, and liked other lakes, to this particular sheet of water there lurked within him an insurmountable antipathy. It was engendered by a variety of associations.

There is a faculty in man that will acknowledge the unseen. He may scout and scare religion from him; but if he does, superstition perches near. His boding was made-up of omens, dreams, and such stuff as he most affected to despise, and there fluttered at his heart a presentiment and disgust.

His foot was on the gunwale of the boat, that was chained to its ring at the margin; but he would not have crossed that water in it for any reason that man could urge.

What was the mischief that sooner or later was to befall him from that lake, he could not define; but that some fatal danger lurked there, was the one idea concerning it that had possession of his fancy.

He was now looking along its still waters, towards the copse and rocks of Snakes Island, thinking of Philip Feltram; and the yellow level sunbeams touched his dark features, that bore a saturnine resemblance to those of Charles II, and marked sharply their firm grim lines, and left his deep-set eyes in shadow.

Who has the happy gift to seize the present, as a child does, and live in it? Who is not often looking far off for his happiness, as Sidney Smith says, like a man looking for his hat when it is upon his head? Sir Bale was brooding over his double hatred, of Feltram and of the lake. It would have been better had he struck down the raven that croaked upon his shoulder, and listened to the harmless birds that were whistling all round among the branches in the golden sunset.

CHAPTER 8
FELTRAM'S PLAN

This horror of the beautiful lake, which other people thought so lovely, was, in that mind which affected to scoff at the unseen, a distinct creation of downright superstition.

The nursery tales which had scared him in his childhood were founded on the tragedy of Snakes Island, and haunted him with an unavowed persistence still. Strange dreams untold had visited him, and a German conjuror, who had made some strangely successful vaticinations, had told him that his worst enemy would come up to him from a lake. He had heard very nearly the same thing from a fortune-teller in France; and once at Lucerne, when he was waiting alone in his room for the hour at which he had appointed to go upon the lake, all being quiet, there came to the window, which was open, a sunburnt, lean, wicked face. Its ragged owner leaned his arm on the window-frame, and with his head in the room, said in his patois, "Ho! waiting are you? You'll have enough of the lake one day. Don't you mind watching; they'll send when you're wanted;" and twisting his yellow face into a malicious distortion, he went on.

This thing had occurred so suddenly, and chimed-in so oddly with his thoughts, which were at that moment at distant Mardykes and the haunted lake, that it disconcerted him. He laughed, he looked out of the window. He would have given that fellow money to tell him why he said that. But there was no good in looking for the scamp; he was gone.

A memory not preoccupied with that lake and its omens, and a presentiment about himself, would not have noted such things. But *his* mind they touched indelibly; and he was ashamed of his childish slavery, but could not help it.

The foundation of all this had been laid in the nursery, in the winter's tales told by its fireside, and which seized upon his fancy and his fears with a strange congeniality.

There is a large bedroom at Mardykes Hall, which tradition assigns to the lady who had perished tragically in the lake. Mrs. Julaper was sure of it; for her aunt, who died a very old woman twenty years before, remembered the time of the lady's death, and when she grew to woman's estate had opportunity in abundance; for the old people who surrounded her could remember forty years farther back, and tell everything connected with the old house in beautiful Miss Feltram's time.

This large old-fashioned room, commanding a view of Snakes Island, the fells, and the lake—somewhat vast and gloomy, and furnished in a stately old fashion—was said to be haunted, especially when the wind blew from the direction of Golden Friars, the point from which it blew on the night of her death in the lake; or when the sky was overcast, and thunder rolled among the lofty fells, and lightning gleamed on the wide sheet of water.

It was on a night like this that a lady visitor, who long after that event occupied, in entire ignorance of its supernatural character, that large room; and being herself a lady of a picturesque turn, and loving the grander melodrama of Nature, bid her maid leave the shutters open, and watched the splendid effects from her bed, until, the storm being still distant, she fell asleep.

It was travelling slowly across the lake, and it was the deep-mouthed clangour of its near approach that startled her, at dead of night, from her slumber, to witness the same phenomena in the tremendous loudness and brilliancy of their near approach.

At this magnificent spectacle she was looking with the awful ecstasy of an observer in whom the sense of danger is subordinated to that of the sublime, when she saw suddenly at the window a woman, whose long hair and dress seemed drenched with water. She was gazing in with a look of terror, and was shaking the sash of the window with vehemence. Having stood there for a few seconds, and before the lady, who beheld all this from her bed, could make up her mind what to do, the storm-beaten figure, wringing her hands, seemed to throw herself backward, and was gone.

Possessed with the idea that she had seen some poor woman overtaken in the storm, who, failing to procure admission there, had gone round to some of the many doors of the mansion, and obtained an entry there, she again fell asleep.

It was not till the morning, when she went to her window to look out upon the now tranquil scene, that she discovered what, being a stranger to the house, she had quite forgotten, that this room was at a great height—some thirty feet—from the ground.

Another story was that of good old Mr. Randal Rymer, who was often a visitor at the house in the late Lady Mardykes' day. In his youth he had been a campaigner; and now that he was a preacher he maintained his hardy habits, and always slept, summer and winter, with a bit of his window up. Being in that room in his bed, and after a short sleep lying awake, the moon shining softly through the window, there passed by that aperture into the room a figure dressed, it seemed to him, in gray that was nearly white. It passed straight to the hearth, where was an expiring wood fire; and cowering over it with outstretched hands, it appeared to be gathering what little heat was to be had. Mr. Rymer, amazed and awestruck, made a movement in his bed; and the figure looked round, with large eyes that in the moonlight looked like melting snow, and stretching its long arms up the chimney, they and the figure itself seemed to blend with the smoke, and so pass up and away.

Sir Bale, I have said, did not like Feltram. His father, Sir William, had left a letter creating a trust, it was said, in favour of Philip Feltram. The document had been found with the will, addressed to Sir Bale in the form of a letter.

"That is mine," said the Baronet, when it dropped out of the will; and he slipped it into his pocket, and no one ever saw it after.

But Mr. Charles Twyne, the attorney of Golden Friars, whenever he got drunk, which was pretty often, used to tell his friends with a grave wink that he knew a thing or two about that letter. It gave Philip Feltram two hundred a-year, charged on Harfax. It was only a direction. It made Sir Bale a trustee, however; and having made away with the "letter," the Baronet had been robbing Philip Feltram ever since.

Old Twyne was cautious, even in his cups, in his choice of an audience, and was a little enigmatical in his revelations. For he was afraid of Sir Bale, though he hated him for employing a lawyer who lived seven miles away, and was a rival. So people were not quite sure whether Mr. Twyne was telling lies or truth, and the principal fact that corroborated his story was Sir Bale's manifest hatred of his secretary. In fact, Sir Bale's retaining him in his house, detesting him as he seemed to do, was not easily to be accounted for, except on the principle of a tacit compromise—a miserable compensation for having robbed him of his rights.

The battle about the banknote proceeded. Sir Bale certainly had doubts, and vacillated; for moral evidence made powerfully in favour of poor Feltram, though the evidence of circumstance made as powerfully against him. But Sir Bale admitted suspicion easily, and in weighing probabilities would count a virtue very lightly against temptation and opportunity; and whatever his doubts might sometimes be, he resisted and quenched them, and never let that ungrateful scoundrel Philip Feltram so much as suspect their existence.

For two days Sir Bale had not spoken to Feltram. He passed by on stair and passage, carrying his head high, and with a thundrous countenance, rolling conclusions and revenges in his soul.

Poor Feltram all this time existed in one long agony. He would have left Mardykes, were it not that he looked vaguely to some just power—to chance itself—against this hideous imputation. To go with this indictment ringing in his ears, would amount to a confession and flight.

Mrs. Julaper consoled him with might and main. She was a sympathetic and trusting spirit, and knew poor Philip Feltram, in her simplicity, better than the shrewdest profligate on earth could have known him. She cried with him in his misery. She was fired with indignation by these suspicions, and still more at what followed.

Sir Bale showed no signs of relenting. It might have been that he was rather glad of so unexceptionable an opportunity of getting rid of Feltram, who, people thought, knew something which it galled the Baronet's pride that he should know.

The Baronet had another shorter and sterner interview with Feltram in his study. The result was, that unless he restored the missing note before ten o'clock next morning, he should leave Mardykes.

To leave Mardykes was no more than Philip Feltram, feeble as he was of will, had already resolved. But what was to become of him? He did not very much care, if he could find any calling, however humble, that would just give him bread.

There was an old fellow and his wife (an ancient dame,) who

lived at the other side of the lake, on the old territories of the Feltrams, and who, from some tradition of loyalty, perhaps, were fond of poor Philip Feltram. They lived somewhat high up on the fells—about as high as trees would grow—and those which were clumped about their rude dwelling were nearly the last you passed in your ascent of the mountain. These people had a multitude of sheep and goats, and lived in their airy solitude a pastoral and simple life, and were childless. Philip Feltram was hardy and active, having passed his early days among that arduous scenery. Cold and rain did not trouble him; and these people being wealthy in their way, and loving him, would be glad to find him employment of that desultory pastoral kind which would best suit him.

This vague idea was the only thing resembling a plan in his mind.

When Philip Feltram came to Mrs. Julaper's room, and told her that he had made up his mind to leave the house forthwith—to cross the lake to the Cloostedd side in Tom Marlin's boat, and then to make his way up the hill alone to Trebeck's lonely farmstead, Mrs. Julaper was overwhelmed.

"Ye'll do no such thing to-night, anyhow. You're not to go like that. Ye'll come into the small room here, where he can't follow; and we'll sit down and talk it over a bit, and ye'll find 'twill all come straight; and this will be no night, anyhow, for such a march. Why, man,'twould take an hour and more to cross the lake, and then a long uphill walk before ye could reach Trebeck's place; and if the night should fall while you were still on the mountain, ye might lose your life among the rocks. It can't be 'tis come to that yet; and the call was in the air, I'm told, all yesterday, and distant thunder today, travelling this way over Blarwyn Fells; and 'twill be a night no one will be out, much less on the mountain side."

CHAPTER 9

THE CRAZY PARSON

Mrs. Julaper had grown weather-wise, living for so long

among this noble and solitary scenery, where people must observe Nature or else nothing—where signs of coming storm or change are almost local, and record themselves on particular cliffs and mountain-peaks, or in the mists, or in mirrored tints of the familiar lake, and are easily learned or remembered. At all events, her presage proved too true.

The sun had set an hour and more. It was dark; and an awful thunder-storm, whose march, like the distant reverberations of an invading army, had been faintly heard beyond the barriers of Blarwyn Fells throughout the afternoon, was near them now, and had burst in deep-mouthed battle among the ravines at the other side, and over the broad lake, that glared like a sheet of burnished steel under its flashes of dazzling blue. Wild and fitful blasts sweeping down the hollows and cloughs of the fells of Golden Friars agitated the lake, and bent the trees low, and whirled away their sere leaves in melancholy drift in their tremendous gusts. And from the window, looking on a scene enveloped in more than the darkness of the night, you saw in the pulsations of the lightning, before "the speedy gleams the darkness swallowed," the tossing trees and the flying foam and eddies on the lake.

In the midst of the hurly-burly, a loud and long knocking came at the hall-door of Mardykes. How long it had lasted before a chance lull made it audible I do not know.

There was nothing picturesquely poor, any more than there were evidences of wealth, anywhere in Sir Bale Mardykes' household. He had no lack of servants, but they were of an inexpensive and homely sort; and the hall-door being opened by the son of an old tenant on the estate—the tempest beating on the other side of the house, and comparative shelter under the gables at the front—he saw standing before him, in the agitated air, a thin old man, who muttering, it might be, a benediction, stepped into the hall, and displayed long silver tresses, just as the storm had blown them, ascetic and eager features, and a pair of large light eyes that wandered wildly. He was dressed in threadbare black; a pair of long leather gaiters, buckled high above his knee, protecting his thin shanks through moss and pool; and the singularity of his appearance was heightened by a wide-leafed felt hat, over which he had tied his handkerchief, so as to bring the leaf of it over his ears, and to secure it from being whirled from his head by the storm.

This odd and storm-beaten figure—tall, and a little stooping, as well as thin—was not unknown to the servant, who saluted him with something of fear as well as of respect as he bid him reverently welcome, and asked him to come in and sit by the fire.

"Get you to your master, and tell him I have a message to him from one he has not seen for two-and-forty years."

As the old man, with his harsh old voice, thus spoke, he un-knotted his handkerchief and bet the rain-drops from his hat upon his knee.

The servant knocked at the library-door, where he found Sir Bale.

"Well, what's the matter?" cried Sir Bale sharply, from his chair before the fire, with angry eyes looking over his shoulder.

"Here's 't sir cumman, Sir Bale," he answered.

"Sir," or "the Sir," is still used as the clergyman's title in the Northumbrian counties.

"What sir?"

"Sir Hugh Creswell, if you please, Sir Bale."

"Ho!—mad Creswell?—O, the crazy parson. Well, tell Mrs. Julaper to let him have some supper—and—and to let him have a bed in some suitable place. That's what he wants. These mad fellows know what they are about."

"No, Sir Bale Mardykes, that is not what he wants," said the loud wild voice of the daft sir over the servant's shoulder. "Often has Mardykes Hall given me share of its cheer and its shelter and the warmth of its fire; and I bless the house that has been an inn to the wayfarer of the Lord. But to-night I go up the lake to Pindar's Bield, three miles on; and there I rest and refresh—not here."

"And why not *here*, Mr. Creswell?" asked the Baronet; for

123

about this crazy old man, who preached in the fields, and appeared and disappeared so suddenly in the orbit of his wide and unknown perambulations of those northern and border counties, there was that sort of superstitious feeling which attaches to the mysterious and the good—an idea that it was lucky to harbour and dangerous to offend him. No one knew whence he came or whither he went. Once in a year, perhaps, he might appear at a lonely farmstead door among the fells, salute the house, enter, and be gone in the morning. His life was austere; his piety enthusiastic, severe, and tinged with the craze which inspired among the rustic population a sort of awe.

"I'll not sleep at Mardykes tonight; neither will I eat, nor drink, nor sit me down—no, nor so much as stretch my hands to the fire. As the man of God came out of Judah to king Jeroboam, so come I to you, sent by a vision, to bear a warning; and as he said, 'If thou wilt give me half thy house, I will not go in with thee, neither will I eat bread nor drink water in this place,' so also say I."

"Do as you please," said Sir Bale, a little sulkily. "Say your say; and you are welcome to stay or go, if go you will on so mad a night as this."

"Leave us," said Creswell, beckoning the servant back with his thin hands; "what I have to say is to your master."

The servant went, in obedience to a gesture from Sir Bale, and shut the door.

The old man drew nearer to the Baronet, and lowering his loud stern voice a little, and interrupting his discourse from time to time, to allow the near thunder-peals to subside, he said,

"Answer me, Sir Bale—what is this that has chanced between you and Philip Feltram?"

The Baronet, under the influence of that blunt and peremptory demand, told him shortly and sternly enough.

"And of all these facts you are sure, else ye would not blast your early companion and kinsman with the name of thief?"

"I *am* sure," said Sir Bale grimly.

"Unlock that cabinet," said the old man with the long white

locks.

"I've no objection," said Sir Bale; and he did unlock an old oak cabinet that stood, carved in high relief with strange figures and gothic grotesques, against the wall, opposite the fireplace. On opening it there were displayed a system of little drawers and pigeon-holes such as we see in more modern escritoires.

"Open that drawer with the red mark of a seal upon it," continued Hugh Creswell, pointing to it with his lank finger.

Sir Bale did so; and to his momentary amazement, and even consternation, there lay the missing note, which now, with one of those sudden caprices of memory which depend on the laws of suggestion and association, he remembered having placed there with his own hand.

"That is it," said old Creswell with a pallid smile, and fixing his wild eyes on the Baronet. The smile subsided into a frown, and said he: "Last night I slept near Haworth Moss; and your father came to me in a dream, and said: 'My son Bale accuses Philip of having stolen a bank-note from his desk. He forgets that he himself placed it in his cabinet. Come with me.' I was, in the spirit, in this room; and he led me to this cabinet, which he opened; and in that drawer he showed me that note. 'Go,' said he, 'and tell him to ask Philip Feltram's pardon, else he will but go in weakness to return in power;' and he said that which it is not lawful to repeat. My message is told. Now a word from myself," he added sternly. "The dead, through my lips, has spoken, and under God's thunder and lightning his words have found ye. Why so uppish wi' Philip Feltram? See how ye threaped, and yet were wrong. He's no tazzle—he's no taggelt. Ask his pardon. Ye must change, or he will no taggelt. Go, in weakness, come in power: mark ye the words. 'Twill make a peal that will be heard in toon and desert, in the swirls o' the mountain, through pikes and valleys, and mak' a waaly man o' thee."

The old man with these words, uttered in the broad northern dialect of his common speech, strode from the room and shut the door. In another minute he was forth into the storm, pursuing what remained of his long march to Pindar's Bield.

"Upon my soul!" said Sir Bale, recovering from his sort of stun which the sudden and strange visit had left, "that's a cool old fellow! Come to rate me and teach me my own business in my own house!" and he rapped out a fierce oath. "Change his mind or no, here he sha'n't stay tonight—not an hour."

Sir Bale was in the lobby in a moment, and thundered to his servants:

"I say, put that fool out of the door—put him out by the shoulder, and never let him put his foot inside it more!"

But the old man's yea was yea, and his nay nay. He had quite meant what he said; and, as I related, was beyond the reach of the indignity of extrusion.

Sir Bale on his return shut his door as violently as if it were in the face of the old prophet.

"Ask Feltram's pardon, by Jove! For what? Why, any jury on earth would have hanged him on half the evidence; and I, like a fool, was going to let him off with his liberty and my hundred pound-note! Ask his pardon indeed!"

Still there were misgivings in his mind; a consciousness that he did owe explanation and apology to Feltram, and an insurmountable reluctance to undertake either. The old dislike—a contempt mingled with fear—not any fear of his malevolence, a fear only of his carelessness and folly; for, as I have said, Feltram knew many things, it was believed, of the Baronet's Continental and Asiatic life, and had even gently remonstrated with him upon the dangers into which he was running. A simple fellow like Philip Feltram is a dangerous depository of a secret. This Baronet was proud, too; and the mere possession of his secrets by Feltram was an involuntary insult, which Sir Bale could not forgive. He wished him far away; and except for the recovery of his bank-note, which he could ill spare, he was sorry that this suspicion was cleared up.

The thunder and storm were unabated; it seemed indeed that they were growing wilder and more awful.

He opened the window-shutter and looked out upon that sublimest of scenes; and so intense and magnificent were its phenomena, that Sir Bale, for a while, was absorbed in this contemplation.

When he turned about, the sight of his L100 note, still between his finger and thumb, made him smile grimly.

The more he thought of it, the clearer it was that he could not leave matters exactly as they were. Well, what should he do? He would send for Mrs. Julaper, and tell her vaguely that he had changed his mind about Feltram, and that he might continue to stay at Mardykes Hall as usual. That would suffice. She could speak to Feltram.

He sent for her; and soon, in the lulls of the great uproar without, he could hear the jingle of Mrs. Julaper's keys and her light tread upon the lobby.

"Mrs. Julaper," said the Baronet, in his dry careless way, "Feltram may remain; your eloquence has prevailed. What have you been crying about?" he asked, observing that his housekeeper's usually cheerful face was, in her own phrase, 'all cried.'

"It is too late, sir; he's gone."

"And when did he go?" asked Sir Bale, a little put out. "He chose an odd evening, didn't he? So like him!"

"He went about half an hour ago; and I'm very sorry, sir; it's a sore sight to see the poor lad going from the place he was reared in, and a hard thing, sir; and on such a night, above all."

"No one asked him to go to-night. Where is he gone to?"

"I don't know, I'm sure; he left my room, sir, when I was upstairs; and Janet saw him pass the window not ten minutes after Mr. Creswell left the house."

"Well, then, there's no good, Mrs. Julaper, in thinking more about it; he has settled the matter his own way; and as he so ordains it—amen, say I. Goodnight."

CHAPTER 10
ADVENTURE IN TOM MARLIN'S BOAT

Philip Feltram was liked very well—a gentle, kindly, and very timid creature, and, before he became so heart-broken, a fellow who liked a joke or a pleasant story, and could laugh heartily.

Where will Sir Bale find so unresisting and respectful a butt and retainer? and whom will he bully now?

Something like remorse was worrying Sir Bale's heart a little; and the more he thought on the strange visit of Hugh Creswell that night, with its unexplained menace, the more uneasy he became.

The storm continued; and even to him there seemed something exaggerated and inhuman in the severity of his expulsion on such a night. It was his own doing, it was true; but would people believe that? and would he have thought of leaving Mardykes at all if it had not been for his kinsman's severity? Nay, was it not certain that if Sir Bale had done as Hugh Creswell had urged him, and sent for Feltram forthwith, and told him how all had been cleared up, and been a little friendly with him, he would have found him still in the house?—for he had not yet gone for ten minutes after Creswell's departure, and thus, all that was to follow might have been averted. But it was too late now, and Sir Bale would let the affair take its own course.

Below him, outside the window at which he stood ruminating, he heard voices mingling with the storm. He could with tolerable certainty perceive, looking into the obscurity, that there were three men passing close under it, carrying some very heavy burden among them.

He did not know what these three black figures in the obscurity were about. He saw them pass round the corner of the building toward the front, and in the lulls of the storm could hear their gruff voices talking.

We have all experienced what a presentiment is, and we all know with what an intuition the faculty of observation is sometimes heightened. It was such an apprehension as sometimes gives its peculiar horror to a dream—a sort of knowledge that what those people were about was in a dreadful way connected with his own fate.

He watched for a time, thinking that they might return; but they did not. He was in a state of uncomfortable suspense.

"If they want me, they won't have much trouble in finding

me, nor any scruple, egad, in plaguing me; they never have."

Sir Bale returned to his letters, a score of which he was that night getting off his conscience—an arrear which would not have troubled him had he not ceased, for two or three days, altogether to employ Philip Feltram, who had been accustomed to take all that sort of drudgery off his hands.

All the time he was writing now he had a feeling that the shadows he had seen pass under his window were machinating some trouble for him, and an uneasy suspense made him lift his eyes now and then to the door, fancying sounds and footsteps; and after a resultless wait he would say to himself, "If anyone is coming, why the devil don't he come?" and then he would apply himself again to his letters.

But on a sudden he heard good Mrs. Julaper's step trotting along the lobby, and the tiny ringing of her keys.

Here was news coming; and the Baronet stood up looking at the door, on which presently came a hurried rapping; and before he had answered, in the midst of a long thunder-clap that suddenly broke, rattling over the house, the good woman opened the door in great agitation, and cried with a tremulous uplifting of her hands.

"O, Sir Bale! O, la, sir! here's poor dear Philip Feltram come home dead!"

Sir Bale stared at her sternly for some seconds.

"Come, now, do be distinct," said Sir Bale; "what has happened?"

"He's lying on the sofa in the old still-room. You never saw—my God!—O, sir—what is life?"

"D—n it, can't you cry by-and-by, and tell me what's the matter now?"

"A bit o' fire there, as luck would have it; but what is hot or cold now? La, sir, they're all doin' what they can; he's drowned, sir, and Tom Warren is on the gallop down to Golden Friars for Doctor Torvey."

"*Is* he drowned, or is it only a ducking? Come, bring me to the place. Dead men don't usually want a fire, or consult doctors.

I'll see for myself."

So Sir Bale Mardykes, pale and grim, accompanied by the light-footed Mrs. Julaper, strode along the passages, and was led by her into the old still-room, which had ceased to be used for its original purpose. All the servants in the house were now collected there, and three men also who lived by the margin of the lake; one of them thoroughly drenched, with rivulets of water still trickling from his sleeves, water along the wrinkles and pockets of his waistcoat and from the feet of his trousers, and pumping and oozing from his shoes, and streaming from his hair down the channels of his cheeks like a continuous rain of tears.

The people drew back a little as Sir Bale entered with a quick step and a sharp pallid frown on his face. There was a silence as he stooped over Philip Feltram, who lay on a low bed next the wall, dimly lighted by two or three candles here and there about the room.

He laid his hand, for a moment, on his cold wet breast.

Sir Bale knew what should be done in order to give a man in such a case his last chance for life. Everybody was speedily put in motion. Philip's drenched clothes were removed, hot blankets enveloped him, warming-pans and hot bricks lent their aid; he was placed at the prescribed angle, so that the water flowed freely from his mouth. The old expedient for inducing artificial breathing was employed, and a lusty pair of bellows did duty for his lungs.

But these helps to life, and suggestions to nature, availed not. Forlorn and peaceful lay the features of poor Philip Feltram; cold and dull to the touch; no breath through the blue lips; no sight in the fish-like eyes; pulseless and cold in the midst of all the hot bricks and warming-pans about him.

At length, everything having been tried, Sir Bale, who had been directing, placed his hand within the clothes, and laid it silently on Philip's shoulder and over his heart; and after a little wait, he shook his head, and looking down on his sunken face, he said,

"I am afraid he's gone. Yes, he's gone, poor fellow! And bear you this in mind, all of you; Mrs. Julaper there can tell you more about it. She knows that it was certainly in no compliance with my wish that he left the house to-night: it was his own obstinate perversity, and perhaps—I forgive him for it—a wish in his un-reasonable resentment to throw some blame upon this house, as having refused him shelter on such a night; than which imputa-tion nothing can be more utterly false. Mrs. Julaper there knows how welcome he was to stay the night; but he would not; he had made up his mind, it seems, without telling any person. Had he told you, Mrs. Julaper?"

"No, sir," sobbed Mrs. Julaper from the centre of a pocket-handkerchief in which her face was buried.

"Not a human being: an angry whim of his own. Poor Fel-tram! and here's the result," said the Baronet. "We have done our best—done everything. I don't think the doctor, when he comes, will say that anything has been omitted; but all won't do. Does anyone here know how it happened?"

Two men knew very well—the man who had been ducked, and his companion, a younger man, who was also in the still-room, and had lent a hand in carrying Feltram up to the house.

Tom Marlin had a queer old stone tenement by the edge of the lake just under Mardykes Hall. Some people said it was the stump of an old tower that had once belonged to Mardykes Castle, of which in the modern building scarcely a relic was discoverable.

This Tom Marlin had an ancient right of fishing in the lake, where he caught pike enough for all Golden Friars; and keeping a couple of boats, he made money beside by ferrying passengers over now and then. This fellow, with a furrowed face and shaggy eyebrows, bald at top, but with long grizzled locks falling upon his shoulders, said,

"He wer wi' me this mornin', sayin' he'd want t' boat to cross the lake in, but he didn't say what hour; and when it came on to thunder and blow like this, ye guess I did not look to see him tonight. Well, my wife was just lightin' a pig-tail—tho' light enough and to spare there was in the lift already—when who should come clatterin' at the latch-pin in the blow o' thunder and wind but Philip, poor lad, himself; and an ill hour for him it was. He's been some time in ill fettle, though he was never frowsy, not he, but always kind and dooce, and canty once, like anither; and he asked me to tak the boat across the lake at once to the Clough o' Cloostedd at t'other side. The woman took the pet and wodn't hear o't; and, 'Dall me, if I go tonight,' quoth I. But he would not be put off so, not he; and dingdrive he went to it, cryin' and putrein' ye'd a-said, poor fellow, he was wrang i' his garrets a'most.

"So at long last I bethought me, there's nout o' a sea to the north o' Snakes Island, so I'll pull him by that side—for the storm is blowin' right up by Golden Friars, ye mind—and when we get near the point, thinks I, he'll see wi' his een how the lake is, and gie it up. For I liked him, poor lad; and seein' he'd set his heart on't, I wouldn't vex nor frump him wi' a no. So down we three—myself, and Bill there, and Philip Feltram—come to the boat; and we pulled out, keeping Snakes Island atwixt us and the wind. 'Twas smooth water wi' us, for 'twas a scug there, but white enough was all beyont the point; and passing the finger-stone, not forty fathom from the shore o' the island, Bill and me pullin' and he sittin' in the stern, poor lad, up he rises, a bit rabblin' to himself, wi' his hands lifted so.

"'Look a-head!' says I, thinkin' something wos comin' atort us.

"But 'twasn't that. The boat was quiet, for while we looked, oo'er our shouthers, oo'er her bows, we didn't pull, so she lay still; and lookin' back again on Philip, he was rabblin' on all the same.

"'It's nobbut a prass wi' himsel'', poor lad,' thinks I.

"But that wasn't it neither; for I sid something white come out o' t' water, by the gunwale, like a hand. By Jen! and he leans oo'er and tuk it; and he sagged like, and so it drew him in, under the mere, before I cud du nout. There was nout to thraa tu him, and no time; down he went, and I followed; and thrice I dived before I found him, and brought him up by the hair at last; and there he is, poor lad! and all one if he lay at the bottom o' t' mere."

As Tom Marlin ended his narrative—often interrupted by the noise of the tempest without, and the peals of thunder that echoed awfully above, like the chorus of a melancholy ballad—the sudden clang of the hall-door bell, and a more faintly-heard knocking, announced a new arrival.

Chapter 11

Sir Bale's Dream

It was Doctor Torvey who entered the old still-room now, buttoned-up to the chin in his greatcoat, and with a muffler of many colours wrapped partly over that feature.

"Well!—hey? So poor Feltram's had an accident?"

The Doctor was addressing Sir Bale, and getting to the bedside as he pulled off his gloves.

"I see you've been keeping him warm—that's right; and a considerable flow of water from his mouth; turn him a little that way. Hey? O, ho!" said the Doctor, as he placed his hand upon Philip, and gently stirred his limbs. "It's more than an hour since this happened. I'm afraid there's very little to be done now;" and in a lower tone, with his hand on poor Philip Feltram's arm, and so down to his fingers, he said in Sir Bale Mardykes' ear, with a shake of his head,

"Here, you see, poor fellow, here's the cadaveric stiffness; it's very melancholy, but it's all over, he's gone; there's no good trying any more. Come here, Mrs. Julaper. Did you ever see any one dead? Look at his eyes, look at his mouth. You ought to have known that, with half an eye. And you know," he added again confidentially in Sir Bale's ear, "trying any more *now* is all my eye."

Then after a few more words with the Baronet, and having heard his narrative, he said from time to time, "Quite right; nothing could be better; capital practice, sir," and so forth. And at the close of all this, amid the sobs of kind Mrs. Julaper and the general whimpering of the humbler handmaids, the Doctor standing by the bed, with his knuckles on the coverlet, and a glance now and then on the dead face beside him, said—by way of 'quieting men's minds,' as the old tract-writers used to say—a few words to the following effect:

"Everything has been done here that the most experienced physician could have wished. Everything has been done in the best way. I don't know anything that has not been done, in fact. If I had been here myself, I don't know—hot bricks—salt isn't a bad thing. I don't know, I say, that anything of any consequence has been omitted." And looking at the body, "You see," and he drew the fingers a little this way and that, letting them return, as they stiffly did, to their former attitude, "you may be sure that the poor gentleman was quite dead by the time he arrived here. So, since he was laid there, nothing has been lost by delay. And, Sir Bale, if you have any directions to send to Golden Friars, sir, I shall be most happy to undertake your message."

"Nothing, thanks; it is a melancholy ending, poor fellow! You must come to the study with me, Doctor Torvey, and talk a little bit more; and—very sad, doctor—and you must have a glass of sherry, or some port—the port used not to be bad here; I don't take it—but very melancholy it is—bring some port and sherry; and, Mrs. Julaper, you'll be good enough to see that everything that should be done here is looked to; and let Marlin and the men have supper and something to drink. You have been too long in your wet clothes, Marlin."

So, with gracious words all round, he led the Doctor to the library where he had been sitting, and was affable and hospitable, and told him his own version of all that had passed between him and Philip Feltram, and presented himself in an amiable point of view, and pleased the Doctor with his port and flatteries—for he could not afford to lose anyone's good word just now; and the Doctor was a bit of a gossip, and in most houses in that region, in one character or another, every three months in the year.

So in due time the Doctor drove back to Golden Friars, with a high opinion of Sir Bale, and higher still of his port, and highest of all of himself: in the best possible humour with the world, not minding the storm that blew in his face, and which he defied in good-humoured mock-heroics spoken in somewhat thick accents, and regarding the thunder and lightning as a lively gala of fireworks; and if there had been a chance of finding his cronies still in the George and Dragon, he would have been among them forthwith, to relate the tragedy of the night, and tell what a good fellow, after all, Sir Bale was; and what a fool, at best, poor Philip Feltram.

But the George was quiet for that night. The thunder rolled over voiceless chambers; and the lights had been put out within the windows, on whose multitudinous small panes the lightning glared. So the Doctor went home to Mrs. Torvey, whom he charmed into good-humoured curiosity by the tale of wonder he had to relate.

Sir Bale's qualms were symptomatic of something a little less sublime and more selfish than conscience. He was not sorry that Philip Feltram was out of the way. His lips might begin to babble inconveniently at any time, and why should not his mouth be stopped? and what stopper so effectual as that plug of clay which fate had introduced? But he did not want to be charged with the odium of the catastrophe. Every man cares something for the opinion of his fellows. And seeing that Feltram had been well liked, and that his death had excited a vehement commiseration, Sir Bale did not wish it to be said that he had made the house too hot to hold him, and had so driven him to extremity.

Sir Bale's first agitation had subsided. It was now late, he had written many letters, and he was tired. It was not wonderful, then, that having turned his lounging-chair to the fire, he should have fallen asleep in it, as at last he did.

The storm was passing gradually away by this time. The thunder was now echoing among the distant glens and gorges of Daulness Fells, and the angry roar and gusts of the tempest were subsiding into the melancholy soughing and piping that soothe like a lullaby.

Sir Bale therefore had his unpremeditated sleep very comfortably, except that his head was hanging a little uneasily; which, perhaps, helped him to this dream.

It was one of those dreams in which the continuity of the waking state that immediately preceded it seems unbroken; for he thought that he was sitting in the chair which he occupied, and in the room where he actually was. It seemed to him that he got up, took a candle in his hand, and went through the passages to the old still-room where Philip Feltram lay. The house seemed perfectly still. He could hear the chirp of the crickets faintly from the distant kitchen, and the tick of the clock sounded loud and hollow along the passage. In the old still-room, as he opened the door, was no light, except what was admitted from the candle he carried.

He found the body of poor Philip Feltram just as he had left it—his gentle face, saddened by the touch of death, was turned upwards, with white lips: with traces of suffering fixed in its outlines, such as caused Sir Bale, standing by the bed, to draw the coverlet over the dead man's features, which seemed silently to upbraid him. "Gone in weakness!" said Sir Bale, repeating the words of the "daft sir," Hugh Creswell; as he did so, a voice whispered near him, with a great sigh, "Come in power!" He looked round, in his dream, but there was no one; the light seemed to fail, and a horror slowly overcame him, especially as he thought he saw the figure under the coverlet stealthily beginning to move.

Backing towards the door, for he could not take his eyes off it, he saw something like a huge black ape creep out at the foot of the bed; and springing at him, it griped him by the throat, so that he could not breathe; and a thousand voices were instantly round him, holloaing, cursing, laughing in his ears; and in this direful plight he waked.

Was it the ring of those voices still in his ears, or a real shriek, and another, and a long peal, shriek after shriek, swelling madly through the distant passages, that held him still, freezing in the horror of his dream?

I will tell you what this noise was.

Chapter 12

Marcella Bligh and Judith Wale Keep Watch

After his bottle of port with Sir Bale, the Doctor had gone down again to the room where poor Philip Feltram lay.

Mrs. Julaper had dried her eyes, and was busy by this time; and two old women were making all their arrangements for a night-watch by the body, which they had washed, and, as their phrase goes, 'laid out' in the humble bed where it had lain while there was still a hope that a spark sufficient to rekindle the fire of life might remain. These old women had points of resemblance: they were lean, sallow, and wonderfully wrinkled, and looked each malign and ugly enough for a witch.

Marcella Bligh's thin hooked nose was now like the beak of a bird of prey over the face of the drowned man, upon whose eyelids she was placing penny-pieces, to keep them from opening; and her one eye was fixed on her work, its sightless companion showing white in its socket, with an ugly leer.

Judith Wale was lifting the pail of hot water with which they had just washed the body. She had long lean arms, a hunched back, a great sharp chin sunk on her hollow breast, and small eyes restless as a ferret's; and she clattered about in great bowls of shoes, old and clouted, that were made for a foot as big as two of hers.

The Doctor knew these two old women, who were often employed in such dismal offices.

"How does Mrs. Bligh? See me with half an eye? Hey—that's rhyme, isn't it?—And, Judy lass—why, I thought you lived nearer the town—here making poor Mr. Feltram's last toilet. You have helped to dress many a poor fellow for his last journey. Not a bad notion of drill either—they stand at attention stiff and straight enough in the sentry-box. Your recruits do you credit, Mrs. Wale."

The Doctor stood at the foot of the bed to inspect, breathing forth a vapour of very fine old port, his hands in his pockets, speaking with a lazy thickness, and looking so comfortable and facetious, that Mrs. Julaper would have liked to turn him out of the room.

But the Doctor was not unkind, only extremely comfortable. He was a good-natured fellow, and had thought and care for the living, but not a great deal of sentiment for the dead, whom he had looked in the face too often to be much disturbed by the spectacle.

"You'll have to keep that bandage on. You should be sharp; you should know all about it, girl, by this time, and not let those muscles stiffen. I need not tell you the mouth shuts as easily as this snuff-box, if you only take it in time.—I suppose, Mrs. Julaper, you'll send to Jos Fringer for the poor fellow's outfit. Fringer is a very proper man—there ain't a properer und-aker in England. I always re-mmend Fringer—in Church-street in Golden Friars. You know Fringer, I daresay."

"I can't say, sir, I'm sure. That will be as Sir Bale may please to direct," answered Mrs. Julaper.

"You've got him very straight—straighter than I thought you could; but the large joints were not so stiff. A very little longer wait, and you'd hardly have got him into his coffin. He'll want a vr-r-ry long one, poor lad. Short cake is life, ma'am. Sad thing this. They'll open their eyes, I promise you, down in the town. 'Twill be cool enough, I'd shay, affre all th-thunr-thunnle, you know. I think I'll take a nip, Mrs. Jool-fr, if you wouldn't mine makin' me out a thimmle-ful bran-band-bran-rand-andy, eh, Mishs Joolfr?"

And the Doctor took a chair by the fire; and Mrs. Julaper, with a dubious conscience and dry hospitality, procured the brandy-flask and wine-glass, and helped the physician in a thin hesitating stream, which left him ample opportunity to cry "Hold—enough!" had he been so minded. But that able physician had no confidence, it would seem, in any dose under a bumper, which he sipped with commendation, and then fell asleep with the firelight on his face—to tender-hearted Mrs. Julaper's disgust—and snored with a sensual disregard of the solemnity of his situation; until with a profound nod, or rather dive, toward the fire, he awoke, got up and shook his ears with a kind of start, and standing with his back to the fire, asked for his muffler and horse; and so took his leave also of the weird sisters, who were still pottering about the body, with croak and whisper, and nod and ogle. He took his leave also of good Mrs. Julaper, who was completing arrangements with teapot and kettle, spiced elderberry wine, and other comforts, to support them through their proposed vigil. And finally, in a sort of way, he took his leave of the body, with a long business-like stare, from the foot of the bed, with his short hands stuffed into his pockets. And so, to Mrs. Julaper's relief, this unseemly doctor, speaking thickly, departed.

And now, the Doctor being gone, and all things prepared for the 'wake' to be observed by withered Mrs. Bligh of the one eye, and yellow Mrs. Wale of the crooked back, the house grew gradually still. The thunder had by this time died into the solid boom of distant battle, and the fury of the gale had subsided to the long sobbing wail that is charged with so eerie a melancholy. Within all was stirless, and the two old women, each a 'Mrs.' by courtesy, who had not much to thank Nature or the world for, sad and cynical, and in a sort outcasts told off by fortune to these sad and grizzly services, sat themselves down by the fire, each perhaps feeling unusually at home in the other's society; and in this soured and forlorn comfort, trimming their fire, quickening the song of the kettle to a boil, and waxing polite and chatty; each treating the other with that deprecatory and formal courtesy which invites a return in kind, and both growing strangely happy in this little world of their own, in the unusual and momentary sense of an importance and consideration which were delightful.

The old still-room of Mardykes Hall is an oblong room wainscoted. From the door you look its full length to the wide stone-shafted Tudor window at the other end. At your left is the ponderous mantelpiece, supported by two spiral stone pillars; and close to the door at the right was the bed in which the two crones had just stretched poor Philip Feltram, who lay as still as an uncoloured wax-work, with a heavy penny-piece on each eye, and a bandage under his jaw, making his mouth look stern. And the two old ladies over their tea by the fire conversed agreeably, compared their rheumatisms and other ailments wordily, and talked of old times, and early recollections, and of sick-beds they had attended, and corpses that "you would not know, so pined and windered" were they; and others so fresh and canny, you'd say the dead had never looked so bonny in life.

Then they began to talk of people who grew tall in their coffins, of others who had been buried alive, and of others who walked after death. Stories as true as holy writ.

"Were you ever down by Hawarth, Mrs. Bligh—hard by Dalworth Moss?" asked crook-backed Mrs. Wale, holding her spoon suspended over her cup.

"Neea whaar sooa far south, Mrs. Wale, ma'am; but ma father was off times down thar cuttin' peat."

"Ah, then ye'll not a kenned farmer Dykes that lived by the Lin-tree Scaur. 'Tweer I that laid him out, poor aad fellow, and a dow man he was when aught went cross wi' him; and he cursed and sweared, twad gar ye dodder to hear him. They said he was a hard man wi' some folk; but he kep a good house, and liked to see plenty, and many a time when I was swaimous about my food, he'd clap t' meat on ma plate, and mak' me eat ma fill. Na, na—there was good as well as bad in farmer Dykes. It was a year after he deed, and Tom Ettles was walking home, down by the Birken Stoop one night, and not a soul nigh, when he sees a big ball, as high as his knee, whirlin' and spangin' away before him on the road. What it wer he could not think; but he never consayted there was a freet or a bo thereaway; so he kep near it, watching every spang and turn it took, till it ran into the gripe by the roadside.

"There was a gravel pit just there, and Tom Ettles wished to take another gliff at it before he went on. But when he keeked into the pit, what should he see but a man attoppa a horse that could not get up or on: and says he, 'I think ye be at a dead-lift there, gaffer.' And wi' the word, up looks the man, and who sud it be but farmer Dykes himsel; and Tom Ettles saw him plain eneugh, and kenned the horse too for Black Captain, the farmer's aad beast, that broke his leg and was shot two years and more before the farmer died. 'Ay,' says farmer Dykes, lookin' very bad; 'forsett-and-backsett, ye'll tak me oot, Tom Ettles, and clap ye doun behint me quick, or I'll claw ho'd o' thee.' Tom felt his hair risin' stiff on his heed, and his tongue so fast to the roof o' his mouth he could scarce get oot a word; but says he, 'If Black Jack can't do it o' noo, he'll ne'er do't and carry double.'

"'I ken my ain business best,' says Dykes. 'If ye gar me gie ye a look, 'twill gie ye the creepin's while ye live; so git ye doun, Tom;' and with that the dobby lifts its neaf, and Tom saw there was a red light round horse and man, like the glow of a peat fire. And says Tom, 'In the name o' God, ye'll let me pass;' and with the word the gooast draws itsel' doun, all a-creaked, like a man wi' a sudden pain; and Tom Ettles took to his heels more deed than alive."

They had approached their heads, and the story had sunk to that mysterious murmur that thrills the listener, when in the brief silence that followed they heard a low odd laugh near the door.

In that direction each lady looked aghast, and saw Feltram sitting straight up in the bed, with the white bandage in his hand, and as it seemed, for one foot was below the coverlet, near the floor, about to glide forth.

Mrs. Bligh, uttering a hideous shriek, clutched Mrs. Wale, and Mrs. Wale, with a scream as dreadful, gripped Mrs. Bligh; and quite forgetting their somewhat formal politeness, they reeled and tugged, wrestling towards the window, each struggling to place her companion between her and the 'dobby,' and both uniting in a direful peal of yells.

This was the uproar which had startled Sir Bale from his dream, and was now startling the servants from theirs.

CHAPTER 13
THE MIST ON THE MOUNTAIN

Doctor Torvey was sent for early next morning, and came full of wonder, learning and scepticism. Seeing is believing, however; and there was Philip Feltram living, and soon to be, in all bodily functions, just as usual.

"Upon my soul, Sir Bale, I couldn't have believed it, if I had not seen it with my eyes," said the Doctor impressively, while sipping a glass of sherry in the 'breakfast parlour,' as the great panelled and pictured room next the dining-room was called. "I don't think there is any similar case on record—no pulse, no more than the poker; no respiration, by Jove, no more than the chimney-piece; as cold as a lead image in the garden there. Well, you'll say all that might possibly be fallacious; but what will you say to the cadaveric stiffness? Old Judy Wale can tell you; and my friend Marcella—Monocula would be nearer the mark—Mrs. Bligh, she knows all those common, and I may say up to this, infallible, signs of death, as well as I do. There is no mystery about them; they'll depose to the literality of the symptoms. You heard how they gave tongue. Upon my honour, I'll send the whole case up to my old chief, Sir Hervey Hansard, to London. You'll hear what a noise it will make among the profession. There never was—and it ain't too much to say there never *will* be—another case like it."

During this lecture, and a great deal more, Sir Bale leaned back in his chair, with his legs extended, his heels on the ground, and his arms folded, looking sourly up in the face of a tall lady in white satin, in a ruff, and with a bird on her hand, who smiled down superciliously from her frame on the Baronet. Sir Bale seemed a little bit high and dry with the Doctor.

"You physicians are unquestionably," he said, "a very learned profession."

The Doctor bowed.

"But there's just one thing you know nothing about——"

"Eh? What's that?" inquired Doctor Torvey.

"Medicine," answered Sir Bale. "I was aware you never knew what was the matter with a sick man; but I didn't know, till now, that you couldn't tell when he was dead."

"Ha, ha!—well—ha, ha!—*yes*—well, you see, you—ha, ha!-

you certainly have me there. But it's a case without a parallel—it is, upon my honour. You'll find it will not only be talked about, but written about; and, whatever papers appear upon it, will come to me; and I'll take care, Sir Bale, you shall have an opportunity of reading them."

"Of which I shan't avail myself," answered Sir Bale. "Take another glass of sherry, Doctor."

The Doctor made his acknowledgments and filled his glass, and looked through the wine between him and the window.

"Ha, ha!—see there, your port, Sir Bale, gives a fellow such habits—looking for the beeswing, by Jove. It isn't easy, in one sense at least, to get your port out of a fellow's head when once he has tasted it."

But if the honest Doctor meant a hint for a glass of that admirable bin, it fell pointless; and Sir Bale had no notion of making another libation of that precious fluid in honour of Doctor Torvey.

"And I take it for granted," said Sir Bale, "that Feltram will do very well; and, should anything go wrong, I can send for you—unless he should die again; and in that case I think I shall take my own opinion."

So he and the Doctor parted.

Sir Bale, although he did not consult the Doctor on his own case, was not particularly well. "That lonely place, those frightful mountains, and that damp black lake"—which features in the landscape he cursed all round—"are enough to give any man blue devils; and when a fellow's spirits go, he's all gone. That's why I'm dyspeptic—that and those d——d debts—and the post, with its flight of croaking and screeching letters from London. I wish there was no post here. I wish it was like Sir Amyrald's time, when they shot the York mercer that came to dun him, and no one ever took anyone to task about it; and now they can pelt you at any distance they please through the post; and fellows lose their spirits and their appetite and any sort of miserable comfort that is possible in this odious abyss."

Was there gout in Sir Bale's case, or 'vapours'? I know not

what the faculty would have called it; but Sir Bale's mode of treatment was simply to work off the attack by long and laborious walking.

This evening his walk was upon the Fells of Golden Friars—long after the landscape below was in the eclipse of twilight, the broad bare sides and angles of these gigantic uplands were still lighted by the misty western sun.

There is no such sense of solitude as that which we experience upon the silent and vast elevations of great mountains. Lifted high above the level of human sounds and habitations, among the wild expanses and colossal features of Nature, we are thrilled in our loneliness with a strange fear and elation—an ascent above the reach of life's vexations or companionship, and the tremblings of a wild and undefined misgiving. The filmy disc of the moon had risen in the east, and was already faintly silvering the shadowy scenery below, while yet Sir Bale stood in the mellow light of the western sun, which still touched also the summits of the opposite peaks of Morvyn Fells.

Sir Bale Mardykes did not, as a stranger might, in prudence, hasten his descent from the heights at which he stood while yet a gleam of daylight remained to him. For he was, from his boyhood, familiar with those solitary regions; and, beside this, the thin circle of the moon, hung in the eastern sky, would brighten as the sunlight sank, and hang like a lamp above his steps.

There was in the bronzed and resolute face of the Baronet, lighted now in the parting beams of sunset, a resemblance to that of Charles the Second—not our "merry" ideal, but the more energetic and saturnine face which the portraits have preserved to us.

He stood with folded arms on the side of the slope, admiring, in spite of his prejudice, the unusual effects of a view so strangely lighted—the sunset tints on the opposite peaks, lost in the misty twilight, now deepening lower down into a darker shade, through which the outlines of the stone gables and tower of Golden Friars and the light of fire or candle in their windows were dimly visible.

As he stood and looked, his more distant sunset went down, and sudden twilight was upon him, and he began to remember the beautiful Homeric picture of a landscape coming out, rock and headland, in the moonlight.

There had hung upon the higher summits, at his right, a heavy fold of white cloud, which on a sudden broke, and, like the smoke of artillery, came rolling down the slopes toward him. Its principal volume, however, unfolded itself in a mighty flood down the side of the mountain towards the lake; and that which spread towards and soon enveloped the ground on which he stood was by no means so dense a fog. A thick mist enough it was; but still, to a distance of twenty or thirty yards, he could discern the outline of a rock or scaur, but not beyond it.

There are few sensations more intimidating than that of being thus enveloped on a lonely mountain-side, which, like this one, here and there breaks into precipice.

There is another sensation, too, which affects the imagination. Overtaken thus on the solitary expanse, there comes a new chill and tremor as this treacherous medium surrounds us, through which unperceived those shapes which fancy conjures up might approach so near and bar our path.

From the risk of being reduced to an actual standstill he knew he was exempt. The point from which the wind blew, light as it was, assured him of that. Still the mist was thick enough seriously to embarrass him. It had overtaken him as he was looking down upon the lake; and he now looked to his left, to try whether in that direction it was too thick to permit a view of the nearest landmarks. Through this white film he saw a figure standing only about five-and-twenty steps away, looking down, as it seemed, in precisely the same direction as he, quite motionless, and standing like a shadow projected upon the smoky vapour. It was the figure of a slight tall man, with his arm extended, as if pointing to a remote object, which no mortal eye certainly could discern through the mist. Sir Bale gazed at this figure, doubtful whether he were in a waking dream, unable to conjecture whence it had come; and as he looked, it moved, and was almost instantly out of sight.

He descended the mountain cautiously. The mist was now thinner, and through the haze he was beginning to see objects more distinctly, and, without danger, to proceed at a quicker pace. He had still a long walk by the uplands towards Mardykes Hall before he descended to the level of the lake.

The mist was still quite thick enough to circumscribe his view and to hide the general features of the landscape; and well was it, perhaps, for Sir Bale that his boyhood had familiarised him with the landmarks on the mountain-side.

He had made nearly four miles on his solitary homeward way, when, passing under a ledge of rock which bears the name of the Cat's Skaitch, he saw the same figure in the short cloak standing within some thirty or forty yards of him—the thin curtain of mist, through which the moonlight touched it, giving to it an airy and unsubstantial character.

Sir Bale came to a standstill. The man in the short cloak nodded and drew back, and was concealed by the angle of the rock.

Sir Bale was now irritated, as men are after a start, and shouting to the stranger to halt, he 'slapped' after him, as the northern phrase goes, at his best pace. But again he was gone, and nowhere could he see him, the mist favouring his evasion.

Looking down the fells that overhang Mardykes Hall, the mountain-side dips gradually into a glen, which, as it descends, becomes precipitous and wooded. A footpath through this ravine conducts the wayfarer to the level ground that borders the lake; and by this dark pass Sir Bale Mardykes strode, in comparatively clear air, along the rocky path dappled with moonlight.

As he emerged upon the lower ground he again encountered the same figure. It approached. It was Philip Feltram.

Chapter 14
A New Philip Feltram

The Baronet had not seen Feltram since his strange escape from death. His last interview with him had been stern and threatening; Sir Bale dealing with appearances in the spirit of an incensed judge, Philip Feltram lamenting in the submission of a helpless despair.

Feltram was full in the moonlight now, standing erect, and smiling cynically on the Baronet.

There was that in the bearing and countenance of Feltram that disconcerted him more than the surprise of the sudden meeting.

He had determined to meet Feltram in a friendly way, whenever that not very comfortable interview became inevitable. But he was confused by the suddenness of Feltram's appearance; and the tone, cold and stern, in which he had last spoken to him came first, and he spoke in it after a brief silence.

"I fancied, Mr. Feltram, you were in your bed; I little expected to find you here. I think the Doctor gave very particular directions, and said that you were to remain perfectly quiet."

"But I know more than the Doctor," replied Feltram, still smiling unpleasantly.

"I think, sir, you would have been better in your bed," said Sir Bale loftily.

"Come, come, come, come!" exclaimed Philip Feltram contemptuously.

"It seems to me," said Sir Bale, a good deal astonished, "you rather forget yourself."

"Easier to forget oneself, Sir Bale, than to forgive others, at times," replied Philip Feltram in his unparalleled mood.

"That's the way fools knock themselves up," continued Sir Bale. "You've been walking ever so far—away to the Fells of Golden Friars. It was you whom I saw there. What d——d folly! What brought you there?"

"To observe you," he replied.

"And have you walked the whole way there and back again? How did you get there?"

"Pooh! how did I come—how did you come—how did the fog come? From the lake, I suppose. We all come up, and then down." So spoke Philip Feltram, with serene insolence.

"You are pleased to talk nonsense," said Sir Bale.

"Because I like it—with a *meaning.*"

Sir Bale looked at him, not knowing whether to believe his eyes and ears. He did not know what to make of him.

"I had intended speaking to you in a conciliatory way; you seem to wish to make that impossible"—Philip Feltram's face wore its repulsive smile;—"and in fact I don't know what to make of you, unless you are ill; and ill you well may be. You can't have walked much less than twelve miles."

"Wonderful effort for me!" said Feltram with the same sneer.

"Rather surprising for a man so nearly drowned," answered Sir Bale Mardykes.

"A dip: you don't like the lake, sir; but I do. And so it is: as Antaeus touched the earth, so I the water, and rise refreshed."

"I think you'd better get in and refresh there. I meant to tell you that all the unpleasantness about that bank-note is over."

"Is it?"

"Yes. It has been recovered by Mr. Creswell, who came here last night. I've got it, and you're not to blame," said Sir Bale.

"But someone *is* to blame," observed Mr. Feltram, smiling still.

"Well, *you* are not, and that ends it," said the Baronet peremptorily.

"Ends it? Really, how good! how very good!"

Sir Bale looked at him, for there was something ambiguous and even derisive in the tone of Feltram's voice.

But before he could quite make up his mind, Feltram spoke again.

"Everything is settled about you and me?"

"There is nothing to prevent your staying at Mardykes now," said Sir Bale graciously.

"I shall be with you for two years, and then I go on my travels," answered Feltram, with a saturnine and somewhat wild look around him.

"Is he going mad?" thought the Baronet.

"But before I go, I'm to put you in a way of paying off your mortgages. That is my business here."

Sir Bale looked at him sharply. But now there was not the unpleasant smile, but the darkened look of a man in secret pain.

"You shall know it all by and by."

And without more ceremony, and with a darkening face, Philip Feltram made his way under the boughs of the thick oaks that grew there, leaving on Sir Bale's mind an impression that he had been watching someone at a distance, and had gone in consequence of a signal.

In a few seconds he followed in the same direction, halloaing after Feltram; for he did not like the idea of his wandering about the country by moonlight, or possibly losing his life among the precipices, and bringing a new discredit upon his house. But no answer came; nor could he in that thick copse gain sight of him again.

When Sir Bale reached Mardykes Hall he summoned Mrs. Julaper, and had a long talk with her. But she could not say that there appeared anything amiss with Philip Feltram; only he seemed more reserved, and as if he was brooding over something he did not intend to tell.

"But, you know, Sir Bale, what happened might well make a thoughtful man of him. If he's ever to think of Death, it should be after looking him so hard in the face; and I'm not ashamed to say, I'm glad to see he has grace to take the lesson, and I hope his experiences may be sanctified to him, poor fellow! Amen."

"Very good song, and very well sung," said Sir Bale; "but it doesn't seem to me that he has been improved, Mrs. Julaper. He seems, on the contrary, in a queer temper and anything but a heavenly frame of mind; and I thought I'd ask you, because if he is ill—I mean feverish—it might account for his eccentricities, as well as make it necessary to send after him, and bring him home, and put him to bed. But I suppose it is as you say,—his adventure has upset him a little, and he'll sober in a day or two, and return to his old ways."

But this did not happen. A change, more comprehensive than

at first appeared, had taken place, and a singular alteration was gradually established.

He grew thin, his eyes hollow, his face gradually forbidding.

His ways and temper were changed: he was a new man with Sir Bale; and the Baronet after a time, people said, began to grow afraid of him. And certainly Feltram had acquired an extraordinary influence over the Baronet, who a little while ago had regarded and treated him with so much contempt.

CHAPTER 15
THE PURSE OF GOLD

The Baronet was very slightly known in his county. He had led a reserved and inhospitable life. He was pressed upon by heavy debts; and being a proud man, held aloof from society and its doings. He wished people to understand that he was nursing his estate; but somehow the estate did not thrive at nurse. In the country other people's business is admirably well known; and the lord of Mardykes was conscious, perhaps, that his neighbours knew as well he did, that the utmost he could do was to pay the interest charged upon it, and to live in a frugal way enough.

The lake measures some four or five miles across, from the little jetty under the walls of Mardykes Hall to Cloostedd.

Philip Feltram, changed and morose, loved a solitary row upon the lake; and sometimes, with no one to aid him in its management, would take the little sailboat and pass the whole day upon those lonely waters.

Frequently he crossed to Cloostedd; and mooring the boat under the solemn trees that stand reflected in that dark mirror, he would disembark and wander among the lonely woodlands, as people thought, cherishing in those ancestral scenes the memory of ineffaceable injuries, and the wrath and revenge that seemed of late to darken his countenance, and to hold him always in a moody silence.

One autumnal evening Sir Bale Mardykes was sourly ruminating after his solitary meal. A very red sun was pouring its last low beams through the valley at the western extremity of the lake, across its elsewhere sombre waters, and touching with a sudden and blood-red tint the sail of the skiff in which Feltram was returning from his lonely cruise.

"Here comes my domestic water-fiend," sneered Sir Bale, as he lay back in his cumbrous armchair. "Cheerful place, pleasant people, delicious fate! The place alone has been enough to set that fool out of his little senses, d——n him!"

Sir Bale averted his eyes, and another subject not pleasanter entered his mind. He was thinking of the races that were coming off next week at Heckleston Downs, and what sums of money might be made there, and how hard it was that he should be excluded by fortune from that brilliant lottery.

"Ah, Mrs. Julaper, is that you?"

Mrs. Julaper, who was still at the door, curtsied, and said, "I came, Sir Bale, to see whether you'd please to like a jug of mulled claret, sir."

"Not I, my dear. I'll take a mug of beer and my pipe; that homely solace better befits a ruined gentleman."

"H'm, sir; you're not that, Sir Bale; you're no worse than half the lords and great men that are going. I would not hear another say that of you, sir."

"That's very kind of you, Mrs. Julaper; but you won't call *me* out for backbiting myself, especially as it is true, d——d true, Mrs. Julaper! Look ye; there never was a Mardykes here before but he could lay his hundred or his thousand pounds on the winner of the Heckleston Cup; and what could I bet? Little more than that mug of beer I spoke of. It was my great-grandfather who opened the course on the Downs of Heckleston, and now *I* can't show there! Well, what must I do? Grin and bear it, that's all. If you please, Mrs. Julaper, I will have that jug of claret you offered. I want spice and hot wine to keep me alive; but I'll smoke my pipe first, and in an hour's time it will do."

When Mrs. Julaper was gone, he lighted his pipe, and drew near the window, through which he looked upon the now fading sky and the twilight landscape.

He smoked his pipe out, and by that time it had grown nearly dark. He was still looking out upon the faint outlines of the view, and thinking angrily what a little bit of luck at the races would do for many a man who probably did not want it half so much as he. Vague and sombre as his thoughts were, they had, like the darkening landscape outside, shape enough to define their general character. Bitter and impious they were—as those of egotistic men naturally are in suffering. And after brooding, and muttering by fits and starts, he said:

"How many tens and hundreds of thousands of pounds will change hands at Heckleston next week; and not a shilling in all the change and shuffle will stick to me! How many a fellow would sell himself, like Dr. Faustus, just for the knowledge of the name of the winner! But he's no fool, and does not buy his own."

Something caught his eye; something moving on the wall. The fire was lighted, and cast a flickering and gigantic shadow upward; the figure of a man standing behind Sir Bale Mardykes, on whose shoulder he placed a lean hand. Sir Bale turned suddenly about, and saw Philip Feltram. He was looking dark and stern, and did not remove his hand from his shoulder as he peered into the Baronet's face with his deep-set mad eyes.

"Ha, Philip, upon my soul!" exclaimed Sir Bale, surprised. "How time flies! It seems only this minute since I saw the boat a mile and a half away from the shore. Well—yes; there has been time; it is dark now. Ha, ha! I assure you, you startled me. Won't you take something? Do. Shall I touch the bell?"

"You have been troubled about those mortgages. I told you I should pay them off, I thought."

Here there was a pause, and Sir Bale looked hard in Feltram's face. If he had been in his ordinary spirits, or perhaps in some of his haunts less solitary than Mardykes, he would have laughed; but here he had grown unlike himself, gloomy and credulous, and was, in fact, a nervous man.

Sir Bale smiled, and shook his head dismally.

"It is very kind of you, Feltram; the idea shows a kindly disposition. I know you would do me a kindness if you could."

As Sir Bale, each looking in the other's eyes, repeated in this sentence the words "kind," "kindly," "kindness," a smile lighted Feltram's face with at each word an intenser light; and Sir Bale grew sombre in its glare; and when he had done speaking, Feltram's face also on a sudden darkened.

"I have found a fortune-teller in Cloostedd Wood. Look here."

And he drew from his pocket a leathern purse, which he placed on the table in his hand; and Sir Bale heard the pleasant clink of coin in it.

"A fortune-teller! You don't mean to say she gave you that?" said Sir Bale.

Feltram smiled again, and nodded.

"It *was* the custom to give the fortuneteller a trifle. It is a great improvement making *her* fee you," observed Sir Bale, with an approach to his old manner.

"He put that in my hand with a message," said Feltram.

"He? O, then it was a male fortune-teller!"

"Gipsies go in gangs, men and women. *He* might lend, though *she* told fortunes," said Feltram.

"It's the first time I ever heard of gipsies lending money;" and he eyed the purse with a whimsical smile.

With his lean fingers still holding it, Feltram sat down at the table. His face contracted as if in cunning thought, and his chin sank upon his breast as he leaned back.

"I think," continued Sir Bale, "ever since they were spoiled, the Egyptians have been a little shy of lending, and leave that branch of business to the Hebrews."

"What would you give to know, now, the winner at Heckleston races?" said Feltram suddenly, raising his eyes.

"Yes; that would be worth something," answered Sir Bale, looking at him with more interest than the incredulity he affected would quite warrant.

"And this money I have power to lend you, to make your game."

"Do you mean that really?" said Sir Bale, with a new energy

in tone, manner, and features.

"That's heavy; there are some guineas there," said Feltram with a dark smile, raising the purse in his hand a little, and letting it drop upon the table with a clang.

"There is *something* there, at all events," said Sir Bale.

Feltram took the purse by the bottom, and poured out on the table a handsome pile of guineas.

"And do you mean to say you got all that from a gipsy in Cloostedd Wood?"

"A friend, who is—*myself*," answered Philip Feltram.

"Yourself! Then it is yours—*you* lend it?" said the Baronet, amazed; for there was no getting over the heap of guineas, and the wonder was pretty equal whence they had come.

"Myself, and not myself," said Feltram oracularly; "as like as voice and echo, man and shadow."

Had Feltram in some of his solitary wanderings and potterings lighted upon hidden treasure? There was a story of two Feltrams of Cloostedd, brothers, who had joined the king's army and fought at Marston Moor, having buried in Cloostedd Wood a great deal of gold and plate and jewels. They had, it was said, intrusted one tried servant with the secret; and that servant remained at home. But by a perverse fatality the three witnesses had perished within a month: the two brothers at Marston Moor; and the confidant, of fever, at Cloostedd. From that day forth treasure-seekers had from time to time explored the woods of Cloostedd; and many a tree of mark was dug beside, and the earth beneath many a stone and scar and other landmark in that solitary forest was opened by night, until hope gradually died out, and the tradition had long ceased to prompt to action, and had become a story and nothing more.

The image of the nursery-tale had now recurred to Sir Bale after so long a reach of years; and the only imaginable way, in his mind, of accounting for penniless Philip Feltram having all that gold in his possession was that, in some of his lonely wanderings, chance had led him to the undiscovered hoard of the two Feltrams who had died in the great civil wars.

"Perhaps those gipsies you speak of found the money where you found them; and in that case, as Cloostedd Forest, and all that is in it is my property, their sending it to me is more like my servant's handing me my hat and stick when I'm going out, than making me a present."

"You will not be wise to rely upon the law, Sir Bale, and to refuse the help that comes unasked. But if you like your mortgages as they are, keep them; and if you like my terms as they are, take them; and when you have made up your mind, let me know."

Philip Feltram dropped the heavy purse into his capacious coat-pocket, and walked, muttering, out of the room.

CHAPTER 16
THE MESSAGE FROM CLOOSTEDD

"Come back, Feltram; come back, Philip!" cried Sir Bale hastily. "Let us talk, can't we? Come and talk this odd business over a little; you must have mistaken what I meant; I should like to hear all about it."

"All is not much, sir," said Philip Feltram, entering the room again, the door of which he had half closed after him. "In the forest of Cloostedd I met today some people, one of whom can foretell events, and told me the names of the winners of the first three races at Heckleston, and gave me this purse, with leave to lend you so much money as you care to stake upon the races. I take no security; you shan't be troubled; and you'll never see the lender, unless you seek him out."

"Well, those are not bad terms," said Sir Bale, smiling wistfully at the purse, which Feltram had again placed upon the table.

"No, not bad," repeated Feltram, in the harsh low tone in which he now habitually spoke.

"You'll tell me what the prophet said about the winners; I should like to hear their names."

"The names I shall tell you if you walk out with me," said Feltram.

"Why not here?" asked Sir Bale.

"My memory does not serve me here so well. Some people, in some places, though they be silent, obstruct thought. Come, let us speak," said Philip Feltram, leading the way.

Sir Bale, with a shrug, followed him.

By this time it was dark. Feltram was walking slowly towards the margin of the lake; and Sir Bale, more curious as the delay increased, followed him, and smiled faintly as he looked after his tall, gaunt figure, as if, even in the dark, expressing a ridicule which he did not honestly feel, and the expression of which, even if there had been light, there was no one near enough to see.

When he reached the edge of the lake, Feltram stooped, and Sir Bale thought that his attitude was that of one who whispers to and caresses a reclining person. What he fancied was a dark figure lying horizontally in the shallow water, near the edge, turned out to be, as he drew near, no more than a shadow on the elsewhere lighter water; and with his change of position it had shifted and was gone, and Philip Feltram was but dabbling his hand this way and that in the water, and muttering faintly to himself. He rose as the Baronet drew near, and standing upright, said,

"I like to listen to the ripple of the water among the grass and pebbles; the tongue and lips of the lake are lapping and whispering all along. It is the merest poetry; but you are so romantic, you excuse me."

There was an angry curve in Feltram's eyebrows, and a cynical smile, and something in the tone which to the satirical Baronet was almost insulting. But even had he been less curious, I don't think he would have betrayed his mortification; for an odd and unavowed influence which he hated was gradually establishing in Feltram an ascendency which sometimes vexed and sometimes cowed him.

"You are not to tell," said Feltram, drawing near him in the dusk. "The secret is yours when you promise."

"Of course I promise," said Sir Bale. "If I believed it, you don't think I could be such an ass as to tell it; and if I didn't believe it, I'd hardly take the trouble."

Feltram stooped, and dipping the hollow of his hand in the water, he raised it full, and said he, "Hold out your hand—the hollow of your hand—like this. I divide the water for a sign-share to me and share to you." And he turned his hand, so as to pour half the water into the hollow palm of Sir Bale, who was smiling, with some uneasiness mixed in his mockery.

"Now, you promise to keep all secrets respecting the teller and the finder, be that who it may?"

"Yes, I promise," said Sir Bale.

"Now do as I do," said Feltram. And he shed the water on the ground, and with his wet fingers touched his forehead and his breast; and then he joined his hand with Sir Bale's, and said, "Now you are my safe man."

Sir Bale laughed. "That's the game they call 'grand mufti,'" said he.

"Exactly; and means nothing," said Feltram, "except that some day it will serve you to remember by. And now the names. Don't speak; listen—you may break the thought else. The winner of the first is *Beeswing*; of the second, *Falcon*; and of the third, *Lightning*."

He had stood for some seconds in silence before he spoke; his eyes were closed; he seemed to bring up thought and speech with difficulty, and spoke faintly and drowsily, both his hands a little raised, and the fingers extended, with the groping air of a man who moves in the dark. In this odd way, slowly, faintly, with many a sigh and scarcely audible groan, he gradually delivered his message and was silent. He stood, it seemed, scarcely half awake, muttering indistinctly and sighing to himself. You would have said that he was exhausted and suffering, like a man at his last hour resigning himself to death.

At length he opened his eyes, looked round a little wildly and languidly, and with another great sigh sat down on a large rock that lies by the margin of the lake, and sighed heavily again and again. You might have fancied that he was a second time recovering from drowning.

Then he got up, and looked drowsily round again, and sighed like a man worn out with fatigue, and was silent.

Sir Bale did not care to speak until he seemed a little more likely to obtain an answer. When that time came, he said, "I wish, for the sake of my believing, that your list was a little less incredible. Not one of the horses you name is the least likely; not one of them has a chance."

"So much the better for you; you'll get what odds you please. You had better seize your luck; on Tuesday Beeswing runs," said Feltram. "When you want money for the purpose, I'm your banker—here is your bank."

He touched his breast, where he had placed the purse, and then he turned and walked swiftly away.

Sir Bale looked after him till he disappeared in the dark. He fluctuated among many surmises about Feltram. Was he insane, or was he practising an imposture? or was he fool enough to believe the predictions of some real gipsies? and had he borrowed this money, which in Sir Bale's eyes seemed the greatest miracle in the matter, from those thriving shepherd mountaineers, the old Trebecks, who, he believed, were attached to him? Feltram had, he thought, borrowed it as if for himself; and having, as Sir Bale in his egotism supposed, "a sneaking regard" for him, had meant the loan for his patron, and conceived the idea of his using his revelations for the purpose of making his fortune. So, seeing no risk, and the temptation being strong, Sir Bale resolved to avail himself of the purse, and use his own judgment as to what horse to back.

About eleven o'clock Feltram, unannounced, walked, with his hat still on, into Sir Bale's library, and sat down at the opposite side of his table, looking gloomily into the Baronet's face for a time.

"Shall you want the purse?" he asked at last.

"Certainly; I always want a purse," said Sir Bale energetically.

"The condition is, that you shall back each of the three horses I have named. But you may back them for much or little, as you like, only the sum must not be less than five pounds in each hundred which this purse contains. That is the condition, and if you violate it, you will make some powerful people very angry, and you will feel it. Do you agree?"

"Of course; five pounds in the hundred—certainly; and how many hundreds are there?"

"Three."

"Well, a fellow with luck may win something with three hundred pounds, but it ain't very much."

"Quite enough, if you use it aright."

"Three hundred pounds," repeated the Baronet, as he emptied the purse, which Feltram had just placed in his hand, upon the table; and contemplating them with grave interest, he began telling them off in little heaps of five-and-twenty each. He might have thanked Feltram, but he was thinking more of the guineas than of the grizzly donor.

"Ay," said he, after a second counting, "I think there *are* exactly three hundred. Well, so you say I must apply three times five—fifteen of these. It is an awful pity backing those queer horses you have named; but if I must make the sacrifice, I must, I suppose?" he added, with a hesitating inquiry in the tone.

"If you don't, you'll rue it," said Feltram coldly, and walked away.

"Penny in pocket's a merry companion," says the old English proverb, and Sir Bale felt in better spirits and temper than he had for many a day as he replaced the guineas in the purse.

It was long since he had visited either the racecourse or any other place of amusement. Now he might face his kind without fear that his pride should be mortified, and dabble in the fascinating agitations of the turf once more.

"Who knows how this little venture may turn out?" he thought. "It is time the luck should turn. My last summer in Germany, my last winter in Paris—d—n me, I'm owed something. It's time I should win a bit."

Sir Bale had suffered the indolence of a solitary and discontented life imperceptibly to steal upon him. It would not do to appear for the first time on Heckleston Lea with any of those signs of negligence which, in his case, might easily be taken for poverty. All his appointments, therefore, were carefully looked after; and on the Monday following, he, followed by his groom, rode away for the Saracen's Head at Heckleston, where he was to put up, for the races that were to begin on the day following, and presented as handsome an appearance as a peer in those days need have cared to show.

CHAPTER 17

ON THE COURSE—BEESWING, FALCON, AND LIGHTNING

As he rode towards Golden Friars, through which his route lay, in the early morning light, in which the mists of night were clearing, he looked back towards Mardykes with a hope of speedy deliverance from that hated imprisonment, and of a return to the continental life in which he took delight. He saw the summits and angles of the old building touched with the cheerful beams, and the grand old trees, and at the opposite side the fells dark, with their backs towards the east; and down the side of the wooded and precipitous clough of Feltram, the light, with a pleasant contrast against the beetling purple of the fells, was breaking in the faint distance. On the lake he saw the white speck that indicated the sail of Philip Feltram's boat, now midway between Mardykes and the wooded shores of Cloostedd.

"Going on the same errand," thought Sir Bale, "I should not wonder. I wish him the same luck. Yes, he's going to Cloostedd Forest. I hope he may meet his gipsies there—the Trebecks, or whoever they are."

And as a momentary sense of degradation in being thus beholden to such people smote him, "Well," thought he, "who knows? Many a fellow will make a handsome sum of a poorer purse than this at Heckleston. It will be a light matter paying them then."

Through Golden Friars he rode. Some of the spectators who did not like him, wondered audibly at the gallant show, hoped it was paid for, and conjectured that he had ridden out in search of a wife. On the whole, however, the appearance of their Baronet in a smarter style than usual was popular, and accepted as a change to the advantage of the town.

Next morning he was on the racecourse of Heckleston, renewing old acquaintance and making himself as agreeable as he could—an object, among some people, of curiosity and even interest. Leaving the carriage-sides, the hoods and bonnets, Sir Bale was soon among the betting men, deep in more serious business.

How did he make his book? He did not break his word. He backed Beeswing, Falcon, and Lightning. But it must be owned not for a shilling more than the five guineas each, to which he stood pledged. The odds were forty-five to one against Beeswing, sixty to one against Lightning, and fifty to one against Falcon.

"A pretty lot to choose!" exclaimed Sir Bale, with vexation. "As if I had money so often, that I should throw it away!"

The Baronet was testy thinking over all this, and looked on Feltram's message as an impertinence and the money as his own.

Let us now see how Sir Bale Mardykes' pocket fared.

Sulkily enough at the close of the week he turned his back on Heckleston racecourse, and took the road to Golden Friars.

He was in a rage with his luck, and by no means satisfied with himself; and yet he had won something. The result of the racing had been curious. In the three principal races the favourites had been beaten: one by an accident, another on a technical point, and the third by fair running. And what horses had won? The names were precisely those which the "fortune-teller" had predicted.

Well, then, how was Sir Bale in pocket as he rode up to his ancestral house of Mardykes, where a few thousand pounds would have been very welcome? He had won exactly 775 guineas; and had he staked a hundred instead of five on each of the names communicated by Feltram, he would have won 15,500 guineas.

He dismounted before his hall-door, therefore, with the discontent of a man who had lost nearly 15,000 pounds. Feltram was upon the steps, and laughed dryly.

"What do you laugh at?" asked Sir Bale tartly.

"You've won, haven't you?"

"Yes, I've won; I've won a trifle."

"On the horses I named?"

"Well, yes; it so turned out, by the merest accident."

Feltram laughed again dryly, and turned away.

Sir Bale entered Mardykes Hall, and was surly. He was in a much worse mood than before he had ridden to Heckleston. But after a week or so ruminating upon the occurrence, he wondered that Feltram spoke no more of it. It was undoubtedly wonderful. There had been no hint of repayment yet, and he had made some hundreds by the loan; and, contrary to all likelihood, the three horses named by the unknown soothsayer had won. Who was this gipsy? It would be worth bringing the soothsayer to Mardykes, and giving his people a camp on the warren, and all the poultry they could catch, and a pig or a sheep every now and then. Why, that seer was worth the philosopher's stone, and could make Sir Bale's fortune in a season. Someone else would be sure to pick him up if he did not.

So, tired of waiting for Feltram to begin, he opened the subject one day himself. He had not seen him for two or three days; and in the wood of Mardykes he saw his lank figure standing among the thick trees, upon a little knoll, leaning on a staff which he sometimes carried with him in his excursions up the mountains.

"Feltram!" shouted Sir Bale.

Feltram turned and beckoned. Sir Bale muttered, but obeyed the signal.

"I brought you here, because you can from this point with unusual clearness today see the opening of the Clough of Feltram at the other side, and the clump of trees, where you will find the way to reach the person about whom you are always thinking."

"Who said I am always thinking about him?" said the Baronet angrily; for he felt like a man detected in a weakness, and resented it.

"*I* say it, because I *know* it; and *you* know it also. See that clump of trees standing solitary in the hollow? Among them, to the left, grows an ancient oak. Cut in its bark are two enormous letters H. F.; so large and bold, that the rugged furrows of the oak bark fail to obscure them, although they are ancient and spread by time. Standing against the trunk of this great tree, with your back to these letters, you are looking up the Glen or Clough of Feltram, that opens northward, where stands Cloostedd Forest spreading far and thick. Now, how do you find our fortune-teller?"

"That is exactly what I wish to know," answered Sir Bale; "because, although I can't, of course, believe that he's a witch, yet he has either made the most marvellous fluke I've heard of, or else he has got extraordinary sources of information; or perhaps he acts partly on chance, partly on facts. Be it which you please, I say he's a marvellous fellow; and I should like to see him, and have a talk with him; and perhaps he could arrange with me. I should be very glad to make an arrangement with him to give me the benefit of his advice about any matter of the same kind again."

"I think he's willing to see you; but he's a fellow with a queer fancy and a pig-head. He'll not come here; you must go to him; and approach him his own way too, or you may fail to find him. On these terms he invites you."

Sir Bale laughed.

"He knows his value, and means to make his own terms."

"Well, there's nothing unfair in that; and I don't see that I should dispute it. How is one to find him?"

"Stand, as I told you, with your back to those letters cut in the oak. Right before you lies an old Druidic altar-stone. Cast your eye over its surface, and on some part of it you are sure to see a black stain about the size of a man's head. Standing, as I suppose you, against the oak, that stain, which changes its place from day to day, will give you the line you must follow through the forest in order to light upon him. Take carefully from it such trees or objects as will guide you; and when the forest thickens, do the best you can to keep to the same line. You are sure to find him."

"You'll come, Feltram. I should lose myself in that wilderness, and probably fail to discover him," said Sir Bale; "and I really wish to see him."

"When two people wish to meet, it is hard if they don't. I can go with you a bit of the way; I can walk a little through the forest by your side, until I see the small flower that grows peeping here and there, that always springs where those people walk; and when I begin to see that sign, I must leave you. And, first, I'll take you across the lake."

"By Jove, you'll do no such thing!" said Sir Bale hastily.

"But that is the way he chooses to be approached," said Philip Feltram.

"I have a sort of feeling about that lake; it's the one childish spot that is left in my imagination. The nursery is to blame for it—old stories and warnings; and I can't think of that. I should feel I had invoked an evil omen if I did. I know it is all nonsense; but we are queer creatures, Feltram. I must only ride there."

"Why, it is five-and-twenty miles round the lake to that; and after all were done, he would not see you. He knows what he's worth, and he'll have his own way," answered Feltram. "The sun will soon set. See that withered branch, near Snakes Island, that looks like fingers rising from the water? When its points grow tipped with red, the sun has but three minutes to live."

"That is a wonder which I can't see; it is too far away."

"Yes, the lake has many signs; but it needs sight to see them," said Feltram.

"So it does," said the Baronet; "more than most men have got. I'll ride round, I say; and I make my visit, for this time, my own way."

"You'll not find him, then; and he wants his money. It would be a pity to vex him."

"It was to you he lent the money," said Sir Bale.

"Yes."

"Well, you are the proper person to find him out and pay him," urged Sir Bale.

"Perhaps so; but he invites you; and if you don't go, he may be offended, and you may hear no more from him."

"We'll try. When can you go? There are races to come off next week, for once and away, at Langton. I should not mind trying my luck there. What do you say?"

"You can go there and pay him, and ask the same question—what horses, I mean, are to win. All the county are to be there; and plenty of money will change hands."

"I'll try," said Feltram.

"When will you go?"

"Tomorrow," he answered.

"I have an odd idea, Feltram, that you are really going to pay off those cursed mortgages."

He laid his hand with at least a gesture of kindness on the thin arm of Feltram, who coldly answered,

"So have I;" and walked down the side of the little knoll and away, without another word or look.

CHAPTER 18
ON THE LAKE, AT LAST

Next day Philip Feltram crossed the lake; and Sir Bale, seeing the boat on the water, guessed its destination, and watched its progress with no little interest, until he saw it moored and its sail drop at the rude pier that affords a landing at the Clough of Feltram. He was now satisfied that Philip had actually gone to seek out the 'cunning man,' and gather hints for the next race.

When that evening Feltram returned, and, later still, entered Sir Bale's library, the master of Mardykes was gladder to see his face and more interested about his news than he would have cared to confess.

Philip Feltram did not affect unconsciousness of that anxiety, but, with great directness, proceeded to satisfy it.

"I was in Cloostedd Forest today, nearly all day—and found the old gentleman in a wax. He did not ask me to drink, nor show me any kindness. He was huffed because you would not take the trouble to cross the lake to speak to him yourself. He took the money you sent him and counted it over, and dropped it into his pocket; and he called you hard names enough and to spare; but I brought him round, and at last he did talk."

"And what did he say?"

"He said that the estate of Mardykes would belong to a Feltram."

"He might have said something more likely," said Sir Bale sourly. "Did he say anything more?"

"Yes. He said the winner at Langton Lea would be Silver Bell."

"Any other name?"

"No."

"Silver Bell? Well, that's not so odd as the last. Silver Bell stands high in the list. He has a good many backers—long odds in his favour against most of the field. I should not mind backing Silver Bell."

The fact is, that he had no idea of backing any other horse from the moment he heard the soothsayer's prediction. He made up his mind to no half measures this time. He would go in to win something handsome.

He was in great force and full of confidence on the racecourse. He had no fears for the result. He bet heavily. There was a good margin still untouched of the Mardykes estate; and Sir Bale was a good old name in the county. He found a ready market for his offers, and had soon staked—such is the growing frenzy of that excitement—about twenty thousand pounds on his favourite, and stood to win seven.

He did not win, however. He lost his twenty thousand pounds.

And now the Mardykes estate was in imminent danger. Sir Bale returned, having distributed I O Us and promissory notes in all directions about him—quite at his wit's end.

Feltram was standing—as on the occasion of his former happier return—on the steps of Mardykes Hall, in the evening sun, throwing eastward a long shadow that was lost in the lake. He received him, as before, with a laugh.

Sir Bale was too much broken to resent this laugh as furiously as he might, had he been a degree less desperate.

He looked at Feltram savagely, and dismounted.

"Last time you would not trust him, and this time he would not trust you. He's huffed, and played you false."

"It was not he. I should have backed that d———d horse in any case," said Sir Bale, grinding his teeth. "What a witch you have discovered! One thing is true, perhaps. If there was a Feltram rich enough, he might have the estate now; but there ain't. They are all beggars. So much for your conjurer."

"He may make amends to you, if you make amends to him."

"He! Why, what can that wretched impostor do? D—n me, I'm past helping now."

"Don't you talk so," said Feltram. "Be civil. You must please the old gentleman. He'll make it up. He's placable when it suits him. Why not go to him his own way? I hear you are nearly ruined. You must go and make it up."

"Make it up! With whom? With a fellow who can't make even a guess at what's coming? Why should I trouble my head about him more?"

"No man, young or old, likes to be frumped. Why did you cross his fancy? He won't see you unless you go to him as he chooses."

"If he waits for that, he may wait till doomsday. I don't choose to go on that water—and cross it I won't," said Sir Bale.

But when his distracting reminders began to pour in upon him, and the idea of dismembering what remained of his property came home to him, his resolution faltered.

"I say, Feltram, what difference can it possibly make to him if I choose to ride round to Cloostedd Forest instead of crossing the lake in a boat?"

Feltram smiled darkly, and answered.

"I can't tell. Can you?"

"Of course I can't—I say I can't; besides, what audacity of a fellow like that presuming to prescribe to me! Utterly ludicrous! And he can't predict—do you really think or believe, Feltram, that he can?"

"I know he can. I know he misled you on purpose. He likes to punish those who don't respect his will; and there is a reason in it, often quite clear—not ill-natured. Now you see he compels you to seek him out, and when you do, I think he'll help you through your trouble. He said he would."

"Then you have seen him since?"

"Yesterday. He has put a pressure on you; but he means to help you."

"If he means to help me, let him remember I want a banker more than a seer. Let him give me a lift, as he did before. He must lend me money."

"He'll not stick at that. When he takes up a man, he carries him through."

"The races of Byermere—I might retrieve at them. But they don't come off for a month nearly; and what is a man like me to do in the meantime?"

"Every man should know his own business best. I'm not like you," said Feltram grimly.

Now Sir Bale's trouble increased, for some people were pressing. Something like panic supervened; for it happened that land was bringing just then a bad price, and more must be sold in consequence.

"All I can tell them is, I am selling land. It can't be done in an hour. I'm selling enough to pay them all twice over. Gentlemen used to be able to wait till a man sold his acres for payment. D—n them! do they want my body, that they can't let me alone for five minutes?"

The end of it was, that before a week Sir Bale told Feltram that he would go by boat, since that fellow insisted on it; and he did not very much care if he were drowned.

It was a beautiful autumnal day. Everything was bright in that mellowed sun, and the deep blue of the lake was tremulous with golden ripples; and crag and peak and scattered wood, faint in the distance, came out with a filmy distinctness on the fells in that pleasant light.

Sir Bale had been ill, and sent down the night before for Doctor Torvey. He was away with a patient. Now, in the morning, he had arrived inopportunely. He met Sir Bale as he issued from the house, and had a word with him in the court, for he would not turn back.

"Well," said the Doctor, after his brief inspection, "you ought to be in your bed; that's all I can say. You are perfectly mad to think of knocking about like this. Your pulse is at a hundred and ten; and, if you go across the lake and walk about Cloostedd, you'll be raving before you come back."

Sir Bale told him, apologetically, as if his life were more to his doctor than to himself, that he would take care not to fatigue himself, and that the air would do him good, and that in any case he could not avoid going; and so they parted.

Sir Bale took his seat beside Feltram in the boat, the sail was spread, and, bending to the light breeze that blew from Golden Friars, she glided from the jetty under Mardykes Hall, and the eventful voyage had begun.

CHAPTER 19
MYSTAGOGUS

The sail was loosed, the boat touched the stone step, and Feltram sprang out and made her fast to the old iron ring. The Baronet followed. So! he had ventured upon that water without being drowned. He looked round him as if in a dream. He had not been there since his childhood. There were no regrets, no sentiment, no remorse; only an odd return of the associations and fresh feelings of boyhood, and a long reach of time suddenly annihilated.

The little hollow in which he stood; the three hawthorn trees at his right; every crease and undulation of the sward, every angle and crack in the lichen-covered rock at his feet, recurred with a sharp and instantaneous recognition to his memory.

"Many a time your brother and I fished for hours together from that bank there, just where the bramble grows. That bramble has not grown an inch ever since, not a leaf altered; we used to pick blackberries off it, with our rods stuck in the bank—it was later in the year than now—till we stript it quite bare after a day or two. The steward used to come over—they were marking timber for cutting and we used to stay here while they rambled through the wood, with an axe marking the trees that were to come down. I wonder whether the big old boat is still anywhere. I suppose she was broken up, or left to rot; I have not seen her since we came home. It was in the wood that lies at the right- the other wood is called the forest; they say in old times it was eight miles long, northward up the shore of the lake, and full of deer; with a forester, and a reeve, and a verderer, and all that. Your brother was older than you; he went to India, or the Colonies; is he living still?"

"I care not."

"That's good-natured, at all events; but do you know?"

"Not I; and what matter? If he's living, I warrant he has his share of the curse, the sweat of his brow and his bitter crust; and if he is dead, he's dust or worse, he's rotten, and smells accordingly."

Sir Bale looked at him; for this was the brother over whom, only a year or two ago, Philip used to cry tears of pathetic long-ing. Feltram looked darkly in his face, and sneered with a cold laugh.

"I suppose you mean to jest?" said Sir Bale.

"Not I; it is the truth. It is what you'd say, if you were honest. If he's alive, let him keep where he is; and if he's dead, I'll have none of him, body or soul. Do you hear that sound?"

"Like the wind moaning in the forest?"

"Yes."

"But I feel no wind. There's hardly a leaf stirring."

"I think so," said Feltram. "Come along."

And he began striding up the gentle slope of the glen, with many a rock peeping through its sward, and tufted ferns and furze, giving a wild and neglected character to the scene; the background of which, where the glen loses itself in a distant turn, is formed by its craggy and wooded side.

Up they marched, side by side, in silence, towards that irregular clump of trees, to which Feltram had pointed from the Mardykes side.

As they approached, it showed more scattered, and two or three of the trees were of grander dimensions than in the distance they had appeared; and as they walked, the broad valley of Cloostedd Forest opened grandly on their left, studding the sides of the valley with solitary trees or groups, which thickened as it descended to the broad level, in parts nearly three miles wide, on which stands the noble forest of Cloostedd, now majestically reposing in the stirless air, gilded and flushed with the melancholy tints of autumn.

I am now going to relate wonderful things; but they rest on the report, strangely consistent, it is true, of Sir Bale Mardykes. That all his senses, however, were sick and feverish, and his brain not quite to be relied on at that moment, is a fact of which sceptics have a right to make all they please and can.

Startled at their approach, a bird like a huge mackaw bounced from the boughs of the trees, and sped away, every now and then upon the ground, toward the shelter of the forest, fluttering and hopping close by the side of the little brook which, emerging from the forest, winds into the glen, and beside the course of which Sir Bale and Philip Feltram had ascended from the margin of the lake.

It fluttered on, as if one of its wings were hurt, and kept hopping and bobbing and flying along the grass at its swiftest, screaming all the time discordantly.

"That must be old Mrs. Amerald's bird, that got away a week ago," said Sir Bale, stopping and looking after it. "Was not it a mackaw?"

"No," said Feltram; "that was a gray parrot; but there are stranger birds in Cloostedd Forest, for my ancestors collected all that would live in our climate, and were at pains to find them the food and shelter they were accustomed to until they grew hardy—that is how it happens."

"By Jove, that's a secret worth knowing," said Sir Bale. "That would make quite a feature. What a fat brute that bird was! and green and dusky-crimson and yellow; but its head is white-age, I suspect; and what a broken beak—hideous bird! splendid plumage; something between a mackaw and a vulture."

Sir Bale spoke jocularly, but with the interest of a bird-fancier; a taste which, when young, he had indulged; and for the moment forgot his cares and the object of his unwonted excursion.

A moment after, a lank slim bird, perfectly white, started from the same boughs, and winged its way to the forest.

"A kite, I think; but its body is a little too long, isn't it?" said Sir Bale again, stopping and looking after its flight also.

"A foreign kite, I daresay?" said Feltram.

All this time there was hopping near them a jay, with the tameness of a bird accustomed to these solitudes. It peered over its slender wing curiously at the visitors; pecking here and nodding there; and thus hopping, it made a circle round them more than once. Then it fluttered up, and perched on a bough of the old oak, from the deep labyrinth of whose branches the other birds had emerged; and from thence it flew down and lighted on the broad druidic stone, that stood like a cyclopean table on its sunken stone props, before the snakelike roots of the oak.

Across this it hopped conceitedly, as over a stage on which it figured becomingly; and after a momentary hesitation, with a little spring, it rose and winged its way in the same direction which the other birds had taken, and was quickly lost in thick forest to the left.

"Here," said Feltram, "this is the tree."

"I remember it well! A gigantic trunk; and, yes, those marks; but I never before read them as letters. Yes, H.F., so they are—very odd I should not have remarked them. They are so large, and so strangely drawn-out in some places, and filled-in in others, and distorted, and the moss has grown about them; I don't wonder I took them for natural cracks and chasms in the bark," said Sir Bale.

"Very like," said Feltram.

Sir Bale had remarked, ever since they had begun their walk from the shore, that Feltram seemed to undergo a gloomy change. Sharper, grimmer, wilder grew his features, and shadow after shadow darkened his face wickedly.

The solitude and grandeur of the forest, and the repulsive gloom of his companion's countenance and demeanour, communicated a tone of anxiety to Sir Bale; and they stood still, side by side, in total silence for a time, looking toward the forest glades; between themselves and which, on the level sward of the valley, stood many a noble tree and fantastic group of forked birch and thorn, in the irregular formations into which Nature had thrown them.

"Now you stand between the letters. Cast your eyes on the stone," said Feltram suddenly, and his low stern tones almost startled the Baronet.

Looking round, he perceived that he had so placed himself that his point of vision was exactly from between the two great letters, now half-obliterated, which he had been scrutinizing just as he turned about to look toward the forest of Cloostedd.

"Yes, so I am," said Sir Bale.

There was within him an excitement and misgiving, akin to the sensation of a man going into battle, and which corresponded with the pale and sombre frown which Feltram wore, and the manifest change which had come over him.

"Look on the stone steadily for a time, and tell me if you see a black mark, about the size of your hand, anywhere upon its surface," said Feltram.

Sir Bale affected no airs of scepticism now; his imagination was stirred, and a sense of some unknown reality at the bottom of that which he had affected to treat before as illusion, inspired a strange interest in the experiment.

"Do you see it?" asked Feltram.

Sir Bale was watching patiently, but he had observed nothing of the kind.

Sharper, darker, more eager grew the face of Philip Feltram, as his eyes traversed the surface of that huge horizontal block.

"Now?" asked Feltram again.

No, he had seen nothing.

Feltram was growing manifestly uneasy, angry almost; he walked away a little, and back again, and then two or three times round the tree, with his hands shut, and treading the ground like a man trying to warm his feet, and so impatiently he returned, and looked again on the stone.

Sir Bale was still looking, and very soon said, drawing his brows together and looking hard,

"Ha!—yes—hush. There it is, by Jove!—wait—yes—there; it is growing quite plain."

It seemed not as if a shadow fell upon the stone, but rather as if the stone became semi-transparent, and just under its surface was something dark—a hand, he thought it—and darker and darker it grew, as if coming up toward the surface, and after some little wavering, it fixed itself movelessly, pointing, as he thought, toward the forest.

"It looks like a hand," said he. "By Jove, it is a hand—pointing towards the forest with a finger."

"Don't mind the finger; look only on that black blurred mark, and from the point where you stand, taking that point for your direction, look to the forest. Take some tree or other landmark for an object, enter the forest there, and pursue the same line, as well as you can, until you find little flowers with leaves like wood-sorrel, and with tall stems and a red blossom, not larger than a drop, such as you have not seen before, growing among the trees, and follow wherever they seem to grow thickest, and there you will find him."

All the time that Feltram was making this little address, Sir Bale was endeavouring to fix his route by such indications as Feltram described; and when he had succeeded in quite es-tablishing the form of a peculiar tree—a melancholy ash, one huge limb of which had been blasted by lightning, and its partly stricken arm stood high and barkless, stretching its white fingers, as it were, in invitation into the forest, and signing the way for him——

"I have it now," said he. "Come Feltram, you'll come a bit of the way with me."

Feltram made no answer, but slowly shook his head, and turned and walked away, leaving Sir Bale to undertake his adventure alone.

The strange sound they had heard from the midst of the forest, like the rumble of a storm or the far-off trembling of a furnace, had quite ceased. Not a bird was hopping on the grass, or visible on bough or in the sky. Not a living creature was in sight—never was stillness more complete, or silence more oppressive.

It would have been ridiculous to give way to the old reluctance which struggled within him. Feltram had strode down the slope, and was concealed by a screen of bushes from his view. So alone, and full of an interest quite new to him, he set out in quest of his adventures.

CHAPTER 20
THE HAUNTED FOREST

Sir Bale Mardykes walked in a straight line, by bush and scaur, over the undulating ground, to the blighted ash-tree; and as he approached it, its withered bough stretched more gigantically into the air, and the forest seemed to open where it pointed.

He passed it by, and in a few minutes had lost sight of it again, and was striding onward under the shadow of the forest, which already enclosed him. He was directing his march with all the care he could, in exactly that line which, according to Feltram's rule, had been laid down for him. Now and then, having, as soldiers say, taken an object, and fixed it well in his memory, he would pause and look about him.

As a boy he had never entered the wood so far; for he was under a prohibition, lest he should lose himself in its intricacies, and be benighted there. He had often heard that it was haunted ground, and that too would, when a boy, have deterred him. It was on this account that the scene was so new to him, and that he cared so often to stop and look about him. Here and there a *vista* opened, exhibiting the same utter desertion, and opening farther perspectives through the tall stems of the trees faintly visible in the solemn shadow. No flowers could he see, but once or twice a wood anemone, and now and then a tiny grove of wood-sorrel.

Huge oak-trees now began to mingle and show themselves more and more frequently among the other timber; and gradually the forest became a great oak wood unintruded upon by any less noble tree. Vast trunks curving outwards to the roots, and expanding again at the branches, stood like enormous columns, striking out their groining boughs, with the dark vaulting of a crypt.

As he walked under the shadow of these noble trees, suddenly his eye was struck by a strange little flower, nodding quite alone by the knotted root of one of those huge oaks.

He stooped and picked it up, and as he plucked it, with a harsh scream just over his head, a large bird with heavy beating wings broke away from the midst of the branches. He could not see it, but he fancied the scream was like that of the huge mackaw whose ill-poised flight he had watched. This conjecture was but founded on the odd cry he had heard.

The flower was a curious one—a stem fine as a hair supported a little bell, that looked like a drop of blood, and never ceased trembling. He walked on, holding this in his fingers; and soon he saw another of the same odd type, then another at a shorter distance, then one a little to the right and another to the left, and farther on a little group, and at last the dark slope was all over trembling with these little bells, thicker and thicker as he descended a gentle declivity to the bank of the little brook, which flowing through the forest loses itself in the lake.

The low murmur of this forest stream was almost the first sound, except the shriek of the bird that startled him a little time ago, which had disturbed the profound silence of the wood since he entered it. Mingling with the faint sound of the brook, he now heard a harsh human voice calling words at intervals, the purport of which he could not yet catch; and walking on, he saw seated upon the grass, a strange figure, corpulent, with a great hanging nose, the whole face glowing like copper. He was dressed in a bottle-green cut-velvet coat, of the style of Queen Anne's reign, with a dusky crimson waistcoat, both over-laid with broad and tarnished gold lace, and his silk stockings on thick swollen legs, with great buckled shoes, straddling on the grass, were rolled up over his knees to his short breeches. This ill-favoured old fellow, with a powdered wig that came down to his shoulders, had a dice-box in each hand, and was apparently playing his left against his right, and calling the throws with a hoarse cawing voice.

Raising his black piggish eyes, he roared to Sir Bale, by name, to come and sit down, raising one of his dice-boxes, and then indicating a place on the grass opposite to him.

Now Sir Bale instantly guessed that this was the man, gipsy, warlock, call him what he might, of whom he had come in search. With a strange feeling of curiosity, disgust, and awe, he drew near. He was resolved to do whatever this old man re-quired of him, and to keep him, this time, in good humour.

Sir Bale did as he bid him, and sat down; and taking the box he presented, they began throwing turn about, with three dice, the copper-faced old man teaching him the value of the throws, as he proceeded, with many a curse and oath; and when he did not like a throw, grinning with a look of such real fury, that the master of Mardykes almost expected him to whip out his sword and prick him through as he sat before him.

After some time spent at this play, in which guineas passed now this way, now that, chucked across the intervening patch of grass, or rather moss, that served them for a green cloth, the old man roared over his shoulder,

"Drink;" and picking up a long-stemmed conical glass which Sir Bale had not observed before, he handed it over to the Bar-onet; and taking another in his fingers, he held it up, while a very tall slim old man, dressed in a white livery, with powdered hair and cadaverous face, which seemed to run out nearly all into a long thin hooked nose, advanced with a flask in each hand. Looking at the unwieldly old man, with his heavy nose, powdered head, and all the bottle-green, crimson, and gold about him, and the long slim serving man, with sharp beak, and white from head to heel, standing by him, Sir Bale was forcibly reminded of the great old macaw and the long and slender kite, whose colours they, after their fashion, reproduced, with something, also indescribable, of the air and character of the birds. Not standing on ceremony, the old fellow held up his own glass first, which the white lackey filled from the flask, and then he filled Sir Bale's glass.

It was a large glass, and might have held about half a pint; and the liquor with which the servant filled it was something of the colour of an opal, and circles of purple and gold seemed to be spreading continually outward from the centre, and running inward from the rim, and crossing one another, so as to form a beautiful rippling net-work.

"I drink to your better luck next time," said the old man, lifting his glass high, and winking with one eye, and leering knowingly with the other; "and you know what I mean."

Sir Bale put the liquor to his lips. Wine? Whatever it was, never had he tasted so delicious a flavour. He drained it to the bottom, and placing it on the grass beside him, and looking again at the old dicer, who was also setting down his glass, he saw, for the first time, the graceful figure of a young woman seated on the grass. She was dressed in deep mourning, had a black hood carelessly over her head, and, strangely, wore a black mask, such as are used at masquerades. So much of her throat and chin as he could see were beautifully white; and there was a prettiness in her air and figure which made him think what a beautiful creature she in all likelihood was. She was reclining slightly against the burly man in bottle-green and gold, and her arm was round his neck, and her slender white hand showed itself over his shoulder.

"Ho! my little Geaiette," cried the old fellow hoarsely; "it will be time that you and I should get home.—So, Bale Mardykes, I have nothing to object to you this time; you've crossed the lake, and you've played with me and won and lost, and drank your glass like a jolly companion, and now we know one another; and an acquaintance is made that will last. I'll let you go, and you'll come when I call for you. And now you'll want to know what horse will win next month at Rindermere races.—Whisper me, lass, and I'll tell him."

So her lips, under the black curtain, crept close to his ear, and she whispered.

"Ay, so it will;" roared the old man, gnashing his teeth; "it will be Rainbow, and now make your best speed out of the forest, or I'll set my black dogs after you, ho, ho, ho! and they may chance to pull you down. Away!"

He cried this last order with a glare so black, and so savage a shake of his huge fist, that Sir Bale, merely making his general bow to the group, clapped his hat on his head, and hastily began his retreat; but the same discordant voice yelled after him:

"You'll want that, you fool; pick it up." And there came hurtling after and beside him a great leather bag, stained, and stuffed with a heavy burden, and bounding by him it stopped with a little wheel that brought it exactly before his feet.

He picked it up, and found it heavy.

Turning about to make his acknowledgments, he saw the two persons in full retreat; the profane old scoundrel in the bottle-green limping and stumbling, yet bowling along at a wonderful rate, with many a jerk and reel, and the slender lady in black gliding away by his side into the inner depths of the forest.

So Sir Bale, with a strange chill, and again in utter solitude, pursued his retreat, with his burden, at a swifter pace, and after an hour or so, had recovered the point where he had entered the forest, and passing by the druidic stone and the mighty oak, saw down the glen at his right, standing by the edge of the lake, Philip Feltram, close to the bow of the boat.

CHAPTER 21
RINDERMERE

Feltram looked grim and agitated when Sir Bale came up to him, as he stood on the flat-stone by which the boat was moored.

"You found him?" said he.

"Yes."

"The lady in black was there?"

"She was."

"And you played with him?"

"Yes."

"And what is that in your hand?"

"A bag of something, I fancy money; it is heavy; he threw it after me. We shall see just now; let us get away."

"He gave you some of his wine to drink?" said Feltram, looking darkly in his face; but there was a laugh in his eyes.

"Yes; of course I drank it; my object was to please him."

"To be sure."

The faint wind that carried them across the lake had quite subsided by the time they had reached the side where they now were.

There was now not wind enough to fill the sail, and it was already evening.

"Give me an oar; we can pull her over in little more than an hour," said Sir Bale; "only let us get away."

He got into the boat, sat down, and placed the leather bag with its heavy freightage at his feet, and took an oar. Feltram loosed the rope and shoved the boat off; and taking his seat also, they began to pull together, without another word, until, in about ten minutes, they had got a considerable way off the Cloostedd shore.

The leather bag was too clumsy a burden to conceal; besides, Feltram knew all about the transaction, and Sir Bale had no need to make a secret. The bag was old and soiled, and tied about the "neck" with a long leather thong, and it seemed to have been sealed with red wax, fragments of which were still sticking to it.

He got it open, and found it full of guineas.

"Halt!" cried Sir Bale, delighted, for he had half apprehended a trick upon his hopes; "gold it is, and a lot of it, by Jove!"

Feltram did not seem to take the slightest interest in the matter. Sulkily and drowsily he was leaning with his elbow on his knee, and it seemed thinking of something far away. Sir Bale could not wait to count them any longer. He reckoned them on the bench, and found two thousand.

It took some time; and when he had got them back into the leather bag, and tied them up again, Feltram, with a sudden start, said sharply,

"Come, take your oar—unless you like the lake by night; and see, a wind will soon be up from Golden Friars!"

He cast a wild look towards Mardykes Hall and Snakes Island, and applying himself to his oar, told Sir Bale to take his also; and nothing loath, the Baronet did so.

It was slow work, for the boat was not built for speed; and by the time they had got about midway, the sun went down, and twilight and the melancholy flush of the sunset tints were upon the lake and fells.

"Ho! here comes the breeze—up from Golden Friars," said Feltram; "we shall have enough to fill the sails now. If you don't fear spirits and Snakes Island, it is all the better for us it should blow from that point. If it blew from Mardykes now, it would be a stiff pull for you and me to get this tub home."

Talking as if to himself, and laughing low, he adjusted the sail and took the tiller, and so, yielding to the rising breeze, the boat glided slowly toward still distant Mardykes Hall.

The moon came out, and the shore grew misty, and the towering fells rose like sheeted giants; and leaning on the gunwale of the boat, Sir Bale, with the rush and gurgle of the water on the boat's side sounding faintly in his ear, thought of his day's adventure, which seemed to him like a dream—incredible but for the heavy bag that lay between his feet.

As they passed Snakes Island, a little mist, like a fragment of a fog, seemed to drift with them, and Sir Bale fancied that whenever it came near the boat's side she made a dip, as if strained toward the water; and Feltram always put out his hand, as if waving it from him, and the mist seemed to obey the gesture; but returned again and again, and the same thing always happened.

It was three weeks after, that Sir Bale, sitting up in his bed, very pale and wan, with his silk night-cap nodding on one side, and his thin hand extended on the coverlet, where the doctor had been feeling his pulse, in his darkened room, related all the wonders of this day to Doctor Torvey. The doctor had attended him through a fever which followed immediately upon his visit to Cloostedd.

"And, my dear sir, by Jupiter, can you really believe all that delirium to be sober fact?" said the doctor, sitting by the bedside, and actually laughing.

"I can't help believing it, because I can't distinguish in any way between all that and everything else that actually happened, and which I must believe. And, except that this is more wonderful, I can find no reason to reject it, that does not as well apply to all the rest."

"Come, come, my dear sir, this will never do—nothing is more common. These illusions accompanying fever frequently antedate the attack, and the man is actually raving before he knows he is ill."

"But what do you make of that bag of gold?"

"Someone has lent it. You had better ask all about it of Feltram when you can see him; for in speaking to me he seemed to know all about it, and certainly did not seem to think the matter at all out of the commonplace. It is just like that fisherman's story, about the hand that drew Feltram into the water on the night that he was nearly drowned. Everyone can see what that was. Why of course it was simply the reflection of his own hand in the water, in that vivid lightning. When you have been out a little and have gained strength you will shake off these dreams."

"I should not wonder," said Sir Bale.

It is not to be supposed that Sir Bale reported all that was in his memory respecting his strange vision, if such it was, at

Cloostedd. He made a selection of the incidents, and threw over the whole adventure an entirely accidental character, and described the money which the old man had thrown to him as amounting to a purse of five guineas, and mentioned nothing of the passages which bore on the coming race.

Good Doctor Torvey, therefore, reported only that Sir Bale's delirium had left two or three illusions sticking in his memory.

But if they were illusions, they survived the event of his recovery, and remained impressed on his memory with the sharpness of very recent and accurately observed fact.

He was resolved on going to the races of Rindermere, where, having in his possession so weighty a guarantee as the leather purse, he was determined to stake it all boldly on Rainbow-against which horse he was glad to hear there were very heavy odds.

The race came off. One horse was scratched, another bolted, the rider of a third turned out to have lost a buckle and three half-pence and so was an ounce and a half under weight, a fourth knocked down the post near Rinderness churchyard, and was held to have done it with his left instead of his right knee, and so had run at the wrong side. The result was that Rainbow came in first, and I should be afraid to say how much Sir Bale won. It was a sum that paid off a heavy debt, and left his affairs in a much more manageable state.

From this time Sir Bale prospered. He visited Cloostedd no more; but Feltram often crossed to that lonely shore as heretofore, and it is believed conveyed to him messages which guided his betting. One thing is certain, his luck never deserted him. His debts disappeared; and his love of continental life seemed to have departed. He became content with Mardykes Hall, laid out money on it, and although he never again cared to cross the lake, he seemed to like the scenery.

In some respects, however, he lived exactly the same odd and unpopular life. He saw no one at Mardykes Hall. He practised a very strict reserve. The neighbours laughed at and disliked him, and he was voted, whenever any accidental contact arose, a very disagreeable man; and he had a shrewd and ready sarcasm that made them afraid of him, and himself more disliked.

Odd rumours prevailed about his household. It was said that his old relations with Philip Feltram had become reversed; and that he was as meek as a mouse, and Feltram the bully now. It was also said that Mrs. Julaper had one Sunday evening when she drank tea at the Vicar's, told his good lady very mysteriously, and with many charges of secrecy, that Sir Bale was none the better of his late-found wealth; that he had a load upon his spirits, that he was afraid of Feltram, and so was everyone else, more or less, in the house; that he was either mad or worse; and that it was an eerie dwelling, and strange company, and she should be glad herself of a change.

Good Mrs. Bedel told her friend Mrs. Torvey; and all Golden Friars heard all this, and a good deal more, in an incredibly short time.

All kinds of rumours now prevailed in Golden Friars, connecting Sir Bale's successes on the turf with some mysterious doings in Cloostedd Forest. Philip Feltram laughed when he heard these stories—especially when he heard the story that a supernatural personage had lent the Baronet a purse full of money.

"You should not talk to Doctor Torvey so, sir," said he grimly; "he's the greatest tattler in the town. It was old Farmer Trebeck, who could buy and sell us all down here, who lent that money. Partly from good-will, but not without acknowledgment. He has my hand for the first, not worth much, and yours to a bond for the two thousand guineas you brought home with you. It seems strange you should not remember that venerable and kind old farmer whom you talked with so long that day. His grandson, who expects to stand well in his will, being a trainer in Lord Varney's stables, has sometimes a tip to give, and he is the source of your information."

"By Jove, I must be a bit mad, then, that's all," said Sir Bale, with a smile and a shrug.

Philip Feltram moped about the house, and did precisely

what he pleased. The change which had taken place in him became more and more pronounced. Dark and stern he always
looked, and often malignant. He was like a man possessed of one
evil thought which never left him.

There was, besides, the good old Gothic superstition of a
bargain or sale of the Baronet's soul to the arch-fiend. This was,
of course, very cautiously whispered in a place where he had influence. It was only a coarser and directer version of a suspicion,
that in a more credulous generation penetrated a level of society
quite exempt from such follies in our day.

One evening at dusk, Sir Bale, sitting after his dinner in his
window, saw the tall figure of Feltram, like a dark streak, standing movelessly by the lake. An unpleasant feeling moved him,
and then an impatience. He got up, and having primed himself
with two glasses of brandy, walked down to the edge of the lake,
and placed himself beside Feltram.

"Looking down from the window," said he, nerved with his
Dutch courage, "and seeing you standing like a post, do you
know what I began to think of?"

Feltram looked at him, but answered nothing.

"I began to think of taking a wife—*marrying*."

Feltram nodded. The announcement had not produced the
least effect.

"Why the devil will you make me so uncomfortable! Can't
you be like yourself—what you *were*, I mean? I won't go on living here alone with you. I'll take a wife, I tell you. I'll choose
a good church-going woman, that will have every man, woman, and child in the house on their marrow-bones twice a day,
morning and evening, and three times on Sundays. How will
you like that?"

"Yes, you will be married," said Feltram, with a quiet decision which chilled Sir Bale, for he had by no means made up his
mind to that desperate step.

Feltram slowly walked away, and that conversation ended.

Now an odd thing happened about this time. There was a
family of Feltram—county genealogists could show how relat-

ed to the vanished family of Cloostedd—living at that time on their estate not far from Carlisle. Three co-heiresses now represented it. They were great beauties—the *belles* of their county in their day.

One was married to Sir Oliver Haworth of Haworth, a great family in those times. He was a knight of the shire, and had refused a baronetage, and, it was said, had his eye on a peerage. The other sister was married to Sir William Walsingham, a wealthy baronet; and the third and youngest, Miss Janet, was still unmarried, and at home at Cloudesly Hall, where her aunt, Lady Harbottle, lived with her, and made a dignified chaperon.

Now it so fell out that Sir Bale, having business at Carlisle, and knowing old Lady Harbottle, paid his respects at Cloudesly Hall; and being no less than five-and-forty years of age, was for the first time in his life, seriously in love.

Miss Janet was extremely pretty—a fair beauty with brilliant red lips and large blue eyes, and ever so many pretty dimples when she talked and smiled. It was odd, but not perhaps against the course of nature, that a man, though so old as he, and quite *blase*, should fall at last under that fascination.

But what are we to say of the strange infatuation of the young lady? No one could tell why she liked him. It was a craze. Her family were against it, her intimates, her old nurse—all would not do; and the oddest thing was, that he seemed to take no pains to please her. The end of this strange courtship was that he married her; and she came home to Mardykes Hall, determined to please everybody, and to be the happiest woman in England.

With her came a female cousin, a good deal her senior, past thirty—Gertrude Mainyard, pale and sad, but very gentle, and with all the prettiness that can belong to her years.

This young lady has a romance. Her hero is far away in India; and she, content to await his uncertain return with means to accomplish the hope of their lives, in that frail chance has long embarked all the purpose and love of her life.

When Lady Mardykes came home, a new leaf was, as the phrase is, turned over. The neighbours and all the country people were willing to give the Hall a new trial. There was visiting and returning of visits; and young Lady Mardykes was liked and admired. It could not indeed have been otherwise. But here the improvement in the relations of Mardykes Hall with other homes ceased. On one excuse or another Sir Bale postponed or evaded the hospitalities which establish intimacies. Some people said he was jealous of his young and beautiful wife. But for the most part his reserve was set down to the old inhospitable cause, some ungenial defect in his character; and in a little time the tramp of horses and roll of carriage-wheels were seldom heard up or down the broad avenue of Mardykes Hall.

Sir Bale liked this seclusion; and his wife, "so infatuated with her idolatry of that graceless old man," as surrounding young ladies said, that she was well content to forego the society of the county people for a less interrupted enjoyment of that of her husband. "What she could see in him" to interest or amuse her so, that for his sake she was willing to be "buried alive in that lonely place," the same critics were perpetually wondering.

A year and more passed thus; for the young wife, happily-*very* happily indeed, had it not been for one topic on which she and her husband could not agree. This was Philip Feltram; and an odd quarrel it was.

CHAPTER 22

SIR BALE IS FRIGHTENED

To Feltram she had conceived, at first sight, a horror. It was not a mere antipathy; fear mingled largely in it. Although she did not see him often, this restless dread grew upon her so, that she urged his dismissal upon Sir Bale, offering to provide, herself, for him a handsome annuity, charged on that part of her property which, by her marriage settlement, had remained in her power. There was a time when Sir Bale was only too anxious to get rid of him. But that was changed now. Nothing could now induce the Baronet to part with him. He at first evaded and resisted quietly. But, urged with a perseverance to which he was unused, he at last broke into fury that appalled her, and swore that if he was worried more upon the subject, he would leave her and the country, and see neither again.

This exhibition of violence affrighted her all the more by reason of the contrast; for up to this he had been an uxorious husband. Lady Mardykes was in hysterics, and thoroughly frightened, and remained in her room for two or three days. Sir Bale went up to London about business, and was not home for more than a week. This was the first little squall that disturbed the serenity of their sky.

This point, therefore, was settled; but soon there came other things to sadden Lady Mardykes. There occurred a little incident, soon after Sir Bale's return from London, which recalled the topic on which they had so nearly quarrelled.

Sir Bale had a dressing-room, remote from the bedrooms, in which he sat and read and sometimes smoked. One night, after the house was all quiet, the Baronet being still up, the bell of this dressing-room rang long and furiously. It was such a peal as a person in extreme terror might ring. Lady Mardykes, with her maid in her room, heard it; and in great alarm she ran in her dressing-gown down the gallery to Sir Bale's room. Mallard the butler had already arrived, and was striving to force the door, which was secured. It gave way just as she reached it, and she rushed through.

Sir Bale was standing with the bell-rope in his hand, in the extremest agitation, looking like a ghost; and Philip Feltram was sitting in his chair, with a dark smile fixed upon him. For a minute she thought he had attempted to assassinate his master. She could not otherwise account for the scene.

There had been nothing of the kind, however; as her husband assured her again and again, as she lay sobbing on his breast, with her arms about his neck.

"To her dying hour," she afterwards said to her cousin, "she never could forget the dreadful look in Feltram's face."

No explanation of that scene did she ever obtain from Sir Bale, nor any clue to the cause of the agony that was so powerfully expressed in his countenance. Thus much only she learned from him, that Feltram had sought that interview for the purpose of announcing his departure, which was to take place within the year.

"You are not sorry to hear that. But if you knew all, you might. Let the curse fly where it may, it will come back to roost. So, darling, let us discuss him no more. Your wish is granted, *dis iratis.*"

Some crisis, during this interview, seemed to have occurred in the relations between Sir Bale and Feltram. Henceforward they seldom exchanged a word; and when they did speak, it was coldly and shortly, like men who were nearly strangers.

One day in the courtyard, Sir Bale seeing Feltram leaning upon the parapet that overlooks the lake, approached him, and said in a low tone,

"I've been thinking if we—that is, I—do owe that money to old Trebeck, it is high time I should pay it. I was ill, and had lost my head at the time; but it turned out luckily, and it ought to be paid. I don't like the idea of a bond turning up, and a lot of interest."

"The old fellow meant it for a present. He is richer than you are; he wished to give the family a lift. He has destroyed the bond, I believe, and in no case will he take payment."

"No fellow has a right to force his money on another," answered Sir Bale. "I never asked him. Besides, as you know, I was not really myself, and the whole thing seems to me quite different from what you say it was; and, so far as my brain is concerned, it was all a phantasmagoria; but, you say, it was he."

"Every man is accountable for what he intends and for what he *thinks* he does," said Feltram cynically.

"Well, I'm accountable for dealing with that wicked old dicer I *thought* I saw—isn't that it? But I must pay old Trebeck all the same, since the money was his. Can you manage a meeting?"

"Look down here. Old Trebeck has just landed; he will sleep tonight at the George and Dragon, to meet his cattle in the morning at Golden Friars fair. You can speak to him yourself."

So saying Feltram glided away, leaving Sir Bale the task of

opening the matter to the wealthy farmer of Cloostedd Fells.

A broad night of steps leads down from the courtyard to the level of the jetty at the lake: and Sir Bale descended, and accosted the venerable farmer, who was bluff, honest, and as frank as a man can be who speaks a *patois* which hardly a living man but himself can understand.

Sir Bale asked him to come to the Hall and take luncheon; but Trebeck was in haste. Cattle had arrived which he wanted to look at, and a pony awaited him on the road, hard by, to Golden Friars; and the old fellow must mount and away.

Then Sir Bale, laying his hand upon his arm in a manner that was at once lofty and affectionate, told in his ears the subject on which he wished to be understood.

The old farmer looked hard at him, and shook his head and laughed in a way that would have been insupportable in a house, and told him, "I hev narra bond o' thoine, mon."

"I know how that is; so does Philip Feltram."

"Well?"

"Well, I must replace the money."

The old man laughed again, and in his outlandish dialect told him to wait till he asked him. Sir Bale pressed it, but the old fellow put it off with outlandish banter; and as the Baronet grew testy, the farmer only waxed more and more hilarious, and at last, mounting his shaggy pony, rode off, still laughing, at a canter to Golden Friars; and when he reached Golden Friars, and got into the hall of the George and Dragon, he asked Richard Turnbull with a chuckle if he ever knew a man refuse an offer of money, or a man want to pay who did not owe; and inquired whether the Squire down at Mardykes Hall mightn't be a bit "wrang in t' garrets." All this, however, other people said, was intended merely to conceal the fact that he really had, through sheer loyalty, lent the money, or rather bestowed it, thinking the old family in jeopardy, and meaning a gift, was determined to hear no more about it. I can't say; I only know people held, some by one interpretation, some by another.

As the caterpillar sickens and changes its hue when it is about to undergo its transformation, so an odd change took place in Feltram. He grew even more silent and morose; he seemed always in an agitation and a secret rage. He used to walk through the woodlands on the slopes of the fells above Mardykes, muttering to himself, picking up the rotten sticks with which the ground was strewn, breaking them in his hands, and hurling them from him, and stamping on the earth as he paced up and down.

One night a thunder-storm came on, the wind blowing gently up from Golden Friars. It was a night black as pitch, illuminated only by the intermittent glare of the lightning. At the foot of the stairs Sir Bale met Feltram, whom he had not seen for some days. He had his cloak and hat on.

"I am going to Cloostedd tonight," he said, "and if all is as I expect, I sha'n't return. We remember all, you and I." And he nodded and walked down the passage.

Sir Bale knew that a crisis had happened in his own life. He felt faint and ill, and returned to the room where he had been sitting. Throughout that melancholy night he did not go to his bed.

In the morning he learned that Marlin, who had been out late, saw Feltram get the boat off, and sail towards the other side. The night was so dark that he could only see him start; but the wind was light and coming up the lake, so that without a tack he could easily make the other side. Feltram did not return. The boat was found fast to the ring at Cloostedd landing-place.

Lady Mardykes was relieved, and for a time was happier than ever. It was different with Sir Bale; and afterwards her sky grew dark also.

CHAPTER 23

A LADY IN BLACK

Shortly after this, there arrived at the George and Dragon a stranger. He was a man somewhat past forty, embrowned by distant travel, and, his years considered, wonderfully good-looking. He had good eyes; his dark-brown hair had no sprinkling of gray in it; and his kindly smile showed very white and even teeth. He made inquiries about neighbours, especially respecting Mardykes Hall; and the answers seemed to interest him profoundly. He inquired after Philip Feltram, and shed tears when he heard that he was no longer at Mardykes Hall, and that Trebeck or other friends could give him no tidings of him.

And then he asked Richard Turnbull to show him to a quiet room; and so, taking the honest fellow by the hand, he said,

"Mr. Turnbull, don't you know me?"

"No, sir," said the host of the George and Dragon, after a puzzled stare, "I can't say I do, sir."

The stranger smiled a little sadly, and shook his head: and with a gentle laugh, still holding his hand in a very friendly way, he said, "I should have known you anywhere, Mr. Turnbull—anywhere on earth or water. Had you turned up on the Himalayas, or in a junk on the Canton River, or as a *dervish* in the mosque of St. Sophia, I should have recognised my old friend, and asked what news from Golden Friars.

"But of course I'm changed. You were a little my senior; and one advantage among many you have over your juniors is that you don't change as we do. I have played many a game of handball in the inn-yard of the George, Mr. Turnbull. You often wagered a pot of ale on my play; you used to say I'd make the best player of fives, and the best singer of a song, within ten miles round the meer. You used to have me behind the bar when I was a boy, with more of an appetite than I have now. I was then at Mardykes Hall, and used to go back in old Marlin's boat. Is old Marlin still alive?"

"Ay, that—he—is," said Turnbull slowly, as he eyed the stranger again carefully. "I don't know who you can be, sir, unless you are—the boy—William Feltram. La! he was seven or eight years younger than Philip. But, lawk!—Well—By Jen, and *be* you Willie Feltram? But no, you can't!"

"Ay, Mr. Turnbull, that very boy—Willie Feltram—even he, and no other; and now you'll shake hands with me, not so formally, but like an old friend."

"Ay, that I will," said honest Richard Turnbull, with a great smile, and a hearty grasp of his guest's hand; and they both laughed together, and the younger man's eyes, for he was an affectionate fool, filled up with tears.

"And I want you to tell me this," said William, after they had talked a little quietly, "now that there is no one to interrupt us, what has become of my brother Philip? I heard from a friend an account of his health that has caused me unspeakable anxiety."

"His health was not bad; no, he was a hardy lad, and liked a walk over the fells, or a pull on the lake; but he was a bit daft, every one said, and a changed man; and, in troth, they say the air o' Mardykes don't agree with every one, no more than him. But that's a tale that's neither here nor there."

"Yes," said William, "that was what they told me—his mind affected. God help and guard us! I have been unhappy ever since; and if I only knew it was well with poor Philip, I think I should be too happy. And where is Philip now?"

"He crossed the lake one night, having took leave of Sir Bale. They thought he was going to old Trebeck's up the Fells. He likes the Feltrams, and likes the folk at Mardykes Hall—though those two families was not always o'er kind to one another. But Trebeck seed nowt o' him, nor no one else; and what has gone wi' him no one can tell."

"*I* heard that also," said William with a deep sigh. "But *I* hoped it had been cleared up by now, and something happier been known of the poor fellow by this time. I'd give a great deal to know—I don't know what I *would* not give to know—I'm so unhappy about him. And now, my good old friend, tell your people to get me a chaise, for I must go to Mardykes Hall; and, first, let me have a room to dress in."

At Mardykes Hall a pale and pretty lady was looking out, alone, from the stone-shafted drawing-room window across the courtyard and the balustrade, on which stood many a great stone cup with flowers, whose leaves were half shed and gone with the winds—emblem of her hopes. The solemn melancholy of the towering fells, the ripple of the lonely lake, deepened her sadness.

The unwonted sound of carriage-wheels awoke her from her reverie.

Before the chaise reached the steps, a hand from its window had seized the handle, the door was thrown open, and William Feltram jumped out.

She was in the hall, she knew not how; and, with a wild scream and a sob, she threw herself into his arms.

Here at last was an end of the long waiting, the dejection which had reached almost the point of despair. And like two rescued from shipwreck, they clung together in an agony of happiness.

William had come back with no very splendid fortune. It was enough, and only enough, to enable them to marry. Prudent people would have thought it, very likely, too little. But he was now home in England, with health unimpaired by his long sojourn in the East, and with intelligence and energies improved by the discipline of his arduous struggle with fortune. He reckoned, therefore, upon one way or other adding something to their income; and he knew that a few hundreds a year would make them happier than hundreds of thousand could other people.

It was five years since they had parted in France, where a journey of importance to the Indian firm, whose right hand he was, had brought him.

The refined tastes that are supposed to accompany gentle blood, his love of art, his talent for music and drawing, had accidentally attracted the attention of the little travelling-party which old Lady Harbottle chaperoned. Miss Janet, now Lady Mardykes, learning that his name was Feltram, made inquiry through a common friend, and learned what interested her still more about him. It ended in an acquaintance, which his manly and gentle nature and his entertaining qualities soon improved into an intimacy.

Feltram had chosen to work his own way, being proud, and also prosperous enough to prevent his pride, in this respect, from being placed under too severe a pressure of temptation. He heard not from but of his brother, through a friend in London, and more lately from Gertrude, whose account of him was sad and even alarming.

When Lady Mardykes came in, her delight knew no bounds. She had already formed a plan for their future, and was not to be put off—William Feltram was to take the great grazing farm that belonged to the Mardykes estate; or, if he preferred it, to farm it for her, sharing the profits. She wanted something to interest her, and this was just the thing. It was hardly half-a-mile away, up the lake, and there was such a comfortable house and garden, and she and Gertrude could be as much together as ever almost; and, in fact, Gertrude and her husband could be nearly always at Mardykes Hall.

So eager and entreating was she, that there was no escape. The plan was adopted immediately on their marriage, and no happier neighbours for a time were ever known.

But was Lady Mardykes content? was she even exempt from the heartache which each mortal thinks he has all to himself? The longing of her life was for children; and again and again had her hopes been disappointed.

One tiny pretty little baby indeed was born, and lived for two years, and then died; and none had come to supply its place and break the childless silence in the great old nursery. That was her sorrow; a greater one than men can understand.

Another source of grief was this: that Sir Bale Mardykes conceived a dislike to William Feltram that was unaccountable. At first suppressed, it betrayed itself negatively only; but with time it increased; and in the end the Baronet made little secret of his wish to get rid of him. Many and ingenious were the annoyances he contrived; and at last he told his wife plainly that he wished William Feltram to find some other abode for himself.

Lady Mardykes pleaded earnestly, and even with tears; for if Gertrude were to leave the neighbourhood, she well knew how utterly solitary her own life would become.

Sir Bale at last vouchsafed some little light as to his motives.

There was an old story, he told her, that his estate would go to a Feltram. He had an instinctive distrust of that family. It was a feeling not given him for nothing; it might be the means of defeating their plotting and strategy. Old Trebeck, he fancied, had a finger in it. Philip Feltram had told him that Mardykes was to pass away to a Feltram. Well, they might conspire; but he would take what care he could that the estate should not be stolen from his family. He did not want his wife stript of her jointure, or his children, if he had any, left without bread.

All this sounded very like madness; but the idea was propounded by Philip Feltram. His own jealousy was at bottom founded on superstition which he would not avow and could hardly define. He bitterly blamed himself for having permitted William Feltram to place himself where he was.

In the midst of these annoyances William Feltram was seriously thinking of throwing up the farm, and seeking similar occupation somewhere else.

One day, walking alone in the thick wood that skirts the lake near his farm, he was discussing this problem with himself; and every now and then he repeated his question, "Shall I throw it up, and give him the lease back if he likes?" On a sudden he heard a voice near him say:

"Hold it, you fool!—hold hard, you fool!—hold it, you fool!"

The situation being lonely, he was utterly puzzled to account for the interruption, until on a sudden a huge parrot, green, crimson, and yellow, plunged from among the boughs over his head to the ground, and partly flying, and partly hopping and tumbling along, got lamely, but swiftly, out of sight among the thick underwood; and he could neither start it nor hear it any more. The interruption reminded him of that which befel Robinson Crusoe. It was more singular, however; for he owned no such bird; and its strangeness impressed the omen all the more.

He related it when he got home to his wife; and as people when living a solitary life, and also suffering, are prone to superstition, she did not laugh at the adventure, as in a healthier state of spirits, I suppose, she would.

They continued, however, to discuss the question together; and all the more industriously as a farm of the same kind, only some fifteen miles away, was now offered to all bidders, under another landlord. Gertrude, who felt Sir Bale's unkindness all the more that she was a distant cousin of his, as it had proved on comparing notes, was very strong in favour of the change, and had been urging it with true feminine ingenuity and persistence upon her husband. A very singular dream rather damped her ardour, however, and it appeared thus:

She had gone to her bed full of this subject; and she thought, although she could not remember having done so, had fallen asleep. She was still thinking, as she had been all the day, about leaving the farm. It seemed to her that she was quite awake, and a candle burning all the time in the room, awaiting the return of her husband, who was away at the fair near Haworth; she saw the interior of the room distinctly. It was a sultry night, and a little bit of the window was raised. A very slight sound in that direction attracted her attention; and to her surprise she saw a jay hop upon the windowsill, and into the room.

Up sat Gertrude, surprised and a little startled at the visit of so large a bird, without presence of mind for the moment even to frighten it away, and staring at it, as they say, with all her eyes. A sofa stood at the foot of the bed; and under this the bird swiftly hopped. She extended her hand now to take the bell-rope at the left side of the bed, and in doing so displaced the curtains, which were open only at the foot.

She was amazed there to see a lady dressed entirely in black, and with the old-fashioned hood over her head. She was young and pretty, and looked kindly at her, but with now and then a slight contraction of lips and eyebrows that indicates pain. This little twitching was momentary, and recurred, it seemed, about once or twice in a minute.

How it was that she was not frightened on seeing this lady, standing like an old friend at her bedside, she could not afterwards understand. Some influence besides the kindness of her look prevented any sensation of terror at the time. With a very white hand the young lady in black held a white handkerchief pressed to her bosom at the top of her bodice.

"Who are you?" asked Gertrude.

"I am a kinswoman, although you don't know me; and I have come to tell you that you must not leave Faxwell" (the name of the place) "or Janet. If you go, I will go with you; and I can make you fear me."

Her voice was very distinct, but also very faint, with something undulatory in it, that seemed to enter Gertrude's head rather than her ear.

Saying this she smiled horribly, and, lifting her handkerchief, disclosed for a moment a great wound in her breast, deep in which Gertrude saw darkly the head of a snake writhing.

Hereupon she uttered a wild scream of terror, and, diving under the bedclothes, remained more dead than alive there, until her maid, alarmed by her cry, came in, and having searched the room, and shut the window at her desire, did all in her power to comfort her.

If this was a nightmare and embodied only by a form of expression which in some states belongs to the imagination, a leading idea in the controversy in which her mind had long been employed, it had at least the effect of deciding her against leaving Faxwell. And so that point was settled; and unpleasant relations continued between the tenants of the farm and the master of Mardykes Hall.

To Lady Mardykes all this was very painful, although Sir Bale did not insist upon making a separation between his wife and her cousin. But to Mardykes Hall that cousin came no more. Even Lady Mardykes thought it better to see her at Faxwell than to risk a meeting in the temper in which Sir Bale then was. And thus several years passed.

No tidings of Philip Feltram were heard; and, in fact, none ever reached that part of the world; and if it had not been highly improbable that he could have drowned himself in the lake without his body sooner or later having risen to the surface, it would have been concluded that he had either accidentally or by design made away with himself in its waters.

Over Mardykes Hall there was a gloom—no sound of children's voices was heard there, and even the hope of that merry advent had died out.

This disappointment had no doubt helped to fix in Sir Bale's mind the idea of the insecurity of his property, and the morbid fancy that William Feltram and old Trebeck were conspiring to seize it; than which, I need hardly say, no imagination more insane could have fixed itself in his mind.

In other things, however, Sir Bale was shrewd and sharp, a clear and rapid man of business, and although this was a strange whim, it was not so unnatural in a man who was by nature so prone to suspicion as Sir Bale Mardykes.

During the years, now seven, that had elapsed since the marriage of Sir Bale and Miss Janet Feltram, there had happened but one event, except the death of their only child, to place them in mourning. That was the decease of Sir William Walsingham, the husband of Lady Mardykes' sister. She now lived in a handsome old dower-house at Islington, and being wealthy, made now and then an excursion to Mardykes Hall, in which she was sometimes accompanied by her sister Lady Haworth. Sir Oliver being a Parliament-man was much in London and deep in politics and intrigue, and subject, as convivial rogues are, to occasional hard hits from gout.

But change and separation had made no alteration in these ladies' mutual affections, and no three sisters were ever more attached.

Was Lady Mardykes happy with her lord? A woman so gentle and loving as she, is a happy wife with any husband who is not an absolute brute. There must have been, I suppose, some good about Sir Bale. His wife was certainly deeply attached to him. She admired his wisdom, and feared his inflexible will, and altogether made of him a domestic idol. To acquire this enviable position, I suspect there must be something not essentially disagreeable about a man. At all events, what her neighbours good-naturedly termed her infatuation continued, and indeed rather improved by time.

CHAPTER 24
AN OLD PORTRAIT

Sir Bale—whom some remembered a gay and convivial man, not to say a profligate one—had grown to be a very gloomy man indeed. There was something weighing upon his mind; and I daresay some of the good gossips of Golden Friars, had there been any materials for such a case, would have believed that Sir Bale had murdered Philip Feltram, and was now the victim of the worm and fire of remorse.

The gloom of the master of the house made his very servants gloomy, and the house itself looked sombre, as if it had been startled with strange and dismal sights.

Lady Mardykes was something of an artist. She had lighted lately, in an out-of-the-way room, upon a dozen or more old portraits. Several of these were full-lengths; and she was—with the help of her maid, both in long aprons, amid sponges and basins, soft handkerchiefs and varnish-pots and brushes—busy in removing the dust and smoke-stains, and in laying-on the varnish, which brought out the colouring, and made the transparent shadows yield up their long-buried treasures of finished detail.

Against the wall stood a full-length portrait as Sir Bale entered the room; having for a wonder, a word to say to his wife.

"O," said the pretty lady, turning to him in her apron, and with her brush in her hand, "we are in such in pickle, Munnings and I have been cleaning these old pictures. Mrs. Julaper says they are the pictures that came from Cloostedd Hall long ago. They were buried in dust in the dark room in the clock-tower. Here is such a characteristic one. It has a long powdered wig-George the First or Second, I don't know which—and such a combination of colours, and such a face. It seems starting out of the canvas, and all but speaks. Do look; that is, I mean, Bale, if you can spare time."

Sir Bale abstractedly drew near, and looked over his wife's shoulder on the full-length portrait that stood before him; and as he did so a strange expression for a moment passed over his face.

The picture represented a man of swarthy countenance, with signs of the bottle glowing through the dark skin; small fierce pig eyes, a rather flat pendulous nose, and a grim forbidding mouth, with a large wart a little above it. On the head hung one of those full-bottomed powdered wigs that look like a cloud of cotton-wadding; a lace cravat was about his neck; he wore short black-velvet breeches with stockings rolled over them, a bottle-green coat of cut velvet and a crimson waistcoat with long flaps; coat and waistcoat both heavily laced with gold. He wore a sword, and leaned upon a crutch-handled cane, and his figure and aspect indicated a swollen and gouty state. He could not be far from sixty.

There was uncommon force in this fierce and forbidding-looking portrait. Lady Mardykes said, "What wonderful dresses they wore! How like a fine magic-lantern figure he looks! What gorgeous colouring! it looks like the plumage of a mackaw; and what a claw his hand is! and that huge broken beak of a nose! Isn't he like a wicked old mackaw?"

"Where did you find that?" asked Sir Bale.

Surprised at his tone, she looked round, and was still more surprised at his looks.

"I told you, dear Bale, I found them in the clock-tower. I hope I did right; it was not wrong bringing them here? I ought to have asked. Are you vexed, Bale?"

"Vexed! not I. I only wish it was in the fire. I must have seen that picture when I was a child. I hate to look at it. I raved about it once, when I was ill. I don't know who it is; I don't remember when I saw it. I wish you'd tell them to burn it."

"It is one of the Feltrams," she answered. "'Sir Hugh Feltram' is on the frame at the foot; and old Mrs. Julaper says he was the father of the unhappy lady who was said to have been drowned near Snakes Island."

"Well, suppose he is; there's nothing interesting in that. It is a disgusting picture. I connect it with my illness; and I think it is the kind of thing that would make any one half mad, if they only looked at it often enough. Tell them to burn it; and come away, come to the next room; I can't say what I want here."

Sir Bale seemed to grow more and more agitated the longer he remained in the room. He seemed to her both frightened and furious; and taking her a little roughly by the wrist, he led her through the door.

When they were in another apartment alone, he again asked the affrighted lady who had told her that picture was there, and who told her to clean it.

She had only the truth to plead. It was, from beginning to end, the merest accident.

"If I thought, Janet, that you were taking counsel of others, talking me over, and trying clever experiments—" he stopped short with his eyes fixed on hers with black suspicion.

His wife's answer was one pleading look, and to burst into tears.

Sir Bale let go her wrist, which he had held up to this; and placing his hand gently on her shoulder, he said,

"You must not cry, Janet; I have given you no excuse for tears. I only wished an answer to a very harmless question; and I am sure you would tell me, if by any chance you have lately seen Philip Feltram; he is capable of arranging all that. No one knows him as I do. There, you must not cry anymore; but tell me truly, has he turned up? is he at Faxwell?"

She denied all this with perfect truth; and after a hesitation of some time, the matter ended. And as soon as she and he were more themselves, he had something quite different to tell her.

"Sit down, Janet; sit down, and forget that vile picture and all I have been saying. What I came to tell you, I think you will like; I am sure it will please you."

And with this little preface he placed his arm about her neck, and kissed her tenderly. She certainly was pleased; and when his little speech was over, she, smiling, with her tears still wet upon her cheeks, put her arms round her husband's neck, and in turn kissed him with the ardour of gratitude, kissed him affectionately; again and again thanking him all the time.

It was no great matter, but from Sir Bale Mardykes it was something quite unusual.

Was it a sudden whim? What was it? Something had prompted Sir Bale, early in that dark shrewd month of December, to tell his wife that he wished to call together some of his county acquaintances, and to fill his house for a week or so, as near Christmas as she could get them to come. He wished her sisters—Lady Haworth (with her husband) and the Dowager Lady Walsingham—to be invited for an early day, before the coming of the other guests, so that she might enjoy their society for a little time quietly to herself before the less intimate guests should assemble.

Glad was Lady Mardykes to hear the resolve of her husband, and prompt to obey. She wrote to her sisters to beg them to arrange to come, together, by the tenth or twelfth of the month, which they accordingly arranged to do. Sir Oliver, it was true, could not be of the party. A minister of state was drinking the waters at Bath; and Sir Oliver thought it would do him no harm to sip a little also, and his fashionable doctor politely agreed, and "ordered" to those therapeutic springs the knight of the shire, who was "consumedly vexed" to lose the Christmas with that jolly dog, Bale, down at Mardykes Hall. But a fellow must have a stomach for his Christmas pudding, and politics takes it out of a poor gentleman deucedly; and health's the first thing, egad!

So Sir Oliver went down to Bath, and I don't know that he tippled much of the waters, but he did drink the burgundy of that haunt of the ailing; and he had the honour of making a fourth not unfrequently in the secretary of state's whist-parties.

It was about the 8th of December when, in Lady Walsingham's carriage, intending to post all the way, that lady, still young, and Lady Haworth, with all the servants that were usual in such expeditions in those days, started from the great Dower House at Islington in high spirits.

Lady Haworth had not been very well—low and nervous; but the clear frosty sun, and the pleasant nature of the excursion, raised her spirits to the point of enjoyment; and expecting nothing but happiness and gaiety—for, after all, Sir Bale was but one of a large party, and even he could make an effort and be agreeable as well as hospitable on occasion—they set out on their northward expedition. The journey, which is a long one, they had resolved to break into a four days' progress; and the inns had been written to, bespeaking a comfortable reception.

CHAPTER 25
THROUGH THE WALL

On the third night they put-up at the comfortable old inn called the Three Nuns. With an effort they might easily have pushed on to Mardykes Hall that night, for the distance is not more than five-and-thirty miles. But, considering her sister's health, Lady Walsingham in planning their route had resolved against anything like a forced march.

Here the ladies took possession of the best sitting-room; and, notwithstanding the fatigue of the journey, Lady Haworth sat up with her sister till near ten o'clock, chatting gaily about a thousand things.

Of the three sisters, Lady Walsingham was the eldest. She had been in the habit of taking the command at home; and now, for advice and decision, her younger sisters, less prompt and courageous than she, were wont, whenever in her neighbourhood, to throw upon her all the cares and agitations of determining what was best to be done in small things and great. It is only fair to say, in addition, that this submission was not by any means exacted; it was the deference of early habit and feebler will, for she was neither officious nor imperious.

It was now time that Lady Haworth, a good deal more fatigued than her sister, should take leave of her for the night.

Accordingly they kissed and bid each other goodnight; and Lady Walsingham, not yet disposed to sleep, sat for some time longer in the comfortable room where they had taken tea, amusing the time with the book that had, when conversation flagged, beguiled the weariness of the journey. Her sister had been in her room nearly an hour, when she became herself a little sleepy. She had lighted her candle, and was going to ring for her maid, when, to her surprise, the door opened, and her sister Lady Haworth entered in a dressing-gown, looking frightened.

"My darling Mary!" exclaimed Lady Walsingham, "what is the matter? Are you well?"

"Yes, darling," she answered, "quite well; that is, I don't know what is the matter—I'm frightened." She paused, listening, with her eyes turned towards the wall. "O, darling Maud, I am so frightened! I don't know what it can be."

"You must not be agitated, darling; there's nothing. You have been asleep, and I suppose you have had a dream. Were you asleep?"

Lady Haworth had caught her sister fast by the arm with both hands, and was looking wildly in her face.

"Have *you* heard nothing?" she asked, again looking towards the wall of the room, as if she expected to hear a voice through it.

"Nonsense, darling; you are dreaming still. Nothing; there has been nothing to hear. I have been awake ever since; if there had been anything to hear, I could not have missed it. Come, sit down. Sip a little of this water; you are nervous, and over-tired; and tell me plainly, like a good little soul, what is the matter; for nothing has happened here; and you ought to know that the Three Nuns is the quietest house in England; and I'm no witch, and if you won't tell me what's the matter, I can't divine it."

"Yes, of course," said Mary, sitting down, and glancing round her wildly. "I don't hear it now; *you* don't?"

"Do, my dear Mary, tell me what you mean," said Lady Walsingham kindly but firmly.

Lady Haworth was holding the still untasted glass of water in her hand.

"Yes, I'll tell you; I have been so frightened! You are right; I had a dream, but I can scarcely remember anything of it, except the very end, when I wakened. But it was not the dream; only it was connected with what terrified me so. I was so tired when I went to bed, I thought I should have slept soundly; and indeed I fell asleep immediately; and I must have slept quietly for a good while. How long is it since I left you?"

"More than an hour."

"Yes, I must have slept a good while; for I don't think I have been ten minutes awake. How my dream began I don't know. I remember only that gradually it came to this: I was standing in a recess in a panelled gallery; it was lofty, and, I thought, belonged to a handsome but old-fashioned house. I was looking straight towards the head of a wide staircase, with a great oak banister. At the top of the stairs, as near to me, about, as that window there, was a thick short column of oak, on top of which was a candlestick. There was no other light but from that one candle; and there was a lady standing beside it, looking down the stairs, with her back turned towards me; and from her gestures I should have thought speaking to people on a lower lobby, but whom from my place I could not see.

"I soon perceived that this lady was in great agony of mind; for she beat her breast and wrung her hands every now and then, and wagged her head slightly from side to side, like a person in great distraction. But one word she said I could not hear. Nor when she struck her hand on the banister, or stamped, as she seemed to do in her pain, upon the floor, could I hear any sound. I found myself somehow waiting upon this lady, and was watching her with awe and sympathy. But who she was I knew not, until turning towards me I plainly saw Janet's face, pale and covered with tears, and with such a look of agony as—O God!—I can never forget."

"Pshaw! Mary darling, what is it but a dream! I have had a thousand more startling; it is only that you are so nervous just now."

"But that is not all—nothing; what followed is so dreadful; for either there is something very horrible going on at Mardykes, or else I am losing my reason," said Lady Haworth in increasing agitation. "I wakened instantly in great alarm, but I suppose no more than I have felt a hundred times on awakening from a frightful dream. I sat up in my bed; I was thinking of ringing for Winnefred, my heart was beating so, but feeling better soon I changed my mind. All this time I heard a faint sound of a voice, as if coming through a thick wall. It came from the wall at the left side of my bed, and I fancied was that of some woman lamenting in a room separated from me by that thick partition. I could only perceive that it was a sound of crying mingled with ejaculations of misery, or fear, or entreaty.

"I listened with a painful curiosity, wondering who it could be, and what could have happened in the neighbouring rooms of the house; and as I looked and listened, I could distinguish my own name, but at first nothing more. That, of course, might have been an accident; and I knew there were many Marys in the world besides myself. But it made me more curious; and a strange thing struck me, for I was now looking at that very wall through which the sounds were coming. I saw that there was a window in it. Thinking that the rest of the wall might nevertheless be covered by another room, I drew the curtain of it and looked out. But there is no such thing. It is the outer wall the entire way along. And it is equally impossible of the other wall, for it is to the front of the house, and has two windows in it; and the wall that the head of my bed stands against has the gallery outside it all the way; for I remarked that as I came to you."

"Tut, tut, Mary darling, nothing on earth is so deceptive as sound; this and fancy account for everything."

"But hear me out; I have not told you all. I began to hear the voice more clearly, and at last quite distinctly. It was Janet's, and she was conjuring you by name, as well as me, to come to her to Mardykes, without delay, in her extremity; yes, *you*, just as vehemently as me. It was Janet's voice. It still seemed separated by the wall, but I heard every syllable now; and I never heard voice or words of such anguish. She was imploring of us to come on, without a moment's delay, to Mardykes; and crying that, if we were not with her, she should go mad."

"Well, darling," said Lady Walsingham, "you see I'm included in this invitation as well as you, and should hate to disappoint Janet just as much; and I do assure you, in the morning you will laugh over this fancy with me; or rather, she will laugh over it with us, when we get to Mardykes. What you do want is rest, and a little *sal volatile.*"

So saying she rang the bell for Lady Haworth's maid. Having comforted her sister, and made her take the nervous specific she recommended, she went with her to her room; and taking possession of the arm-chair by the fire, she told her that she would keep her company until she was asleep, and remain long enough to be sure that the sleep was not likely to be interrupted. Lady Haworth had not been ten minutes in her bed, when she raised herself with a start to her elbow, listening with parted lips and wild eyes, her trembling fingers behind her ears. With an exclamation of horror, she cried,

"There it is again, upbraiding us! I can't stay longer."

She sprang from the bed, and rang the bell violently.

"Maud," she cried in an ecstasy of horror, "nothing shall keep me here, whether you go or not. I will set out the moment the horses are put to. If you refuse to come, Maud, mind the responsibility is yours—listen!" and with white face and starting eyes she pointed to the wall. "Have you ears; don't you hear?"

The sight of a person in extremity of terror so mysterious, might have unnerved a ruder system than Lady Walsingham's. She was pale as she replied; for under certain circumstances those terrors which deal with the supernatural are more contagious than any others. Lady Walsingham still, in terms, held to her opinion; but although she tried to smile, her face showed that the panic had touched her.

"Well, dear Mary," she said, "as you will have it so, I see no good in resisting you longer. Here, it is plain, your nerves will not suffer you to rest. Let us go then, in heaven's name; and when you get to Mardykes Hall you will be relieved."

All this time Lady Haworth was getting on her things, with the careless hurry of a person about to fly for her life; and Lady

Walsingham issued her orders for horses, and the general preparations for resuming the journey.

It was now between ten and eleven; but the servant who rode armed with them, according to the not unnecessary usage of the times, thought that with a little judicious bribing of postboys they might easily reach Mardykes Hall before three o'clock in the morning.

When the party set forward again, Lady Haworth was comparatively tranquil. She no longer heard the unearthly mimickry of her sister's voice; there remained only the fear and suspense which that illusion or visitation had produced.

Her sister, Lady Walsingham, after a brief effort to induce something like conversation, became silent. A thin sheet of snow had covered the darkened landscape, and some light flakes were still dropping. Lady Walsingham struck her repeater often in the dark, and inquired the distances frequently. She was anxious to get over the ground, though by no means fatigued. Something of the anxiety that lay heavy at her sister's heart had touched her own.

CHAPTER 26
PERPLEXED

The roads even then were good, and very good horses the posting-houses turned out; so that by dint of extra pay the rapid rate of travelling undertaken by the servant was fully accomplished in the first two or three stages.

While Lady Walsingham was continually striking her repeater in her ear, and as they neared their destination, growing in spite of herself more anxious, her sister's uneasiness showed itself in a less reserved way; for, cold as it was, with snowflakes actually dropping, Lady Haworth's head was perpetually out at the window, and when she drew it up, sitting again in her place, she would audibly express her alarms, and apply to her sister for consolation and confidence in her suspense.

Under its thin carpet of snow, the pretty village of Golden Friars looked strangely to their eyes. It had long been fast asleep, and both ladies were excited as they drew up at the steps of the George and Dragon, and with bell and knocker roused the slumbering household.

What tidings awaited them here? In a very few minutes the door was opened, and the porter staggered down, after a word with the driver, to the carriage-window, not half awake.

"Is Lady Mardykes well?" demanded Lady Walsingham.

"Is Sir Bale well?"

"Are all the people at Mardykes Hall quite well?"

With clasped hands Lady Haworth listened to the successive answers to these questions which her sister hastily put. The answers were all satisfactory. With a great sigh and a little laugh, Lady Walsingham placed her hand affectionately on that of her sister; who, saying, "God be thanked!" began to weep.

"When had you last news from Mardykes?" asked Lady Walsingham.

"A servant was down here about four o'clock."

"O! no one since?" said she in a disappointed tone.

No one had been from the great house since, but all were well then.

"They are early people, you know, dear; and it is dark at four, and that is as late as they could well have heard, and nothing could have happened since—very unlikely. We have come very fast; it is only a few minutes past two, darling."

But each felt the chill and load of their returning anxiety.

While the people at the George were rapidly getting a team of horses to, Lady Walsingham contrived a moment for an order from the other window to her servant, who knew Golden Friars perfectly, to knock-up the people at Doctor Torvey's, and to inquire whether all were well at Mardykes Hall.

There he learned that a messenger had come for Doctor Torvey at ten o'clock, and that the Doctor had not returned since. There was no news, however, of any one's being ill; and the Doctor himself did not know what he was wanted about. While Lady Haworth was talking to her maid from the window next the steps, Lady Walsingham was, unobserved, receiving this information at the other.

It made her very uncomfortable.

In a few minutes more, however, with a team of fresh horses, they were again rapidly passing the distance between them and Mardykes Hall.

About two miles on, their drivers pulled-up, and they heard a voice talking with them from the roadside. A servant from the Hall had been sent with a note for Lady Walsingham, and had been ordered, if necessary, to ride the whole way to the Three Nuns to deliver it. The note was already in Lady Walsingham's hand; her sister sat beside her, and with the corner of the open note in her fingers, she read it breathlessly at the same time by the light of a carriage-lamp which the man held to the window. It said:

My dearest love—my darling sister—dear sisters both!— in God's name, lose not a moment. I am so overpowered and *terrified*. I cannot explain; I can only implore of you to come with all the haste you can make. Waste no time, dar- lings. I hardly understand what I write. Only this, dear sis- ters; I feel that my reason will desert me, unless you come soon. You will not fail me now. Your poor distracted

JANET

The sisters exchanged a pale glance, and Lady Haworth grasped her sister's hand.

"Where is the messenger?" asked Lady Walsingham.

A mounted servant came to the window.

"Is any one ill at home?" she asked.

"No, all were well—my lady, and Sir Bale—no one sick."

"But the Doctor was sent for; what was that for?"

"I can't say, my lady."

"You are quite certain that no one—think—*no* one is ill?"

"There is no one ill at the Hall, my lady, that I have heard of."

"Is Lady Mardykes, my sister, still up?"

"Yes, my lady; and her maid is with her."

"And Sir Bale, are you certain he is quite well?"

"Sir Bale is quite well, my lady; he has been busy settling papers tonight, and was as well as usual."

"That will do, thanks," said the perplexed lady; and to her own servant she added, "On to Mardykes Hall with all the speed they can make. I'll pay them well, tell them."

And in another minute they were gliding along the road at a pace which the muffled beating of the horses' hoofs on the thin sheet of snow that covered the road showed to have broken out of the conventional trot, and to resemble something more like a gallop.

And now they were under the huge trees, that looked black as hearse-plumes in contrast with the snow. The cold gleam of the lake in the moon which had begun to shine out now met their gaze; and the familiar outline of Snakes Island, its solemn timber bleak and leafless, standing in a group, seemed to watch Mardykes Hall with a dismal observation across the water. Through the gate and between the huge files of trees the carriage seemed to fly; and at last the steaming horses stood panting, nodding and snorting, before the steps in the courtyard.

There was a light in an upper window, and a faint light in the hall, the door of which was opened; and an old servant came down and ushered the ladies into the house.

CHAPTER 27

THE HOUR

Lightly they stepped over the snow that lay upon the broad steps, and entering the door saw the dim figure of their sister, already in the large and faintly-lighted hall. One candle in the hand of her scared maid, and one burning on the table, leaving the distant parts of that great apartment in total darkness, touched the figures with the odd sharp lights in which Schalken delights; and a streak of chilly moonlight, through the open door, fell upon the floor, and was stretched like a white sheet at her feet. Lady Mardykes, with an exclamation of agitated relief, threw her arms, in turn, round the necks of her sisters, and hugging them, kissed them again and again, murmuring her thanks, calling them her "blessed sisters," and praising God for his mercy in having sent them to her in time, and altogether in a rapture of agitation and gratitude.

Taking them each by a hand, she led them into a large room, on whose panels they could see the faint twinkle of the tall gilded frames, and the darker indication of the old portraits, in which that interesting house abounds. The moonbeams, entering obliquely through the Tudor stone-shafts of the window and thrown upon the floor, reflected an imperfect light; and the candle which the maid who followed her mistress held in her hand shone dimly from the sideboard, where she placed it. Lady Mardykes told her that she need not wait.

"They don't know; they know only that we are in some great confusion; but—God have mercy on me!—nothing of the reality. Sit down, darlings; you are tired."

She sat down between them on a sofa, holding a hand of each. They sat opposite the window, through which appeared the magnificent view commanded from the front of the house: in the foreground the solemn trees of Snakes Island, one great branch stretching upward, bare and moveless, from the side, like an arm raised to heaven in wonder or in menace towards the house; the lake, in part swept by the icy splendour of the moon, trembling with a dazzling glimmer, and farther off lost in blackness; the Fells rising from a base of gloom, into ribs and peaks white with snow, and looking against the pale sky, thin and transparent as a haze. Right across to the storied woods of Cloostedd, and the old domains of the Feltrams, this view extended.

Thus alone, their mufflers still on, their hands clasped in hers, they breathlessly listened to her strange tale.

Connectedly told it amounted to this: Sir Bale seemed to have been relieved of some great anxiety about the time when, ten days before, he had told her to invite her friends to Mardykes Hall. This morning he had gone out for a walk with Trevor, his under-steward, to talk over some plans about thinning the woods at this side; and also to discuss practically a proposal, lately made by a wealthy merchant, to take a very long lease, on advantageous terms to Sir Bale as he thought, of the old park and chase of Cloostedd, with the intention of building there, and making it once more a handsome residence.

In the improved state of his spirits, Sir Bale had taken a shrewd interest in this negotiation; and was actually persuaded to cross the lake that morning with his adviser, and to walk over the grounds with him.

Sir Bale had seemed unusually well, and talked with great animation. He was more like a young man who had just attained his majority, and for the first time grasped his estates, than the grim elderly Baronet who had been moping about Mardykes, and as much afraid as a cat of the water, for so many years.

As they were returning toward the boat, at the roots of that same scathed elm whose barkless bough had seemed, in his former visit to this old wood, to beckon him from a distance, like a skeleton arm, to enter the forest, he and his companion on a sudden missed an old map of the grounds which they had been consulting.

"We must have left it in the corner tower of Cloostedd House, which commands that view of the grounds, you remember; it would not do to lose it. It is the most accurate thing we have. I'll sit down here and rest a little till you come back."

The man was absent little more than twenty minutes. When he returned, he found that Sir Bale had changed his position, and was now walking to and fro, around and about, in what, at a distance, he fancied was mere impatience, on the open space a couple of hundred paces nearer to the turn in the valley towards the boat. It was not impatience. He was agitated. He looked pale, and he took his companion's arm—a thing he had never thought of doing before—and said, "Let us away quickly. I've something to tell at home,—and I forgot it."

Not another word did Sir Bale exchange with his companion. He sat in the stern of the boat, gloomy as a man about to glide under traitor's-gate. He entered his house in the same sombre and agitated state. He entered his library, and sat for a long time as if stunned.

At last he seemed to have made-up his mind to something; and applied himself quietly and diligently to arranging papers, and docketing some and burning others. Dinner-time arrived. He sent to tell Lady Mardykes that he should not join her at dinner, but would see her afterwards.

"It was between eight and nine," she continued, "I forget the exact time, when he came to the tower drawing-room where I was. I did not hear his approach. There is a stone stair, with a thick carpet on it. He told me he wished to speak to me there. It is an out-of-the-way place—a small old room with very thick walls, and there is a double door, the inner one of oak—I suppose he wished to guard against being overheard.

"There was a look in his face that frightened me; I saw he had something dreadful to tell. He looked like a man on whom a lot had fallen to put someone to death," said Lady Mardykes. "O, my poor Bale! my husband, my husband! he knew what it would be to me."

Here she broke into the wildest weeping, and it was some time before she resumed.

"He seemed very kind and very calm," she said at last; "he said but little; and, I think, these were his words: 'I find, Janet, I have made a great miscalculation—I thought my hour of danger had passed. We have been many years together, but a parting must sooner or later be, and my time has come.'

"I don't know what I said. I would not have so much minded—for I could not have believed, if I had not seen him—but there was that in his look and tone which no one could doubt.

"'I shall die before tomorrow morning,' he said. 'You must command yourself, Janet; it can't be altered now.'

"'O, Bale,' I cried nearly distracted, 'you would not kill yourself!'

"'Kill myself! poor child! no, indeed,' he said; 'it is simply that I shall die. No violent death—nothing but the common subsidence of life—I have made up my mind; what happens to everybody can't be so very bad; and millions of worse men than

I die every year. You must not follow me to my room, darling; I shall see you by and by.'

"His language was collected and even cold; but his face looked as if it was cut in stone; you never saw, in a dream, a face like it."

Lady Walsingham here said, "I am certain he is ill; he's in a fever. You must not distract and torture yourself about his predictions. You sent for Doctor Torvey; what did he say?"

"I could not tell him all."

"O, no; I don't mean that; they'd only say he was mad, and we little better for minding what he says. But did the Doctor see him? and what did he say of his health?"

"Yes; he says there is nothing wrong—no fever—nothing whatever. Poor Bale has been so kind; he saw him to please me," she sobbed again wildly. "I wrote to implore of him. It was my last hope, strange as it seems; and O, would to God I could think it! But there is nothing of that kind. Wait till you have seen him. There is a frightful calmness about all he says and does; and his directions are all so clear, and his mind so perfectly collected, it is quite impossible."

And poor Lady Mardykes again burst into a frantic agony of tears.

CHAPTER 28
SIR BALE IN THE GALLERY

"Now, Janet darling, you are yourself low and nervous, and you treat this fancy of Bale's as seriously as he does himself. The truth is, he is a hypochondriac, as the doctors say; and you will find that I am right; he will be quite well in the morning, and I daresay a little ashamed of himself for having frightened his poor little wife as he has. I will sit up with you. But our poor Mary is not, you know, very strong; and she ought to lie down and rest a little. Suppose you give me a cup of tea in the drawing-room. I will run up to my room and get these things off, and meet you in the drawing-room; or, if you like it better, you can sit with me in my own room; and for goodness' sake let us have candles enough and a bright fire; and I promise you, if you will only exert your own good sense, you shall be a great deal more cheerful in a very little time."

Lady Walsingham's address was kind and cheery, and her air confident. For a moment a ray of hope returned, and her sister Janet acknowledged at least the possibility of her theory. But if confidence is contagious, so also is panic; and Lady Walsingham experienced a sinking of the heart which she dared not confess to her sister, and vainly strove to combat.

Lady Walsingham went up with her sister Mary, and having seen her in her room, and spoken again to her in the same cheery tone in which she had lectured her sister Lady Mardykes, she went on; and having taken possession of her own room, and put off her cloaks and shawls, she was going downstairs again, when she heard Sir Bale's voice, as he approached along the gallery, issuing orders to a servant, as it seemed, exactly in his usual tone.

She turned, with a strange throb at her heart, and met him.

A little sterner, a little paler than usual he looked; she could perceive no other change. He took her hand kindly and held it, as with dilated eyes he looked with a dark inquiry for a moment in her face. He signed to the servant to go on, and said, "I'm glad you have come, Maud. You have heard what is to happen; and I don't know how Janet could have borne it without your support. You did right to come; and you'll stay with her for a day or two, and take her away from this place as soon as you can."

She looked at him with the embarrassment of fear. He was speaking to her with the calmness of a leave-taking in the press-room—the serenity that overlies the greatest awe and agony of which human nature is capable.

"I am glad to see you, Bale," she began, hardly knowing what she said, and she stopped short.

"You are come, it turns out, on a sad mission," he resumed; "you find all about to change. Poor Janet! it is a blow to her. I shall not live to see tomorrow's sun."

"Come," she said, startled, "you must not talk so. No, Bale, you have no right to speak so; you can have no reason to justify it. It is cruel and wicked to trifle with your wife's feelings. If you are under a delusion, you must make an effort and shake it off, or, at least, cease to talk of it. You are not well; I know by your looks you are ill; but I am very certain we shall see you much better by tomorrow, and still better the day following."

"No, I'm not ill, sister. Feel that pulse, if you doubt me; there is no fever in it. I never was more perfectly in health; and yet I know that before the clock, that has just struck three, shall have struck five, I, who am talking to you, shall be dead."

Lady Walsingham was frightened, and her fear irritated her.

"I have told you what I think and believe," she said vehemently. "I think it wrong and cowardly of you to torture my poor sister with your whimsical predictions. Look into your own mind, and you will see you have absolutely no reason to support what you say. How *can* you inflict all this agony upon a poor creature foolish enough to love you as she does, and weak enough to believe in your idle dreams?"

"Stay, sister; it is not a matter to be debated so. If to-morrow I can hear you, it will be time enough to upbraid me. Pray return now to your sister; she needs all you can do for her. She is much to be pitied; her sufferings afflict me. I shall see you and her again before my death. It would have been more cruel to leave her unprepared. Do all in your power to nerve and tranquillise her. What is past cannot now be helped."

He paused, looking hard at her, as if he had half made up his mind to say something more. But if there was a question of the kind, it was determined in favour of silence.

He dropped her hand, turned quickly, and left her.

CHAPTER 29
DR. TORVEY'S OPINION

When Lady Walsingham reached the head of the stairs, she met her maid, and from her learned that her sister, Lady Mardykes, was downstairs in the same room. On approaching, she heard her sister Mary's voice talking with her, and found them together. Mary, finding that she could not sleep, had put on her clothes again, and come down to keep her sister company. The room looked more comfortable now. There were candles lighted, and a good fire burnt in the grate; tea-things stood on a little table near the fire, and the two sisters were talking, Lady Mardykes appearing more collected, and only they two in the room.

"Have you seen him, Maud?" cried Lady Mardykes, rising and hastily approaching her the moment she entered.

"Yes, dear; and talked with him, and——"

"Well?"

"And I think very much as I did before. I think he is nervous, he says he is not ill; but he is nervous and whimsical, and as men always are when they happen to be out of sorts, very positive; and of course the only thing that can quite undeceive him is the lapse of the time he has fixed for his prediction, as it is sure to pass without any tragic result of any sort. We shall then all see alike the nature of his delusion."

"O, Maud, if I were only sure you thought so! if I were sure you really had hopes! Tell me, Maud, for God's sake, what you really think."

Lady Walsingham was a little disconcerted by the unexpected directness of her appeal.

"Come, darling, you must not be foolish," she said; "we can only talk of impressions, and we are imposed upon by the solemnity of his manner, and the fact that he evidently believes in his own delusion; everyone does believe in his own delusion-there is nothing strange in that."

"O, Maud, I see you are not convinced; you are only trying to comfort me. You have no hope—none, none, none!" and she covered her face with her hands, and wept again convulsively.

Lady Walsingham was silent for a moment, and then with an effort said, as she placed her hand on her sister's arm, "You see, dear Janet, there is no use in my saying the same thing over and over again; an hour or two will show who is right. Sit down again, and be like yourself. My maid told me that you had sent to the parlour for Doctor Torvey; he must not find you so. What would he think? Unless you mean to tell him of Bale's strange fancy; and a pretty story that would be to set afloat in Golden Friars. I think I hear him coming."

So, in effect, he was. Doctor Torvey—with the florid gravity of a man who, having just swallowed a bottle of port, besides some glasses of sherry, is admitted to the presence of ladies whom he respects—entered the room, made what he called his "leg and his compliments," and awaited the ladies' commands.

"Sit down, Doctor Torvey," said Lady Walsingham, who in the incapacity of her sister undertook the doing of the honours. "My sister, Lady Mardykes, has got it into her head somehow that Sir Bale is ill. I have been speaking to him; he certainly does not look very well, but he says he is quite well. Do you think him well?—that is, we know you don't think there is anything of importance amiss—but she wishes to know whether you think him *perfectly* well."

The Doctor cleared his voice and delivered his lecture, a little thickly at some words, upon Sir Bale's case; the result of which was that it was no case at all; and that if he would only live something more of a country gentleman's life, he would be as well as any man could desire—as well as any man, gentle or simple, in the country.

"The utmost I should think of doing for him would be, perhaps, a little quinine, nothing mo'—shurely—he is really and toory a very shoun' shtay of health."

Lady Walsingham looked encouragingly at her sister and nodded.

"I've been shen' for, La'y Walsh—Walse—Walsing—*ham*; old Jack Amerald—he likshe his glass o' port," he said roguishly, "and shuvversh accord'n'ly," he continued, with a compassionating paddle of his right hand; "one of thoshe aw—odd feels in his stomach; and as I have pretty well done all I can man-n'ge down here, I must be off, ye shee. Wind up from Golden Friars, and a little flutter ovv zhnow, thazh all;" and with some remarks about the extreme cold of the weather, and the severity of their night journey, and many respectful and polite parting speeches, the Doctor took his leave; and they soon heard the wheels of his gig and the tread of his horse, faint and muffled from the snow in the courtyard, and the Doctor, who had connected that melancholy and agitated household with the outer circle of humanity, was gone.

There was very little snow falling, half-a-dozen flakes now and again, and their flight across the window showed, as the Doctor had in a manner boasted, that the wind was in his face as he returned to Golden Friars. Even these desultory snow-flakes ceased, at times, altogether; and returning, as they say, "by fits and starts," left for long intervals the landscape, under the brilliant light of the moon, in its wide white shroud. The curtain of the great window had not been drawn. It seemed to Lady Walsingham that the moonbeams had grown more dazzling, that Snakes Island was nearer and more distinct, and the outstretched arm of the old tree looked bigger and angrier, like the uplifted arm of an assassin, who draws silently nearer as the catastrophe approaches.

Cold, dazzling, almost repulsive in this intense moonlight and white sheeting, the familiar landscape looked in the eyes of Lady Walsingham. The sisters gradually grew more and more silent, an unearthly suspense overhung them all, and Lady Mardykes rose every now and then and listened at the open door for step or voice in vain. They all were overpowered by the intenser horror that seemed gathering around them. And thus an hour or more passed.

CHAPTER 30

HUSH

Pale and silent those three beautiful sisters sat. The horrible quietude of a suspense that had grown all but insupportable oppressed the guests of Lady Mardykes, and something like the numbness of despair had reduced her to silence, the dreadful counterfeit of peace.

Sir Bale Mardykes on a sudden softly entered the room. Reflected from the floor near the window, the white moonlight somehow gave to his fixed features the character of a smile. With a warning gesture, as he came in, he placed his finger to his lips, as if to enjoin silence; and then, having successively pressed the hands of his two sisters-in-law, he stooped over his almost fainting wife, and twice pressed her cold forehead with his lips; and so, without a word, he went softly from the room.

Some seconds elapsed before Lady Walsingham, recovering her presence of mind, with one of the candlesticks from the table in her hand, opened the door and followed.

She saw Sir Bale mount the last stair of the broad flight visible from the hall, and candle in hand turn the corner of the massive banister, and as the light thrown from his candle showed, he continued, without hurry, to ascend the second flight.

With the irrepressible curiosity of horror she continued to follow him at a distance.

She saw him enter his own private room, and close the door.

Continuing to follow she placed herself noiselessly at the door of the apartment, and in breathless silence, with a throbbing heart, listened for what should pass.

She distinctly heard Sir Bale pace the floor up and down for some time, and then, after a pause, a sound as if someone had thrown himself heavily on the bed. A silence followed, during which her sisters, who had followed more timidly, joined her. She warned them with a look and gesture to be silent.

Lady Haworth stood a little behind, her white lips moving, and her hands clasped in a silent agony of prayer. Lady Mardykes leaned against the massive oak door-case.

With her hand raised to her ear, and her lips parted, Lady Walsingham listened for some seconds—for a minute, two minutes, three. At last, losing heart, she seized the handle in her panic, and turned it sharply. The door was locked on the inside, but someone close to it said from within, "Hush, hush!"

Much alarmed now, the same lady knocked violently at the door. No answer was returned.

She knocked again more violently, and shook the door with all her fragile force. It was something of horror in her countenance as she did so, that, no doubt, terrified Lady Mardykes, who with a loud and long scream sank in a swoon upon the floor.

The servants, alarmed by these sounds, were speedily in the gallery. Lady Mardykes was carried to her room, and laid upon her bed; her sister, Lady Haworth, accompanying her. In the meantime the door was forced. Sir Bale Mardykes was found stretched upon his bed.

Those who have once seen it, will not mistake the aspect of death. Here, in Sir Bale Mardykes' room, in his bed, in his clothes, is a stranger, grim and awful; in a few days to be insupportable, and to pass alone into the prison-house, and to be seen no more.

Where is Sir Bale Mardykes now, whose roof-tree and whose place at board and bed will know him no more? Here lies a chap-fallen, fish-eyed image, chilling already into clay, and stiffening in every joint.

There is a marble monument in the pretty church of Golden Friars. It stands at the left side of what antiquarians call "the high altar." Two pillars at each end support an arch with several armorial bearings on as many shields sculptured above. Beneath, on a marble flooring raised some four feet, with a cornice round, lies Sir Bale Mardykes, of Mardykes Hall, ninth Baronet of that ancient family, chiselled in marble with knee-breeches and buckled-shoes, and *ailes de pigeon*, and single-breasted coat and long waist-coat, ruffles and sword, such as gentlemen wore about the year 1770, and bearing a strong resemblance to the features of the second Charles. On the broad marble which forms the background is inscribed an epitaph, which has perpetuated to our times the estimate formed by his "inconsolable widow," the Dowager Lady Mardykes, of the virtues and accomplishments of her deceased lord.

Lady Walsingham would have qualified two or three of the more highly-coloured hyperboles, at which the Golden Friars of those days sniffed and tittered. They don't signify now; there is no contemporary left to laugh or whisper. And if there be not much that is true in the letter of that inscription, it at least perpetuates something that *is* true—that wonderful glorificaion of partisanship, the affection of an idolising wife.

Lady Mardykes, a few days after the funeral, left Mardykes Hall for ever. She lived a great deal with her sister, Lady Walsingham; and died, as a line cut at the foot of Sir Bale Mardykes' epitaph records, in the year 1790; her remains being laid beside those of her beloved husband in Golden Friars.

The estates had come to Sir Bale Mardykes free of entail. He had been pottering over a will, but it was never completed, nor even quite planned; and after much doubt and scrutiny, it was at last ascertained that, in default of a will and of issue, a clause in the marriage-settlement gave the entire estates to the Dowager Lady Mardykes.

By her will she bequeathed the estates to "her cousin, also a kinsman of the late Sir Bale Mardykes her husband," William Feltram, on condition of his assuming the name and arms of Mardykes, the arms of Feltram being quartered in the shield.

Thus was oddly fulfilled the prediction which Philip Feltram had repeated, that the estates of Mardykes were to pass into the hands of a Feltram.

About the year 1795 the baronetage was revived, and William Feltram enjoyed the title for fifteen years, as Sir William Mardykes.

The Evil Guest

(Aka: Some Account of the Latter Days of Richard Marston of Dunoran and later reworked into the novel *A Lost Name.)*

1895

When Lust hath conceived, it bringeth forth Sin: and Sin, when it is finished, bringeth forth Death.

About sixty years ago, and somewhat more than twenty miles from the ancient town of Chester, in a southward direction, there stood a large, and, even then, an old-fashioned mansion-house. It lay in the midst of a demesne of considerable extent, and richly wooded with venerable timber; but, apart from the sombre majesty of these giant groups, and the varieties of the undulating ground on which they stood, there was little that could be deemed attractive in the place. A certain air of neglect and decay, and an indescribable gloom and melancholy, hung over it. In darkness, it seemed darker than any other tract; when the moonlight fell upon its glades and hollows, they looked spectral and awful, with a sort of churchyard loneliness; and even when the blush of the morning kissed its broad woodlands, there was a melancholy in the salute that saddened rather than cheered the heart of the beholder.

This antique, melancholy, and neglected place, we shall call, for distinctness sake, Gray Forest. It was then the property of the younger son of a nobleman, once celebrated for his ability and his daring, but who had long since passed to that land where human wisdom and courage avail naught. The representative of this noble house resided at the family mansion in Sussex, and the cadet, whose fortunes we mean to sketch in these pages, lived upon the narrow margin of an encumbered income, in a reserved and unsocial discontent, deep among the solemn shadows of the old woods of Gray Forest.

The Hon. Richard Marston was now somewhere between forty and fifty years of age—perhaps nearer the latter; he still, however, retained, in an eminent degree, the traits of manly beauty, not the less remarkable for its unquestionably haughty and passionate character. He had married a beautiful girl, of good family, but without much money, somewhere about eighteen years before; and two children, a son and a daughter, had been the fruit of this union. The boy, Harry Marston, was at this time at Cambridge; and his sister, scarcely fifteen, was at home with her parents, and under the training of an accomplished governess, who had been recommended to them by a noble relative of Mrs. Marston.

She was a native of France, but thoroughly mistress of the English language, and, except for a foreign accent, which gave a certain prettiness to all she said, she spoke it as perfectly as any native Englishwoman. This young Frenchwoman was eminently handsome and attractive. Expressive, dark eyes, a clear olive complexion, small even teeth, and a beautifully-dimpling smile, more perhaps than a strictly classic regularity of features, were the secrets of her unquestionable influence, at first sight, upon the fancy of every man of taste who beheld her.

Mr. Marston's fortune, never very large, had been shattered by early dissipation. Naturally of a proud and somewhat exacting temper, he actively felt the mortifying consequences of his poverty. The want of what he felt ought to have been his position and influence in the county in which he resided, fretted and galled him; and he cherished a resentful and bitter sense of every slight, imaginary or real, to which the same fruitful source of annoyance and humiliation had exposed him. He held, therefore, but little intercourse with the surrounding gentry, and that little not of the pleasantest possible kind; for, not being himself in a condition to entertain, in that style which accorded with his own ideas of his station, he declined, as far as was compatible with good breeding, all the proffered hospitalities of the neighbourhood; and, from his wild and neglected park, looked out upon the surrounding world in a spirit of moroseness and defiance, very unlike, indeed, to that of neighbourly goodwill.

In the midst, however, of many of the annoyances attendant upon crippled means, he enjoyed a few of those shadowy indications of hereditary importance, which are all the more dearly prized, as the substantial accessories of wealth have disappeared. The mansion in which he dwelt was, though old-fashioned, imposing in its aspect, and upon a scale unequivocally aristocratic; its walls were hung with ancestral portraits, and he managed to maintain about him a large and tolerably respectable staff of servants. In addition to these, he had his extensive demesne, his deer-park, and his unrivalled timber, wherewith to console himself; and, in the consciousness of these possessions, he found some imperfect assuagement of those bitter feelings of suppressed scorn and resentment, which a sense of lost station and slighted importance engendered.

Mr. Marston's early habits had, unhappily, been of a kind to aggravate, rather than alleviate, the annoyances incidental to reduced means. He had been a gay man, a voluptuary, and a gambler. His vicious tastes had survived the means of their gratification. His love for his wife had been nothing more than one of those vehement and headstrong fancies, which, in self-indulgent men, sometimes result in marriage, and which seldom outlive the first few months of that life-long connection. Mrs. Marston was a gentle, noble-minded woman. After agonies or disappointment, which none ever suspected, she had at length learned to submit, in sad and gentle acquiescence, to her fate. Those feelings, which had been the charm of her young days, were gone, and, as she bitterly felt, forever. For them there was no recall they could not return; and, without complaint or reproach, she yielded to what she felt was inevitable.

It was impossible to look at Mrs. Marston, and not to discern, at a glance, the ruin of a surpassingly beautiful woman; a good deal wasted, pale, and chastened with a deep, untold sorrow, but still possessing the outlines, both in face and form, of that noble beauty and matchless grace, which had made her, in happier days, the admired of all observers. But equally impossible was it to converse with her, for even a minute, without hearing, in the gentle and melancholy music of her voice, the sad echoes of those griefs to which her early beauty had been sacrificed, an undying sense of lost love, and happiness departed, never to come again.

One morning, Mr. Marston had walked, as was his custom when he expected the messenger who brought from the neighbouring post office his letters, some way down the broad, straight avenue, with its double rows of lofty trees at each side, when he encountered the nimble emissary on his return. He took the letter-bag in silence. It contained but two letters—one addressed to "*Mademoiselle de Barras, chez M. Marston,*" and the other to himself. He took them both, dismissed the messenger, and opening that addressed to himself, read as follows, while he slowly retraced his steps towards the house:—

Dear Richard,

I am a whimsical fellow, as you doubtless remember, and have lately grown, they tell me, rather hippish besides. I do not know to which infirmity I am to attribute a sudden fancy that urges me to pay you a visit, if you will admit me. To say truth, my dear Dick, I wish to see a little of your part of the world, and, I will confess it, en passant, to see a little of you too. I really wish to make acquaintance with your family; and though they tell me my health is very much shaken, I must say, in self-defence, I am not a troublesome inmate.

I can perfectly take care of myself, and need no nursing or caudling whatever. Will you present this, my petition, to Mrs. Marston, and report her decision thereon to me. Seriously, I know that your house may be full, or some other contretemps may make it impracticable for me just now to invade you. If it be so, tell me, my dear Richard, frankly, as my movements are perfectly free, and my time all my own, so that I can arrange my visit to suit your

228

convenience.

Yours, &c.,

WYNSTON E. BERKLEY

P.S.—Direct to me at —— Hotel, in Chester, as I shall probably be there by the time this reaches you.

"Ill-bred and pushing as ever," quoth Mr. Marston, angrily, as he thrust the unwelcome letter into his pocket. "This fellow, wallowing in wealth, without one nearer relative on earth than I, and associated more nearly still with me the—pshaw! not affection—the recollections of early and intimate companionship, leaves me unaided, for years of desertion and suffering, to the buffetings of the world, and the troubles of all but overwhelming pecuniary difficulties, and now, with the cool confidence of one entitled to respect and welcome, invites himself to my house. Coming here," he continued, after a gloomy pause, and still pacing slowly towards the house, "to collect amusing materials for next season's gossip—stories about the married Benedick—the bankrupt *beau*—the outcast tenant of a Cheshire wilderness"; and, as he said this, he looked at the neglected prospect before him with an eye almost of hatred. "Aye, to see the nakedness of the land is he coming, but he shall be disappointed. His money may buy him a cordial welcome at an inn, but curse me if it shall purchase him a reception here."

He again opened and glanced through the letter.

"Aye, purposely put in such a way that I can't decline it without affronting him," he continued doggedly. "Well, then, he has no one to blame but himself—affronted he shall be; I shall effectually put an end to this humorous excursion. Egad, it is rather hard if a man cannot keep his poverty to himself."

Sir Wynston Berkley was a baronet of large fortune—a selfish, fashionable man, and an inveterate bachelor. He and Marston had been schoolfellows, and the violent and implacable temper of the latter had as little impressed his companion with feelings of regard, as the frivolity and selfishness of the baronet had won the esteem of his relative. As boys, they had little in common upon which to rest the basis of a friendship, or even a mu-

229

tual liking. Berkley was gay, cold, and satirical; his cousin—for cousins they were—was jealous, haughty, and relentless. Their negative disinclination to one another's society, not unnaturally engendered by uncongenial and unamiable dispositions, had for a time given place to actual hostility, while the two young men were at Oxford. In some intrigue, Marston discovered in his cousin a too-successful rival; the consequence was, a bitter and furious quarrel, which, but for the prompt and peremptory interference of friends, Marston would undoubtedly have pushed to a bloody issue. Time had, however, healed this rupture, and the young men came to regard one another with the same feelings, and eventually to re-establish the same sort of cold and indifferent intimacy which had subsisted between them before their angry collision.

Under these circumstances, whatever suspicion Marston might have felt on the receipt of the unexpected, and indeed unaccountable proposal, which had just reached him, he certainly had little reason to complain of any violation of early friendship in the neglect with which Sir Wynston had hitherto treated him. In deciding to decline his proposed visit, however, Marston had not consulted the impulses of spite or anger. He knew the baronet well; he knew that he cherished no good will towards him, and that in the project which he had thus unexpectedly broached, whatever indirect or selfish schemes might possibly be at the bottom of it, no friendly feeling had ever mingled. He was therefore resolved to avoid the trouble and the expense of a visit in all respects distasteful to him, and in a gentlemanlike way, but, at the same time, as the reader may suppose, with very little anxiety as to whether or not his gay correspondent should take offence at his reply, to decline, once for all, the proposed distinction.

With this resolution, he entered the spacious and somewhat dilapidated mansion which called him master; and entering a sitting room, appropriated to his daughter's use, he found her there, in company with her beautiful French governess. He kissed his child, and saluted her young preceptress with formal courtesy.

"*Mademoiselle*," said he, "I have got a letter for you; and, Rhoda," he continued, addressing his pretty daughter, "bring this to your mother, and say, I request her to read it."

He gave her the letter he himself had just received, and the girl tripped lightly away upon her mission.

Had he narrowly scrutinised the countenance of the fair Frenchwoman, as she glanced at the direction of that which he had just placed in her hand, he might have seen certain transient, but very unmistakable evidences of excitement and agitation. She quickly concealed the letter, however, and with a sigh, the momentary flush which it had called to her cheek subsided, and she was tranquil as usual.

Mr. Marston remained for some minutes—five, eight, or ten, we cannot say precisely—pretty much where he had stood on first entering the chamber, doubtless awaiting the return of his messenger, or the appearance of his wife. At length, however, he left the room himself to seek her; but, during his brief stay, his previous resolution had been removed. By what influence we cannot say; but removed completely it unquestionably was, and a final determination that Sir Wynston Berkley should become his guest had fixedly taken its place.

As Marston walked along the passages which led from this room, he encountered Mrs. Marston and his daughter.

"Well," said he, "you have read Wynston's letter?"

"Yes," she replied, returning it to him; "and what answer, Richard, do you purpose giving him?"

She was about to hazard a conjecture, but checked herself, remembering that even so faint an evidence of a disposition to advise might possibly be resented by her cold and imperious lord.

"I have considered it, and decided to receive him," he replied.

"Ah! I am afraid—that is, I hope—he may find our housekeeping such as he can enjoy," she said, with an involuntary expression of surprise; for she had scarcely had a doubt that her husband would have preferred evading the visit of his fine

231

friend, under his gloomy circumstances.

"If our modest fare does not suit him," said Marston, with sullen bitterness, "he can depart as easily as he came. We, poor gentlemen, can but do our best. I have thought it over, and made up my mind."

"And how soon, my dear Richard, do you intend fixing his arrival?" she inquired, with the natural uneasiness of one upon whom, in an establishment whose pretensions considerably exceeded its resources, the perplexing cares of housekeeping devolved.

"Why, as soon as he pleases," replied he, "I suppose you can easily have his room prepared by tomorrow or next day. I shall write by this mail, and tell him to come down at once."

Having said this in a cold, decisive way, he turned and left her, as it seemed, not caring to be teased with further questions. He took his solitary way to a distant part of his wild park, where, far from the likelihood of disturbance or intrusion, he was often wont to amuse himself for the live-long day, in the sedentary sport of shooting rabbits. And there we leave him for the present, signifying to the distant inmates of his house the industrious pursuit of his unsocial occupation, by the dropping fire that sullenly, from hour to hour, echoed from the remote woods.

Mrs. Marston issued her orders; and having set on foot all the necessary preparations for so unwonted an event as a stranger's visit of some duration, she betook herself to her little boudoir-the scene of many an hour of patient but bitter suffering, unseen by human eye, and unknown, except to the just Searcher of hearts, to whom belongs mercy—and vengeance.

Mrs. Marston had but two friends to whom she had ever spoken upon the subject nearest her heart—the estrangement of her husband, a sorrow to which even time had failed to reconcile her. From her children this grief was carefully concealed. To them she never uttered the semblance of a complaint. Anything that could by possibility have reflected blame or dishonour upon their father, she would have perished rather than have allowed them so much as to suspect. The two friends who did understand her feelings, though in different degrees, were, one, a good and venerable clergyman, the Rev. Doctor Danvers, a frequent visitor and occasional guest at Gray Forest, where his simple manners and unaffected benignity and tenderness of heart had won the love of all, with the exception of its master, and commanded even his respect. The second was no other than the young French governess, Mademoiselle de Barras, in whose ready sympathy and consolatory counsels she found no small happiness. The society of this young lady had indeed become, next to that of her daughter, her greatest comfort and pleasure.

Mademoiselle de Barras was of a noble though ruined French family, and a certain nameless elegance and dignity attested, spite of her fallen condition, the purity of her descent. She was accomplished—possessed of that fine perception and sensitiveness, and that ready power of self-adaptation to the peculiarities and moods of others, which we term tact—and was, moreover, gifted with a certain natural grace, and manners the most winning imaginable. In short, she was a fascinating companion; and when the melancholy circumstances of her own situation, and the sad history of her once rich and noble family, were taken into account, with her striking attractions of person and air, the combination of all these associations and impressions rendered her one of the most interesting persons that could well be imagined. The circumstances of Mademoiselle de Barras's history and descent seemed to warrant, on Mrs. Marston's part, a closer intimacy and confidence than usually subsists between parties mutually occupying such a relation.

Mrs. Marston had hardly established herself in this little apartment, when a light foot approached, a gentle tap was given at the door, and Mademoiselle de Barras entered.

"Ah, *mademoiselle*, so kind—such pretty flowers. Pray sit down," said the lady, with a sweet and grateful smile, as she took from the tapered fingers of the foreigner the little bouquet, which she had been at the pains to gather.

Mademoiselle sat down, and gently took the lady's hand and kissed it. A small matter will overflow a heart charged with sorrow—a chance word, a look, some little office of kindness-and so it was with mademoiselle's bouquet and gentle kiss. Mrs. Marston's heart was touched; her eyes filled with bright tears; she smiled gratefully upon her fair and humble companion, and as she smiled, her tears overflowed, and she wept in silence for some minutes.

"My poor *mademoiselle*," she said, at last, "you are so very, very kind."

Mademoiselle said nothing; she lowered her eyes, and pressed the poor lady's hand.

Apparently to interrupt an embarrassing silence, and to give a more cheerful tone to their little interview, the governess, in a gay tone, on a sudden said—

"And so, *madame*, we are to have a visitor, Miss Rhoda tells me—a baronet, is he not?"

"Yes, indeed, *mademoiselle*—Sir Wynston Berkley, a gay London gentleman, and a cousin of Mr. Marston's," she replied.

"Ha—a cousin!" exclaimed the young lady, with a little more surprise in her tone than seemed altogether called for—"a cousin? oh, then, that is the reason of his visit. Do, pray, *madame*, tell me all about him; I am so much afraid of strangers, and what you call men of the world. Oh, dear Mrs. Marston, I am not worthy to be here, and he will see all that in a moment; indeed, indeed, I am afraid. Pray tell me all about him."

She said this with a simplicity which made the elder lady smile, and while *mademoiselle* readjusted the tiny flowers which formed the bouquet she had just presented to her, Mrs. Marston good-naturedly recounted to her all she knew of Sir Wynston Berkley, which, in substance, amounted to no more than we have already stated. When she concluded, the young Frenchwoman continued for some time silent, still busy with her flowers. But, suddenly, she heaved a deep sigh, and shook her head.

"You seem disquieted, *mademoiselle*," said Mrs. Marston, in a tone of kindness.

"I am thinking, *madame*," she said, still looking upon the flowers which she was adjusting, and again sighing profoundly, "I am thinking of what you said to me a week ago; alas!"

"I do not remember what it was, my good *mademoiselle*—nothing, I am sure, that ought to grieve you—at least nothing that was intended to have that effect," replied the lady, in a tone of gentle encouragement.

"No, not intended, *madame*," said the young Frenchwoman, sorrowfully.

"Well, what was it? Perhaps you misunderstood; perhaps I can explain what I said," replied Mrs. Marston, affectionately.

"Ah, *madame*, you think—you think I am unlucky," answered the young lady, slowly and faintly.

"Unlucky! Dear *mademoiselle*, you surprise me," rejoined her companion.

"I mean—what I mean is this, *madame*; you date unhappiness—if not its beginning, at least its great aggravation and increase," she answered, dejectedly, "from the time of my coming here, *madame*; and though I know you are too good to dislike me on that account, yet I must, in your eyes, be ever connected with calamity, and look like an ominous thing."

"Dear *mademoiselle*, allow no such thought to enter your mind. You do me great wrong, indeed you do," said Mrs. Marston, laying her hand upon the young lady's, kindly.

There was a silence for a little time, and the elder lady resumed:—"I remember now what you allude to, dear *mademoiselle*—the increased estrangement, the widening separation which severs me from one unutterably dear to me—the first and bitter disappointment of my life, which seems to grow more hopelessly incurable day by day."

Mrs. Marston paused, and, after a brief silence, the governess said:—

"I am very superstitious myself, dear *madame*, and I thought I must have seemed to you an inauspicious inmate—in short, unlucky—as I have said; and the thought made me very unhappy—so unhappy, that I was going to leave you, *madame*—I may now tell you frankly—going away; but you have set my doubts at rest, and I am quite happy again."

"Dear *mademoiselle*," cried the lady, tenderly, and rising, as she spake, to kiss the cheek of her humble friend; "never—never speak of this again. God knows I have too few friends on earth, to spare the kindest and tenderest among them all. No, no. You little think what comfort I have found in your warm-hearted and ready sympathy, and how dearly I prize your affection, my poor *mademoiselle*."

The young Frenchwoman rose, with downcast eyes, and a dimpling, happy smile; and, as Mrs. Marston drew her affectionately toward her, and kissed her, she timidly returned the embrace of her kind patroness. For a moment her graceful arms encircled her, and she whispered to her, "Dear *madame*, how happy—how very happy you make me."

Had Ithuriel touched with his spear the beautiful young woman, thus for a moment, as it seemed, lost in a trance of gratitude and love, would that angelic form have stood the test unscathed? A spectator, marking the scene, might have observed a strange gleam in her eyes—a strange expression in her face—an influence for a moment not angelic, like a shadow of some passing spirit, cross her visibly, as she leaned over the gentle lady's neck, and murmured, "Dear *madame*, how happy—how very happy you make me." Such a spectator, as he looked at that gentle lady, might have seen, for one dreamy moment, a lithe and painted serpent, coiled round and round, and hissing in her ear.

A few minutes more, and *mademoiselle* was in the solitude of her own apartment. She shut and bolted the door, and taking from her desk the letter which she had that morning received, threw herself into an armchair, and studied the document profoundly. Her actual revision and scrutiny of the letter itself was interrupted by long intervals of profound abstraction; and, after a full hour thus spent, she locked it carefully up again, and with a clear brow, and a gay smile, rejoined her pretty pupil for a walk.

We must now pass over an interval of a few days, and come at once to the arrival of Sir Wynston Berkley, which duly occurred upon the evening of the day appointed. The baronet descended from his chaise but a short time before the hour at which the little party, which formed the family at Gray Forest were wont to assemble for the social meal of supper. A few minutes devoted to the mysteries of the toilet, with the aid of an accomplished valet, enabled him to appear, as he conceived, without disadvantage at this domestic reunion.

Sir Wynston Berkley was a particularly gentleman-like person. He was rather tall, and elegantly made, with gay, easy manners, and something indefinably aristocratic in his face, which, however, was a little more worn than his years would have strictly accounted for. But Sir Wynston had been a *roué*, and, spite of the cleverest possible making up, the ravages of excess were very traceable in the lively *beau* of fifty. Perfectly well dressed, and with a manner that was ease and gaiety itself, he was at home from the moment he entered the room. Of course, anything like genuine cordiality was out of the question; but Mr. Marston embraced his relative with perfect good breeding, and the baronet appeared determined to like everybody, and be pleased with everything. He had not been five minutes in the parlour, chatting gaily with Mr. and Mrs. Marston and their pretty daughter, when *Mademoiselle* de Barras entered the room. As she moved towards Mrs. Marston, Sir Wynston rose, and, observing her with evident admiration, said in an undertone, inquiringly, to Marston, who was beside him—

"And this?"

"That is Mademoiselle de Barras, my daughter's governess, and Mrs. Marston's companion," said Marston, drily.

"Ha!" said Sir Wynston; "I thought you were but three at home just now, and I was right. Your son is at Cambridge; I heard so from our old friend, Jack Manbury. Jack has his boy there too. Egad, Dick, it seems but last week that you and I were there together."

"Yes," said Marston, looking gloomily into the fire, as if he saw, in its smoke and flicker, the phantoms of murdered time and opportunity; "but I hate looking back, Wynston. The past is to me but a medley of ill-luck and worse management."

"Why what an ungrateful dog you are!" returned Sir Wynston, gaily, turning his back upon the fire, and glancing round the spacious and handsome, though somewhat faded apartment. "I was on the point of congratulating you on the possession of the finest park and noblest demesne in Cheshire, when you begin to grumble. Egad, Dick, all I can say to your complaint is, that I don't pity you, and there are dozens who may honestly envy you—that is all."

In spite of this cheering assurance, Marston remained sullenly silent. Supper, however, had now been served, and the little party assumed their places at the table.

"I am sorry, Wynston, I have no sport of any kind to offer you here," said Marston, "except, indeed, some good trout-fishing, if you like it. I have three miles of excellent fishing at your command."

"My dear fellow, I am a mere cockney," rejoined Sir Wynston; "I am not a sportsman; I never tried it, and should not like to begin now. No, Dick, what I much prefer is, abundance of your fresh air, and the enjoyment of your scenery. When I was at Rouen three years ago—"

"Ha!—Rouen? *Mademoiselle* will feel an interest in that; it is her birth-place," interrupted Marston, glancing at the Frenchwoman.

"Yes—Rouen—ah—yes!" said *mademoiselle*, with very evident embarrassment.

Sir Wynston appeared for a moment a little disconcerted too, but rallied speedily, and pursued his detail of his doings at that fair town of Normandy.

Marston knew Sir Wynston well; and he rightly calculated that whatever effect his experience of the world might have had in intensifying his selfishness or hardening his heart, it certainly could have had none in improving a character originally worthless and unfeeling. He knew, moreover, that his wealthy cousin was gifted with a great deal of that small cunning which is available for masking the little scheming of frivolous and worldly men; and that Sir Wynston never took trouble of any kind without a sufficient purpose, having its centre in his own personal gratification.

This visit greatly puzzled Marston; it gave him even a vague sense of uneasiness. Could there exist any flaw in his own title to the estate of Gray Forest? He had an unpleasant, doubtful sort of remembrance of some apprehensions of this kind, when he was but a child, having been whispered in the family. Could this really be so, and could the baronet have been led to make this unexpected visit merely for the purpose of personally examining into the condition or a property of which he was about to become the legal invader? The nature of this suspicion affords, at all events, a fair gauge of Marston's estimate of his cousin's character.

And as he revolved these doubts from time to time, and as he thought of Mademoiselle de Barras's transient, but unaccountable embarrassment at the mention of Rouen by Sir Wynston—an embarrassment which the baronet himself appeared for a moment to reciprocate—undefined, glimmering suspicions of another kind flickered through the darkness of his mind. He was effectually puzzled; his surmises and conjectures baffled; and he more than half repented that he had acceded to his cousin's proposal, and admitted him as an inmate of his house.

Although Sir Wynston comported himself as if he were conscious of being the very most welcome visitor who could possibly have established himself at Gray Forest, he was, doubtless, fully aware of the real feelings with which he was regarded by his host. If he had in reality an object in prolonging his stay, and wished to make the postponement of his departure the direct interest of his entertainer, he unquestionably took effectual measures for that purpose.

The little party broke up every evening at about ten o'clock, and Sir Wynston retired to his chamber at the same hour. He found little difficulty in inducing Marston to amuse him there with a quiet game of piquet. In his own room, therefore, in the luxurious ease of dressing gown and slippers he sat at cards with his host, often until an hour or two past midnight. Sir Wynston was exorbitantly wealthy, and very reckless in expenditure. The stakes for which they played, although they gradually became in reality pretty heavy, were in his eyes a very unimportant consideration. Marston, on the other hand, was poor, and played with the eye of a lynx and the appetite of a shark.

The ease and perfect good-humour with which Sir Wynston lost were not unimproved by his entertainer, who, as may readily be supposed, was not sorry to reap this golden harvest, provided without the slightest sacrifice, on his part, of pride or independence. If, indeed, he sometimes suspected that his guest was a little more anxious to lose than to win, he was also quite resolved not to perceive it, but calmly persisted in, night after night, giving Sir Wynston, as he termed it, his revenge; or, in other words, treating him to a repetition of his losses. All this was very agreeable to Marston, who began to treat his visitor with, at all events, more external cordiality and distinction than at first.

An incident, however, occurred, which disturbed these amicable relations in an unexpected way. It becomes necessary here to mention that Mademoiselle de Barras's sleeping apartment opened from a long corridor. It was *en suite* with two dressing rooms, each opening also upon the corridor, but wholly unused and unfurnished. Some five or six other apartments also opened at either side, upon the same passage. These little local details being premised, it so happened that one day Marston, who had gone out with the intention of angling in the trout-stream which flowed through his park, though at a considerable distance from the house, having unexpectedly returned to procure some tackle which he had forgotten, was walking briskly through the corridor in question to his own apartment, when, to his surprise, the door of one of the deserted dressing-rooms, of which we have spoken, was cautiously pushed open, and Sir Wynston Berkley issued from it.

Marston was almost beside him as he did so, and Sir Wynston made a motion as if about instinctively to draw back again, and at the same time the keen ear of his host distinctly caught the sound of rustling silks and a tiptoe tread hastily withdrawing from the deserted chamber. Sir Wynston looked nearly as much confused as a man of the world can look. Marston stopped short, and scanned his visitor for a moment with a very peculiar expression.

"You have caught me peeping, Dick. I am an inveterate explorer," said the baronet, with an effectual effort to shake off his embarrassment. "An open door in a fine old house is a temptation which—"

"That door is usually closed, and ought to be kept so," interrupted Marston, drily; "there is nothing whatever to be seen in the room but dust and cobwebs."

"Pardon me," said Sir Wynston, more easily, "you forget the view from the window."

"Aye, the view, to be sure; there is a good view from it," said Marston, with as much of his usual manner as he could resume so soon; and, at the same time, carelessly opening the door again, he walked in, accompanied by Sir Wynston, and both stood at the window together, looking out in silence upon a prospect which neither of them saw.

"Yes, I do think it is a good view," said Marston; and as he turned carelessly away, he darted a swift glance round the chamber. The door opening toward the French lady's apartment was closed, but not actually shut. This was enough; and as they left the room, Marston repeated his invitation to his guest to accompany him; but in a tone which showed that he scarcely followed the meaning of what he himself was saying.

He walked undecidedly toward his own room, then turned and went down stairs. In the hall he met his pretty child.

"Ha! Rhoda," said he, "you have not been out today?"

"No, papa; but it is so very fine, I think I shall go now."

"Yes; go, and *mademoiselle* can accompany you. Do you hear, Rhoda, *mademoiselle* goes with you, and you had better go at once."

A few minutes more, and Marston, from the parlour-window, beheld Rhoda and the elegant French girl walking together towards the woodlands. He watched them gloomily, himself unseen, until the crowding underwood concealed their receding figures. Then, with a sigh, he turned, and reascended the great staircase.

"I shall sift this mystery to the bottom," thought he. "I shall foil the conspirators, if so they be, with their own weapons; art with art; chicane with chicane; duplicity with duplicity."

He was now in the long passage, which we have just spoken of, and glancing back and before him, to ascertain that no chance eye discerned him, he boldly entered *mademoiselle's* chamber. Her writing desk lay upon the table. It was locked; and coolly taking it in his hands, Marston carried it into his own room, bolted his chamber-door, and taking two or three bunches of keys, he carefully tried nearly a dozen in succession, and when almost despairing of success, at last found one which fitted the lock, turned, and opened the desk.

Sustained throughout his dishonourable task by some strong and angry passion, the sight of the open *escritoire* checked and startled him for a moment. Violated privilege, invaded secrecy, base, perfidious espionage upbraided and stigmatized him, as the intricacies of the outraged sanctuary opened upon his intrusive gaze. He felt for a moment shocked and humbled. He was impelled to lock and replace the desk where he had originally found it, without having effected his meditated treason; but this hesitation was transient; the fiery and reckless impulse which had urged him to the act returned to enforce its consummation. With a guilty eye and eager hands, he searched the contents of this tiny repository of the fair Norman's written secrets.

"Ha! the very thing," he muttered, as he detected the identical letter which he himself had handed to Mademoiselle de Barras but a few days before. "The handwriting struck me, ill-disguised; I thought I knew it; we shall see."

He had opened the letter; it contained but a few lines: he held his breath while he read it. First he grew pale, then a shadow came over his face, and then another, and another, darker and darker, shade upon shade, as if an exhalation from the pit was momentarily blackening the air about him. He said nothing; there was but one long, gentle sigh, and in his face a mortal sternness, as he folded the letter again, replaced it, and locked the desk.

Of course, when Mademoiselle de Barras returned from her accustomed walk, she found everything in her room, to all appearances, undisturbed, and just as when she left it. While this young lady was making her toilet for the evening, and while Sir Wynston Berkley was worrying himself with conjectures as to whether Marston's evil looks, when he encountered him that morning in the passage, existed only in his own fancy, or were, in good truth, very grim and significant realities, Marston himself was striding alone through the wildest and darkest solitudes of his park, haunted by his own unholy thoughts, and, it may be, by those other evil and unearthly influences which wander, as we know, "in desert places."

Darkness overtook him, and the chill of night, in these lonely tracts. In his solitary walk, what fearful company had he been keeping! As the shades of night deepened round him, the sense of the neighborhood of ill, the consciousness of the foul fancies or which, where he was now treading, he had been for hours the sport, oppressed him with a vague and unknown terror; a certain horror of the thoughts which had been his comrades through the day, which he could not now shake off, and which haunted him with a ghastly and defiant pertinacity, scared, while they half-enraged him. He stalked swiftly homewards, like a guilty man pursued.

Marston was not perfectly satisfied, though very nearly, with the evidence now in his possession. The letter, the stolen perusal of which had so agitated him that day, bore no signature; but, independently of the handwriting, which seemed, spite of the constraint of an attempted disguise, to be familiar to his eye, there existed, in the matter of the letter, short as it was, certain internal evidences, which, although not actually conclusive, raised, in conjunction with all the other circumstances, a powerful presumption in aid of his suspicions. He resolved, however, to sift the matter further, and to bide his time.

Meanwhile his manner must indicate no trace of his dark

surmises and bitter thoughts. Deception, in its two great branches, simulation and dissimulation, was easy to him. His habitual
reserve and gloom would divest any accidental and momentary
disclosure of his inward trouble of everything suspicious or unaccountable, which would have characterized such displays and
eccentricities in another man.

His rapid and reckless ramble, a kind of physical vent for the
paroxysm which had so agitated him throughout the greater
part of the day, had soiled and disordered his dress, and thus had
helped to give to his whole appearance a certain air of haggard
wildness, which, in the privacy of his chamber, he hastened carefully and entirely to remove.

At supper, Marston was apparently in unusually good spirits. Sir Wynston and he chatted gaily and fluently upon many
subjects, grave and gay. Among them the inexhaustible topic of
popular superstition happened to turn up, and especially the
subject of strange prophecies of the fates and fortunes of individuals, singularly fulfilled in the events of their afterlife.

"By-the-by, Dick, this is rather a nervous topic for me to
discuss," said Sir Wynston.

"How so?" asked his host.

"Why, don't you remember?" urged the baronet.

"No, I don't recollect what you allude to," replied Marston,
in all sincerity.

"Why, don't you remember Eton?" pursued Sir Wynston.

"Yes, to be sure," said Marston.

"Well?" continued his visitor.

"Well, I really don't recollect the prophecy," replied
Marston.

"What! do you forget the gypsy who predicted that you were
to murder me, Dick—eh?"

"Ah-ha, ha!" laughed Marston, with a start.

"Don't you remember it now?" urged his companion.

"Ah, why yes, I believe I do," said Marston; "but another
prophecy was running in my mind; a gypsy prediction, too. At
Ascot, do you recollect the girl told me I was to be Lord Chan-

cellor of England, and a duke besides?"

"Well, Dick," rejoined Sir Wynston, merrily, "if both are to be fulfilled, or neither, I trust you may never sit upon the woolsack of England."

The party soon after broke up: Sir Wynston and his host, as usual, to pass some hours at piquet; and Mrs. Marston, as was her wont, to, spend some time in her own *boudoir*, over notes and accounts, and the worrying details of housekeeping.

While thus engaged, she was disturbed by a respectful tap at her door, and an elderly servant, who had been for many years in the employment of Mr. Marston, presented himself.

"Well, Merton, do you want anything?" asked the lady.

"Yes, ma'am, please, I want to give warning; I wish to leave the service, ma'am;" replied he, respectfully, but doggedly.

"To leave us, Merton!" echoed his mistress, both surprised and sorry for the man had been long her servant, and had been much liked and trusted.

"Yes, ma'am," he repeated.

"And why do you wish to do so, Merton? Has anything occurred to make the place unpleasant to you?" urged the lady.

"No, ma'am—no, indeed," said he, earnestly, "I have nothing to complain of—nothing, indeed, ma'am."

"Perhaps, you think you can do better, if you leave us?" suggested his mistress.

"No, indeed, ma'am, I have no such thought," he said, and seemed on the point of bursting into tears; "but—but, somehow—ma'am, there is something come over me, lately, and I can't help, but think, if I stay here, ma'am—some—some—misfortune will happen to us all—and that is the truth, ma'am."

"This is very foolish, Merton—a mere childish fancy," replied Mrs. Marston; "you like your place, and have no better prospect before you; and now, for a mere superstitious fancy, you propose giving it up, and leaving us. No, no, Merton, you had better think the matter over—and if you still, upon reflection, prefer going away, you can then speak to your master."

"Thank you ma'am—God bless you," said the man, withdrawing.

Mrs. Marston rang the bell for her maid, and retired to her room. "Has anything occurred lately," she asked, "to annoy Merton?"

"No, ma'am, I don't know of anything; but he is very changed, indeed, of late," replied the maid.

"He has not been quarrelling?" inquired she.

"Oh, no, ma'am, he never quarrels; he is very quiet, and keeps to himself always; he thinks a wonderful deal of himself," replied the servant.

"But, you said that he is much changed—did you not?" continued the lady; for there was something strangely excited and unpleasant in the man's manner, in this little interview, which struck Mrs. Marston, and alarmed her curiosity. He had seemed like one charged with some horrible secret—intolerable, and which he yet dared not reveal.

"What," proceeded Mrs. Marston, "is the nature of the change of which you speak?"

"Why, ma'am, he is like one frightened, and in sorrow," she replied; "he will sit silent, and now and then shaking his head, as if he wanted to get rid of something that is teasing him, for an hour together."

"Poor man!" said she.

"And, then, when we are at meals, he will, all on a sudden, get up, and leave the table; and Jem Boulter, that sleeps in the next room to him, says, that, almost as often as he looks through the little window between the two rooms, no matter what hour in the night, he sees Mr. Merton on his knees by the bedside, praying or crying, he don't know which; but, any way, he is not happy—poor man!—and that is plain enough."

"It is very strange," said the lady, after a pause; "but, I think, and hope, after all, it will prove to have been no more than a little nervousness."

"Well, ma'am, I do hope it is not his conscience that is coming against him, now," said the maid.

"We have no reason to suspect anything of the kind," said

Mrs. Marston, gravely, "quite the reverse; he has been always a particularly proper man."

"Oh, indeed," responded the attendant, "goodness forbid I should say or think anything against him; but I could not help telling you my mind, ma'am, meaning no harm."

"And, how long is it since you observed this sad change in poor Merton?" persisted the lady.

"Not, indeed, to say very long, ma'am," replied the girl; "somewhere about a week, or very little more—at least, as we remarked, ma'am."

Mrs. Marston pursued her inquiries no further that night. But, although she affected to treat the matter thus lightly, it had, somehow, taken a painful hold upon her imagination, and left in her mind those undefinable and ominous sensations, which, in certain mental temperaments, seem to foreshadow the approach of unknown misfortune.

For two or three days, everything went on smoothly, and pretty much as usual. At the end of this brief interval, however, the attention of Mrs. Marston was recalled to the subject of her servant's mysterious anxiety to leave, and give up his situation. Merton again stood before her, and repeated the intimation he had already given.

"Really, Merton, this is very odd," said the lady. "You like your situation, and yet you persist in desiring to leave it. What am I to think?"

"Oh, ma'am," said he, "I am unhappy; I am tormented, ma'am. I can't tell you, ma'am; I can't indeed ma'am!"

"If anything weighs upon your mind, Merton, I would advise you to consult our good clergyman, Dr. Danvers," urged the lady.

The servant hung his head, and mused for a time gloomily; and then said decisively—"No, ma'am; no use."

"And pray, Merton, how long is it since you first entertained this desire?" asked Mrs. Marston.

"Since Sir Wynston Berkley came, ma'am," answered he.

"Has Sir Wynston annoyed you in any way?" continued she.

"Far from it, ma'am," he replied; "he is a very kind gentleman."

"Well, his man, then; is he a respectable, inoffensive person?" she inquired.

"I never met one more so," said the man, promptly, and raising his head.

"What I wish to know is, whether your desire to go is connected with Sir Wynston and his servant?" said Mrs. Marston.

The man hesitated, and shifted his position uneasily.

"You need not answer, Merton, if you don't wish it," she said kindly.

"Why, ma'am, yes, it has something to say to them both," he replied, with some agitation.

"I really cannot understand this," said she.

Merton hesitated for some time, and appeared much troubled. "It was something, ma'am—something that Sir Wynston's man said to me; and there it is out," he said at last, with an effort.

"Well, Merton," said she, "I won't press you further; but I must say, that as this communication, whatever it may be, has caused you, unquestionably, very great uneasiness, it seems to me but probable that it affects the safety or the interests of some person—I cannot say of whom; and, if so, there can be no doubt that it is your duty to acquaint those who are so involved in the disclosure, with its purport."

"No, ma'am, there is nothing in what I heard that could touch anybody but myself. It was nothing but what others heard, without remarking it, or thinking about it. I can't tell you anymore, ma'am; but I am very unhappy, and uneasy in my mind."

As the man said this, he began to weep bitterly.

The idea that his mind was affected now seriously occurred to Mrs. Marston, and she resolved to convey her suspicions to her husband, and to leave him to deal with the case as to him should seem good.

"Don't agitate yourself so, Merton; I shall speak to your master upon what you have said; and you may rely upon it, that no surmise to the prejudice of your character has entered my mind," said Mrs. Marston, very kindly.

"Oh, ma'am, you are too good," sobbed the poor man, vehemently. "You don't know me, ma'am; I never knew myself till lately. I am a miserable man. I am frightened at myself, ma'am—frightened terribly. Christ knows, it would be well for me I was dead this minute."

"I am very sorry for your unhappiness, Merton," said Mrs. Marston; "and, especially, that I can do nothing to alleviate it; I can but speak, as I have said, to your master, and he will give you your discharge, and arrange whatever else remains to be done."

"God bless you, ma'am," said the servant, still much agitated, and left her.

Mr. Marston usually passed the early part of the day in active exercise, and she, supposing that he was, in all probability, at that moment far from home, went to "*mademoiselle's*" chamber, which was at the other end of the spacious house, to confer with her in the interval upon the strange application thus urged by poor Merton.

Just as she reached the door of Mademoiselle de Barras's chamber, she heard voices within exerted in evident excitement. She stopped in amazement. They were those of her husband and *mademoiselle*. Startled, confounded, and amazed, she pushed open the door, and entered. Her husband was sitting, one hand clutched upon the arm of the chair he occupied, and the other extended, and clenched, as it seemed, with the emphasis of rage, upon the desk that stood upon the table. His face was darkened with the stormiest passions, and his gaze was fixed upon the Frenchwoman, who was standing with a look half-guilty, half-imploring, at a little distance.

There was something, to Mrs. Marston, so utterly unexpected, and even so shocking, in this *tableau*, that she stood for some seconds pale and breathless, and gazing with a vacant stare of fear and horror from her husband to the French girl, and from her to her husband again. The three figures in this strange group remained fixed, silent, and aghast, for several seconds. Mrs. Marston endeavoured to speak; but, though her lips moved, no sound escaped her; and, from very weakness, she sank, half-fainting, into a chair.

Marston rose, throwing, as he did so, a guilty and furious glance at the young Frenchwoman, and walked a step or two toward the door; he hesitated, however, and turned, just as *mademoiselle*, bursting into tears, threw her arms round Mrs. Marston's neck, and passionately exclaimed, "Protect me, *madame*, I implore, from the insults and suspicions of your husband."

Marston stood a little behind his wife, and he and the governess exchanged a glance of keen significance, as the latter sank, sobbing, like an injured child into its mother's embrace, upon the poor lady's tortured bosom.

"*Madame, madame!* he says—Mr. Marston says—I have presumed to give you advice, and to meddle, and to interfere; that I am endeavouring to make you despise his authority. *Madame*, speak for me. Say, *madame*, have I ever done so?—say, *madame*, am I the cause of bitterness and contumacy? Ah, *mon Dieu! c'est trop*—it is too much, *madame*. I shall go—I must go, *madame*. Why, ah! why, did I stay for this?"

As she thus spoke, *mademoiselle* again burst into a paroxysm of weeping, and again the same significant glance was interchanged.

"Go; yes, you shall go," said Marston, striding toward the window. "I will have no whispering or conspiring in my house: I have heard of your confidences and consultations. Mrs. Marston, I meant to have done this quietly," he continued, addressing his wife; "I meant to have given Mademoiselle de Barras my opinion and her dismissal without your assistance; but it seems you wish to interpose. You are sworn friends, and never fail one another, of course, at a pinch. I take it for granted that I owe your presence at our interview which I am resolved shall be, as respects *mademoiselle*, a final one, to a message from that intriguing young lady—eh?"

"I have had no message, Richard," said Mrs. Marston; "I don't know—do tell me, for God's sake, what is all this about?" And as the poor lady thus spoke, her overwrought feelings found vent in a violent flood of tears.

"Yes, *madame*, that is the question. I have asked him frequently what is all this anger, all these reproaches about; what have
I done?" interposed *mademoiselle*, with indignant vehemence,
standing erect, and viewing Marston with a flashing eye and a
flushed cheek. "Yes, I am called conspirator, meddler, intrigant.
Ah, *madame*, it is intolerable."

"But what have I done, Richard?" urged the poor lady,
stunned and bewildered; "how have I offended you?"

"Yes, yes," continued the Frenchwoman, with angry volubil-
ity, "what has she done that you call contumacy and disrespect?
Yes, dear *madame*, there is the question; and if he cannot answer,
is it not most cruel to call me conspirator, and spy, and intrigant,
because I talk to my dear *madame*, who is my only friend in this
place?"

"Mademoiselle de Barras, I need no declamation from you;
and, pardon me, Mrs. Marston, nor from you either," retorted he;
"I have my information from one on whom I can rely; let that
suffice. Of course you are both agreed in a story. I dare say you
are ready to swear you never so much as canvassed my conduct,
and my coldness and estrangement—eh? These are the words,
are not they?"

"I have done you no wrong, sir; *madame* can tell you. I am no
mischief-maker; no, I never was such a thing. Was I, *madame*?"
persisted the governess—"bear witness for me?"

"I have told you my mind, Mademoiselle de Barras," interrupted Marston; "I will have no altercation, if you please. I think,
Mrs. Marston, we have had enough of this; may I accompany
you hence?"

So saying, he took the poor lady's passive hand, and led her
from the room. *Mademoiselle* stood in the centre of the apartment, alone, erect, with heaving breast and burning cheek-
beautiful, thoughtful, guilty—the very type of the fallen angelic.
There for a time, her heart all confusion, her mind darkened, we
must leave her; various courses before her, and as yet without
resolution to choose among them; a lost spirit, borne on the

eddies of the storm; fearless and self-reliant, but with no star to guide her on her dark, malign, and forlorn way.

Mrs. Marston, in her own room, reviewed the agitating scene through which she had just been so unexpectedly carried. The tremendous suspicion which, at the first disclosure of the *tableau* we have described, smote the heart and brain of the poor lady with the stun of a thunderbolt, had been, indeed, subsequently disturbed, and afterwards contradicted; but the shock of her first impression remained still upon her mind and heart. She felt still through every nerve the vibrations of that maddening terror and despair which had overcome her senses for a moment. The surprise, the shock, the horror, outlived the obliterating influence of what followed.

She was in this agitation when Mademoiselle de Barras entered her chamber, resolved with all her art to second and support the success of her prompt measures in the recent critical emergency. She had come, she said, to bid her dear *madame* farewell, for she was resolved to go. Her own room had been invaded, that insult and reproach might be heaped upon her; how utterly unmerited Mrs. Marston knew. She had been called by every foul name which applied to the spy and the maligner; she could not bear it. Someone had evidently been endeavouring to procure her removal, and had but too effectually succeeded. *Mademoiselle* was determined to go early the next morning; nothing should prevent or retard her departure; her resolution was taken. In this strain did *mademoiselle* run on, but in a subdued and melancholy tone, and weeping profusely.

The wild and ghastly suspicions which had for a moment flashed terribly upon the mind of Mrs. Marston, had faded away under the influences of reason and reflection, although, indeed, much painful excitement still remained, before Mademoiselle de Barras had visited her room. Marston's temper she knew but too well; it was violent, bitter, and impetuous; and though he cared little, if at all, for her, she had ever perceived that he was angrily jealous of the slightest intimacy or confidence by which any other than himself might establish an influence over her mind. That he had learned the subject of some of her most interesting conversations with *mademoiselle* she could not doubt, for he had violently upbraided that young lady in her presence with having discussed it, and here now was *mademoiselle* herself taking refuge with her from galling affront and unjust reproach, incensed, wounded, and weeping. The whole thing was consistent; all the circumstances bore plainly in the same direction; the evidence was conclusive; and Mrs. Marston's thoughts and feelings respecting her fair young confidante quickly found their old level, and flowed on tranquilly and sadly in their accustomed channel.

While Mademoiselle de Barras was thus, with the persevering industry of the spider, repairing the meshes which a chance breath had shattered, she would, perhaps, have been in her turn shocked and startled, could she have glanced into Marston's mind, and seen, in what was passing there, the real extent of her danger.

Marston was walking, as usual, alone, and in the most solitary region of his lonely park. One hand grasped his walking stick, not to lean upon it, but as if it were the handle of a battle-axe; the other was buried in his bosom; his dark face looked upon the ground, and he strode onward with a slow but energetic step, which had the air of deep resolution. He found himself at last in a little churchyard, lying far among the wild forest of his demesne, and in the midst of which, covered with ivy and tufted plants, now ruddy with autumnal tints, stood the ruined walls of a little chapel. In the dilapidated vault close by lay buried many of his ancestors, and under the little wavy hillocks of fern and nettles, slept many an humble villager.

He sat down upon a worn tombstone in this lowly ruin, and with his eyes fixed upon the ground, he surrendered his spirit to the stormy and evil thoughts which he had invited. Long and motionless he sat there, while his foul fancies and schemes began to assume shape and order. The wind rushing through the ivy roused him for a moment, and as he raised his gloomy eye it alighted accidentally upon a skull, which some wanton hand had fixed in a crevice of the wall. He averted his glance quickly, but almost as quickly refixed his gaze upon the impassive symbol of death, with an expression glowering and contemptuous, and with an angry gesture struck it down among the weeds with his stick. He left the place, and wandered on through the woods.

"Men can't control the thoughts that flit across their minds," he muttered, as he went along, "anymore than they can direct the shadows of the clouds that sail above them. They come and pass, and leave no stain behind. What, then, of omens, and that wretched effigy of death? Stuff—pshaw! Murder, indeed! I'm incapable of murder. I have drawn my sword upon a man in fair duel; but murder! Out upon the thought, out upon it."

He stamped upon the ground with a pang at once of fury and horror. He walked on a little, stopped again, and folding his arms, leaned against an ancient tree.

"Mademoiselle de Barras, *vous êtes une traîtresse*, and you shall go. Yes, go you shall; you have deceived me, and we must part."

He said this with melancholy bitterness; and, after a pause, continued:

"I will have no other revenge. No; though, I dare say, she will care but little for this; very little, if at all."

"And then, as to the other person," he resumed, after a pause, "it is not the first time he has acted like a trickster. He has crossed me before, and I will choose an opportunity to tell him my mind. I won't mince matters with him either, and will not spare him one insulting syllable that he deserves. He wears a sword, and so do I; if he pleases, he may draw it; he shall have the opportunity; but, at all events, I will make it impossible for him to prolong his disgraceful visit at my house."

On reaching home and his own study, the servant, Merton, presented himself, and his master, too deeply excited to hear him then, appointed the next day for the purpose. There was no contending against Marston's peremptory will, and the man reluctantly withdrew. Here was, apparently, a matter of no imaginable moment; whether this menial should be discharged on that day, or on the morrow; and yet mighty things were involved in the alternative.

There was a deeper gloom than usual over the house. The servants seemed to know that something had gone wrong, and looked grave and mysterious. Marston was more than ever dark and moody. Mrs. Marston's dimmed and swollen eyes showed that she had been weeping. *Mademoiselle* absented herself from supper, on the plea of a bad headache. Rhoda saw that something, she knew not what, had occurred to agitate her elders, and was depressed and anxious. The old clergyman, whom we have already mentioned, had called, and stayed to supper. Dr. Danvers was a man of considerable learning, strong sense, and remarkable simplicity of character. His thoughtful blue eye, and well-marked countenance, were full of gentleness and benevolence, and elevated by a certain natural dignity, of which purity and goodness, without one debasing shade of self-esteem and arrogance, were the animating spirit.

Mrs. Marston loved and respected this good minister of God; and many a time had sought and found, in his gentle and earnest counsels, and in the overflowing tenderness of his sympathy, much comfort and support in the progress of her sore and protracted earthly trial. Most especially at one critical period in her history had he endeared himself to her, by interposing, and successfully, to prevent a formal separation which (as ending forever the one hope that cheered her on, even in the front of despair) she would probably not long have survived.

With Mr. Marston, however, he was far from being a favourite. There was that in his lofty and simple purity which abashed and silently reproached the sensual, bitter, disappointed man of the world. The angry pride of the scornful man felt its own meanness in the grand presence of a simple and humble Christian minister. And the very fact that all his habits had led him to hold such a character in contempt, made him but the more unreasonably resent the involuntary homage which its exhibition in Dr. Danvers's person invariably extorted from him. He felt in this good man's presence under a kind of irritating restraint; that he was in the presence of one with whom he had, and could have, no sympathy whatever, and yet one whom he could not help both admiring and respecting; and in these conflicting feelings were involved certain gloomy and humbling inferences about himself, which he hated, and almost feared to contemplate.

It was well, however, for the indulgence of Sir Wynston's conversational propensities, that Dr. Danvers had happened to drop in; for Marston was doggedly silent and sullen, and Mrs. Marston was herself scarcely more disposed than he to maintain her part in a conversation; so that, had it not been for the opportune arrival of the good clergyman, the supper must have been dispatched with a very awkward and unsocial taciturnity.

Marston thought, and, perhaps, not erroneously, that Sir Wynston suspected something of the real state of affairs, and he was, therefore, incensed to perceive, as he thought, in his manner, very evident indications of his being in unusually good spirits. Thus disposed, the party sat down to supper.

"One of our number is missing," said Sir Wynston, affecting a slight surprise, which, perhaps, he did not feel.

"Mademoiselle de Barras—I trust she is well?" said Doctor Danvers, looking towards Marston.

"I suppose she is; I don't know," said Marston, drily.

"Why! how should he know," said the baronet, gaily, but with something almost imperceptibly sarcastic in his tone. "Our friend, Marston, is privileged to be as ungallant as he pleases, except where he has the happy privilege to owe allegiance; but I, a gay young bachelor of fifty, am naturally curious. I really do trust that our charming French friend is not unwell."

He addressed his inquiry to Mrs. Marston, who, with some slight confusion, replied:—

"No; nothing, at least, serious; merely a slight headache. I am sure she will be quite well enough to come down to breakfast."

"She is, indeed, a very charming and interesting young person," said Doctor Danvers. "There is a certain simplicity about her which argues a good and kind heart, and an open nature."

"Very true, indeed, doctor," observed Berkley, with the same faint, but, to Marston, exquisitely provoking approximation to sarcasm. "There is, as you say, a very charming simplicity. Don't you think so, Marston?"

Marston looked at him for a moment, but continued silent.

"Poor *mademoiselle!*—she is, indeed, a most affectionate creature," said Mrs. Marston, who felt called upon to say something.

"Come, Marston, will you contribute nothing to the general fund of approbation?" said Sir Wynston, who was gifted by nature with an amiable talent for teasing, which he was fond of exercising in a quiet way. "We have all, but you, said something handsome of our absent young friend."

"I never praise anybody, Wynston; not even you," said Marston, with an obvious sneer.

"Well, well, I must comfort myself with the belief that your silence covers a great deal of goodwill, and, perhaps, a little admiration, too," answered his cousin, significantly.

"Comfort yourself in any honest way you will, my dear Wynston," retorted Marston, with a degree of asperity, which, to all but the baronet himself, was unaccountable. "You may be right, you may be wrong; on a subject so unimportant it matters very little which; you are at perfect liberty to practice delusions, if you will, upon yourself."

"By-the-bye, Mr. Marston, is not your son about to come down here?" asked Doctor Danvers, who perceived that the altercation was becoming, on Marston's part, somewhat testy, if not positively rude.

"Yes; I expect him in a few days," replied he, with a sudden gloom.

"You have not seen him, Sir Wynston?" asked the clergyman.

"I have that pleasure yet to come," said the baronet.

"A pleasure it is, I do assure you," said Doctor Danvers, heartily. "He is a handsome lad, with the heart of a hero—a fine, frank, generous lad, and as merry as a lark."

"Yes, yes," interrupted Marston; "he is well enough, and has done pretty well at Cambridge. Doctor Danvers, take some wine."

It was strange, but yet mournfully true, that the praises which the good Doctor Danvers thus bestowed upon his son were bitter to the soul of the unhappy Marston. They jarred upon his ear, and stung his heart; for his conscience converted them into so many latent insults and humiliations to himself.

"Your wine is very good, Marston. I think your clarets are many degrees better than any I can get," said Sir Wynston, sipping a glass of his favourite wine. "You country gentlemen are sad selfish dogs; and, with all your grumbling, manage to collect the best of whatever is worth having about you."

"We sometimes succeed in collecting a pleasant party," retorted Marston, with ironical courtesy, "though we do not always command the means of entertaining them quite as we would wish."

It was the habit of Doctor Danvers, without respect of persons or places, to propose, before taking his departure from whatever domestic party he chanced to be thrown among for the evening, to read some verses from that holy Book, on which his own hopes and peace were founded, and to offer up a prayer for all to the throne of grace. Marston, although he usually absented himself from such exercises, did not otherwise discourage them; but upon the present occasion, starting from his gloomy reverie, he himself was the first to remind the clergyman of his customary observance. Evil thoughts loomed upon the mind of Marston, like measureless black mists upon a cold, smooth sea. They rested, grew, and darkened there; and no heaven-sent breath came silently to steal them away.

Under this dread shadow his mind lay waiting, like the deep, before the Spirit of God moved upon its waters, passive and awful. Why for the first time now did religion interest him? The unseen, intangible, was even now at work within him. A dreadful power shook his very heart and soul. There was some strange, ghastly wrestling going on in his own immortal spirit, a struggle that made him faint, which he had no power to determine. He looked upon the holy influence of the good man's prayer—a prayer in which he could not join—with a dull, superstitious hope that the words, inviting better influence, though uttered by another, and with other objects, would, like a spell, chase away the foul fiend that was busy with his soul. Marston sate, looking into the fire, with a countenance of stern gloom, upon which the wayward lights of the flickering hearth sported fitfully; while at a distant table Doctor Danvers sate down, and, taking his well-worn Bible from his pocket, turned over its leaves, and began, in gentle but impressive tones, to read.

Sir Wynston was much too well bred to evince the slightest disposition to aught but the most proper and profound attention. The faintest imaginable gleam of ridicule might, perhaps, have been discerned in his features, as he leaned back in his chair, and, closing his eyes, composed himself to at least an attitude of attention. No man could submit with more cheerfulness to an inevitable bore.

In these things, then, thou hast no concern; the judgment troubles thee not; thou hast no fear of death, Sir Wynston Berkley; yet there is a heart beating near thee, the mysteries of which, could they glide out and stand before thy face, would perchance appal thee, cold, easy man of the world. Aye, couldst thou but see with those cunning eyes of thine, but twelve brief hours into futurity, each syllable that falls from that good man's lips unheeded would peal through thy heart and brain like maddening thunder. Hearken, hearken, Sir Wynston Berkley, perchance these are the farewell words of thy better angel—the last pleadings of despised mercy!

The party broke up. Doctor Danvers took his leave, and rode homeward, down the broad avenue, between the gigantic ranks of elm that closed it in. The full moon was rising above the distant hills; the mists lay like sleeping lakes in the laps of the hollows; and the broad demesne looked tranquil and sad under this chastened and silvery glory. The good old clergyman thought, as he pursued his way, that here at least, in a spot so beautiful and sequestered, the stormy passions and fell contentions of the outer world could scarcely penetrate. Yet, in that calm secluded spot, and under the cold, pure light which fell so holily, what a hell was weltering and glaring!—what a spectacle was that moon to go down upon! As Sir Wynston was leaving the parlour for his own room, Marston accompanied him to the hall, and said—"I shan't play tonight, Sir Wynston."

"Ah, ha! very particularly engaged?" suggested the baronet, with a faint, mocking smile. "Well, my dear fellow, we must endeavour to make up for it tomorrow—eh?"

"I don't know that," said Marston, "and—in a word, there is no use, sir, in our masquerading with one another. Each knows the other; each understands the other. I wish to have a word or two with you in your room tonight, when we shan't be interrupted."

Marston spoke in a fierce and grating whisper, and his countenance, more even than his accents, betrayed the intensity of his bridled fury. Sir Wynston, however, smiled upon his cousin as if his voice had been melody, and his looks all sunshine.

"Very good, Marston, just as you please," he said; "only don't be later than one, as I shall be getting into bed about that hour."

"Perhaps, upon second thoughts, it is as well to defer what I have to say," said Marston, musingly. "Tomorrow will do as well; so, perhaps, Sir Wynston, I may not trouble you tonight."

"Just as suits you best, my dear Marston," replied the baronet, with a tranquil smile; "only don't come after the hour I have stipulated."

So saying, the baronet mounted the stairs, and made his way to his chamber. He was in excellent spirits, and in high good-humour with himself: the object of his visit to Gray Forest had been, as he now flattered himself, attained. He had conducted an affair requiring the profoundest mystery in its prosecution, and the nicest tactic in its management, almost to a triumphant issue. He had perfectly masked his design, and completely outwitted Marston; and to a person who piqued himself upon his clever diplomacy, and vaunted that he had never yet sustained a defeat in any object which he had seriously proposed to himself, such a combination of successes was for the moment quite intoxicating.

Sir Wynston not only enjoyed his own superiority with all the vanity of a selfish nature, but he no less enjoyed, with a keen and malicious relish, the intense mortification which, he was well assured, Marston must experience; and all the more acutely, because of the utter impossibility, circumstanced as he was, of his taking any steps to manifest his vexation, without compromising himself in a most unpleasant way.

Animated by these amiable feelings, Sir Wynston Berkley sate down, and wrote the following short letter, addressed to Mrs. Gray, Wynston Hall:—

Mrs. Gray,
On receipt of this have the sitting rooms and several bedrooms put in order, and thoroughly aired. Prepare for my use the suite of three rooms over the library and drawing room; and have the two great wardrobes, and the cabinet in the state bedroom, removed into the large dressing room which opens upon the bedroom I have named. Make everything as comfortable as possible. If anything is wanted in the way of furniture, drapery, ornament, &c., you need only write to John Skelton, Esq., Spring-garden, London, stating what is required, and he will order and send them down. You must be expeditious, as I shall probably go down to Wynston, with two or three friends, at the beginning of next month.
                    WYNSTON BERKLEY
P.S.—I have written to direct Arkins and two or three of the other servants to go down at once. Set them all to work immediately.

He then applied himself to another letter of considerably greater length, and from which, therefore, we shall only offer a few extracts. It was addressed to John Skelton, Esq., and began as follows.—

My Dear Skelton,

You are, doubtless, surprised at my long silence, but I have had nothing very particular to say. My visit to this dull and uncomfortable place was (as you rightly surmise) not without its object—a little bit of wicked romance; the pretty *demoiselle* of Rouen, whom I mentioned to you more than once—*la belle de Barras*—was, in truth, the attraction that drew me hither; and I think (for, as yet, she affects hesitation), I shall have no further trouble with her. She is a fine creature, and you will admit, when you have seen her, well worth taking some trouble about.

She is, however, a very knowing little minx, and evidently suspects me of being a sad, fickle dog—and, as I surmise, has some plans, moreover, respecting my morose cousin, Marston, a kind of wicked Penruddock, who has carried all his London tastes into his savage retreat, a paradise of bogs and bushes. There is, I am very confident, a liaison in that quarter. The young lady is evidently a good deal afraid of him, and insists upon such precautions in our interviews, that they have been very few, and far between, indeed.

Today, there has been a fracas of some kind. I have no doubt that Marston, poor devil, is jealous. His situation is really pitiably comic—with an intriguing mistress, a saintly wife, and a devil of a jealous temper of his own. I shall meet Mary on reaching town. Has Clavering (shabby dog!) paid his I.O.U. yet? Tell the little opera woman she had better be quiet. She ought to know me by this time; I shall do what is right, but won't submit to be bullied. If she is troublesome, snap your fingers at her, on my behalf, and leave her to her remedy. I have written to Gray, to get things at Wynston in order. She will draw upon you for what money she requires. Send down two or three of the servants, if they have not already gone.

The place is very dusty and dingy, and needs a great deal of brushing and scouring. I shall see you in town very soon. By the way, has the claret I ordered from the Dublin house arrived yet? It is consigned to you, and goes by the 'Lizard'; pay the freightage, and get Edwards to pack it; ten dozen or so may as well go down to Wynston, and send other wines in proportion. I leave details to you. . . .

Some further directions upon other subjects followed; and having subscribed the dispatch, and addressed it to the gentlemanlike scoundrel who filled the onerous office of *factotum* to this profligate and exacting man of the world, Sir Wynston Berkley rang his bell, and gave the two letters into the hand of his man, with special directions to carry them himself in person, to the post office in the neighbouring village, early next morning. These little matters completed, Sir Wynston stirred his fire, leaned back in his easy chair, and smiled blandly over the sunny prospect of his imaginary triumphs.

It here becomes necessary to describe, in a few words, some of the local relations of Sir Wynston's apartments. The bedchamber which he occupied opened from the long passage of which we have already spoken—and there were two other smaller apartments opening from it in train. In the further of these, which was entered from a lobby, communicating by a back stair with the kitchen and servants' apartments, lay Sir Wynston's valet, and the intermediate chamber was fitted up as a dressing room for the baronet himself. These circumstances it is necessary to mention, that what follows may be clearly intelligible.

While the baronet was penning these records of vicious schemes—dire waste of wealth and time—irrevocable time!- Marston paced his study in a very different frame of mind. There were a gloom and disorder in the room accordant with those of his own mind. Shelves of ancient tomes, darkened by time, and upon which the dust of years lay sleeping—dark oaken cabinets, filled with piles of deeds and papers, among which the nimble spiders were crawling—and, from the dusky walls, several stark, pale ancestors, looking down coldly from their tarnished frames.

An hour, and another hour passed—and still Marston paced

this melancholy chamber, a prey to his own fell passions and dark thoughts. He was not a superstitious man, but, in the visions which haunted him, perhaps, was something which made him unusually excitable—for, he experienced a chill of absolute horror, as, standing at the farther end of the room, with his face turned towards the entrance, he beheld the door noiselessly and slowly pushed open, by a pale, thin hand, and a figure dressed in a loose white robe, glide softly in. He stood for some seconds gazing upon this apparition, as it moved hesitatingly towards him from the dusky extremity of the large apartment, before he perceived that the form was that of Mrs. Marston.

"Hey, ha!—Mrs. Marston—what on earth has called you hither?" he asked, sternly. "You ought to have been at rest an hour ago; get to your chamber, and leave me, I have business to attend to."

"Now, dear Richard, you must forgive me," she said, drawing near, and looking up into his haggard face with a sweet and touching look of timidity and love; "I could not rest until I saw you again; your looks have been all this night so unlike yourself; so strange and terrible, that I am afraid some great misfortune threatens you, which you fear to tell me of."

"My looks! Why, curse it, must I give an account of my looks?" replied Marston, at once disconcerted and wrathful. "Misfortune! What misfortune can befall us more? No, there is nothing, nothing, I say, but your own foolish fancy; go to your room—go to sleep—my looks, indeed; pshaw!"

"I came to tell you, dear Richard, that I will do, in all respects, just as you desire. If you continue to wish it, I will part with poor *mademoiselle*; though, indeed, Richard, I shall miss her more than you can imagine; and all your suspicions have wronged her deeply," said Mrs. Marston. Her husband darted a sudden flashing glance of suspicious scrutiny upon her face; but its expression was frank, earnest, noble. He was disarmed; he hung his head gloomily upon his breast, and was silent for a time. She came nearer, and laid her hand upon his arm. He looked darkly into her upturned eyes, and a feeling which had not touched his heart for many a day—an emotion of pity, transient, indeed, but vivid, revisited him. He took her hand in his, and said, in gentler terms than she had heard him use for a long time—

"No, indeed, Gertrude, you have deceived yourself; no misfortune has happened, and if I am gloomy, the source of all my troubles is within. Leave me, Gertrude, for the present. As to the other matter, the departure of Mademoiselle de Barras, we can talk of that tomorrow—now I cannot; so let us part. Go to your room; good night."

She was withdrawing, and he added, in a subdued tone— "Gertrude, I am very glad you came—very glad. Pray for me tonight."

He had followed her a few steps toward the door, and now stopped short, turned about, and walked dejectedly back again—

"I am right glad she came," he muttered, as soon as he was once more alone. "Wynston is provoking and fiery, too. Were I, in my present mood, to seek a *tête-à-tête* with him, who knows what might come of it? Blood; my own heart whispers—blood! I'll not trust myself."

He strode to the study door, locked it, and taking out the key, shut it in the drawer of one of the cabinets.

"Now it will need more than accident or impulse to lead me to him. I cannot go, at least, without reflection, without premeditation. *Avaunt*, fiend. I have baffled you."

He stood in the centre of the room, cowering and scowling as he said this, and looked round with a glance half-defiant, half-fearful, as if he expected to see some dreadful form in the dusky recesses of the desolate chamber. He sat himself by the smouldering fire, in sombre and agitated rumination. He was restless; he rose again, unbuckled his sword, which he had not loosed since evening, and threw it hastily into a corner. He looked at his watch, it was half-past twelve; he glanced at the door, and thence at the cabinet in which he had placed the key; then he turned hastily, and sate down again. He leaned his elbows on his knees, and his chin upon his clenched hand; still he was restless and excited. Once more he arose, and paced up and down. He consulted his watch again; it was now but a quarter to one.

Sir Wynston's man having received the letters, and his master's permission to retire to rest, got into his bed, and was soon beginning to dose. We have already mentioned that his and Sir Wynston's apartments were separated by a small dressing room, so that any ordinary noise or conversation could be heard but imperfectly from one to the other. The servant, however, was startled by a sound of something falling on the floor of his master's apartment, and broken to pieces by the violence of the shock. He sate up in his bed, listened, and heard some sentences spoken vehemently, and gabbled very fast. He thought he distinguished the words "wretch" and "God"; and there was something so strange in the tone in which they were spoken, that the man got up and stole noiselessly through the dressing room, and listened at the door.

He heard him, as he thought, walking in his slippers through the room, and making his customary arrangements previously to getting into bed. He knew that his master had a habit of speaking when alone, and concluded that the accidental breakage of some glass or chimney-ornament had elicited the volley of words he had heard. Well knowing that, except at the usual hours, or in obedience to Sir Wynston's bell, nothing more displeased his master than his presuming to enter his sleeping-apartment while he was there, the servant quietly retreated, and, perfectly satisfied that all was right, composed himself to slumber, and was soon beginning to dose again.

The adventures of the night, however, were not yet over. Waking, as men sometimes do, without any ascertainable cause; without a start or an uneasy sensation; without even a disturbance of the attitude of repose, he opened his eyes and beheld Merton, the servant of whom we have spoken, standing at a little distance from his bed. The moonlight fell in a clear flood upon this figure: the man was ghastly pale; there was a blotch of blood on his face; his hands were clasped upon something which they nearly concealed; and his eyes, fixed on the servant who had just awakened, shone in the cold light with a wild and lifeless glitter. This spectre drew close to the side of the bed, and stood for a few moments there with a look of agony and menace, which startled the newly-awakened man, who rose upright, and said—

"Mr. Merton, Mr. Merton—in God's name, what is the matter?"

Merton recoiled at the sound of his voice; and, as he did so, dropped something on the floor, which rolled away to a distance; and he stood gazing silently and horribly upon his interrogator.

"Mr. Merton, I say, what is it?" urged the man. "Are you hurt? Your face is bloody."

Merton raised his hand to his face mechanically, and Sir Wynston's man observed that it, too, was covered with blood.

"Why, man," he said, vehemently, and actually freezing with horror," you are all bloody; hands and face; all over blood."

"My hand is cut to the bone," said Merton, in a harsh whisper; and speaking to himself, rather than addressing the servant—"I wish it was my neck; I wish to God I bled to death."

"You have hurt your hand, Mr. Merton," repeated the man, scarce knowing what he said.

"Aye," whispered Merton, wildly drawing toward the bedside again; "who told you I hurt my hand? It is cut to the bone, sure enough."

He stooped for a moment over the bed, and then cowered down toward the floor to search for what he had dropped.

"Why, Mr. Merton, what brings you here at this hour?" urged the man, after a pause of a few seconds. "It is drawing toward morning."

"Aye, aye," said Merton, doubtfully, and starting upright again, while he concealed in his bosom what he had been in search of. "Near morning, is it? Night and morning, it is all one to me. I believe I am going mad, by—"

"But what do you want? What did you come here for at this hour?" persisted the man.

"What! Aye, that is it; why, his boots and spurs, to be sure. I

267

forgot them. His—his—Sir Wynston's boots and spurs; I forgot to take them, I say," said Merton, looking toward the dressing room, as if about to enter it.

"Don't mind them tonight, I say, don't go in there," said the man, peremptorily, and getting out upon the floor. "I say, Mr. Merton, this is no hour to be going about searching in the dark for boots and spurs. You'll waken the master. I can't have it, I say; go down, and let it be for tonight."

Thus speaking, in a resolute and somewhat angry under-key, the valet stood between Merton and the entrance of the dressing-room; and, signing with his hand toward the other door of the apartment, continued—

"Go down, I say, Mr. Merton, go down; you may as well quietly, for, I tell you plainly, you shall neither go a step further, nor stay here a moment longer."

The man drew his shoulders up, and made a sort of shivering moan, and clasping his hands together, shook them, as it seemed, in great agony. He then turned abruptly, and hurried from the room by the door leading to the kitchen.

"By my faith," said the servant, "I am glad he is gone. The poor chap is turning crazy, as sure as I am a living man. I'll not have him prowling about here anymore, however; that I am resolved on."

In pursuance of this determination, by no means an imprudent one, as it seemed, he fastened the door communicating with the lower apartments upon the inside. He had hardly done this, when he heard a step traversing the stable-yard, which lay under the window of his apartment. He looked out, and saw Merton walking hurriedly across, and into a stable at the farther end.

Feeling no very particular curiosity about his movements, the man hurried back to his bed. Merton's eccentric conduct of late had become so generally remarked and discussed among the servants, that Sir Wynston's man was by no means surprised at the oddity of the visit he had just had; nor, after the first few moments of doubt, before the appearance of blood had been accounted for, had he entertained any suspicions whatever connected with the man's unexpected presence in the room. Merton was in the habit of coming up every night to take down Sir Wynston's boots, whenever the baronet had ridden in the course of the day; and this attention had been civilly undertaken as a proof of goodwill toward the valet, whose duty this somewhat soiling and ungentlemanlike process would otherwise have been. So far, the nature of the visit was explained; and the remembrance of the friendly feeling and good offices which had been mutually interchanged, as well as of the inoffensive habits for which Merton had earned a character for himself, speedily calmed the uneasiness, for a moment amounting to actual alarm, with which the servant had regarded his appearance.

We must now pass on to the morrow, and ask the reader's attention for a few moments to a different scene.

In contact with Gray Forest upon the northern side, and divided by a common boundary, lay a demesne, in many respects presenting a very striking contrast to its grander neighbour. It was a comparatively modern place. It could not boast the towering timber which enriched and overshadowed the vast and varied expanse of its aristocratic rival; but, if it was inferior in the advantages of antiquity, and, perhaps, also in some of those of nature, its superiority in other respects was striking, and important. Gray Forest was not more remarkable for its wild and neglected condition, than was Newton Park for the care and elegance with which it was kept. No one could observe the contrast, without, at the same time, divining its cause. The proprietor of the one was a man of wealth, fully commensurate with the extent and pretensions of the residence he had chosen; the owner of the other was a man of broken fortunes.

Under a green shade, which nearly met above, a very young man, scarcely one-and-twenty, of a frank and sensible, rather than a strictly handsome countenance, was walking, followed by half a dozen dogs of as many breeds and sizes. This young man was George Mervyn, the only son of the present proprietor of the place. As he approached the great gate, the clank of a horse's hoofs in quick motion upon the sequestered road which ran outside it, reached him; and hardly had he heard these sounds, when a young gentleman rode briskly by, directing his look into the demesne as he passed. He had no sooner seen him, than wheeling his horse about, he rode up to the iron gate, and dismounting, threw it open, and let his horse in.

"Ha! Charles Marston, I protest!" said the young man, quickening his pace to meet his friend. "Marston, my dear fellow," he called aloud, "how glad I am to see you."

There was another entrance into Newton Park, opening from the same road, about half a mile further on; and Charles Marston made his way lie through this. Thus the young people walked on, talking of a hundred things as they proceeded, in the mirth of their hearts.

Between the fathers of the two young men, who thus walked so affectionately together, there subsisted unhappily no friendly feelings. There had been several slight disagreements between them, touching their proprietary rights, and one of these had ripened into a formal and somewhat expensive litigation, respecting a certain right of fishing claimed by each. This legal encounter had terminated in the defeat of Marston. Mervyn, however, promptly wrote to his opponent, offering him the free use of the waters for which they had thus sharply contested, and received a curt and scarcely civil reply, declining the proposed courtesy.

This exhibition of resentment on Marston's part had been followed by some rather angry collisions, where chance or duty happened to throw them together. It is but justice to say that, upon all such occasions, Marston was the aggressor. But Mervyn was a somewhat testy old gentleman, and had a certain pride of his own, which was not to be trifled with. Thus, though near neighbours, the parents of the young friends were more than strangers to each other. On Mervyn's side, however, this estrangement was unalloyed with bitterness, and simply of that kind which the great moralist would have referred to "defensive pride." It did not include any member of Marston's family, and

Charles, as often as he desired it, which was, in truth, as often as his visits could escape the special notice of his father, was a welcome guest at Newton Park.

These details respecting the mutual relation in which the two families stood, it was necessary to state, for the purpose of making what follows perfectly clear. The young people had now reached the further gate, at which they were to part. Charles Marston, with a heart beating happily in the anticipation of many a pleasant meeting, bid him farewell for the present, and in a few minutes more was riding up the broad, straight avenue, towards the gloomy mansion which closed in the hazy and sombre perspective. As he moved onward, he passed a labourer, with whose face, from his childhood, he had been familiar.

"How do you do, Tom?" he cried.

"At your service, sir," replied the man, uncovering, "and welcome home, sir."

There was something dark and anxious in the man's looks, which ill-accorded with the welcome he spoke, and which suggested some undefined alarm.

"The master, and mistress, and Miss Rhoda—are all well?" he asked eagerly.

"All well, sir, thank God," replied the man.

Young Marston spurred on, filled with vague apprehensions, and observing the man still leaning upon his spade, and watching his progress with the same gloomy and curious eye.

At the hall-door he met with one of the servants, booted and spurred.

"Well, Daly," he said, as he dismounted, "how are all at home?"

This man, like the former, met his smile with a troubled countenance, and stammered—

"All, sir—that is, the master, and mistress, and Miss Rhoda—quite well, sir; but—"

"Well, well," said Charles, eagerly, "speak on—what is it?"

"Bad work, sir," replied the man, lowering his voice. "I am going off this minute for—"

"For what?" urged the young gentleman.

"Why, sir, for the coroner," replied he.

"The coroner—the coroner! Why, good God, what has happened?" cried Charles, aghast with horror.

"Sir Wynston," commenced the man, and hesitated.

"Well?" pursued Charles, pale and breathless.

"Sir Wynston—he—it is he," said the man.

"He? Sir Wynston? Is he dead, or who is?—Who is dead?" demanded the young man, almost fiercely.

"Sir Wynston, sir; it is he that is dead. There is bad work, sir—very bad, I'm afraid," replied the man.

Charles did not wait to inquire further, but, with a feeling of mingled horror and curiosity, entered the house.

He hurried up the stairs, and entered his mother's sitting room. She was there, perfectly alone, and so deadly pale, that she scarcely looked like a living being. In an instant they were locked in one another's arms.

"Mother—my dear mother, you are ill," said the young man, anxiously.

"Oh, no, no, dear Charles, but frightened, horrified;" and as she said this, the poor lady burst into tears.

"What is this horrible affair? Something about Sir Wynston. He is dead, I know, but is it—is it suicide?" he asked.

"Oh, no, not suicide," said Mrs. Marston, greatly agitated.

"Good God! Then he is murdered," whispered the young man, growing very pale.

"Yes, Charles—horrible—dreadful! I can scarcely believe it," replied she, shuddering while she wept.

"Where is my father?" inquired the young man, after a pause.

"Why, why, Charles, darling—why do you ask for him?" she said, wildly, grasping him by the arm, as she looked into his face with a terrified expression.

"Why—why, he could tell me the particulars of this horrible tragedy," answered he, meeting her agonized look with one of alarm and surprise, "as far as they have been as yet collected.

How is he, mother—is he well?"

"Oh, yes, quite well, thank God," she answered, more collect-edly—"quite well, but, of course, greatly, dreadfully shocked."

"I will go to him, mother; I will see him," said he, turning towards the door.

"He has been wretchedly depressed and excited for some days," said Mrs. Marston, dejectedly, "and this dreadful occur-rence will, I fear, affect him most deplorably."

The young man kissed her tenderly and affectionately, and hurried down to the library, where his father usually sat when he desired to be alone, or was engaged in business. He opened the door softly. His father was standing at one of the windows, his face haggard as from a night's watching, unkempt and un-shorn, and with his hands thrust into his pockets. At the sound of the revolving door he started, and seeing his son, first recoiled a little, with a strange, doubtful expression, and then rallying, walked quickly towards him with a smile, which had in it some-thing still more painful.

"Charles, I am glad to see you," he said, shaking him with an agitated pressure by both hands, "Charles, this is a great calamity, and what makes it still worse, is that the murderer has escaped; it looks badly, you know."

He fixed his gaze for a few moments upon his son, turned abruptly, and walked a little way into the room then, in a discon-certed manner, he added, hastily turning back—

"Not that it signifies to us, of course—but I would fain have justice satisfied."

"And who is the wretch—the murderer?" inquired Charles.

"Who? Why, everyone knows!—that scoundrel, Merton," answered Marston, in an irritated tone—"Merton murdered him in his bed, and fled last night; he is gone—escaped—and I suspect Sir Wynston's man of being an accessory."

"Which was Sir Wynston's bedroom?" asked the young man.

"The room that old Lady Mostyn had—the room with the portrait of Grace Hamilton in it."

"I know—I know," said the young man, much excited. "I

should wish to see it."

"Stay," said Marston; "the door from the passage is bolted on the inside, and I have locked the other; here is the key, if you choose to go, but you must bring Hughes with you, and do not disturb anything; leave all as it is; the jury ought to see, and examine for themselves."

Charles took the key, and, accompanied by the awestruck servant, he made his way by the back stairs to the door opening from the dressing-room, which, as we have said, intervened between the valet's chamber and Sir Wynston's. After a momentary hesitation, Charles turned the key in the door, and stood.

"In the dark chamber of white death."

The shutters lay partly open, as the valet had left them some hours before, on making the astounding discovery, which the partially admitted light revealed. The corpse lay in the silk-embroidered dressing gown, and other habiliments, which Sir Wynston had worn, while taking his ease in his chamber, on the preceding night. The coverlet was partially dragged over it. The mouth was gaping, and filled with clotted blood; a wide gash was also visible in the neck, under the ear; and there was a thickening pool of blood at the bedside, and quantities of blood, doubtless from other wounds, had saturated the bedclothes under the body. There lay Sir Wynston, stiffened in the attitude in which the struggle of death had left him, with his stern, stony face, and dim, terrible gaze turned up.

Charles looked breathlessly for more than a minute upon this mute and unchanging spectacle, and then silently suffered the curtain to fall back again, and stepped, with the light tread of awe, again to the door. There he turned back, and pausing for a minute, said, in a whisper, to the attendant—

"And Merton did this?"

"Troth, I'm afeard he did, sir," answered the man, gloomily.

"And has made his escape?" continued Charles.

"Yes, sir; he stole away in the night-time," replied the servant, "after the murder was done" (and he glanced fearfully toward the bed); "God knows where he's gone."

"The villain!" muttered Charles; "but what was his motive? why did he do all this—what does it mean?"

"I don't know exactly, sir, but he was very queer for a week and more before it," replied the man; "there was something bad over him for a long time."

"It is a terrible thing," said Charles, with a profound sigh; "a terrible and shocking occurrence."

He hesitated again at the door, but his feelings had sustained a terrible revulsion at sight of the corpse, and he was no longer disposed to prosecute his purposed examination of the chamber and its contents; with a view to conjecturing the probable circumstances of the murder.

"Observe, Hughes, that I have moved nothing in the chamber from the place it occupied when we entered," he said to the servant, as they withdrew.

He locked the door, and as he passed through the hall, on his return, he encountered his father, and, restoring the key, said—

"I could not stay there; I am almost sorry I have seen it; I am overpowered; what a determined, ferocious murder it was; the place is all in a pool of gore; he must have received many wounds."

"I can't say; the particulars will be elicited soon enough; those details are for the inquest; as for me, I hate such spectacles," said Marston, gloomily; "go now, and see your sister; you will find her there."

He pointed to the small room where we have first seen her and her fair governess; Charles obeyed the direction, and Marston proceeded himself to his wife's sitting room.

The young man, dispirited and horrified by the awful spectacle he had just contemplated, hurried to the little study occupied by his sister. Marston himself ascended, as we have said, the great staircase leading to his wife's private sitting room.

"Mrs. Marston," he said, entering, "this is a hateful occurrence, a dreadful thing to have taken place here; I don't mean to affect grief which I don't feel; but the thing is very shocking, and particularly so, as having occurred under my roof; but that cannot now be helped. I have resolved to spare no exertions, and no influence, to bring the assassin to justice; and a coroner's jury will, within a few hours, sift the evidence which we have succeeded in collecting. But my purpose in seeking you now is, to recur to the conversation we yesterday had, respecting a member of this establishment."

"Mademoiselle de Barras?" suggested the lady.

"Yes, Mademoiselle de Barras," echoed Marston; "I wish to say, that, having reconsidered the circumstances affecting her, I am absolutely resolved that she shall not continue to be an inmate of this house."

He paused, and Mrs. Marston said—

"Well, Richard, I am sorry, very sorry for it; but your decision shall never be disputed by me."

"Of course," said Marston, drily; "and, therefore, the sooner you acquaint her with it, and let her know that she must go, the better."

Having said this, he left her, and went to his own chamber, where he proceeded to make his toilet with elaborate propriety, in preparation for the scene which was about to take place under his roof.

Mrs. Marston, meanwhile, suffered from a horrible uncertainty. She never harboured, it is true, one doubt as to her husband's perfect innocence of the ghastly crime which filled their house with fear and gloom; but at the same time that she thoroughly and indignantly scouted the possibility of his, under any circumstances, being accessory to such a crime, she experienced a nervous and agonizing anxiety lest anyone else should possibly suspect him, however obliquely and faintly, of any participation whatever in the foul deed. This vague fear tortured her; it had taken possession of her mind; and it was the more acutely painful, because it was of a kind which precluded the possibility of her dispelling it, as morbid fears so often are dispelled, by taking counsel upon its suggestions with a friend.

The day wore on, and strange faces began to fill the great parlour. The coroner, accompanied by a physician, had arrived. Several of the gentry in the immediate vicinity had been summoned as jurors, and now began to arrive in succession. Marston, in a handsome and sober suit, received these visitors with a stately and melancholy courtesy, befitting the occasion. Mervyn and his son had both been summoned, and, of course, were in attendance. There being now a sufficient number to form a jury, they were sworn, and immediately proceeded to the chamber where the body of the murdered man was lying.

Marston accompanied them, and with a pale and stern countenance, and in a clear and subdued tone, called their attention successively to every particular detail which he conceived important to be noted. Having thus employed some minutes, the jury again returned to the parlour, and the examination of the witnesses commenced.

Marston, at his own request, was first sworn and examined. He deposed merely to the circumstance of his parting, on the night previous, with Sir Wynston, and to the state in which he had seen the room and the body in the morning. He mentioned also the fact, that on hearing the alarm in the morning, he had hastened from his own chamber to Sir Wynston's, and found, on trying to enter, that the door opening upon the passage was secured on the inside. This circumstance showed that the murderer must have made his egress at least through the valet's chamber, and by the back-stairs. Marston's evidence went no further.

The next witness sworn was Edward Smith, the servant of the late Sir Wynston Berkley. His evidence was a narrative of the occurrences we have already stated. He described the sounds which he had overheard from his master's room, the subsequent appearance of Merton, and the conversation which had passed between them. He then proceeded to mention, that it was his master's custom to have himself called at seven o'clock, at which hour he usually took some medicine, which it was the valet's duty to bring to him; after which he either settled again to rest, or rose in a short time, if unable to sleep. Having measured and prepared the dose in the dressing room, the servant went on to say, he had knocked at his master's door, and receiving no answer, had entered the room, and partly unclosed the shutters. He perceived the blood on the carpet, and on opening the curtains, saw his master lying with his mouth and eyes open, perfectly dead, and weltering in gore.

He had stretched out his hand, and seized that of the dead man, which was quite stiff and cold; then, losing heart, he had run to the door communicating with the passage, but found it locked, and turned to the other entrance, and ran down the back-stairs, crying "murder." Mr. Hughes, the butler, and James Carney, another servant, came immediately, and they all three went back into the room. The key was in the outer door, upon the inside, but they did not unlock it until they had viewed the body. There was a great pool of blood in the bed, and in it was lying a red-handled case knife, which was produced, and identified by the witness. Just then they heard Mr. Marston calling for admission, and they opened the door with some difficulty, for the lock was rusty. Mr. Marston had ordered them to leave the things as they were, and had used very stern language to the witness. They had then left the room, securing both doors.

This witness underwent a severe and searching examination, but his evidence was clear and consistent.

In conclusion, Marston produced a dagger, which was stained with blood, and asked the man whether he recognized it.

Smith at once stated this to have been the property of his late master, who, when traveling, carried it, together with his pistols, along with him. Since his arrival at Gray Forest, it had lain upon the chimney-piece in his bedroom, where he believed it to have been upon the previous night.

James Carney, one of Marston's servants, was next sworn and examined. He had, he said, observed a strange and unaccountable agitation and depression in Merton's manner for some days past; he had also been several times disturbed at night by his talking aloud to himself, and walking to and fro in his room. Their bedrooms were separated by a thin partition, in which was a window, through which Carney had, on the night of the murder, observed a light in Merton's room, and, on looking in, had seen him dressing hastily. He also saw him twice take up, and again lay down, the red-hafted knife which had been found in the bed of the murdered man. He knew it by the handle being broken near the end. He had no suspicion of Merton having any mischievous intentions, and lay down again to rest. He afterwards heard him pass out of his room, and go slowly up the back-stairs leading to the upper story. Shortly after this he had fallen asleep, and did not hear or see him return. He then described, as Smith had already done, the scene which presented itself in the morning, on his accompanying him into Sir Wynston's bedchamber.

The next witness examined was a little Irish boy, who described himself as "a poor scholar." His testimony was somewhat singular. He deposed that he had come to the house on the preceding evening, and had been given some supper, and was afterwards permitted to sleep among the hay in one of the lofts. He had, however, discovered what he considered a snugger berth. This was an unused stable, in the further end of which lay a quantity of hay. Among this he had lain down, and gone to sleep. He was, however, awakened in the course of the night by the entrance of a man, whom he saw with perfect distinctness in the moonlight, and his description of his dress and appearance tallied exactly with those of Merton.

This man occupied himself for sometime in washing his hands and face in a stable bucket, which happened to stand by the door; and, during the whole of this process, he continued to moan and mutter, like one in woeful perturbation. He said, distinctly, twice or thrice, "by ——, I am done for;" and every now and then he muttered, "and nothing for it, after all." When he had done washing his hands, he took something from his coat-pocket, and looked at it, shaking his head; at this time he was standing with his back turned toward the boy, so that he could not see what this object might be. The man, however, put it into his breast, and then began to search hurriedly, as it seemed, for some hiding place for it. After looking at the pavement, and poking at the chinks of the wall, he suddenly went to the window, and forced up the stone which formed the sill. Under this he threw the object which the boy had seen him examine with so much perplexity, and then he readjusted the stone, and removed the evidences of its having been recently stirred.

The boy was a little frightened, but very curious about all that he saw; and when the man left the stable in which he lay, he got up, and following to the door, peeped after him. He saw him putting on an outside-coat and hat, near the yard gate; and then, with great caution, unbolt the wicket, constantly looking back towards the house, and so let himself out. The boy was uneasy, and sat in the hay, wide-awake, until morning. He then told the servants what he had seen, and one of the men having raised the stone, which he had not strength to lift, they found the dagger, which Smith had identified as belonging to his master. This weapon was stained with blood; and some hair, which was found to correspond in colour with Sir Wynston's, was sticking in the crevice between the blade and the handle.

"It appears very strange that one man should have employed two distinct instruments of this kind," observed Mervyn, after a pause. A silence followed.

"Yes, strange; it does seem strange," said Marston, clearing his voice.

"Yet, it is clear," said another of the jury, "that the same hand did employ them. It is proved that the knife was in Merton's possession just as he left his chamber; and proved, also, that the dagger was secreted by him after he quitted the house."

"Yes," said Marston, with a grisly sort of smile, and glancing sarcastically at Mervyn, while he addressed the last speaker—"I thank you for recalling my attention to the facts. It certainly is not a very pleasant suggestion, that there still remains within my household an undetected murderer."

Mervyn ruminated for a time, and said he should wish to put a few more questions to Smith and Carney. They were accordingly recalled, and examined in great detail, with a view to ascertain whether any indication of the presence of a second person having visited the chamber with Merton was discoverable. Nothing, however, appeared, except that the valet mentioned the noise and the exclamations which he had indistinctly heard.

"You did not mention that before, sir," said Marston, sharply.

"I did not think of it, sir," replied the man, "the gentlemen were asking me so many questions; but I told you, sir, about it in the morning."

"Oh, ah—yes, yes—I believe you did," said Marston; "but you then said that Sir Wynston often talked when he was alone; eh, sir?"

"Yes, sir, and so he used, which was the reason I did not go into the room when I heard it," replied the man.

"How long afterwards was it when you saw Merton in your own room?" asked Mervyn.

"I could not say, sir," answered Smith; "I was soon asleep, and can't say how long I slept before he came."

"Was it an hour?" pursued Mervyn.

"I can't say," said the man, doubtfully.

"Was it five hours?" asked Marston.

"No, Sir; I am sure it was not five."

"Could you swear it was more than half-an-hour?" persisted Marston.

"No, I could not swear that," answered he.

"I am afraid, Mr. Mervyn; you have found a mare's nest," said Marston, contemptuously.

"I have done my duty, sir," retorted Mervyn, cynically; "which plainly requires that I shall have no doubt, which the evidence of the witness can clear up, unsifted and unsatisfied. I happened to think it of some moment to ascertain, if possible, whether more persons than one were engaged in this atrocious murder. You don't seem to think the question so important a one; different men, sir, take different views."

"Views, sir, in matters of this sort, especially where they tend to multiply suspicions, and to implicate others, ought to be supported by something more substantial than mere fancies," retorted Marston.

"I don't know what you call fancies," replied Mervyn, testily; "but here are two deadly weapons, a knife and a dagger, each, it would seem, employed in doing this murder; if you see nothing odd in that, I can't enable you to do so."

"Well, sir," said Marston, grimly, "the whole thing is, as you term it, odd; and I can see no object in your picking out this particular singularity for long-winded criticism, except to cast scandal upon my household, by leaving a hideous and vague imputation floating among the members of it. Sir, sir, this is a foul way," he cried, sternly, "to gratify a paltry spite."

"Mr. Marston," said Mervyn, rising, and thrusting his hands into his pockets, while he confronted him to the full as sternly, "the country knows in which of our hearts the spite, if any there be between us, is harboured. I owe you no friendship, but, sir, I cherish no malice, either; and against the worst enemy I have on earth I am incapable of perverting an opportunity like this, and inflicting pain, under the pretence of discharging a duty."

Marston was on the point of retorting, but the coroner interposed, and besought them to confine their attention strictly to the solemn inquiry which they were summoned together to prosecute.

There remained still to be examined the surgeon who had accompanied the coroner, for the purpose of reporting upon the extent and nature of the injuries discoverable upon the person of the deceased. He, accordingly, deposed, that having examined the body, he found no less than three deep wounds, inflicted with some sharp instrument; two of them had actually penetrated the heart, and were, of course, supposed to cause instant death. Besides these, there were two contusions, one upon the back of the head, the other upon the forehead, with a slight abrasion of the eyebrow. There was a large lock of hair torn out by the roots at the front of the head, and the palm and fingers of the right hand were cut. This evidence having been taken, the jury once more repaired to the chamber where the body lay, and proceeded with much minuteness to examine the room, with a view to ascertain, if possible, more particularly the exact circumstances of the murder.

The result of this elaborate scrutiny was as follows:—The deceased, they conjectured, had fallen asleep in his easy chair, and, while he was unconscious, the murderer had stolen into the room, and, before attacking his victim, had secured the bedroom-door upon the inside. This was argued from the non-discovery of blood upon the handle, or any other part of the door. It was supposed that he had then approached Sir Wynston, with the view either of robbing, or of murdering him while he slept, and that the deceased had awakened just after he had reached him; that a brief and desperate struggle had ensued, in which the assailant had struck his victim with his fist upon the forehead, and having stunned him, had hurriedly clutched him by the hair, and stabbed him with the dagger, which lay close by upon the chimneypiece, forcing his head violently against the back of the chair.

This part of the conjecture was supported by the circumstance of there being discovered a lock of hair upon the ground at the spot, and a good deal of blood. The carpet, too, was tumbled, and a water-decanter, which had stood upon the table close by, was lying in fragments upon the floor. It was supposed that the murderer had then dragged the half-lifeless body to the bed, where, having substituted the knife, which he had probably brought to the room in the same pocket from which the boy afterwards saw him take the dagger, he dispatched him; and either hearing some alarm—perhaps the movement of the valet in the adjoining room, or from some other cause—he dropped the knife in the bed, and was not able to find it again.

The wounds upon the hand of the dead man indicated his having caught and struggled to hold the blade of the weapon with which he was assailed. The impression of a bloody hand thrust under the bolster, where it was Sir Wynston's habit to place his purse and watch, when making his arrangements for the night, supplied the motive of this otherwise unaccountable atrocity.

After some brief consultation, the jury agreed upon a verdict of wilful murder against John Merton, a finding of which the coroner expressed his entire approbation.

Marston, as a justice of the peace, had informations, embodying the principal part of the evidence given before the coroner, sworn against Merton, and transmitted a copy of them to the Home Office. A reward for the apprehension of the culprit was forthwith offered, but for some months without effect.

Marston had, in the interval, written to several of Sir Wynston's many relations, announcing the catastrophe, and requesting that steps might immediately be taken to have the body removed. Meanwhile undertakers were busy in the chamber of death. The corpse was enclosed in lead, and that again in cedar, and a great oak shell, covered with crimson cloth and goldheaded nails, and with a gilt plate, recording the age, title, &c. &c., of the deceased, was screwed down firmly over all.

Nearly a fortnight elapsed before any reply to Marston's letters was received. A short epistle at last arrived from Lord H——, the late Sir Wynston's uncle, deeply regretting the "sad and inexplicable occurrence," and adding, that the will, which, on receipt of the "distressing intelligence," was immediately opened and read, contained no direction whatever respecting the sepulture of the deceased, which had therefore better be completed as modestly and expeditiously as possible, in the neighbourhood; and, in conclusion, he directed that the accounts of the undertakers, &c., employed upon the melancholy occasion, might be sent in to Mr. Skelton, who had kindly undertaken to leave London without any delay, for the purpose of completing these last arrangements, and who would, in any matter of business connected with the deceased, represent him, Lord H——, as executor of the late baronet.

This letter was followed, in a day or two, by the arrival of Skelton, a well-dressed, languid, impertinent London tuft-hunter, a good deal faded, with a somewhat sallow and puffy face, charged with a pleasant combination at once of meanness, insolence, and sensuality—just such a person as Sir Wynston's parasite might have been expected to prove.

However well disposed to impress the natives with high notions of his extraordinary refinement and importance, he very soon discovered that, in Marston, he had stumbled upon a man of the world, and one thoroughly versed in the ways and characters of London life. After some ineffectual attempts, therefore, to overawe and astonish his host, Mr. Skelton became aware of the fruitlessness of the effort, and condescended to abate somewhat of his pretensions. Marston could not avoid inviting this person to pass the night at his house, an invitation which was accepted, of course; and next morning, after a late breakfast, Mr. Skelton observed, with a yawn—"And now, about this body—poor Berkley!—what do you propose to do with him?"

"I have no proposition to make," said Marston, drily. "It is no affair of mine, except that the body may be removed without more delay. I have no suggestion to offer."

"H——'s notion was to have him buried as near the spot as may be," said Skelton.

Marston nodded.

"There is a kind of vault, is not there, in the demesne, a family burial-place?" inquired the visitor.

"Yes, sir," replied Marston, curtly.

"Well?" drawled Skelton.

"Well, sir, what then?" responded Marston.

"Why, as the wish of the parties is to have him buried—poor fellow!—as quietly as possible, I think he might just as well be laid there as anywhere else!"

"Had I desired it, Mr. Skelton, I should myself have made the offer," said Marston, abruptly.

"Then you don't wish it?" said Skelton.

"No, sir; certainly not—most peremptorily not," answered Marston, with more sharpness than, in his early days, he would have thought quite consistent with politeness.

"Perhaps," replied Skelton, for want of something better to say, and with a callous sort of levity; "perhaps you hold the idea—some people do—that murdered men can't rest in their graves until their murderers have expiated their guilt?"

Marston made no reply, but shot two or three lurid glances from under his brow at the speaker.

"Well, then, at all events," continued Skelton, indolently resuming his theme, "if you decline your assistance, may I, at least, hope for your advice? Knowing nothing of this country, I would ask you whither you would recommend me to have the body conveyed?"

"I don't care to advise in the matter," said Marston; "but if I were directing, I should have the remains buried in Chester. It is not more than twenty miles from this; and if, at any future time, his family should desire to remove the body, it could be effected more easily from thence. But you can decide."

"Egad! I believe you are right," said Skelton, glad to be relieved of the trouble of thinking about the matter; "and I shall take your advice."

In accordance with this declaration the body was, within four-and-twenty hours, removed to Chester, and buried there, Mr. Skelton attending on behalf of Sir Wynston's numerous and afflicted friends and relatives.

There are certain heartaches for which time brings no healing; nay, which grow but the sorer and fiercer as days and years roll on; of this kind, perhaps, were the stern and bitter feelings which now darkened the face of Marston with an almost perpetual gloom. His habits became even more unsocial than before. The society of his son he no longer seemed to enjoy. Long and solitary rambles in his wild and extensive demesne consumed the listless hours or his waking existence; and when the weather prevented this, he shut himself up, upon pretence of business, in his study.

He had not, since the occasion we have already mentioned, referred to the intended departure of Mademoiselle de Barras. Truth to say, his feelings with respect to that young lady were of a conflicting and mysterious kind; and as often as his dark thoughts wandered to her (which, indeed, was frequently enough), his muttered exclamation seemed to imply some painful and horrible suspicions respecting her.

"Yes," he would mutter, "I thought I heard your light foot upon the lobby, on that accursed night. Fancy! Well, it may have been, but assuredly a strange fancy. I cannot comprehend that woman. She baffles my scrutiny. I have looked into her face with an eye she might well understand, were it indeed as I sometimes suspect, and she has been calm and unmoved. I have watched and studied her; still—doubt, doubt, hideous doubt!—is she what she seems, or—a tigress?"

Mrs. Marston, on the other hand, procrastinated from day to day the painful task of announcing to Mademoiselle de Barras the stern message with which she had been charged by her husband. And thus several weeks had passed, and she began to think that his silence upon the subject, notwithstanding his seeing the young French lady at breakfast every morning, amounted to a kind of tacit intimation that the sentence of banishment was not to be carried into immediate execution, but to be kept suspended over the unconscious offender.

It was now six or eight weeks since the hearse carrying away the remains of the ill-fated Sir Wynston Berkley had driven down the dusky avenue; the autumn was deepening into winter, and as Marston gloomily trod the woods of Gray Forest, the withered leaves whirled drearily along his pathway, and the gusts that swayed the mighty branches above him were rude and ungenial. It was a bleak and sombre day, and as he broke into a long and picturesque *vista*, deep among the most sequestered woods, he suddenly saw before him, and scarcely twenty paces from the spot on which he stood, an apparition, which for some moments absolutely froze him to the earth.

Travel-soiled, tattered, pale, and wasted, John Merton, the murderer, stood before him. He did not exhibit the smallest disposition to turn about and make his escape. On the contrary, he remained perfectly motionless, looking upon his former master with a wild and sorrowful gaze. Marston twice or thrice essayed to speak; his face was white as death, and had he beheld the spectre of the murdered baronet himself, he could not have met the sight with a countenance of ghastlier horror.

"Take me, sir," said Merton, doggedly.

Still Marston did not stir.

"Arrest me, sir, in God's name! here I am," he repeated, dropping his arms by his side; "I'll go with you wherever you tell me."

"Murderer!" cried Marston, with a sudden burst of furious horror, "murderer—assassin—miscreant—take that!"

And, as he spoke, he discharged one of the pistols he always carried about him full at the wretched man. The shot did not take effect, and Merton made no other gesture but to clasp his hands together, with an agonized pressure, while his head sunk upon his breast.

"Shoot me; shoot me," he said hoarsely; "kill me like a dog: better for me to be dead than what I am."

The report of Marston's pistol had, however, reached another ear; and its ringing echoes had hardly ceased to vibrate among the trees, when a stern shout was heard not fifty yards away, and, breathless and amazed, Charles Marston sprang to the place. His father looked from Merton to him, and from him again to Merton, with a guilty and stupefied scowl, still holding the smoking pistol in his hand.

"What—how! Good God—Merton!" ejaculated Charles.

"Aye, sir, Merton; ready to go to gaol, or wherever you will," said the man, recklessly.

"A murderer; a madman; don't believe him," muttered Marston, scarce audibly, with lips as white as wax.

"Do you surrender yourself, Merton?" demanded the young man, sternly, advancing toward him.

"Yes, sir; I desire nothing more; God knows I wish to die," responded he, despairingly, and advancing slowly to meet Charles.

"Come, then," said young Marston, seizing him by the collar, "come quietly to the house. Guilty and unhappy man, you are now my prisoner, and, depend upon it, I shall not let you go."

"I don't want to go, I tell you, sir. I have travelled fifteen miles today, to come here and give myself up to the master."

"Accursed madman," said Marston unconsciously, gazing at the prisoner; and then suddenly rousing himself, he said, "Well, miscreant, you wish to die, and, by ——, you are in a fair way to have your wish."

"So best," said the man, doggedly. "I don't want to live; I wish I was in my grave; I wish I was dead a year ago."

Some fifteen minutes afterwards, Merton, accompanied by Marston and his son Charles, entered the hall of the mansion which, not ten weeks before, he had quitted under circumstances so guilty and terrible. When they reached the house, Merton seemed much agitated, and wept bitterly on seeing two or three of his former fellow servants, who looked on him in silence as they passed, with a gloomy and fearful curiosity. These, too, were succeeded by others, peeping and whispering, and upon one pretence or another crossing and re-crossing the hall, and stealing hurried glances at the criminal.

Merton sate with his face buried in his hands, sobbing, and taking no note of the humiliating scrutiny of which he was the subject. Meanwhile Marston, pale and agitated, made out his committal, and having sworn in several of his labourers and servants as special constables, dispatched the prisoner in their charge to the county gaol, where, under lock and key, we leave him in safe custody for the present.

After this event Marston became excited and restless. He scarcely ate or slept, and his health seemed now as much scattered as his spirits had been before. One day he glided into the room in which, as we have said, it was Mrs. Marston's habit frequently to sit alone. His wife was there, and, as he entered, she uttered an exclamation of doubtful joy and surprise. He sate down near her in silence, and for some time looked gloomily on the ground. She did not care to question him, and anxiously waited until he should open the conversation. At length he raised his eyes, and, looking full at her, asked abruptly—"Well, what about *mademoiselle*?"

Mrs. Marston was embarrassed, and hesitated.

"I told you what I wished with respect to that young lady

some time ago, and commissioned you to acquaint her with my pleasure; and yet I find her still here, and apparently as much established as ever."

Again Mrs. Marston hesitated. She scarcely knew how to confess to him that she had not conveyed his message.

"Don't suppose, Gertrude, that I wish to find fault. I merely wanted to know whether you had told Mademoiselle de Barras that we were agreed as to the necessity or expediency, or what you please, of dispensing henceforward with her services, I perceive by your manner that you have not done so. I have no doubt your motive was a kind one, but my decision remains unaltered; and I now assure you again that I wish you to speak to her; I wish you explicitly to let her know my wishes and yours."

"Not mine, Richard," she answered faintly.

"Well, mine, then," he replied, roughly; "we shan't quarrel about that."

"And when—how soon—do you wish me to speak to her on this, to both of us, most painful subject?" asked she, with a sigh.

"Today—this hour—this minute, if you can; in short the sooner the better," he replied, rising. "I see no reason for holding it back any longer. I am sorry my wishes were not complied with immediately. Pray, let there be no further hesitation or delay. I shall expect to learn this evening that all is arranged."

Marston having thus spoken, left her abruptly, went down to his study with a swift step, shut himself in, and throwing himself into a great chair, gave a loose to his agitation, which was extreme.

Meanwhile Mrs. Marston had sent for Mademoiselle de Barras, anxious to get through her painful task as speedily as possible. The fair French girl quickly presented herself.

"Sit down, *mademoiselle*," said Mrs. Marston, taking her hand kindly, and drawing her to the *prie-dieu* chair beside herself.

Mademoiselle de Barras sate down, and, as she did so, read the countenance of her patroness with one rapid glance of her flashing eyes. These eyes, however, when Mrs. Marston looked at her the next moment, were sunk softly and sadly upon the floor. There was a heightened colour, however, in her cheek, and a quicker heaving of her bosom, which indicated the excitement of an anticipated and painful disclosure. The outward contrast of the two women, whose hands were so lovingly locked together, was almost as striking as the moral contrast of their hearts. The one, so chastened, sad, and gentle; the other, so capable of pride and passion; so darkly excitable, and yet so mysteriously beautiful. The one, like a Niobe seen in the softest moonshine; the other, a Venus, lighted in the glare of distant conflagration.

"*Mademoiselle*, dear *mademoiselle*, I am so much grieved at what I have to say, that I hardly know how to speak to you," said poor Mrs. Marston, pressing her hand; "but Mr. Marston has twice desired me to tell you, what you will hear with far less pain than it costs me to say it."

Mademoiselle de Barras stole another flashing glance at her companion, but did not speak.

"Mr. Marston still persists, *mademoiselle*, in desiring that we shall part."

"*Est-il possible?*" cried the Frenchwoman, with a genuine start.

"Indeed, *mademoiselle*, you may well be surprised," said Mrs. Marston, encountering her full and dilated gaze, which, however, dropped again in a moment to the ground. "You may, indeed, naturally be surprised and shocked at this, to me, most severe decision."

"When did he speak last of it?" said she, rapidly.

"But a few moments since," answered Mrs. Marston.

"Ha," said *mademoiselle*, and remained silent and motionless for more than a minute.

"*Madame*," she cried at last, mournfully, "I suppose, then, I must go; but it tears my heart to leave you and dear Miss Rhoda. I would be very happy if, before departing, you would permit me, dear *madame*, once more to assure Mr. Marston of my innocence, and, in his presence, to call heaven to witness how unjust are all his suspicions."

"Do so, *mademoiselle*, and I will add my earnest assurances again; though, heaven knows," she said, despondingly, "I anticipate little success; but it is well to leave no chance untried."

Marston was sitting, as we have said, in his library. His agitation had given place to a listless gloom, and he leaned back in his chair, his head supported by his hand, and undisturbed, except by the occasional fall of the embers upon the hearth. There was a knock at the chamber door. His back was towards it, and, without turning or moving, he called to the applicant to enter. The door opened—closed again: a light tread was audible—a tall shadow darkened the wall: Marston looked round, and Mademoiselle de Barras was standing before him. Without knowing how or why, he rose, and stood gazing upon her in silence.

"Mademoiselle de Barras!" he said, at last, in a tone of cold surprise.

"Yes, poor Mademoiselle de Barras," replied the sweet voice of the young Frenchwoman, while her lips hardly moved as the melancholy tones passed them.

"Well, *mademoiselle*, what do you desire?" he asked, in the same cold accents, and averting his eyes.

"Ah, *monsieur*, do you ask?—can you pretend to be ignorant? Have you not sent me a message, a cruel, cruel message?"

She spoke so low and gently, that a person at the other end of the room could hardly have heard her words.

"Yes, Mademoiselle de Barras, I did send you a message," he replied, doggedly. "A cruel one you will scarcely presume to call it, when you reflect upon your own conduct, and the circumstances which have provoked the measures I have taken."

"What have I done, *Monsieur*?—what circumstances do you mean?" asked she, plaintively.

"What have you done! A pretty question, truly. Ha, ha!" he repeated, bitterly, and then added, with suppressed vehemence, "ask your own heart, *mademoiselle*."

"I have asked, I do ask, and my heart answers—nothing," she replied, raising her fine melancholy eyes for a moment to his face.

"It lies, then," he retorted, with a fierce scoff.

"*Monsieur*, before heaven I swear, you wrong me foully," she said, earnestly, clasping her hands together.

"Did ever woman say she was accused rightly, *mademoiselle?*" retorted Marston, with a sneer.

"I don't know—I don't care. I only know that I am innocent," continued she, piteously. "I call heaven to witness you have wronged me."

"Wronged you!—why, after all, with what have I charged you?" said he, scoffingly; "but let that pass. I have formed my opinions, arrived at my conclusions. If I have not named them broadly, you at least seem to understand their nature thoroughly. I know the world. I am no novice in the arts of women, *mademoiselle*. Reserve your vows and attestations for schoolboys and simpletons; they are sadly thrown away upon me."

Marston paced to and fro, with his hands thrust into his pockets, as he thus spoke.

"Then you don't, or rather you will not believe what I tell you?" said she, imploringly. "No," he answered, drily and slowly, as he passed her. "I don't, and I won't (as you say) believe one word of it; so, pray spare yourself further trouble about the matter."

She raised her head, and darted after him a glance that seemed absolutely to blaze, and at the same time smote her little hand fast clenched upon her breast. The words, however, that trembled on her pale lips were not uttered; her eyes were again cast down, and her fingers played with the little locket that hung round her neck.

"I must make, before I go," she said, with a deep sigh and a melancholy voice, "one confidence—one last confidence: judge me by it. You cannot choose but believe me now: it is a secret, and it must even here be whispered, whispered, whispered!"

As she spoke, the colour fled from her face, and her tones became so strange and resolute, that Marston turned short upon his heel, and stopped before her. She looked in his face; he frowned, but lowered his eyes. She drew nearer, laid her hand upon his shoulder, and whispered for a few moments in his ear. He raised his face suddenly: its features were sharp and fixed; its hue was changed; it was livid and moveless, like a face cut in gray stone. He staggered back a little and a little more, and then a little more, and fell backward. Fortunately, the chair in which he had been sitting received him, and he lay there insensible as a corpse.

When at last his eyes opened, there was no gleam of triumph, no shade of anger, nothing perceptible of guilt or menace, in the young woman's countenance. The flush had returned to her cheeks; her dimpled chin had sunk upon her full white throat; sorrow, shame, and pride seemed struggling in her handsome face, and she stood before him like a beautiful penitent, who has just made a strange and humbling shrift to her father confessor.

Next day, Marston was mounting his horse for a solitary ride through his park, when Doctor Danvers rode abruptly into the courtyard from the back entrance. Marston touched his hat, and said—

"I don't stand on forms with you, doctor, and you, I know, will waive ceremony with me. You will find Mrs. Marston at home."

"Nay, my dear sir," interrupted the clergyman, sitting firm in his saddle, "my business lies with you today."

"The devil it does!" said Marston, with discontented surprise.

"Truly it does, sir," repeated he, with a look of gentle reproof, for the profanity of Marston's ejaculation, far more than the rudeness of his manner, offended him; "and I grieve that your surprise should have somewhat carried you away—"

"Well, then, Doctor Danvers," interrupted Marston, drily, and without heeding his concluding remark, "if you really have business with me, it is, at all events, of no very pressing kind, and may be as well told after supper as now. So, pray, go into the house and rest yourself: we can talk together in the evening."

"My horse is not tired," said the clergyman, patting his steed's neck; "and if you do not object, I will ride by your side for a short time, and as we go, I can say out what I have to tell."

"Well, well, be it so," said Marston, with suppressed impatience, and without more ceremony, he rode slowly along the avenue, and turned off upon the soft sward in the direction of the wildest portion of his wooded demesne, the clergyman keeping close beside him. They proceeded some little way at a walk before Doctor Danvers spoke.

"I have been twice or thrice with that unhappy man," at length he said.

"What unhappy man? Unhappiness is no distinguishing singularity, is it?" said Marston, sharply.

"No, truly, you have well said," replied Doctor Danvers. "True it is that man is born unto trouble as the sparks fly upward. I speak, however, of your servant, Merton—a most unhappy wretch."

"Ha! you have been with him, you say?" replied Marston, with evident interest and anxiety.

"Yes, several times, and conversed with him long and gravely," continued the clergyman.

"Humph! I thought that had been the chaplain's business, not yours, my good friend," observed Marston.

"He has been unwell," replied Dr. Danvers; "and thus, for a day or two, I took his duty, and this poor man, Merton, having known something of me, preferred seeing me rather than a stranger; and so, at the chaplain's desire and his, I continued my visits."

"Well, and you have taught him to pray and sing psalms, I suppose; and what has come of it all?" demanded Marston, testily.

"He does pray, indeed, poor man! and I trust his prayers are heard with mercy at the throne of grace," said his companion, in his earnestness disregarding the sneering tone of his companion. "He is full of compunction, and admits his guilt."

"Ho! that is well—well for himself—well for his soul, at least; you are sure of it; he confesses; confesses his guilt?"

Marston put his question so rapidly and excitedly, that the

clergyman looked with a slight expression of surprise; and recovering himself, he added, in an unconcerned tone—

"Well, well—it was just as well he did so; the evidence is too clear for doubt or mystification; he knew he had no chance, and has taken the seemliest course; and, doubtless, the best for his hopes hereafter."

"I did not question him upon the subject," said Doctor Danvers; "I even declined to hear him speak upon it at first; but he told me he was resolved to offer no defence, and that he saw the finger of God in the fate which had overtaken him."

"He will plead guilty, then, I suppose?" suggested Marston, watching the countenance of his companion with an anxious and somewhat sinister eye.

"His words seem to imply so much," answered he; "and having thus frankly owned his guilt, and avowed his resolution to let the law take its due course in his case, without obstruction or evasion, I urged him to complete the grand work he had begun, and to confess to you, or to some other magistrate fully, and in detail, every circumstance connected with the perpetration of the dreadful deed."

Marston knit his brows, and rode on for some minutes in silence. At length he said, abruptly—

"In this, it seems to me, sir, you a little exceeded your commission."

"How so, my dear sir?" asked the clergyman.

"Why, sir," answered Marston, "the man may possibly change his mind before the day of trial, and it is the hangman's office, not yours, my good sir, to fasten the halter about his neck. You will pardon my freedom; but, were this deposition made as you suggest, it would undoubtedly hang him."

"God forbid, Mr. Marston," rejoined Danvers, "that I should induce the unhappy man to forfeit his last chances of escape, and to shut the door of human mercy against himself, but on this he seems already resolved; he says so; he has solemnly declared his resolution to me; and even against my warning, again and again reiterated the same declaration."

"That I should have thought quite enough, were I in your place, without inviting a detailed description of the whole process by which this detestable butchery was consummated. What more than the simple knowledge of the man's guilt does any mortal desire; guilty, or not guilty, is the plain question which the law asks, and no more; take my advice, sir, as a poor Protestant layman, and leave the acts of the confessional and inquisition to Popish priests."

"Nay, Mr. Marston, you greatly misconceive me; as matters stand, there exists among the coroner's jury, and thus among the public, some faint and unfounded suspicion of the possibility of Merton's having had an accessory or accomplice in the perpetration of this foul murder."

"It is a lie, sir—a malignant, d——d lie—the jury believe no such thing, nor the public neither," said Marston, starting in his saddle, and speaking in a voice of thunder; "you have been crammed with lies, sir; malicious, unmeaning, vindictive lies; lies invented to asperse my family, and torture my feelings; suggested in my presence by that scoundrel Mervyn, and scouted by the common sense of the jury."

"I do assure you," replied Doctor Danvers, in a voice which seemed scarcely audible, after the stunning and passionate explosion of Marston's wrath, "I did not imagine that you could feel thus sorely upon the point; nay, I thought that you yourself were not without such painful doubts."

"Again, I tell you, sir," said Marston, in a tone somewhat calmer, but no less stern, "such doubts as you describe have no existence; your unsuspecting ear has been alarmed by a vindictive wretch, an old scoundrel who has scarce a passion left but spite towards me; few such there are, thank God; few such villains as would, from a man's very calamities, distil poison to kill the peace and character of his family."

"I am sorry, Mr. Marston," said the clergyman, "you have formed so ill an opinion of a neighbour, and I am very sure that Mr. Mervyn meant you no ill in frankly expressing whatever doubts still rested on his mind, after the evidence was taken."

"He did—the scoundrel!" said Marston, furiously striking his hand, in which his whip was clutched, upon his thigh; "he did mean to wound and torture me; and with the same object he persists in circulating what he calls his doubts. Meant me no ill, forsooth! why, my great God, sir, could any man be so stupid as not to perceive that the suggestion of such suspicions—absurd, contradictory, incredible as they were—was precisely the thing to exasperate feelings sufficiently troubled already, and not content with raising the question, where it was scouted, as I said, as soon as named, the vindictive slanderer proceeds to propagate and publish his pretended surmises—d——n him."

"Mr. Marston, you will pardon me when I say that, as a Christian minister, I cannot suffer a spirit so ill as that you manifest, and language so unseemly as that you have just uttered, to pass unreproved," said Danvers, solemnly. "If you will cherish those bitter and unchristian feelings, at least for the brief space that I am with you, command your fierce, unbecoming words."

Marston was about to make a sneering retort, but restrained himself, and turned his head away.

"The wretched man himself appears now very anxious to make some further disclosures," resumed Doctor Danvers, after a pause, "and I recommended him to make them to you, Mr. Marston, as the most natural depository of such a statement."

"Well, Mr. Danvers, to cut the matter short, as it appears that a confession of some sort is to be made, be it so. I will attend and receive it. The judges will not be here for eight or ten weeks to come, so there is no great hurry about it. I shall ride down to the town, and see him in the jail sometime in the next week."

With this assurance Marston parted from the old clergyman, and rode on alone through the furze and fern of his wild and sombre park.

After supper that evening Marston found himself alone in the parlour with his wife. Mrs. Marston availed herself of the opportunity to redeem her pledge to Mademoiselle de Barras. She was not aware of the strange interview which had taken place between him and the lady for whom she pleaded. The result of her renewed entreaties perhaps the reader has anticipated. Marston listened, doubted, listened, hesitated again, put questions, pondered the answers; debated the matter inwardly, and at last gruffly consented to give the young lady another trial, and permit her to remain some time longer. Poor Mrs. Marston, little suspecting the dreadful future, overwhelmed her husband with gratitude for granting to her entreaties (as he had predetermined to do) this fatal boon.

Not caring to protract this scene—either from a disinclination to listen to expressions of affection, which had long lost their charm for him, and had become even positively distasteful, or perhaps from some instinctive recoil from the warm expression of gratitude from lips which, were the truth revealed, might justly have trembled with execration and reproach—he abruptly left the room, and Mrs. Marston, full of her good news, hastened, in the kindness of her heart, to communicate the fancied result of her advocacy to Mademoiselle de Barras.

It was about a week after this, that Marston was one evening surprised in his study by the receipt of the following letter from Dr. Danvers:—

My Dear Sir,
You will be shocked to hear that Merton is most dangerously ill, and at this moment in imminent peril. He is thoroughly conscious of his situation, and himself regards it as a merciful interposition of Providence to spare him the disgrace and terror of the dreadful fate, which he anticipated. The unhappy man has twice repeated his anxious desire, this day, to state some facts connected with the murder of the late Sir Wynston Berkley, which, he says, it is of the utmost moment that you should hear. He says that he could not leave the world in peace without having made this disclosure, which he especially desires to make to yourself, and entreats that you will come to receive his communication as early as you can in the morning. This is indeed needful, as the physician says that he is fast sinking. I offer no apology for adding my earnest solicitations to

those or the dying man; and am, dear sir, your very obedient servant,

J. Danvers

"He regards it as a merciful interposition of Providence," muttered Marston, as he closed the letter, with a sneer. "Well, some men have odd notions of mercy and providence, to be sure; but if it pleases him, certainly I shall not complain for one."

Marston was all this evening in better spirits than he had enjoyed for months, or even years. A mountain seemed to have been lifted from his heart. He joined in the conversation during and after supper, listened with apparent interest, talked with animation, and even laughed and jested. It is needless to say all this flowed not from the healthy cheer of a heart at ease, but from the excited and almost feverish sense of sudden relief.

Next morning, Marston rode into the old-fashioned town, at the further end of which the dingy and grated front of the jail looked warningly out upon the rustic passengers. He passed the sentries and made his inquiries of the official at the hatch. He was relieved from the necessity of pushing these into detail, however, by the appearance of the physician, who at that moment passed from the interior of the prison.

"Dr. Danvers told me he expected to see you here this morning," said the medical man, after the customary salutation had been interchanged. "Your call, I believe, is connected with the prisoner, John Merton?"

"Yes, sir, so it is," said Marston. "Is he in a condition, pray, to make a statement of considerable length?"

"Far from it, Mr. Marston; he has but a few hours to live," answered the physician, "and is now insensible; but I believe he last night saw Dr. Danvers, and told him whatever was weighing upon his mind."

"Ha!—And can you say where Dr. Danvers now is?" inquired Marston, anxiously and hurriedly. "Not here, is he?"

"No; but I saw him, as I came here, not ten minutes since, ride into the town. It is market-day, and you will probably find him somewhere in the high street for an hour or two to come," answered he.

Marston thanked him, and, lost in abstraction, rode down to the little inn, entered a sitting room, and wrote a hurried line to Dr. Danvers, entreating his attendance there, as a place where they might converse less interruptedly than in the street; and committing this note to the waiter, with the injunction to deliver it at once, and an intimation of where Dr. Danvers was probably to be found, he awaited, with intense and agitating anxiety, the arrival of the clergyman.

It was not for nearly ten minutes, however, which his impatience magnified into an eternity, that the well-known voice of Dr. Danvers reached him from the little hall. It was in vain that Marston strove to curb his violent agitation: his heart swelled as if it would smother him; he felt, as it were, the chill of death pervade his frame, and he could scarcely see the door through which he momentarily expected the entrance of the clergyman.

A few minutes more, and Dr. Danvers entered the little apartment.

"My dear sir," said he, gravely and earnestly, as he grasped the cold hand of Marston, "I am rejoiced to see you. I have matters of great moment and the strangest mystery to lay before you."

"I dare say—I was sure—that is, I suspected so much," answered Marston, breathing fast, and looking very pale. "I heard at the prison that the murderer, Merton, was fast dying, and now is in an unconscious state; and from the physician, that you had seen him, at his urgent entreaty, last night. My mind misgives me, sir, I fear I know not what. I long, yet dread, to hear the wretched man's confession. For God's sake tell me, does it implicate anybody else in the guilt?"

"No; no one specifically; but it has thrown a hideous additional mystery over the occurrence. Listen to me, my dear sir, and the whole narrative, as he stated it to me, shall be related now to you," said Dr. Danvers.

Marston had closed the door carefully, and they sate down together at the further end of the apartment. Marston, breathless and ghastly pale; his lips compressed—his brows knit—and his dark, dilated gaze fixed immovably upon the speaker. Dr. Danvers, on the other hand, tranquil and solemn, and with, perhaps, some shade of awe overcasting the habitual sweetness of his countenance.

"His confession was a strange one," renewed Dr. Danvers, shaking his head gravely. "He said that the first idea of the crime was suggested by Sir Wynston's man accidentally mentioning, a few days after their arrival, that his master slept with his bank-notes, to the amount of some hundreds of pounds, in a pocket-book under his pillow. He declared that as the man mentioned this circumstance, something muttered the infernal suggestion in his ear, and from that moment he was the slave of that one idea; it was ever present with him. He contended against it in vain; he dreaded and abhorred it; but still it possessed him; he felt his power of resistance yielding.

"This horrible stranger which had stolen into his heart, waxed in power and importunity, and tormented him day and night. He resolved to fly from the house. He gave notice to you and Mrs. Marston of his intended departure; but accident protracted his stay until that fatal night which sealed his doom. The influence which had mastered him forced him to rise from his bed, and take the knife—the discovery of which afterwards helped to convict him—and led him to Sir Wynston's chamber; he entered; it was a moonlight night."

Here the clergyman, glancing round the room, lowered his voice, and advanced his lips so near to Marston, that their heads nearly touched. In this tone and attitude he continued his narrative for a few minutes. At the end of this brief space, Marston rose up slowly, and with a movement backward, every feature strung with horror, and saying, in a long whisper, the one word, "yes," which seemed like the hiss of a snake before he makes his last deadly spring. Both were silent for a time. At last Marston broke out with hoarse vehemence.

"Dreadful—horrible—oh, God! God!—My God! How frightful!"

And throwing himself into a chair, he clasped his hands across his eyes and forehead, while the sweat of agony literally poured down his pale face.

"Truly it is so," said the clergyman, scarcely above his breath; and, after a long interval—"horrible indeed!"

"Well," said Marston, rising suddenly to his feet, wiping the dews of horror from his face, and looking wildly round, like one newly awoke from a nightmare, "I must make the most of this momentous and startling disclosure. I shall spare no pains to come at the truth," said he, energetically. "Meanwhile, my dear sir, for the sake of justice and of mercy, observe secrecy. Leave me to sift this matter; give no note anywhere that we suspect. Observe this reserve and security, and with it detection will follow. Breathe but one word, and you arm the guilty with double caution, and turn licentious gossip loose upon the fame of an innocent and troubled family. Once more I entreat—I expect—I implore silence—silence, at least, for the present—silence!"

"I quite agree with you, my dear Mr. Marston," answered Dr. Danvers. "I have not divulged one syllable of that poor wretch's confession, save to yourself alone. You, as a magistrate, a relative of the murdered gentleman, and the head of that establishment among whom the guilt rests, are invested with an interest in detecting, and powers of sifting the truth in this matter, such as none other possesses. I clearly see, with you, too, the inexpediency and folly of talking, for talking's sake, of this affair. I mean to keep my counsel, and shall most assuredly, irrespectively even of your request—which should, however, of course, have weight with me—maintain a strict and cautious silence upon this subject."

Some little time longer they remained together, and Marston, buried in strange thoughts, took his leave, and rode slowly back to Gray Forest.

Months passed away—a year, and more—and though no new character appeared upon the stage, the relations which had subsisted among the old ones became, in some respects, very materially altered. A gradual and disagreeable change came over

Mademoiselle de Barras's manner; her affectionate attentions to Mrs. Marston became less and less frequent; nor was the change merely confined to this growing coldness; there was something of a positive and still more unpleasant kind in the alteration we have noted. There was a certain independence and carelessness, conveyed in a hundred intangible but significant little incidents and looks—a something which, without being open to formal rebuke or remonstrance, yet bordered, in effect, upon impertinence, and even insolence.

This indescribable and provoking self-assertion, implied in glances, tones, emphasis, and general bearing, surprised Mrs. Marston far more than it irritated her. As often as she experienced one of these studied slights or insinuated impertinences, she revolved in her own mind all the incidents of their past intercourse, in the vain endeavour to recollect someone among them which could possibly account for the offensive change so manifest in the conduct of the young Frenchwoman.

Mrs. Marston, although she sometimes rebuked these artful affronts by a grave look, a cold tone, or a distant manner, yet had too much dignity to engage in a petty warfare of annoyance, and had, in reality, no substantial and well-defined ground of complaint against her, such as would have warranted her either in taking the young lady herself to task, or in bringing her conduct under the censure of Marston.

One evening, it happened that Mrs. Marston and Mademoiselle de Barras had been left alone together. After the supper-party had dispersed, they had been for a long time silent. Mrs. Marston resolved to improve the *Tate-à-Tate*, for the purpose of eliciting from *mademoiselle* an explanation of her strange behaviour.

"*Mademoiselle*," said she, "I have lately observed a very marked change in your conduct to me."

"Indeed!" said the Frenchwoman.

"Yes, *mademoiselle*; you must be yourself perfectly aware of that change; it is a studied and intentional one," continued Mrs. Marston, in a gentle but dignified tone. "Although I have felt some doubt as to whether it were advisable, so long as you observe toward me the forms of external respect, and punctually discharge the duties you have undertaken, to open any discussion whatever upon the subject; yet I have thought it better to give you a fair opportunity of explaining frankly, should you desire to do so, the feelings and impressions under which you are acting."

"Ah, you are very obliging, *madame*," said she, coolly.

"It is quite clear, *mademoiselle*, that you have either misunderstood me, or that you are dissatisfied with your situation among us: your conduct cannot otherwise be accounted for," said Mrs. Marston, gravely.

"My conduct—*ma foi!* what conduct?" retorted the handsome Frenchwoman, confidently, and with a disdainful glance.

"If you question the fact, *mademoiselle*," said the elder lady, "it is enough. Your ungracious manner and ungentle looks, I presume, arise from what appears to you a sufficient and well-defined cause, of which, however, I know nothing."

"I really was not aware," said Mademoiselle de Barras, with a supercilious smile, "that my looks and my manner were subjected to so strict a criticism, or that it was my duty to regulate both according to so nice and difficult a standard."

"Well, *mademoiselle*," continued Mrs. Marston, "it is plain that whatever may be the cause of your dissatisfaction, you are resolved against confiding it to me. I only wish to know frankly from your own lips, whether you have formed a wish to leave this situation. If so, I entreat you to declare it freely."

"You are very obliging, indeed, *madame*," said the pretty foreigner, drily, "but I have no such wish, at least at present."

"Very well, *mademoiselle*," replied Mrs. Marston, with gentle dignity; "I regret your want of candour, on your own account. You would, I am sure, be much happier, were you to deal frankly with me."

"May I now have your permission, *madame*, to retire to my room?" asked the French girl, rising, and making a low courtesy—"that is, if *madame* has nothing further to censure."

"Certainly, *mademoiselle*; I have nothing further to say," replied the elder lady.

The Frenchwoman made another and a deeper courtesy, and withdrew. Mrs. Marston, however, heard, as she was designed to do, the young lady tittering and whispering to herself, as she lighted her candle in the hall. This scene mortified and grieved poor Mrs. Marston inexpressibly. She was little, if at all, accessible to emotions of anger and certainly, none such mingled in the feelings with which she regarded Mademoiselle de Barras. But she had found in this girl a companion, and even a confidante in her melancholy solitude; she had believed her affectionate, sympathetic, tender, and the disappointment was as bitter as un-imagined.

The annoyances which she was fated to receive from Mad-emoiselle de Barras were destined, however, to grow in number and in magnitude. The Frenchwoman sometimes took a fan-cy, for some unrevealed purpose, to talk a good deal to Mrs. Marston, and on such occasions would persist, notwithstanding that lady's marked reserve and discouragement, in chatting away, as if she were conscious that her conversation was the most wel-come entertainment possible to her really unwilling auditor. No one of their interviews did she ever suffer to close without in some way or other suggesting or insinuating something mysteri-ous and untold to the prejudice of Mr. Marston.

Those vague and intangible hints, the meaning of which, for an instant legible and terrific, seemed in another moment to dissolve and disappear, tortured Mrs. Marston like the intrusion of a spectre; and this, along with the portentous change, rather felt than visible, in *mademoiselle's* conduct toward her, invested the beautiful Frenchwoman, in the eyes of her former friend and patroness, with an indefinable character that was not only repulsive but formidable.

Mrs. Marston's feelings with respect to this person were still further disturbed by the half-conveyed hints and innuendoes of her own maid, who never lost an opportunity of insinuating her intense dislike of the Frenchwoman, and appeared perpetually to be upon the very verge of making some explicit charges, or some shocking revelations, respecting her, which, however, she as invariably evaded; and even when Mrs. Marston once or twice insisted upon her explaining her meaning distinctly, she eluded her mistress's desire, and left her still in the same uneasy uncertainty.

Marston, on his part, however much his conduct might tend to confirm suspicion, certainly did nothing to dissipate the painful and undefined apprehension respecting himself, which Mademoiselle de Barras, with such malign and mysterious industry, laboured to raise. His spirits and temper were liable to strange fluctuations. In the midst of that excited gaiety, to which, until lately, he had been so long a stranger, would sometimes intervene paroxysms of the blackest despair, all the ghastlier for the contrast, and with a suddenness so abrupt and overwhelming, that one might have fancied him crossed by the shadow of some terrific apparition.

Sometimes for a whole day, or even more, he would withdraw himself from the society of his family, and, in morose and moody solitude, take his meals alone in his library, and steal out unattended to wander among the thickets and glades of his park. Sometimes, again, he would sit for hours in the room which had been Sir Wynston's, and, with a kind of horrible resolution, often loiter there till after nightfall. In such hours, the servants would listen with curious awe, as they heard his step, pacing to and fro, in that deserted and inauspicious chamber, while his voice, in broken sentences, was also imperfectly audible, as if maintaining a muttered dialogue.

These eccentric practices gradually invested him, in the eyes of his domestics, with a certain preternatural mystery, which enhanced the fear with which they habitually regarded him, and was subsequently confirmed by his giving orders to have the furniture taken out of the ominous suite of rooms, and the doors nailed up and secured. He gave no reason for this odd and abrupt measure, and gossip of course reported that the direction had originated in his having encountered the spectre of the murdered baronet, in one of these strange and unseasonable visits to the scene of the fearful catastrophe.

In addition to all this, Marston's conduct towards his wife became strangely capricious. He avoided her society more than ever; and when he did happen to exchange a few words with her, they were sometimes harsh and violent, and at others remorsefully gentle and sad, and this without any changes of conduct upon her part to warrant the wayward uncertainty of his treatment. Under all these circumstances, Mrs. Marston's unhappiness and uneasiness greatly increased. Mademoiselle de Barras, too, upon several late occasions, had begun to assume a tone of authority and dictation, which justly offended the mistress of the establishment. Meanwhile Charles Marston had returned to Cambridge; and Rhoda, no longer enjoying happy walks with her brother, pursued her light and easy studies with Mademoiselle de Barras, and devoted her leisure hours to the loved society of her mother.

One day Mrs. Marston, sitting in her room with Rhoda, had happened to call her own maid, to take down and carefully dust some richly bound volumes which filled a bookcase in the little chamber.

"You have been crying, Willett," said Mrs. Marston, observing that the young woman's eyes were red and swollen.

"Indeed, and I was, ma'am," she replied, reluctantly, "and I could not help it, so I could not."

"Why, what has happened to vex you? Has anyone ill-treated you?" said Mrs. Marston, who had an esteem for the poor girl. "Come, come, you must not fret about it; only tell me what has vexed you."

"Oh! Ma'am, no one has ill-used me, ma'am; but I can't but be vexed sometimes, ma'am, and fretted to see how things is going on. I have one wish, just one wish, ma'am, and if I got that, I'd ask no more," said the girl.

"And what is it?" asked Mrs. Marston; "what do you wish for? Speak plainly, Willett; what is it?"

"Ah! Ma'am, if I said it, maybe you might not be pleased.

Don't ask me, ma'am," said the girl dusting the books very hard, and tossing them down again with angry emphasis. "I don't desire anybody's harm, God knows; but, for all that, I wish what I wish, and that is the truth."

"Why, Willett, I really cannot account for your strange habit of lately hinting, and insinuating, and always speaking riddles, and refusing to explain your meaning. What do you mean? Speak plainly. If there are any dishonest practices going on, it is your duty to say so distinctly."

"Oh! Ma'am, it is just a wish I have. I wish—; but it's no matter. If I could once see the house clear of that Frenchwoman—"

"If you mean Mademoiselle de Barras, she is a lady," interrupted Mrs. Marston.

"Well, ma'am, I beg pardon," continued the woman; "lady or no lady, it is all one to me; for I am very sure, ma'am, she'll never leave the house till there is something bad comes about; and—and—. I can't bring myself to talk to you about her, ma'am. I can't say what I want to tell you: but—but—. Oh, ma'am, for God's sake, try and get her out, any way, no matter how; try and get rid of her."

As she said this, the poor girl burst into a passionate agony of tears, and Mrs. Marston and Rhoda looked on in silent amazement, while she for some minutes continued to sob and weep.

The party were suddenly recalled from their various reveries by a knock at the chamber-door. It opened, and the subject of the girl's deprecatory entreaty entered. There was something unusually excited and assured in Mademoiselle de Barras's air and countenance; perhaps she had a suspicion that she had been the topic of their conversation. At all events, she looked round upon them with a smile, in which there was something supercilious, and even defiant; and, without waiting to be invited, sate herself down, with a haughty air.

"I was about to ask you to sit down, *mademoiselle*, but you have anticipated me," said Mrs. Marston, gravely. "You have something to say to me, I suppose; I am quite at leisure, so pray let me hear it now."

"Thank you, thank you, *madame*," replied she, with a sharp, and even scornful glance; "I ought to have asked your permission to sit; I forgot; but you have condescended to give it without my doing so; that was very kind, very kind, indeed."

"But I wish to know, *mademoiselle*, whether you have anything very particular to say to me?" said Mrs. Marston.

"You wish to know!—and why, pray *madame*?" asked Mademoiselle de Barras, sharply.

"Because, unless it is something very urgent, I should prefer your talking to me some other time; as, at present, I desire to be alone with my daughter."

"Oh, ho! I ought to ask pardon again," said *mademoiselle*, with the same glance, and the same smile. "I find I am *de trop*☐quite in the way. *Hélas*! I am very unfortunate today."

Mademoiselle de Barras made not the slightest movement, and it was evident that she was resolved to prolong her stay, in sheer defiance of Mrs. Marston's wishes.

"*Mademoiselle*, I conclude from your silence that you have nothing very pressing to say, and, therefore, must request that you will have the goodness to leave me for the present," said Mrs. Marston, who felt that the spirit of the French girl's conduct was too apparent not to have been understood by Rhoda and the servant, and that it was of a kind, for example sake, impossible to be submitted to, or tolerated.

Mademoiselle de Barras darted a fiery and insolent glance at Mrs. Marston, and was, doubtless, upon the point of precipitating the open quarrel which was impending, by setting her authority at defiance; but she checked herself, and changed her line of operations.

"We are not alone *madame*," she said, with a heightened colour, and a slight toss of the head. "I was about to speak of Mr. Marston. I had something, not much, I confess, to say; but before servants I shan't speak; nor, indeed, now at all. So, *madame*, as you desire it, I shall no further interrupt you. Come, Miss Rhoda, come to the music-room, if you please, and finish your practice for today."

"You forget, *mademoiselle*, that I wish to have my daughter with me at present," said Mrs. Marston.

"I am very sorry, *madame*," said the French lady, with the same heightened colour and unpleasant smile, and her finely-penciled brows just discernibly knit, so as to give a novel and menacing expression to her beautiful face—"I am very sorry, *madame*, but she must, so long as I remain accountable for her education, complete her allotted exercises at the appointed hours; and nothing shall, I assure you, with my consent, interfere with these duties. Come, Miss Rhoda, precede me, if you please, to the music-room. Come, come."

"Stay where you are, Rhoda," said Mrs. Marston, firmly and gently, and betraying no symptom of excitement, except in a slight tremor of her voice, and a faint flush upon her cheek- "Stay where you are, my dear child. I am your mother, and, next to your father, have the first claim upon your obedience. *Mademoiselle*," she continued, addressing the Frenchwoman, calmly but firmly, "my daughter will remain here for some time longer, and you will have the goodness to withdraw. I insist upon it, Mademoiselle de Barras."

"I will not leave the room, I assure you, *madame*, without my pupil," retorted *mademoiselle*, with resolute insolence. "Your husband, *madame*, has invested me with this authority, and she shall obey me. Miss Rhoda, I say again, go down to the music-room."

"Remain where you are, Rhoda," said Mrs. Marston again. "*Mademoiselle*; you have long been acting as if your object were to provoke me to part with you. I find it impossible any longer to overlook this grossly disrespectful conduct; conduct of which I had, indeed, believed you absolutely incapable. Willett," she continued, addressing the maid, who was evidently bursting with rage at the scene she had just witnessed, "your master is, I believe, in the library; go down, and tell him that I entreat him to come here immediately."

The maid started on her mission with angry alacrity, dart-ing a venomous glance at the handsome Frenchwoman as she passed.

Mademoiselle de Barras, meanwhile, sate, listless and defiant, in her chair, and tapping her little foot with angry excitement upon the floor. Rhoda sate close by her mother, holding her hand fast, and looking frightened, perplexed, and as if she were on the point of weeping. Mrs. Marston, though flushed and excited, yet maintained her dignified and grave demeanour. And thus, in silence, did they all three await the arrival of the arbiter to whom Mrs. Marston had so promptly appealed.

A few minutes more, and Marston entered the room. *Mademoiselle's* expression changed as he did so to one of dejected and sorrowful submission; and, as Marston's eye lighted upon her, his brow darkened and his face grew pale.

"Well, well—what is it?—What is all this?" he said, glancing with a troubled eye from one to the other. "Speak, someone. Mrs. Marston, you sent for me; what is it?"

"I want to know, Mr. Marston, from your own lips," said the lady, in reply, "whether Rhoda is to obey me or Mademoiselle de Barras?"

"Bah!—A question of women's prerogative," said Marston, with muttered vehemence.

"Of a wife's and a mother's prerogative, Richard," said Mrs. Marston, with gentle emphasis. "A very simple question, and one I should have thought needing no deliberation to decide it."

"Well, child," sad he, turning to Rhoda, with angry irony, "pray what is all this fuss about? You are a very ill used young lady, I dare aver. Pray what cruelties does Mademoiselle de Barras propose inflicting upon you, that you need to appeal thus to your mother for protection?"

"You quite mistake me, Richard," interposed Mrs. Marston; "Rhoda is perfectly passive in the matter. I simply wish to learn from you, in *mademoiselle's* presence, whether I or she is to command my daughter?"

"Command!" said Marston, evading the direct appeal; "and

pray what is all this commanding about?—What do you want the girl to do?"

"I wish her to remain here with me for a little time, and *mademoiselle*, knowing this, desires her instantly to go to the music-room, and leave me. That is all," said Mrs. Marston.

"And pray, is there nothing to make her going to the music-room advisable or necessary? Has she no music to learn, or studies to pursue? Pshaw! Mrs. Marston, what needs all this noise about nothing? Go, miss," he added, sharply and peremptorily, addressing Rhoda, "go this moment to the music-room."

The girl glided from the room, and *mademoiselle*, as she followed, shot a glance at Mrs. Marston which wounded and humbled her in the dust.

"Oh! Richard, Richard, if you knew all, you would not have subjected me to this indignity," she said; and throwing her arms about his neck, she wept, for the first time for many a long year, upon his breast.

Marston was embarrassed and agitated. He disengaged her arms from his neck, and placed her gently in a chair. She sobbed on for some time in silence—a silence which Marston himself did not essay to break. He walked to the door, apparently with the intention of leaving her. He hesitated however, and returned; took a hurried turn through the room; hesitated again; sat down; then returned to the door, not to depart, but to close it carefully, and walked gloomily to the window, whence he looked forth, buried in agitating and absorbing thoughts.

"Richard, to you this seems a trifling thing; but, indeed it is not so," said Mrs. Marston, sadly.

"You are very right, Gertrude," he said, quickly, and almost with a start; "it is very far from a trifling thing; it is very important."

"You don't blame me, Richard?" said she.

"I blame nobody," said he.

"Indeed, I never meant to offend you, Richard," she urged.

"Of course not; no, no; I never said so," he interrupted, sarcastically; "what could you gain by that?"

"Oh! Richard, better feelings have governed me," she said, in a melancholy and reproachful tone.

"Well, well, I suppose so," he said; and after an interval, he added abstractedly, "This cannot, however, go on; no, no—it cannot. Sooner or later it must have come; better at once-better now."

"What do you mean, Richard?" she said, greatly alarmed, she knew not why. "What are you resolving upon? Dear Richard, in mercy tell me. I implore of you, tell me."

"Why, Gertrude, you seem to me to fancy that, because I don't talk about what is passing, that I don't see it either. Now this is quite a mistake," said Marston, calmly and resolutely—"I have long observed your growing dislike of Mademoiselle de Barras. I have thought it over; this fracas of today has determined me; it is decisive. I suppose you now wish her to go, as earnestly as you once wished her to stay. You need not answer. I know it. I neither ask nor care to whose fault I am to attribute these changed feelings—female caprice accounts sufficiently for it; but whatever the cause, the effect is undeniable; and the only way to deal satisfactorily with it is, to dismiss *mademoiselle* at once. You need take no part in the matter; I take it upon myself. Tomorrow morning she shall have left this house. I have said it, and am perfectly resolved."

As he thus spoke, as if to avoid the possibility of any further discussion, he turned abruptly from her, and left the room.

The extreme agitation which she had just undergone combined with her physical delicacy to bring on an hysterical attack; and poor Mrs. Marston, with an aching head and a heavy heart, lay down upon her bed. She had swallowed an opiate, and before ten o'clock upon that night, an eventful one as it proved, she had sunk into a profound slumber.

Some hours after this, she became in a confused way conscious of her husband's presence in the room. He was walking, with an agitated mien, up and down the chamber, and casting from time to time looks of great trouble toward the bed where she lay. Though the presence of her husband was a strange and long unwonted occurrence there, at such an hour, and though she felt the strangeness of the visit, the power of the opiate overwhelmed her so, that she could only see this apparition gliding slowly back and forward before her, with the passive wonder and curiosity with which one awaits the issue of an interesting dream.

For a time she lay once more in an uneasy sleep; but still, throughout even this, she was conscious of his presence; and when, a little while after, she again saw him, he was not walking to and fro before the foot of the bed, but sitting beside her, with one hand laid upon the pillow on which her head was resting, the other supporting his chin. He was looking steadfastly upon her, with a changed face, an expression of bitter sorrow, compunction, and tenderness. There was not one trace of sternness; all was softened. The look was what she fancied he might have turned upon her had she lain there dead, ere yet the love of their early and ill-fated union had grown cold in his heart.

There was something in it which reminded her of days and feelings gone, never to return. And while she looked in his face with a sweet and mournful fascination, tears unconsciously wet the pillow on which her poor head was resting. Unable to speak, unable to move, she heard him say—"It was not your fault, Gertrude—it was not yours, nor mine. There is a destiny in these things too strong for us. Past is past—what is done, is done forever; and even were it all to do over again, what power have I to mend it? No, no; how could I contend against the combined power of passions, circumstances, influences—in a word, of fate? You have been good and patient, while I—; but no matter. Your lot, Gertrude, is a happier one than mine."

Mrs. Marston heard him and saw him, but she had not the power, nor even the will, herself to speak or move. He appeared before her passive sense like the phantasm of a dream. He stood up at the bedside, and looked on her steadfastly, with the same melancholy expression. For a moment he stooped over her, as if about to kiss her face, but checked himself, stood erect again at the bedside, then suddenly turned; the curtain fell back into its place, and she saw him no more.

With a strange mixture of sweet and bitter feelings this vision rested upon the memory of Mrs. Marston, until, gradually, deep slumber again overcame her senses, and the incident and all its attendant circumstances faded into oblivion.

It was past eight o'clock when Mrs. Marston awoke next morning. The sun was shining richly and cheerily in at the windows; and as the remembrance of Marston's visit to her chamber, and the unwonted manifestations of tenderness and compunction which accompanied it, returned, she felt something like hope and happiness, to which she had long been a stranger, flutter her heart. The pleasing reverie to which she was yielding was, however, interrupted. The sound of stifled sobbing in the room reached her ear, and, pushing back the bed-curtains, and leaning forward to look, she saw her maid, Willett, sitting with her back to the wall, crying bitterly, and striving, as it seemed, to stifle her sobs with her apron, which was wrapped about her face.

"Willet, Willett, is it you who are sobbing? What is the matter with you, child?" said Mrs. Marston, anxiously.

The girl checked herself, dried her eyes hastily, and walking briskly to a little distance, as if engaged in arranging the chamber, she said, with an affectation of carelessness—

"Oh, ma'am, it is nothing; nothing at all, indeed, ma'am."

Mrs. Marston remained silent for a time, while all her vague apprehensions returned. Meantime the girl continued to shove the chairs hither and thither, and to arrange and disarrange everything in the room with a fidgety industry, intended to cover her agitation. A few minutes, however, served to weary her of this, for she abruptly stopped, stood by the bedside, and, looking at her mistress, burst into tears.

"Good God! What is it?" said Mrs. Marston, shocked and even terrified, while new alarms displaced her old ones. "Is Miss Rhoda—can it be—is she—is my darling well?"

"Oh, yes, ma'am," answered the maid, "very well, ma'am; she is up, and out walking and knows nothing of all this."

"All what?" urged Mrs. Marston. "Tell me, tell me, Willett,

what has happened. What is it? Speak, child; say what it is?"

"Oh, ma'am! Oh my poor dear mistress!" continued the girl, and stopped, almost stifled with sobs.

"Willett, you must speak; you must say what is the matter. I implore of you—desire you!" urged the distracted lady. Still the girl, having made one or two ineffectual efforts to speak, continued to sob.

"Willett, you will drive me mad. For mercy's sake, for God's sake, speak—tell me what it is!" cried the unhappy lady.

"Oh, ma'am, it is—it is about the master," sobbed the girl.

"Why he can't—he has not—oh, merciful God! He has not hurt himself," she almost screamed.

"No, ma'am, no; not himself; no, no, but—" and again she hesitated.

"But what? Speak out, Willett; dear Willett have mercy on me, and speak out," cried her wretched mistress.

"Oh, ma'am, don't be fretted; don't take it to heart, ma'am," said the maid, clasping her hands together in anguish.

"Anything, anything, Willett; only speak at once," she answered.

"Well, ma'am, it is soon said—it is easy told. The master, ma'am—the master is gone with the Frenchwoman; they went in the travelling coach last night, ma'am; he is gone away with her, ma'am; that is all."

Mrs. Marston looked at the girl with a gaze of stupefied, stony terror; not a muscle of her face moved; not one heaving respiration showed that she was living. Motionless, with this fearful look fixed upon the girl, and her thin hands stretched towards her, she remained, second after second. At last her outstretched hands began to tremble more and more violently; and as if for the first time the knowledge of this calamity had reached her, with a cry, as though body and soul were parting, she fell back motionless in her bed.

Several hours had passed before Mrs. Marston was restored to consciousness. To this state of utter insensibility, one of silent, terrified stupor succeeded; and it was not until she saw her daughter Rhoda standing at her bedside, weeping, that she found voice and recollection to speak.

"My child; my darling, my poor child," she cried, sobbing piteously, as she drew her to her heart and looked in her face alternately—"my darling, my darling child!"

Rhoda could only weep, and return her poor mother's caresses in silence. Too young and inexperienced to understand the full extent and nature of this direful calamity, the strange occurrence, the general and apparent consternation of the whole household, and the spectacle of her mother's agony, had filled her with fear, perplexity, and anguish. Scared and stunned with a vague sense of danger, like a young bird that, for the first time, cowers under a thunderstorm, she nestled in her mother's bosom; there, with a sense of protection, and of boundless love and tenderness, she lay frightened, wondering, and weeping.

Two or three days passed, and Dr. Danvers came and sate for several hours with poor Mrs. Marston. To comfort and console were, of course, out of his power. The nature of the bereavement, far more terrible than death—its recent occurrence—the distracting consciousness of all its complicated consequences-rendered this a hopeless task. She bowed herself under the blow with the submission of a broken heart. The hope to which she had clung for years had vanished; the worst that ever her imagination feared had come in earnest.

One idea was now constantly present in her mind. She felt a sad, but immovable assurance, that she should not live long, and the thought, "what will become of my darling when I am gone; who will guard and love my child when I am in my grave; to whom is she to look for tenderness and protection then?" perpetually haunted her, and superadded the pangs of a still wilder despair to the desolation of a broken heart.

It was not for more than a week after this event, that one day Willett, with a certain air of anxious mystery, entered the silent and darkened chamber where Mrs. Marston lay. She had a letter in her hand; the seal and handwriting were Mr. Marston's. It was long before the injured wife was able to open it; when she did so, the following sentences met her eye:—

Gertrude,

You can be ignorant neither of the nature nor of the consequences of the decisive step I have taken: I do not seek to excuse it. For the censure of the world, its meddling and mouthing hypocrisy, I care absolutely nothing; I have long set it at defiance. And you yourself, Gertrude, when you deliberately reconsider the circumstances of estrangement and coldness under which, though beneath the same roof, we have lived for years, without either sympathy or confidence, can scarcely, if at all, regret the rupture of a tie which had long ceased to be anything better than an irksome and galling formality. I do not desire to attribute to you the smallest blame.

There was an incompatibility, not of temper but of feelings, which made us strangers though calling one another man and wife. Upon this fact I rest my own justification; our living together under these circumstances was, I dare say, equally undesired by us both. It was, in fact, but a deference to the formal hypocrisy of the world. At all events, the irrevocable act which separates us forever is done, and I have now merely to state so much of my intentions as may relate in anywise to your future arrangements. I have written to your cousin, and former guardian, Mr. Latimer, telling him how matters stand between us.

You, I told him, shall have, without opposition from me, the whole of your own fortune to your own separate use, together with whatever shall be mutually agreed upon as reasonable, from my income, for your support and that of my daughter. It will be necessary to complete your arrangements with expedition, as I purpose returning to Gray Forest in about three weeks; and as, of course, a meeting between you and those by whom I shall be accompanied is wholly out of the question, you will see the expediency of losing no time in adjusting everything for yours and my daughter's departure. In the details, of course,

I shall not interfere. I think I have made myself clearly intelligible, and would recommend your communicating at once with Mr. Latimer, with a view to completing temporary arrangements, until your final plans shall have been decided upon.

RICHARD MARSTON

The reader can easily conceive the feelings with which this letter was perused. We shall not attempt to describe them; nor shall we weary his patience by a detail of all the circumstances attending Mrs. Marston's departure. Suffice it to mention that, in less than a fortnight after the receipt of the letter which we have just copied, she had forever left the mansion of Gray Forest.

In a small house, in a sequestered part of the rich county of Warwick, the residence of Mrs. Marston and her daughter was for the present fixed. And there, for a time, the heart-broken and desolate lady enjoyed, at least, the privilege of an immunity from the intrusions of all external trouble. But the blow, under which the feeble remains of her health and strength were gradually to sink, had struck too surely home; and, from month to month—almost from week to week—the progress of decay was perceptible.

Meanwhile, though grieved and humbled, and longing to comfort his unhappy mother Charles Marston, for the present absolutely dependent upon his father, had no choice but to remain at Cambridge, and to pursue his studies there.

At Gray Forest Marston and the partner of his guilt continued to live. The old servants were all gradually dismissed, and new ones hired by Mademoiselle de Barras. There they dwelt, shunned by everybody, in a stricter and more desolate seclusion than ever. The novelty of the unrestraint and licence of their new mode of life speedily passed away, and with it the excited and guilty sense of relief which had for a time produced a false and hollow gaiety. The sense of security prompted in *mademoiselle* a hundred indulgences which, in her former precarious position, she would not have dreamed of.

Outbreaks of temper, sharp and sometimes violent, began to

manifest themselves on her part, and renewed disappointment and blacker remorse to darken the soul of Marston himself. Often, in the dead of the night, the servants would overhear their bitter and fierce altercations ringing through the melancholy mansion, and often the reckless use of terrible and mysterious epithets of crime. Their quarrels increased in violence and in frequency, and, before two years had passed, feelings of bitterness, hatred, and dread, alone seemed to subsist between them. Yet upon Marston she continued to exercise a powerful and mysterious influence. There was a dogged, apathetic submission on his part, and a growing insolence on hers, constantly more and more strikingly visible. Neglect, disorder, and decay, too, were more than ever apparent in the dreary air of the place.

Doctor Danvers, save by rumour and conjecture, knew nothing of Marston and his abandoned companion. He had, more than once, felt a strong disposition to visit Gray Forest, and expostulate, face to face, with its guilty proprietor. This idea, however, he had, upon consideration, dismissed; not on account of any shrinking from the possible repulses and affronts to which the attempt might subject him, but from a thorough conviction that the endeavour would be utterly fruitless for good, while it might, very obviously, expose him to painful misinterpretation and suspicion, and leave it to be imagined that he had been influenced, if by no meaner motive, at least by the promptings of a coarse curiosity.

Meanwhile he maintained a correspondence with Mrs. Marston, and had even once or twice since her departure visited her. Latterly, however, this correspondence had been a good deal interrupted, and its intervals had been supplied occasionally by Rhoda, whose letters, although she herself appeared unconscious of the mournful event the approach of which they too plainly indicated, were painful records of the rapid progress of mortal decay.

He had just received one of those ominous letters, at the little post office in the town we have already mentioned, and, full of the melancholy news it contained, Dr. Danvers was returning slowly towards his home. As he rode into a lonely road, traversing an undulating tract of some three miles in length, the singularity, it may be, of his costume attracted the eye of another passenger, who was, as it turned out, no other than Marston himself. For two or three miles of this desolate road, their ways happened to lie together. Marston's first impulse was to avoid the clergyman; his second, which he obeyed, was to join company, and ride along with him, at all events, for so long as would show that he shrank from no encounter which fortune or accident presented. There was a spirit of bitter defiance in this, which cost him a painful effort.

"How do you do, Parson Danvers?" said Marston, touching his hat with the handle of his whip.

Danvers thought he had seldom seen a man so changed in so short a time. His face had grown sallow and wasted, and his figure slightly stooped, with an appearance almost of feebleness.

"Mr. Marston," said the clergyman, gravely, and almost sternly, though with some embarrassment, "it is a long time since you and I have seen one another, and many and painful events have passed in the interval. I scarce know upon what terms we meet. I am prompted to speak to you, and in a tone, perhaps, which you will hardly brook; and yet, if we keep company, as it seems likely we may, I cannot, and I ought not, to be silent."

"Well, Mr. Danvers, I accept the condition—speak what you will," said Marston, with a gloomy promptitude. "If you exceed your privilege, and grow uncivil, I need but use my spurs, and leave you behind me preaching to the winds."

"Ah! Mr. Marston," said Dr. Danvers, almost sadly, after a considerable pause, "when I saw you close beside me, my heart was troubled within me."

"You looked on me as something from the nether world, and expected to see the cloven hoof," said Marston, bitterly, and raising his booted foot a little as he spoke; "but, after all, I am but a vulgar sinner of flesh and blood, without enough of the preternatural about me to frighten an old nurse, much less to agitate a pillar of the Church."

"Mr. Marston, you talk sarcastically, but you feel that recent circumstances, as well as old recollections, might well disturb and trouble me at sight of you," answered Dr. Danvers.

"Well—yes—perhaps it is so," said Marston, hastily and sullenly, and became silent for a while.

"My heart is full, Mr. Marston; charged with grief, when I think of the sad history of those with whom, in my mind, you must ever be associated," said Doctor Danvers.

"Aye, to be sure," said Marston, with stern impatience; "but, then, you have much to console you. You have got your comforts and your respectability; all the dearer, too, from the contrast of other people's misfortunes and degradations; then you have your religion moreover—"

"Yes," interrupted Danvers, earnestly, and hastening to avoid a sneer upon this subject; "God be blessed, I am an humble follower of his gracious Son, our Redeemer; and though, I trust, I should bear with patient submission whatever chastisement in his wisdom and goodness he might see fit to inflict upon me, yet I do praise and bless him for the mercy which has hitherto spared me, and I do feel that mercy all the more profoundly, from the afflictions and troubles with which I daily see others overtaken."

"And in the matter of piety and decorum, doubtless, you bless God also," said Marston, sarcastically, "that you are not as other men are, nor even as this publican."

"Nay, Mr. Marston; God forbid I should harden my sinful heart with the wicked pride of the Pharisee. Evil and corrupt am I already over much. Too well I know the vileness of my heart, to make myself righteous in my own eyes," replied Dr. Danvers, humbly. "But, sinner as I am, I am yet a messenger of God, whose mission is one of authority to his fellow-sinners; and woe is me if I speak not the truth at all seasons, and in all places where my words may be profitably heard."

"Well, Doctor Danvers, it seems you think it your duty to speak to me, of course, respecting my conduct and my spiritual state. I shall save you the pain and trouble of opening the subject;

I shall state the case for you in two words," said Marston, almost fiercely. "I have put away my wife without just cause, and am living in sin with another woman. Come, what have you to say on this theme? Speak out. Deal with me as roughly as you will, I will hear it, and answer you again."

"Alas, Mr. Marston! And do not these things trouble you?" exclaimed Dr. Danvers, earnestly. "Do they not weigh heavy upon your conscience? Ah, sir, do you not remember that, slowly and surely, you are drawing towards the hour of death, and the Day of Judgment?"

"The hour or death! Yes, I know it is coming, and I await it with indifference. But, for the Day of Judgment, with its books and trumpets! My dear doctor, pray don't expect to frighten me with that."

Marston spoke with an angry scorn, which had the effect of interrupting the conversation for some moments.

They rode on, side by side, for a long time, without speaking. At length, however, Marston unexpectedly broke the silence—

"Doctor Danvers," said he, "you asked me some time ago if I feared the hour of death, and the Day of Judgement. I answered you truly, I do not fear them; nay death, I think, I could meet with a happier and a quieter heart than any other chance that can befall me; but there are other fears; fears that do trouble me much."

Doctor Danvers looked inquiringly at him; but neither spoke for a time.

"You have not seen the catastrophe of the tragedy yet," said Marston, with a stern, stony look, made more horrible by a forced smile and something like a shudder. "I wish I could tell you—you, Doctor Danvers—for you are honourable and gentle-hearted. I wish I durst tell you what I fear; the only, only thing I really do fear. No mortal knows it but myself, and I see it coming upon me with slow, but unconquerable power. Oh, God—dreadful Spirit—spare me!"

Again they were silent, and again Marston resumed—

"Doctor Danvers, don't mistake me," he said, turning sharply, and fixing his eyes with a strange expression upon his companion. "I dread nothing human; I fear neither death, nor disgrace, nor eternity; I have no secrets to keep—no exposures to apprehend; but I dread—I dread—"

He paused, scowled darkly, as if stung with pain, turned away, muttering to himself, and gradually became much excited.

"I can't tell you now, sir, and I won't," he said, abruptly and fiercely, and with a countenance darkened with a wild and appalling rage that was wholly unaccountable. "I see you searching me with your eyes. Suspect what you will, sir, you shan't inveigle me into admissions. Aye, pry—whisper—stare—question, conjecture, sir—I suppose I must endure the world's impertinence, but d——n me if I gratify it."

It would not be easy to describe Dr. Danvers' astonishment at this unaccountable explosion of fury. He was resolved, however, to bear his companion's violence with temper.

They rode on slowly for fully ten minutes in utter silence, except that Marston occasionally muttered to himself, as it seemed, in excited abstraction. Danvers had at first felt naturally offended at the violent and insulting tone in which he had been so unexpectedly and unprovokedly addressed; but this feeling of irritation was but transient, and some fearful suspicions as to Marston's sanity flitted through his mind. In a calmer and more dogged tone, his companion now addressed him:—

"There is little profit you see, doctor, in worrying me about your religion," said Marston. "it is but sowing the wind, and reaping the whirlwind; and, to say the truth, the longer you pursue it, the less I am in the mood to listen. If ever you are cursed and persecuted as I have been, you will understand how little tolerant of gratuitous vexations and contradictions a man may become. We have squabbled over religion long enough, and each holds his own faith still. Continue to sun yourself in your happy delusions, and leave me untroubled to tread the way of my own dark and cheerless destiny."

Thus saying, he made a sullen gesture of farewell, and spurring his horse, crossed the broken fence at the roadside, and so, at a listless pace, through gaps and by farm-roads, penetrated towards his melancholy and guilty home.

Two years had now passed since the decisive event which had forever separated Marston from her who had loved him so devotedly and so fatally; two years to him of disappointment, abasement, and secret rage; two years to her of gentle and heart-broken submission to the chastening hand of heaven. At the end of this time she died. Marston read the letter that announced the event with a stern look, and silently, but the shock he felt was terrific. No man is so self-abandoned to despair and degradation, that at some casual moment thoughts of amendment— some gleams of hope, however faint and transient, from the distant future—will not visit him.

With Marston, those thoughts had somehow ever been associated with vague ideas of a reconciliation with the being whom he had forsaken—good and pure, and looking at her from the darkness and distance of his own fallen state, almost angelic as she seemed. But she was now dead; he could make her no atonement; she could never smile forgiveness upon him. This long-familiar image—the last that had reflected for him one ray of the lost peace and love of happier times—had vanished, and henceforward there was before him nothing but storm and fear.

Marston's embarrassed fortunes made it to him an object to resume the portion of his income heretofore devoted to the separate maintenance of his wife and daughter. In order to effect this it became, of course, necessary to recall his daughter, Rhoda, and fix her residence once more at Gray Forest. No more dreadful penalty could have been inflicted upon the poor girl—no more agonizing ordeal than that she was thus doomed to undergo. She had idolized her mother, and now adored her memory. She knew that Mademoiselle de Barras had betrayed and indirectly murdered the parent she had so devotedly loved; she knew that that woman had been the curse, the fate of her family, and she regarded her naturally with feelings of mingled terror and abhorrence, the intensity of which was indescribable.

The few scattered friends and relatives, whose sympathies had been moved by the melancholy fate of poor Mrs. Marston, were unanimously agreed that the intended removal of the young and innocent daughter to the polluted mansion of sin and shame, was too intolerably revolting to be permitted. But each of these virtuous individuals unhappily thought it the duty of the others to interpose; and with a running commentary of wonder and reprobation, and much virtuous criticism, events were suffered uninterruptedly to take their sinister and melancholy course.

It was about two months after the death of Mrs. Marston, and on a bleak and ominous night at the wintry end of autumn, that poor Rhoda, in deep mourning, and pale with grief and agitation, descended from a chaise at the well-known door of the mansion of Gray Forest. Whether from consideration for her feelings, or, as was more probable, from pure indifference, Rhoda was conducted, on her arrival, direct to her own chamber, and it was not until the next morning that she saw her father. He entered her room unexpectedly, he was very pale, and as she thought, greatly altered, but he seemed perfectly collected, and free from agitation.

The marked and even shocking change in his appearance, and perhaps even the trifling though painful circumstance that he wore no mourning for the beloved being who was gone, caused her, after a moment's mute gazing in his face, to burst into an irrepressible flood of tears. Marston waited stoically until the paroxysm had subsided, and then taking her hand, with a look in which a dogged sternness was contending with something like shame, he said:—

"There, there; you can weep when I am gone. I shan't say very much to you at present, Rhoda, and only wish you to attend to me for one minute. Listen, Rhoda; the lady whom you have been in the habit (here he slightly averted his eyes) of calling Mademoiselle de Barras, is no longer so; she is married; she is my wife, and consequently you will treat her with the respect due to"—he would have said "a mother," but could not, and supplied the phrase by adding, "to that relation."

Rhoda was unable to speak, but almost unconsciously bowed her head in token of attention and submission, and her father pressed her hand more kindly, as he continued:—

"I have always found you a dutiful and obedient child, Rhoda, and expected no other conduct from you. Mrs. Marston will treat you with proper kindness and consideration, and desires me to say that you can, whenever you please, keep strictly to yourself, and need not, unless you feel so disposed, attend the regular meals of the family. This privilege may suit your present depressed spirits, and you must not scruple to use it."

After a few words more, Marston withdrew, leaving his daughter to her reflections, and bleak and bitter enough they were.

Some weeks passed away, and perhaps we shall best consult our readers' ease by substituting for the formal precision of narrative, a few extracts from the letters which Rhoda wrote to her brother, still at Cambridge. These will convey her own impressions respecting the scenes and personages among whom she was now to move.

The house and place are much neglected, and the former in some parts suffered almost to go to decay. The windows broken in the last storm, nearly eight months ago, they tell me, are still unmended, and the roof, too, unrepaired. The pretty garden, near the well, among the lime trees, that our darling mother was so fond of, is all but obliterated with weeds and grass, and since my first visit I have not had heart to go near it again. All the old servants are gone; new faces everywhere.

I have been obliged several times, through fear of offending my father, to join the party in the drawing room. You may conceive what I felt at seeing *mademoiselle* in the place once filled by our dear mamma, I was so choked with sorrow, bitterness, and indignation, and my heart so palpitated, that I could not speak, and I believe they thought I was going to faint. *Mademoiselle* looked very angry, but my father pretending to show me, heaven knows what, from the window, led me to it, and the air revived me a little.

Mademoiselle (for I cannot call her by her new name) is altered a good deal—more, however, in the character than in the contour of her face and figure.

Certainly, however, she has grown a good deal fuller, and her colour is higher; and whether it is fancy or not, I cannot say, but certainly to me it seems that the expression of her face has acquired something habitually lowering and malicious, and which, I know not how, inspires me with an undefinable dread. She has, however, been tolerably civil to me, but seems contemptuous and rude to my father, and I am afraid he is very wretched, I have seen them exchange such looks, and overheard such intemperate and even appalling altercations between them, as indicate something worse and deeper than ordinary ill-will.

This makes me additionally wretched, especially as I cannot help thinking that some mysterious cause enables her to frighten and tyrannise over my poor father. I sometimes think he absolutely detests her; yet, though fiery altercations ensue, he ultimately submits to this bad and cruel woman. Oh, my dear Charles, you have no idea of the shocking, or rather the terrifying, reproaches I have heard interchanged between them, as I accidently passed the room where they were sitting—such terms as have sent me to my room, feeling as if I were in a horrid dream, and made me cry and tremble for hours after I got there. . . . I see my father very seldom, and when I do, he takes but little notice of me. . . . Poor Willett, you know, returned with me. She accompanies me in my walks, and is constantly dropping hints about *mademoiselle*, from which I know not what to gather. . . .

I often fear that my father has some secret and mortal ailment. He generally looks ill, and sometimes quite wretchedly. He came twice lately to my room, I think to speak to me on some matter of importance; but he said only a sentence or two, and even these broken and incoherent. He seemed unable to command spirits for the interview;

and, indeed, he grew so agitated and strange, that I was alarmed, and felt greatly relieved when he left me....

I do not, you see, disguise my feelings, dear Charles; I do not conceal from you the melancholy and anguish of my present situation. How intensely I long for your promised arrival. I have not a creature to whom I can say one word in confidence, except poor Willett; who, though very good-natured, and really dear to me, is yet far from being a companion. I sometimes think my intense anxiety to see you here is almost selfish; for I know you will feel as acutely as I do, the terrible change observable everywhere. But I cannot help longing for your return, dear Charles, and counting the days and the very hours till you arrive. .

Be cautious, in writing to me, not to say anything which you would not wish *mademoiselle* to see; for Willett tells me that she knows that she often examines, and even intercepts the letters that arrive; and, though Willett may be mistaken, and I hope she is, yet it is better that you should be upon your guard. Ever since I heard this, I have brought my letters to the post office myself, instead of leaving them with the rest upon the hall table; and you know it is a long walk for me. . . .

I go to church every Sunday, and take Willett along with me. No one from this seems to think of doing so but ourselves. I see the Mervyns there. Mrs. Mervyn is particularly kind; and I know that she wishes to offer me an asylum at Newton Park; and you cannot think with how much tenderness and delicacy she conveys the wish. But I dare not hint the subject to my father; and, earnestly as I desire it, I could not but feel that I should go there, not to visit, but to reside. And so even in this, in many respects, delightful project, is mingled the bitter apprehension of dependence—something so humiliating, that, kindly and delicately as the offer is made, I could not bring myself to embrace it. I have a great deal to say to you, and long to see you.. . .

These extracts will enable the reader to form a tolerably accurate idea of the general state of affairs at Gray Forest. Some particulars must, however, be added.

Marston continued to be the same gloomy and joyless being as heretofore. Sometimes moody and apathetic, sometimes wayward and even savage, but never for a moment at ease, never social—an isolated, disdainful, ruined man.

One day as Rhoda sate and read under the shade of some closely-interwoven evergreens, in a lonely and sheltered part of the neglected pleasure-grounds, with her honest maid Willett in attendance, she was surprised by the sudden appearance of her father, who stood unexpectedly before her. Though his attitude for some time was fixed, his countenance was troubled with anxiety and pain, and his sunken eyes rested upon her with a fiery and fretted gaze. He seemed lost in thought for a while, and then, touching Willett sharply on the shoulder, said abruptly:

"Go; I shall call you when you are wanted. Walk down that alley." And, as he spoke, he indicated with his walking-cane the course he desired her to take.

When the maid was sufficiently distant to be quite out of hearing, Marston sate down beside Rhoda upon the bench, and took her hand in silence. His grasp was cold, and alternately relaxed and contracted with an agitated uncertainty, while his eyes were fixed upon the ground, and he seemed meditating how to open the conversation. At last, as if suddenly awaking from a fearful reverie, he said—"You correspond with Charles?"

"Yes, sir," she replied, with the respectful formality prescribed by the usages of the time, "we correspond regularly."

"Aye, aye; and, pray, when did you last hear from him?" he continued.

"About a month since, sir," she replied.

"Ha—and—and—was there nothing strange—nothing—nothing mysterious and menacing in his letter? Come, come, you know what I speak of." He stopped abruptly, and stared in her face with an agitated gaze.

"No, indeed, sir; there was not anything of the kind," she

replied.

"I have been greatly shocked, I may say incensed," said Marston excitedly, "by a passage in his last letter to me. Not that it says anything specific; but—but it amazes me—it enrages me."

He again checked himself, and Rhoda, much surprised, and even shocked, said, stammeringly—

"I am sure, sir, that dear Charles would not intentionally say or do anything that could offend you."

"Ah, as to that, I believe so, too. But it is not with him I am indignant; no, no. Poor Charles! I believe he is, as you say, disposed to conduct himself as a son ought to do, respectfully and obediently. Yes, yes, Charles is very well; but I fear he is leading a bad life, notwithstanding—a very bad life. He is becoming subject to influences which never visit or torment the good; believe me, he is."

Marston shook his head, and muttered to himself, with a look of almost craven anxiety, and then whispered to his daughter—

"Just read this, and then tell me is it not so. Read it, read it, and pronounce."

As he thus spoke, he placed in her hand the letter of which he had spoken, and with the passage to which he invited her attention folded down. It was to the following effect:—

I cannot tell you how shocked I have been by a piece of scandal, as I must believe it, conveyed to me in an anonymous letter, and which is of so very delicate a nature, that without your special command I should hesitate to pain you by its recital. I trust it may be utterly false. Indeed I assume it to be so. It is enough to say that it is of a very distressing nature, and affects the lady (Mademoiselle de Barras) whom you have recently honoured with your hand.

"Now you see," cried Marston, with a shuddering fierceness, as she returned the letter with a blanched cheek and trembling hand—"now you see it all. Are you stupid?—the stamp of the cloven hoof—eh?"

Rhoda, unable to gather his meaning, but, at the same time, with a heart full and trembling very much, stammered a few frightened words, and became silent.

"It is he, I tell you, that does it all; and if Charles were not living an evil life, he could not have spread his nets for him," said Marston, vehemently. "He can't go near anything good; but, like a scoundrel, he knows where to find a congenial nature; and when he does, he has skill enough to practice upon it. I know him well, and his arts and his smiles; aye, and his scowls and his grins, too. He goes, like his master, up and down, and to and fro upon the earth, for ceaseless mischief. There is not a friend of mine he can get hold of, but he whispered in his ear some damned slander of me. He is drawing them all into a common understanding against me; and he takes an actual pleasure in telling me how the thing goes on—how, one after the other, he has converted my friends into conspirators and libellers, to blast my character, and take my life, and now the monster essays to lure my children into the hellish confederation."

"Who is he, father, who is he?" faltered Rhoda.

"You never saw him," retorted Marston, sternly.

"No, no; you can't have seen him, and you probably never will; but if he does come here again, don't listen to him. He is half-fiend and half-idiot, and no good comes of his mouthing and muttering. Avoid him, I warn you, avoid him. Let me see: how shall I describe him? Let me see. You remember—you remember Berkley—Sir Wynston Berkley. Well, he greatly resembles that dead villain: he has all the same grins, and shrugs, and monkey airs, and his face and figure are like. But he is a grimed, ragged, wasted piece of sin, little better than a beggar—a shrunken, malignant libel on the human shape. Avoid him, I tell you, avoid him: he is steeped in lies and poison, like the very serpent that betrayed us. Beware of him, I say, for if he once gains your ear, he will delude you, spite of all your vigilance; he will make you his accomplice, and thenceforth, inevitably, there is nothing but mortal and implacable hatred between us!"

Frightened at this wild language, Rhoda did not answer, but

looked up in his face in silence. A fearful transformation was there—a scowl so livid and maniacal, that her very senses seemed leaving her with terror. Perhaps the sudden alteration observable in her countenance, as this spectacle so unexpectedly encountered her, recalled him to himself; for he added, hurriedly, and in a tone of gentler meaning—

"Rhoda, Rhoda, watch and pray. My daughter, my child! keep your heart pure, and nothing bad can approach you for ill. No, no; you are good, and the good need not fear!"

Suddenly Marston burst into tears, as he ended this sentence, and wept long and convulsively. She did not dare to speak, or even to move; but after a while he ceased, appeared uneasy, half ashamed and half angry; and looking with a horrified and bewildered glance into her face, he said—

"Rhoda, child, what—what have I said? My God! what have I been saying? Did I—do I look ill? Oh, Rhoda, Rhoda, may you never feel this!"

He turned away from her without awaiting her answer, and walked away with the appearance of intense agitation, as if to leave her. He turned again, however, and with a face pallid and sunken as death, approached her slowly—

"Rhoda," said he, "don't tell what I have said to anyone-don't, I conjure you, even to Charles. I speak too much at random, and say more than I mean—a foolish, rambling habit: so do not repeat one word of it, not one word to any living mortal. You and I, Rhoda, must have our little secrets."

He ended with an attempt at a smile, so obviously painful and fear-stricken that as he walked hurriedly away, the astounded girl burst into a bitter flood of tears. What was, what could be, the meaning of the shocking scene she had then been forced to witness? She dared not answer the question. Yet one ghastly doubt haunted her like her shadow—a suspicion that the malignant and hideous light of madness was already glaring upon his mind. As, leaning upon the arm of her astonished attendant, she retracted her steps, the trees, the flowers, the familiar hall-door, the echoing passages—every object that met her eye—seemed strange and unsubstantial, and she gliding on among them in a horrid dream.

Time passed on: there was no renewal of the painful scene which dwelt so sensibly in the affrighted imagination of Rhoda. Marston's manner was changed towards her; he seemed shy, cowed, and uneasy in her presence, and thenceforth she saw less than ever of him. Meanwhile the time approached which was to witness the long expected, and, by Rhoda, the intensely prayed for arrival of her brother.

Some four or five days before this event, Mr. Marston, having, as he said, some business in Chester, and further designing to meet his son there, took his departure from Gray Forest, leaving poor Rhoda to the guardianship of her guilty stepmother; and although she had seen so little of her father, yet the very consciousness of his presence had given her a certain confidence and sense of security, which vanished at the moment of his departure. Fear-stricken and wretched as he had been, his removal, nevertheless, seemed to her to render the lonely and inauspicious mansion still more desolate and ominous than before.

She had, with a vague and instinctive antipathy, avoided all contact and intercourse with Mrs. Marston, or as, for distinctness sake, we shall continue to call her, "*Mademoiselle*," since her return; and she on her part had appeared to acquiesce with a sort of scornful nonchalance, in the tacit understanding that she and her former pupil should see and hear as little as might be of one another.

Meanwhile poor Willett, with her good-natured honesty and her inexhaustible gossip, endeavoured to amuse and reassure her young mistress, and sometimes even with some partial success.

We must now follow Mr. Marston in his solitary expedition to Chester. When he took his place in the stagecoach he had the whole interior of the vehicle to himself, and thus continued to be its solitary occupant for several miles. The coach, however, was eventually hailed, brought to, and the door being opened, Dr. Danvers got in, and took his place opposite to the passenger already established there. The worthy man was so busied in directing the disposition of his luggage from the window, and in arranging the sundry small parcels with which he was charged, that he did not recognize his companion until they were in motion.

When he did so it was with no very pleasurable feeling; and it is probable that Marston, too, would have gladly escaped the coincidence which thus reduced them once more to the temporary necessity of a *tête-à-tête*. Embarrassing as each felt the situation to be, there was, however, no avoiding it, and, after a recognition and a few forced attempts at conversation, they became, by mutual consent, silent and uncommunicative.

The journey, though in point of space a mere trifle, was, in those slowcoach days, a matter of fully five hours' duration; and before it was completed the sun had set, and darkness began to close. Whether it was that the descending twilight dispelled the painful constraint under which Marston had seemed to labour, or that some more purely spiritual and genial influence had gradually dissipated the repulsion and distrust with which, at first, he had shrunk from a renewal of intercourse with Dr. Danvers, he suddenly accosted him thus.

"Dr. Danvers, I have been fifty times on the point of speaking to you—confidentially of course—while sitting here opposite to you, what I believe I could scarcely bring myself to hint to any other man living; yet I must tell it, and soon, too, or I fear it will have told itself."

Dr. Danvers intimated his readiness to hear and advise, if desired; and Marston resumed abruptly, after a pause—

"Pray, Doctor Danvers, have you heard any stories of an odd kind; any surmises—I don't mean of a moral sort, for those I hold very cheap—to my prejudice? Indeed I should hardly say to my prejudice; I mean—I ought to say—in short, have you heard people remark upon any fancied eccentricities, or that sort of thing, about me?"

He put the question with obvious difficulty, and at last seemed to overcome his own reluctance with a sort of angry and excited self-contempt and impatience. Doctor Danvers was a little puzzled by the interrogatory, and admitted, in reply, that he did not comprehend its drift.

"Doctor Danvers," he resumed, sternly and dejectedly, "I told you, in the chance interview we had some months ago, that I was haunted by a certain fear. I did not define it, nor do I think you suspect its nature. It is a fear of nothing mortal, but of the immortal tenant of this body. My mind; sir, is beginning to play me tricks; my guide mocks and terrifies me."

There was a perceptible tinge of horror in the look of astonishment with which Dr. Danvers listened.

"You are a gentleman, sir, and a Christian clergyman; what I have said and shall say is confided to your honour; to be held sacred as the confession of misery, and hidden from the coarse gaze of the world. I have become subject to a hideous delusion. It comes at intervals. I do not think any mortal suspects it, except, maybe, my daughter Rhoda. It comes and disappears, and comes again. I kept my pleasant secret for a long time, but at last I let it slip, and committed myself fortunately, to but one person, and that my daughter; and, even so, I hardly think she understood me. I recollected myself before I had disclosed the grotesque and infernal chimera that haunts me."

Marston paused. He was stooped forward, and looking upon the floor of the vehicle, so that his companion could not see his countenance. A silence ensued, which was interrupted by Marston, who once more resumed.

"Sir," said he, "I know not why, but I have longed, intensely longed, for some trustworthy ear into which to pour this horrid secret; why I repeat, I cannot tell, for I expect no sympathy, and hate compassion. It is, I suppose, the restless nature of the devil that is in me; but, be it what it may, I will speak to you, but to you only, for the present, at least, to you alone."

Doctor Danvers again assured him that he might repose the most entire confidence in his secrecy.

"The human mind, I take it, must have either comfort in the past or hope in the future," he continued, "otherwise it is in danger. To me, sir, the past is intolerably repulsive; one boundless, barren, and hideous Golgotha of dead hopes and murdered opportunities; the future, still blacker and more furious, peopled with dreadful features of horror and menace, and losing itself in utter darkness. Sir, I do not exaggerate. Between such a past and such a future I stand upon this miserable present; and the only comfort I still am capable of feeling is, that no human being pities me; that I stand aloof from the insults of compassion and the hypocrisies of sympathetic morality; and that I can safely defy all the respectable scoundrels in Christendom to enhance, by one feather's weight, the load which I myself have accumulated, and which I myself hourly and unaided sustain."

Doctor Danvers here introduced a word or two in the direction of their former conversation.

"No, sir, there is no comfort from that quarter either," said Marston, bitterly; "you but cast your seeds, as the parable terms your teaching, upon the barren sea, in wasting them on me. My fate, be it what it may, is as irrevocably fixed, as though I were dead and judged a hundred years ago.

"This cursed dream," he resumed abruptly, "that everyday enslaves me more and more, has reference to that—that occurrence about Wynston Berkley—he is the hero of the hellish illusion. At certain times, sir, it seems to me as if he, though dead, were still invested with a sort of spurious life; going about unrecognized, except by me, in squalor and contempt, and whispering away my fame and life; labouring with the malignant industry of a fiend to involve me in the meshes of that special perdition from which alone I shrink, and to which this emissary of hell seems to have predestined me. Sir, this is a monstrous and hideous extravagance, a delusion, but, after all, no more than a trick of the imagination; the reason, the judgment, is untouched. I cannot choose but see all the damned phantasmagoria, but I do not believe it real, and this is the difference between my case and—and—madness!"

They were now entering the suburbs of Chester, and Doctor Danvers, pained and shocked beyond measure by this unlooked-for disclosure, and not knowing what remark or comfort to offer, relieved his temporary embarrassment by looking from the window, as though attracted by the flash of the lamps, among which the vehicle was now moving. Marston, however, laid his hand upon his arm, and thus recalled him, for a moment, to a forced attention.

"It must seem strange to you, Doctor, that I should trust this cursed secret to your keeping," he said; "and, truth to say, it seems so to myself. I cannot account for the impulse, the irresistible power of which has forced me to disclose the hateful mystery to you, but the fact is this, beginning like a speck, this one idea has gradually darkened and dilated, until it has filled my entire mind. The solitary consciousness of the gigantic mastery it has established there had grown intolerable; I must have told it. The sense of solitude under this aggressive and tremendous delusion was agony, hourly death to my soul. That is the secret of my talkativeness; my sole excuse for plaguing you with the dreams of a wretched hypochondriac."

Doctor Danvers assured him that no apologies were needed, and was only restrained from adding the expression of that pity which he really felt, by the fear of irritating a temper so full of bitterness, pride and defiance. A few minutes more, and the coach having reached its destination, they bid one another farewell, and parted.

At that time there resided in a decent mansion about a mile from the town of Chester, a dapper little gentleman, whom we shall call Doctor Parkes. This gentleman was the proprietor and sole professional manager of a private asylum for the insane and enjoyed a high reputation, and a proportionate amount of business, in his melancholy calling. It was about the second day after the conversation we have just sketched, that this little gentleman, having visited, according to his custom, all his domestic patients, was about to take his accustomed walk in his somewhat restricted pleasure grounds, when his servant announced a visitor.

"A gentleman," he repeated; "you have seen him before-eh?"

"No, sir," replied the man; "he is in the study, sir."

"Ha! a professional call. Well, we shall see."

So saying, the little gentleman summoned his gravest look, and hastened to the chamber of audience.

On entering he found a man dressed well, but gravely, having in his air and manner something of high breeding. In countenance striking, dark-featured, and stern, furrowed with the lines of pain or thought, rather than of age, although his dark hairs were largely mingled with white.

The physician bowed, and requested the stranger to take a chair; he, however, nodded slightly and impatiently, as if to intimate an intolerance of ceremony, and, advancing a step or two, said abruptly—

"My name, sir, is Marston; I have come to give you a patient."

The doctor bowed with a still deeper inclination, and paused for a continuance of the communication thus auspiciously commenced.

"You are Dr. Parkes, I take it for granted," said Marston, in the same tone.

"Your most obedient, humble servant, sir," replied he, with the polite formality of the day, and another grave bow.

"Doctor," demanded Marston, fixing his eye upon him sternly, and significantly tapping his own forehead, "can you stay execution?"

The physician looked puzzled, hesitated, and at last requested his visitor to be more explicit.

"Can you," said Marston, with the same slow and stern articulation, and after a considerable pause—"can you prevent the malady you profess to cure?—can you meet and defeat the enemy halfway?—can you scare away the spirit of madness before it takes actual possession, and while it is still only hovering about its threatened victim?"

"Sir," he replied, "in certain cases—in very many, indeed—the enemy, as you well call it, may thus be met, and effectually worsted at a distance. Timely interposition, in ninety cases out of a hundred, is everything; and, I assure you, I hear your question with much pleasure, inasmuch as I assume it to have reference to the case of the patient about whom you desire to consult me; and who is, therefore, I hope, as yet merely menaced with the misfortune from which you would save him."

"I, myself, am that patient, sir," said Marston, with an effort; "your surmise is right. I am not mad, but unequivocally menaced with madness; it is not to be mistaken. Sir, there is no misunderstanding the tremendous and intolerable signs that glare upon my mind."

"And pray, sir, have you consulted your friends or your family upon the course best to be pursued?" inquired Dr. Parkes, with grave interest.

"No, sir," he answered sharply, and almost fiercely; "I have no fancy to make myself the subject of a writ *de lunatico inquirendo*; I don't want to lose my liberty and my property at a blow. The course I mean to take has been advised by no one but myself—is known to no other. I now disclose it, and the causes of it, to you, a gentleman, and my professional adviser, in the expectation that you will guard with the strictest secrecy my spontaneous revelations; this you promise me?"

"Certainly, Mr. Marston; I have neither the disposition nor the right to withhold such a promise," answered the physician.

"Well, then, I will first tell you the arrangement I propose, with your permission, to make, and then I shall answer all your questions, respecting my own case," resumed Marston, gloomily. "I wish to place myself under your care, to live under your roof, reserving my full liberty of action. I must be free to come and to go as I will; and on the other hand, I undertake that you shall find me an amenable and docile patient enough. In addition, I stipulate that there shall be no attempt whatever made to communicate with those who are connected with me: these terms agreed upon, I place myself in your hands. You will find in me, as I said before, a deferential patient, and I trust not a troublesome one. I hope you will excuse my adding, that I shall myself pay the charge of my sojourn here from week to week, in advance."

The proposed arrangement was a strange one; and although Dr. Parkes dimly foresaw some of the embarrassments which might possibly arise from his accepting it, there was yet so much that was reasonable as well as advantageous in the proposal, that he could not bring himself to decline it.

The preliminary arrangement concluded, Dr. Parkes proceeded to his more strictly professional investigation. It is, of course, needless to recapitulate the details of Marston's tormenting fancies, with which the reader has indeed been already sufficiently acquainted. Doctor Parkes, having attentively listened to the narrative, and satisfied himself as to the physical health of his patient, was still sorely puzzled as to the probable issue of the awful struggle already but too obviously commenced between the mind and its destroyer in the strange case before him. One satisfactory symptom unquestionably was, the as yet transitory nature of the delusion, and the evident and energetic tenacity with which reason contended for her vital ascendancy. It was a case, however, which for many reasons sorely perplexed him, but of which, notwithstanding, he was disposed, whether rightly or wrongly the reader will speedily see, to take by no means a decidedly gloomy view.

Having disburdened his mind of this horrible secret, Marston felt for a time a sense of relief amounting almost to elation. With far less of apprehension and dismay than he had done so for months before, he that night repaired to his bedroom. There was nothing in his case, Doctor Parkes believed, to warrant his keeping any watch upon Marston's actions, and accordingly he bid him good-night, in the full confidence of meeting him, if not better, at least not worse, on the ensuing morning.

He miscalculated, however. Marston had probably himself been conscious of some coming crisis in his hideous malady, when he took the decisive step of placing himself under the care of Doctor Parkes. Certain it is, that upon that very night the disease broke forth in a new and appalling development. Doctor Parkes, whose bedroom was next to that occupied by Marston, was awakened in the dead of night by a howling, more like that of a beast than a human voice, and which gradually swelled into an absolute yell; then came some horrid laughter and entreaties, thick and frantic; then again the same unearthly howl. The practiced ear of Doctor Parkes recognized but too surely the terrific import of those sounds. Springing from his bed, and seizing the candle which always burned in his chamber, in anticipation of such sudden and fearful emergencies, he hurried with a palpitating heart, and spite of his long habituation to such scenes as he expected, with a certain sense of horror, to the chamber of his aristocratic patient.

Late as it was, Marston had not yet gone to bed; his candle was still burning, and he himself, half dressed, stood in the centre of the floor, shaking and livid, his eyes burning with the preterhuman fires of insanity. As Doctor Parkes entered the chamber, another shout, or rather yell, thundered from the lips of this demoniac effigy; and the mad-doctor stood freezing with horror in the doorway, and yet exerting what remained to him of presence of mind, in the vain endeavour, in the flaring light of the candle, to catch and fix with his own practiced eye the gaze of the maniac.

Second after second, and minute after minute, he stood confronting this frightful slave of Satan, in the momentary expectation that he would close with and destroy him. On a sudden, however, this brief agony of suspense was terminated; a change like an awakening consciousness of realities, or rather like the withdrawal of some hideous and visible influence from within, passed over the tense and darkened features of the wretched being; a look of horrified perplexity, doubt, and inquiry, supervened, and he at last said, in a subdued and sullen tone, to Doctor Parkes:

"Who are you, sir? What do you want here? Who are you, sir, I say?"

"Who am I? Why, your physician, sir; Doctor Parkes, sir; the owner of this house, sir," replied he, with all the sternness he could command, and yet white as a spectre with agitation. "For shame, sir, for shame, to give way thus. What do you mean by creating this causeless alarm, and disturbing the whole household at so unseasonable an hour? For shame, sir; go to your bed; undress yourself this moment; for shame."

Doctor Parkes, as he spoke, was reassured by the arrival of one of his servants, alarmed by the unmistakable sounds of violent frenzy; he signed, however, to the man not to enter, feeling confident, as he did, that the paroxysm had spent itself.

"Aye, aye," muttered Marston, looking almost sheepishly; "Doctor Parkes, to be sure. What was I thinking of? how cursedly absurd! And this," he continued, glancing at his sword, which he threw impatiently upon a sofa as he spoke. "Folly—nonsense! A false alarm, as you say, doctor. I beg your pardon."

As Marston spoke, he proceeded with much agitation slowly to undress himself. He had, however, but commenced the process, when, turning abruptly to Doctor Parkes, he said, with a countenance of horror, and in a whisper—

"By ——, doctor, it has been upon me worse than ever, I would have sworn I had the villain with me for hours—hours, sir—torturing me with his damned sneering threats; till, by ——, I could stand it no longer, and took my sword. Oh, doctor, can't you save me? can nothing be done for me?"

Pale, covered with the dews of horror, he uttered these last words in accents of such imploring despair, as might have borne across the dreadful gulf the prayer of Dives for that one drop of water which never was to cool his burning tongue.

When Rhoda learned that her father, on leaving Gray Forest, had fixed no definite period for his return, she began to feel her situation at home so painful and equivocal, that, having taken honest Willett to counsel, she came at last to the resolution of accepting the often conveyed invitation of Mrs. Mervyn and sojourning, at all events until her father's return, at Newton Park.

"My dear young friend," said the kind lady, as soon as she heard Rhoda's little speech to its close, "I can scarcely describe the gratification with which I see you here; the happiness with which I welcome you to Newton Park; nor, indeed, the anxiety with which I constantly contemplated your trying and painful position at Gray Forest. Indeed I ought to be angry with you for having refused me this happiness so long; but you have made amends at last; though, indeed, it was impossible to have deferred it longer. You must not fancy, however, that I will consent to lose you so soon as you seem to have intended. No, no; I have found it too hard to catch you, to let you take wing so easily; besides, I have others to consult as well as myself, and persons, too, who are just as anxious as I am to make a prisoner of you here."

The good Mrs. Mervyn accompanied these words with looks so sly, and emphasis so significant, that Rhoda was fain to look down, to hide her blushes; and compassionating the confusion she herself had caused, the kind old lady led her to the chamber which was henceforward, so long as she consented to remain, to be her own apartment.

How that day was passed, and how fleetly its hours sped away, it is needless to tell. Old Mervyn had his gentle as well as his grim aspect; and no welcome was ever more cordial and tender than that with which he greeted the unprotected child of his morose and repulsive neighbour. It would be impossible to convey any idea of the countless assiduities and the secret delight with which young Mervyn attended their rambles.

The party were assembled at supper. What a contrast did this cheerful, happy—unutterably happy—gathering, present, in the mind of Rhoda, to the dull, drear, fearful evenings which she had long been wont to pass at Gray Forest.

As they sate together in cheerful and happy intercourse, a chaise drove up to the hall-door, and the knocking had hardly ceased to reverberate, when a well-known voice was heard in the hall.

Young Mervyn started to his feet, and merrily ejaculating, "Charles Marston! this is delightful!" disappeared, and in an instant returned with Charles himself.

We pass over all the embraces of brother and sister; the tears and smiles of reunited affection. We omit the cordial shaking of hands; the kind looks; the questions and answers; all these, and all the little attentions of that good old-fashioned hospitality, which was never weary of demonstrating the cordiality of its welcome, we abandon to the imagination of the good-natured reader.

Charles Marston, with the advice of his friend, Mr. Mervyn, resolved to lose no time in proceeding to Chester, whither it was ascertained his father had gone, with the declared intention of meeting and accompanying him home. He arrived in that town in the evening; and having previously learned that Doctor Danvers had been for some time in Chester, he at once sought him at his usual lodgings, and found the worthy old gentleman at his solitary "dish" of tea.

"My dear Charles," said he, greeting his young friend with earnest warmth, "I am rejoiced beyond measure to see you. Your father is in town, as you supposed; and I have just had a note from him, which has, I confess, not a little agitated me, referring, as it does, to a subject of painful and horrible interest; one with which, I suppose, you are familiar, but upon which I myself have never yet spoken fully to any person, excepting your father only."

"And pray, my dear sir, what is this topic?" inquired Charles, with marked interest.

"Read this note," answered the clergyman, placing one at the same time in his young visitor's hand.

Charles read as follows:

My Dear Sir,

I have a singular communication to make to you, but in the strictest privacy, with reference to a subject which, merely to name, is to awaken feelings of doubt and horror; I mean the confession of Merton, with respect to the murder of Wynston Berkley. I will call upon you this evening after dark; for I have certain reasons for not caring to meet old acquaintances about town; and if you can afford me half an hour, I promise to complete my intended disclosure within that time. Let us be strictly private; this is my only *proviso*.

Yours with much respect,
Richard Marston

"Your father has been sorely troubled in mind," said Doctor Danvers, as soon as the young man had read this communication; "he has told me as much; it may be that the discovery he has now made may possibly have relieved him from certain galling anxieties. The fear that unjust suspicion should light upon himself, or those connected with him, has, I dare say, tormented him sorely. God grant, that as the providential unfolding of all the details of this mysterious crime comes about, he maybe brought to recognize, in the just and terrible process, the hand of heaven. God grant, that at last his heart may be softened, and his spirit illuminated by the blessed influence he has so long and so sternly rejected."

As the old man thus spake—as if in symbolic answering to his prayer—a sudden glory from the setting sun streamed through the funereal pile of clouds which filled the western horizon, and flooded the chamber where they were.

After a silence, Charles Marston said, with some little embarrassment—"It may be a strange confession to make, though, indeed, hardly so to you—for you know but too well the gloomy reserve with which my father has uniformly treated me—that the exact nature of Merton's confession never reached my ears; and once or twice, when I approached the subject, in conversation with you, it seemed to me that the subject was one which, for some reason, it was painful to you to enter upon."

"And so it was, in truth, my young friend—so it was; for that confession left behind it many fearful doubts, proving, indeed, nothing but the one fact, that, morally, the wretched man was guilty of the murder."

Charles, urged by a feeling of the keenest interest, requested Dr. Danvers to detail to him the particulars of the dying man's narration.

"Willingly," answered Dr. Danvers, with a look of gloom, and heaving a profound sigh—"willingly, for you have now come to an age when you may safely be entrusted with secrets affecting your own family, and which, although, thank God, as I believe they in no respect involve the honour of anyone of its members,

347

yet might deeply involve its peace and its security against the assaults of vague and horrible slander. Here, then, is the narrative: Merton, when he was conscious of the approach of death, qualified, by a circumstantial and detailed statement, the absolute confession of guilt which he had at first sullenly made. In this he declared that the guilt of design and intention only was his—that in the act itself he had been anticipated.

"He stated, that from the moment when Sir Wynston's servant had casually mentioned the circumstance of his master's usually sleeping with his watch and pocketbook under his pillow, the idea of robbing him had taken possession of his mind. With the idea of robbing him (under the peculiar circumstances, his servant sleeping in the apartment close by, and the slightest alarm being, in all probability, sufficient to call him to the spot) the idea of anticipating resistance by murder had associated itself. He had contended against these haunting and growing solicitations of Satan, with an earnest agony.

"He had intended to leave his place, and fly from the mysterious temptation which he felt he wanted power to combat, but accident or fate prevented him. In a state of ghastly excitement he had, on the memorable night of Sir Wynston's murder, proceeded, as had afterwards appeared in evidence, by the back stair to the baronet's chamber; he had softly stolen into it, and gone to the bedside, with the weapon in his hand. He drew his breath for the decisive stroke, which was to bereave the (supposedly) sleeping man of life, and when stretching his left hand under the clothes, it rested upon a dull, cold corpse, and, at the same moment, his right hand was immersed in a pool of blood. He dropped the knife, recoiled a pace or so.

"With a painful effort, however, he again grasped with his hand to recover the weapon he had suffered to escape, and secured, as it afterwards turned out, not the knife with which he had meditated the commission of his crime, but the dagger which was afterwards found where he had concealed it. He was now fully alive to the horror of his situation; he was compromised as fully as if he had in very deed driven home the weapon. To be found under such circumstances, would convict him as surely as if fifty eyes had seen him strike the blow. He had nothing now for it but flight; and in order to guard himself against the contingency of being surprised from the door opening upon the corridor, he bolted it; then groped under the murdered man's pillow for the booty which had so fatally fascinated his imagination. Here he was disappointed. What further happened you already know."

Charles listened with breathless attention to this recital, and, after a painful interval, said—

"Then the actual murderer is, after all, unascertained. This is, indeed, horrible; it was very natural that my father should have felt the danger to which such a disclosure would have exposed the reputation of our family, yet I should have preferred encountering it, were it ten times as great, to the equivocal prudence of suppressing the truth with respect to a murder committed under my own roof."

"He has, however, it would seem, arrived at some new conclusions," said Dr. Danvers, "and is now prepared to throw some unanticipated light upon the whole transaction."

Even as they were talking, a knocking was heard at the hall-door, and after a brief and hurried consultation, it was agreed, that, considering the strict condition of privacy attached to this visit by Mr. Marston himself, as well as his reserved and wayward temper, it might be better for Charles to avoid presenting himself to his father on this occasion. A few seconds afterwards the door opened, and Mr. Marston entered the apartment. It was now dark, and the servant, unbidden, placed candles upon the table. Without answering one word to Dr. Danvers' greeting, Marston sat down, as it seemed, in agitated abstraction. Removing his hat suddenly (for he had not even made this slight homage to the laws of courtesy), he looked round with a careworn, fiery eye, and a pale countenance, and said—

"We are quite alone, Dr. Danvers—no one anywhere near?"

Dr. Danvers assured him that all was secure. After a long and agitated pause, Marston said—

"You remember Merton's confession. He admitted his intention to kill Berkley, but denied that he was the actual murderer. He spoke truth—no one knew it better than I; for I am the murderer."

Dr. Danvers was so shocked and overwhelmed that he was utterly unable to speak.

"Aye, sir, in point of law and of morals, literally and honestly, the murderer of Wynston Berkley. I am resolved you shall know it all. Make what use of it you will—I care for nothing now, but to get rid of the d——d, unsustainable secret, and that is done. I did not intend to kill the scoundrel when I went to his room; but with the just feelings of exasperation with which I regarded him, it would have been wiser had I avoided the interview; and I meant to have done so. But his candle was burning; I saw the light through the door, and went in. It was his evil fortune to indulge in his old strain of sardonic impertinence. He provoked me; I struck him—he struck me again—and with his own dagger I stabbed him three times.

"I did not know what I had done; I could not believe it. I felt neither remorse nor sorrow—why should I?—but the thing was horrible, astounding. There he sat in the corner of his cushioned chair, with the old fiendish smile on still. Sir, I never thought that any human shape could look so dreadful. I don't know how long I stayed there, freezing with horror and detestation, and yet unable to take my eyes from the face. Did you see it in the coffin? Sir, there was a sneer of triumph on it that was diabolic and prophetic."

Marston was fearfully agitated as he spoke, and repeatedly wiped from his face the cold sweat that gathered there.

"I could not leave the room by the back stairs," he resumed, "for the valet slept in the intervening chamber. I felt such an appalled antipathy to the body, that I could scarcely muster courage to pass it. But, sir, I am not easily cowed—I mastered this repugnance in a few minutes—or, rather, I acted spite of it, I knew not how; but instinctively it seemed to me that it was better to lay the body in the bed, than leave it where it was, shewing, as its position might, that the thing occurred in an altercation. So, sir, I raised it, and bore it softly across the room, and laid it in the bed; and, while I was carrying it, it swayed forward, the arms glided round my neck, and the head rested against my cheek—that was a parody upon a brotherly embrace!

"I do not know at what moment it was, but some time when I was carrying Wynston, or laying him in the bed," continued Marston, who spoke rather like one pursuing a horrible reverie, than as a man relating facts to a listener, "I heard a light tread, and soft breathing in the lobby. A thunderclap would have stunned me less that minute. I moved softly, holding my breath, to the door. I believe, in moments of strong excitement, men hear more acutely than at other times; but I thought I heard the rustling of a gown, going from the door again. I waited—it ceased; I waited until all was quiet.

"I then extinguished the candle, and groped my way to the door; there was a faint light in the corridor, and I thought I saw a head projected from the chamber-door, next to the French-woman's—*mademoiselle's*. As I came on, it was softly withdrawn, and the door not quite noiselessly closed. I could not be absolutely certain, but I learned all afterward. And now, sir, you have the story of Sir Wynston's murder."

Dr. Danvers groaned in spirit, being wrung alike with fear and sorrow. With hands clasped, and head bowed down, in an exceeding bitter agony of soul, he murmured only the words of the Litany—*Lord, have mercy upon us; Christ, have mercy upon us; Lord, have mercy upon us.*

Marston had recovered his usual lowering aspect and gloomy self-possession in a few moments, and was now standing erect and defiant before the humbled and afflicted minister of God. The contrast was terrible—almost sublime.

Doctor Danvers resolved to keep this dreadful secret, at least for a time, to himself. He could not make up his mind to inflict upon those whom he loved so well as Charles and Rhoda the shame and agony of such a disclosure; yet he was sorely troubled, for his was a conflict of duty and mercy, of love and justice.

He told Charles Marston, when urged with earnest inquiry, that what he had heard that evening was intended solely for his own ear, and gently but peremptorily declined telling, at least until some future time, the substance of his father's communication.

Charles now felt it necessary to see his father, for the purpose of letting him know the substance of the letter respecting *"mademoiselle"* and the late Sir Wynston which had reached him. Accordingly, he proceeded, accompanied by Doctor Danvers, on the next morning, to the hotel where Marston had intimated his intention of passing the night.

On their inquiring for him in the hall, the porter appeared much perplexed and disturbed, and as they pressed him with questions, his answers became conflicting and mysterious. Mr. Marston was there—he had slept there last night; he could not say whether or not he was then in the house; but he knew that no one could be admitted to see him. He would, if the gentlemen wished it, send their cards to (not Mr. Marston, but) the proprietor. And, finally, he concluded by begging that they would themselves see "the proprietor," and dispatched a waiter to apprise him of the circumstances of the visit. There was something odd and even sinister in all this, which, along with the whispering and the curious glances of the waiters, who happened to hear the errand on which they came, inspired the two companions with vague misgivings, which they did not care mutually to disclose.

In a few moments they were shown into a small sitting room upstairs, where the proprietor, a fussy little gentleman, and apparently very uneasy and frightened, received them.

"We have called here to see Mr. Marston," said Doctor Danvers, "and the porter has referred us to you."

"Yes, sir, exactly—precisely so," answered the little man, fidgeting excessively, and as it seemed, growing paler every instant; "but—but, in fact, sir, there is, there has been—in short, have you not heard of the—the accident?"

He wound up with a prodigious effort, and wiped his forehead when he had done.

"Pray, sir, be explicit: we are near friends of Mr. Marston; in fact, sir, this is his son," said Doctor Danvers, pointing to Charles Marston; "and we are both uneasy at the reserve with which our inquiries have been met. Do, I entreat of you, say what has happened?"

"Why—why," hesitated the man, "I really—I would not for five hundred pounds it had happened in my house. The—the unhappy gentleman has, in short—"

He glanced at Charles, as if afraid of the effect of the disclosure he was on the point of making, and then hurriedly said-
"He is dead, sir; he was found dead in his room, this morning, at eight o'clock. I assure you I have not been myself ever since."

Charles Marston was so stunned by this sudden blow, that he was upon the point of fainting. Rallying, however, with a strong effort, he demanded to be conducted to the chamber where the body lay. The man assented, but hesitated on reaching the door, and whispered something in the ear of Doctor Danvers, who, as he heard it, raised his hands and eyes with a mute expression of horror, and turning to Charles, said—

"My dear young friend, remain where you are for a few moments. I will return to you immediately, and tell you whatever I have ascertained. You are in no condition for such a scene at present."

Charles, indeed, felt that the fact was so, and, sick and giddy, suffered Doctor Danvers, with gentle compulsion, to force him into a seat.

In silence the venerable clergyman followed his conductor. With a palpitating heart he advanced to the bedside, and twice essayed to draw the curtain, and twice lost courage; but gathering resolution at last, he pulled the drapery aside, and beheld all he was to see again of Richard Marston.

The bedclothes were drawn so as nearly to cover the mouth.

"There is the wound, sir," whispered the man, as with coarse officiousness he drew back the bedclothes from the throat of the corpse, and exhibited a gash, as it seemed, nearly severing the head from the body. With sickening horror Doctor Danvers turned away from the awful spectacle. He covered his face in his hands, and it seemed to him as if a soft, solemn voice whispered in his ear the mystic words, "*Whoso sheddeth man's blood, by man shall his blood be shed.*"

The hand which, but a few years before, had, unsuspected, consigned a fellow-mortal to the grave, had itself avenged the murder—Marston had perished by his own hand.

Naturally ambitious and intriguing, the perilous tendencies of such a spirit in Mademoiselle de Barras had never been schooled by the mighty and benignant principles of religion; of her accidental acquaintance at Rouen with Sir Wynston Berkley, and her subsequent introduction, in an evil hour, into the family at Gray Forest, it is unnecessary to speak. The unhappy terms on which she found Marston living with his wife, suggested, in their mutual alienation, the idea of founding a double influence in the household; and to conceive the idea, and to act upon it, were, in her active mind, the same. Young, beautiful, fascinating, she well knew the power of her attractions, and determined, though probably without one thought of transgressing the limits of literal propriety, to bring them to bear upon the discontented, retired *roué*, for whom she cared absolutely nothing, except as the instrument, and in part the victim of her schemes.

Thus yielding to the double instinct that swayed her, she gratified, at the same time, her love of intrigue and her love of power. At length, however, came the hour which demanded a sacrifice to the evil influence she had hitherto worshipped on such easy terms. She found that her power must now be secured by crime, and she fell. Then came the arrival of Sir Wynston—his murder—her elopement with Marston, and her guilty and joyless triumph. At last, however, came the blow, long suspended and terrific, which shattered all her hopes and schemes, and drove her once again upon the world. The catastrophe we have just described.

After it she made her way to Paris. Arrived in the capital of

France, she speedily dissipated whatever remained of the money and valuables which she had taken with her from Gray Forest; and Madame Marston, as she now styled herself, was glad to place herself once more as a governess in an aristocratic family. So far her good fortune had prevailed in averting the punishment but too well earned by her past life. But a day of reckoning was to come. A few years later France was involved in the uproar and conflagration of revolution.

Noble families were scattered, beggared, decimated; and their dependants, often dragged along with them into the flaming abyss, in many instances suffered the last dire extremities of human ill. It was at this awful period that a retribution so frightful and extraordinary overtook Madame Marston, that we may hereafter venture to make it the subject of a separate narrative. Until then the reader will rest satisfied with what he already knows of her history; and meanwhile bid a long, and as it may possibly turn out, an eternal farewell to that beautiful embodiment of an evil and disastrous influence.

The concluding chapter in a novel is always brief, though seldom so short as the world would have it. In a tale like this, the "winding up" must be proportionately contracted. We have scarcely a claim to so many lines as the formal novelist may occupy pages, in the distribution of poetic justice, and the final grouping of his characters into that effective tableau upon which, at last, the curtain gracefully descends. We, too, may be all the briefer, inasmuch as the reader has doubtless anticipated the little we have to say. It amounts, then, to this:—

Within two years after the fearful event which we have just recorded, an alliance had drawn together, in nearer and dearer union, the inmates of Gray Forest and Newton Park. Rhoda had given her hand to young Mervyn, of ulterior consequences we say nothing—the nursery is above our province. And now, at length, after this Christmas journey through somewhat stern and gloomy scenery, in this long-deferred flood of golden sunshine we bid thee, gentle reader, a fond farewell.

A Chapter in the History of a Tyrone Family

(Later rewritten as the novel *The Wyvern Mystery*.)

INTRODUCTION

In the following narrative, I have endeavoured to give as nearly as possible the *ipsissima verba* of the valued friend from whom I received it, conscious that any aberration from HER mode of telling the tale of her own life would at once impair its accuracy and its effect.

Would that, with her words, I could also bring before you her animated gesture, her expressive countenance, the solemn and thrilling air and accent with which she related the dark passages in her strange story; and, above all, that I could communicate the impressive consciousness that the narrator had seen with her own eyes, and personally acted in the scenes which she described; these accompaniments, taken with the additional circumstance that she who told the tale was one far too deeply and sadly impressed with religious principle to misrepresent or fabricate what she repeated as fact, gave to the tale a depth of interest which the events recorded could hardly, themselves, have produced.

I became acquainted with the lady from whose lips I heard this narrative nearly twenty years since, and the story struck my fancy so much that I committed it to paper while it was still fresh in my mind; and should its perusal afford you entertainment for a listless half hour, my labour shall not have been bestowed in vain.

I find that I have taken the story down as she told it, in the first person, and perhaps this is as it should be.

She began as follows:

My maiden name was Richardson,[1] the designation of a family of some distinction in the county of Tyrone. I was the younger of two daughters, and we were the only children. There was a difference in our ages of nearly six years, so that I did not, in my childhood, enjoy that close companionship which sisterhood, in other circumstances, necessarily involves; and while I was still a child, my sister was married.

The person upon whom she bestowed her hand was a Mr. Carew, a gentleman of property and consideration in the north of England.

I remember well the eventful day of the wedding; the thronging carriages, the noisy menials, the loud laughter, the merry faces, and the gay dresses. Such sights were then new to me, and harmonised ill with the sorrowful feelings with which I regarded the event which was to separate me, as it turned out, forever from a sister whose tenderness alone had hitherto more than supplied all that I wanted in my mother's affection.

The day soon arrived which was to remove the happy couple from Ashtown House. The carriage stood at the hall-door, and my poor sister kissed me again and again, telling me that I should see her soon.

The carriage drove away, and I gazed after it until my eyes filled with tears, and, returning slowly to my chamber, I wept more bitterly and, so to speak, more desolately, than ever I had done before.

My father had never seemed to love or to take an interest in me. He had desired a son, and I think he never thoroughly forgave me my unfortunate sex.

---

1. I have carefully altered the names as they appear in the original MSS., for the reader will see that some of the circumstances recorded are not of a kind to reflect honour upon those involved in them; and as many are still living, in every way honoured and honourable, who stand in close relation to the principal actors in this drama, the reader will see the necessity of the course which we have adopted.

My having come into the world at all as his child he regarded as a kind of fraudulent intrusion, and as his antipathy to me had its origin in an imperfection of mine, too radical for removal, I never even hoped to stand high in his good graces.

My mother was, I dare say, as fond of me as she was of anyone; but she was a woman of a masculine and a worldly cast of mind. She had no tenderness or sympathy for the weaknesses, or even for the affections, of woman's nature and her demeanour towards me was peremptory, and often even harsh.

It is not to be supposed, then, that I found in the society of my parents much to supply the loss of my sister. About a year after her marriage, we received letters from Mr. Carew, containing accounts of my sister's health, which, though not actually alarming, were calculated to make us seriously uneasy. The symptoms most dwelt upon were loss of appetite and cough.

The letters concluded by intimating that he would avail himself of my father and mother's repeated invitation to spend some time at Ashtown, particularly as the physician who had been consulted as to my sister's health had strongly advised a removal to her native air.

There were added repeated assurances that nothing serious was apprehended, as it was supposed that a deranged state of the liver was the only source of the symptoms which at first had seemed to intimate consumption.

In accordance with this announcement, my sister and Mr. Carew arrived in Dublin, where one of my father's carriages awaited them, in readiness to start upon whatever day or hour they might choose for their departure

It was arranged that Mr. Carew was, as soon as the day upon which they were to leave Dublin was definitely fixed, to write to my father, who intended that the two last stages should be performed by his own horses, upon whose speed and safety far more reliance might be placed than upon those of the ordinary posthorses, which were at that time, almost without exception, of the very worst order. The journey, one of about ninety miles, was to be divided; the larger portion being reserved for the second day.

On Sunday a letter reached us, stating that the party would leave Dublin on Monday, and, in due course, reach Ashtown upon Tuesday evening.

Tuesday came the evening closed in, and yet no carriage; darkness came on, and still no sign of our expected visitors.

Hour after hour passed away, and it was now past twelve; the night was remarkably calm, scarce a breath stirring, so that any sound, such as that produced by the rapid movement of a vehicle, would have been audible at a considerable distance. For some such sound I was feverishly listening.

It was, however, my father's rule to close the house at night-fall, and the window-shutters being fastened, I was unable to reconnoitre the avenue as I would have wished. It was nearly one o'clock, and we began almost to despair of seeing them upon that night, when I thought I distinguished the sound of wheels, but so remote and faint as to make me at first very uncertain. The noise approached; it became louder and clearer; it stopped for a moment.

I now heard the shrill screaming of the rusty iron, as the avenue-gate revolved on its hinges; again came the sound of wheels in rapid motion.

'It is they,' said I, starting up; 'the carriage is in the avenue.'

We all stood for a few moments breathlessly listening. On thundered the vehicle with the speed of a whirlwind; crack went the whip, and clatter went the wheels, as it rattled over the uneven pavement of the court. A general and furious barking from all the dogs about the house, hailed its arrival.

We hurried to the hall in time to hear the steps let down with the sharp clanging noise peculiar to the operation, and the hum of voices exerted in the bustle of arrival. The hall-door was now thrown open, and we all stepped forth to greet our visitors.

The court was perfectly empty; the moon was shining broadly and brightly upon all around; nothing was to be seen but the tall trees with their long spectral shadows, now wet with the dews of midnight.

We stood gazing from right to left, as if suddenly awakened

from a dream; the dogs walked suspiciously, growling and snuff-
ing about the court, and by totally and suddenly ceasing their
former loud barking, expressing the predominance of fear.

We stared one upon another in perplexity and dismay, and I
think I never beheld more pale faces assembled. By my father's
direction, we looked about to find anything which might indicate or account for the noise which we had heard; but no such
thing was to be seen—even the mire which lay upon the avenue
was undisturbed. We returned to the house, more panic-struck
than I can describe.

On the next day, we learned by a messenger, who had ridden hard the greater part of the night, that my sister was dead.
On Sunday evening, she had retired to bed rather unwell, and,
on Monday, her indisposition declared itself unequivocally to
be malignant fever. She became hourly worse and, on Tuesday
night, a little after midnight, she expired[2]

---

2. The residuary legatee of the late Frances Purcell, who has the honour of select-
ing such of his lamented old friend's manuscripts as may appear fit for publication,
in order that the lore which they contain may reach the world before scepticism
and utility have robbed our species of the precious gift of credulity, and scorn-
fully kicked before them, or trampled into annihilation those harmless fragments
of picturesque superstition which it is our object to preserve, has been subjected to
the charge of dealing too largely in the marvellous; and it has been half insinuated
that such is his love for *diablerie*, that he is content to wander a mile out of his way,
in order to meet a fiend or a goblin, and thus to sacrifice all regard for truth and
accuracy to the idle hope of affrighting the imagination, and thus pandering to the
bad taste of his reader. He begs leave, then, to take this opportunity of asserting his
perfect innocence of all the crimes laid to his charge, and to assure his reader that
he never PANDERED TO HIS BAD TASTE, nor went one inch out of his way
to introduce witch, fairy, devil, ghost, or any other of the grim fraternity of the re-
doubted Raw-head-and-bloody-bones. His province, touching these tales, has been
attended with no difficulty and little responsibility; indeed, he is accountable for
nothing more than an alteration in the names of persons mentioned therein, when
such a step seemed necessary, and for an occasional note, whenever he conceived it
possible, innocently, to edge in a word. These tales have been WRITTEN DOWN,
as the heading of each announces, by the Rev. Francis Purcell, P.P., of Drumcool-
agh; and in all the instances, which are many, in which the present writer has had
an opportunity of comparing the manuscript of his departed friend with the actual
traditions which are current amongst the families whose fortunes they pretend to il-
lustrate, he has uniformly found that whatever of supernatural occurred in the story,
so far from having been exaggerated by him, had been rather softened down, and,
wherever it could be attempted, accounted for.

I mention this circumstance, because it was one upon which a thousand wild and fantastical reports were founded, though one would have thought that the truth scarcely required to be improved upon; and again, because it produced a strong and lasting effect upon my spirits, and indeed, I am inclined to think, upon my character.

I was, for several years after this occurrence, long after the violence of my grief subsided, so wretchedly low-spirited and nervous, that I could scarcely be said to live; and during this time, habits of indecision, arising out of a listless acquiescence in the will of others, a fear of encountering even the slightest opposition, and a disposition to shrink from what are commonly called amusements, grew upon me so strongly, that I have scarcely even yet altogether overcome them.

We saw nothing more of Mr. Carew. He returned to England as soon as the melancholy rites attendant upon the event which I have just mentioned were performed; and not being altogether inconsolable, he married again within two years; after which, owing to the remoteness of our relative situations, and other circumstances, we gradually lost sight of him.

I was now an only child; and, as my elder sister had died without issue, it was evident that, in the ordinary course of things, my father's property, which was altogether in his power, would go to me; and the consequence was, that before I was fourteen, Ashtown House was besieged by a host of suitors. However, whether it was that I was too young, or that none of the aspirants to my hand stood sufficiently high in rank or wealth, I was suffered by both parents to do exactly as I pleased; and well was it for me, as I afterwards found, that fortune, or rather Providence, had so ordained it, that I had not suffered my affections to become in any degree engaged, for my mother would never have suffered any SILLY FANCY of mine, as she was in the habit of styling an attachment, to stand in the way of her ambitious views—views which she was determined to carry into effect, in defiance of every obstacle, and in order to accomplish which she would not have hesitated to sacrifice anything so unreasonable and contemptible as a girlish passion.

When I reached the age of sixteen, my mother's plans began to develop themselves; and, at her suggestion, we moved to Dublin to sojourn for the winter, in order that no time might be lost in disposing of me to the best advantage.

I had been too long accustomed to consider myself as of no importance whatever, to believe for a moment that I was in reality the cause of all the bustle and preparation which surrounded me, and being thus relieved from the pain which a consciousness of my real situation would have inflicted, I journeyed towards the capital with a feeling of total indifference.

My father's wealth and connection had established him in the best society, and, consequently, upon our arrival in the metropolis we commanded whatever enjoyment or advantages its gaieties afforded.

The tumult and novelty of the scenes in which I was involved did not fail considerably to amuse me, and my mind gradually recovered its tone, which was naturally cheerful.

It was almost immediately known and reported that I was an heiress, and of course my attractions were pretty generally acknowledged.

Among the many gentlemen whom it was my fortune to please, one, ere long, established himself in my mother's good graces, to the exclusion of all less important aspirants. However, I had not understood or even remarked his attentions, nor in the slightest degree suspected his or my mother's plans respecting me, when I was made aware of them rather abruptly by my mother herself.

We had attended a splendid ball, given by Lord M——, at his residence in Stephen's Green, and I was, with the assistance of my waiting-maid, employed in rapidly divesting myself of the rich ornaments which, in profuseness and value, could scarcely have found their equals in any private family in Ireland.

I had thrown myself into a lounging-chair beside the fire, listless and exhausted, after the fatigues of the evening, when I was aroused from the reverie into which I had fallen by the sound of footsteps approaching my chamber, and my mother entered.

'Fanny, my dear,' said she, in her softest tone, 'I wish to say a word or two with you before I go to rest. You are not fatigued, love, I hope?'

'No, no, madam, I thank you,' said I, rising at the same time from my seat, with the formal respect so little practised now.

'Sit down, my dear,' said she, placing herself upon a chair beside me; 'I must chat with you for a quarter of an hour or so. Saunders' (to the maid) 'you may leave the room; do not close the room-door, but shut that of the lobby.'

This precaution against curious ears having been taken as directed, my mother proceeded.

'You have observed, I should suppose, my dearest Fanny-indeed, you MUST have observed Lord Glenfallen's marked attentions to you?'

'I assure you, madam——' I began.

'Well, well, that is all right,' interrupted my mother; 'of course you must be modest upon the matter; but listen to me for a few moments, my love, and I will prove to your satisfaction that your modesty is quite unnecessary in this case. You have done better than we could have hoped, at least so very soon. Lord Glenfallen is in love with you. I give you joy of your conquest;' and saying this, my mother kissed my forehead.

'In love with me!' I exclaimed, in unfeigned astonishment.

'Yes, in love with you,' repeated my mother; 'devotedly, distractedly in love with you. Why, my dear, what is there wonderful in it? Look in the glass, and look at these,' she continued, pointing with a smile to the jewels which I had just removed from my person, and which now lay a glittering heap upon the table.

'May there not,' said I, hesitating between confusion and real alarm—'is it not possible that some mistake may be at the bottom of all this?'

'Mistake, dearest! none,' said my mother. 'None; none in the world. Judge for yourself; read this, my love.' And she placed in my hand a letter, addressed to herself, the seal of which was broken. I read it through with no small surprise. After some very fine complimentary flourishes upon my beauty and perfections, as also upon the antiquity and high reputation of our family, it went on to make a formal proposal of marriage, to be communicated or not to me at present, as my mother should deem expedient; and the letter wound up by a request that the writer might be permitted, upon our return to Ashtown House, which was soon to take place, as the spring was now tolerably advanced, to visit us for a few days, in case his suit was approved.

'Well, well, my dear,' said my mother, impatiently; 'do you know who Lord Glenfallen is?'

'I do, madam,' said I rather timidly, for I dreaded an altercation with my mother.

'Well, dear, and what frightens you?' continued she. 'Are you afraid of a title? What has he done to alarm you? he is neither old nor ugly.'

I was silent, though I might have said, 'He is neither young nor handsome.'

'My dear Fanny,' continued my mother, 'in sober seriousness you have been most fortunate in engaging the affections of a nobleman such as Lord Glenfallen, young and wealthy, with first-rate—yes, acknowledged FIRST-RATE abilities, and of a family whose influence is not exceeded by that of any in Ireland. Of course you see the offer in the same light that I do—indeed I think you MUST.'

This was uttered in no very dubious tone. I was so much astonished by the suddenness of the whole communication that I literally did not know what to say.

'You are not in love?' said my mother, turning sharply, and fixing her dark eyes upon me with severe scrutiny.

'No, madam,' said I, promptly; horrified, as what young lady would not have been, at such a query.

'I'm glad to hear it,' said my mother, drily. 'Once, nearly twenty years ago, a friend of mine consulted me as to how he should deal with a daughter who had made what they call a love-match—beggared herself, and disgraced her family; and I said, without hesitation, take no care for her, but cast her off. Such punishment I awarded for an offence committed against the reputation of a family not my own; and what I advised respecting the child of another, with full as small compunction I would DO with mine. I cannot conceive anything more unreasonable or intolerable than that the fortune and the character of a family should be marred by the idle caprices of a girl.'

She spoke this with great severity, and paused as if she expected some observation from me.

I, however, said nothing.

'But I need not explain to you, my dear Fanny,' she continued, 'my views upon this subject; you have always known them well, and I have never yet had reason to believe you likely, voluntarily, to offend me, or to abuse or neglect any of those advantages which reason and duty tell you should be improved. Come hither, my dear; kiss me, and do not look so frightened. Well, now, about this letter, you need not answer it yet; of course you must be allowed time to make up your mind. In the meantime I will write to his lordship to give him my permission to visit us at Ashtown. Good night, my love.'

And thus ended one of the most disagreeable, not to say astounding, conversations I had ever had. It would not be easy to describe exactly what were my feelings towards Lord Glenfallen;—whatever might have been my mother's suspicions, my heart was perfectly disengaged—and hitherto, although I had not been made in the slightest degree acquainted with his real views, I had liked him very much, as an agreeable, well-informed man, whom I was always glad to meet in society. He had served in the navy in early life, and the polish which his manners received in his after intercourse with courts and cities had not served to obliterate that frankness of manner which belongs proverbially to the sailor.

Whether this apparent candour went deeper than the outward bearing, I was yet to learn. However, there was no doubt that, as far as I had seen of Lord Glenfallen, he was, though perhaps not so young as might have been desired in a lover, a singularly pleasing man; and whatever feeling unfavourable to him had found its way into my mind, arose altogether from the dread, not an unreasonable one, that constraint might be practised upon my inclinations. I reflected, however, that Lord Glenfallen was a wealthy man, and one highly thought of; and although I could never expect to love him in the romantic sense of the term, yet I had no doubt but that, all things considered, I might be more happy with him than I could hope to be at home.

When next I met him it was with no small embarrassment, his tact and good breeding, however, soon reassured me, and effectually prevented my awkwardness being remarked upon. And I had the satisfaction of leaving Dublin for the country with the full conviction that nobody, not even those most intimate with me, even suspected the fact of Lord Glenfallen's having made me a formal proposal.

This was to me a very serious subject of self-gratulation, for, besides my instinctive dread of becoming the topic of the speculations of gossip, I felt that if the situation which I occupied in relation to him were made publicly known, I should stand committed in a manner which would scarcely leave me the power of retraction.

The period at which Lord Glenfallen had arranged to visit Ashtown House was now fast approaching, and it became my mother's wish to form me thoroughly to her will, and to obtain my consent to the proposed marriage before his arrival, so that all things might proceed smoothly, without apparent opposition or objection upon my part. Whatever objections, therefore, I had entertained were to be subdued; whatever disposition to resistance I had exhibited or had been supposed to feel, were to be completely eradicated before he made his appearance; and my mother addressed herself to the task with a decision and energy against which even the barriers, which her imagination had created, could hardly have stood.

If she had, however, expected any determined opposition from me, she was agreeably disappointed. My heart was perfectly free, and all my feelings of liking and preference were in favour of Lord Glenfallen; and I well knew that in case I refused to dispose of myself as I was desired, my mother had alike the power and the will to render my existence as utterly miserable as even the most ill-assorted marriage could possibly have done.

You will remember, my good friend, that I was very young and very completely under the control of my parents, both of whom, my mother particularly, were unscrupulously determined in matters of this kind, and willing, when voluntary obedience on the part of those within their power was withheld, to compel a forced acquiescence by an unsparing use of all the engines of the most stern and rigorous domestic discipline.

All these combined, not unnaturally, induced me to resolve upon yielding at once, and without useless opposition, to what appeared almost to be my fate.

The appointed time was come, and my now accepted suitor arrived; he was in high spirits, and, if possible, more entertaining than ever.

I was not, however, quite in the mood to enjoy his sprightliness; but whatever I wanted in gaiety was amply made up in the triumphant and gracious good-humour of my mother, whose smiles of benevolence and exultation were showered around as bountifully as the summer sunshine.

I will not weary you with unnecessary prolixity. Let it suffice to say, that I was married to Lord Glenfallen with all the attendant pomp and circumstance of wealth, rank, and grandeur. According to the usage of the times, now humanely reformed, the ceremony was made, until long past midnight, the season of wild, uproarious, and promiscuous feasting and revelry.

Of all this I have a painfully vivid recollection, and particularly of the little annoyances inflicted upon me by the dull and coarse jokes of the wits and wags who abound in all such places, and upon all such occasions.

I was not sorry when, after a few days, Lord Glenfallen's carriage appeared at the door to convey us both from Ashtown; for any change would have been a relief from the irksomeness of ceremonial and formality which the visits received in honour of my newly-acquired titles hourly entailed upon me.

It was arranged that we were to proceed to Cahergillagh, one of the Glenfallen estates, lying, however, in a southern county, so that, owing to the difficulty of the roads at the time, a tedious journey of three days intervened.

I set forth with my noble companion, followed by the regrets of some, and by the envy of many; though God knows I little deserved the latter. The three days of travel were now almost spent, when, passing the brow of a wild heathy hill, the domain of Cahergillagh opened suddenly upon our view.

It formed a striking and a beautiful scene. A lake of considerable extent stretching away towards the west, and reflecting from its broad, smooth waters, the rich glow of the setting sun, was overhung by steep hills, covered by a rich mantle of velvet sward, broken here and there by the grey front of some old rock, and exhibiting on their shelving sides, their slopes and hollows, every variety of light and shade; a thick wood of dwarf oak, birch, and hazel skirted these hills, and clothed the shores of the lake, running out in rich luxuriance upon every promontory, and spreading upward considerably upon the side of the hills.

'There lies the enchanted castle,' said Lord Glenfallen, pointing towards a considerable level space intervening between two of the picturesque hills, which rose dimly around the lake.

This little plain was chiefly occupied by the same low, wild wood which covered the other parts of the domain; but towards the centre a mass of taller and statelier forest trees stood darkly grouped together, and among them stood an ancient square tower, with many buildings of a humbler character, forming together the manor-house, or, as it was more usually called, the Court of Cahergillagh.

As we approached the level upon which the mansion stood, the winding road gave us many glimpses of the time-worn castle and its surrounding buildings; and seen as it was through the long *vistas* of the fine old trees, and with the rich glow of evening upon it, I have seldom beheld an object more picturesquely striking.

I was glad to perceive, too, that here and there the blue curling smoke ascended from stacks of chimneys now hidden by the rich, dark ivy which, in a great measure, covered the building. Other indications of comfort made themselves manifest as we approached; and indeed, though the place was evidently one of considerable antiquity, it had nothing whatever of the gloom of decay about it.

'You must not, my love,' said Lord Glenfallen, 'imagine this place worse than it is. I have no taste for antiquity—at least I should not choose a house to reside in because it is old. Indeed I do not recollect that I was even so romantic as to overcome my aversion to rats and rheumatism, those faithful attendants upon your noble relics of feudalism; and I much prefer a snug, modern, unmysterious bedroom, with well-aired sheets, to the waving tapestry, mildewed cushions, and all the other interesting appliances of romance. However, though I cannot promise you all the discomfort generally belonging to an old castle, you will find legends and ghostly lore enough to claim your respect; and if old Martha be still to the fore, as I trust she is, you will soon have a supernatural and appropriate anecdote for every closet and corner of the mansion; but here we are—so, without more ado, welcome to Cahergillagh!'

We now entered the hall of the castle, and while the domestics were employed in conveying our trunks and other luggage which we had brought with us for immediate use to the apartments which Lord Glenfallen had selected for himself and me, I went with him into a spacious sitting-room, wainscoted with finely polished black oak, and hung round with the portraits of various worthies of the Glenfallen family.

This room looked out upon an extensive level covered with the softest green sward, and irregularly bounded by the wild wood I have before mentioned, through the leafy arcade formed by whose boughs and trunks the level beams of the setting sun were pouring. In the distance a group of dairy-maids were plying their task, which they accompanied throughout with snatches of Irish songs which, mellowed by the distance, floated not unpleasingly to the ear; and beside them sat or lay, with all the grave importance of conscious protection, six or seven large dogs of various kinds. Farther in the distance, and through the cloisters of the arching wood, two or three ragged urchins were employed in driving such stray kine as had wandered farther than the rest to join their fellows.

As I looked upon this scene which I have described, a feeling of tranquillity and happiness came upon me, which I have never experienced in so strong a degree; and so strange to me was the sensation that my eyes filled with tears.

Lord Glenfallen mistook the cause of my emotion, and taking me kindly and tenderly by the hand, he said:

'Do not suppose, my love, that it is my intention to SETTLE here. Whenever you desire to leave this, you have only to let me know your wish, and it shall be complied with; so I must entreat of you not to suffer any circumstances which I can control to give you one moment's uneasiness. But here is old Martha; you must be introduced to her, one of the heirlooms of our family.'

A hale, good-humoured, erect old woman was Martha, and an agreeable contrast to the grim, decrepid hag which my fancy had conjured up, as the depository of all the horrible tales in which I doubted not this old place was most fruitful.

She welcomed me and her master with a profusion of gratulations, alternately kissing our hands and apologising for the liberty, until at length Lord Glenfallen put an end to this somewhat fatiguing ceremonial by requesting her to conduct me to my chamber if it were prepared for my reception.

I followed Martha up an old-fashioned oak staircase into a long, dim passage, at the end of which lay the door which communicated with the apartments which had been selected for our use; here the old woman stopped, and respectfully requested me to proceed.

I accordingly opened the door, and was about to enter, when something like a mass of black tapestry, as it appeared, disturbed by my sudden approach, fell from above the door, so as completely to screen the aperture; the startling unexpectedness of the occurrence, and the rustling noise which the drapery made in its descent, caused me involuntarily to step two or three paces backwards. I turned, smiling and half-ashamed, to the old servant, and said:

'You see what a coward I am.'

The woman looked puzzled, and, without saying any more, I was about to draw aside the curtain and enter the room, when, upon turning to do so, I was surprised to find that nothing whatever interposed to obstruct the passage.

I went into the room, followed by the servant-woman, and was amazed to find that it, like the one below, was wainscoted, and that nothing like drapery was to be found near the door.

'Where is it?' said I; 'what has become of it?'

'What does your ladyship wish to know?' said the old woman.

'Where is the black curtain that fell across the door, when I attempted first to come to my chamber?' answered I.

'The cross of Christ about us!' said the old woman, turning suddenly pale.

'What is the matter, my good friend?' said I; 'you seem frightened.'

'Oh no, no, your ladyship,' said the old woman, endeavouring to conceal her agitation; but in vain, for tottering towards a chair, she sank into it, looking so deadly pale and horror-struck that I thought every moment she would faint.

'Merciful God, keep us from harm and danger!' muttered she at length.

'What can have terrified you so?' said I, beginning to fear that she had seen something more than had met my eye. 'You appear ill, my poor woman!'

'Nothing, nothing, my lady,' said she, rising. 'I beg your ladyship's pardon for making so bold. May the great God defend us from misfortune!'

'Martha,' said I, 'something HAS frightened you very much, and I insist on knowing what it is; your keeping me in the dark upon the subject will make me much more uneasy than anything you could tell me. I desire you, therefore, to let me know what agitates you; I command you to tell me.'

'Your ladyship said you saw a black curtain falling across the door when you were coming into the room,' said the old woman.

'I did,' said I; 'but though the whole thing appears somewhat strange, I cannot see anything in the matter to agitate you so excessively.'

'It's for no good you saw that, my lady,' said the crone; 'something terrible is coming. It's a sign, my lady—a sign that never fails.'

'Explain, explain what you mean, my good woman,' said I, in spite of myself, catching more than I could account for, of her superstitious terror.

'Whenever something—something BAD is going to happen to the Glenfallen family, some one that belongs to them sees a black handkerchief or curtain just waved or falling before their faces. I saw it myself,' continued she, lowering her voice, 'when I was only a little girl, and I'll never forget it. I often heard of it before, though I never saw it till then, nor since, praised be God. But I was going into Lady Jane's room to waken her in the morning; and sure enough when I got first to the bed and began to draw the curtain, something dark was waved across the division, but only for a moment; and when I saw rightly into the bed, there was she lying cold and dead, God be merciful to me! So, my lady, there is small blame to me to be daunted when any one of the family sees it; for it's many's the story I heard of it, though I saw it but once.'

I was not of a superstitious turn of mind, yet I could not resist a feeling of awe very nearly allied to the fear which my companion had so unreservedly expressed; and when you consider my situation, the loneliness, antiquity, and gloom of the place, you will allow that the weakness was not without excuse.

In spite of old Martha's boding predictions, however, time flowed on in an unruffled course. One little incident however, though trifling in itself, I must relate, as it serves to make what follows more intelligible.

Upon the day after my arrival, Lord Glenfallen of course desired to make me acquainted with the house and domain; and accordingly we set forth upon our ramble. When returning, he became for some time silent and moody, a state so unusual with him as considerably to excite my surprise.

I endeavoured by observations and questions to arouse him-but in vain. At length, as we approached the house, he said, as if speaking to himself:

''Twere madness—madness—madness,' repeating the words bitterly—'sure and speedy ruin.'

There was here a long pause; and at length, turning sharply towards me, in a tone very unlike that in which he had hitherto addressed me, he said:

'Do you think it possible that a woman can keep a secret?'

'I am sure,' said I, 'that women are very much belied upon the score of talkativeness, and that I may answer your question with the same directness with which you put it—I reply that I DO think a woman can keep a secret.'

'But I do not,' said he, drily.

We walked on in silence for a time. I was much astonished at his unwonted abruptness—I had almost said rudeness.

After a considerable pause he seemed to recollect himself, and with an effort resuming his sprightly manner, he said:

'Well, well, the next thing to keeping a secret well is, not to desire to possess one—talkativeness and curiosity generally go together. Now I shall make test of you, in the first place, respecting the latter of these qualities. I shall be your BLUEBEARD-tush, why do I trifle thus? Listen to me, my dear Fanny; I speak now in solemn earnest. What I desire is intimately, inseparably, connected with your happiness and honour as well as my own; and your compliance with my request will not be difficult. It will impose upon you a very trifling restraint during your sojourn here, which certain events which have occurred since our arrival have determined me shall not be a long one.

'You must promise me, upon your sacred honour, that you

will visit ONLY that part of the castle which can be reached from the front entrance, leaving the back entrance and the part of the building commanded immediately by it to the menials, as also the small garden whose high wall you see yonder; and never at any time seek to pry or peep into them, nor to open the door which communicates from the front part of the house through the corridor with the back. I do not urge this in jest or in caprice, but from a solemn conviction that danger and misery will be the certain consequences of your not observing what I prescribe. I cannot explain myself further at present. Promise me, then, these things, as you hope for peace here, and for mercy hereafter.'

I did make the promise as desired, and he appeared relieved; his manner recovered all its gaiety and elasticity: but the recollection of the strange scene which I have just described dwelt painfully upon my mind.

More than a month passed away without any occurrence worth recording; but I was not destined to leave Cahergillagh without further adventure. One day, intending to enjoy the pleasant sunshine in a ramble through the woods, I ran up to my room to procure my bonnet and shawl. Upon entering the chamber, I was surprised and somewhat startled to find it occupied. Beside the fireplace, and nearly opposite the door, seated in a large, old-fashioned elbow-chair, was placed the figure of a lady. She appeared to be nearer fifty than forty, and was dressed suitably to her age, in a handsome suit of flowered silk; she had a profusion of trinkets and jewellery about her person, and many rings upon her fingers. But although very rich, her dress was not gaudy or in ill taste. But what was remarkable in the lady was, that although her features were handsome, and upon the whole pleasing, the pupil of each eye was dimmed with the whiteness of cataract, and she was evidently stone-blind. I was for some seconds so surprised at this unaccountable apparition, that I could not find words to address her.

'Madam,' said I, 'there must be some mistake here—this is my bed-chamber.'

'Marry come up,' said the lady, sharply; 'YOUR chamber! Where is Lord Glenfallen?'

'He is below, madam,' replied I; 'and I am convinced he will be not a little surprised to find you here.'

'I do not think he will,' said she; 'with your good leave, talk of what you know something about. Tell him I want him. Why does the minx dilly-dally so?'

In spite of the awe which this grim lady inspired, there was something in her air of confident superiority which, when I considered our relative situations, was not a little irritating.

'Do you know, madam, to whom you speak?' said I.

'I neither know nor care,' said she; 'but I presume that you are someone about the house, so again I desire you, if you wish to continue here, to bring your master hither forthwith.'

'I must tell you, madam,' said I, 'that I am Lady Glenfallen.'

'What's that?' said the stranger, rapidly.

'I say, madam,' I repeated, approaching her that I might be more distinctly heard, 'that I am Lady Glenfallen.'

'It's a lie, you trull!' cried she, in an accent which made me start, and at the same time, springing forward, she seized me in her grasp, and shook me violently, repeating, 'It's a lie—it's a lie!' with a rapidity and vehemence which swelled every vein of her face. The violence of her action, and the fury which convulsed her face, effectually terrified me, and disengaging myself from her grasp, I screamed as loud as I could for help. The blind woman continued to pour out a torrent of abuse upon me, foaming at the mouth with rage, and impotently shaking her clenched fists towards me.

I heard Lord Glenfallen's step upon the stairs, and I instantly ran out; as I passed him I perceived that he was deadly pale, and just caught the words: 'I hope that demon has not hurt you?'

I made some answer, I forget what, and he entered the chamber, the door of which he locked upon the inside. What passed within I know not; but I heard the voices of the two speakers raised in loud and angry altercation.

I thought I heard the shrill accents of the woman repeat the words, 'Let her look to herself;' but I could not be quite sure. This short sentence, however, was, to my alarmed imagination, pregnant with fearful meaning.

The storm at length subsided, though not until after a conference of more than two long hours. Lord Glenfallen then returned, pale and agitated.

'That unfortunate woman,' said he, 'is out of her mind. I daresay she treated you to some of her ravings; but you need not dread any further interruption from her: I have brought her so far to reason. She did not hurt you, I trust.'

'No, no,' said I; 'but she terrified me beyond measure.'

'Well,' said he, 'she is likely to behave better for the future; and I dare swear that neither you nor she would desire, after what has passed, to meet again.'

This occurrence, so startling and unpleasant, so involved in mystery, and giving rise to so many painful surmises, afforded me no very agreeable food for rumination.

All attempts on my part to arrive at the truth were baffled; Lord Glenfallen evaded all my inquiries, and at length peremptorily forbid any further allusion to the matter. I was thus obliged to rest satisfied with what I had actually seen, and to trust to time to resolve the perplexities in which the whole transaction had involved me.

Lord Glenfallen's temper and spirits gradually underwent a complete and most painful change; he became silent and abstracted, his manner to me was abrupt and often harsh, some grievous anxiety seemed ever present to his mind; and under its influence his spirits sunk and his temper became soured.

I soon perceived that his gaiety was rather that which the stir and excitement of society produce, than the result of a healthy habit of mind; every day confirmed me in the opinion, that the considerate good-nature which I had so much admired in him was little more than a mere manner; and to my infinite grief and surprise, the gay, kind, open-hearted nobleman who had for months followed and flattered me, was rapidly assuming the form of a gloomy, morose, and singularly selfish man. This was a bitter discovery, and I strove to conceal it from myself as long as I could; but the truth was not to be denied, and I was forced to believe that Lord Glenfallen no longer loved me, and that he was at little pains to conceal the alteration in his sentiments.

One morning after breakfast, Lord Glenfallen had been for some time walking silently up and down the room, buried in his moody reflections, when pausing suddenly, and turning towards me, he exclaimed:

'I have it—I have it! We must go abroad, and stay there too; and if that does not answer, why—why, we must try some more effectual expedient. Lady Glenfallen, I have become involved in heavy embarrassments. A wife, you know, must share the fortunes of her husband, for better for worse; but I will waive my right if you prefer remaining here—here at Cahergillagh. For I would not have you seen elsewhere without the state to which your rank entitles you; besides, it would break your poor mother's heart,' he added, with sneering gravity. 'So make up your mind—Cahergillagh or France. I will start if possible in a week, so determine between this and then.'

He left the room, and in a few moments I saw him ride past the window, followed by a mounted servant. He had directed a domestic to inform me that he should not be back until the next day.

I was in very great doubt as to what course of conduct I should pursue, as to accompanying him in the continental tour so suddenly determined upon. I felt that it would be a hazard too great to encounter; for at Cahergillagh I had always the consciousness to sustain me, that if his temper at any time led him into violent or unwarrantable treatment of me, I had a remedy within reach, in the protection and support of my own family, from all useful and effective communication with whom, if once in France, I should be entirely debarred.

As to remaining at Cahergillagh in solitude, and, for aught I knew, exposed to hidden dangers, it appeared to me scarcely less objectionable than the former proposition; and yet I feared that with one or other I must comply, unless I was prepared to come to an actual breach with Lord Glenfallen. Full of these unpleasing doubts and perplexities, I retired to rest.

I was wakened, after having slept uneasily for some hours, by some person shaking me rudely by the shoulder; a small lamp burned in my room, and by its light, to my horror and amazement, I discovered that my visitant was the self-same blind old lady who had so terrified me a few weeks before.

I started up in the bed, with a view to ring the bell, and alarm the domestics; but she instantly anticipated me by saying:

'Do not be frightened, silly girl! If I had wished to harm you I could have done it while you were sleeping; I need not have wakened you. Listen to me, now, attentively and fearlessly, for what I have to say interests you to the full as much as it does me. Tell me here, in the presence of God, did Lord Glenfallen marry you—ACTUALLY MARRY you? Speak the truth, woman.'

'As surely as I live and speak,' I replied, 'did Lord Glenfallen marry me, in presence of more than a hundred witnesses.'

'Well,' continued she, 'he should have told you THEN, before you married him, that he had a wife living, which wife I am. I feel you tremble—tush! do not be frightened. I do not mean to harm you. Mark me now—you are NOT his wife. When I make my story known you will be so neither in the eye of God nor of man. You must leave this house upon to-morrow. Let the world know that your husband has another wife living; go you into retirement, and leave him to justice, which will surely overtake him. If you remain in this house after tomorrow you will reap the bitter fruits of your sin.'

So saying, she quitted the room, leaving me very little disposed to sleep.

Here was food for my very worst and most terrible suspicions; still there was not enough to remove all doubt. I had no proof of the truth of this woman's statement.

Taken by itself, there was nothing to induce me to attach weight to it; but when I viewed it in connection with the extraordinary mystery of some of Lord Glenfallen's proceedings, his strange anxiety to exclude me from certain portions of the mansion, doubtless lest I should encounter this person—the strong influence, nay, command which she possessed over him, a circumstance clearly established by the very fact of her residing in the very place where, of all others, he should least have desired to find her—her thus acting, and continuing to act in direct contradiction to his wishes; when, I say, I viewed her disclosure in connection with all these circumstances, I could not help feeling that there was at least a fearful verisimilitude in the allegations which she had made.

Still I was not satisfied, nor nearly so. Young minds have a reluctance almost insurmountable to believing, upon anything short of unquestionable proof, the existence of premeditated guilt in anyone whom they have ever trusted; and in support of this feeling I was assured that if the assertion of Lord Glenfallen, which nothing in this woman's manner had led me to disbelieve, were true, namely that her mind was unsound, the whole fabric of my doubts and fears must fall to the ground.

I determined to state to Lord Glenfallen freely and accurately the substance of the communication which I had just heard, and in his words and looks to seek for its proof or refutation. Full of these thoughts, I remained wakeful and excited all night, every moment fancying that I heard the step or saw the figure of my recent visitor, towards whom I felt a species of horror and dread which I can hardly describe.

There was something in her face, though her features had evidently been handsome, and were not, at first sight, unpleasing, which, upon a nearer inspection, seemed to indicate the habitual prevalence and indulgence of evil passions, and a power of expressing mere animal anger, with an intenseness that I have seldom seen equalled, and to which an almost unearthly effect was given by the convulsive quivering of the sightless eyes.

You may easily suppose that it was no very pleasing reflection to me to consider that, whenever caprice might induce her to return, I was within the reach of this violent and, for aught I knew, insane woman, who had, upon that very night, spoken to me in a tone of menace, of which her mere words, divested of the manner and look with which she uttered them, can convey but a faint idea.

Will you believe me when I tell you that I was actually afraid to leave my bed in order to secure the door, lest I should again encounter the dreadful object lurking in some corner or peeping from behind the window-curtains, so very a child was I in my fears.

The morning came, and with it Lord Glenfallen. I knew not, and indeed I cared not, where he might have been; my thoughts were wholly engrossed by the terrible fears and suspicions which my last night's conference had suggested to me. He was, as usual, gloomy and abstracted, and I feared in no very fitting mood to hear what I had to say with patience, whether the charges were true or false.

I was, however, determined not to suffer the opportunity to pass, or Lord Glenfallen to leave the room, until, at all hazards, I had unburdened my mind.

'My lord,' said I, after a long silence, summoning up all my firmness—'my lord, I wish to say a few words to you upon a matter of very great importance, of very deep concernment to you and to me.'

I fixed my eyes upon him to discern, if possible, whether the announcement caused him any uneasiness; but no symptom of any such feeling was perceptible.

'Well, my dear,' said he, 'this is no doubt a very grave preface, and portends, I have no doubt, something extraordinary. Pray let us have it without more ado.'

He took a chair, and seated himself nearly opposite to me.

'My lord,' said I, 'I have seen the person who alarmed me so much a short time since, the blind lady, again, upon last night.' His face, upon which my eyes were fixed, turned pale; he hesitated for a moment, and then said:

'And did you, pray, madam, so totally forget or spurn my express command, as to enter that portion of the house from which your promise, I might say your oath, excluded you?-answer me that!' he added fiercely.

'My lord,' said I, 'I have neither forgotten your COMMANDS, since such they were, nor disobeyed them. I was, last night, wakened from my sleep, as I lay in my own chamber, and accosted by the person whom I have mentioned. How she found access to the room I cannot pretend to say.'

'Ha! this must be looked to,' said he, half reflectively; 'and pray,' added he, quickly, while in turn he fixed his eyes upon me, 'what did this person say? since some comment upon her communication forms, no doubt, the sequel to your preface.'

'Your lordship is not mistaken,' said I; 'her statement was so extraordinary that I could not think of withholding it from you. She told me, my lord, that you had a wife living at the time you married me, and that she was that wife.'

Lord Glenfallen became ashy pale, almost livid; he made two or three efforts to clear his voice to speak, but in vain, and turning suddenly from me, he walked to the window. The horror and dismay which, in the olden time, overwhelmed the woman of Endor when her spells unexpectedly conjured the dead into her presence, were but types of what I felt when thus presented with what appeared to be almost unequivocal evidence of the guilt whose existence I had before so strongly doubted.

There was a silence of some moments, during which it were hard to conjecture whether I or my companion suffered most.

Lord Glenfallen soon recovered his self-command; he returned to the table, again sat down and said:

'What you have told me has so astonished me, has unfolded such a tissue of motiveless guilt, and in a quarter from which I had so little reason to look for ingratitude or treachery, that your announcement almost deprived me of speech; the person in question, however, has one excuse, her mind is, as I told you before, unsettled. You should have remembered that, and hesitated to receive as unexceptionable evidence against the honour of your husband, the ravings of a lunatic. I now tell you that this is the last time I shall speak to you upon this subject, and, in the presence of the God who is to judge me, and as I hope for mercy in the day of judgment, I swear that the charge thus brought against me is utterly false, unfounded, and ridiculous; I defy the world in any point to taint my honour; and, as I have never taken the opinion of madmen touching your character or morals, I think it but fair to require that you will evince a like tenderness for me; and now, once for all, never again dare to repeat to me your insulting suspicions, or the clumsy and infamous calumnies of fools. I shall instantly let the worthy lady who contrived this somewhat original device, understand fully my opinion upon the matter. Good morning;' and with these words he left me again in doubt, and involved in all horrors of the most agonising suspense.

I had reason to think that Lord Glenfallen wreaked his vengeance upon the author of the strange story which I had heard, with a violence which was not satisfied with mere words, for old Martha, with whom I was a great favourite, while attending me in my room, told me that she feared her master had ill-used the poor blind Dutch woman, for that she had heard her scream as if the very life were leaving her, but added a request that I should not speak of what she had told me to any one, particularly to the master.

'How do you know that she is a Dutch woman?' inquired I, anxious to learn anything whatever that might throw a light upon the history of this person, who seemed to have resolved to mix herself up in my fortunes.

'Why, my lady,' answered Martha, 'the master often calls her the Dutch hag, and other names you would not like to hear, and I am sure she is neither English nor Irish; for, whenever they talk together, they speak some queer foreign lingo, and fast enough, I'll be bound. But I ought not to talk about her at all; it might be as much as my place is worth to mention her—only you saw her first yourself, so there can be no great harm in speaking of her now.'

'How long has this lady been here?' continued I.

'She came early on the morning after your ladyship's arrival,' answered she; 'but do not ask me anymore, for the master would think nothing of turning me out of doors for daring to speak of her at all, much less to you, my lady.'

I did not like to press the poor woman further, for her reluctance to speak on this topic was evident and strong.

You will readily believe that upon the very slight grounds which my information afforded, contradicted as it was by the solemn oath of my husband, and derived from what was, at best, a very questionable source, I could not take any very decisive measure whatever; and as to the menace of the strange woman who had thus unaccountably twice intruded herself into my chamber, although, at the moment, it occasioned me some uneasiness, it was not, even in my eyes, sufficiently formidable to induce my departure from Cahergillagh.

A few nights after the scene which I have just mentioned, Lord Glenfallen having, as usual, early retired to his study, I was left alone in the parlour to amuse myself as best I might.

It was not strange that my thoughts should often recur to the agitating scenes in which I had recently taken a part.

The subject of my reflections, the solitude, the silence, and the lateness of the hour, as also the depression of spirits to which I had of late been a constant prey, tended to produce that nervous excitement which places us wholly at the mercy of the imagination.

In order to calm my spirits I was endeavouring to direct my thoughts into some more pleasing channel, when I heard, or thought I heard, uttered, within a few yards of me, in an odd, half-sneering tone, the words,

'There is blood upon your ladyship's throat.'

So vivid was the impression that I started to my feet, and involuntarily placed my hand upon my neck.

I looked around the room for the speaker, but in vain.

I went then to the room-door, which I opened, and peered into the passage, nearly faint with horror lest some leering, shapeless thing should greet me upon the threshold.

When I had gazed long enough to assure myself that no strange object was within sight, 'I have been too much of a rake lately; I am racking out my nerves,' said I, speaking aloud, with a view to reassure myself.

I rang the bell, and, attended by old Martha, I retired to settle for the night.

While the servant was—as was her custom—arranging the lamp which I have already stated always burned during the night in my chamber, I was employed in undressing, and, in doing so, I had recourse to a large looking-glass which occupied a considerable portion of the wall in which it was fixed, rising from the ground to a height of about six feet—this mirror filled the space of a large panel in the wainscoting opposite the foot of the bed.

I had hardly been before it for the lapse of a minute when something like a black pall was slowly waved between me and it.

'Oh, God! there it is,' I exclaimed, wildly. 'I have seen it again, Martha—the black cloth.'

'God be merciful to us, then!' answered she, tremulously crossing herself. 'Some misfortune is over us.'

'No, no, Martha,' said I, almost instantly recovering my collectedness; for, although of a nervous temperament, I had never been superstitious. 'I do not believe in omens. You know I saw, or fancied I saw, this thing before, and nothing followed.'

'The Dutch lady came the next morning,' replied she.

'But surely her coming scarcely deserved such a dreadful warning,' I replied.

'She is a strange woman, my lady,' said Martha; 'and she is not GONE yet—mark my words.'

'Well, well, Martha,' said I, 'I have not wit enough to change your opinions, nor inclination to alter mine; so I will talk no more of the matter. Goodnight,' and so I was left to my reflections.

After lying for about an hour awake, I at length fell into a kind of doze; but my imagination was still busy, for I was startled from this unrefreshing sleep by fancying that I heard a voice close to my face exclaim as before:

'There is blood upon your ladyship's throat.'

The words were instantly followed by a loud burst of laughter.

Quaking with horror, I awakened, and heard my husband enter the room. Even this was it relief.

Scared as I was, however, by the tricks which my imagination had played me, I preferred remaining silent, and pretending to sleep, to attempting to engage my husband in conversation, for I well knew that his mood was such, that his words would not, in all probability, convey anything that had not better be unsaid and unheard.

Lord Glenfallen went into his dressing-room, which lay upon the right-hand side of the bed. The door lying open, I could see him by himself, at full length upon a sofa, and, in about half an hour, I became aware, by his deep and regularly drawn respiration, that he was fast asleep.

When slumber refuses to visit one, there is something peculiarly irritating, not to the temper, but to the nerves, in the consciousness that someone is in your immediate presence, actually enjoying the boon which you are seeking in vain; at least, I have always found it so, and never more than upon the present occasion.

A thousand annoying imaginations harassed and excited me; every object which I looked upon, though ever so familiar, seemed to have acquired a strange phantom-like character, the varying shadows thrown by the flickering of the lamplight, seemed shaping themselves into grotesque and unearthly forms, and whenever my eyes wandered to the sleeping figure of my husband, his features appeared to undergo the strangest and most demoniacal contortions.

Hour after hour was told by the old clock, and each succeeding one found me, if possible, less inclined to sleep than its predecessor.

It was now considerably past three; my eyes, in their involuntary wanderings, happened to alight upon the large mirror which was, as I have said, fixed in the wall opposite the foot of the bed. A view of it was commanded from where I lay, through the curtains. As I gazed fixedly upon it, I thought I perceived the broad sheet of glass shifting its position in relation to the bed; I riveted my eyes upon it with intense scrutiny; it was no deception, the mirror, as if acting of its own impulse, moved slowly aside, and disclosed a dark aperture in the wall, nearly as large as an ordinary door; a figure evidently stood in this, but the light was too dim to define it accurately.

It stepped cautiously into the chamber, and with so little noise, that had I not actually seen it, I do not think I should have been aware of its presence. It was arrayed in a kind of woollen nightdress, and a white handkerchief or cloth was bound tightly about the head; I had no difficulty, spite of the strangeness of the attire, in recognising the blind woman whom I so much dreaded.

She stooped down, bringing her head nearly to the ground, and in that attitude she remained motionless for some moments, no doubt in order to ascertain if any suspicious sound were stirring.

She was apparently satisfied by her observations, for she immediately recommenced her silent progress towards a ponderous mahogany dressing-table of my husband's. When she had reached it, she paused again, and appeared to listen attentively for some minutes; she then noiselessly opened one of the drawers, from which, having groped for some time, she took something, which I soon perceived to be a case of razors. She opened it, and tried the edge of each of the two instruments upon the skin of her hand; she quickly selected one, which she fixed firmly in her grasp. She now stooped down as before, and having listened for a time, she, with the hand that was disengaged, groped her way into the dressing-room where Lord Glenfallen lay fast asleep.

I was fixed as if in the tremendous spell of a nightmare. I could not stir even a finger; I could not lift my voice; I could not even breathe; and though I expected every moment to see the sleeping man murdered, I could not even close my eyes to shut out the horrible spectacle, which I had not the power to avert.

I saw the woman approach the sleeping figure, she laid the

unoccupied hand lightly along his clothes, and having thus ascertained his identity, she, after a brief interval, turned back and again entered my chamber; here she bent down again to listen.

I had now not a doubt but that the razor was intended for my throat; yet the terrific fascination which had locked all my powers so long, still continued to bind me fast.

I felt that my life depended upon the slightest ordinary exertion, and yet I could not stir one joint from the position in which I lay, nor even make noise enough to waken Lord Glenfallen.

The murderous woman now, with long, silent steps, approached the bed; my very heart seemed turning to ice; her left hand, that which was disengaged, was upon the pillow; she gradually slid it forward towards my head, and in an instant, with the speed of lightning, it was clutched in my hair, while, with the other hand, she dashed the razor at my throat.

A slight inaccuracy saved me from instant death; the blow fell short, the point of the razor grazing my throat. In a moment, I know not how, I found myself at the other side of the bed, uttering shriek after shriek; the wretch was, however, determined if possible to murder me.

Scrambling along by the curtains, she rushed round the bed towards me; I seized the handle of the door to make my escape. It was, however, fastened. At all events, I could not open it. From the mere instinct of recoiling terror, I shrunk back into a corner. She was now within a yard of me. Her hand was upon my face.

I closed my eyes fast, expecting never to open them again, when a blow, inflicted from behind by a strong arm, stretched the monster senseless at my feet. At the same moment the door opened, and several domestics, alarmed by my cries, entered the apartment.

I do not recollect what followed, for I fainted. One swoon succeeded another, so long and death-like, that my life was considered very doubtful.

At about ten o'clock, however, I sunk into a deep and refreshing sleep, from which I was awakened at about two, that I might swear my deposition before a magistrate, who attended for that purpose.

I accordingly did so, as did also Lord Glenfallen, and the woman was fully committed to stand her trial at the ensuing assizes.

I shall never forget the scene which the examination of the blind woman and of the other parties afforded.

She was brought into the room in the custody of two servants. She wore a kind of flannel wrapper which had not been changed since the night before. It was torn and soiled, and here and there smeared with blood, which had flowed in large quantities from a wound in her head. The white handkerchief had fallen off in the scuffle, and her grizzled hair fell in masses about her wild and deadly pale countenance.

She appeared perfectly composed, however, and the only regret she expressed throughout, was at not having succeeded in her attempt, the object of which she did not pretend to conceal.

On being asked her name, she called herself the Countess Glenfallen, and refused to give any other title.

'The woman's name is Flora Van-Kemp,' said Lord Glenfallen.

'It WAS, it WAS, you perjured traitor and cheat!' screamed the woman; and then there followed a volley of words in some foreign language. 'Is there a magistrate here?' she resumed; 'I am Lord Glenfallen's wife—I'll prove it—write down my words. I am willing to be hanged or burned, so HE meets his deserts. I did try to kill that doll of his; but it was he who put it into my head to do it—two wives were too many; I was to murder her, or she was to hang me; listen to all I have to say.'

Here Lord Glenfallen interrupted.

'I think, sir,' said he, addressing the magistrate, 'that we had better proceed to business; this unhappy woman's furious recriminations but waste our time. If she refuses to answer your questions, you had better, I presume, take my depositions.'

'And are you going to swear away my life, you black-perjured murderer?' shrieked the woman. 'Sir, sir, sir, you must hear me,' she continued, addressing the magistrate; 'I can convict him—he bid me murder that girl, and then, when I failed, he came behind me, and struck me down, and now he wants to swear away my life. Take down all I say.'

'If it is your intention,' said the magistrate, 'to confess the crime with which you stand charged, you may, upon producing sufficient evidence, criminate whom you please.'

'Evidence!—I have no evidence but myself,' said the woman. 'I will swear it all—write down my testimony—write it down, I say—we shall hang side by side, my brave lord—all your own handy-work, my gentle husband.'

This was followed by a low, insolent, and sneering laugh, which, from one in her situation, was sufficiently horrible.

'I will not at present hear anything,' replied he, 'but distinct answers to the questions which I shall put to you upon this matter.'

'Then you shall hear nothing,' replied she sullenly, and no inducement or intimidation could bring her to speak again.

Lord Glenfallen's deposition and mine were then given, as also those of the servants who had entered the room at the moment of my rescue.

The magistrate then intimated that she was committed, and must proceed directly to gaol, whither she was brought in a carriage; of Lord Glenfallen's, for his lordship was naturally by no means in-different to the effect which her vehement accusations against himself might produce, if uttered before every chance hearer whom she might meet with between Cahergillagh and the place of confinement whither she was despatched.

During the time which intervened between the committal and the trial of the prisoner, Lord Glenfallen seemed to suffer agonies of mind which baffle all description; he hardly ever slept, and when he did, his slumbers seemed but the instruments of new tortures, and his waking hours were, if possible, exceeded in intensity of terrors by the dreams which disturbed his sleep.

Lord Glenfallen rested, if to lie in the mere attitude of repose were to do so, in his dressing-room, and thus I had an opportunity of witnessing, far oftener than I wished it, the fearful workings of his mind. His agony often broke out into such fearful paroxysms that delirium and total loss of reason appeared to be impending. He frequently spoke of flying from the country, and bringing with him all the witnesses of the appalling scene upon which the prosecution was founded; then, again, he would fiercely lament that the blow which he had inflicted had not ended all.

The assizes arrived, however, and upon the day appointed Lord Glenfallen and I attended in order to give our evidence.

The cause was called on, and the prisoner appeared at the bar.

Great curiosity and interest were felt respecting the trial, so that the court was crowded to excess.

The prisoner, however, without appearing to take the trouble of listening to the indictment, pleaded guilty, and no representations on the part of the court availed to induce her to retract her plea.

After much time had been wasted in a fruitless attempt to prevail upon her to reconsider her words, the court proceeded, according to the usual form, to pass sentence.

This having been done, the prisoner was about to be removed, when she said, in a low, distinct voice:

'A word—a word, my lord!—Is Lord Glenfallen here in the court?'

On being told that he was, she raised her voice to a tone of loud menace, and continued:

'Hardress, Earl of Glenfallen, I accuse you here in this court of justice of two crimes,—first, that you married a second wife, while the first was living; and again, that you prompted me to the murder, for attempting which I am to die. Secure him—chain him—bring him here.'

There was a laugh through the court at these words, which were naturally treated by the judge as a violent extemporary recrimination, and the woman was desired to be silent.

'You won't take him, then?' she said; 'you won't try him? You'll let him go free?'

It was intimated by the court that he would certainly be allowed 'to go free,' and she was ordered again to be removed.

Before, however, the mandate was executed, she threw her arms wildly into the air, and uttered one piercing shriek so full of preternatural rage and despair, that it might fitly have ushered a soul into those realms where hope can come no more.

The sound still rang in my ears, months after the voice that had uttered it was forever silent.

The wretched woman was executed in accordance with the sentence which had been pronounced.

For some time after this event, Lord Glenfallen appeared, if possible, to suffer more than he had done before, and altogether his language, which often amounted to half confessions of the guilt imputed to him, and all the circumstances connected with the late occurrences, formed a mass of evidence so convincing that I wrote to my father, detailing the grounds of my fears, and imploring him to come to Cahergillagh without delay, in order to remove me from my husband's control, previously to taking legal steps for a final separation.

Circumstanced as I was, my existence was little short of intolerable, for, besides the fearful suspicions which attached to my husband, I plainly perceived that if Lord Glenfallen were not relieved, and that speedily, insanity must supervene. I therefore expected my father's arrival, or at least a letter to announce it, with indescribable impatience.

About a week after the execution had taken place, Lord Glenfallen one morning met me with an unusually sprightly air.

'Fanny,' said he, 'I have it now for the first time in my power to explain to your satisfaction everything which has hitherto appeared suspicious or mysterious in my conduct. After breakfast come with me to my study, and I shall, I hope, make all things clear.'

This invitation afforded me more real pleasure than I had experienced for months. Something had certainly occurred to tranquillize my husband's mind in no ordinary degree, and I thought it by no means impossible that he would, in the proposed interview, prove himself the most injured and innocent of men.

Full of this hope, I repaired to his study at the appointed hour. He was writing busily when I entered the room, and just raising his eyes, he requested me to be seated.

I took a chair as he desired, and remained silently awaiting his leisure, while he finished, folded, directed, and sealed his letter. Laying it then upon the table with the address downward, he said,

'My dearest Fanny, I know I must have appeared very strange to you and very unkind—often even cruel. Before the end of this week I will show you the necessity of my conduct—how impossible it was that I should have seemed otherwise. I am conscious that many acts of mine must have inevitably given rise to painful suspicions—suspicions which, indeed, upon one occasion, you very properly communicated to me. I have got two letters from a quarter which commands respect, containing information as to the course by which I may be enabled to prove the negative of all the crimes which even the most credulous suspicion could lay to my charge. I expected a third by this morning's post, containing documents which will set the matter for ever at rest, but owing, no doubt, to some neglect, or, perhaps, to some difficulty in collecting the papers, some inevitable delay, it has not come to hand this morning, according to my expectation.

'I was finishing one to the very same quarter when you came in, and if a sound rousing be worth anything, I think I shall have a special messenger before two days have passed. I have been anxiously considering with myself, as to whether I had better imperfectly clear up your doubts by submitting to your inspection the two letters which I have already received, or wait till I can triumphantly vindicate myself by the production of the documents which I have already mentioned, and I have, I think, not unnaturally decided upon the latter course. However, there is a person in the next room whose testimony is not without its value excuse me for one moment.'

So saying, he arose and went to the door of a closet which opened from the study; this he unlocked, and half opening the door, he said, 'It is only I,' and then slipped into the room and carefully closed and locked the door behind him.

I immediately heard his voice in animated conversation. My curiosity upon the subject of the letter was naturally great, so, smothering any little scruples which I might have felt, I resolved to look at the address of the letter which lay, as my husband had left it, with its face upon the table. I accordingly drew it over to me and turned up the direction.

For two or three moments I could scarce believe my eyes, but there could be no mistake—in large characters were traced the words, 'To the Archangel Gabriel in Heaven.'

I had scarcely returned the letter to its original position, and in some degree recovered the shock which this unequivocal proof of insanity produced, when the closet door was unlocked, and Lord Glenfallen re-entered the study, carefully closing and locking the door again upon the outside.

'Whom have you there?' inquired I, making a strong effort to appear calm.

'Perhaps,' said he, musingly, 'you might have some objection to seeing her, at least for a time.'

'Who is it?' repeated I.

'Why,' said he, 'I see no use in hiding it—the blind Dutch-woman. I have been with her the whole morning. She is very anxious to get out of that closet; but you know she is odd, she is scarcely to be trusted.'

A heavy gust of wind shook the door at this moment with a sound as if something more substantial were pushing against it.

'Ha, ha, ha!—do you hear her?' said he, with an obstreperous burst of laughter.

The wind died away in a long howl, and Lord Glenfallen, suddenly checking his merriment, shrugged his shoulders, and muttered:

'Poor devil, she has been hardly used.'

'We had better not tease her at present with questions,' said I, in as unconcerned a tone as I could assume, although I felt every moment as if I should faint.

'Humph! maybe so,' said he. 'Well, come back in an hour or two, or when you please, and you will find us here.'

He again unlocked the door, and entered with the same precautions which he had adopted before, locking the door upon the inside; and as I hurried from the room, I heard his voice again exerted as if in eager parley.

I can hardly describe my emotions; my hopes had been raised to the highest, and now, in an instant, all was gone—the dreadful consummation was accomplished—the fearful retribution had fallen upon the guilty man—the mind was destroyed—the power to repent was gone.

The agony of the hours which followed what I would still call my AWFUL interview with Lord Glenfallen, I cannot describe; my solitude was, however, broken in upon by Martha, who came to inform me of the arrival of a gentleman, who expected me in the parlour.

I accordingly descended, and, to my great joy, found my father seated by the fire.

This expedition upon his part was easily accounted for: my communications had touched the honour of the family. I speedily informed him of the dreadful malady which had fallen upon the wretched man.

My father suggested the necessity of placing some person to watch him, to prevent his injuring himself or others.

I rang the bell, and desired that one Edward Cooke, an attached servant of the family, should be sent to me.

I told him distinctly and briefly the nature of the service required of him, and, attended by him, my father and I proceeded at once to the study. The door of the inner room was still closed, and everything in the outer chamber remained in the same order in which I had left it. We then advanced to the closet-door, at which we knocked, but without receiving any answer.

We next tried to open the door, but in vain—it was locked upon the inside. We knocked more loudly, but in vain.

Seriously alarmed, I desired the servant to force the door, which was, after several violent efforts, accomplished, and we entered the closet.

Lord Glenfallen was lying on his face upon a sofa.

'Hush!' said I, 'he is asleep.' We paused for a moment.

'He is too still for that,' said my father.

We all of us felt a strong reluctance to approach the figure.

'Edward,' said I, 'try whether your master sleeps.'

The servant approached the sofa where Lord Glenfallen lay. He leant his ear towards the head of the recumbent figure, to ascertain whether the sound of breathing was audible. He turned towards us, and said:

'My lady, you had better not wait here; I am sure he is dead!'

'Let me see the face,' said I, terribly agitated; 'you MAY be mistaken.'

The man then, in obedience to my command, turned the body round, and, gracious God! what a sight met my view. He was, indeed, perfectly dead.

The whole breast of the shirt, with its lace frill, was drenched with gore, as was the couch underneath the spot where he lay.

The head hung back, as it seemed, almost severed from the body by a frightful gash, which yawned across the throat. The instrument which had inflicted it was found under his body.

All, then, was over; I was never to learn the history in whose termination I had been so deeply and so tragically involved.

The severe discipline which my mind had undergone was not bestowed in vain. I directed my thoughts and my hopes to that place where there is no more sin, nor danger, nor sorrow.

Thus ends a brief tale whose prominent incidents many will recognise as having marked the history of a distinguished family; and though it refers to a somewhat distant date, we shall be found not to have taken, upon that account, any liberties with the facts, but in our statement of all the incidents to have rigorously and faithfully adhered to the truth.

A Debt of Honour, a Ghost Story

Hush! what was that cry, so low but yet so piercing, so strange but yet so sorrowful? It was not the marmot upon the side of the Righi—it was not the heron down by the lake; no, it was distinctively human. Hush! there it is again—from the churchyard which I have just left!

Not ten minutes have elapsed since I was sitting on the low wall of the churchyard of Weggis, watching the calm glories of the moonlight illuminating with silver splendour the lake of Lucerne; and I am certain there was no one within the inclosure but myself.

I am mistaken, surely. What a silence there is upon the night! Not a breath of air now to break up into a thousand brilliant ripples the long reflection of the August moon, or to stir the foliage of the chestnuts; not a voice in the village; no splash of oar upon the lake. All life seems at perfect rest, and the solemn stillness that reigns about the topmost glaciers of S. Gothard has spread its mantle over the warmer world below.

I must not linger; as it is, I shall have to wake up the porter to let me into the hotel. I hurry on.

Not ten paces, though. Again I hear the cry. This time it sounds to me like the long, sad sob of a wearied and broken heart. Without staying to reason with myself, I quickly retrace my steps.

I stumble about among the iron crosses and the graves, and displace in my confusion wreaths of immortelles and fresher flowers. A huge mausoleum stands between me and the wall upon which I had been sitting not a quarter of an hour ago. The mausoleum casts a deep shadow upon the side nearest to me. Ah! something is stirring there. I strain my eyes—the figure of a man passes slowly out of the shade, and silently occupies my place upon the wall. It must have been his lips that gave out that miserable sound.

What shall I do? Compassion and curiosity are strong. The man whose heart can be rent so sorely ought not to be allowed to linger here with his despair. He is gazing, as I did, upon the lake. I mark his profile—clear-cut and symmetrical; I catch the lustre of large eyes. The face, as I can see it, seems very still and placid. I may be mistaken; he may merely be a wanderer like myself; perhaps he heard the three strange cries, and has also come to seek the cause. I feel impelled to speak to him.

I pass from the path by the church to the east side of the mausoleum, and so come toward him, the moon full upon his features. Great heaven! how pale his face is!

"Good-evening, sir. I thought myself alone here, and wondered that no other travellers had found their way to this lovely spot. Charming, is it not?"

For a moment he says nothing, but his eyes are full upon me. At last he replies:

"It is charming, as you say, Mr. Reginald Westcar."

"You know me?" I exclaim, in astonishment.

"Pardon me, I can scarcely claim a personal acquaintance. But yours is the only English name entered today in the *Livre des Etrangers*."

"You are staying at the Hotel de la Concorde, then?"

An inclination of the head is all the answer vouchsafed.

"May I ask," I continue, "whether you heard just now a very strange cry repeated three times?"

A pause. The lustrous eyes seem to search me through and through—I can hardly bear their gaze. Then he replies.

"I fancy I heard the echoes of some such sounds as you describe."

The *echoes*! Is this, then, the man who gave utterance to those cries of woe! is it possible? The face seems so passionless; but the pallor of those features bears witness to some terrible agony within.

"I thought someone must be in distress," I rejoin, hastily; "and I hurried back to see if I could be of any service."

"Very good of you," he answers, coldly; "but surely such a place as this is not unaccustomed to the voice of sorrow."

"No doubt. My impulse was a mistaken one."

"But kindly meant. You will not sleep less soundly for acting on that impulse, Reginald Westcar."

He rises as he speaks. He throws his cloak round him, and stands motionless. I take the hint. My mysterious countryman wishes to be alone. Some one that he has loved and lost lies buried here.

"Goodnight, sir," I say, as I move in the direction of the little chapel at the gate. "Neither of us will sleep the less soundly for thinking of the perfect repose that reigns around this place."

"What do you mean?" he asks.

"The dead," I reply, as I stretch my hand toward the graves. "Do you not remember the lines in 'King Lear'?

"'*After life's fitful fever he sleeps well.*'"

"But *you* have never died, Reginald Westcar. You know nothing of the sleep of death."

For the third time he speaks my name almost familiarly, and—I know not why—a shudder passes through me. I have no time, in my turn, to ask him what he means; for he strides silently away into the shadow of the church, and I, with a strange sense of oppression upon me, returned to my hotel.

★ ★ ★ ★ ★

The events which I have just related passed in vivid recollection through my mind as I travelled northward one cold November day in the year 185—. About six months previously I had taken my degree at Oxford, and had since been enjoying a trip upon the continent; and on my return to London I found a letter awaiting me from my lawyers, informing me somewhat to my astonishment, that I had succeeded to a small estate in Cumberland. I must tell you exactly how this came about. My mother was a Miss Ringwood, and she was the youngest of three children: the eldest was Aldina, the second was Geoffrey, and the third (my mother) Alice. Their mother (who had been a widow since my mother's birth) lived at this little place in Cumberland, and which was known as The Shallows; she died shortly after my mother's marriage with my father, Captain Westcar.

My aunt Aldina and my uncle Geoffrey—the one at that time aged twenty-eight, and the other twenty-six—continued to reside at The Shallows. My father and mother had to go to India, where I was born, and where, when quite a child, I was left an orphan. A few months after my mother's marriage my aunt disappeared; a few weeks after that event, and my uncle Geoffrey dropped down dead, as he was playing at cards with Mr. Maryon, the proprietor of a neighboring mansion known as The Mere. A fortnight after my uncle's death, my aunt Aldina returned to The Shallows, and never left it again till she was carried out in her coffin to her grave in the churchyard. Ever since her return from her mysterious disappearance she maintained an impenetrable reserve.

As a schoolboy I visited her twice or thrice, but these visits depressed my youthful spirits to such an extent, that as I grew older I excused myself from accepting my aunt's not very pressing invitations; and at the time I am now speaking of I had not seen her for eight or ten years. I was rather surprised, therefore, when she bequeathed me The Shallows, which, as the surviving child, she inherited under her mother's marriage settlement.

But The Shallows had always exercised a grim influence over me, and the knowledge that I was now going to it as my home oppressed me. The road seemed unusually dark, cold, and lonely. At last I passed the lodge, and two hundred yards more brought me to the porch. Very soon the door was opened by an elderly female, whom I well remembered as having been my aunt's housekeeper and cook. I had pleasant recollections of her, and was glad to see her. To tell the truth, I had not anticipated my visit to my newly acquired property with any great degree of enthusiasm; but a very tolerable dinner had an inspiriting effect, and I was pleased to learn that there was a bin of old Madeira in the cellar. Naturally I soon grew cheerful, and consequently talkative; and summoned Mrs. Balk for a little gossip. The substance of what I gathered from her rather diffusive conversation was as follows:

My aunt had resided at The Shallows ever since the death of my uncle Geoffrey, but she had maintained a silent and reserved habit; and Mrs. Balk was of opinion that she had had some great misfortune. She had persistently refused all intercourse with the people at The Mere. Squire Maryon, himself a cold and taciturn man, had once or twice showed a disposition to be friendly, but she had sternly repulsed all such overtures. Mrs. Balk was of opinion that Miss Ringwood was not "quite right," as she expressed it, on some topics; especially did she seem impressed with the idea that The Mere ought to belong to her. It appeared that the Ringwoods and Maryons were distant connections; that

The Mere belonged in former times to a certain Sir Henry Benet; that he was a bachelor, and that Squire Maryon's father and old Mr. Ringwood were cousins of his, and that there was some doubt as to which was the real heir; that Sir Henry, who disliked old Maryon, had frequently said he had set any chance of dispute at rest, by bequeathing the Mere property by will to Mr. Ringwood, my mother's father; that, on his death, no such will could be found; and the family lawyers agreed that Mr. Maryon was the legal inheritor, and my uncle Geoffrey and his sisters must be content to take the Shallows, or nothing at all. Mr. Maryon was comparatively rich, and the Ringwoods poor, consequently they were advised not to enter upon a costly lawsuit.

My aunt Aldina maintained to the last that Sir Henry had made a will, and that Mr. Maryon knew it, but had destroyed or suppressed the document. I did not gather from Mrs. Balk's narrative that Miss Ringwood had any foundation for her belief, and I dismissed the notion at once as baseless.

"And my uncle Geoffrey died of apoplexy, you say, Mrs. Balk?"

"I don't say so, sir, no more did Miss Ringwood; but *they* said so."

"Whom do you mean by *they*?"

"The people at The Mere—the young doctor, a friend of Squire Maryon's, who was brought over from York, and the rest; he fell heavily from his chair, and his head struck against the fender."

"Playing at cards with Mr. Maryon, I think you said."

"Yes, sir; he was too fond of cards, I believe, was Mr. Geoffrey."

"Is Mr. Maryon seen much in the county—is he hospitable?"

"Well, sir, he goes up to London a good deal, and has some friends down from town occasionally; but he does not seem to care much about the people in the neighbourhood."

"He has some children, Mrs. Balk?"

"Only one daughter, sir; a sweet pretty thing she is. Her mother died when Miss Agnes was born."

"You have no idea, Mrs. Balk, what my aunt Aldina's great misfortune was?"

"Well, sir, I can't help thinking it must have been a love affair. She always hated men so much."

"Then why did she leave The Shallows to me, Mrs. Balk?"

"Ah, you are laughing, sir. No doubt she considered that The Mere ought to belong to you, as the heir of the Ringwoods, and she placed you here, as near as might be to the place."

"In hopes that I might marry Miss Maryon, eh, Mrs. Balk?"

"You are laughing again, sir. I don't imagine she thought so much of that, as of the possibility of your discovering something about the missing will."

I bade the communicative Mrs. Balk good night and retired to my bedroom—a low, wide, sombre, oak-panellèd chamber. I must confess that family stories had no great interest for me, living apart from them at school and college as I had done; and as I undressed I thought more of the probabilities of sport the eight hundred acres of wild shooting belonging to The Shallows would afford me, than of the supposed will my poor aunt had evidently worried herself about so much. Thoroughly tired after my long journey, I soon fell fast asleep amid the deep shadows of the huge four-poster I mentally resolved to chop up into firewood at an early date, and substitute for it a more modern iron bedstead.

How long I had been asleep I do not know, but I suddenly started up, the echo of a long, sad cry ringing in my ears.

I listened eagerly—sensitive to the slightest sound—painfully sensitive as one is only in the deep silence of the night.

I heard the old-fashioned clock I had noticed on the stairs strike three. The reverberation seemed to last a long time, then all was silent again. "A dream," I muttered to myself, as I lay down upon the pillow; "Madeira is a heating wine. But what can I have been dreaming of?"

Sleep seemed to have gone altogether, and the busy mind wandered among the continental scenes I had lately visited. By and by I found myself in memory once more within the Weggis churchyard. I was satisfied; I had traced my dream to the cries that I had heard there. I turned round to sleep again. Perhaps I fell into a doze—I cannot say; but again I started up at the repetition, as it seemed outside my window, of that cry of sadness and despair. I hastily drew aside the heavy curtains of my bed—at that moment the room seemed to be illuminated with a dim, unearthly light—and I saw, gradually growing into human shape, the figure of a woman. I recognized in it my aunt, Miss Ringwood. Horror-struck, I gazed at the apparition; it advanced a little—the lips moved—I heard it distinctly say:

"*Reginald Westcar, The Mere belongs to you. Compel John Maryon to pay the debt of honor!*"

I fell back senseless.

When next I returned to consciousness, it was when I was called in the morning; the shutters were opened, and I saw the red light of the dawning winter sun.

★ ★ ★ ★ ★

There is a strange sympathy between the night and the mind.

402

All one's troubles represent themselves as increased a hundred-fold if one wakes in the night, and begins to think about them. A muscular pain becomes the certainty of an incurable internal disease; and a headache suggests incipient softening of the brain. But all these horrors are dissipated with the morning light, and the after-glow of a cold bath turns them into jokes. So it was with me on the morning after my arrival at The Shallows. I accounted most satisfactorily for all that had occurred, or seemed to have occurred, during the night; and resolved that, though the old Madeira was uncommonly good, I must be careful in future not to drink more than a couple of glasses after dinner.

I need scarcely say that I said nothing to Mrs. Balk of my bad dreams, and shortly after breakfast I took my gun, and went out in search of such game as I might chance to meet with. At three o'clock I sent the keeper home, as his capacious pockets were pretty well filled, telling him that I thought I knew the country, and should stroll back leisurely. The gray gloom of the November evening was spreading over the sky as I came upon a small plantation which I believed belonged to me. I struck straight across it; emerging from its shadows, I found myself by a small stream and some marshy land; on the other side another small plantation.

A snipe got up, I fired, and tailored it. I marked the bird into this other plantation, and followed. Up got a covey of partridges—bang, bang—one down by the side of an oak. I was about to enter this covert, when a lady and gentleman emerged, and, struck with the unpleasant thought that I was possibly trespassing, I at once went forward to apologize.

Before I could say a word, the gentleman addressed me.

"May I ask, sir, if I have given you permission to shoot over my preserves?"

"I beg to express my great regret, sir," I replied, as I lifted my hat in acknowledgment of the lady's presence, "that I should have trespassed upon your land. I can only plead, as my excuse, that I fully believed I was still upon the manor belonging to The Shallows."

"Gentlemen who go out shooting ought to know the limits of their estates," he answered harshly; "the boundaries of The Shallows are well defined, nor is the area they contain so very extensive. You have no right upon this side the stream, sir; oblige me by returning."

I merely bowed, for I was nettled by his tone, and as I turned away I noticed that the young lady whispered to him.

"One moment, sir," he said, "my daughter suggests the possibility of your being the new owner of The Shallows. May I ask if this is so?"

It had not occurred to me before, but I understood in a moment to whom I had been speaking, and I replied:

"Yes, Mr. Maryon—my name is Westcar."

Such was my introduction to Mr. and Miss Maryon. The proprietor of The Mere appeared to be a gentleman, but his manners were cold and reserved, and a careful observer might have remarked a perpetual restlessness in the eyes, as if they were physically incapable of regarding the same object for more than a moment. He was about sixty years of age, apparently; and though he now and again made an effort to carry himself upright, the head and shoulders soon drooped again, as if the weight of years, and, it might be, the memory of the past, were a heavy load to carry. Of Miss Maryon it is sufficient to say that she was nineteen or twenty, and it did not need a second glance to satisfy me that her beauty was of no ordinary kind.

I must hurry over the records of the next few weeks. I became a frequent visitor at The Mere. Mr. Maryon's manner never became cordial, but he did not seem displeased to see me; and as to Agnes,—well, she certainly was not displeased either.

I think it was on Christmas Day that I suddenly discovered that I was desperately in love. Miss Maryon had been for two or three days confined to her room by a bad cold, and I found myself in a great state of anxiety to see her again. I am sorry to say that my thoughts wandered a good deal when I was at church upon that festival, and I could not help thinking what ample room there was for a bridal procession up the spacious aisle.

Suddenly my eyes rested upon a mural tablet, inscribed, "To the memory of Aldina Ringwood."

Then with a cold thrill there came back upon me what I had almost forgotten, the dream, or whatever it was, that had occurred on that first night at The Shallows; and those strange words—"The Mere belongs to you. Compel John Maryon to pay the debt of honour!" Nothing but the remembrance of Agnes' sweet face availed for the time to banish the vision, the statement, and the bidding.

Miss Maryon was soon downstairs again. Did I flatter myself too much in thinking that she was as glad to see me as I was to see her? No—I felt sure that I did not. Then I began to reflect seriously upon my position. My fortune was small, quite enough for me, but not enough for two; and as she was heiress of The Mere and a comfortable rent-roll of some six or eight thousand a year, was it not natural that Mr. Maryon expected her to make what is called a "good match"? Still, I could not conceal from myself the fact, that he evinced no objection whatever to my frequent visits at his house, nor to my taking walks with his daughter when he was unable to accompany us.

One bright, frosty day I had been down to the lake with Miss Maryon, and had enjoyed the privilege of teaching her to skate; and on returning to the house, we met Mr. Maryon upon the terrace, He walked with us to the conservatory; we went in to examine the plants, and he remained outside, pacing up and down the terrace. Both Agnes and myself were strangely silent; perhaps my tongue had found an eloquence upon the ice which was well met by a shy thoughtfulness upon her part. But there was a lovely colour upon her cheeks, and I experienced a very considerable and unusual fluttering about my heart.

It happened as we were standing at the door of the conservatory, both of us silently looking away from the flowers upon the frosty view, that our eyes lighted at the same time upon Mr. Maryon. He, too, was apparently regarding the prospect, when suddenly he paused and staggered back, as if something unexpected met his gaze.

"Oh, poor papa! I hope he is not going to have one of his fits!" exclaimed Agnes.

"Fits! Is he subject to such attacks?" I inquired.

"Not ordinary fits," she answered hurriedly; "I hardly know how to explain them. They come upon him occasionally, and generally at this period of the year."

"Shall we go to him?" I suggested.

"No; you cannot help him; and he cannot bear that they should be noticed."

We both watched him. His arms were stretched up above his head, and again he recoiled a step or two. I sought for an explanation in Agnes' face.

"A stranger!" she exclaimed. "Who can it be?"

I looked toward Mr. Maryon. A tall figure of a man had come from the farther side of the house; he wore a large, loose coat and a kind of military cap upon his head.

"Doubtless you are surprised to see me, John," we heard the new-comer say, in a confident voice, "but I am not the devil, man, that you should greet me with such a peculiar attitude." He held out his hand, and continued, "Come, don't let the warmth of old fellowship be all on one side, this wintry day."

We could see that Mr. Maryon took the proffered right hand with his left for an instant, then seemed to shrink away, but exchanged no word of this greeting.

"I don't understand this," said Agnes, and we both hurried forward. The stranger, seeing Agnes approach, lifted his cap.

"Ah, your daughter, John, no doubt. I see the likeness to her lamented mother. Pray introduce me."

Mr. Maryon's usually pallid features had assumed a still paler hue, and he said in a low voice:

"Colonel Bludyer—my daughter." Agnes barely bowed.

"Charmed to renew your acquaintance, Miss Maryon. When last I saw you, you were quite a baby; but your father and I are very old friends—are we not, John?"

Mr. Maryon vaguely nodded his head.

"Well, John, you have often pressed your hospitality upon me, but till now I have never had an opportunity of availing myself of your kind offers; so I have brought my bag, and intend at last to give you the pleasure of my company for a few days."

I certainly should have thought that a man of Mr. Maryon's disposition would have resented such conduct as this, or, at all events, have given this self-invited guest a chilling welcome. Mr. Maryon, however, in a confused and somewhat stammering tone, said that he was glad Colonel Bludyer had come at last, and bade his daughter go and make the necessary arrangements. Agnes, in silent astonishment, entered the house, and then Mr. Maryon turned to me hastily and bade me goodbye. In a by no means comfortable frame of mind I returned to The Shallows.

The sudden advent of this miscellaneous colonel was naturally somewhat irritating to me. Not only did I regard the man as an intolerable bore, but I could not help fancying that he was something more than an old friend of Mr. Maryon's; in fact, I was led to judge, by Mr. Maryon's strange conduct, that this Bludyer had some power over him which might be exercised to the detriment of the Maryon family, and I was convinced there was some mystery it was my business to penetrate.

The following day I went up to The Mere to see if Miss Maryon was desirous of renewing her skating lesson. I found the party in the billiard-room, Agnes marking for her father and the Colonel. Mr. Maryon, whom I knew to be an exceptionally good player, seemed incapable of making a decent stroke; the Colonel, on the other hand, could evidently give a professional fifteen, and beat him easily. We all went down to the lake together. I had no chance of any quiet conversation with Agnes; the Colonel was perpetually beside us.

I returned home disgusted. For two whole days I did not go near The Mere. On the third day I went up, hoping that the horrid Colonel would be gone. It was beginning to snow when I left The Shallows at about two o'clock in the afternoon, and Mrs. Balk foretold a heavy storm, and bade me not be late returning.

The black winter darkness in the sky deepened as I approached The Mere. I was ushered again into the billiard-room. Agnes was marking, as upon the previous occasion, but two days had worked a sad difference in her face. Mr. Maryon hardly noticed my entrance; he was flushed, and playing eagerly; the Colonel was boisterous, declaring that John had never played better twenty years ago. I relieved Agnes of the duty of marking. The snow fell in a thick layer upon the skylight, and the Colonel became seriously anxious about my return home.

As I did not think he was the proper person to give me hints, I resolutely remained where I was, encouraged in my behaviour by the few words I gained from Agnes, and by the looks of entreaty she gave me. I had always considered Mr. Maryon to be an abstemious man, but he drank a good deal of brandy and soda during the long game of seven hundred up, and when he succeeded in beating the Colonel by forty-three, he was in roaring spirits, and insisted upon my staying to dinner. Need I say that I accepted the invitation?

I made such toilet as I could in a most unattainable chamber that was allotted to me, and hurried back to the drawing-room in the hope that I might get a few private words with Agnes. I was not disappointed. She, too, had hurried down, and in a few words I learned that this abominable Bludyer was paying her his coarse attentions, and with, apparently, the full consent of Mr. Maryon. My indignation was unbounded. Was it possible that Mr. Maryon intended to sacrifice this fair creature to that repulsive man?

Mr. Maryon had appeared in excellent spirits when dinner began, and the first glass or two of champagne made him merrier than I thought it possible for him to be. But by the time the dessert was on the table he had grown silent and thoughtful; nor did he respond to the warm eulogiums the Colonel passed upon the magnum of claret which was set before us.

After dinner we sat in the library. The Colonel left the room to fetch some cigars he had been loudly extolling. Then Agnes had an opportunity of whispering to me.

"Look at papa—see how strangely he sits—his hands clenching the arms of the chair, his eyes fixed upon the blazing coals! How old he seems to be tonight! His terrible fits are coming on—he is always like this toward the end of January!"The Colonel's return put an end to any further confidential talk.

When we separated for the night, I felt that my going to bed would be purposeless. I felt most painfully wide awake. I threw myself down upon my bed, and worried myself by trying to imagine what secret there could be between Maryon and Bludyer—for that a secret of some kind existed, I felt certain. I tossed about till I heard the stroke of one. A dreadful restlessness had come upon me. It seemed as if the solemn night-side of life was busy waking now, but the silence and solitude of my antique chamber became too much for me. I rose from my bed, and paced up and down the room. I raked up the dying embers of the fire, and drew an armchair to the hearth.

I fell into a doze. By and by I woke up suddenly, and I was conscious of stealthy footsteps in the passage. My sense of hearing became painfully acute. I heard the footsteps retreating down the corridor, until they were lost in the distance. I cautiously opened the door, and, shading the candle with my hand, looked out—there was nothing to be seen; but I felt that I could not remain quietly in my room, and, closing the door behind me, I went out in search of I knew not what.

The sitting-rooms and bedrooms in ordinary use at The Mere were in the modern part of the house; but there was an old Elizabethan wing which I had often longed to explore, and in this strange ramble of mine I soon had reason to be satisfied that I was well within it. At the end of an oak-panelled narrow passage a door stood open, and I entered a low, sombre apartment fitted with furniture in the style of two hundred years ago. There was something awfully ghostly about the look of this room. A great four-post bedstead, with heavy hangings, stood in a deep recess; a round oak table and two high-backed chairs were in the centre of the room. Suddenly, as I gazed on these things, I heard stealthy footsteps in the passage, and saw a dim light advancing.

Acting on a sudden impulse, I extinguished my candle and

withdrew into the shadow of the recess, watching eagerly. The footsteps came nearer. My heart seemed to stand still with expectation. They paused outside the door, for a moment really-for an age it seemed to me. Then, to my astonishment, I saw Mr. Maryon enter. He carried a small night-lamp in his hand. Another glance satisfied me that he was walking in his sleep. He came straight to the round table, and set down the lamp. He seated himself in one of the high-backed chairs, his vacant eyes staring at the chair opposite; then his lips began to move quickly, as if he were addressing someone. Then he rose, went to the bureau, and seemed to take something from it; then he sat down again. What a strange action of his hands! At first I could not understand it; then it flashed upon me that in this dream of his he must be shuffling cards. Yes, he began to deal; then he was playing with his adversary—his lips moving anxiously at times.

A look of terrible eagerness came over the sleepwalker's countenance. With nimble fingers he dealt the cards, and played. Suddenly with a sweep of his hand he seemed to fling the pack into the fireplace, started from his seat, grappled with his unseen adversary, raised his powerful right hand, and struck a tremendous blow. Hush! more footsteps along the passage! Am I deceived? From my concealment I watch for what is to follow. Colonel Bludyer comes in, half dressed, but wide awake.

"You maniac!" I hear him mutter: "I expected you were given to such tricks as these. Lucky for you no eyes but mine have seen your abject folly. Come back to your room."

Mr. Maryon is still gazing, his arms lifted wildly above his head, upon the imagined foe whom he had felled to the ground. The Colonel touches him on the shoulder, and leads him away, leaving the lamp. My reasoning faculties had fully returned to me. I held a clue to the secret, and for Agnes' sake it must be followed up. I took the lamp away, and placed it on a table where the chamber candlesticks stood, relit my own candle, and found my way back to my bedroom.

The next morning, when I came down to breakfast, I found Colonel Bludyer warming himself satisfactorily at the blazing fire. I learned from him that our host was far from well, and that Miss Maryon was in attendance upon her father; that the Colonel was charged with all kinds of apologies to me, and good wishes for my safe return home across the snow. I thanked him for the delivery of the message, while I felt perfectly convinced that he had never been charged with it. However that might be, I never saw Mr. Maryon that morning; and I started back to The Shallows through the snow.

For the next two or three days the weather was very wild, but I contrived to get up to The Mere, and ask after Mr. Maryon. Better, I was told, but unable to see any one. Miss Maryon, too, was fatigued with nursing her father. So there was nothing to do but to trudge home again.

"*Reginald Westcar, The Mere is yours. Compel John Maryon to pay the debt of honour!*"

Again and again these words forced themselves upon me, as I listlessly gazed out upon the white landscape. The strange scene that I had witnessed on that memorable night I passed beneath Mr. Maryon's roof had brought them back to my memory with redoubled force, and I began to think that the apparition I had seen—or dreamed of—on my first night at The Shallows had more of truth in it than I had been willing to believe.

Three more days passed away, and a carter-boy from The Mere brought me a note. It was Agnes' handwriting. It said:

DEAR MR. WESTCAR: Pray come up here, if you possibly can. I cannot understand what is the matter with papa; and he wishes me to do a dreadful thing. Do come. I feel that I have no friend but you. I am obliged to send this note privately.

I need scarcely say that five minutes afterward I was plunging through the snow toward The Mere. It was already late on that dark February evening as I gained the shrubbery; and as I was pondering upon the best method of securing admittance, I became aware that the figure of a man was hurrying on some yards in front of me. At first I thought it must be one of the gardeners, but all of a sudden I stood still, and my blood seemed to freeze with horror, as I remarked that the figure in front of me *left no trace of footmarks on the snow*! My brain reeled for a moment, and I thought I should have fallen; but I recovered my nerves, and when I looked before me again, it had disappeared. I pressed on eagerly. I arrived at the front door—it was wide open; and I passed through the hall to the library. I heard Agnes' voice.

"No, no, papa. You must not force me to this! I cannot—will not—marry Colonel Bludyer!"

"You *must*," answered Mr. Maryon, in a hoarse voice; "you *must* marry him, and save your father from something worse than disgrace!"

Not feeling disposed to play the eavesdropper, I entered the room. Mr. Maryon was standing at the fireplace. Agnes was crouching on the ground at his feet. I saw at once that it was no use for me to dissemble the reason of my visit, and, without a word of greeting, I said:

"Miss Maryon, I have come, in obedience to your summons. If I can prevent any misfortune from falling upon you I am ready to help you, with my life. You have guessed that I love you. If my love is returned I am prepared to dispute my claim with any man."

Agnes, with a cry of joy, rose from her knees, and rushed toward me. Ah! how strong I felt as I held her in my arms!

"I have my answer," I continued. "Mr. Maryon, I have reason to believe that your daughter is in fear of the future you have forecast for her. I ask you to regard those fears, and to give her to me, to love and cherish as my wife."

Mr. Maryon covered his face with his hands; and I could hear him murmur, "Too late—too late!"

"No, not too late," I echoed. "What is this Bludyer to you, that you should sacrifice your daughter to a man whose very look proclaims him a villain? Nothing can compel you to such a deed—not even a *debt of honour*!"

What it was impelled me to say these last words I know not, but they had an extraordinary effect upon Mr. Maryon. He started toward me, then checked himself; his face was livid, his eyeballs glaring, and he threw up his arms in the strange manner I had already witnessed.

"What is all this?" exclaimed a harsh voice behind me. "Mr. Westcar insulting Miss Maryon and her father! it is time for me to interfere." And Colonel Bludyer approached me menacingly. All his jovial manner and fulsome courtesy was gone; and in his flushed face and insolent look the savage rascal was revealed.

"You will interfere at your peril," I replied. "I am a younger man than you are, and my strength has not been weakened by drink and dissipation. Take care."

The villain drew himself up to his full height; and, though he must have been at least some sixty years of age, I felt assured that I should meet no ordinary adversary if a personal struggle should ensue. Agnes fainted, and I laid her on a sofa.

"Miss Maryon wants air," said the Colonel, in a calmer voice. "Excuse me, Mr. Maryon, if I open a window." He tore open the shutters, and threw up the sash. "And now, Mr. Westcar, unless you are prepared to be sensible, and make your exit by the door, I shall be under the unpleasant necessity of throwing you out of the window."

The ruffian advanced toward me as he spoke. Suddenly he paused. His jaw dropped; his hair seemed literally to stand on end; his white lips quivered; he shook, as with an ague; his whole form appeared to shrink. I stared in amazement at the awful change. A strange thrill shot through me, as I heard a quiet voice say:

"Richard Bludyer, your grave is waiting for you. Go."

The figure of a man passed between me and him. The wretched man shrank back, and, with a wild cry, leaped from the window he had opened.

All this time Mr. Maryon was standing like a lifeless statue.

In helpless wonder I gazed at the figure before me. I saw clearly the features in profile, and, swift as lightning, my memory was carried back to the unforgotten scene in the churchyard upon the Lake of Lucerne, and I recognized the white face of the young man with whom I there had spoken.

"John Maryon," said the voice, "this is the night upon which, a quarter of a century ago, you killed me. It is your last night on earth. You must go through the tragedy again."

Mr. Maryon, still statue-like, beckoned to the figure, and opened a half-concealed door which led into his study. The strange but opportune visitant seemed to motion to me with a gesture of his hand, which I felt I must obey, and I followed in this weird procession. From the study we mounted by a private staircase to a large, well-furnished bedchamber. Here we paused. Mr. Maryon looked tremblingly at the stranger, and said, in a low, stammering voice:

"This is my room. In this room, on this night, twenty-five years ago, you told me that you were certain Sir Henry Benet's will was in existence, and that you had made up your mind to dispute my possession to this property. You had discovered letters from Sir Henry to your father which gave you a clue to the spot where that will might be found. You, Geoffrey Ringwood, of generous and extravagant nature, offered to find the will in my presence. It was late at night, as now; all the household slept. I accepted your invitation, and followed you."

Mr. Maryon ceased; he seemed physically unable to continue. The terrible stranger, in his low, echoing voice, replied:

"Go on; confess all."

"You and I, Geoffrey, had been what the world calls friends. We had been much in London together; we were both passionately fond of cards. We had a common acquaintance, Richard Bludyer. He was present on the 2nd of February, when I lost a large sum of money to you at *ecarte*. He hinted to me that you might possibly use these sums in instituting a lawsuit against me for the recovery of this estate. Your intimation that you knew of the existence of the will alarmed me, as it had become necessary for me to remain owner of The Mere. As I have said, I accepted your invitation, and followed you to Sir Henry Benet's room; and now I follow you again."

As he said these words, Geoffrey Ringwood, or his ghost,

passed silently by Mr. Maryon, and led the way into the corridor. At the end of the corridor all three paused outside an oak door which I remembered well. A gesture from the leader made Mr. Maryon continue:

"On this threshold you told me suddenly that Bludyer was a villain, and had betrayed your sister Aldina; that she had fled with him that night; that he could never marry her, as you had reason to know he had a wife alive. You made me swear to help you in your vengeance against him. We entered the room, as we enter it now."

Our leader had opened the door of the room, and we were in the same chamber I had wandered to when I had slept at The Mere. The figure of Geoffrey Ringwood paused at the round table, and looked again at Mr. Maryon, who proceeded:

"You went straight to the fifth panel from the fireplace, and then touched a spring, and the panel opened. You said that the will giving this property to your father and his heirs was to be found there. I was convinced that you spoke the truth, but, suddenly remembering your love of gambling, I suggested that we should play for it. You accepted at once. We searched among the papers, and found the will. We placed the will upon the table, and began to play. We agreed that we would play up to ten thousand pounds.

"Your luck was marvellous. In two hours the limit was reached. I owed you ten thousand pounds, and had lost The Mere. You laughed, and said, 'Well, John, you have had a fair chance. At ten o'clock this morning I shall expect you to pay me *your debt of honour.*' I rose; the devil of despair strong upon me. With one hand I swept the cards from the table into the fire, and with the other seized you by the throat, and dealt you a blow upon the temple. You fell dead upon the floor."

Need I say that as I heard this fearful narrative, I recognized the actions of the sleepwalker, and understood them all?

"To the end!" said the hollow voice. "Confess to the end!"

"The doctor who examined your body gave his opinion, at the inquest, that you had died of apoplexy, caused by strong cerebral excitement. My evidence was to the effect that I believed you had lost a very large sum of money to Captain Bludyer, and that you had told me you were utterly unable to pay it. The jury found their verdict accordingly, and I was left in undisturbed possession of The Mere. But the memory of my crime haunted me as only such memories can haunt a criminal, and I became a morose and miserable man.

"One thing bound me to life—my daughter. When Reginald Westcar appeared upon the scene I thought that the debt of honour would be satisfied if he married Agnes. Then Bludyer reappeared, and he told me that he knew that I had killed you. He threatened to revive the story, to exhume your body, and to say that Aldina Ringwood had told him all about the will. I could purchase his silence only by giving him my daughter, the heiress of The Mere. To this I consented."

As he said these last words, Mr. Maryon sunk heavily into the chair.

The figure of Geoffrey Ringwood placed one ghostly hand upon his left temple, and then passed silently out of the room. I started up, and followed the phantom along the corridor-down the staircase—out at the front door, which still stood open—across the snow-covered lawn—into the plantation; and then it disappeared as strangely as I first had seen it; and, hardly knowing whether I was mad or dreaming, I found my way back to The Shallows.

★ ★ ★ ★ ★

For some weeks I was ill with brain-fever. When I recovered I was told that terrible things had happened at The Mere. Mr. Maryon had been found dead in Sir Henry Benet's room—an effusion of blood upon the brain, the doctors said—and the body of Colonel Bludyer had been discovered in the snow in an old disused gravel-pit not far from the house.

★ ★ ★ ★ ★

A year afterward I married Agnes Maryon; and, if all that I had seen and heard upon that 3rd of February was not merely the invention of a fevered brain, the debt of honour was at last discharged, for I, the nephew of the murdered Geoffrey Ringwood, became the owner of The Mere.

An Account of Some Strange Disturbances in Aungier Street

It is not worth telling, this story of mine—at least, not worth writing. Told, indeed, as I have sometimes been called upon to tell it, to a circle of intelligent and eager faces, lighted up by a good after-dinner fire on a winter's evening, with a cold wind rising and wailing outside, and all snug and cosy within, it has gone off—though I say it, who should not—indifferent well. But it is a venture to do as you would have me. Pen, ink, and paper are cold vehicles for the marvellous, and a "reader" decidedly a more critical animal than a "listener." If, however, you can induce your friends to read it after nightfall, and when the fireside talk has run for a while on thrilling tales of shapeless terror; in short, if you will secure me the *mollia tempora fandi*, I will go to my work, and say my say, with better heart. Well, then, these conditions presupposed, I shall waste no more words, but tell you simply how it all happened.

My cousin (Tom Ludlow) and I studied medicine together. I think he would have succeeded, had he stuck to the profession; but he preferred the Church, poor fellow, and died early, a sacrifice to contagion, contracted in the noble discharge of his duties. For my present purpose, I say enough of his character when I mention that he was of a sedate but frank and cheerful nature; very exact in his observance of truth, and not by any means like myself—of an excitable or nervous temperament.

My Uncle Ludlow—Tom's father—while we were attending lectures, purchased three or four old houses in Aungier Street, one of which was unoccupied. *He* resided in the country, and Tom proposed that we should take up our abode in the untenanted house, so long as it should continue unlet; a move which would accomplish the double end of settling us nearer alike to our lecture-rooms and to our amusements, and of relieving us from the weekly charge of rent for our lodgings.

Our furniture was very scant—our whole equipage remarkably modest and primitive; and, in short, our arrangements pretty nearly as simple as those of a bivouac. Our new plan was, therefore, executed almost as soon as conceived. The front drawing-room was our sitting-room. I had the bedroom over it, and Tom the back bedroom on the same floor, which nothing could have induced me to occupy.

The house, to begin with, was a very old one. It had been, I believe, newly fronted about fifty years before; but with this exception, it had nothing modern about it. The agent who bought it and looked into the titles for my uncle, told me that it was sold, along with much other forfeited property, at Chichester House, I think, in 1702; and had belonged to Sir Thomas Hacket, who was Lord Mayor of Dublin in James II.'s time. How old it was *then*, I can't say; but, at all events, it had seen years and changes enough to have contracted all that mysterious and saddened air, at once exciting and depressing, which belongs to most old mansions.

There had been very little done in the way of modernising details; and, perhaps, it was better so; for there was something queer and by-gone in the very walls and ceilings—in the shape of doors and windows—in the odd diagonal site of the chimney-pieces—in the beams and ponderous cornices—not to mention the singular solidity of all the woodwork, from the banisters to the windowframes, which hopelessly defied disguise, and would have emphatically proclaimed their antiquity through any conceivable amount of modern finery and varnish.

An effort had, indeed, been made, to the extent of papering the drawing-rooms; but somehow, the paper looked raw and out of keeping; and the old woman, who kept a little dirt-pie of a shop in the lane, and whose daughter—a girl of two and fifty-was our solitary handmaid, coming in at sunrise, and chastely receding again as soon as she had made all ready for tea in our state apartment;—this woman, I say, remembered it, when old Judge Horrocks (who, having earned the reputation of a particularly "hanging judge," ended by hanging himself, as the coroner's jury found, under an impulse of "temporary insanity," with a child's skipping-rope, over the massive old banisters) resided there, entertaining good company, with fine venison and rare old port. In those halcyon days, the drawing-rooms were hung with gilded leather, and, I dare say, cut a good figure, for they were really spacious rooms.

The bedrooms were wainscoted, but the front one was not gloomy; and in it the cosiness of antiquity quite overcame its sombre associations. But the back bedroom, with its two queer-ly-placed melancholy windows, staring vacantly at the foot of the bed, and with the shadowy recess to be found in most old houses in Dublin, like a large ghostly closet, which, from congeniality of temperament, had amalgamated with the bedchamber, and dissolved the partition. At night-time, this "alcove"—as our "maid" was wont to call it—had, in my eyes, a specially sinister and suggestive character. Tom's distant and solitary candle glimmered vainly into its darkness. *There* it was always overlooking him—always itself impenetrable. But this was only part of the effect.

The whole room was, I can't tell how, repulsive to me. There was, I suppose, in its proportions and features, a latent discord—a certain mysterious and indescribable relation, which jarred indistinctly upon some secret sense of the fitting and the safe, and raised indefinable suspicions and apprehensions of the imagination. On the whole, as I began by saying, nothing could have induced me to pass a night alone in it.

I had never pretended to conceal from poor Tom my superstitious weakness; and he, on the other hand, most unaffectedly ridiculed my tremors. The sceptic was, however, destined to receive a lesson, as you shall hear.

We had not been very long in occupation of our respective dormitories, when I began to complain of uneasy nights and disturbed sleep. I was, I suppose, the more impatient under this annoyance, as I was usually a sound sleeper, and by no means prone to nightmares. It was now, however, my destiny, instead of enjoying my customary repose, every night to "sup full of horrors." After a preliminary course of disagreeable and frightful dreams, my troubles took a definite form, and the same vision, without an appreciable variation in a single detail, visited me at least (on an average) every second night in the week.

Now, this dream, nightmare, or infernal illusion—which you please—of which I was the miserable sport, was on this wise:—

I saw, or thought I saw, with the most abominable distinctness, although at the time in profound darkness, every article of furniture and accidental arrangement of the chamber in which I lay. This, as you know, is incidental to ordinary nightmare. Well, while in this clairvoyant condition, which seemed but the lighting up of the theatre in which was to be exhibited the monotonous tableau of horror, which made my nights insupportable, my attention invariably became, I know not why, fixed upon the windows opposite the foot of my bed; and, uniformly with the same effect, a sense of dreadful anticipation always took slow but sure possession of me.

I became somehow conscious of a sort of horrid but undefined preparation going forward in some unknown quarter, and by some unknown agency, for my torment; and, after an interval, which always seemed to me of the same length, a picture suddenly flew up to the window, where it remained fixed, as if by an electrical attraction, and my discipline of horror then commenced, to last perhaps for hours. The picture thus mysteriously glued to the window-panes, was the portrait of an old man, in a crimson flowered silk dressing-gown, the folds of which I could now describe, with a countenance embodying a strange mixture of intellect, sensuality, and power, but withal sinister and full of malignant omen.

His nose was hooked, like the beak of a vulture; his eyes

large, grey, and prominent, and lighted up with a more than mortal cruelty and coldness. These features were surmounted by a crimson velvet cap, the hair that peeped from under which was white with age, while the eyebrows retained their original blackness. Well I remember every line, hue, and shadow of that stony countenance, and well I may! The gaze of this hellish visage was fixed upon me, and mine returned it with the inexplicable fascination of nightmare, for what appeared to me to be hours of agony. At last——

The cock he crew, away then flew

the fiend who had enslaved me through the awful watches of the night; and, harassed and nervous, I rose to the duties of the day.

I had—I can't say exactly why, but it may have been from the exquisite anguish and profound impressions of unearthly horror, with which this strange phantasmagoria was associated—an insurmountable antipathy to describing the exact nature of my nightly troubles to my friend and comrade. Generally, however, I told him that I was haunted by abominable dreams; and, true to the imputed materialism of medicine, we put our heads together to dispel my horrors, not by exorcism, but by a tonic.

I will do this tonic justice, and frankly admit that the accursed portrait began to intermit its visits under its influence. What of that? Was this singular apparition—as full of character as of terror—therefore the creature of my fancy, or the invention of my poor stomach? Was it, in short, *subjective* (to borrow the technical slang of the day) and not the palpable aggression and intrusion of an external agent? That, good friend, as we will both admit, by no means follows. The evil spirit, who enthralled my senses in the shape of that portrait, may have been just as near me, just as energetic, just as malignant, though I saw him not.

What means the whole moral code of revealed religion regarding the due keeping of our own bodies, soberness, temperance, etc.? here is an obvious connexion between the material and the invisible; the healthy tone of the system, and its unimpaired energy, may, for aught we can tell, guard us against influences which would otherwise render life itself terrific. The mesmerist and the electro-biologist will fail upon an average with nine patients out of ten—so may the evil spirit. Special conditions of the corporeal system are indispensable to the production of certain spiritual phenomena. The operation succeeds sometimes—sometimes fails—that is all.

I found afterwards that my would-be sceptical companion had his troubles too. But of these I knew nothing yet. One night, for a wonder, I was sleeping soundly, when I was roused by a step on the lobby outside my room, followed by the loud clang of what turned out to be a large brass candlestick, flung with all his force by poor Tom Ludlow over the banisters, and rattling with a rebound down the second flight of stairs; and almost concurrently with this, Tom burst open my door, and bounced into my room backwards, in a state of extraordinary agitation.

I had jumped out of bed and clutched him by the arm before I had any distinct idea of my own whereabouts. There we were—in our shirts—standing before the open door—staring through the great old banister opposite, at the lobby window, through which the sickly light of a clouded moon was gleaming.

"What's the matter, Tom? What's the matter with you? What the devil's the matter with you, Tom?" I demanded shaking him with nervous impatience.

He took a long breath before he answered me, and then it was not very coherently.

"It's nothing, nothing at all—did I speak?—what did I say?—where's the candle, Richard? It's dark; I—I had a candle!"

"Yes, dark enough," I said; "but what's the matter?—what *is* it?—why don't you speak, Tom?—have you lost your wits?-what is the matter?"

"The matter?—oh, it is all over. It must have been a dream—nothing at all but a dream—don't you think so? It could not be anything more than a dream."

"Of *course*" said I, feeling uncommonly nervous, "it *was* a dream."

"I thought," he said, "there was a man in my room, and—and I jumped out of bed; and—and—where's the candle?"

"In your room, most likely," I said, "shall I go and bring it?"

"No; stay here—don't go; it's no matter—don't, I tell you; it was all a dream. Bolt the door, Dick; I'll stay here with you—I feel nervous. So, Dick, like a good fellow, light your candle and open the window—I am in a *shocking state.*"

I did as he asked me, and robing himself like Granuaile in one of my blankets, he seated himself close beside my bed.

Everybody knows how contagious is fear of all sorts, but more especially that particular kind of fear under which poor Tom was at that moment labouring. I would not have heard, nor I believe would he have recapitulated, just at that moment, for half the world, the details of the hideous vision which had so unmanned him.

"Don't mind telling me anything about your nonsensical dream, Tom," said I, affecting contempt, really in a panic; "let us talk about something else; but it is quite plain that this dirty old house disagrees with us both, and hang me if I stay here any longer, to be pestered with indigestion and—and—bad nights, so we may as well look out for lodgings—don't you think so?-at once."

Tom agreed, and, after an interval, said—

"I have been thinking, Richard, that it is a long time since I saw my father, and I have made up my mind to go down tomorrow and return in a day or two, and you can take rooms for us in the meantime."

I fancied that this resolution, obviously the result of the vision which had so profoundly scared him, would probably vanish next morning with the damps and shadows of night. But I was mistaken. Off went Tom at peep of day to the country, having agreed that so soon as I had secured suitable lodgings, I was to recall him by letter from his visit to my Uncle Ludlow.

Now, anxious as I was to change my quarters, it so happened, owing to a series of petty procrastinations and accidents, that nearly a week elapsed before my bargain was made and my letter of recall on the wing to Tom; and, in the meantime, a trifling adventure or two had occurred to your humble servant, which, absurd as they now appear, diminished by distance, did certainly at the time serve to whet my appetite for change considerably.

A night or two after the departure of my comrade, I was sitting by my bedroom fire, the door locked, and the ingredients of a tumbler of hot whisky-punch upon the crazy spider-table; for, as the best mode of keeping the

Black spirits and white,
Blue spirits and grey,

with which I was environed, at bay, I had adopted the practice recommended by the wisdom of my ancestors, and "kept my spirits up by pouring spirits down." I had thrown aside my volume of Anatomy, and was treating myself by way of a tonic, preparatory to my punch and bed, to half-a-dozen pages of the *Spectator*, when I heard a step on the flight of stairs descending from the attics. It was two o'clock, and the streets were as silent as a churchyard—the sounds were, therefore, perfectly distinct. There was a slow, heavy tread, characterised by the emphasis and deliberation of age, descending by the narrow staircase from above; and, what made the sound more singular, it was plain that the feet which produced it were perfectly bare, measuring the descent with something between a pound and a flop, very ugly to hear.

I knew quite well that my attendant had gone away many hours before, and that nobody but myself had any business in the house. It was quite plain also that the person who was coming down stairs had no intention whatever of concealing his movements; but, on the contrary, appeared disposed to make even more noise, and proceed more deliberately, than was at all necessary. When the step reached the foot of the stairs outside my room, it seemed to stop; and I expected every moment to see my door open spontaneously, and give admission to the original of my detested portrait. I was, however, relieved in a few seconds by hearing the descent renewed, just in the same manner, upon the staircase leading down to the drawing-rooms, and thence, after another pause, down the next flight, and so on to the hall, whence I heard no more.

Now, by the time the sound had ceased, I was wound up, as they say, to a very unpleasant pitch of excitement. I listened, but there was not a stir. I screwed up my courage to a decisive experiment—opened my door, and in a stentorian voice bawled over the banisters, "Who's there?" There was no answer but the ringing of my own voice through the empty old house,—no renewal of the movement; nothing, in short, to give my unpleasant sensations a definite direction. There is, I think, something most disagreeably disenchanting in the sound of one's own voice under such circumstances, exerted in solitude, and in vain. It redoubled my sense of isolation, and my misgivings increased on perceiving that the door, which I certainly thought I had left open, was closed behind me; in a vague alarm, lest my retreat should be cut off, I got again into my room as quickly as I could, where I remained in a state of imaginary blockade, and very uncomfortable indeed, till morning.

Next night brought no return of my barefooted fellow-lodger; but the night following, being in my bed, and in the dark—somewhere, I suppose, about the same hour as before, I distinctly heard the old fellow again descending from the garrets.

This time I had had my punch, and the *morale* of the garrison was consequently excellent. I jumped out of bed, clutched the poker as I passed the expiring fire, and in a moment was upon the lobby. The sound had ceased by this time—the dark and chill were discouraging; and, guess my horror, when I saw, or thought I saw, a black monster, whether in the shape of a man or a bear I could not say, standing, with its back to the wall, on the lobby, facing me, with a pair of great greenish eyes shining dimly out. Now, I must be frank, and confess that the cupboard which displayed our plates and cups stood just there, though at the moment I did not recollect it.

At the same time I must honestly say, that making every allowance for an excited imagination, I never could satisfy myself that I was made the dupe of my own fancy in this matter; for this apparition, after one or two shiftings of shape, as if in the act of incipient transformation, began, as it seemed on second thoughts, to advance upon me in its original form. From an instinct of terror rather than of courage, I hurled the poker, with all my force, at its head; and to the music of a horrid crash made my way into my room, and double-locked the door. Then, in a minute more, I heard the horrid bare feet walk down the stairs, till the sound ceased in the hall, as on the former occasion.

If the apparition of the night before was an ocular delusion of my fancy sporting with the dark outlines of our cupboard, and if its horrid eyes were nothing but a pair of inverted teacups, I had, at all events, the satisfaction of having launched the poker with admirable effect, and in true "fancy" phrase, "knocked its two daylights into one," as the commingled fragments of my tea-service testified. I did my best to gather comfort and courage from these evidences; but it would not do. And then what could I say of those horrid bare feet, and the regular tramp, tramp, tramp, which measured the distance of the entire staircase through the solitude of my haunted dwelling, and at an hour when no good influence was stirring? Confound it!—the whole affair was abominable. I was out of spirits, and dreaded the approach of night.

It came, ushered ominously in with a thunder-storm and dull torrents of depressing rain. Earlier than usual the streets grew silent; and by twelve o'clock nothing but the comfortless pattering of the rain was to be heard.

I made myself as snug as I could. I lighted *two* candles instead of one. I forswore bed, and held myself in readiness for a sally, candle in hand; for, *coute qui coute*, I was resolved to *see* the being, if visible at all, who troubled the nightly stillness of my mansion. I was fidgety and nervous and tried in vain to interest myself with my books. I walked up and down my room, whistling in turn martial and hilarious music, and listening ever and anon for the dreaded noise. I sate down and stared at the square label on the solemn and reserved-looking black bottle, until "FLANAGAN & CO'S BEST OLD MALT WHISKY" grew into a sort of subdued accompaniment to all the fantastic and horrible speculations which chased one another through my brain.

Silence, meanwhile, grew more silent, and darkness darker. I listened in vain for the rumble of a vehicle, or the dull clamour of a distant row. There was nothing but the sound of a rising wind, which had succeeded the thunder-storm that had travelled over the Dublin mountains quite out of hearing. In the middle of this great city I began to feel myself alone with nature, and Heaven knows what beside. My courage was ebbing. Punch, however, which makes beasts of so many, made a man of me again—just in time to hear with tolerable nerve and firmness the lumpy, flabby, naked feet deliberately descending the stairs again.

I took a candle, not without a tremor. As I crossed the floor I tried to extemporise a prayer, but stopped short to listen, and never finished it. The steps continued. I confess I hesitated for some seconds at the door before I took heart of grace and opened it. When I peeped out the lobby was perfectly empty—there was no monster standing on the staircase; and as the de-tested sound ceased, I was reassured enough to venture forward nearly to the banisters. Horror of horrors! within a stair or two beneath the spot where I stood the unearthly tread smote the floor. My eye caught something in motion; it was about the size of Goliah's foot—it was grey, heavy, and flapped with a dead weight from one step to another. As I am alive, it was the most monstrous grey rat I ever beheld or imagined.

Shakespeare says—"*Some men there are cannot abide a gaping pig, and some that are mad if they behold a cat.*" I went well-nigh out of my wits when I beheld this *rat*; for, laugh at me as you may, it fixed upon me, I thought, a perfectly human expression of mal-ice; and, as it shuffled about and looked up into my face almost from between my feet, I saw, I could swear it—I felt it then, and know it now, the infernal gaze and the accursed countenance of my old friend in the portrait, transfused into the visage of the bloated vermin before me.

I bounced into my room again with a feeling of loathing and horror I cannot describe, and locked and bolted my door as if a lion had been at the other side. D——n him or *it*; curse the portrait and its original! I felt in my soul that the rat—yes, the *rat*, the RAT I had just seen, was that evil being in masquerade, and rambling through the house upon some infernal night lark.

Next morning I was early trudging through the miry streets; and, among other transactions, posted a peremptory note recalling Tom. On my return, however, I found a note from my absent "chum," announcing his intended return next day. I was doubly rejoiced at this, because I had succeeded in getting rooms; and because the change of scene and return of my comrade were rendered specially pleasant by the last night's half ridiculous half horrible adventure.

I slept extemporaneously in my new quarters in Digges' Street that night, and next morning returned for breakfast to the haunted mansion, where I was certain Tom would call immediately on his arrival.

I was quite right—he came; and almost his first question referred to the primary object of our change of residence.

"Thank God," he said with genuine fervour, on hearing that all was arranged. "On *your* account I am delighted. As to myself, I assure you that no earthly consideration could have induced me ever again to pass a night in this disastrous old house."

"Confound the house!" I ejaculated, with a genuine mixture of fear and detestation, "we have not had a pleasant hour since we came to live here"; and so I went on, and related incidentally my adventure with the plethoric old rat.

"Well, if that were *all*," said my cousin, affecting to make light of the matter, "I don't think I should have minded it very much."

"Ay, but its eye—its countenance, my dear Tom," urged I; "if you had seen *that*, you would have felt it might be *anything* but what it seemed."

"I inclined to think the best conjurer in such a case would be an able-bodied cat," he said, with a provoking chuckle.

"But let us hear your own adventure," I said tartly.

At this challenge he looked uneasily round him. I had poked

up a very unpleasant recollection.

"You shall hear it, Dick; I'll tell it to you," he said. "Begad, sir, I should feel quite queer, though, telling it *here*, though we are too strong a body for ghosts to meddle with just now."

Though he spoke this like a joke, I think it was serious calculation. Our Hebe was in a corner of the room, packing our cracked delft tea and dinner-services in a basket. She soon suspended operations, and with mouth and eyes wide open became an absorbed listener. Tom's experiences were told nearly in these words:—

"I saw it three times, Dick—three distinct times; and I am perfectly certain it meant me some infernal harm. I was, I say, in danger—in *extreme* danger; for, if nothing else had happened, my reason would most certainly have failed me, unless I had escaped so soon. Thank God. I *did* escape.

"The first night of this hateful disturbance, I was lying in the attitude of sleep, in that lumbering old bed. I hate to think of it. I was really wide awake, though I had put out my candle, and was lying as quietly as if I had been asleep; and although accidentally restless, my thoughts were running in a cheerful and agreeable channel.

"I think it must have been two o'clock at least when I thought I heard a sound in that—that odious dark recess at the far end of the bedroom. It was as if someone was drawing a piece of cord slowly along the floor, lifting it up, and dropping it softly down again in coils. I sate up once or twice in my bed, but could see nothing, so I concluded it must be mice in the wainscot. I felt no emotion graver than curiosity, and after a few minutes ceased to observe it.

"While lying in this state, strange to say; without at first a suspicion of anything supernatural, on a sudden I saw an old man, rather stout and square, in a sort of roan-red dressing-gown, and with a black cap on his head, moving stiffly and slowly in a diagonal direction, from the recess, across the floor of the bedroom, passing my bed at the foot, and entering the lumber-closet at the left. He had something under his arm; his head hung a little at one side; and, merciful God! when I saw his face."

Tom stopped for a while, and then said—

"That awful countenance, which living or dying I never can forget, disclosed what he was. Without turning to the right or left, he passed beside me, and entered the closet by the bed's head.

"While this fearful and indescribable type of death and guilt was passing, I felt that I had no more power to speak or stir than if I had been myself a corpse. For hours after it had disappeared, I was too terrified and weak to move. As soon as daylight came, I took courage, and examined the room, and especially the course which the frightful intruder had seemed to take, but there was not a vestige to indicate anybody's having passed there; no sign of any disturbing agency visible among the lumber that strewed the floor of the closet.

"I now began to recover a little. I was fagged and exhausted, and at last, overpowered by a feverish sleep. I came down late; and finding you out of spirits, on account of your dreams about the portrait, whose *original* I am now certain disclosed himself to me, I did not care to talk about the infernal vision. In fact, I was trying to persuade myself that the whole thing was an illusion, and I did not like to revive in their intensity the hated impressions of the past night—or to risk the constancy of my scepticism, by recounting the tale of my sufferings.

"It required some nerve, I can tell you, to go to my haunted chamber next night, and lie down quietly in the same bed," continued Tom. "I did so with a degree of trepidation, which, I am not ashamed to say, a very little matter would have sufficed to stimulate to downright panic. This night, however, passed off quietly enough, as also the next; and so too did two or three more. I grew more confident, and began to fancy that I believed in the theories of spectral illusions, with which I had at first vainly tried to impose upon my convictions.

"The apparition had been, indeed, altogether anomalous. It had crossed the room without any recognition of my presence: I had not disturbed *it*, and *it* had no mission to *me*. What, then, was the imaginable use of its crossing the room in a visible shape at all? Of course it might have *been* in the closet instead of *going* there, as easily as it introduced itself into the recess without entering the chamber in a shape discernible by the senses. Besides, how the deuce *had* I seen it? It was a dark night; I had no candle; there was no fire; and yet I saw it as distinctly, in colouring and outline, as ever I beheld human form! A cataleptic dream would explain it all; and I was determined that a dream it should be.

"One of the most remarkable phenomena connected with the practice of mendacity is the vast number of deliberate lies we tell ourselves, whom, of all persons, we can least expect to deceive. In all this, I need hardly tell you, Dick, I was simply lying to myself, and did not believe one word of the wretched humbug. Yet I went on, as men will do, like persevering charlatans and impostors, who tire people into credulity by the mere force of reiteration; so I hoped to win myself over at last to a comfortable scepticism about the ghost.

"He had not appeared a second time—that certainly was a comfort; and what, after all, did I care for him, and his queer old toggery and strange looks? Not a fig! I was nothing the worse for having seen him, and a good story the better. So I tumbled into bed, put out my candle, and, cheered by a loud drunken quarrel in the back lane, went fast asleep.

"From this deep slumber I awoke with a start. I knew I had had a horrible dream; but what it was I could not remember. My heart was thumping furiously; I felt bewildered and feverish; I sate up in the bed and looked about the room. A broad flood of moonlight came in through the curtainless window; everything was as I had last seen it; and though the domestic squabble in the back lane was, unhappily for me, allayed, I yet could hear a pleasant fellow singing, on his way home, the then popular comic ditty called, 'Murphy Delany.' Taking advantage of this diversion I lay down again, with my face towards the fireplace, and closing my eyes, did my best to think of nothing else but the song, which was every moment growing fainter in the distance:—

"' *Twas Murphy Delany, so funny and frisky,*

Stept into a shebeen shop to get his skin full;
He reeled out again pretty well lined with whiskey,
As fresh as a shamrock, as blind as a bull.

"The singer, whose condition I dare say resembled that of his hero, was soon too far off to regale my ears anymore; and as his music died away, I myself sank into a doze, neither sound nor refreshing. Somehow the song had got into my head, and I went meandering on through the adventures of my respectable fellow-countryman, who, on emerging from the 'shebeen shop,' fell into a river, from which he was fished up to be 'sat upon' by a coroner's jury, who having learned from a 'horse-doctor' that he was 'dead as a door-nail, so there was an end,' returned their verdict accordingly, just as he returned to his senses, when an angry altercation and a pitched battle between the body and the coroner winds up the lay with due spirit and pleasantry.

"Through this ballad I continued with a weary monotony to plod, down to the very last line, and then *da capo*, and so on, in my uncomfortable half-sleep, for how long, I can't conjecture. I found myself at last, however, muttering, '*dead* as a door-nail, so there was an end'; and something like another voice within me, seemed to say, very faintly, but sharply, 'dead! dead! *dead*! and may the Lord have mercy on your soul!' and instantaneously I was wide awake, and staring right before me from the pillow.

"Now—will you believe it, Dick?—I saw the same accursed figure standing full front, and gazing at me with its stony and fiendish countenance, not two yards from the bedside."

Tom stopped here, and wiped the perspiration from his face. I felt very queer. The girl was as pale as Tom; and, assembled as we were in the very scene of these adventures, we were all, I dare say, equally grateful for the clear daylight and the resuming bustle out of doors.

"For about three seconds only I saw it plainly; then it grew indistinct; but, for a long time, there was something like a column of dark vapour where it had been standing, between me and the wall; and I felt sure that he was still there. After a good while, this appearance went too. I took my clothes downstairs to the hall, and dressed there, with the door half open; then went out into the street, and walked about the town till morning, when I came back, in a miserable state of nervousness and exhaustion. I was such a fool, Dick, as to be ashamed to tell you how I came to be so upset. I thought you would laugh at me; especially as I had always talked philosophy, and treated *your* ghosts with contempt. I concluded you would give me no quarter; and so kept my tale of horror to myself.

"Now, Dick, you will hardly believe me, when I assure you, that for many nights after this last experience, I did not go to my room at all. I used to sit up for a while in the drawing-room after you had gone up to your bed; and then steal down softly to the hall-door, let myself out, and sit in the 'Robin Hood' tavern until the last guest went off; and then I got through the night like a sentry, pacing the streets till morning.

"For more than a week I never slept in bed. I sometimes had a snooze on a form in the 'Robin Hood,' and sometimes a nap in a chair during the day; but regular sleep I had absolutely none.

"I was quite resolved that we should get into another house; but I could not bring myself to tell you the reason, and I somehow put it off from day to day, although my life was, during every hour of this procrastination, rendered as miserable as that of a felon with the constables on his track. I was growing absolutely ill from this wretched mode of life.

"One afternoon I determined to enjoy an hour's sleep upon your bed. I hated mine; so that I had never, except in a stealthy visit every day to unmake it, lest Martha should discover the secret of my nightly absence, entered the ill-omened chamber.

"As ill-luck would have it, you had locked your bedroom, and taken away the key. I went into my own to unsettle the bedclothes, as usual, and give the bed the appearance of having been slept in. Now, a variety of circumstances concurred to bring about the dreadful scene through which I was that night to pass. In the first place, I was literally overpowered with fatigue, and longing for sleep; in the next place, the effect of this extreme exhaustion upon my nerves resembled that of a narcotic, and rendered me less susceptible than, perhaps, I should in any other condition have been, of the exciting fears which had become habitual to me. Then again, a little bit of the window was open, a pleasant freshness pervaded the room, and, to crown all, the cheerful sun of day was making the room quite pleasant. What was to prevent my enjoying an hour's nap *here*? The whole air was resonant with the cheerful hum of life, and the broad matter-of-fact light of day filled every corner of the room.

"I yielded—stifling my qualms—to the almost overpowering temptation; and merely throwing off my coat, and loosening my cravat, I lay down, limiting myself to *half*-an-hour's doze in the unwonted enjoyment of a feather bed, a coverlet, and a bolster.

"It was horribly insidious; and the demon, no doubt, marked my infatuated preparations. Dolt that I was, I fancied, with mind and body worn out for want of sleep, and an arrear of a full week's rest to my credit, that such measure as *half*-an-hour's sleep, in such a situation, was possible. My sleep was death-like, long, and dreamless.

"Without a start or fearful sensation of any kind, I waked gently, but completely. It was, as you have good reason to remember, long past midnight—I believe, about two o'clock. When sleep has been deep and long enough to satisfy nature thoroughly, one often wakens in this way, suddenly, tranquilly, and completely.

"There was a figure seated in that lumbering, old sofa-chair, near the fireplace. Its back was rather towards me, but I could not be mistaken; it turned slowly round, and, merciful heavens! there was the stony face, with its infernal lineaments of malignity and despair, gloating on me. There was now no doubt as to its consciousness of my presence, and the hellish malice with which it was animated, for it arose, and drew close to the bedside. There was a rope about its neck, and the other end, coiled up, it held stiffly in its hand.

"My good angel nerved me for this horrible crisis. I remained for some seconds transfixed by the gaze of this tremendous phantom. He came close to the bed, and appeared on the point of mounting upon it. The next instant I was upon the floor at the far side, and in a moment more was, I don't know how, upon the lobby.

"But the spell was not yet broken; the valley of the shadow of death was not yet traversed. The abhorred phantom was before me there; it was standing near the banisters, stooping a little, and with one end of the rope round its own neck, was poising a noose at the other, as if to throw over mine; and while engaged in this baleful pantomime, it wore a smile so sensual, so unspeakably dreadful, that my senses were nearly overpowered. I saw and remember nothing more, until I found myself in your room.

"I had a wonderful escape, Dick—there is no disputing *that*—an escape for which, while I live, I shall bless the mercy of heaven. No one can conceive or imagine what it is for flesh and blood to stand in the presence of such a thing, but one who has had the terrific experience. Dick, Dick, a shadow has passed over me—a chill has crossed my blood and marrow, and I will never be the same again—never, Dick—never!"

Our handmaid, a mature girl of two-and-fifty, as I have said, stayed her hand, as Tom's story proceeded, and by little and little drew near to us, with open mouth, and her brows contracted over her little, beady black eyes, till stealing a glance over her shoulder now and then, she established herself close behind us. During the relation, she had made various earnest comments, in an undertone; but these and her ejaculations, for the sake of brevity and simplicity, I have omitted in my narration.

"It's often I heard tell of it," she now said, "but I never believed it rightly till now—though, indeed, why should not I? Does not my mother, down there in the lane, know quare stories, God bless us, beyant telling about it? But you ought not to have slept in the back bedroom. She was loath to let me be going in and out of that room even in the day time, let alone for any Christian to spend the night in it; for sure she says it was his own bedroom."

"*Whose* own bedroom?" we asked, in a breath.

"Why, *his*—the ould Judge's—Judge Horrock's, to be sure,

God rest his sowl"; and she looked fearfully round.

"Amen!" I muttered. "But did he die there?"

"Die there! No, not quite *there*," she said. "Shure, was not it over the banisters he hung himself, the ould sinner, God be merciful to us all? and was not it in the alcove they found the handles of the skipping-rope cut off, and the knife where he was settling the cord, God bless us, to hang himself with? It was his housekeeper's daughter owned the rope, my mother often told me, and the child never throve after, and used to be starting up out of her sleep, and screeching in the night time, wid dhrames and frights that cum an her; and they said how it was the speerit of the ould Judge that was tormentin' her; and she used to be roaring and yelling out to hould back the big ould fellow with the crooked neck; and then she'd screech 'Oh, the master! the master! he's stampin' at me, and beckoning to me! Mother, darling, don't let me go!' And so the poor crathure died at last, and the docthers said it was wather on the brain, for it was all they could say."

"How long ago was all this?" I asked.

"Oh, then, how would I know?" she answered. "But it must be a wondherful long time ago, for the housekeeper was an ould woman, with a pipe in her mouth, and not a tooth left, and better nor eighty years ould when my mother was first married; and they said she was a rale buxom, fine-dressed woman when the ould Judge come to his end; an', indeed, my mother's not far from eighty years ould herself this day; and what made it worse for the unnatural ould villain, God rest his soul, to frighten the little girl out of the world the way he did, was what was mostly thought and believed by everyone. My mother says how the poor little crathure was his own child; for he was by all accounts an ould villain every way, an' the hangin'est judge that ever was known in Ireland's ground."

"From what you said about the danger of sleeping in that bedroom," said I, "I suppose there were stories about the ghost having appeared there to others."

"Well, there was things said—quare things, surely," she answered, as it seemed, with some reluctance. "And why would not there? Sure was it not up in that same room he slept for more than twenty years? and was it not in the *alcove* he got the rope ready that done his own business at last, the way he done many a betther man's in his lifetime?—and was not the body lying in the same bed after death, and put in the coffin there, too, and carried out to his grave from it in Pether's churchyard, after the coroner was done? But there was quare stories—my mother has them all—about how one Nicholas Spaight got into trouble on the head of it."

"And what did they say of this Nicholas Spaight?" I asked.

"Oh, for that matther, it's soon told," she answered.

And she certainly did relate a very strange story, which so piqued my curiosity, that I took occasion to visit the ancient lady, her mother, from whom I learned many very curious particulars. Indeed, I am tempted to tell the tale, but my fingers are weary, and I must defer it. But if you wish to hear it another time, I shall do my best.

When we had heard the strange tale I have *not* told you, we put one or two further questions to her about the alleged spectral visitations, to which the house had, ever since the death of the wicked old Judge, been subjected.

"No one ever had luck in it," she told us. "There was always cross accidents, sudden deaths, and short times in it. The first that tuck, it was a family—I forget their name—but at any rate there was two young ladies and their papa. He was about sixty, and a stout healthy gentleman as you'd wish to see at that age. Well, he slept in that unlucky back bedroom; and, God between us an' harm! sure enough he was found dead one morning, half out of the bed, with his head as black as a sloe, and swelled like a puddin', hanging down near the floor. It was a fit, they said. He was as dead as a mackerel, and so *he* could not say what it was; but the ould people was all sure that it was nothing at all but the ould Judge, God bless us! that frightened him out of his senses and his life together.

"Sometime after there was a rich old maiden lady took the

house. I don't know which room *she* slept in, but she lived alone; and at any rate, one morning, the servants going down early to their work, found her sitting on the passage-stairs, shivering and talkin' to herself, quite mad; and never a word more could any of *them* or her friends get from her ever afterwards but, 'Don't ask me to go, for I promised to wait for him.' They never made out from her who it was she meant by *him*, but of course those that knew all about the ould house were at no loss for the meaning of all that happened to her.

"Then afterwards, when the house was let out in lodgings, there was Micky Byrne that took the same room, with his wife and three little children; and sure I heard Mrs. Byrne myself telling how the children used to be lifted up in the bed at night, she could not see by what mains; and how they were starting and screeching every hour, just all as one as the housekeeper's little girl that died, till at last one night poor Micky had a dhrop in him, the way he used now and again; and what do you think in the middle of the night he thought he heard a noise on the stairs, and being in liquor, nothing less id do him but out he must go himself to see what was wrong. Well, after that, all she ever heard of him was himself sayin', 'Oh, God!' and a tumble that shook the very house; and there, sure enough, he was lying on the lower stairs, under the lobby, with his neck smashed double undher him, where he was flung over the banisters."

Then the handmaiden added—

"I'll go down to the lane, and send up Joe Gavvey to pack up the rest of the taythings, and bring all the things across to your new lodgings."

And so we all sallied out together, each of us breathing more freely, I have no doubt, as we crossed that ill-omened threshold for the last time.

Now, I may add thus much, in compliance with the immemorial usage of the realm of fiction, which sees the hero not only through his adventures, but fairly out of the world. You must have perceived that what the flesh, blood, and bone hero of romance proper is to the regular compounder of fiction, this old house of brick, wood, and mortar is to the humble recorder of this true tale. I, therefore, relate, as in duty bound, the catastrophe which ultimately befell it, which was simply this—that about two years subsequently to my story it was taken by a quack doctor, who called himself Baron Duhlstoerf, and filled the parlour windows with bottles of indescribable horrors preserved in brandy, and the newspapers with the usual grandiloquent and mendacious advertisements. This gentleman among his virtues did not reckon sobriety, and one night, being overcome with much wine, he set fire to his bed curtains, partially burned himself, and totally consumed the house. It was afterwards rebuilt, and for a time an undertaker established himself in the premises.

I have now told you my own and Tom's adventures, together with some valuable collateral particulars; and having acquitted myself of my engagement, I wish you a very goodnight, and pleasant dreams.

An Adventure of Hardress Fitzgerald, a Royalist Captain

The following brief narrative contains a faithful account of one of the many strange incidents which chequered the life of Hardress Fitzgerald—one of the now-forgotten heroes who flourished during the most stirring and, though the most disastrous, by no means the least glorious period of our eventful history.

He was a captain of horse in the army of James, and shared the fortunes of his master, enduring privations, encountering dangers, and submitting to vicissitudes the most galling and ruinous, with a fortitude and a heroism which would, if coupled with his other virtues have rendered the unhappy monarch whom he served, the most illustrious among unfortunate princes.

I have always preferred, where I could do so with any approach to accuracy, to give such relations as the one which I am about to submit to you, in the first person, and in the words of the original narrator, believing that such a form of recitation not only gives freshness to the tale, but in this particular instance, by bringing before me and steadily fixing in my mind's eye the veteran royalist who himself related the occurrence which I am about to record, furnishes an additional stimulant to my memory, and a proportionate check upon my imagination.

As nearly as I can recollect then, his statement was as follows:

After the fatal battle of the Boyne, I came up in disguise to

Dublin, as did many in a like situation, regarding the capital as furnishing at once a good central position of observation, and as secure a lurking-place as I cared to find.

I would not suffer myself to believe that the cause of my royal master was so desperate as it really was; and while I lay in my lodgings, which consisted of the garret of a small dark house, standing in the lane which runs close by Audoen's Arch, I busied myself with continual projects for the raising of the country, and the recollecting of the fragments of the defeated army—plans, you will allow, sufficiently magnificent for a poor devil who dared scarce show his face abroad in the daylight.

I believe, however, that I had not much reason to fear for my personal safety, for men's minds in the city were greatly occupied with public events, and private amusements and debaucheries, which were, about that time, carried to an excess which our country never knew before, by reason of the raking together from all quarters of the empire, and indeed from most parts of Holland, the most dissolute and desperate adventurers who cared to play at hazard for their lives; and thus there seemed to be but little scrutiny into the characters of those who sought concealment.

I heard much at different times of the intentions of King James and his party, but nothing with certainty.

Some said that the king still lay in Ireland; others, that he had crossed over to Scotland, to encourage the Highlanders, who, with Dundee at their head, had been stirring in his behoof; others, again, said that he had taken ship for France, leaving his followers to shift for themselves, and regarding his kingdom as wholly lost, which last was the true version, as I afterwards learned.

Although I had been very active in the wars in Ireland, and had done many deeds of necessary but dire severity, which have often since troubled me much to think upon, yet I doubted not but that I might easily obtain protection for my person and property from the Prince of Orange, if I sought it by the ordinary submissions; but besides that my conscience and my affections resisted such time-serving concessions, I was resolved in my own mind that the cause of the royalist party was by no means desperate, and I looked to keep myself unimpeded by any pledge or promise given to the usurping Dutchman, that I might freely and honourably take a share in any struggle which might yet remain to be made for the right.

I therefore lay quiet, going forth from my lodgings but little, and that chiefly under cover of the dusk, and conversing hardly at all, except with those whom I well knew.

I had like once to have paid dearly for relaxing this caution; for going into a tavern one evening near the Tholsel, I had the confidence to throw off my hat, and sit there with my face quite exposed, when a fellow coming in with some troopers, they fell a-boozing, and being somewhat warmed, they began to drink 'Confusion to popery,' and the like, and to compel the peaceable persons who happened to sit there, to join them in so doing.

Though I was rather hot-blooded, I was resolved to say nothing to attract notice; but, at the same time, if urged to pledge the toasts which they were compelling others to drink, to resist doing so.

With the intent to withdraw myself quietly from the place, I paid my reckoning, and putting on my hat, was going into the street, when the countryman who had come in with the soldiers called out:

'Stop that popish tom-cat!'

And running across the room, he got to the door before me, and, shutting it, placed his back against it, to prevent my going out.

Though with much difficulty, I kept an appearance of quietness, and turning to the fellow, who, from his accent, I judged to be northern, and whose face I knew—though, to this day, I cannot say where I had seen him before—I observed very calmly:

'Sir, I came in here with no other design than to refresh myself, without offending any man. I have paid my reckoning, and now desire to go forth. If there is anything within reason that I can do to satisfy you, and to prevent trouble and delay to myself, name your terms, and if they be but fair, I will frankly comply with them.'

He quickly replied:

'You are Hardress Fitzgerald, the bloody popish captain, that hanged the twelve men at Derry.'

I felt that I was in some danger, but being a strong man, and used to perils of all kinds, it was not easy to disconcert me.

I looked then steadily at the fellow, and, in a voice of much confidence, I said:

'I am neither a Papist, a Royalist, nor a Fitzgerald, but an honester Protestant, mayhap, than many who make louder professions.'

'Then drink the honest man's toast,' said he. 'Damnation to the pope, and confusion to skulking Jimmy and his runaway crew.'

'Yourself shall hear me,' said I, taking the largest pewter pot that lay within my reach. 'Tapster, fill this with ale; I grieve to say I can afford nothing better.'

I took the vessel of liquor in my hand, and walking up to him, I first made a bow to the troopers who sat laughing at the sprightliness of their facetious friend, and then another to himself, when saying, 'G— damn yourself and your cause!' I flung the ale straight into his face; and before he had time to recover himself, I struck him with my whole force and weight with the pewter pot upon the head, so strong a blow, that he fell, for aught I know, dead upon the floor, and nothing but the handle of the vessel remained in my hand.

I opened the door, but one of the dragoons drew his sabre, and ran at me to avenge his companion. With my hand I put aside the blade of the sword, narrowly escaping what he had intended for me, the point actually tearing open my vest. Without allowing him time to repeat his thrust, I struck him in the face with my clenched fist so sound a blow that he rolled back into the room with the force of a tennis ball.

It was well for me that the rest were half drunk, and the evening dark; for otherwise my folly would infallibly have cost me my life. As it was, I reached my garret in safety, with a resolution to frequent taverns no more until better times.

My little patience and money were well-nigh exhausted, when, after much doubt and uncertainty, and many conflicting reports, I was assured that the flower of the Royalist army, under the Duke of Berwick and General Boisleau, occupied the city of Limerick, with a determination to hold that fortress against the prince's forces; and that a French fleet of great power, and well freighted with arms, ammunition, and men, was riding in the Shannon, under the walls of the town. But this last report was, like many others then circulated, untrue; there being, indeed, a promise and expectation of such assistance, but no arrival of it till too late.

The army of the Prince of Orange was said to be rapidly approaching the town, in order to commence the siege.

On hearing this, and being made as certain as the vagueness and unsatisfactory nature of my information, which came not from any authentic source, would permit; at least, being sure of the main point, which all allowed—namely, that Limerick was held for the king—and being also naturally fond of enterprise, and impatient of idleness, I took the resolution to travel thither, and, if possible, to throw myself into the city, in order to lend what assistance I might to my former companions in arms, well knowing that any man of strong constitution and of some experience might easily make himself useful to a garrison in their straitened situation.

When I had taken this resolution, I was not long in putting it into execution; and, as the first step in the matter, I turned half of the money which remained with me, in all about seventeen pounds, into small wares and merchandise such as travelling traders used to deal in; and the rest, excepting some shillings which I carried home for my immediate expenses, I sewed carefully in the lining of my breeches waistband, hoping that the sale of my commodities might easily supply me with subsistence upon the road.

I left Dublin upon a Friday morning in the month of September, with a tolerably heavy pack upon my back.

I was a strong man and a good walker, and one day with another travelled easily at the rate of twenty miles in each day, much time being lost in the towns of any note on the way, where, to avoid suspicion, I was obliged to make some stay, as if to sell my wares.

I did not travel directly to Limerick, but turned far into Tipperary, going near to the borders of Cork.

Upon the sixth day after my departure from Dublin I learned, CERTAINLY, from some fellows who were returning from trafficking with the soldiers, that the army of the prince was actually encamped before Limerick, upon the south side of the Shannon.

In order, then, to enter the city without interruption, I must needs cross the river, and I was much in doubt whether to do so by boat from Kerry, which I might have easily done, into the Earl of Clare's land, and thus into the beleaguered city, or to take what seemed the easier way, one, however, about which I had certain misgivings—which, by the way, afterwards turned out to be just enough. This way was to cross the Shannon at O'Brien's Bridge, or at Killaloe, into the county of Clare.

I feared, however, that both these passes were guarded by the prince's forces, and resolved, if such were the case, not to essay to cross, for I was not fitted to sustain a scrutiny, having about me, though pretty safely secured, my commission from King James—which, though a dangerous companion, I would not have parted from but with my life.

I settled, then, in my own mind, that if the bridges were guarded I would walk as far as Portumna, where I might cross, though at a considerable sacrifice of time; and, having determined upon this course, I turned directly towards Killaloe.

I reached the foot of the mountain, or rather high hill, called Keeper—which had been pointed out to me as a landmark—lying directly between me and Killaloe, in the evening, and, having ascended some way, the darkness and fog overtook me.

The evening was very chilly, and myself weary, hungry, and

much in need of sleep, so that I preferred seeking to cross the hill, though at some risk, to remaining upon it throughout the night. Stumbling over rocks and sinking into bog-mire, as the nature of the ground varied, I slowly and laboriously plodded on, making very little way in proportion to the toil it cost me.

After half an hour's slow walking, or rather rambling, for, owing to the dark, I very soon lost my direction, I at last heard the sound of running water, and with some little trouble reached the edge of a brook, which ran in the bottom of a deep gully. This I knew would furnish a sure guide to the low grounds, where I might promise myself that I should speedily meet with some house or cabin where I might find shelter for the night.

The stream which I followed flowed at the bottom of a rough and swampy glen, very steep and making many abrupt turns, and so dark, owing more to the fog than to the want of the moon (for, though not high, I believe it had risen at the time), that I continually fell over fragments of rock and stumbled up to my middle into the rivulet, which I sought to follow.

In this way, drenched, weary, and with my patience almost exhausted, I was toiling onward, when, turning a sharp angle in the winding glen, I found myself within some twenty yards of a group of wild-looking men, gathered in various attitudes round a glowing turf fire.

I was so surprised at this rencontre that I stopped short, and for a time was in doubt whether to turn back or to accost them.

A minute's thought satisfied me that I ought to make up to the fellows, and trust to their good faith for whatever assistance they could give me.

I determined, then, to do this, having great faith in the impulses of my mind, which, whenever I have been in jeopardy, as in my life I often have, always prompted me aright.

The strong red light of the fire showed me plainly enough that the group consisted, not of soldiers, but of Irish kernes, or countrymen, most of them wrapped in heavy mantles, and with no other covering for their heads than that afforded by their long, rough hair.

There was nothing about them which I could see to intimate whether their object were peaceful or warlike; but I afterwards found that they had weapons enough, though of their own rude fashion.

There were in all about twenty persons assembled around the fire, some sitting upon such blocks of stone as happened to lie in the way; others stretched at their length upon the ground.

'God save you, boys!' said I, advancing towards the party.

The men who had been talking and laughing together instantly paused, and two of them—tall and powerful fellows— snatched up each a weapon, something like a short halberd with a massive iron head, an instrument which they called among themselves a rapp, and with two or three long strides they came up with me, and laying hold upon my arms, drew me, not, you may easily believe, making much resistance, towards the fire.

When I reached the place where the figures were seated, the two men still held me firmly, and some others threw some handfuls of dry fuel upon the red embers, which, blazing up, cast a strong light upon me.

When they had satisfied themselves as to my appearance, they began to question me very closely as to my purpose in being upon the hill at such an unseasonable hour, asking me what was my occupation, where I had been, and whither I was going.

These questions were put to me in English by an old half-military looking man, who translated into that language the suggestions which his companions for the most part threw out in Irish.

I did not choose to commit myself to these fellows by telling them my real character and purpose, and therefore I represented myself as a poor travelling chapman who had been at Cork, and was seeking his way to Killaloe, in order to cross over into Clare and thence to the city of Galway.

My account did not seem fully to satisfy the men.

I heard one fellow say in Irish, which language I understood, 'Maybe he is a spy.'

They then whispered together for a time, and the little man who was their spokesman came over to me and said:

'Do you know what we do with spies? we knock their brains out, my friend.'

He then turned back to them with whom he had been whispering, and talked in a low tone again with them for a considerable time.

I now felt very uncomfortable, not knowing what these savages—for they appeared nothing better—might design against me.

Twice or thrice I had serious thoughts of breaking from them, but the two guards who were placed upon me held me fast by the arms; and even had I succeeded in shaking them off, I should soon have been overtaken, encumbered as I was with a heavy pack, and wholly ignorant of the lie of the ground; or else, if I were so exceedingly lucky as to escape out of their hands, I still had the chance of falling into those of some other party of the same kind.

I therefore patiently awaited the issue of their deliberations, which I made no doubt affected me nearly.

I turned to the men who held me, and one after the other asked them, in their own language, 'Why they held me?' adding, 'I am but a poor pedlar, as you see. I have neither money nor money's worth, for the sake of which you should do me hurt. You may have my pack and all that it contains, if you desire it-but do not injure me.'

To all this they gave no answer, but savagely desired me to hold my tongue.

I accordingly remained silent, determined, if the worst came, to declare to the whole party, who, I doubted not, were friendly, as were all the Irish peasantry in the south, to the Royal cause, my real character and design; and if this avowal failed me, I was resolved to make a desperate effort to escape, or at least to give my life at the dearest price I could.

I was not kept long in suspense, for the little veteran who had spoken to me at first came over, and desiring the two men

449

to bring me after him, led the way along a broken path, which wound by the side of the steep glen.

I was obliged willy nilly to go with them, and, half-dragging and half-carrying me, they brought me by the path, which now became very steep, for some hundred yards without stopping, when suddenly coming to a stand, I found myself close before the door of some house or hut, I could not see which, through the planks of which a strong light was streaming.

At this door my conductor stopped, and tapping gently at it, it was opened by a stout fellow, with buff-coat and jack-boots, and pistols stuck in his belt, as also a long cavalry sword by his side.

He spoke with my guide, and to my no small satisfaction, in French, which convinced me that he was one of the soldiers whom Louis had sent to support our king, and who were said to have arrived in Limerick, though, as I observed above, not with truth.

I was much assured by this circumstance, and made no doubt but that I had fallen in with one of those marauding parties of native Irish, who, placing themselves under the guidance of men of courage and experience, had done much brave and essential service to the cause of the king.

The soldier entered an inner door in the apartment, which opening disclosed a rude, dreary, and dilapidated room, with a low plank ceiling, much discoloured by the smoke which hung suspended in heavy masses, descending within a few feet of the ground, and completely obscuring the upper regions of the chamber.

A large fire of turf and heath was burning under a kind of rude chimney, shaped like a large funnel, but by no means discharging the functions for which it was intended. Into this inauspicious apartment was I conducted by my strange companions. In the next room I heard voices employed, as it seemed, in brief questioning and answer; and in a minute the soldier re-entered the room, and having said, '*Votre prisonnier—le general veut le voir,*' he led the way into the inner room, which in point of comfort and cleanliness was not a whit better than the first.

Seated at a clumsy plank table, placed about the middle of the floor, was a powerfully built man, of almost colossal stature— his military accoutrements, cuirass and rich regimental clothes, soiled, deranged, and spattered with recent hard travel; the flowing wig, surmounted by the cocked hat and plume, still rested upon his head. On the table lay his sword-belt with its appendage, and a pair of long holster pistols, some papers, and pen and ink; also a stone jug, and the fragments of a hasty meal. His attitude betokened the languor of fatigue. His left hand was buried beyond the lace ruffle in the breast of his cassock, and the elbow of his right rested upon the table, so as to support his head. From his mouth protruded a tobacco-pipe, which as I entered he slowly withdrew.

A single glance at the honest, good-humoured, comely face of the soldier satisfied me of his identity, and removing my hat from my head I said, 'God save General Sarsfield!'

The general nodded.

'I am a prisoner here under strange circumstances,' I continued 'I appear before you in a strange disguise. You do not recognise Captain Hardress Fitzgerald!'

'Eh, how's this?' said he, approaching me with the light.

'I am that Hardress Fitzgerald,' I repeated, 'who served under you at the Boyne, and upon the day of the action had the honour to protect your person at the expense of his own.' At the same time I turned aside the hair which covered the scar which you well know upon my forehead, and which was then much more remarkable than it is now.

The general on seeing this at once recognised me, and embracing me cordially, made me sit down, and while I unstrapped my pack, a tedious job, my fingers being nearly numbed with cold, sent the men forth to procure me some provision.

The general's horse was stabled in a corner of the chamber where we sat, and his war-saddle lay upon the floor. At the far end of the room was a second door, which stood half open; a bogwood fire burned on a hearth somewhat less rude than the one which I had first seen, but still very little better appointed with a chimney, for thick wreaths of smoke were eddying, with every fitful gust, about the room. Close by the fire was strewed a bed of heath, intended, I supposed, for the stalwart limbs of the general.

'Hardress Fitzgerald,' said he, fixing his eyes gravely upon me, while he slowly removed the tobacco-pipe from his mouth, 'I remember you, strong, bold and cunning in your warlike trade; the more desperate an enterprise, the more ready for it, you. I would gladly engage you, for I know you trustworthy, to perform a piece of duty requiring, it may be, no extraordinary quality to fulfil; and yet perhaps, as accidents may happen, demanding every attribute of daring and dexterity which belongs to you.'

Here he paused for some moments.

I own I felt somewhat flattered by the terms in which he spoke of me, knowing him to be but little given to compliments; and not having any plan in my head, farther than the rendering what service I might to the cause of the king, caring very little as to the road in which my duty might lie, I frankly replied:

'Sir, I hope, if opportunity offers, I shall prove to deserve the honourable terms in which you are pleased to speak of me. In a righteous cause I fear not wounds or death; and in discharging my duty to my God and my king, I am ready for any hazard or any fate. Name the service you require, and if it lies within the compass of my wit or power, I will fully and faithfully perform it. Have I said enough?'

'That is well, very well, my friend; you speak well, and manfully,' replied the general. 'I want you to convey to the hands of General Boisleau, now in the city of Limerick, a small written packet; there is some danger, mark me, of your falling in with some outpost or straggling party of the prince's army. If you are taken unawares by any of the enemy you must dispose of the packet inside your person, rather than let it fall into their hands—that is, you must eat it. And if they go to question you with thumb-screws, or the like, answer nothing; let them knock your brains out first.' In illustration, I suppose, of the latter alternative, he knocked the ashes out of his pipe upon the table as he uttered it.

'The packet,' he continued, 'you shall have tomorrow morning. Meantime comfort yourself with food, and afterwards with sleep; you will want, mayhap, all your strength and wits on the morrow.'

I applied myself forthwith to the homely fare which they had provided, and I confess that I never made a meal so heartily to my satisfaction.

It was a beautiful, clear, autumn morning, and the bright beams of the early sun were slanting over the brown heath which clothed the sides of the mountain, and glittering in the thousand bright drops which the melting hoar-frost had left behind it, and the white mists were lying like broad lakes in the valleys, when, with my pedlar's pack upon my back, and General Sarsfield's precious despatch in my bosom, I set forth, refreshed and courageous.

As I descended the hill, my heart expanded and my spirits rose under the influences which surrounded me. The keen, clear, bracing air of the morning, the bright, slanting sunshine, the merry songs of the small birds, and the distant sounds of awakening labour that floated up from the plains, all conspired to stir my heart within me, and more like a mad-cap boy, broken loose from school, than a man of sober years upon a mission of doubt and danger, I trod lightly on, whistling and singing alternately for very joy.

As I approached the object of my early march, I fell in with a countryman, eager, as are most of his kind, for news.

I gave him what little I had collected, and professing great zeal for the king, which, indeed, I always cherished, I won upon his confidence so far, that he became much more communicative than the peasantry in those quarters are generally wont to be to strangers.

From him I learned that there was a company of dragoons in William's service, quartered at Willaloe; but he could not tell whether the passage of the bridge was stopped by them or not.

With a resolution, at all events, to make the attempt to cross, I approached the town. When I came within sight of the river, I quickly perceived that it was so swollen with the recent rains, as, indeed, the countryman had told me, that the fords were wholly impassable.

I stopped then, upon a slight eminence overlooking the village, with a view to reconnoitre and to arrange my plans in case of interruption. While thus engaged, the wind blowing gently from the west, in which quarter Limerick lay, I distinctly heard the explosion of the cannon, which played from and against the city, though at a distance of eleven miles at the least.

I never yet heard the music that had for me half the attractions of that sullen sound, and as I noted again and again the distant thunder that proclaimed the perils, and the valour, and the faithfulness of my brethren, my heart swelled with pride, and the tears rose to my eyes; and lifting up my hands to heaven, I prayed to God that I might be spared to take a part in the righteous quarrel that was there so bravely maintained.

I felt, indeed, at this moment a longing, more intense than I have the power to describe, to be at once with my brave companions in arms, and so inwardly excited and stirred up as if I had been actually within five minutes' march of the field of battle.

It was now almost noon, and I had walked hard since morning across a difficult and broken country, so that I was a little fatigued, and in no small degree hungry. As I approached the hamlet, I was glad to see in the window of a poor hovel several large cakes of meal displayed, as if to induce purchasers to enter.

I was right in regarding this exhibition as an intimation that entertainment might be procured within, for upon entering and inquiring, I was speedily invited by the poor woman, who, it appeared, kept this humble house of refreshment, to lay down my pack and seat myself by a ponderous table, upon which she promised to serve me with a dinner fit for a king; and indeed, to my mind, she amply fulfilled her engagement, supplying me abundantly with eggs, bacon, and wheaten cakes, which I discussed with a zeal which almost surprised myself.

Having disposed of the solid part of my entertainment, I was proceeding to regale myself with a brimming measure of strong waters, when my attention was arrested by the sound of horses' hoofs in brisk motion upon the broken road, and evidently approaching the hovel in which I was at that moment seated.

The ominous clank of sword scabbards and the jingle of brass accoutrements announced, unequivocally, that the horsemen were of the military profession.

'The red-coats will stop here undoubtedly,' said the old woman, observing, I suppose, the anxiety of my countenance; 'they never pass us without coming in for half an hour to drink or smoke. If you desire to avoid them, I can hide you safely; but don't lose a moment. They will be here before you can count a hundred.'

I thanked the good woman for her hospitable zeal; but I felt a repugnance to concealing myself as she suggested, which was enhanced by the consciousness that if by any accident I were detected while lurking in the room, my situation would of itself inevitably lead to suspicions, and probably to discovery.

I therefore declined her offer, and awaited in suspense the entrance of the soldiers.

I had time before they made their appearance to move my seat hurriedly from the table to the hearth, where, under the shade of the large chimney, I might observe the coming visitors with less chance of being myself remarked upon.

As my hostess had anticipated, the horsemen drew up at the door of the hut, and five dragoons entered the dark chamber where I awaited them.

Leaving their horses at the entrance, with much noise and clatter they proceeded to seat themselves and call for liquor.

Three of these fellows were Dutchmen, and, indeed, all belonged, as I afterwards found, to a Dutch regiment, which had been recruited with Irish and English, as also partly officered from the same nations.

Being supplied with pipes and drink they soon became

merry; and not suffering their smoking to interfere with their conversation, they talked loud and quickly, for the most part in a sort of barbarous language, neither Dutch nor English, but compounded of both.

They were so occupied with their own jocularity that I had very great hopes of escaping observation altogether, and remained quietly seated in a corner of the chimney, leaning back upon my seat as if asleep.

My taciturnity and quiescence, however, did not avail me, for one of these fellows coming over to the hearth to light his pipe, perceived me, and looking me very hard in the face, he said:

'What countryman are you, brother, that you sit with a covered head in the room with the prince's soldiers?'

At the same time he tossed my hat off my head into the fire. I was not fool enough, though somewhat hot-blooded, to suffer the insolence of this fellow to involve me in a broil so dangerous to my person and ruinous to my schemes as a riot with these soldiers must prove. I therefore, quietly taking up my hat and shaking the ashes out of it, observed:

'Sir, I crave your pardon if I have offended you. I am a stranger in these quarters, and a poor, ignorant, humble man, desiring only to drive my little trade in peace, so far as that may be done in these troublous times.'

'And what may your trade be?' said the same fellow.

'I am a travelling merchant,' I replied; 'and sell my wares as cheap as any trader in the country.'

'Let us see them forthwith,' said he; 'mayhap I or my comrades may want something which you can supply. Where is thy chest, friend? Thou shalt have ready money' (winking at his companions), 'ready money, and good weight, and sound metal; none of your rascally pinchbeck. Eh, my lads? Bring forth the goods, and let us see.'

Thus urged, I should have betrayed myself had I hesitated to do as required; and anxious, upon any terms, to quiet these turbulent men of war, I unbuckled my pack and exhibited its contents upon the table before them.

'A pair of lace ruffles, by the Lord!' said one, unceremoniously seizing upon the articles he named.

'A phial of perfume,' continued another, tumbling over the farrago which I had submitted to them, 'wash-balls, combs, stationery, slippers, small knives, tobacco; by ———, this merchant is a prize! Mark me, honest fellow, the man who wrongs thee shall suffer—'fore Gad he shall; thou shalt be fairly dealt with' (this he said while in the act of pocketing a small silver tobacco-box, the most valuable article in the lot). 'You shall come with me to head-quarters; the captain will deal with you, and never haggle about the price. I promise thee his good will, and thou wilt consider me accordingly. You'll find him a profitable customer—he has money without end, and throws it about like a gentleman. If so be as I tell thee, I shall expect, and my comrades here, a piece or two in the way of a compliment—but of this anon. Come, then, with us; buckle on thy pack quickly, friend.'

There was no use in my declaring my willingness to deal with themselves in preference to their master; it was clear that they had resolved that I should, in the most expeditious and advantageous way, turn my goods into money, that they might excise upon me to the amount of their wishes.

The worthy who had taken a lead in these arrangements, and who by his stripes I perceived to be a corporal, having insisted on my taking a dram with him to cement our newly-formed friendship, for which, however, he requested me to pay, made me mount behind one of his comrades; and the party, of which I thus formed an unwilling member, moved at a slow trot towards the quarters of the troop.

They reined up their horses at the head of the long bridge, which at this village spans the broad waters of the Shannon connecting the opposite counties of Tipperary and Clare.

A small tower, built originally, no doubt, to protect and to defend this pass, occupied the near extremity of the bridge, and in its rear, but connected with it, stood several straggling buildings rather dilapidated.

A dismounted trooper kept guard at the door, and my con-

ductor having, dismounted, as also the corporal, the latter inquired:

'Is the captain in his quarters?'

'He is,' replied the sentinel.

And without more ado my companion shoved me into the
entrance of the small dark tower, and opening a door at the extremity of the narrow chamber into which we had passed from
the street, we entered a second room in which were seated some
half-dozen officers of various ranks and ages, engaged in drinking, and smoking, and play.

I glanced rapidly from man to man, and was nearly satisfied
by my inspection, when one of the gentlemen whose back had
been turned towards the place where I stood, suddenly changed
his position and looked towards me.

As soon as I saw his face my heart sank within me, and I
knew that my life or death was balanced, as it were, upon a razor's edge.

The name of this man whose unexpected appearance thus
affected me was Hugh Oliver, and good and strong reason had I
to dread him, for so bitterly did he hate me, that to this moment
I do verily believe he would have compassed my death if it lay
in his power to do so, even at the hazard of his own life and soul,
for I had been—though God knows with many sore strugglings
and at the stern call of public duty—the judge and condemner
of his brother; and though the military law, which I was called
upon to administer, would permit no other course or sentence
than the bloody one which I was compelled to pursue, yet even
to this hour the recollection of that deed is heavy at my breast.

As soon as I saw this man I felt that my safety depended upon
the accident of his not recognising me through the disguise
which I had assumed, an accident against which were many
chances, for he well knew my person and appearance.

It was too late now to destroy General Sarsfield's instructions;
any attempt to do so would ensure detection. All then depended
upon a cast of the die.

When the first moment of dismay and heart-sickening agitation had passed, it seemed to me as if my mind acquired a collectedness and clearness more complete and intense than I had ever experienced before.

I instantly perceived that he did not know me, for turning from me to the soldier with all air of indifference, he said,

'Is this a prisoner or a deserter? What have you brought him here for, sirra?'

'Your wisdom will regard him as you see fit, may it please you,' said the corporal. 'The man is a travelling merchant, and, overtaking him upon the road, close by old Dame MacDonagh's cot, I thought I might as well make a sort of prisoner of him that your honour might use him as it might appear most convenient; he has many commododies which are not unworthy of price in this wilderness, and some which you may condescend to make use of yourself. May he exhibit the goods he has for sale, an't please you?'

'Ay, let us see them,' said he.

'Unbuckle your pack,' exclaimed the corporal, with the same tone of command with which, at the head of his guard, he would have said 'Recover your arms.' 'Unbuckle your pack, fellow, and show your goods to the captain—here, where you are.'

The conclusion of his directions was suggested by my endeavouring to move round in order to get my back towards the windows, hoping, by keeping my face in the shade, to escape detection.

In this manoeuvre, however, I was foiled by the imperiousness of the soldier; and inwardly cursing his ill-timed interference, I proceeded to present my merchandise to the loving contemplation of the officers who thronged around me, with a strong light from an opposite window full upon my face.

As I continued to traffic with these gentlemen, I observed with no small anxiety the eyes of Captain Oliver frequently fixed upon me with a kind of dubious inquiring gaze.

'I think, my honest fellow,' he said at last, 'that I have seen you somewhere before this. Have you often dealt with the military?'

459

'I have traded, sir,' said I, 'with the soldiery many a time, and always been honourably treated. Will your worship please to buy a pair of lace ruffles?—very cheap, your worship.'

'Why do you wear your hair so much over your face, sir?' said Oliver, without noticing my suggestion. 'I promise you, I think no good of thee; throw back your hair, and let me see thee plainly. Hold up your face, and look straight at me; throw back your hair, sir.'

I felt that all chance of escape was at an end; and stepping forward as near as the table would allow me to him, I raised my head, threw back my hair, and fixed my eyes sternly and boldly upon his face.

I saw that he knew me instantly, for his countenance turned as pale as ashes with surprise and hatred. He started up, placing his hand instinctively upon his sword-hilt, and glaring at me with a look so deadly, that I thought every moment he would strike his sword into my heart. He said in a kind of whisper: 'Hardress Fitzgerald?'

'Yes;' said I, boldly, for the excitement of the scene had effectually stirred my blood, 'Hardress Fitzgerald is before you. I know you well, Captain Oliver. I know how you hate me. I know how you thirst for my blood; but in a good cause, and in the hands of God, I defy you.'

'You are a desperate villain, sir,' said Captain Oliver; 'a rebel and a murderer! Holloa, there! guard, seize him!'

As the soldiers entered, I threw my eyes hastily round the room, and observing a glowing fire upon the hearth, I suddenly drew General Sarsfield's packet from my bosom, and casting it upon the embers, planted my foot upon it.

'Secure the papers!' shouted the captain; and almost instantly I was laid prostrate and senseless upon the floor, by a blow from the butt of a carbine.

I cannot say how long I continued in a state of torpor; but at length, having slowly recovered my senses, I found myself lying firmly handcuffed upon the floor of a small chamber, through a narrow loophole in one of whose walls the evening sun was shining. I was chilled with cold and damp, and drenched in blood, which had flowed in large quantities from the wound on my head. By a strong effort I shook off the sick drowsiness which still hung upon me, and, weak and giddy, I rose with pain and difficulty to my feet.

The chamber, or rather cell, in which I stood was about eight feet square, and of a height very disproportioned to its other dimensions; its altitude from the floor to the ceiling being not less than twelve or fourteen feet. A narrow slit placed high in the wall admitted a scanty light, but sufficient to assure me that my prison contained nothing to render the sojourn of its tenant a whit less comfortless than my worst enemy could have wished.

My first impulse was naturally to examine the security of the door, the loop-hole which I have mentioned being too high and too narrow to afford a chance of escape. I listened attentively to ascertain if possible whether or not a guard had been placed upon the outside.

Not a sound was to be heard. I now placed my shoulder to the door, and sought with all my combined strength and weight to force it open. It, however, resisted all my efforts, and thus baffled in my appeal to mere animal power, exhausted and disheartened, I threw myself on the ground.

It was not in my nature, however, long to submit to the apathy of despair, and in a few minutes I was on my feet again.

With patient scrutiny I endeavoured to ascertain the nature of the fastenings which secured the door.

The planks, fortunately, having been nailed together fresh, had shrunk considerably, so as to leave wide chinks between each and its neighbour.

By means of these apertures I saw that my dungeon was secured, not by a lock, as I had feared, but by a strong wooden bar, running horizontally across the door, about midway upon the outside.

'Now,' thought I, 'if I can but slip my fingers through the opening of the planks, I can easily remove the bar, and then——'

My attempts, however, were all frustrated by the manner in

which my hands were fastened together, each embarrassing the other, and rendering my efforts so hopelessly clumsy, that I was obliged to give them over in despair.

I turned with a sigh from my last hope, and began to pace my narrow prison floor, when my eye suddenly encountered an old rusty nail or holdfast sticking in the wall.

All the gold of Plutus would not have been so welcome as that rusty piece of iron.

I instantly wrung it from the wall, and inserting the point between the planks of the door into the bolt, and working it backwards and forwards, I had at length the unspeakable satisfaction to perceive that the beam was actually yielding to my efforts, and gradually sliding into its berth in the wall.

I have often been engaged in struggles where great bodily strength was required, and every thew and sinew in the system taxed to the uttermost; but, strange as it may appear, I never was so completely exhausted and overcome by any labour as by this comparatively trifling task.

Again and again was I obliged to desist, until my cramped finger-joints recovered their power; but at length my perseverance was rewarded, for, little by little, I succeeded in removing the bolt so far as to allow the door to open sufficiently to permit me to pass.

With some squeezing I succeeded in forcing my way into a small passage, upon which my prison-door opened.

This led into a chamber somewhat more spacious than my cell, but still containing no furniture, and affording no means of escape to one so crippled with bonds as I was.

At the far extremity of this room was a door which stood ajar, and, stealthily passing through it, I found myself in a room containing nothing but a few raw hides, which rendered the atmosphere nearly intolerable.

Here I checked myself, for I heard voices in busy conversation in the next room.

I stole softly to the door which separated the chamber in which I stood from that from which the voices proceeded.

A moment served to convince me that any attempt upon it would be worse than fruitless, for it was secured upon the outside by a strong lock, besides two bars, all which I was enabled to ascertain by means of the same defect in the joining of the planks which I have mentioned as belonging to the inner door.

I had approached this door very softly, so that, my proximity being wholly unsuspected by the speakers within, the conversation continued without interruption.

Planting myself close to the door, I applied my eye to one of the chinks which separated the boards, and thus obtained a full view of the chamber and its occupants.

It was the very apartment into which I had been first conducted. The outer door, which faced the one at which I stood, was closed, and at a small table were seated the only tenants of the room—two officers, one of whom was Captain Oliver. The latter was reading a paper, which I made no doubt was the document with which I had been entrusted.

'The fellow deserves it, no doubt' said the junior officer. 'But, methinks, considering our orders from head-quarters, you deal somewhat too hastily.'

'Nephew, nephew,' said Captain Oliver, 'you mistake the tenor of our orders. We were directed to conciliate the peasantry by fair and gentle treatment, but not to suffer spies and traitors to escape. This packet is of some value, though not, in all its parts, intelligible to me. The bearer has made his way hither under a disguise, which, along with the other circumstances of his appearance here, is sufficient to convict him as a spy.'

There was a pause here, and after a few minutes the younger officer said:

'Spy is a hard term, no doubt, uncle; but it is possible—nay, likely, that this poor devil sought merely to carry the parcel with which he was charged in safety to its destination. Pshaw! he is sufficiently punished if you duck him, for ten minutes or so, between the bridge and the mill-dam.'

'Young man,' said Oliver, somewhat sternly, 'do not obtrude your advice where it is not called for; this man, for whom you plead, murdered your own father!'

I could not see how this announcement affected the person to whom it was addressed, for his back was towards me; but I conjectured, easily, that my last poor chance was gone, for a long silence ensued. Captain Oliver at length resumed:

'I know the villain well. I know him capable of any crime; but, by ——, his last card is played, and the game is up. He shall not see the moon rise tonight.'

There was here another pause.

Oliver rose, and going to the outer door, called:

'Hewson! Hewson!'

A grim-looking corporal entered.

'Hewson, have your guard ready at eight o'clock, with their carbines clean, and a round of ball-cartridge each. Keep them sober; and, further, plant two upright posts at the near end of the bridge, with a cross one at top, in the manner of a gibbet. See to these matters, Hewson: I shall be with you speedily.'

The corporal made his salutations, and retired.

Oliver deliberately folded up the papers with which I had been commissioned, and placing them in the pocket of his vest, he said:

'Cunning, cunning Master Hardress Fitzgerald hath made a false step; the old fox is in the toils. Hardress Fitzgerald, Hardress Fitzgerald, I will blot you out.'

He repeated these words several times, at the same time rubbing his finger strongly upon the table, as if he sought to erase a stain:

'I WILL BLOT YOU OUT!'

There was a kind of glee in his manner and expression which chilled my very heart.

'You shall be first shot like a dog, and then hanged like a dog: shot tonight, and hung tomorrow; hung at the bridge-head— hung, until your bones drop asunder!'

It is impossible to describe the exultation with which he seemed to dwell upon, and to particularise the fate which he intended for me.

I observed, however, that his face was deadly pale, and felt assured that his conscience and inward convictions were struggling against his cruel resolve. Without further comment the two officers left the room, I suppose to oversee the preparations which were being made for the deed of which I was to be the victim.

A chill, sick horror crept over me as they retired, and I felt, for the moment, upon the brink of swooning. This feeling, however, speedily gave place to a sensation still more terrible. A state of excitement so intense and tremendous as to border upon literal madness, supervened; my brain reeled and throbbed as if it would burst; thoughts the wildest and the most hideous flashed through my mind with a spontaneous rapidity that scared my very soul; while, all the time, I felt a strange and frightful impulse to burst into uncontrolled laughter.

Gradually this fearful paroxysm passed away. I kneeled and prayed fervently, and felt comforted and assured; but still I could not view the slow approaches of certain death without an agitation little short of agony.

I have stood in battle many a time when the chances of escape were fearfully small. I have confronted foemen in the deadly breach. I have marched, with a constant heart, against the cannon's mouth. Again and again has the beast which I bestrode been shot under me; again and again have I seen the comrades who walked beside me in an instant laid for ever in the dust; again and again have I been in the thick of battle, and of its mortal dangers, and never felt my heart shake, or a single nerve tremble: but now, helpless, manacled, imprisoned, doomed, forced to watch the approaches of an inevitable fate—to wait, silent and moveless, while death as it were crept towards me, human nature was taxed to the uttermost to bear the horrible situation.

I returned again to the closet in which I had found myself upon recovering from the swoon.

The evening sunshine and twilight was fast melting into darkness, when I heard the outer door, that which communicated with the guard-room in which the officers had been amusing themselves, opened and locked again upon the inside.

A measured step then approached, and the door of the wretched cell in which I lay being rudely pushed open, a soldier entered, who carried something in his hand; but, owing to the obscurity of the place, I could not see what.

'Art thou awake, fellow?' said he, in a gruff voice. 'Stir thyself; get upon thy legs.'

His orders were enforced by no very gentle application of his military boot.

'Friend,' said I, rising with difficulty, 'you need not insult a dying man. You have been sent hither to conduct me to death. Lead on! My trust is in God, that He will forgive me my sins, and receive my soul, redeemed by the blood of His Son.'

There here intervened a pause of some length, at the end of which the soldier said, in the same gruff voice, but in a lower key:

'Look ye, comrade, it will be your own fault if you die this night. On one condition I promise to get you out of this hobble with a whole skin; but if you go to any of your d——d gammon, by G——, before two hours are passed, you will have as many holes in your carcase as a target.'

'Name your conditions,' said I, 'and if they consist with honour, I will never balk at the offer.'

'Here they are: you are to be shot tonight, by Captain Oliver's orders. The carbines are cleaned for the job, and the cartridges served out to the men. By G——, I tell you the truth!'

Of this I needed not much persuasion, and intimated to the man my conviction that he spoke the truth.

'Well, then,' he continued, 'now for the means of avoiding this ugly business. Captain Oliver rides this night to headquarters, with the papers which you carried. Before he starts he will pay you a visit, to fish what he can out of you with all the fine promises he can make. Humour him a little, and when you find an opportunity, stab him in the throat above the *cuirass*.'

'A feasible plan, surely,' said I, raising my shackled hands, 'for a man thus completely crippled and without a weapon.'

'I will manage all that presently for you,' said the soldier. 'When you have thus dealt with him, take his cloak and hat, and so forth, and put them on; the papers you will find in the pocket of his vest, in a red leather case. Walk boldly out. I am appointed to ride with Captain Oliver, and you will find me holding his horse and my own by the door. Mount quickly, and I will do the same, and then we will ride for our lives across the bridge. You will find the holster-pistols loaded in case of pursuit; and, with the devil's help, we shall reach Limerick without a hair hurt. My only condition is, that when you strike Oliver, you strike home, and again and again, until he is FINISHED; and I trust to your honour to remember me when we reach the town.'

I cannot say whether I resolved right or wrong, but I thought my situation, and the conduct of Captain Oliver, warranted me in acceding to the conditions propounded by my visitant, and with alacrity I told him so, and desired him to give me the power, as he had promised to do, of executing them.

With speed and promptitude he drew a small key from his pocket, and in an instant the manacles were removed from my hands.

How my heart bounded within me as my wrists were released from the iron gripe of the shackles! The first step toward freedom was made—my self-reliance returned, and I felt assured of success.

'Now for the weapon,' said I.

'I fear me, you will find it rather clumsy,' said he; 'but if well handled, it will do as well as the best Toledo. It is the only thing I could get, but I sharpened it myself; it has an edge like a skean.'

He placed in my hand the steel head of a halberd. Grasping it firmly, I found that it made by no means a bad weapon in point of convenience; for it felt in the hand like a heavy dagger, the portion which formed the blade or point being crossed nearly at the lower extremity by a small bar of metal, at one side shaped into the form of an axe, and at the other into that of a hook. These two transverse appendages being muffled by the folds of my cravat, which I removed for the purpose, formed a perfect guard or hilt, and the lower extremity formed like a tube, in which the pike-handle had been inserted, afforded ample space for the grasp of my hand; the point had been made as sharp as a needle, and the metal he assured me was good.

Thus equipped he left me, having observed, 'The captain sent me to bring you to your senses, and give you some water that he might find you proper for his visit. Here is the pitcher; I think I have revived you sufficiently for the captain's purpose.'

With a low savage laugh he left me to my reflections.

Having examined and adjusted the weapon, I carefully bound the ends of the cravat, with which I had secured the cross part of the spear-head, firmly round my wrist, so that in case of a struggle it might not easily be forced from my hand; and having made these precautionary dispositions, I sat down upon the ground with my back against the wall, and my hands together under my coat, awaiting my visitor.

The time wore slowly on; the dusk became dimmer and dimmer, until it nearly bordered on total darkness.

'How's this?' said I, inwardly; 'Captain Oliver, you said I should not see the moon rise tonight. Methinks you are somewhat tardy in fulfilling your prophecy.'

As I made this reflection, a noise at the outer door announced the entrance of a visitant. I knew that the decisive moment was come, and letting my head sink upon my breast, and assuring myself that my hands were concealed, I waited, in the attitude of deep dejection, the approach of my foe and betrayer.

As I had expected, Captain Oliver entered the room where I lay. He was equipped for instant duty, as far as the imperfect twilight would allow me to see; the long sword clanked upon the floor as he made his way through the lobbies which led to my place of confinement; his ample military cloak hung upon his arm; his cocked hat was upon his head, and in all points he was prepared for the road.

This tallied exactly with what my strange informant had told me.

I felt my heart swell and my breath come thick as the awful moment which was to witness the death-struggle of one or other of us approached.

Captain Oliver stood within a yard or two of the place where I sat, or rather lay; and folding his arms, he remained silent for a minute or two, as if arranging in his mind how he should address me.

'Hardress Fitzgerald,' he began at length, 'are you awake? Stand up, if you desire to hear of matters nearly touching your life or death. Get up, I say.'

I arose doggedly, and affecting the awkward movements of one whose hands were bound,

'Well,' said I, 'what would you of me? Is it not enough that I am thus imprisoned without a cause, and about, as I suspect, to suffer a most unjust and violent sentence, but must I also be disturbed during the few moments left me for reflection and repentance by the presence of my persecutor? What do you want of me?'

'As to your punishment, sir,' said he, 'your own deserts have no doubt suggested the likelihood of it to your mind; but I now am with you to let you know that whatever mitigation of your sentence you may look for, must be earned by your compliance with my orders. You must frankly and fully explain the contents of the packet which you endeavoured this day to destroy; and further, you must tell all that you know of the designs of the popish rebels.'

'And if I do this I am to expect a mitigation of my punishment—is it not so?'

Oliver bowed.

'And what IS this mitigation to be? On the honour of a soldier, what is it to be?' inquired I.

'When you have made the disclosure required,' he replied, 'you shall hear. 'Tis then time to talk of indulgences.'

'Methinks it would then be too late,' answered I. 'But a chance is a chance, and a drowning man will catch at a straw. You are an honourable man, Captain Oliver. I must depend, I suppose, on your good faith. Well, sir, before I make the desired communication I have one question more to put. What is to befall me in case that I, remembering the honour of a soldier and a gentleman, reject your infamous terms, scorn your mitigations, and defy your utmost power?'

'In that case,' replied he, coolly, 'before half an hour you shall be a corpse.'

'Then God have mercy on your soul!' said I; and springing forward, I dashed the weapon which I held at his throat.

I missed my aim, but struck him full in the mouth with such force that most of his front teeth were dislodged, and the point of the spear-head passed out under his jaw, at the ear.

My onset was so sudden and unexpected that he reeled back to the wall, and did not recover his equilibrium in time to prevent my dealing a second blow, which I did with my whole force. The point unfortunately struck the cuirass, near the neck, and glancing aside it inflicted but a flesh wound, tearing the skin and tendons along the throat.

He now grappled with me, strange to say, without uttering any cry of alarm; being a very powerful man, and if anything rather heavier and more strongly built than I, he succeeded in drawing me with him to the ground. We fell together with a heavy crash, tugging and straining in what we were both conscious was a mortal struggle. At length I succeeded in getting over him, and struck him twice more in the face; still he struggled with an energy which nothing but the tremendous stake at issue could have sustained.

I succeeded again in inflicting several more wounds upon him, any one of which might have been mortal. While thus contending he clutched his hands about my throat, so firmly that I felt the blood swelling the veins of my temples and face almost to bursting. Again and again I struck the weapon deep into his face and throat, but life seemed to adhere in him with an almost INSECT tenacity.

My sight now nearly failed, my senses almost forsook me; I felt upon the point of suffocation when, with one desperate effort, I struck him another and a last blow in the face. The weapon which I wielded had lighted upon the eye, and the point penetrated the brain; the body quivered under me, the deadly grasp relaxed, and Oliver lay upon the ground a corpse!

As I arose and shook the weapon and the bloody cloth from my hand, the moon which he had foretold I should never see rise, shone bright and broad into the room, and disclosed, with ghastly distinctness, the mangled features of the dead soldier; the mouth, full of clotting blood and broken teeth, lay open; the eye, close by whose lid the fatal wound had been inflicted, was not, as might have been expected, bathed in blood, but had started forth nearly from the socket, and gave to the face, by its fearful unlikeness to the other glazing orb, a leer more hideous and unearthly than fancy ever saw. The wig, with all its rich curls, had fallen with the hat to the floor, leaving the shorn head exposed, and in many places marked by the recent struggle; the rich lace cravat was drenched in blood, and the gay uniform in many places soiled with the same.

It is hard to say, with what feelings I looked upon the unsightly and revolting mass which had so lately been a living and a comely man. I had not any time, however, to spare for reflection; the deed was done—the responsibility was upon me, and all was registered in the book of that God who judges rightly.

With eager haste I removed from the body such of the military accoutrements as were necessary for the purpose of my disguise. I buckled on the sword, drew off the military boots, and donned them myself, placed the brigadier wig and cocked hat upon my head, threw on the cloak, drew it up about my face, and proceeded, with the papers which I found as the soldier had foretold me, and the key of the outer lobby, to the door of the guard-room; this I opened, and with a firm and rapid tread walked through the officers, who rose as I entered, and passed without question or interruption to the street-door. Here I was met by the grim looking corporal, Hewson, who, saluting me, said:

'How soon, captain, shall the file be drawn out and the prisoner despatched?'

'In half an hour,' I replied, without raising my voice.

The man again saluted, and in two steps I reached the soldier who held the two horses, as he had intimated.

'Is all right?' said he, eagerly.

'Ay,' said I, 'which horse am I to mount?'

He satisfied me upon this point, and I threw myself into the saddle; the soldier mounted his horse, and dashing the spurs into the flanks of the animal which I bestrode, we thundered along the narrow bridge. At the far extremity a sentinel, as we approached, called out, 'Who goes there? stand, and give the word!' Heedless of the interruption, with my heart bounding with excitement, I dashed on, as did also the soldier who accompanied me.

'Stand, or I fire! give the word!' cried the sentry.

'God save the king, and to hell with the prince!' shouted I, flinging the cocked hat in his face as I galloped by.

The response was the sharp report of a carbine, accompanied by the whiz of a bullet, which passed directly between me and my comrade, now riding beside me.

'Hurrah!' I shouted; 'try it again, my boy.'

And away we went at a gallop, which bid fair to distance anything like pursuit.

Never was spur more needed, however, for soon the clatter of horses' hoofs, in full speed, crossing the bridge, came sharp and clear through the stillness of the night.

Away we went, with our pursuers close behind; one mile was passed, another nearly completed. The moon now shone forth, and, turning in the saddle, I looked back upon the road we had passed.

One trooper had headed the rest, and was within a hundred yards of us.

I saw the fellow throw himself from his horse upon the ground.

I knew his object, and said to my comrade:

'Lower your body—lie flat over the saddle; the fellow is going to fire.'

I had hardly spoken when the report of a carbine startled the echoes, and the ball, striking the hind leg of my companion's horse, the poor animal fell headlong upon the road, throwing his rider head-foremost over the saddle.

My first impulse was to stop and share whatever fate might await my comrade; but my second and wiser one was to spur on, and save myself and my despatch.

I rode on at a gallop, turning to observe my comrade's fate. I saw his pursuer, having remounted, ride rapidly up to him, and, on reaching the spot where the man and horse lay, rein in and dismount.

He was hardly upon the ground, when my companion shot him dead with one of the holster-pistols which he had drawn from the pipe; and, leaping nimbly over a ditch at the side of the road, he was soon lost among the ditches and thorn-bushes which covered that part of the country.

Another mile being passed, I had the satisfaction to perceive that the pursuit was given over, and in an hour more I crossed Thomond Bridge, and slept that night in the fortress of Limerick, having delivered the packet, the result of whose safe arrival was the destruction of William's great train of artillery, then upon its way to the besiegers.

Years after this adventure, I met in France a young officer, who I found had served in Captain Oliver's regiment; and he explained what I had never before understood—the motives of the man who had wrought my deliverance. Strange to say, he was the foster-brother of Oliver, whom he thus devoted to death, but in revenge for the most grievous wrong which one man can inflict upon another!

An Authentic Narrative of a Haunted House

[The Editor of the University Magazine submits the following very remarkable statement, with every detail of which he has been for some years acquainted, upon the ground that it affords the most authentic and ample relation of a series of marvellous phenomena, in nowise connected with what is technically termed "spiritualism," which he has anywhere met with. All the persons—and there are many of them living—upon whose separate evidence some parts, and upon whose united testimony others, of this most singular recital depend, are, in their several walks of life, respectable, and such as would in any matter of judicial investigation be deemed wholly unexceptionable witnesses. There is not an incident here recorded which would not have been distinctly deposed to on oath had any necessity existed, by the persons who severally, and some of them in great fear, related their own distinct experiences.]

[The Editor begs most pointedly to meet in limine the suspicion, that he is elaborating a trick, or vouching for another ghost of Mrs. Veal. As a mere story the narrative is valueless: its sole claim to attention is its absolute truth. For the good faith of its relater he pledges his own and the character of this Magazine. With the Editor's concurrence, the name of the watering-place, and some special circumstances in no essential way bearing upon the peculiar character of the story, but which might have indicated the locality, and possibly annoyed persons interested in house property there, have been suppressed by the narrator. Not the slightest liberty has been taken with the narrative, which is presented precisely in the terms in which the writer of it, who employs throughout the first person, would, if need were, fix it in the form of an affidavit.]

Within the last eight years—the precise date I purposely omit—!, I was ordered by my physician, my health being in an unsatisfactory state, to change my residence to one upon the sea-coast; and accordingly, I took a house for a year in a fashionable watering-place, at a moderate distance from the city in which I had previously resided, and connected with it by a railway.

Winter was setting in when my removal thither was decided upon; but there was nothing whatever dismal or depressing in the change. The house I had taken was to all appearance, and in point of convenience, too, quite a modern one. It formed one in a cheerful row, with small gardens in front, facing the sea, and commanding sea air and sea views in perfection. In the rear it had coach-house and stable, and between them and the house a considerable grass-plot, with some flowerbeds, interposed.

Our family consisted of my wife and myself, with three children, the eldest about nine years old, she and the next in age being girls; and the youngest, between six and seven, a boy. To these were added six servants, whom, although for certain reasons I decline giving their real names, I shall indicate, for the sake of clearness, by arbitrary ones. There was a nurse, Mrs. Southerland; a nursery-maid, Ellen Page; the cook, Mrs. Greenwood; and the housemaid, Ellen Faith; a butler, whom I shall call Smith, and his son, James, about two-and-twenty.

We came out to take possession at about seven o'clock in the evening; everything was comfortable and cheery; good fires lighted, the rooms neat and airy, and a general air of preparation and comfort, highly conducive to good spirits and pleasant anticipations.

The sitting-rooms were large and cheerful, and they and the bedrooms more than ordinarily lofty, the kitchen and servants' rooms, on the same level, were well and comfortably furnished, and had, like the rest of the house, an air of recent painting and fitting up, and a completely modern character, which imparted a very cheerful air of cleanliness and convenience.

There had been just enough of the fuss of settling agreeably to occupy us, and to give a pleasant turn to our thoughts after we had retired to our rooms. Being an invalid, I had a small bed to myself—resigning the four-poster to my wife. The candle was extinguished, but a night-light was burning. I was coming up stairs, and she, already in bed, had just dismissed her maid, when we were both startled by a wild scream from her room; I found her in a state of the extremest agitation and terror. She insisted that she had seen an unnaturally tall figure come beside her bed and stand there. The light was too faint to enable her to define anything respecting this apparition, beyond the fact of her having most distinctly seen such a shape, colourless from the insufficiency of the light to disclose more than its dark outline.

We both endeavoured to reassure her. The room once more looked so cheerful in the candlelight, that we were quite uninfluenced by the contagion of her terrors. The movements and voices of the servants down stairs still getting things into their places and completing our comfortable arrangements, had also their effect in steeling us against any such influence, and we set the whole thing down as a dream, or an imperfectly-seen outline of the bed-curtains. When, however, we were alone, my wife reiterated, still in great agitation, her clear assertion that she had most positively seen, being at the time as completely awake as ever she was, precisely what she had described to us. And in this conviction she continued perfectly firm.

A day or two after this, it came out that our servants were under an apprehension that, somehow or other, thieves had established a secret mode of access to the lower part of the house. The butler, Smith, had seen an ill-looking woman in his room on the first night of our arrival; and he and other servants constantly saw, for many days subsequently, glimpses of a retreating figure, which corresponded with that so seen by him, passing through a passage which led to a back area in which were some coal-vaults.

This figure was seen always in the act of retreating, its back turned, generally getting round the corner of the passage into the area, in a stealthy and hurried way, and, when closely followed, imperfectly seen again entering one of the coal-vaults, and when pursued into it, nowhere to be found.

The idea of anything supernatural in the matter had, strange to say, not yet entered the mind of any one of the servants. They had heard some stories of smugglers having secret passages into houses, and using their means of access for purposes of pillage, or with a view to frighten superstitious people out of houses which they needed for their own objects, and a suspicion of similar practices here, caused them extreme uneasiness. The apparent anxiety also manifested by this retreating figure to escape observation, and her always appearing to make her egress at the same point, favoured this romantic hypothesis. The men, however, made a most careful examination of the back area, and of the coal-vaults, with a view to discover some mode of egress, but entirely without success. On the contrary, the result was, so far as it went, subversive of the theory; solid masonry met them on every hand.

I called the man, Smith, up, to hear from his own lips the particulars of what he had seen; and certainly his report was very curious. I give it as literally as my memory enables me:—

His son slept in the same room, and was sound asleep; but he lay awake, as men sometimes will on a change of bed, and having many things on his mind. He was lying with his face towards the wall, but observing a light and some little stir in the room, he turned round in his bed, and saw the figure of a woman, squalid, and ragged in dress; her figure rather low and broad; as well as I recollect, she had something—either a cloak or shawl—on, and wore a bonnet. Her back was turned, and she appeared to be searching or rummaging for something on the floor, and, without appearing to observe him, she turned in doing so towards him. The light, which was more like the intense glow of a coal, as he described it, being of a deep red colour, proceeded from the hollow of her hand, which she held beside her head, and he saw her perfectly distinctly. She appeared middle-aged, was deeply pitted with the smallpox, and blind of one eye. His phrase in describing her general appearance was, that she was "a miserable, poor-looking creature."

He was under the impression that she must be the woman who had been left by the proprietor in charge of the house, and who had that evening, after having given up the keys, remained for some little time with the female servants. He coughed, therefore, to apprize her of his presence, and turned again towards the wall. When he again looked round she and the light were gone; and odd as was her method of lighting herself in her search, the circumstances excited neither uneasiness nor curiosity in his mind, until he discovered next morning that the woman in question had left the house long before he had gone to his bed.

I examined the man very closely as to the appearance of the person who had visited him, and the result was what I have described. It struck me as an odd thing, that even then, considering how prone to superstition persons in his rank of life usually are, he did not seem to suspect anything supernatural in the occurrence; and, on the contrary, was thoroughly persuaded that his visitant was a living person, who had got into the house by some hidden entrance.

On Sunday, on his return from his place of worship, he told me that, when the service was ended, and the congregation making their way slowly out, he saw the very woman in the crowd, and kept his eye upon her for several minutes, but such was the crush, that all his efforts to reach her were unavailing, and when he got into the open street she was gone. He was quite positive as to his having distinctly seen her, however, for several minutes, and scouted the possibility of any mistake as to identity; and fully impressed with the substantial and living reality of his visitant, he was very much provoked at her having escaped him. He made inquiries also in the neighbourhood, but could procure no information, nor hear of any other persons having seen any woman corresponding with his visitant.

The cook and the housemaid occupied a bedroom on the

kitchen floor. It had whitewashed walls, and they were actually terrified by the appearance of the shadow of a woman passing and repassing across the side wall opposite to their beds. They suspected that this had been going on much longer than they were aware, for its presence was discovered by a sort of accident, its movements happening to take a direction in distinct contrariety to theirs.

This shadow always moved upon one particular wall, returning after short intervals, and causing them extreme terror. They placed the candle, as the most obvious specific, so close to the infested wall, that the flame all but touched it; and believed for some time that they had effectually got rid of this annoyance; but one night, notwithstanding this arrangement of the light, the shadow returned, passing and repassing, as heretofore, upon the same wall, although their only candle was burning within an inch of it, and it was obvious that no substance capable of casting such a shadow could have interposed; and, indeed, as they described it, the shadow seemed to have no sort of relation to the position of the light, and appeared, as I have said, in manifest defiance of the laws of optics.

I ought to mention that the housemaid was a particularly fearless sort of person, as well as a very honest one; and her companion, the cook, a scrupulously religious woman, and both agreed in every particular in their relation of what occurred.

Meanwhile, the nursery was not without its annoyances, though as yet of a comparatively trivial kind. Sometimes, at night, the handle of the door was turned hurriedly as if by a person trying to come in, and at others a knocking was made at it. These sounds occurred after the children had settled to sleep, and while the nurse still remained awake. Whenever she called to know "who is there," the sounds ceased; but several times, and particularly at first, she was under the impression that they were caused by her mistress, who had come to see the children, and thus impressed she had got up and opened the door, expecting to see her, but discovering only darkness, and receiving no answer to her inquiries.

With respect to this nurse, I must mention that I believe no more perfectly trustworthy servant was ever employed in her capacity; and, in addition to her integrity, she was remarkably gifted with sound common sense.

One morning, I think about three or four weeks after our arrival, I was sitting at the parlour window which looked to the front, when I saw the little iron door which admitted into the small garden that lay between the window where I was sitting and the public road, pushed open by a woman who so exactly answered the description given by Smith of the woman who had visited his room on the night of his arrival as instantaneously to impress me with the conviction that she must be the identical person. She was a square, short woman, dressed in soiled and tattered clothes, scarred and pitted with smallpox, and blind of an eye. She stepped hurriedly into the little enclosure, and peered from a distance of a few yards into the room where I was sitting. I felt that now was the moment to clear the matter up; but there was something stealthy in the manner and look of the woman which convinced me that I must not appear to notice her until her retreat was fairly cut off.

Unfortunately, I was suffering from a lame foot, and could not reach the bell as quickly as I wished. I made all the haste I could, and rang violently to bring up the servant Smith. In the short interval that intervened, I observed the woman from the window, who having in a leisurely way, and with a kind of scrutiny, looked along the front windows of the house, passed quickly out again, closing the gate after her, and followed a lady who was walking along the footpath at a quick pace, as if with the intention of begging from her. The moment the man entered I told him—"the blind woman you described to me has this instant followed a lady in that direction, try to overtake her." He was, if possible, more eager than I in the chase, but returned in a short time after a vain pursuit, very hot, and utterly disappointed. And, thereafter, we saw her face no more.

All this time, and up to the period of our leaving the house, which was not for two or three months later, there occurred at intervals the only phenomenon in the entire series having any resemblance to what we hear described of "Spiritualism." This was a knocking, like a soft hammering with a wooden mallet, as it seemed in the timbers between the bedroom ceilings and the roof. It had this special peculiarity, that it was always rythmical, and, I think, invariably, the emphasis upon the last stroke. It would sound rapidly "one, two, three, *four*—one, two, three, *four*;" or "one, two, *three*—one, two, *three*," and sometimes "one, *two*—one, *two*," &c., and this, with intervals and resumptions, monotonously for hours at a time.

At first this caused my wife, who was a good deal confined to her bed, much annoyance; and we sent to our neighbours to inquire if any hammering or carpentering was going on in their houses but were informed that nothing of the sort was taking place. I have myself heard it frequently, always in the same inaccessible part of the house, and with the same monotonous emphasis. One odd thing about it was, that on my wife's calling out, as she used to do when it became more than usually troublesome, "stop that noise," it was invariably arrested for a longer or shorter time.

Of course none of these occurrences were ever mentioned in hearing of the children. They would have been, no doubt, like most children, greatly terrified had they heard anything of the matter, and known that their elders were unable to account for what was passing; and their fears would have made them wretched and troublesome.

They used to play for some hours every day in the back garden—the house forming one end of this oblong inclosure, the stable and coach-house the other, and two parallel walls of considerable height the sides. Here, as it afforded a perfectly safe playground, they were frequently left quite to themselves; and in talking over their days' adventures, as children will, they happened to mention a woman, or rather the woman, for they had long grown familiar with her appearance, whom they used to see in the garden while they were at play. They assumed that she came in and went out at the stable door, but they never actually saw her enter or depart.

They merely saw a figure—that of a very poor woman, soiled and ragged—near the stable wall, stooping over the ground, and apparently grubbing in the loose clay in search of something. She did not disturb, or appear to observe them; and they left her in undisturbed possession of her nook of ground. When seen it was always in the same spot, and similarly occupied; and the description they gave of her general appearance—for they never saw her face—corresponded with that of the one-eyed woman whom Smith, and subsequently as it seemed, I had seen.

The other man, James, who looked after a mare which I had purchased for the purpose of riding exercise, had, like everyone else in the house, his little trouble to report, though it was not much. The stall in which, as the most comfortable, it was decided to place her, she peremptorily declined to enter. Though a very docile and gentle little animal, there was no getting her into it. She would snort and rear, and, in fact, do or suffer any thing rather than set her hoof in it. He was fain, therefore, to place her in another. And on several occasions he found her there, exhibiting all the equine symptoms of extreme fear. Like the rest of us, however, this man was not troubled in the particular case with any superstitious qualms. The mare had evidently been frightened; and he was puzzled to find out how, or by whom, for the stable was well-secured, and had, I am nearly certain, a lock-up yard outside.

One morning I was greeted with the intelligence that robbers had certainly got into the house in the night; and that one of them had actually been seen in the nursery. The witness, I found, was my eldest child, then, as I have said, about nine years of age. Having awoke in the night, and lain awake for some time in her bed, she heard the handle of the door turn, and a person whom she distinctly saw—for it was a light night, and the window-shutters unclosed—but whom she had never seen before, stepped in on tiptoe, and with an appearance of great caution.

He was a rather small man, with a very red face; he wore an oddly cut frock coat, the collar of which stood up, and trousers, rough and wide, like those of a sailor, turned up at the ankles, and either short boots or clumsy shoes, covered with mud. This man listened beside the nurse's bed, which stood next the door, as if to satisfy himself that she was sleeping soundly; and having done so for some seconds, he began to move cautiously in a diagonal line, across the room to the chimney-piece, where he stood for a while, and so resumed his tiptoe walk, skirting the wall, until he reached a chest of drawers, some of which were open, and into which he looked, and began to rummage in a hurried way, as the child supposed, making search for something worth taking away.

He then passed on to the window, where was a dressing-table, at which he also stopped, turning over the things upon it, and standing for some time at the window as if looking out, and then resuming his walk by the side wall opposite to that by which he had moved up to the window, he returned in the same way toward the nurse's bed, so as to reach it at the foot. With its side to the end wall, in which was the door, was placed the little bed in which lay my eldest child, who watched his proceedings with the extremest terror.

As he drew near she instinctively moved herself in the bed, with her head and shoulders to the wall, drawing up her feet; but he passed by without appearing to observe, or, at least, to care for her presence. Immediately after the nurse turned in her bed as if about to waken; and when the child, who had drawn the clothes about her head, again ventured to peep out, the man was gone.

The child had no idea of her having seen anything more formidable than a thief. With the prowling, cautious, and noise-less manner of proceeding common to such marauders, the air and movements of the man whom she had seen entirely cor-responded. And on hearing her perfectly distinct and consistent account, I could myself arrive at no other conclusion than that a stranger had actually got into the house. I had, therefore, in the first instance, a most careful examination made to discover any traces of an entrance having been made by any window into the house.

The doors had been found barred and locked as usual; but no sign of any thing of the sort was discernible. I then had the various articles—plate, wearing apparel, books, &c., counted; and after having conned over and reckoned up everything, it became quite clear that nothing whatever had been removed from the house, nor was there the slightest indication of anything having been so much as disturbed there. I must here state that this child was remarkably clear, intelligent, and observant; and that her description of the man, and of all that had occurred, was most exact, and as detailed as the want of perfect light rendered possible.

I felt assured that an entrance had actually been effected into the house, though for what purpose was not easily to be conjectured. The man, Smith, was equally confident upon this point; and his theory was that the object was simply to frighten us out of the house by making us believe it haunted; and he was more than ever anxious and on the alert to discover the conspirators. It often since appeared to me odd. Every year, indeed, more odd, as this cumulative case of the marvellous becomes to my mind more and more inexplicable—that underlying my sense of mystery and puzzle, was all along the quiet assumption that all these occurrences were one way or another referable to natural causes.

I could not account for them, indeed, myself; but during the whole period I inhabited that house, I never once felt, though much alone, and often up very late at night, any of those tremors and thrills which everyone has at times experienced when situation and the hour are favourable. Except the cook and housemaid, who were plagued with the shadow I mentioned crossing and recrossing upon the bedroom wall, we all, without exception, experienced the same strange sense of security, and regarded these phenomena rather with a perplexed sort of interest and curiosity, than with any more unpleasant sensations.

The knockings which I have mentioned at the nursery door, preceded generally by the sound of a step on the lobby, meanwhile continued. At that time (for my wife, like myself, was an invalid) two eminent physicians, who came out occasionally by rail, were attending us. These gentlemen were at first only amused, but ultimately interested, and very much puzzled by the occurrences which we described. One of them, at last, recommended that a candle should be kept burning upon the lobby. It was in fact a recurrence to an old woman's recipe against ghosts—of course it might be serviceable, too, against impostors; at all events, seeming, as I have said, very much interested and puzzled, he advised it, and it was tried. We fancied that it was successful; for there was an interval of quiet for, I think, three or four nights. But after that, the noises—the footsteps on the lobby—the knocking at the door, and the turning of the handle recommenced in full force, notwithstanding the light upon the table outside; and these particular phenomena became only more perplexing than ever.

The alarm of robbers and smugglers gradually subsided after a week or two; but we were again to hear news from the nursery. Our second little girl, then between seven and eight years of age, saw in the night time—she alone being awake—a young woman, with black, or very dark hair, which hung loose, and with a black cloak on, standing near the middle of the floor, opposite the hearthstone, and fronting the foot of her bed. She appeared quite unobservant of the children and nurse sleeping in the room. She was very pale, and looked, the child said, both "sorry and frightened," and with something very peculiar and terrible about her eyes, which made the child conclude that she was dead. She was looking, not at, but in the direction of the child's bed, and there was a dark streak across her throat, like a scar with blood upon it.

This figure was not motionless; but once or twice turned slowly, and without appearing to be conscious of the presence of the child, or the other occupants of the room, like a person in vacancy or abstraction. There was on this occasion a night-light burning in the chamber; and the child saw, or thought she saw, all these particulars with the most perfect distinctness. She got her head under the bed-clothes; and although a good many years have passed since then, she cannot recall the spectacle without feelings of peculiar horror.

One day, when the children were playing in the back garden, I asked them to point out to me the spot where they were accustomed to see the woman who occasionally showed herself as I have described, near the stable wall. There was no division of opinion as to this precise point, which they indicated in the most distinct and confident way. I suggested that, perhaps, something might be hidden there in the ground; and advised them digging a hole there with their little spades, to try for it. Accordingly, to work they went, and by my return in the evening they had grubbed up a piece of a jawbone, with several teeth in it. The bone was very much decayed, and ready to crumble to pieces, but the teeth were quite sound. I could not tell whether they were human grinders; but I showed the fossil to one of the physicians I have mentioned, who came out the next evening, and he pronounced them human teeth.

The same conclusion was come to a day or two later by the other medical man. It appears to me now, on reviewing the whole matter, almost unaccountable that, with such evidence before me, I should not have got in a labourer, and had the spot effectually dug and searched. I can only say, that so it was. I was quite satisfied of the moral truth of every word that had been related to me, and which I have here set down with scrupulous accuracy. But I experienced an apathy, for which neither then nor afterwards did I quite know how to account. I had a vague, but immovable impression that the whole affair was referable to natural agencies. It was not until some time after we had left the house, which, by-the-by, we afterwards found had had the reputation of being haunted before we had come to live in it, that on reconsideration I discovered the serious difficulty of accounting satisfactorily for all that had occurred upon ordinary principles.

A great deal we might arbitrarily set down to imagination. But even in so doing there was, *in limine*, the oddity, not to say improbability, of so many different persons having nearly simultaneously suffered from different spectral and other illusions during the short period for which we had occupied that house, who never before, nor so far as we learned, afterwards were troubled by any fears or fancies of the sort. There were other things, too, not to be so accounted for. The odd knockings in the roof I frequently heard myself.

There were also, which I before forgot to mention, in the daytime, rappings at the doors of the sitting-rooms, which constantly deceived us; and it was not till our "come in" was unanswered, and the hall or passage outside the door was discovered to be empty, that we learned that whatever else caused them, human hands did not. All the persons who reported having seen the different persons or appearances here described by me, were just as confident of having literally and distinctly seen them, as I was of having seen the hard-featured woman with the blind eye, so remarkably corresponding with Smith's description.

About a week after the discovery of the teeth, which were found, I think, about two feet under the ground, a friend, much advanced in years, and who remembered the town in which we had now taken up our abode, for a very long time, happened to pay us a visit. He good-humouredly pooh-poohed the whole thing; but at the same time was evidently curious about it. "We might construct a sort of story," said I (I am giving, of course, the substance and purport, not the exact words, of our dialogue), "and assign to each of the three figures who appeared their respective parts in some dreadful tragedy enacted in this house.

The male figure represents the murderer; the ill-looking, one-eyed woman his accomplice, who, we will suppose, buried the body where she is now so often seen grubbing in the earth, and where the human teeth and jawbone have so lately been disinterred; and the young woman with dishevelled tresses, and black cloak, and the bloody scar across her throat, their victim. A difficulty, however, which I cannot get over, exists in the cheerfulness, the great publicity, and the evident very recent date of the house."

"Why, as to that," said he, "the house is *not* modern; it and those beside it formed an old government store, altered and fitted up recently as you see. I remember it well in my young days, fifty years ago, before the town had grown out in this direction, and a more entirely lonely spot, or one more fitted for the commission of a secret crime, could not have been imagined."

I have nothing to add, for very soon after this my physician pronounced a longer stay unnecessary for my health, and we took our departure for another place of abode. I may add, that although I have resided for considerable periods in many other houses, I never experienced any annoyances of a similar kind elsewhere; neither have I made (stupid dog! you will say), any inquiries respecting either the antecedents or subsequent history of the house in which we made so disturbed a sojourn. I was content with what I knew, and have here related as clearly as I could, and I think it a very pretty puzzle as it stands.

Billy Malowney's Taste
of Love and Glory

Let the reader fancy a soft summer evening, the fresh dews falling on bush and flower. The sun has just gone down, and the thrilling vespers of thrushes and blackbirds ring with a wild joy through the saddened air; the west is piled with fantastic clouds, and clothed in tints of crimson and amber, melting away into a wan green, and so eastward into the deepest blue, through which soon the stars will begin to peep.

Let him fancy himself seated upon the low mossy wall of an ancient churchyard, where hundreds of grey stones rise above the sward, under the fantastic branches of two or three half-withered ash-trees, spreading their arms in everlasting love and sorrow over the dead.

The narrow road upon which I and my companion await the tax-cart that is to carry me and my basket, with its rich fruitage of speckled trout, away, lies at his feet, and far below spreads an undulating plain, rising westward again into soft hills, and traversed (every here and there visibly) by a winding stream which, even through the mists of evening, catches and returns the funereal glories of the skies.

As the eye traces its wayward wanderings, it loses them for a moment in the heaving verdure of white-thorns and ash, from among which floats from some dozen rude chimneys, mostly unseen, the transparent blue film of turf smoke. There we know, although we cannot see it, the steep old bridge of Carrickadrum spans the river; and stretching away far to the right the valley of

Lisnamoe: its steeps and hollows, its straggling hedges, its fair-green, its tall scattered trees, and old grey tower, are disappearing fast among the discoloured tints and haze of evening.

Those landmarks, as we sit listlessly expecting the arrival of our modest conveyance, suggest to our companion—a bare-legged Celtic brother of the gentle craft, somewhat at the wrong side of forty, with a turf-coloured caubeen, patched frieze, a clear brown complexion, dark-grey eyes, and a right pleasant dash of roguery in his features—the tale, which, if the reader pleases, he is welcome to hear along with me just as it falls from the lips of our humble comrade.

His words I can give, but your own fancy must supply the advantages of an intelligent, expressive countenance, and, what is perhaps harder still, the harmony of his glorious brogue, that, like the melodies of our own dear country, will leave a burden of mirth or of sorrow with nearly equal propriety, tickling the diaphragm as easily as it plays with the heart-strings, and is in itself a national music that, I trust, may never, never—scouted and despised though it be—never cease, like the lost tones of our harp, to be heard in the fields of my country, in welcome or endearment, in fun or in sorrow, stirring the hearts of Irish men and Irish women.

My friend of the caubeen and naked shanks, then, com-menced, and continued his relation, as nearly as possible, in the following words:—

Av coorse ye often heerd talk of Billy Malowney, that lived by the bridge of Carrickadrum. 'Leum-a-rinka' was the name they put on him, he was sich a beautiful dancer. An' faix, it's he was the rale sportin' boy, every way—killing the hares, and gaff-ing the salmons, an' fightin' the men, an' funnin' the women, and coortin' the girls; an' be the same token, there was not a colleen inside iv his jurisdiction but was breakin' her heart wid the fair love iv him.

Well, this was all pleasant enough, to be sure, while it lasted; but inhuman beings is born to misfortune, an' Bill's divarshin was not to last always. A young boy can't be continially coortin' and kissin' the girls (an' more's the pity) without exposin' himself to the most eminent parril; an' so signs all' what should happen Billy Malowney himself, but to fall in love at last wid little Molly Donovan, in Coolnamoe.

I never could ondherstand why in the world it was Bill fell in love wid HER, above all the girls in the country. She was not within four stone weight iv being as fat as Peg Brallaghan; and as for redness in the face, she could not hould a candle to Judy Flaherty. (Poor Judy! she was my sweetheart, the darlin', an' co-orted me constant, ever antil she married a boy of the Butlers; an' it's twenty years now since she was buried under the ould white-thorn in Garbally. But that's no matther!)

Well, at any rate, Molly Donovan tuck his fancy, an' that's everything! She had smooth brown hair—as smooth as silk-an' a pair iv soft coaxin' eyes—an' the whitest little teeth you ever seen; an', bedad, she was every taste as much in love wid himself as he was.

Well, now, he was raly stupid wid love: there was not a bit of fun left in him. He was good for nothin' an airth bud sittin' under bushes, smokin' tobacky, and sighin' till you'd wonder how in the world he got wind for it all.

An', bedad, he was an illigant scholar, moreover; an', so signs, it's many's the song he made about her; an' if you'd be walkin' in the evening, a mile away from Carrickadrum, begorra you'd hear him singing out like a bull, all across the country, in her praises.

Well, ye may be sure, ould Tim Donovan and the wife was not a bit too well plased to see Bill Malowney coortin' their daughter Molly; for, do ye mind, she was the only child they had, and her fortune was thirty-five pounds, two cows, and five illigant pigs, three iron pots and a skillet, an' a trifle iv poultry in hand; and no one knew how much besides, whenever the Lord id be plased to call the ould people out of the way into glory!

So, it was not likely ould Tim Donovan id be fallin' in love wid poor Bill Malowney as aisy as the girls did; for, barrin' his beauty, an' his gun, an' his dhudheen, an' his janius, the divil a taste of property iv any sort or description he had in the wide world!

Well, as bad as that was, Billy would not give in that her father and mother had the smallest taste iv a right to intherfare, good or bad.

'An' you're welcome to rayfuse me,' says he, 'whin I ax your lave,' says he; 'an' I'll ax your lave,' says he, 'whenever I want to coort yourselves,' says he; 'but it's your daughter I'm coortin' at the present,' says he, 'an that's all I'll say,' says he; 'for I'd as soon take a doase of salts as be discoursin' ye,' says he.

So it was a rale blazin' battle betune himself and the ould people; an', begorra, there was no soart iv blaguardin' that did not pass betune them; an' they put a solemn injection on Molly again seein' him or meetin' him for the future.

But it was all iv no use. You might as well be pursuadin' the birds agin flying, or sthrivin' to coax the stars out iv the sky into your hat, as be talking common sinse to them that's fairly bothered and burstin' wid love. There's nothin' like it. The toothache an' cholic together id compose you betther for an argyment than itself. It leaves you fit for nothin' bud nansinse.

It's stronger than whisky, for one good drop iv it will make you drunk for one year, and sick, begorra, for a dozen.

It's stronger than the say, for it'll carry you round the world an' never let you sink, in sunshine or storm; an,' begorra, it's stronger than Death himself, for it is not afeard iv him, bedad, but dares him in every shape.

But lovers has quarrels sometimes, and, begorra, when they do, you'd a'most imagine they hated one another like man and wife. An' so, signs an, Billy Malowney and Molly Donovan fell out one evening at ould Tom Dundon's wake; an' whatever came betune them, she made no more about it but just draws her cloak round her, and away wid herself and the sarvant-girl home again, as if there was not a corpse, or a fiddle, or a taste of divarsion in it.

Well, Bill Malowney follied her down the boreen, to try could he deludher her back again; but, if she was bitther before, she gave it to him in airnest when she got him alone to herself, and to that degree that he wished her safe home, short and sulky enough, an' walked back again, as mad as the devil himself, to the wake, to pay a respect to poor Tom Dundon.

Well, my dear, it was aisy seen there was something wrong avid Billy Malowney, for he paid no attintion the rest of the evening to any soart of divarsion but the whisky alone; an' every glass he'd drink it's what he'd be wishing the divil had the women, an' the worst iv bad luck to all soarts iv courting, until, at last, wid the goodness iv the sperits, an' the badness iv his temper, an' the constant flusthration iv cursin', he grew all as one as you might say almost, saving your presince, bastely drunk!

Well, who should he fall in wid, in that childish condition, as he was deploying along the road almost as straight as the letter S, an' cursin' the girls, an' roarin' for more whisky, but the recruiting-sargent iv the Welsh Confusileers.

So, cute enough, the sargent begins to convarse him, an' it was not long until he had him sitting in Murphy's public-house, wid an elegant dandy iv punch before him, an' the king's money safe an' snug in the lowest wrinkle of his breeches-pocket.

So away wid him, and the dhrums and fifes playing, an' a dozen more unforthunate bliggards just listed along with him, an' he shakin' hands wid the sargent, and swearin' agin the women every minute, until, be the time he kem to himself, begorra, he was a good ten miles on the road to Dublin, an' Molly and all behind him.

It id be no good tellin' you iv the letters he wrote to her from the barracks there, nor how she was breaking her heart to go and see him just wanst before he'd go; but the father an' mother would not allow iv it be no manes.

An' so in less time than you'd be thinkin' about it, the colonel had him polished off into it rale elegant soger, wid his gun exercise, and his bagnet exercise, and his small sword, and broad sword, and pistol and dagger, an' all the rest, an' then away wid him on boord a man-a-war to furrin parts, to fight for King George agin Bonyparty, that was great in them times.

Well, it was very soon in everyone's mouth how Billy Malowney was batin' all before him, astonishin' the ginerals, an frightenin' the inimy to that degree, there was not a Frinchman dare say parley voo outside of the rounds iv his camp.

You may be sure Molly was proud iv that same, though she never spoke a word about it; until at last the news kem home that Billy Malowney was surrounded an' murdered by the Frinch army, under Napoleon Bonyparty himself. The news was brought by Jack Brynn Dhas, the peddlar, that said he met the corporal iv the regiment on the quay iv Limerick, an' how he brought him into a public-house and thrated him to a naggin, and got all the news about poor Billy Malowney out iv him while they war dhrinkin' it; an' a sorrowful story it was.

The way it happened, accordin' as the corporal tould him, was jist how the Jook iv Wellington detarmined to fight a rale tarin' battle wid the Frinch, and Bonyparty at the same time was aiqually detarmined to fight the divil's own scrimmidge wid the British foorces.

Well, as soon as the business was pretty near ready at both sides, Bonyparty and the general next undher himself gets up behind a bush, to look at their inimies through spy-glasses, and thry would they know any iv them at the distance.

'Bedadad!' says the gineral, afther a divil iv a long spy, 'I'd bet half a pint,' says he, 'that's Bill Malowney himself,' says he, 'down there,' says he.

'Och!' says Bonypart, 'do you tell me so?' says he—'I'm fairly heart-scalded with that same Billy Malowney,' says he; 'an' I think if I was wanst shut iv him I'd bate the rest iv them aisy,' says he.

'I'm thinking so myself,' says the gineral, says he; 'but he's a tough bye,' says he.

'Tough!' says Bonypart, 'he's the divil,' says he.

'Begorra, I'd be better plased.' says the gineral, says he, 'to take himself than the Duke iv Willinton,' says he, 'an' Sir Edward Blakeney into the bargain,' says he.

'The Duke of Wellinton and Gineral Blakeney,' says Bonypart, 'is great for planning, no doubt,' says he; 'but Billy Malowney's the boy for ACTION,' says he—'an' action's everything, just now,' says he.

So wid that Bonypart pushes up his cocked hat, and begins scratching his head, and thinning and considherin' for the bare life, and at last says he to the gineral:

'Gineral Commandher iv all the Foorces,' says he, 'I've hot it,' says he: 'ordher out the forlorn hope,' says he, 'an' give them as much powdher, both glazed and blasting,' says he, 'an' as much bullets do ye mind, an' swan-dhrops an' chain-shot,' says he, 'an' all soorts iv waipons an' combustables as they can carry; an' let them surround Bill Malowney,' says he, 'an' if they can get any soort iv an advantage,' says he, 'let them knock him to smithereens,' says he, 'an' then take him presner,' says he; 'an' tell all the bandmen iv the Frinch army,' says he, 'to play up "Garryowen," to keep up their sperits,' says he, 'all the time they're advancin'. An' you may promise them anything you like in my name,' says he; for, by my sowl, I don't think its many iv them 'ill come back to throuble us,' says he, winkin' at him.

So away with the gineral, an' he ordhers out the forlorn hope, all' tells the band to play, an' everything else, just as Bonypart desired him. An' sure enough, whin Billy Malowney heerd the music where he was standin' taking a blast of the dhudheen to compose his mind for murdherin' the Frinchmen as usual, being mighty partial to that tune intirely, he cocks his ear a one side, an' down he stoops to listen to the music; but, begorra, who should be in his rare all the time but a Frinch grannideer behind a bush, and seeing him stooped in a convanient forum, bedad he let flies at him sthraight, and fired him right forward between the legs an' the small iv the back, glory be to God! with what they call (saving your presence) a bum-shell.

Well, Bill Malowney let one roar out iv him, an' away he rowled over the field iv battle like a slitther (as Bonypart and the Duke iv Wellington, that was watching the manoeuvres from a distance, both consayved) into glory.

An' sure enough the Frinch was overjoyed beyant all bounds, an' small blame to them—an' the Duke of Wellington, I'm toult, was never all out the same man sinst.

At any rate, the news kem home how Billy Malowney was murdhered by the Frinch in furrin parts.

Well, all this time, you may be sure, there was no want iv boys comin' to coort purty Molly Donovan; but one way ar another, she always kept puttin' them off constant. An' though her father and mother was nathurally anxious to get rid of her respickably, they did not like to marry her off in spite iv her teeth.

An' this way, promising one while and puttin' it off another, she conthrived to get on from one Shrove to another, until near seven years was over and gone from the time when Billy Malowney listed for furrin sarvice.

It was nigh hand a year from the time whin the news iv Leum-a-rinka bein' killed by the Frinch came home, an' in place iv forgettin' him, as the saisins wint over, it's what Molly was growin' paler and more lonesome every day, antil the neighbours thought she was fallin' into a decline; and this is the way it was with her whin the fair of Lisnamoe kem round.

It was a beautiful evenin', just at the time iv the reapin' iv the oats, and the sun was shinin' through the red clouds far away over the hills iv Cahirmore.

Her father an' mother, an' the boys an' girls, was all away down in the fair, and Molly Sittin' all alone on the step of the stile, listening to the foolish little birds whistlin' among the leaves—and the sound of the mountain-river flowin' through the stones an' bushes—an' the crows flyin' home high overhead to the woods iv Glinvarlogh—an' down in the glen, far away, she could see the fair-green iv Lisnamoe in the mist, an' sunshine among the grey rocks and threes—an' the cows an' the horses, an' the blue frieze, an' the red cloaks, an' the tents, an' the smoke, an' the ould round tower—all as soft an' as sorrowful as a dhrame iv ould times.

An' while she was looking this way, an' thinking iv Leum-a-rinka—poor Bill iv the dance, that was sleepin' in his lonesome glory in the fields iv Spain—she began to sing the song he used to like so well in the ould times—

Shule, shule, shale a-roon;

an' when she ended the verse, what do you think but she heard a manly voice just at the other side iv the hedge, singing the last words over again!

Well she knew it; her heart flutthered up like a little bird that id be wounded, and then dhropped still in her breast. It was himself. In a minute he was through the hedge and standing before her.

'Leum!' says she.

'Mavourneen cuishla machree!' says he; and without another word they were locked in one another's arms.

Well, it id only be nansinse for me thryin' an' tell ye all the foolish things they said, and how they looked in one another's faces, an' laughed, an' cried, an' laughed again; and how, when they came to themselves, and she was able at last to believe it was raly Billy himself that was there, actially holdin' her hand, and lookin' in her eyes the same way as ever, barrin' he was browner and boulder, an' did not, maybe, look quite as merry in himself as he used to do in former times—an' fondher for all, an' more lovin' than ever—how he tould her all about the wars wid the Frinchmen—an' how he was wounded, and left for dead in the field iv battle, bein' shot through the breast, and how he was discharged, an' got a pinsion iv a full shillin' a day—and how he was come back to liv the rest iv his days in the sweet glen iv Lisnamoe, an' (if only SHE'D consint) to marry herself in spite iv them all.

Well, ye may aisily think they had plinty to talk about, afther seven years without once seein' one another; and so signs on, the time flew by as swift an' as pleasant as a bird on the wing, an' the sun wint down, an' the moon shone sweet an' soft instead, an' they two never knew a ha'porth about it, but kept talkin' an' whisperin', an' whisperin' an' talkin'; for it's wondherful how often a tinder-hearted girl will bear to hear a purty boy tellin' her the same story constant over an' over; ontil at last, sure enough, they heerd the ould man himself comin' up the boreen, singin' the 'Colleen Rue'—a thing he never done barrin' whin he had a dhrop in; an' the misthress walkin' in front iv him, an' two illigant Kerry cows he just bought in the fair, an' the sarvint boys dhriving them behind.

'Oh, blessed hour!' says Molly, 'here's my father.'

'I'll spake to him this minute,' says Bill.

'Oh, not for the world,' says she; 'he's singin' the "Colleen Rue," ' says she, 'and no one dar raison with him,' says she.

'An' where'll I go, thin?' says he, 'for they're into the haggard an top iv us,' says he, 'an' they'll see me iv I lep through the hedge,' says he.

'Thry the pig-sty,' says she, 'mavourneen,' says she, 'in the name iv God,' says she.

'Well, darlint,' says he, 'for your sake,' says he, 'I'll condescend to them animals,' says he.

An' wid that he makes a dart to get in; bud, begorra, it was too late—the pigs was all gone home, and the pig-sty was as full as the Burr coach wid six inside.

'Och! blur-an'-agers,' says he, 'there is not room for a suckin'-pig,' says he, 'let alone a Christian,' says he.

'Well, run into the house, Billy,' says she, 'this minute,' says she, 'an' hide yourself antil they're quiet,' says she, 'an' thin you can steal out,' says she, 'anknownst to them all,' says she.

'I'll do your biddin', says he, 'Molly asthore,' says he.

'Run in thin,' says she, 'an' I'll go an' meet them,' says she.

So wid that away wid her, and in wint Billy, an' where 'id he hide himself bud in a little closet that was off iv the room where the ould man and woman slep'. So he closed the doore, and sot down in an ould chair he found there convanient.

Well, he was not well in it when all the rest iv them comes into the kitchen, an' ould Tim Donovan singin' the 'Colleen Rue' for the bare life, an' the rest iv them sthrivin' to humour him, and doin' exactly everything he bid them, because they seen he was foolish be the manes iv the liquor.

Well, to be sure all this kep' them long enough, you may be sure, from goin' to bed, so that Billy could get no manner iv an advantage to get out iv the house, and so he sted sittin' in the dark closet in state, cursin' the 'Colleen Rue,' and wondherin' to the divil whin they'd get the ould man into his bed. An', as if that was not delay enough, who should come in to stop for the night but Father O'Flaherty, of Cahirmore, that was buyin' a horse at the fair! An' av course, there was a bed to be med down for his raverence, an' some other attintions; an' a long discoorse himself an' ould Mrs. Donovan had about the slaughter iv Billy Malowney, an' how he was buried on the field iv battle; an' his raverence hoped he got a dacent funeral, an' all the other convaniences iv religion. An' so you may suppose it was pretty late in the night before all iv them got to their beds.

Well, Tim Donovan could not settle to sleep at all at all, an' so he kep' discoorsin' the wife about the new cows he bought, an' the strippers he sould, an' so an for better than an hour, ontil from one thing to another he kem to talk about the pigs, an' the poulthry; and at last, having nothing betther to discoorse about, he begun at his daughter Molly, an' all the heartscald she was to him be raison iv refusin' the men. An' at last says he:

'I onderstand,' says he, 'very well how it is,' says he. 'It's how she was in love,' says he, 'wid that bliggard, Billy Malowney,' says he, 'bad luck to him!' says he; for by this time he was coming to his raison.

'Ah!' says the wife, says she, 'Tim darlint, don't be cursin' them that's dead an' buried,' says she.

'An' why would not I,' says he, 'if they desarve it?' says he.

'Whisht,' says she, 'an' listen to that,' says she. 'In the name of the Blessed Vargin,' says she, 'what IS it?' says she.

An' sure enough what was it but Bill Malowney that was dhroppin' asleep in the closet, an' snorin' like a church organ.

'Is it a pig,' says he, 'or is it a Christian?'

'Arra! listen to the tune iv it,' says she; 'sure a pig never done the like is that,' says she.

'Whatever it is,' says he, 'it's in the room wid us,' says he. 'The Lord be marciful to us!' says he.

'I tould you not to be cursin',' says she; 'bad luck to you,' says she, 'for an ommadhaun!' for she was a very religious woman in herself.

'Sure, he's buried in Spain,' says he; 'an' it is not for one little innocent expression,' says he, 'he'd be comin' all that a way to annoy the house,' says he.

Well, while they war talkin', Bill turns in the way he was sleepin' into an aisier imposture; and as soon as he stopped snorin' ould Tim Donovan's courage riz agin, and says he:

'I'll go to the kitchen,' says he, 'an' light a rish,' says he.

An' with that away wid him, an' the wife kep' workin' the beads all the time, an' before he kem back Bill was snorin' as loud as ever.

'Oh! bloody wars—I mane the blessed saints about us!—that deadly sound,' says he; 'it's going on as lively as ever,' says he.

'I'm as wake as a rag,' says his wife, says she, 'wid the fair anasiness,' says she. 'It's out iv the little closet it's comin',' says she.

'Say your prayers,' says he, 'an' hould your tongue,' says he, 'while I discoorse it,' says he. 'An' who are ye,' says he, 'in the name iv of all the holy saints?' says he, givin' the door a dab iv a crusheen that wakened Bill inside. 'I ax,' says he, 'who are you?' says he.

Well, Bill did not rightly remember where in the world he was, but he pushed open the door, an' says he:

'Billy Malowney's my name,' says he, 'an' I'll thank ye to tell me a betther,' says he.

Well, whin Tim Donovan heard that, an' actially seen that it was Bill himself that was in it, he had not strength enough to let a bawl out iv him, but he dhropt the candle out iv his hand, an' down wid himself on his back in the dark.

Well, the wife let a screech you'd hear at the mill iv Killraghlin, an'—

'Oh,' says she, 'the spirit has him, body an' bones!' says she. 'Oh, holy St. Bridget—oh, Mother iv Marcy—oh, Father O'Flaherty!' says she, screechin' murdher from out iv her bed.

Well, Bill Malowney was not a minute remimberin' himself, an' so out wid him quite an' aisy, an' through the kitchen; bud in place iv the door iv the house, it's what he kem to the door iv Father O'Flaherty's little room, where he was jist wakenin' wid the noise iv the screechin' an' battherin'; an' bedad, Bill makes no more about it, but he jumps, wid one boult, clever an' clane into his raverance's bed.

'What do ye mane, you uncivilised bliggard?' says his raverance. 'Is that a venerable way,' says he, 'to approach your clargy?' says he.

'Hould your tongue,' says Bill, 'an' I'll do ye no harum,' says he.

'Who are you, ye scoundhrel iv the world?' says his raverance.

'Whisht!' says he? 'I'm Billy Malowney,' says he.

'You lie!' says his raverance for he was frightened beyont all bearin'—an' he makes but one jump out iv the bed at the wrong side, where there was only jist a little place in the wall for a press, an' his raverance could not as much as turn in it for the wealth iv kingdoms. 'You lie,' says he; 'but for feared it's the truth you're tellin',' says he, 'here's at ye in the name iv all the blessed saints together!' says he.

An' wid that, my dear, he blazes away at him wid a Latin prayer iv the strongest description, an', as he said himself afterwards, that was iv a nature that id dhrive the divil himself up the chimley like a puff iv tobacky smoke, wid his tail betune his legs.

'Arra, what are ye sthrivin' to say,' says Bill; says he, 'if ye don't hould your tongue,' says he, 'wid your parly voo;' says he, 'it's what I'll put my thumb on your windpipe,' says he, 'an' Billy Malowney never wint back iv his word yet,' says he.

'Thundher-an-owns,' says his raverance, says he—seein' the Latin took no infect on him, at all at all an' screechin' that you'd think he'd rise the thatch up iv the house wid the fair fright-'and thundher and blazes, boys, will none iv yes come here wid a candle, but lave your clargy to be choked by a spirit in the dark?' says he.

Well, be this time the sarvint boys and the rest iv them wor up an' half dressed, an' in they all run, one on top iv another, wid pitchforks and spades, thinkin' it was only what his raverence

501

slep' a dhrame iv the like, by means of the punch he was afther takin' just before he rowl'd himself into the bed. But, begorra, whin they seen it was raly Bill Malowney himself that was in it, it was only who'd be foremost out agin, tumblin' backways, one over another, and his raverence roarin' an' cursin' them like mad for not waitin' for him.

Well, my dear, it was betther than half an hour before Billy Malowney could explain to them all how it raly was himself, for begorra they were all iv them persuadin' him that he was a spirit to that degree it's a wondher he did not give in to it, if it was only to put a stop to the argiment.

Well, his raverence tould the ould people then, there was no use in sthrivin' agin the will iv Providence an' the vagaries iv love united; an' whin they kem to undherstand to a sartinty how Billy had a shillin' a day for the rest iv his days, begorra they took rather a likin' to him, and considhered at wanst how he must have riz out of all his nansinse entirely, or his gracious Majesty id never have condescinded to show him his countenance that way every day of his life, on a silver shillin'.

An' so, begorra, they never stopt till it was all settled—an' there was not sich a weddin' as that in the counthry sinst. It's more than forty years ago, an' though I was no more nor a gossoon myself, I remimber it like yestherday. Molly never looked so purty before, an' Billy Malowney was plisant beyont all hearin', to that degree that half the girls in it was fairly tarin' mad—only they would not let on—they had not him to themselves in place iv her. An' begorra I'd be afeared to tell ye, because you would not believe me, since that blessid man Father Mathew put an end to all soorts of sociality, the Lord reward him, how many gallons iv pottieen whisky was dhrank upon that most solemn and tindher occasion.

Pat Hanlon, the piper, had a faver out iv it; an' Neddy Shawn Heigue, mountin' his horse the wrong way, broke his collar-bone, by the manes iv fallin' over his tail while he was feelin' for his head; an' Payther Brian, the horse-docther, I am tould, was never quite right in the head ever afther; an' ould Tim Donovan was singin' the 'Colleen Rue' night and day for a full week; an' begorra the weddin' was only the foundation iv fun, and the beginning iv divarsion, for there was not a year for ten years afther, an' more, but brought round a christenin' as regular as the sasins revarted.

Borrhomeo the Astrologer

At the period of the famous plague of Milan in 1630, a frenzy of superstition seized upon the population high and low. Old prophecies of a diabolical visitation reserved for their city, in that particular year of grace, prepared the way for this wild panic of the imagination. When the plague broke out terror seems to have acted to a degree scarcely paralleled upon the fancy or the credulity of the people. Excitement in very many cases produced absolutely the hallucinations of madness. Persons deposed, in the most solemn and consistent terms, to having themselves witnessed diabolical processions, spoken with an awful impersonation of Satan, and been solicited amidst scenes and personages altogether supernatural, to lend their human agency to the nefarious designs of the fiend, by consenting to disseminate by certain prescribed means, the virus of the pestilence.

Some of the stories related of persons possessed by these awful fancies are in print; and by no means destitute of a certain original and romantic horror. That which I am about to tell, however, has I believe, never been printed. At all events I saw it only in MSS., sewed up in vellum, with a psaltery and half-a-dozen lives of saints, in the library of the old Dominican monastery which stands about two leagues to the north-east of the city. With your permission I am about to give you the best translation I was able to make of this short but odd story, of the truth of which, judging from the company in which I found it, the honest monks entertained no sort of doubt. You are to remember that all sorts of tales of wonder were at that time flying about and believed in Milan, and that many of these were authenticated in such a way as to leave no doubt as to the *bona fides* of those who believed themselves to have been eyewitnesses of what they told. Monks and country *padres* of course believed; but so did men who stood highest in the church, and who, unless fame belied them, believed little else.

In the year of our Lord, 1630, when Satan, by divine permission, appearing among us in person, afflicted, our beautiful city of Milan with a pestilence unheard of in its severity, there lived in the *Strada Piaña*, which has lately been pulled down, an astrologer calling himself Borrhomeo. Some say he came from Perrugia, others from Venice; I know not. He it was who first predicted, in the year of our Lord, 1628, by means of his art. that the pale comet which then appeared would speedily be followed, not by war or by famine, but by pestilence; which accordingly came to pass. Beside his skill in astrology, which was wonderful, he was profoundly versed in alchymy. He was a man great in stature, and strong, though old in years, and with a most reverent beard. But though seemingly austere in his life, it is said that he was given up, in secret, to enormous wickedness.

Having shut himself up in his house for more than a month, with his furnace and crucibles (truly he had made repeated and near approaches to the grand *arcanum*) he had arrived, as he supposed, at the moment of projection.

He collects the powder and tries it on molten lead; it was a failure. He was too wise to be angry; the long pursuit of his art had taught him patience. But while he is pondering in a profound and gloomy reverie, a retort, which he had forgotten in the furnace, explodes.

He sees in the smoke a pale young man, dressed in mourning, with black hair, and viewing him with a sad and reproachful countenance.

Borrhomeo who lived among *chimæras*, is not utterly overcome, as another man might be, and confronts him, amazed, indeed, but not terrified.

The stranger shook his head like a holy young confessor, who hears an evil shrift; and says he, rather sternly—"Borrhomeo! Beware of covetousness which is idolatry. On this sordid pursuit which you call a science, have you wasted your days on earth and your peace hereafter."

"Young man," says the alchymist, too much struck by the manner and reproof of the stranger to ask himself how he came there—"Wealth is power to do good as well as evil. To seek it is, therefore, an ambition as honourable as any other."

"We both know why you seek it, and how you would employ it," answers the young man gravely.

The old man's face flushed with anger at this rebuke, and he looked down frowningly to the table whereon lay the book of his spells. But he bethought him this must be a good spirit, and he was abashed. Nevertheless, he roused his courage, and shook his white mane back, and was on the point of answering sternly, when the young man said with a melancholy smile—

"Besides, you will never discover the grand *arcanum*—the elixir *vitæ*, or the philosopher's stone."

His words, which were as soft as snowflakes, fell like an iron mace upon the heart of the seer.

"Perhaps not," said the astrologer frigidly.

"Not perhaps," said the stranger.

"At all events, young man—for as such you appear—and I know what spirits seek who take that shape, the science has its charms for me; and when the pleasures of the young are as harmless as the amusements of the aged I'll hear you question mine."

"You know not what spirit you are of. As for me, I am contrite and humble—well I may," says the stranger faintly with a sigh. "Besides, what you have pursued in vain, and will never by your own researches find, I have discovered."

"What! the"—

"Yes, the tincture that can prolong life to virtual immortality, and the dust that can change that lead into gold; but I care for neither."

"Why, young man, if this be true," says Borrhomeo in a rap-

506

ture of wonder, "you stand before me an angel of wisdom, in power and immortality like a god!"

"No," says the stranger, "a long-lived fellow, with along purse—that's all."

"All?—everything?" cries the old man. "Will you—*will* you"

"Yes, sir, you shall see," says the young man in black. "Give me that crucible. It is all a matter of proportions. Water, clay, and air are the material of all the vegetable world—the flowers and forests, the wines and the fruits—the seed is both the laboratory and the chemist, and knows how, with the sun's help, to apportion and combine."

While he said this with the abstracted manner of one whose mind is mazed in a double reverie, while his hands work out some familiar problem, he tumbled over the alchymist's papers, and unstopped and stopped his bottles of crystals, precipitates, and elixirs—taking a little from this and a little from that, and throwing all into a small gold cup that stood on the table; but like a juggler, he moved those bottles so deftly, that the quick eyes and retentive soul of the old man vainly sought to catch or keep the order of the process. When he had done there was hardly a thimble-full.

"Is that it?" whispered the old man, twinkling with greedy eyes.

"No," said the stranger, with a sly smile, "there is one very simple ingredient which you have forgotten."

He took a large, flat, oval gold box, with some hair set under a crystal in the lid of it, and looking at it for a moment, he seemed to sigh. He tapped it like a snuff-box—there was within it a powder like vermilion, and on the inside of the lid, in the centre, was the small enamel portrait of a beautiful but sinister female face. The features were so very beautiful, and the expression so strangely blended with horror, that it fixed the gaze of the old man for a moment; and—was it illusion?—he thought he saw the face steadily dilating as if it would gradually fill the lid of the box, and even expand to human dimensions.

"Yes," said the stranger, as having taken some of the red pow-

507

der, he shut the cover down again with a snap, "she was beautiful, and her lineaments are still clear and bright—nothing like darkness to keep them from fading, and so the poor little miniature is again in prison;" and he dropped the box back into his pocket.

Then he took two iron ladles, and heating in the one his powder to a white heat, and bidding the alchymist melt a pellet of lead in the other, and pour it into the ladle which held the powder, there arose a beautiful purple fire in the bottom of it, with an intense fringe of green and yellow; and when it subsided, there was a little nut of gold there of the bigness of the leaden pellet.

The fiery eyes of the alchymist almost leaped from their sockets into the iron cup, and he could have clasped his marvelous visitor round the knees and worshipped him.

"And now," says the stranger very gently and earnestly, "in return for satisfying your curiosity, I ask only your solemn promise to prosecute this dread science no more. Ha! you'll not give it. Take, then, my warning, and remember the wages of this knowledge is sorrow."

"But won't you tell me how to commute—and—and—you have not produced the elixir," the old man cried.

"'Tis folly—and, as I've told you, worse—a snare," answered the young man, sighing heavily. "I came not to satisfy but to rebuke your dangerous though fruitless frenzy. Besides, I hear my friend still pacing the street. Hark! he taps at the window."

Then came a sharp rattle as of a cane tapping angrily on the window.

The young man bowed, smiling sadly, and somehow got himself away, though without hurry, yet so quickly that the old man could not reach the door till after it had closed and he was gone.

"Oaf that I am!" cried the astrologer, losing patience and stamping on the ground, "how have I let him go? He hesitated—he would have yielded—his scruples, benevolent perhaps, I could have quieted—and yet in the very crisis I was tongue-tied and motionless, and let him go !"

He pushed open the little window, from which he observed the street, and thought he saw the stranger walking round the corner, conversing with a little hunchback in a red cloak, and followed by an ugly dog.

At sight of the great white head and beard, and the fierce features of the alchymist, bleared and tanned in the smoke of his furnace, people stopped and looked. So he withdrew, and in haste got him ready for the street, waiting for no refreshment, though he had fasted long; for he had the strength as well as the stature of a giant, and forth he went.

By this time the twilight had passed into night. He had his mantle about him, and his rapier and dagger—for the streets were dangerous, and a feather in his cap, and his white beard hidden behind the fold of his cloak. So he might have passed for a tall soldier of the guard.

The pestilence kept people much within doors, and the streets more solitary than was customary. He had walked through the town two hours and more, before he met with anything to speak of. Then—lo!—on a sudden, near the Fountain of the Lion—it being then moonlight—he discovers, in a solitude, the figure of his visitor, standing with the hunchback and the dog, which he knew by its ungainly bones, and its carrying its huge head so near the ground.

So he shouts along the silent street, "Stay a moment, *signor*," and he mends his pace.

But they were parting company there, it seemed, and away went the deformed, with his unsightly beast at his heels, and this way came the youth in black.

So standing full in his way, and doffing his cap, and throwing back his cloak, that his snowy beard and head might appear, and the stranger recognize him when he drew nigh. He cried—

"Borrhomeo implores thee to take pity on his ignorance."

"What! still mad?" said the young man. "This man will waste the small remnant of his years in godless search after gold and immortality; better he should know all, and feel their vanity."

"Better a thousand times!" cried the old man, in ecstasy.

"There is in this city, *signor*, at this time, in great secrecy, the master who taught me," says the youth, "the master of all alchymists. Many centuries since he found out the elixir *vitæ*. From him I've learned the few secrets that I know, and without his leave I dare not impart them. If you desire it, I will bring you before him; but, once in his presence, you cannot recede, and his conditions you must accept."

"All, all, with my whole heart. But some reasonable pleasures"—

"With your pleasures he will not interfere; he cannot change your heart," said the young man, with one of his heavy sighs; "but you know what gold is, and what the elixir is, and power and immortality are not to be had for nothing."

"Lead on, *signor*, I'm ready," cries the old man, whose face flushed, and his eyes burned with the fires of an evil rapture.

"Take my hand," said the young man, more stern and pale than he had yet appeared. So he did, and his conductor seized it with a cold gripe, and they walked swiftly on.

Now he led him through several streets, and on their way Borrhomeo passes his notary, and, lingering a moment, asks him whether he has a bond, signed by a certain merchant, with whom he had contracted for a loan. The notary, who was talking to another, says, suddenly, to that other—

"*Per Baccho*! I've just called to mind a matter that must be looked after for Signor Borrhomeo;" and he called him a nickname, which incensed the astrologer, who struck him a lusty box upon the ear.

"There's a humming in my ear tonight," said the notary, going into his house; "I hope it is no sign of the plague."

So on they walked, side by side, till they reached the shop of a *vintner* of no good repute. It was well known to Borrhomeo—a house of evil resort, where the philosopher sometimes stole, disguised, by night, to be no longer a necromancer, but a man, and, so, from a man to become a beast.

They passed through the shop. The host, with a fat pale face, and a villainous smile, was drawing wine, which a handsome damsel was waiting to take away with her. He kissed her as she paid, and she gave him a cuff on his fat white chops, and laughed.

"What's become of Signor Borrhomeo," said the girl, "that he never comes here now."

"Why, here he is !" cries Borrhomeo, with a saturnine smile, and he slaps his broad palm on her shoulder.

But the girl only shrugged, with a little shiver, and said, "What a chill down my back—they're walking over my grave now."

[The Italian phrase here is very nearly equivalent].

"Why they neither hear nor see me !" said the astrologer, amazed.

They went into the inner room, where guests used to sit and drink. But the plague had stopped all that, and the room was empty.

"He's in there," said the young man; "you'll see him presently."

Borrhomeo was filled with an awful curiosity. He knew the room, he thought, well; and there never had been, he thought, a door where the young man had pointed; but there was now a drapery there like what covers a doorway, and it swelled and swayed slowly in the wind.

"Some centuries?" said the astrologer, looking on the dark drapery. "Geber, perhaps, or Alfarabi"

"It matters not a pin's point what his name; you'll call him ' my lord,' simply; and—observe—we alchymists are a potent order, and it behoves you to keep your word with us."

"I will be true," said Borrhomeo.

"And use the powers you gain, beneficently," repeated his guide.

"I'm but a sinner. I will strive, with only an exception, in favour of such things as make wealth and lifeworth having," answered the philosopher.

"See, take this, and do as I bidyou," said the youth, giving him a thin round film of human skin.

[*How the honest monk who wrote the tale, or even Borrhomeo him-self, knew this and many other matters he describes, 'tis for him to say.*]

"Breathe on it," said he.

And when he did so he made him stretch it to the size of a sheet of paper, which he did quite easily.

"Now cover your face with it as with a napkin."

So he did.

"'Twill do; give it to me. It is but a picture. See."

And it slowly shrunk until its disc was just the same as that of the lady's miniature in the lid of the box, over which he fixed it.

Borrhomeo beheld his own picture.

"Every adept has his portrait here," said the young man. "So good a likeness is always pleasant; but these have a power beside, and establish a sympathy between their originals and their possessor which secures discipline and silence."

"How does it work?" asked Borrhomeo.

"Have I not been your good angel?" said the young man, sitting before him. He extends his legs—pushing out his feet, and letting his chin sink on his chest—he fixes his eyes upon him with a horrible and sarcastic glare, and one of his feet contracts and divides into a goatish stump.

Borrhomeo would have burst into a yell, but he could not.

"It is a nightmare, is it not?" said the stranger, who seemed delighted to hold him, minute after minute, in that spell. At last the shoe and hose that seemed to have shrunk apart like burning parchment, closed over the goatish shin and hoof; and rising, he shook him by the shoulder. With a gasp, the astrologer started to his feet.

"There, I told you it was a nightmare, or—or what you please. I could not have done it but through the picture. You see how fast we have you. You must for once resemble a Christian, Borrhomeo, and with us deal truly and honestly."

"You've promised me the elixir *vitæ*," the old man said, fearful lest the secret should escape him.

"And you shall have it. Go, bring a cup of wine. He'll not see you, nor the wine, nor the cup."

So he brought a cup of Falernian, which he loved the best.

"There's fifty years of life for every drop," said the youth.

"Let me live a thousand years, to begin with," cries Borrhomeo.

"Beware.You'll tire of it"—

"Nay. Give me the twenty drops."

So he took the cup, and measured the drops; and as they fell, the wine was agitated with a gentle simmer all over, and threw out ring after ring of purple, green, and gold. And Borrhomeo drank it, and sucked in the last drop in ecstasy, and cried out, blaspheming, with joy and sensual delight—

"And I'm to have this secret, too."

"This and all others, when you claim them," said the young man.

"See, 'tis time," he added.

And Borrhomeo saw that the great misshapen dog he had seen in the street, was sniffing by the stranger's feet.

When they went into the inner room there was a large table, and many men at either side; and at the head a gigantic man, with a face like the face of a beast, but the flesh was as of a man. Borrhomeo quaked in his presence.

"I am aware of what hath passed, Borrhomeo," he said. "The condition is this :—You take this vial, and with the fluid it contains and the sponge trace the letter S on every door of every church and religious house within the walls of Milan. The dog will go with you."

It was a fiend in dog's shape, says the monkish writer; and had he failed in his task would have torn him in pieces.

So Borrhomeo, that old arch-villain, undertook this office cheerfully, well knowing what its purpose was. For it was a thing notorious, that Satan was himself in a bodily, though phantasmal, shape seen before in Milan, and that he had tempted others to a like fascinorous action; but, happily for their souls, in vain. The Stygian satellites of the fiend had power to smear the door of every unconsecrated house in Milan with that pestilential virus, as, indeed, the citizens with their own eyes, when first the plague broke out, beheld upon their own doors. But they could not defile the church gates, nor the doors of the monasteries; and according to the conditions under which their infernal malice is bound, they could in nowise effect it save by the hand of one who was baptized, which, to the baleful abuse of that holy sacrament, the wretch, Borrhomeo, had been.

He did his accursed and murderous office well and fearlessly. His reward mammon and indefinite lone life. The hell-dog by his side compelling him, and the belief in his invisibility making him confident withal. But therein was shown forth to all the world the craft of the fiend, and the just judgement of heaven; for he was plainly seen in the very act by the Sexton of the Church of Saint Mary of the Passion, and by the Pastor of the convent of Saint Justina of Padua, and the same officer of the Olivetans of Saint Victor. So, finding in the morning the only too plain and fatal traces of what he had been doing, with a mob at their heels, who would have had his life but for the guard, they arrested him in his house next morning, and the mob breaking in, smashed all the instruments of his infernal art, and would have burnt the house had they been allowed.

He being duly arraigned was, according to law, put to the torture, and forthwith confessed all the particulars I have related. So he was cast into a dungeon to await execution, which secretly he dreaded not, being confident in the efficacy of the elixir he had swallowed.

He was not to be put to death by decapitation. It was justly thought too honourable for so sordid a miscreant. He was sentenced to be hanged, and after hanging a day and a night he was to be laid in an open grave outside the gate on the Roman road, and there impaled, and after three days' exposure to be covered in, and so committed to the keeping of the earth, no more to groan under his living enormities.

The night before his execution, thinking deeply on the virtue of the elixir, and having assured himself, by many notable instances, which he easily brought to remembrance, that they could not deprive him, even by this severity, of his life, he lifted up his eyes and beheld the young man, in mourning suit, whose visit had been his ruin, standing near him in the cell.

This slave of Satan affected a sad countenance at first; and said he, "We are cast down, Borrhomeo, by reason of thy sentence."

"But we've cheated them," answers he, pretending, maybe, more confidence than he had; "they can't kill me."

"That's certain," rejoins the fiend.

"I shall live for a thousand years," says he.

"Ay, you must continue to live for full one thousand years; 'tis a fair term—Is it not?"

"A great deal may be done in that time," says the old man, while beads of perspiration covered his puckered forehead, and he thought that, perhaps, he might cheat *him* too, and make his peace with heaven.

"They can't hang me," says Borrhomeo.

"Oh! yes, they will certainly hang you; but, then, you'll live through it."

"Ay, the elixir," cried the prisoner.

"Thus stands the case: when an ordinary man is hanged he dies outright; but you can't die."

"No—ha, ha !—I can't die !"

"Therefore, when you are hanged, you feel, think, hear, and so forth during the process."

"St. Anthony! But then 'tis only an hour—one hour of agony—and it ends."

"You are to hang for a whole day and night," continued the fiend; "but that don't signify. Then when they take you down, you continue to feel, hear, think, and, if they leave your eyes open, to see, just as usual."

"Why, yes, certainly, I'm alive," cries Borrhomeo.

"Yes, alive, quite alive, although you appear to be dead," says the daemon with a smile.

"Ay; but what's the best moment to make my escape?" says Borrhomeo.

"Escape! why, you *have* escaped. They can't kill you. No one can kill you, until your time is out. Then you know they lay you in an open grave and impale you."

"What! ah, ha!" roared the old sinner, "you are jesting."

"Hush! depend upon it they will go through with it."

The old man shook in every joint.

"Then, after three days and" nights, they bury you," said his visitor.

"I'll lose my life, or I'll break from them!" shouts the gigantic astrologer.

"But you can't lose your life, and you can't break from them," says the fiend, softly.

"Why not? Oh! blessed saints! I'm stronger than you think."

"Ay, muscle, bones—you are an old giant !"

"Surely," cries the old man, "and the terror of a dead man rising; ha! don't you see? They fly before me, and so I escape."

"But you can't rise."

"Say—say in heaven's name what you mean," thundered old Borrhomeo.

"Do you remember, *signor*, that nightmare, as we jocularly called it, at the sign of the 'Red Hat'?"

"Yes."

"Well, a man who having swallowed the elixir *vitæ*, suffers that sort of shock which in other mortals is a violent death, is afflicted during the remainder of his period of life, whether he be decapitated, or dismembered, or is laid unmutilated in the grave, with that sort of catalepsy, which you experienced for a minute—a catalepsy that does not relax or intermit. For that reason you ought to have carefully avoided this predicament."

"'Tis a lie," roared the old man, and he ground his teeth, *that's* not living."

"You'll find, upon my honour, that it is living," answered the fiend, with a gentle smile, and withdrawing from the cell.

Borrhomeo told all this to a priest, not under seal of confession, but to induce him to plead for his life. But the good man seeing he had already made himself the liegeman and accomplice of Satan, refused. Nor would his intercession have prevailed in any wise.

So Borrhomeo was hanged, impaled, and buried, according to his sentence; and it came to pass that fourteen years afterwards, that grave was opened in making a great drain from the group of houses thereby, and Borrhomeo was found just as he was laid therein, in no wise decayed, but fresh and sound, which, indeed, showed that there did remain in him that sort of life which was supposed to ward off the common consequences of death.

So he was thrown into a great pit, and with many curses, covered in with stones and earth, where his stupendous punishment proceeds.

Get thee hence, Satan.

Catherine's Quest

Imagine to yourself an old, rambling, red-brick house, with odd corners and gables here and there, all bound and clasped together with ivy, and you have Craymoor Grange. It was built long before Queen Elizabeth's time, and that illustrious monarch is said to have slept in it in one of her royal progresses—as where has she not slept?

There still remain some remnants of bygone ages, although it has been much modernized and added to in later days. Among these are the brewhouse and laundry—formerly, it is said, dining-hall and ball-room. The latter of these is chiefly remarkable for an immense arched window, such as you see in churches, with five lights.

When we came to the Grange this window had been partially blocked up, and in front of it, up to one-third of its height, was a wooden dais, or platform, on which stood a cumbrous mangle, left there, I suppose, by the last tenants of the house.

Of these last tenants we knew very little, for it was so long since it had been inhabited that the oldest authority in the village could not remember it.

There were, however, some half-defaced monuments in the village church of Craymoor, bearing the figures and escutcheons of knights and dames of "the old family," as the villagers said; but the inscriptions were worn and almost illegible, and for some time we none of us took the pains to decipher them.

We first came to Craymoor Grange in the summer of 1849, my husband having discovered the place in one of his rambles, and taken a fancy to it. At first I certainly thought we could never make it our home, it was so dilapidated and tumble-down; but by the time winter came on we had had several repairs done and alterations made, and the rooms really became quite presentable.

As our family was small we confined ourselves chiefly to the newest part of the house, leaving the older rooms to the mice, dust, and darkness. We made use of two of the old rooms, however, one as a servants' bedroom and the other as an extra spare chamber, in case of many visitors. For myself, though I hope I am neither nervous nor superstitious, I confess that I would rather sleep in "our wing," as we called the part of the house we inhabited, than in any of the old rooms.

When Catherine l'Estrange came to us, however, during our first Christmas at Craymoor, I found that she was troubled with no such fancies, but declared that she delighted in queer old rooms, with raftered ceilings and deep window-seats, such as ours, and begged to be allowed to occupy the spare chamber. This I readily acceded to, as we had several visitors, and needed all the available rooms.

As my story has principally to do with Catherine l'Estrange, I suppose I ought to speak more fully about her. She was an old school-friend of my daughter Ella, and at the time of which I am speaking was just one-and-twenty, and the merriest girl I ever knew. She had stayed with us once or twice before we came to the Grange, but we then knew no other particulars concerning her family, than that her father had been an Indian officer, and that he and her mother had both died in India when she was about six years old, leaving her to the care of an aunt living in England.

I now, after a long, and I fear a tedious, preamble, come to my story.

On the eve of the new year of 1850, Catherine had a very bad sore throat, and was obliged, though sorely against her inclination, to stay in bed all day, and forego our small evening gayety.

At about 6 o'clock p.m., Ella took her some tea, and fearing she would be dull, offered to stay with her during the evening. This, however, Catherine would not hear of. "You go and entertain your company," said she laughingly, "and leave me to my own devices; I feel very lazy, and I dare say I shall go to sleep." As she had not slept much on the preceding night, Ella thought it was the best thing she could do; so she went out by the door leading on to the corridor, first placing the night-lamp on a table behind the door opening on to the laundry, so that it might not shine in her face.

She did not again visit Catherine's room until reminded to do so by my son George, at about half-past ten. She then rapped at the door, and receiving no answer, opened it softly, and approached the bed. Catherine lay quite still, and Ella imagined her to be asleep. She therefore returned to the drawing-room without disturbing her.

As it was New Year's eve, we stayed up "to see the old year out and the new year in," and at a few minutes to twelve we all gathered round the open window on the stairs to hear the chimes ring out from the village church.

We were all listening breathlessly as the hall-clock struck twelve, when a piercing cry suddenly echoed through the house, causing us all to start in alarm. I knew that it could only proceed from Catherine's room, for the servants were all assembled at the window beneath us, listening, like ourselves, for the chimes. Thither therefore I flew, followed by Ella, and we found poor Catherine in a truly pitiable state.

She was deadly pale, in an agony of terror, and the perspiration stood in large drops upon her forehead. It was some time before we could succeed at all in composing her, and her first words were to implore us to take her into another room.

She was too weak to stand, so we wrapped her in blankets, and carried her into Ella's bedroom. I noticed that as she was taken through the laundry she shuddered, and put her hands before her eyes. When she was laid on Ella's bed she grew calmer, and apologized for the trouble she had caused, saying that she had had a dreadful dream.

With this explanation we were fain to be content, though I thought it hardly accounted for her excessive terror. I had observed, however, that any allusion to what had passed caused her to tremble and turn pale again, and I thought it best to refrain from exciting her further.

When morning came I found Catherine almost her usual self again; but I persuaded her to remain in bed until the evening, as her cold was not much better. Ella's curiosity to hear the dream which had so much excited her friend could now no longer be restrained; but whenever she asked to hear it, Catherine said, "Not now; another time, perhaps, I may tell you."

When she came down to dinner in the evening, we noticed that she was peculiarly silent, and we endeavoured to rally her into her usual spirits, but in vain. She tried to laugh and to appear merry, poor child; but there was evidently something on her mind.

At last, as we all sat round the fire after dinner, she spoke. She addressed herself to my husband, but the tone of her voice caused us all to listen.

"Mr. Fanshawe, I have something to ask of you," said she, and then paused.

"Ask on," said Mr. Fanshawe.

"I know that you will think the request I am going to make a peculiar one; but I have a particular reason for making it," continued she. "It is that you will have the wooden dais in front of the laundry window removed."

Mr. Fanshawe certainly was taken aback, as were we all. When he had mastered his bewilderment, and assured himself that he had heard aright—

"It is, indeed, a strange request, my dear Catherine," said he; "what can be your reason for asking such a thing?"

"If you will only have it done, and not question me, you will understand my reason," answered Catherine.

Mr. Fanshawe demurred, however, thinking it some foolish whim, and at last Catherine said:

"I must tell you why I wish it done, then: I am sure we shall discover something underneath."

At this we all looked at one another in extreme bewilderment.

"Discover something underneath? No doubt we should—cobwebs, probably, and dust and spiders," answered Mr. Fanshawe, much amused.

But Catherine was not to be laughed down.

"Only do as I wish," said she beseechingly, "and you will see. If you find nothing underneath the dais but cobwebs and dust, then you may laugh at me as much as you like." And I saw that she was serious, for tears were actually gathering in her eyes. Of course we were all very anxious to know what Catherine expected to find, and how she came to suspect that there was anything to be found; but she would not say, and begged us all not to question her.

And now George took upon himself to interfere.

"Let us do as Catherine wishes, father," said he; "the dais spoils the laundry, and would be much better away."

"Well, well," said Mr. Fanshawe, "do as you like, only I shall expect my share of the treasure that is found.—And now," added he, "you must have a glass of wine to warm you, Catherine, for you look sadly pale, child."

Here the conversation changed, though we often alluded to the subject again during the evening.

The next morning the first thing in all our thoughts was Catherine's singular request.

I think Mr. Fanshawe had hoped she would have forgotten it, but such was not the case; on the contrary, she enlisted George's services the first thing after breakfast to carry out her design, and they left the room together, accompanied by Ella.

It was a snowy morning, and Mr. Fanshawe was obliged to be away from home all day on business, so I was quite at a loss how to entertain my numerous guests successfully. Happily for me, however, the mystery attendant on the removal of the dais in the laundry charmed them all; and I have to thank Catherine for contributing to their amusement much better than I could possibly have done.

Not long after the disappearance of Catherine, Ella, and George, a message was sent to us in the drawing-room requesting our presence in the laundry; and on all flocking there with more or less eagerness, we found a fire burning on the old-fashioned hearth and chairs arranged round it.

It appeared that with the help of Sam, our factotum, who was a kind of Jack-of-all-trades, George had succeeded in loosening the planks of the dais, which, although strongly put together, were rotten and worm-eaten, and that we were now summoned to be witnesses of its removal. We found Catherine trembling with a strange eagerness, and her face quite pale with excitement. This was shared by Ella and George; and, judging by the important expression on their faces, I fancied they were let further into the secret than anyone else.

We all sat down in the chairs placed for our accommodation, and the wild whistling of the wind in the huge chimney, together with the sheets of snow which darkened the window-panes, enhanced the mystery of the whole affair, while George and his coadjutor worked lustily on.

At length, after a great deal of panting and puffing, George was heard to exclaim, "Now for the tug of war!" and there followed a minute's pause, and then a crash as the loosened planks were torn asunder, and a cloud of dust enveloped both workmen and spectators.

Involuntarily we all started forward, and a moment of the direst confusion ensued, during which the boys of our party greatly endangered their limbs among the broken boards.

"By George!" exclaimed my son at last—in his eagerness invoking his patron saint—as he stumbled upon something, "there is something here and no mistake;" and, hastily clearing away the rubbish and clinging cobwebs, he disclosed to view what proved on examination to be an immense oaken chest, about four feet in height, heavily carved, and ornamented with brass mouldings corroded with age and damp.

Here was a piece of excitement indeed; never in my most imaginative moments had I thought of anything so mysterious as this. The most sceptical among us grew interested.

"Oh, do open it!" cried Ella, when the first exclamations of surprise were over.

"Easier to say than to do, miss," replied Sam, exerting his Herculean strength in vain. With the aid of a hammer and the kitchen-poker, however, he at last succeeded in forcing it open. We all pressed forward eagerly to peer inside. There was something in it certainly, but we none of us could determine what, until Sam, who was the boldest of us all, thrust in his hand and brought forth—something which caused the bravest to start with horror, while poor Catherine sank down, white and trembling, upon the littered floor. It was a bone, to which adhered fragments of decaying silk.

The consternation and conjectures which followed can be better imagined than described. Seeing the effects of the discovery upon Catherine, and indeed upon all, I bade Sam replace it in the chest, which George closed again, to be left until Mr. Fanshawe came home and could investigate the matter.

The rest of the day I passed in attending to Catherine, who seemed much shocked and overcome by what she had seen, and in trying to divert my guests' thoughts from the subject, and dispel the gloom which had gathered over all. In this I succeeded only partially, and never did I welcome my husband's return more gladly than on that evening.

On his arrival I would not let him be disturbed by the relation of what had happened until he had finished his dinner, and it was not till we were gathered as usual round the fire that George related the whole story to him.

When he ended the two gentlemen left the room together, in order that Mr. Fanshawe might verify by his own eyes what he would hardly believe.

They were some time gone, and on their return I noticed that my husband held in his hand an old piece of soiled parchment, with mouldy seals affixed to it.

"We certainly have discovered much more than I thought for, Catherine," said he, "and possibly more than you thought for either." Here he paused for her to reply, but she did not.

"The bones are most probably those of some animal," added he—I fancied I could detect a certain anxiety in his tone that belied what he said; "but in order to quell the active imaginations which I can see are running away with some of you"—here he looked round with a smile—"I will send for Dr. Driscoll to come and examine them tomorrow. I have also found a piece of parchment in the chest," he added; "but I have not yet looked at its contents."

"Before you do that, Mr. Fanshawe, and before you send for the surgeon," interrupted Catherine suddenly in a clear voice, "I think I can tell you all about the bones found in the chest, and how I guessed them to be there."

"I should certainly be very glad to be told," my husband admitted, much surprised; "though how you can possibly know, I cannot surmise."

"Listen, and I will tell you," answered Catherine; and feeling very glad that our curiosity was at last to be gratified, we all "pricked up our ears," as George would say, to listen.

I here transcribe Catherine's story word for word, as my son George subsequently wrote it down from her dictation.

★ ★ ★ ★ ★

"You all remember," she began, "my alarming you on New Year's eve at midnight, and that I told you I was disturbed by a dreadful dream.

"I said so because I thought you would make fun of me if I called it a vision; and yet it was much more like a vision, for I seemed to see it waking, and it was more vivid and consecutive than any dream I ever had.

"Before I try to describe it, I want you all to understand that I seemed intuitively to comprehend what I saw, and to recognize all the figures which appeared before me, and their relation to one another, though I am sure I never beheld them before in my life.

"When Ella left me that night, I lay propped up with pillows, staring idly at the strange shadows thrown by the hidden lamp across the laundry ceiling and over the floor. As I looked it seemed to me that a change came over the room—a most unaccountable change.

"Instead of the blocked-up window, the rusty mangle, and the dais at the farther end, I saw the window clear and distinct from top to bottom, and in front of a deep window-seat at its base stood an oaken chest, exactly corresponding to the one discovered this morning. The room seemed brilliantly lighted, and everything was clearly and distinctly visible; and not only was it changed, but also peopled.

"Many figures passed up and down; brocaded silks swept the floor, and old-world forms of men in strange costumes bowed in courtly style to the dames by their side. Among all these figures I noticed only one couple particularly, and I knew them to be bride and bridegroom. The man was tall and broad, with dark hair and eyes, and a sensual and cruel face. He seemed, however, to be quite enslaved by the woman by his side, whom I hardly even now like to think of, there was something to me so repellent in her presence.

"She was tall and of middle age, and would have been handsome were it not for a sinister expression in her dark flashing eyes, which was enhanced by the black eyebrows which met over them.

"She reminded me irresistibly of the effigy on the stone monument in Craymoor church, which Ella and I named "the wicked woman."

"As I gazed on the strange scene before me I presently became aware of three other figures which I had not noticed before. They were standing in a small arched doorway in one corner of the room (where the servants' bedroom now is) furtively watching the gay company. One was a pale, careworn woman, apparently of about five-and-thirty, still beautiful, though haggard and mournful-looking, with blue eyes and a fair complexion.

"Her hands rested on the shoulders of two children, one a

526

boy and the other a girl, of about ten and eleven years of age respectively. They much resembled their mother, and, like her, they were meanly dressed, though no poverty of attire could hide the nobility of their aspect. I noticed that the mother's eyes rested chiefly on the face of the tall stately man before mentioned, who seemed unaware or careless of her presence; and instinctively I knew him to be the father of her children and the blighter of her life.

"As I looked and beheld all this, the lights vanished, the company disappeared, and the room became dark and deserted. No, not quite deserted, for I presently distinguished, seated on the window-seat by the old oaken chest, the fair woman and her children again.

"The moonlight now streamed through the window upon the woman's face, making it appear more ghastly and haggard than before. In her long thin fingers she was holding up to the light a necklace of large pearls, curiously interwoven in a diamond pattern, and on this the children's eyes were fixed.

"She then hung it on the girl's fair neck, who hid it in her bosom. Both children then twined their arms round their mother and kissed her repeatedly, while her head sank lower and lower, and the paleness of death overspread her features.

"This scene faded away as the other had done, and I saw the fair woman no more.

"Then it seemed to me that many figures passed and repassed before the window—the wicked woman (as I shall call her to distinguish her), accompanied by a boy the image of herself, whom I knew to be her son. He was apparently older than the fair-haired children, who also passed to and fro, attired as servants, and generally employed in some menial work.

"At last the wicked woman's son, with haughty gestures, ordered the other boy to pick up something that lay on the ground, and when he refused, he raised his cane as though to strike him. Before he could do so, however, the boy flew at him, and they engaged in a fierce struggle.

"In the midst of this the wicked woman, whom I had learned

to dread, came forward and separated them; after which she pointed imperiously to the door, and signed to the younger boy to go out.

"He obeyed her mandate, but first threw his arms round his sister in a last embrace, and she detached the pearl necklace from off her neck and gave it to him. He then went out, waving a last *adieu* to her, and I saw him no more.

"Confused images seemed to crowd before me after this, and I remember nothing clearly until I beheld an infirm and tottering figure led away through the arched doorway, in whom I recognized the tall and stately man I had first seen in company with the wicked woman, but who was now an old man, apparently being supported to his bed to die. As he passed out he laid one trembling hand upon the head of the fair girl, now a blooming woman, and a softer shade came over his face. This the wicked woman noted, and she marked her disapproval by a vindictive frown.

"She also was older-looking, but age had in no degree softened her features; on the contrary, they appeared to me to wear a harsher expression than before.

"In the next scene which came before me, the wicked woman's son was evidently making love to the girl. Both were standing by the old window-seat, but her face was resolutely turned away from him, and when she at last looked at him it was with an expression of uncontrollable horror and dislike.

"Again this scene changed as those before it had done; the young man was gone, and only the light of a grated lantern illumined the room, or rather made darkness visible. The wicked woman was the only occupant of the laundry; she was kneeling by the oaken chest, trying to raise the heavy lid. In her left hand she held a piece of parchment, with large red seals pendent from it. I knew it to be the old man's will which she was hiding, thus defrauding the just claimants of their rights.

"Her hands trembled, and her whole appearance denoted guilty trepidation. At length, however, the lid was raised, but just as she was about to replace the parchment in the chest, a figure glided silently from a dark corner of the window-seat and confronted her. It was the fair girl, pale, resolute, and extending her hand to claim the will.

"After the first guilty start, which caused her to drop the parchment into the chest, the wicked woman hurriedly tried to close the lid. Her efforts were frustrated, however, by the girl, who leaned with all her force upon it, keeping it back, and still held out her hand as before.

"There followed a pause, which seemed to me very long, but which could in reality have only lasted a minute.

"It was broken by the wicked woman, who, hastily casting a glance behind her into the gloom of the darkened chamber, then seized the girl by the arm and dragged her with all her force into the chest. It was but the work of a moment, for the woman was much the more powerful of the two, and the poor victim was too much taken by surprise to make much resistance. I saw one despairing look in her face as her murderess flashed the lantern before it with a hideous gleam of triumph.

"Then the lid was pressed down upon her, and I saw no more, only I felt an unutterable terror, and tried in vain to scream.

"This was not all the vision, however, for before I had mastered my terror the scene was superseded by another.

"This time it was twilight, and the wicked woman and her son were together. The son seemed to be talking eagerly, and grew more and more excited, while the mother stood still and erect, with a malicious smile upon her lips. Presently she moved toward the chest with a fell purpose in her eyes, unlocked it with a key which hung from her girdle, raised the lid and disclosed the contents.

"I understood it all now: the son was asking for the girl whom he had loved, and whom on his return home he missed, and the wicked woman, enraged at hearing for the first time that he had loved her, was determined to have her revenge.

"He should see her again.

"On beholding the dread contents of the chest, the man staggered back horrified; then, doubtless comprehending the case, he turned suddenly upon the murderess, and threw his arm around her, and there ensued a struggle terrible to witness.

"Her proud triumphant glance of malice was now succeeded by one of abject fear, and, as his strength began to gain the mastery, of despair.

"His iron frame heaved for a moment with the violence of his efforts, the next he had forced her down into the chest upon the mouldering body of her victim. I saw her eyes light up with the terror of death for one second, and then her screams were stifled forever beneath the massive lid.

"The horror of this scene was too much for me; I found voice to scream at last, and I suppose it was my cry which alarmed you all."

When Catherine ceased speaking there was a profound silence for a minute, which Mr. Fanshawe was the first to break as he said with a peculiar intonation in his voice, "It is very strange, very unaccountable," re-echoing all our thoughts.

Now it happened that Mr. Fleet, our family lawyer, was among our guests that Christmas-time, and since the discovery of the chest and bones had taken a great interest in the whole affair. He now questioned and cross-questioned Catherine, and seemed quite satisfied with the result.

"This would have made a fine case," said he, "if only it had been a question of the right of succession, for any lawyer to make out; but unfortunately the events are too long past to have any bearing upon the present." (There Mr. Fleet was wrong, though we none of us knew it at the time.)

We now all launched forth into conjectures and opinions, during which Catherine lay still and weary upon the sofa. I saw this, and thought it quite time to put an end to the day's adventures by suggesting a retirement for the night, and we were soon all dispersed to dream of the mysterious vision and discovery.

* * * * *

I think we were none of us sorry when morning dawned without any further tragedy (by *us*, I mean the female part of the establishment).

When I came down to breakfast I found Mr. Fleet very active on the subject of the night before.

"A surgeon ought to be immediately sent for to pronounce an opinion on the contents of the chest," he said; and Dr. Driscoll presently came, and after examining the bones minutely, decided that they were, as we thought, those of two females, who might have been from one to two hundred years dead.

Mr. Fleet next offered to decipher the will, for such he imagined the parchment to be, and he and Mr. Fanshawe were closeted together for some time.

When they at last appeared again, they looked much interested and excited, and led me away to inform me of the result of their examination.

They told me that the document had proved to be a will, but that there was a circumstance connected with it which greatly added to the mystery of the whole business. This was the mention of the name of L'Estrange. I was, of course, as much surprised as they, and heard the will read with great interest.

I cannot remember the technical terms in which it was expressed. Mr. Fleet read me the translation he had made, for the original was in old English; but it was to this effect:

It purported to be the will of Reginald, Viscount St. Aubyn, in which he bequeathed all his inheritance to his lawful son Francis St. Aubyn—commonly known by the name of Francis l'Estrange—and to his heirs forever. It was signed Reginald, Viscount St. Aubyn, and the witnesses were John Murray and Phoebe Brett, who in the old copy had each affixed their mark.

Mr. Fleet affirmed that it was a perfectly legal document, but this was not all it contained.

There was an appendix which our lawyer translated as follows:

"In order to avoid all disputes and doubts which might otherwise arise, I do hereby declare that my lawful wife was Editha, youngest daughter of Francis l'Estrange, Baronet, and that the register of our marriage may be seen in the church of St. Andrew, Haslet. By this marriage we had two children, a son

Francis, and a daughter Catherine, commonly called Francis and Catherine l'Estrange. And I hereby declare that Agatha Thornhaugh was not legally married to me as she imagined, my lawful wife being alive at the time; neither do I leave to her son by her first husband, Ralph Thornhaugh, any part or share in my inheritance."

Both the will and the writing at the foot of it were dated the 14th of May, 1668.

This accumulation of mysteries caused me for a time to feel quite bewildered and unable to think, but Mr. Fleet was in his element.

"Here is a case worth entering into," said he, and he further went on to state that he had no doubt that the L'Estranges mentioned in the will were our Catherine's ancestors, the Christian names being similar rendering it more than probable. She was most likely a direct descendant of Francis l'Estrange, the heir mentioned in the will, who was no doubt also the fair-haired boy Catherine had seen in her vision.

The bones were those of his sister, the murdered Catherine l'Estrange, and of her murderess Agatha Thornhaugh, herself immured by her own son; but the matter ought not to rest on mere surmise, and the first place to go to for corroborating evidence was Craymoor church.

The rapidity with which Mr. Fleet came to his conclusions increased my bewilderment, and I was at a loss to know what evidence he expected to gain from Craymoor church. He reminded me, however, of Catherine's statement that "the wicked woman" of her vision resembled the effigy on the monument there.

Thither, then, the lawyer repaired, accompanied by Mr. Fanshawe and George. It was thought best to keep the sequel of the story from Catherine and the others until it was explained more fully, as Mr. Fleet boldly affirmed it should be. I awaited anxiously the result of their researches, and they exceeded I think even our good investigator's hopes.

Not only had they deciphered the inscription round the old

monument, but with leave from the clergyman and the assistance of the sexton they had disinterred the coffin and found it to be filled with stones.

I am aware that this was rather an illegal proceeding, but as Mr. Fleet was only acting *en amateur* and not professionally, he did not stick at trifles.

The inscription was in Latin, and stated that the tomb was erected in memory of Agatha, wife of Reginald, Viscount St. Aubyn, who was buried beneath, and who died on the 31st day of December, 1649—exactly two hundred years before the day on which Catherine had seen the vision.

I could not help thinking it shocking that the villagers had for two centuries been worshipping in the presence of a perpetual lie, but Mr. Fleet thought only of the grand corroboration of his "case." He applied to Mr. Fanshawe to take the next step, namely, to write to Catherine's aunt and only living relative, to tell her the whole story, and beg her to assist in elucidating matters by giving all the information she could respecting the L'Estrange family.

This was done, and we anxiously awaited the answer. Meantime, all my guests were clamorous to hear the contents of the will, and I had to appease them as best I could, by promising that they should know all soon.

In a few days, old Miss l'Estrange's answer came. She said her brother, father, and grandfather had all served in India, and that she believed her great-grandfather, who was a Francis l'Estrange, to have passed most of his life abroad, there having been a cloud over his early youth. What this was, however, she could not say. She affirmed that the L'Estranges had in old times resided in ——shire; and she further stated that her father's family had consisted of herself and her brother, whose only child Catherine was.

This was certainly not much information, but it was enough for our purpose. We no longer remained in doubt as to the truth of Mr. Fleet's version of the story, and when he himself told it to all our family-party one evening, everyone agreed that he had certainly succeeded in making out a very clever case.

As for Catherine, on being told that the figures she had be-held in the vision were thought to be those of her ancestors, she was not so much surprised as I expected, but said that she had had a presentiment all along that the tragedies she had witnessed were in some way connected with her own family.

I must not forget to say that on ascertaining that the parish church of Haslet was still standing, we searched the register, and another link of evidence was made clear by the finding of the looked-for entry.

There remains little more to be told. The charge of the old will was committed to Mr. Fleet, and Catherine's story has been carefully laid up among the archives of our family. I say advis-edly of *our* family, for the line of the L'Estranges, alias St. Aubyns, has been united to ours by the marriage of Catherine to my son George, which took place in 1850.

I who write this am an old woman now, but I still live with my son and daughter-in-law.

George has bought Craymoor Grange, thus rendering justice after the lapse of two centuries, and restoring the inheritance of her fathers to the rightful owner.

I have but one more incident to relate, and I have done. A short time ago, old Miss l'Estrange died, bequeathing all her worldly possessions to Catherine. Among these were some old family relics. Catherine was looking over them as George un-packed them, and she presently came to a miniature of a young and beautiful girl with fair hair and blue eyes, and a wistful ex-pression, and with it a necklace of pearls strung in a diamond pattern. On seeing these she became suddenly grave, and hand-ing them to me, said: "They are the same; the young girl, and the pearl necklace I told you of." No more was said at the time, for the children were present, and we had always avoided alluding to the horrible family tragedy before them; but if we had still retained any doubt about its truth—which we had not—this would have set it at rest.

If you were to visit Craymoor Grange now, you would find

no old laundry. The part of the house containing it has been pulled down, and children play and chickens peckett on the ground where it once stood.

The oaken chest has also long since been destroyed.

Devereux's Dream

I give you this story only at second-hand; but you have it in substance—and he wasted few words over it—as Paul Devereux told it me.

It was not the only queer story he could have told about himself if he had chosen, by a good many, I should say. Paul's life had been an eminently unconventional one: the man's face certified to that—hard, bronzed, war-worn, seamed and scarred with strange battle-marks—the face of a man who had dared and done most things.

It was not his custom to speak much of what he had done, however. Probably only because he and I were little likely to meet again that he told me this I am free to tell you now.

We had come across one another for the first time for years that afternoon on the Italian Boulevart. Paul had landed a couple of weeks previously at Marseilles from a long yacht-cruise in southern waters, the monotony of which we heard had been agreeably diversified by a little pirate-hunting and slaver-chasing—the evil tongues called it piracy and slave-running; and certainly Devereux was quite equal to either *metier*, and he was about starting on a promising little filibustering expedition across the Atlantic, where the chances were he would be shot, and the certainty was that he would be starved. So perhaps he felt inclined to be a trifle more communicative than usual, as we sat late that night over a blazing pyre of logs and in a cloud of Cavendish. At all events he was, and after this fashion.

I forget now exactly how the subject was led up to. Expression of some philosophic incredulity on my part regarding certain matters, followed by a ten-minutes' silence on his side pregnant with unwonted words to come—that was it, perhaps. At last he said, more to himself, it seemed, than to me:

"'Such stuff as dreams are made of.' Well, who knows? You're a Sadducee, Bertie; you call this sort of thing, politely, indigestion. Perhaps you're right. But yet I had a queer dream once."

"Not unlikely," I assented.

"You're wrong; I never dream, as a rule. But, as I say, I had a queer dream once; and queer because it came literally true three years afterward."

"Queer indeed, Paul."

"Happens to be true. What's queerer still, my dream was the means of my finding a man I owed a long score, and a heavy one, and of my paying him in full."

"Bad for the payee!" I thought.

Paul's face had grown terribly eloquent as he spoke those last words. On a sudden the expression of it changed—another memory was stirring in him. Wonderfully tender the fierce eyes grew; wonderfully tender the faint, sad smile, that was like sunshine on storm-scathed granite. That smile transfigured the man before me.

"Ah, poor child—poor Lucille!" I heard him mutter.

That was it, was it? So I let him be. Presently he lifted his head. If he had let himself get the least thing out of hand for a moment, he had got back his self-mastery the next.

"I'll tell you that queer story, Bertie, if you like," he said.

The proposition was flatteringly unusual, but the voice was quite his own.

"Somehow I'd sooner talk than think about—*her*," he went on after a pause.

I nodded. He might talk about this, you see, but *I* couldn't. He began with a question—an odd one:

"Did you ever hear I'd been married?"

Paul Devereux and a wife had always seemed and been to me a most unheard-of conjunction. So I laconically said:

"No."

"Well, I was once, years ago. She was my wife—that child—for a week. And then——"

I easily filled up the pause; but, as it happened, I filled it up wrongly; for he added:

"And then she was murdered."

I was not unused to our Paul's stony style of talk; but this last sentence was sufficiently startling.

"Eh?"

"Murdered—in her sleep. They never found the man who did it either, though I had Durbec and all the Rue de Jerusalem at work. But I forgave them that, for I found the man myself, and killed him."

He was filling his pipe again as he told me this, and he perhaps rammed the Cavendish in a little tighter, but that was all. The thing was a matter of course; I knew my Paul, well enough to know that. Of course he killed him.

"Mind you," he continued, kindling the black *brule-gueule* the while—"mind you, I'd never seen this man before, never known of his existence, except in a way that—however, it was this way."

He let his grizzled head drop back on the cushions of his chair, and his eyes seemed to see the queer story he was telling enacted once more before him in the red hollows of the fire.

"As I said, it was years ago. I was waiting here in Paris for some fellows who were to join me in a campaign we'd arranged against the African big game. I never was more fit for anything of that sort than I was then. I only tell you this to show you that the thing can't be accounted for by my nerves having been out of order at all.

"Well: I was dining alone that day, at the Cafe Anglais. It was late when I sat down to my dinner in the little salon as usual. Only two other men were still lingering over theirs. All the time they stayed they bored me so persistently with some confounded story of a murder they were discussing, that I was once or twice more than half-inclined to tell them so. At last, though, they went away.

"But their talk kept buzzing abominably in my head. When the waiter brought me the evening paper, the first thing that caught my eye was a circumstantial account of the *probable* way the fellow did his murder. I say probable, for they never caught him; and, as you will see directly, they could only suppose how it occurred.

"It seemed that a well-known Paris banker, who was ascertained beyond doubt to have left one station alive and well, and with a couple of hundred thousand *francs* in a leathern *sac* under his seat, arrived at the next station the train stopped at with his throat cut and *minus* all his money, except a few banknotes to no great amount, which the assassin had been wise enough to leave behind him. The train was a night express on one of the southern lines; the banker travelled quite alone, in a first-class carriage; and the murder must have taken place between midnight and 1 a.m. next morning. The newspapers supposed-rightly enough, I think—that the murderer must have entered the carriage *from without*, stabbed his victim in his sleep—there were no signs of any struggle—opened the *sac*, taken what he wanted, and retreated, loot and all, by the way he came. I fully indorsed my particular writer's opinion that the murderer was an uncommonly cool and clever individual, especially as I fancy he got clear off and was never afterward laid hands on.

"When I had done that I thought I had done with the affair altogether. Not at all. I was regularly ridden with this confounded murder. You see the banker was rather a swell; everybody knew him: and that, of course, made it so shocking. So everybody kept talking about him: they were talking about him at the Opera, and over the *baccarat* and *bouillotte* at La Topaze's later. To escape him I went to bed and smoked myself to sleep. And then a queer thing came to pass: I had a dream—I who never dream; and this is what I dreamed:

"I saw a wide, rich country that I knew. A starless night hung over it like a pall. I saw a narrow track running through it, straight, both ways, for leagues. Something sped along this track with a hurtling rush and roar. This something that at first had looked like a red-eyed devil, with dark sides full of dim fire, resolved itself, as I watched it, presently, into a more conventional night express-train. It flew along, though, as no express-train ever travelled yet; for all that, I was able to keep it quite easily in view. I could count the carriages as they whirled by. One— two—three—four—five—six; but I could only see distinctly into one. Into that one with perfect distinctness. Into that one I seemed forced to look.

"It was the fourth carriage. Two people were in it. They sat in opposite corners; both were sleeping. The one who sat facing forward was a woman—a girl, rather. I could see that; but I couldn't see her face. The blind was drawn across the lamp in the roof, and the light was very dim; moreover, this girl lay back in the shadow. Yet I seemed to know her, and I knew that her face was very fair. She wore a cloak that shrouded her form completely, yet her form was familiar to me.

"The figure opposite to her was a man's. Strangely familiar to me too this figure was. But, as he slept, his head had sunk upon his breast, and the shadow cast upon his face by the low-drawn travelling-cap he wore hid it from me. Yet if I had seemed to know the girl's face, I was certain I knew the man's. But as I could see, so I could remember, neither. And there was an absolute torture in this which I can't explain to you,—in this inability, and in my inability to wake them from their sleep.

"From the first I had been conscious of a desire to do that. This desire grew stronger every second. I tried to call to them, and my tongue wouldn't move. I tried to spring toward them, to thrust out my arms and touch them, and my limbs were paralyzed. And then I tried to shut my eyes to what I *knew* must happen, and my eyes were held open and dragged to look on in spite of me. And I saw this:

"I saw the door of the carriage where these two sleepers, whose sleep was so horribly sound, were sitting—I saw this door open, and out of the thick darkness another face look in.

"The light, as I have said, was very dim, but I could see his face as plainly as I can see yours. A large yellow face it was, like a wax mask. The lips were full, and lustful and cruel. The eyes were little eyes of an evil gray. Thin yellow streaks marked the absence of the eyebrows; thin yellow hair showed itself under a huge fur travelling-cap. The whole face seemed to grow slowly into absolute distinctness as I looked, by the sort of devilish light that it, as it were, radiated. I had chanced upon a good many damnable visages before then; but there was a cold fiendishness about this one such as I had seen on no man's face, alive or dead, till then.

"The next moment the man this face belonged to was standing in the carriage, that seemed to plunge and sway more furiously, as though to waken them that still slept on. He wore a long fur travelling-robe, girt about the waist with a fur girdle. Abnormally tall and broad as he was, he looked in this dress gigantic. Yet there was a marvellous cat-like lightness and agility about all his movements.

"He bent over the girl lying there helpless in her sleep. I don't make rash bargains as a rule, but I felt I would have given years of my life for five minutes of my lost freedom of limb just then. I tell you the torture was infernal.

"The assassin—I knew he was an assassin—bent awhile, gloatingly, over the girl. His great yellow hands were both bare, and on the forefinger of the right hand I could see some great stone blazing like an evil eye. In that right hand there gleamed something else. I saw him draw it slowly from his sleeve, and, as he drew it, turn round and look at the other sleeper with an infernal triumphant malignity and hate the Devil himself might have envied. But the man he looked at slept heavily on. And then—God! I feel the agony I felt in my dream then now!-then I saw the great yellow hand, with the great evil eye upon it, lifted murderously, and the bright steel it held shimmer as the assassin turned again and bent his yellow face down closer to that other face hidden from me in the shadow—the girl's face, that I knew was so fair.

"How can I tell this?. . . The blade flashed and fell. . . . There was the sound of a heavy sigh stifled under a heavy hand. . . .

"Then the huge form of the assassin was reared erect, and the bloated yellow face seemed to laugh silently, while the hand that held the steel pointed at the sleeping man in diabolical menace.

"And so the huge form and the bloated yellow face seemed to fade away while I watched.

"The express rushed and roared through the blinding darkness without; the sleeping man slept on still; till suddenly a strong light fell full upon him, and he woke.

"And then I saw why I had been so certain that I knew him. For as he lifted his head, I saw his face in the strong light.

"*And the face was my own face; and the sleeper was myself!*"

Paul Devereux made a pause in his queer story here. Except when he had spoken of the girl, he had spoken in his usual cool, hard way. The pipe he had been smoking all the time was smoked out. He took time to fill another before he went on. I said never a word, for I guessed who the sleeping girl was.

"Well," Paul remarked presently, "that was a devilish queer dream, wasn't it? You'll account for it by telling me I'd been so pestered with the story of the banker's murder that I naturally had nightmare; perhaps, too, that my digestion was out of order. Call it a nightmare, call it dyspepsia, if you like. I *don't*, because— But you'll see why I don't directly.

"At the same moment that my dream-self awoke in my dream, my actual self woke in reality, and with the same ghastly horror.

"I say the *same* horror, for neither then nor afterward could I separate my oneself from my other self. They seemed identical; so that this queer dream made a more lasting impression upon me than you'd think. However, in the life I led that sort of thing couldn't last very long. Before I came back from Africa I had utterly forgotten all about it. Before I left Paris, though, and while it was quite fresh in my memory, I sketched the big murderer just as I had seen him in my dream. The great yellow face, the great broad frame in the fur travelling-robe, the great hand with the great evil eye upon it—everything, carefully and minutely, as though I had been going to paint a portrait that I wanted to make lifelike. I think at the time I had some such intention. If I had, I never fulfilled it. But I made the sketch, as I say, carefully; and then I forgot all about it.

"Time passed—three years nearly. I was wintering in the south of France that year. There it was that I met her—Lucille. Old D'Avray, her father, and I had met before in Algeria. He was dying now. He left the child on his deathbed to me. The end was I married her.

"Poor little thing! I think I might have made her happy—who knows? She used to tell me often she was happy with me. Poor little thing!

"Well, we were to come straight to London. That was Lucille's notion. She wanted to go to my London first—nowhere else. Now I would rather have gone anywhere else; but, naturally, I let the child have her way. She seemed nervously eager about it, I remembered afterward; seemed to have a nervous objection to every other place I proposed. But I saw or suspected nothing to make me question her very closely, or the reasons for her preference for our grimy old Pandemonium. What could I suspect? Not the truth. If I only had! If I had only guessed what it was that made her, as she said, long to be safe there already. Safe? What had she to fear with me? Ah, what indeed!

"So we started on our journey to England. It was a cold, dark night, early in March. We reached Lyons somewhere about seven. I should have stayed there that night but for Lucille. She entreated me so earnestly and with such strange vehemence to go on by the night-mail to Paris, that at last, to satisfy her, I consented; though it struck me unpleasantly at the time that I had let her travel too long already, and that this feverishness was the consequence of over-fatigue. But she became pacified at once when I told her it should be as she wanted; and declared she should sleep perfectly well in the carriage with me beside her. She should feel quite safe then, she said.

"Safe! Where safer? you might ask. Nowhere, I believe. Alone with me—surely nowhere safer. The Paris express was a short train that night; but I managed to secure a compartment for ourselves. I left Lucille in her corner there while I went across to the *buffet* to fill a flask. I was gone barely five minutes; but when I came back the change in the child's face fairly startled me. I had seen it last with the smile it always wore for me on it, looking so childishly happy in the lamp-light. Now it was all gray-pale and distorted; and the great blue eyes told me directly with what.

"Fear—sudden, terrible fear—I thought. But *fear*? Fear of what? I asked her. She clung close to me half-sobbing awhile before she could answer; and then she told me—nothing. There was nothing the matter; only she had felt a pain—a cruel pain—at her heart; and it had frightened her. Yes, that was it; it had frightened her, but it had passed; and she was well, quite well again now.

"All this time her eyes seemed to be telling me another story; but I said nothing; she was obviously too excited already. I did my best to soothe her, and I succeeded. She told me she felt quite well once more before we started. No, she had rather, much rather go on to Paris, as I had promised her she should. She should sleep all the way, if no one came into the carriage to disturb her. No one could come in? Then nothing could be better.

"And so it was that she and I started that night by the Paris mail.

"I made her up a bed of rugs and wraps upon the cushions; but she had rather rest her head upon my shoulder, she said, and feel my arm about her; nothing could hurt her then. Ah, strange how she harped on that.

"She lay there, then, as she loved best—with her head resting on my shoulder, not sleeping much or soundly; uneasily, with sudden waking starts, and with glances round her; till I would speak to her. And then she would look up into my face and smile; and so drop into that uneasy sleep again. And I would think she was over-tired, that was all; and reproach myself with having let her come on. And three or four hours passed like this; and then we had got as far as Dijon.

"But the child was fairly worn out now; and she offered no

opposition when I asked her to let me pillow her head on something softer than my shoulder. So I folded, a great thick shawl she was too well cloaked to need, and she made that her pillow.

"We were rushing full swing through the wild, dark night, when she lifted up her face and bade me kiss her and bid her sleep well. And I put my arm round her, and kissed the child's loving lips—for the last time while she lived. Then I flung myself on the seat opposite her; and, watching her till she slept soundly and peacefully, slept at last myself also. I had drawn the blind across the lamp in the roof, and the light in the carriage was very dim.

"How long I slept I don't know; it couldn't have been more than an hour and a half, because the express was slackening speed for its first halt beyond Dijon. I had slept heavily I knew; but I woke with a sudden, sharp sense of danger that made me broad awake, and strung every nerve in a moment. The sort of feeling you have when you wake on a prairie, where you have come across 'Indian sign;' on outpost-duty, when your *feldwebel* plucks gently at your cloak. You know what I mean.

"I was on my feet at once. As I said, the light in the carriage was very dim, and the shadow was deepest where Lucille lay. I looked there instinctively. She must have moved in her sleep, for her face was turned away from me; and the cloak I had put so carefully about her had partly fallen off. But she slept on still. Only soundly, very soundly; she scarcely seemed to breathe. And—*did* she breathe?

"A ghastly fear ran through my blood, and froze it. I understood why I had wakened. In my nostrils was an awful odour that I knew well enough. I bent over her; I touched her. Her face was very cold; her eyes glared glassily at me; my hands were wet with something. My hands were wet with blood—her blood!

"I tore away the blind from the lamp, and then I could see that my wife of a week lay there stabbed straight to the heart—dead—dead beyond doubting; murdered in her sleep."

Devereux's stern, low voice shook ever so little as he spoke those last words; and we both sat very silent after them for a good while. Only when he could trust his utterance again he went on.

"A curious piece of devilry, wasn't it? That child—whom had she ever harmed? Who could hate her like this? I remember I thought that, in a dull, confused sort of way, when I found myself alone in that carriage with her lying dead on the cushions before me. *Alone* with her—you understand? It was confusing.

"I pass over what immediately followed. The express came duly to a halt; and then I called people to me, and—and the Paris express went on without that particular carriage.

"The inquiry began before some local authority next day. Very little came of it. What could come of it, unless they had convicted *me* of the murder of this child I would have given my own life to save?

"They might have done that at home; but they knew better here, and didn't. They couldn't find me the actual assassin, however; though I believe they did their best. All they found was his weapon, which he most purposely have left behind. I asked for this, and got it. It gave their police no clue; and it gave me none. But I had a fancy for it.

"It was a plain, double-edged, admirably-tempered dagger—a very workmanlike article indeed. On the cross hilt of it I swore one day that I would live thenceforth for one thing alone-the discovery of the murderer of old D'Avray's child, whom I had promised him to care for before all. When I had found this man, whoever he was, I also swore that I would kill him. Kill him myself, you understand; without any of the law's delay or uncertainty, without troubling *bourreau* or hangman. Kill him as he had killed her—to do this was what I meant to live for. There was war to the knife between him and me.

"I started, of course, under one heavy disadvantage. He knew me, probably, whereas I didn't know him at all. When he found that his amiable intention of fixing the crime on me had been frustrated, it must, I imagined, have occurred to him that the said crime might eventually be fixed by me on him. And he had proved himself to be a person who didn't stick at trifles. It behooved me, therefore, to go to work cautiously. But I hadn't fought Indians for nothing; and I *was* very cautious. I waited quiet till I got a clue. It was a curious one; and I got it in this way. It struck me one day, suddenly, that I had heard of a murder precisely similar to this already. I could not at first call the thing to mind; but presently I remembered—my dream. And then I asked myself this: *Had not this murder been done before my eyes three years ago?*

"I came to the conclusion that the circumstances of the murder in my dream were absolutely identical with the circumstances of the actual crime. Yes; the girl whose face in that dream I had never been able to see was Lucille. Yes; the assassin whose face I had seen so plainly in that dream was the real assassin. In short, I believe that the murder had been *rehearsed* before me three years previous to its actual committal.

"Now this sounds rather wild. Yet I came to this conviction quite coolly and deliberately. It *was* a conviction. Assuming it to be true, the odds against me grew shorter directly; *for I had the portrait of the man I wanted drawn by myself the day after I had seen him in my dream.* And the original of that portrait was a man not to be easily mistaken, supposing him to exist at all. The day I came across that sketch of him in that old forgotten sketch-book of mine, I was as sure he did exist as that I was alive myself. What I had to do was to find this man, and then I never doubted I should find the man I wanted. You see how the odds had shortened. If he knew me I knew him now, and he had no notion that I did know him. It was a good deal fairer fight between us.

"I fought it out alone. My story was hardly one the Rue de Jerusalem would have acted upon; and, besides, I wanted no interference. So, with the portrait before me, I sat down and began to consider who this man was, and why he had murdered that child. The big, burly frame, the heavy yellow face, the sandy-yellow hair, the physiognomy generally, was Teutonic. My man I put down as a North German. Now there were, and are probably, plenty of men who would have no objection whatever to put a knife into me, if they got the chance; but this man, whom I had never met, could have had no such quarrel as theirs with me. His quarrel with me must have been, then, Lucille. Yes, that was it—Lucille. I began to see clearly: a thwarted, devilish passion—a cool, infernal revenge. The child had feared something of this sort; had perhaps seen him that night.

"This explained her nervous terror, her nervous anxiety to stop nowhere, to travel on. In that carriage of that express-train, alone with me—where could she be safer? This accounted, too, for her anxiety to reach England. He would not dare follow her there, she had thought, or, at least, could not without my noticing him. And then she would have told me. She had not told me before evidently because she had feared for *me* too, in a quarrel with this man. She must, innocent child as she was, have had some instinctive knowledge of what he was capable. . . . Ay, a cool, infernal revenge, indeed. To kill her; to fix the murder on me. That dagger he had left behind. . . . The apparent impossibility of any one's entering the carriage as he must have entered it at all, to say nothing of the almost absolute impossibility of his doing so without disturbing either of us,—you see it might have gone hard with me if a British jury had had to decide on the case.

"Well, to cut this as short as may be, I made up my mind that the man I wanted was a North German; that he had conceived a hideous passion for Lucille before I knew her; that she had shrunk from it and him so unmistakably, that he knew he had no chance; that my taking her away as my wife, to which he might have been a witness, drove him to as hideous a revenge; that, hearing we were going to England, and seeing that we were likely to stop nowhere on the way, and so give him a chance of doing what he had made up his mind to do, he had decided to do what he had done as he had done it,—counting on finding us asleep as he had found us, or on his strength if it came to a fight between him and me; but coolly reckless enough to brave everything in any case.

"And the devil aiding, he had in great part and only too well succeeded. He was now either so far satisfied that, if I made no move against him—and how, he might think, could I?—he, feeling himself all safe, would let me be; or, on the other hand, he did not feel safe, and was not satisfied, and was arranging for my being disposed of by and by. I considered the latter frame of mind as his most probable one; I went to work cautiously, as I say. I ascertained that Lucille had made no mention of any obnoxious *pretendant* at any time; I didn't expect to find she had, her terror of the man was too intense. But this man must have met her somewhere—where?

"When old D'Avray came home to die, his daughter was just leaving her Paris *pensionnat*. All through his last illness he had seen no visitor but me, and Lucille had never quitted him. Besides, I had been there all the time. I presumed, then, that this man and she had met in Paris; and I believe they were only likely to have met at one of the half-dozen houses where the child would now and again be asked. I got a list of all these. One name only struck me; it happened to be a German name-Steinmetz. I wondered if Monsieur Steinmetz was my man. In the meantime, who was he? I had no trouble in finding that out: Monsieur Steinmetz was a German banker of good standing and repute, reasonably well off, and recently left a widower.

"Personally? *Dame*, personally Monsieur Steinmetz was a great man and a fat, with a big face and blond hair, and the appearance of what he really was—a *bon vivant* and a *bon enfant* yet *n'avait jamais fait de mal a personne—allez!*—All, yes; in effect, *Madame* had died about a year ago, and *Monsieur* had been inconsolable for a long time. He had changed his residence now, and inhabited a house in one of the new streets off the Champs Elysees.

"From another source I discovered that in the lifetime of Madame Steinmetz Lucille was frequently at the house. She had ceased to come there about the date of the commencement of *Madame's* sudden illness. I got this information by degrees, while I lay *perdu* in an old haunt of mine in the Pays Latin yonder; for I had always had an idea that I should find the man I wanted in Paris. When I had got it, I thought I should like to see Monsieur Steinmetz, the agreeable banker. One night I strolled up as far as his new residence in the street off the Champs Elysees. Monsieur Steinmetz lived on the first-floor. There was a brilliant light there: Monsieur Steinmetz was entertaining friends, it seemed.

"It was a fine night; I established myself out of sight under the doorway of an unfinished house opposite, and waited. I don't know why; perhaps I fancied that when his friends were gone, the fineness of the night might induce Monsieur Steinmetz to take a stroll, and that then I should be able to gratify my curiosity. You see, I knew that if he were my man, I should know him directly. I waited a good while: shadows crossed the lighted blinds; once a big, broad shadow appeared there, that made me fancy I mightn't have been waiting for nothing after all, somehow.

"Presently Monsieur Steinmetz's guests departed, and in a little while after there appeared on the little balcony of Monsieur Steinmetz's apartment *the man I wanted*. There was a moon that night, and the cold white light fell on the great yellow face, with the full lustful lips, and the full cruel chin, just as I had seen the light fall on it in my dream. It was the same face, Bertie; the same face, the same man. I couldn't be mistaken. I had no doubt; I *knew* that the assassin of my wife, of that tender, innocent, helpless child, stood there, twenty yards from me, on that balcony.

"I had got myself pretty well in hand; and it was as well. I never moved. The face I knew turned presently toward the spot where I stood hidden,—the face I had seen in my dream, beyond all doubting. The evil gray eyes glanced carelessly into the shadow, and up and down the quiet street; and then Monsieur Steinmetz, humming an air, got inside the window again, and closed it after him. Once more the great burly shadow that had at first told me I should not wait in that dark doorway in vain crossed the blinds; and then it disappeared. I saw my man no more that night; but I had seen enough. I knew who he was now, and where to find him.

"As I walked along home I thought what I would do. I quite

meant to kill Monsieur Steinmetz; but I also meant to have no *demeles* with an Imperial *Procureur* and the *Cour d'Assizes* for doing so. I didn't want to murder him, either. I thought I would wait a little for the chance of a suitable opportunity for settling my business satisfactorily. And I did wait. I turned this delay to account, and got together a case of circumstantial evidence against my man that, though perhaps it might have broken down in a law-court, would have been alone amply sufficient for me.

"The reason why Lucille's visits to the banker's house ceased was, it appeared, because Madame Steinmetz had conceived all at once a jealous dislike to her. How far this was owing to Lucille herself I could well understand; but I could understand *Madame's* jealousy equally well. *Madame's* illness, strangely sudden, dated from the cessation of Lucille's visits. Was it hard to find a *cause* for that illness—a cause for the wife's subsequent suspected death? I thought not. Then had followed Lucille's departure from Paris. The child's anxiety for her father hid her *other fear* from his eyes and mine; but that fear must have been on her then. With us she forgot it in time; yet it or another reason had always prevented all mention of what had occasioned it. She became my wife.

"At that very time I easily ascertained that Steinmetz was absent from Paris; less easily, but indubitably, that he had, at all events, been as far south as Lyons. At Lyons it must have been that Lucille first discovered he was dogging us. Hence her alarm, which I had remembered, and her anxiety to proceed on our journey without stopping for the night, as I had previously arranged. The morning after the murder Steinmetz reappeared in Paris. From the hour at which he was seen at the *gare*, it was certain that he had travelled by the night express train in which Lucille and I had started from Lyons; and he wore that morning a travelling-coat of fur in all respects similar to the one I remembered so well.

"If I had ever had any doubt of my man after actually seeing him, I should probably have convinced myself that he was my man by the general tendency of these facts, which I got at slowly and one by one. But I had no need of such evidence; and of course no case, even with such evidence, for a court of law. However, courts of law I had never intended to trouble in the matter.

"The opportunity I was waiting was some time before it offered. Monsieur Steinmetz was a man of regular habits, I found—from his first-floor in the street off the Champs Elysees, every morning at eleven, to the Bourse; thence to his bureau hard by till four; from his bureau to his cafe, where he read papers and played dominoes till six; and then home slowly by the Boulevarts. He might consider himself tolerably safe from me while he led this sort of life, even supposing he was aware he was incurring any danger. I don't think he troubled much about that; till one night, when, over the count of the beloved domino-points, his eyes met mine fixed right upon him. I had arranged this little surprise to see how it would affect him.

"Perhaps my gaze may have expressed something more than the mere distraction I intended; but I noticed—though a more indifferent observer might easily have failed to notice—how the great yellow face, expanded in childish interest in the childish game, seemed suddenly to grow gray and harden; how the fat smile became a cruel baring of sharp white teeth; how the fat chin squared itself. The man knew me, and scented danger.

"A moment's reflection convinced Monsieur Steinmetz, though, that it could be by no means so certain that I knew him; five minutes' observation of me more than half satisfied him that I did not. Yet what did I want there? What was I doing in Paris? This might concern him nearly, he must have thought.

"I kept my own face in order, and watched his. It wasn't an easy one to read; but you see I had studied it closely, and in a way he couldn't have dreamed of. Monsieur Steinmetz was outwardly his wonted self, but inwardly not quite comfortable when he rose; and I saw the evil eye gleam on his great yellow finger as he took out his purse to pay the *garcon*, just as I had seen it when that finger pointed at *myself* in my dream. I felt curious sensations, Bertie, as I sat there and looked abstractedly at Monsieur Steinmetz.

"I wondered how long it would be before—But my time hadn't come yet. He went out without another glance at me. I saw his huge form on the other side of the street when I left the cafe in my turn. This I had expected. Monsieur Steinmetz was naturally curious. It was hardly possible that I could know him; but it was quite certain that he ought to know all about me. So, when I moved on, he moved on; in short, Monsieur Steinmetz dogged me up one street and down another, till he finally dogged me home to my hiding-place in the Pays Latin. He did it very well, too—much better than you would have expected from so apparently unwieldy a *mouchard*. But I *remembered* how lightly he could move.

"Next day I had, of course, disappeared from my old quarters, and gone no one knew where. I suppose Monsieur Steinmetz didn't like this fact when he heard of it. It might have seemed suspicious. Suppose I *had* recognized him? In that case I had evidently a little game of my own, and was as evidently desirous to keep it dark. He was a cool hand; but I fancy my man began to get a little uneasy. He took some trouble to find me again. After a while I permitted him to do that. Once found, he seemed determined that I should not be lost sight of again for want of watching.

"I permitted that, too; it helped play my game, and I wanted to bring it to an end. To which intent, Monsieur Steinmetz got to hear from sources best known to himself as much of my plans as should bring him to the state I wanted. That was a murderous state. I wanted to get him to think that I was dangerous enough to be worth putting out of the way. I presume he was aware there were, or would be, weak joints in his armour, impenetrable as it seemed; and he preferred not risking the ordeal of legal battle if he could help it. At all events, he elected at last to rid himself of a person who might be dangerous, and was troublesome, by the shortest and the simplest means.

"I say so because when, believing my man was ripe for this, I left Paris about midday for a certain secluded little spot on the sea-coast, I saw one of Monsieur Steinmetz's employees on the platform; and because, two days after my arrival in my secluded spot, I met Monsieur Steinmetz in person, newly arrived also. Now this was exactly what I had intended and anticipated. Monsieur Steinmetz had come down there to put me out of his way, if he could. He passed me, leisurely strolling in the opposite direction, humming his favourite *aria*, bigger and yellower than ever, the evil eye fiery on his finger. His own eyes shot me as evil fire; but he said nothing. . . . I saw he was ripe, though. . . . My time was close at hand.

"It came. Monsieur Steinmetz and I met once more in the very place where I, knowing my ground, had intended we should meet. It was a dip in the cliffs like a hollowed palm, and just there the cliff jutted out a good bit, with a sheer fall on to the rocks below. It was a gray afternoon, at the end of summer. The wind was rising fast; there was a thunder of heavy waves already.

"I think he had been dogging me; but I hadn't chosen to let him get up to me till now. We were quite out of sight when he had reached the level bottom of the dip, where I had halted—quite out of sight, and quite alone. To do him justice, he came on steadily enough. His face was liker the sketch I had made of it, liker the face I had seen in my dream, than it had ever looked before. Evidently he had made up his mind. . . . At last, then!... Well, I had been waiting long!. . . He was close beside me.

"'*Ah! bon jour, cher Monsieur Steinmetz.*'

"'So?' he said, his little eyes contracting like a cobra's. 'Ah! *Monsieur* knows my name?'

"'Among other things about you—yes.'

"'So!' The yellow face was turning grayer and harder every minute—liker and liker to my likeness of it. 'And what other things? Has it never appeared to you that this you do, have been doing—this meddling, may be dangerous, *hein*?'

"He had changed his tone, as he had changed the person in which he addressed me. Yes, he had certainly made up his mind. And his big right hand was hidden inside his waistcoat, so that I could not see the evil eye I knew was on his finger.

"'Dangerous?' he repeated slowly.

"'Possibly.'

"'Ay, surely; I shall crush you!'

"'Try.'

"'In good time; wait. You plot against me. Take care; I am strong; I warn you. There must be an end of this, you understand, or———'

"He nodded his big head significantly.

"'You are right,' I told him; 'there must be an end. It is coming.'

"'So?'

"'Yes; I know you. You know me now.'

"'I know you. What do you want?'

"'To kill you.'

"'So?'

"'Yes; as you killed her.'

"'As I killed her? That is it, then? You know that?'

"'I know that.'

"'Well, it is true. I killed her. Now you can guess what I am going to do to you—to you, curse you!—whom she loved.'

"The very face I had seen in my dream now, Bertie, the very face! There was something besides the evil eye that gleamed in his right hand when he drew it from his breast. Once more he spoke.

"'Yes, I killed her. I meant worse for you. You escaped that; but you will not escape me now. Fool! were you mad to do this? Did not I hate you enough? And I would have let you be. Ah, die, then, if you will have it so!'

"His heavy right arm swung high as he spoke, and I saw the sharp steel gleam as it turned to fall. And I twisted from his grip, and caught the falling arm, and bent it till the dagger dropped to the ground. And then, for a fierce, desperate, devilish minute, I had him in my clutch, dragging him nearer the smooth, slippery edge. He was no match for me at this I knew, and he knew; but he held me with the hold of his despair, and I could not loose myself. Both of us together, he meant; but not I. Yet I only freed myself just as he rolled exhausted, but clutching at the tough, short bushes wildly, toward the brink, and partly over it.... Only the hold of his hands between him and his death. And I knelt above him, with the knife in my hand that was stained with *her* blood.

"The great yellow face, ashen now in its mortal agony, looked silently up at me—for three or four awful seconds; and then—then it disappeared.

"Bah!" Paul concluded, "that was the end of it."

Doctor Feversham's Story

"I have made a point all my life," said the doctor, "of believing nothing of the kind."

Much ghost-talk by firelight had been going on in the library at Fordwick Chase, when Doctor Feversham made this remark.

"As much as to say," observed Amy Fordwick, "that you are afraid to tackle the subject, because you pique yourself on being strong-minded, and are afraid of being convinced against your will."

"Not precisely, young lady. A man convinced against his will is in a different state of mind from mine in matters like these. But it is true that cases in which the supernatural element appears at first sight to enter are so numerous in my profession, that I prefer accepting only the solutions of science, so far as they go, to entering on any wild speculations which it would require more time than I should care to devote to them to trace to their origin."

"But without entering fully into the why and wherefore, how can you be sure that the proper treatment is observed in the numerous cases of mental hallucination which must come under your notice?" inquired Latimer Fordwick, who was studying for the Bar.

"I content myself, my young friend, with following the rules laid down for such cases, and I generally find them successful," answered the old Doctor.

"Then you admit that cases have occurred within your knowledge of which the easiest apparent solution could be one which involved a belief in supernatural agencies?" persisted Latimer, who was rather prolix and pedantic in his talk.

"I did not say so," said the Doctor.

"But of course he meant us to infer it," said Amy. "Now, my dear old Doctor, do lay aside professional dignity, and give us one good ghost-story out of your personal experience. I believe you have been dying to tell one for the last hour, if you would only confess it."

"I would rather not help to fill that pretty little head with idle fancies, dear child," answered the old man, looking fondly at Amy, who was his especial pet and darling.

"Nonsense! You know I am even painfully unimaginative and matter-of-fact; and as for idle fancies, is it an idle fancy to think you like to please me?" said Amy coaxingly.

"Well, after all, you have been frightening each other with so many thrilling tales for the last hour or two, that I don't suppose I should do much harm by telling you a circumstance which happened to me when I was a young man, and has always rather puzzled me."

A murmur of approval ran round the party. All disposed themselves to listen; and Doctor Feversham, after a prefatory pinch of snuff, began.

"In my youth I resided for some time with a family in the north of England, in the double capacity of secretary and physician. While I was going through the hospitals of Paris I became acquainted with my employer, whom I will call Sir James Collingham, under rather peculiar circumstances, which have nothing to do with my story. He had an only daughter, who was about sixteen when I first entered the family, and it was on her account that Sir James wished to have some person with a competent knowledge of medicine and physiology as one of his household. Miss Collingham was subject to fits of a very peculiar kind, which threw her into a sort of trance, lasting from half an hour to three or even four days, according to the severity of the visitation.

"During these attacks she occasionally displayed that extraordinary phenomenon which goes by the name of clairvoyance. She saw scenes and persons who were far distant, and described them with wonderful accuracy. Though quite unconscious of all outward things, and apparently in a state of the deepest insensibility, she would address remarks to those present which bore reference to the thoughts then occupying their minds, though they had given them no outward expression; and her remarks showed an insight into matters which had perhaps been carefully kept secret, which might truly be termed preternatural.

"Under these circumstances, Sir James was very unwilling to bring her into contact with strangers when it could possibly be avoided; and the events which first brought us together, having also led to my treating Miss Collingham rather successfully in a severe attack of her malady, induced her father to offer me a position in his household which, as a young, friendless man, I was very willing to accept.

"Collingham-Westmore was a very ancient house of great extent, and but indifferently kept in repair. The country surrounding it is of great natural beauty, thinly inhabited, and, especially at the time I speak of, before railways had penetrated so far north, somewhat lonely and inaccessible. A group of small houses clustered round the village church of Westmorton, distant about three miles from the mansion of the Collingham family; and a solitary posting-house, on what was then the great north road, could be reached by a horseman in about an hour, though the only practicable road for carriages was at least fifteen miles from the highway to Collingham-Westmore. Wild and lovely in the eyes of an admirer of nature were the hills and 'cloughs' among which I pursued my botanical studies for many a long, silent summer day. My occupations at the mansion—everybody called it the mansion, and I must do so from force of habit, though it sounds rather like a house-agent's advertisement—were few and light; the society was not particularly to my taste, and the fine old library only attracted me on rainy days, of which, truth to say, we had our full share.

"The Collingham family circle comprised a maiden aunt of

Sir James, Miss Patricia, a stern and awful specimen of the female sex in its fossil state; her ward, Miss Henderson, who, having long passed her pupilage, remained at Collingham-Westmore in the capacity of *gouvernante* and companion to the young heiress; the heiress aforesaid, and myself. A priest—did I say that the Collinghams still professed the old religion?—came on Sundays and holydays to celebrate mass in the gloomy old chapel; but neighbours there were none, and only about half-a-dozen times during the four years I was an inmate of the mansion were strangers introduced into the family party."

"How dreadfully dull it must have been!" exclaimed Amy sympathetically.

"It *was* dull," answered the Doctor. "Even with my naturally cheerful disposition, and the course of study with which I methodically filled up all my leisure hours except those devoted to out-of-door exercise, the gloom of the old mansion weighed upon me till I sometimes felt that I must give up my situation at all risks, and return to the world, though it were to struggle with poverty and friendlessness.

"There was no lack of dismal legends and superstitions connected with the mansion, and every trifling circumstance that occurred was twisted into an omen or presage, whether of good or evil, by the highly wrought fancy of Miss Patricia. These absurdities, together with the past grandeur of their house, and the former glories of their religion, formed the staple subjects of conversation when the family was assembled; and as I became more intimately acquainted with the state of my patient, I felt convinced that the atmosphere of gloomy superstition in which she had been reared had fostered, even if it had not altogether been the cause of, her morbid mental and bodily condition.

"Among the many legends connected with the mansion, one seemed to have a peculiar fascination for Miss Collingham, perhaps because it was the most ghastly and repulsive. One wing of the house was held to be haunted by the spirit of an ancestress of the family, who appeared in the shape of a tall woman, with one hand folded in her white robe and the other pointing upward. It was said, that in a room at the end of the haunted wing this lady had been foully murdered by her jealous husband. The window of the apartment overhung the wild wooded side of one of the 'cloughs' common in the country; and tradition averred that the victim was thrown from this window by her murderer. As she caught hold of the sill in a last frantic struggle for life, he severed her hand at the wrist, and the mutilated body fell, with one fearful shriek, into the depth below.

"Since then, a white shadowy form has forever been sitting at the fatal window, or wandering along the deserted passages of the haunted wing with the bleeding stump folded in her robe; and in moments of danger or approaching death to any member of the Collingham family, the same long, wild shriek rises slowly from the wooded cliff and peals through the mansion; while to different individuals of the house, a pale hand has now and then been visible, laid on themselves or some other of the family, a never-failing omen of danger or death.

"I need not tell you how false and foolish all this dreary superstition appeared to me; and I exerted all my powers of persuasion to induce Miss Patricia to dwell less on these and similar themes in the presence of Miss Collingham. But there seemed to be something in the very air of the gloomy old mansion which fostered such delusions; for when I spoke to Father O'Connor the priest, and urged on him the pernicious effect which was thus produced on my patient's mind, I found him as fully imbued with the spirit of credulity as the most hysterical housemaid of them all. He solemnly declared to me that he had himself repeatedly seen the pale lady sitting at the fatal window, when on his way to and from his home beyond the hills; and moreover, that on the death of Lady Collingham, which occurred at her daughter's birth, he had heard the long, shrill death-scream echo through the mansion while engaged in the last offices of the Church by the bedside of the dying lady.

"So I found it impossible to fight single-handed against these adverse influences, and could only endeavour to divert the mind of my patient into more healthy channels of thought. In this I succeeded perfectly. She became an enthusiastic botanist, and our rambles in search of the rare and lovely specimens which were to be found among the woods and moors surrounding her dwelling did more for her health, both of body and mind, than all the medical skill I could bring to bear on her melancholy case.

"Four years had elapsed since I first took up my abode at Collingham-Westmore. Miss Collingham had grown from a sickly child into a singularly graceful young woman, full of bright intelligence, eager for information, and with scarcely an outward trace remaining of her former fragile health. Still those mysterious swoons occasionally visited her, forming an insurmountable obstacle to her mingling in general society, which she was in all other respects so well fitted to adorn. They occurred without any warning or apparent cause; one moment she would be engaged in animated conversation, and the next, white and rigid as a statue, she would fall back in her chair insensible to all outward objects, but rapt and carried away into a world of her own, whose visions she would sometimes describe in glowing language, although she retained no recollection whatever of them when she returned, as suddenly and at as uncertain a period, to her normal condition.

"On one of these occasions we were sitting, after dinner, in a large apartment called the summer dining-room. Fruit and wine were on the table, and the last red beams of the setting sun lighted up the distant woods, which were in the first flush of their autumn glory. I turned to remark on the beautiful effect of light to Miss Collingham, and at the very moment I did so she fell back in one of her strange swoons. But instead of the death-like air which her features usually assumed, a lovely smile lighted them up, and an expression of ecstasy made her beauty appear for the moment almost superhuman. Slowly she raised her right hand, and pointed in the direction of the setting sun. 'He is coming,' she said in soft, clear tones; 'life and light are coming with him,—life and light and liberty!'

"Her hand fell gently by her side; the rapt expression faded from her countenance, and the usual death-like blank over-spread it. This trance passed away like others, and by midnight the house was profoundly still. Soon after that hour a vociferous peal at the great hall-bell roused most of the inmates from sleep. My rooms were in a distant quarter of the house, and a door opposite to that of my bedroom led to the haunted wing, but was always kept locked. I started up on hearing a second ring, and looked out, in hopes of seeing a servant pass, and ascertaining the cause of this unusual disturbance.

"I saw no one, and after listening for a while to the opening of the hall-door, and the sound of distant voices, I made up my mind that I should be sent for if wanted, and re-entered my room. As I was closing the door, I was rather startled to see a tall object, of grayish-white colour and indistinct form, issue from the gallery whose door, as I said before, had always been locked in my recollection. For a moment I felt as though rooted to the spot, and a strange sensation crept over me. The next, all trace of the appearance had vanished, and I persuaded myself that what I had seen must have been some effect of light from the open door of my room.

"The cause of the nightly disturbance appeared at breakfast on the following morning in the shape of a remarkably handsome young man, who was introduced by Sir James as his nephew, Don Luis de Cabral, the son of an only sister long dead, who had married a Spaniard of high rank. Don Luis showed but little trace of his southern parentage. If I may so express it, all the depth and warmth of colouring in that portion of his blood which he inherited from his Spanish ancestors came out in the raven-black hair and large lustrous dark eyes, which impressed you at once with their uncommon beauty.

"For the rest, he was a fine well-grown young man, no darker in complexion than an Englishman might well be, and with a careless, happy boyishness of manner, which won immediately on the regard of strangers, and rendered his presence in the house like that of a perpetual sunbeam. We all wondered, after a little while, what we had done before Luis came among us. He was as a son to Sir James; Miss Patricia softened to this new and pleasing interest in her colourless existence as I could not have believed it was in her fossilized nature to do; Miss Henderson became animated, almost young, under the reviving influence of the youth and joyousness of our new inmate; and I own that I speedily attached myself with a warm and affectionate regard to the happy, unselfish nature that seemed to brighten all who came near it.

"But the most remarkable effect of the presence of Don Luis de Cabral among us was visible in Miss Collingham. 'Love at first sight,' often considered as a mere phrase, was, in the case of these two young creatures, an unmistakable reality. From the moment of their first meeting, the cousins were mutually drawn toward each other; and seeing the bright and wonderful change wrought by the presence of Don Luis in Blanche Collingham, I could not but remember, with the interest that attaches to a curious psychological phenomenon, the words she uttered in her trance on the eve of his arrival. 'Life, light, and liberty,' indeed, appeared given to all that was best and brightest in her nature. Her health improved visibly, and her beauty, always touching, became radiant in its full development.

"My duties toward her were now merely nominal; and when, about two months later, Sir James announced to me her approaching marriage, and confessed that it was with this object he had invited Don Luis to come and make the acquaintance of his English relations, the strong opinions I entertained against the marriage of first cousins, and also on the especial inadvisability of any project of marriage in the case of Miss Collingham, could not prevent my hearty rejoicing in the fair prospect of happiness in which two persons who deeply interested me were indulging.

"Winter set in early and severely that year among our northern hills, and with a view to Blanche's removal from its withering influence, which I always considered prejudicial to her, the preparations for the marriage were hurried on, and the ceremony was fixed to take place about the middle of December.

The travelling-carriage which was to convey the young couple on their way southward was to arrive at the nearest railway-station—then more than thirty miles distant—a week before the marriage; and as some important portions of the trousseau, together with a valuable package of jewels intended by Don Luis as presents for his bride, were expected at the same time, the young man announced his intention of riding across the hills to ——, in order to superintend the conveyance of the carriage and its contents along the rough mountain roads that it must traverse.

"We were all sitting around the great fireplace in the winter parlour on the evening before his departure. Miss Collingham had been languid and depressed throughout the day, and often adverted to the long wintry ride he was to undertake in a strain of apprehension at which Don Luis laughed gayly. To divert her mind, he recounted various adventures which had befallen him in foreign lands, with a vigorous simplicity of description which enchained her attention and interested us all.

"Suddenly, so sitting, Miss Collingham leaned forward, and in a changed, eager voice exclaimed, 'Luis, take away your hand from your throat!'

"We looked. Luis' hands were lying one over the other on his knee in a careless attitude that was habitual to him.

"'Take it away, I say! Oh, take it away!'

"Miss Collingham started to her feet as she uttered these words almost in a shriek, and then fell back rigid and senseless, her outstretched hand still pointing to her betrothed.

"The fit was a severe one, but by morning it had yielded to remedies, and Luis set off early on his ride, to make the most of the short daylight, and intending to return with the carriage on the morrow. All that day Miss Collingham remained in a half-conscious state. It was a dreary day of gloom, with a piercing north wind, and toward evening the snow began to fall in those close, compact flakes which forebode a heavy storm. We were glad to think that Luis must have reached his destination before it began; but when the next morning dawned on a wide expanse of snow, and the air was still thick with fast-falling flakes, it was feared that the state of the roads would preclude all hope of the arrival of the carriage on that day.

"My patient took no heed of the untoward state of the weather. She was still in a drowsy condition, very unlike that which usually succeeded her attacks, and Miss Henderson, who had watched by her through the night, told me she spoke more than once in a strange, excited manner, as though carrying on a conversation with someone whom she appeared to see by her bedside. As the good lady, however, could give but a very imperfect and incoherent account of what had passed, I was left in some doubt as to whether Miss Collingham had seen more or Miss Henderson less than there really was to be seen, as I had before had reason to believe that she was not a very vigilant nurse.

"So the hours went on, and night closed in. Sir James began to feel some uneasiness at the non-appearance, not only of Don Luis, but also of the priest, who was to have arrived at Collingham-Westmore on that day.

"On questioning some of the servants who had been out of the house, the absence of Father O'Connor at least was satisfactorily accounted for: they all declared that it would be quite impossible for those best acquainted with the hills to find their way across them in the blinding drifts which had never ceased throughout the day. We concluded that Father O'Connor and Don Luis were alike storm-stayed, and had no remedy but patience.

"Late in the evening—it must have been near midnight—I was in Miss Collingham's dressing-room with Miss Patricia, who intended to watch by her through the night. We were talking by the fire, of the snow-storm which still continued, and of the hindrance it might prove to the marriage—the day fixed for which was now less than a week distant—when we heard a voice in the adjoining room, where we imagined the object of our care to be sleeping. We went in. Miss Collingham was sitting up in bed, her eyes wide open, in one of her rigid fits. She was speaking rapidly in a low tone, unlike her usual voice.

"'You cannot get through all that snow,' she said. 'Get help; there are men not far off with spades. Oh, be careful! You are off the road! Stop, stop! that is the way to Armstrong's Clough. Does not the postboy know the road? He is bewildered. I tell you it is madness to go on. See, one of the horses has fallen; he kicks—he will hit you! Oh, how dark it is! And the snow covers your lantern, and you cannot see the edge. Now the horse is up again, but he cannot go on. Do not beat him, Luis; it is not his fault, poor beast; the snow is too thick, and you are on rough ground. Now he rears—he backs—the other one backs also—the wheel of the carriage is over the edge—ah!'

"The scream with which these wild, hurried words ended seemed to be taken up and echoed from a distance. Miss Patricia stared at me with a ghastly white face of horror, and I felt my blood curdle as that long, shrill, unearthly shriek pealed through the silent passages. It grew louder and nearer, and seemed to sweep through the room, dying away in the opposite direction. Miss Patricia fell forward without a word in a dead faint.

"I looked at Miss Collingham; she had not moved, or shown any sign of hearing or heeding that awful sound. In a few seconds the room was filled with terrified women, roused from their sleep by the weird cry which rang through the house. Miss Patricia was conveyed by some of them to her own room, where, after much difficulty, we restored her to consciousness. Her first act was to grasp me by the arm.

"'Mr. Feversham, for the love of the Holy Virgin do not leave me! I have seen that which I cannot look upon and live.'

"I soothed her as best I might, and at last persuaded her to allow me to leave her with her own maid in order to visit my other patient, promising to return shortly.

"I found no change whatever in Miss Collingham. Sir James was in the room trying to establish some degree of calmness and order among the terrified women. We succeeded in persuading most of them to take a restorative and return to bed, and leaving two of the most self-possessed to watch beside Miss Collingham, who was still completely insensible, we went together to Miss Patricia's room.

"'Brother, I have seen her!' she exclaimed on Sir James' entrance.

"'Seen who, my dear Patricia?'

"'The pale lady—the spectre of our house,' she replied, shuddering from head to foot. 'She passed through the room, her hand upraised, and the blood-spots on her garment. Oh, James! my time is come, and Father O'Connor is not here.'

"Sir James did not attempt to combat his sister's superstitious terrors, but appeared, on the contrary, almost as deeply impressed as herself, and questioned her closely about the apparition. Her answers led to some mention of the strange vision which Miss Collingham was describing in her trance just before the scream was heard. At Sir James' request I put down in writing, as nearly as I could remember, all she had said, and so great was the impression it made on my mind that I believe I recalled her very words. Knowing all we did of her abnormal condition while in a state of trance, it was impossible not to fear that she might have been describing a scene that was actually occurring at the time; and Sir James determined to send out a party, as soon as daylight came, on the road by which Don Luis must arrive.

"The morning dawned brightly, with a keen frost, and several men were sent off along the road to —— with the first rays of light.

"Some hours afterward Father O'Connor arrived, having made his way with considerable difficulty across the hill. Miss Patricia claimed his first attention, for my unhappy charge remained senseless and motionless as ever.

"After a long conference, he came to me with grave looks.

"'She is at the window this day,' he said, shaking his head sorrowfully, when I had told him my share of the last night's singular experiences. 'The pale lady is there; I saw her as I came by the bridge as plainly as now I see you. We shall have evil tidings of that poor lad before nightfall, or I am strangely mistaken.'

"Evil tidings indeed they were that reached us on the return of some of the exploring-party. They were first attracted from following as nearly as they could the line of road, blocked as it was with drifts of snow by hearing the howling of a dog at some little distance, in the direction of the precipitous ravine which went by the name of 'Armstrong's Clough.' Following the sound, they came upon traces of wheels in the hill-side, where no carriage could have gone had it not been for the deep snow which concealed and smoothed away the inequalities of the ground. These marks were traced here and there till they led to the verge of the precipice, where a struggle had evidently taken place, and masses of snow had been dislodged and fallen into the ravine.

"Looking below, the only thing they could see in the waste of snow was a little dog, who was known to be in the habit of running with the post-horses from ——, which was scraping wildly in the snow and filling the air with its dismal howlings. A considerable circuit had to be made before the bottom of the clough could be reached, and then the whole tragedy was revealed. There lay the broken carriage, the dead horses, and two stiffened corpses under the snow, that had drifted over and around them.

"I need not pursue the melancholy story; I was an old fool for telling it to you," said the Doctor.

"But Miss Collingham—what became of her?" asked an eager listener.

"Well, she did not recover," answered the Doctor with a slight trembling in his voice. "It was a sad matter altogether; and within a short time she lay beside her betrothed in the family vault below the chapel. Sir James broke up his establishment and went abroad, and I never saw any of the family again."

"And what did you do, Doctor?"

"I went to London, to seek my fortune as best I might; and I hope you may all prosper as well, my young friends."

"And is it all really true?" asked Amy, who had listened with breathless attention.

"That is the worst of it; it really is," said the Doctor.

The Little Red Man
From Stories of Lough Guir

The good governess had a particular liking for the old castle, and when lessons were over, would take her book or her work into a large room in the ancient building, called the Earl's Hall. Here she caused a table and chair to be placed for her use, and in the *chiaroscuro* would so sit at her favourite occupations, with just a little ray of subdued light, admitted through one of the glassless windows above her, and falling upon her table.

The Earl's Hall is entered by a narrow arched door, opening close to the winding stair. It is a very large and gloomy room, pretty nearly square, with a lofty vaulted ceiling, and a stone floor. Being situated high in the castle, the walls of which are immensely thick, and the windows very small and few, the silence that reigns here is like that of a subterranean cavern. You hear nothing in this solitude, except perhaps twice a day, the twitter of a swallow in one of the small windows high in the wall. This good lady, having one day retired to her accustomed solitude, was missed from the house at her wonted hour of return.

This in a country house, such as Irish houses were in those days, excited little surprise, and no harm. But when the dinner hour came, which was then, in country houses, five o'clock, and the governess had not appeared, some of her young friends, it being not yet winter, and sufficient light remaining to guide them through the gloom of the dim ascent and passages, mounted the old stone stair to the level of the Earl's Hall, gaily calling to her as they approached.

There was no answer. On the stone floor, outside the door of the Earl's Hall, to their horror, they found her lying insensible. By the usual means she was restored to consciousness; but she continued very ill, and was conveyed to the house, where she took to her bed.

It was there and then that she related what had occurred to her. She had placed herself, as usual, at her little work table, and had been either working or reading—I forget which—for some time, and felt in her usual health and serene spirits. Raising her eyes, and looking toward the door, she saw a horrible-looking little man enter. He was dressed in red, was very short, had a singularly dark face, and a most atrocious countenance. Having walked some steps into the room, with his eyes fixed on her, he stopped, and beckoning to her to follow, moved back toward the door. About halfway, again he stopped once more and turned. She was so terrified that she sat staring at the apparition without moving or speaking.

Seeing that she had not obeyed him, his face became more frightful and menacing, and as it underwent this change, he raised his hand and stamped on the floor. Gesture, look, and all, expressed diabolical fury. Through sheer extremity of terror she did rise, and, as he turned again, followed him a step or two in the direction of the door. He again stopped, and with the same mute menace, compelled her again to follow him.

She reached the narrow stone doorway of the Earl's Hall, through which he had passed; from the threshold she saw him standing a little way off, with his eyes still fixed on her. Again he signed to her, and began to move along the short passage that leads to the winding stair.

But instead of following him further, she fell on the floor in a fit.

The poor lady was thoroughly persuaded that she was not long to survive this vision, and her foreboding proved true. From her bed she never rose.

LEONAUR

ALSO FROM LEONAUR
AVAILABLE IN SOFTCOVER OR HARDCOVER WITH DUST JACKET

THE LONG PATROL *by George Berrie*—A Novel of Light Horsemen from Gallipoli to the Palestine campaign of the First World War.

NAPOLEONIC WAR STORIES *by Arthur Quiller-Couch*—Tales of soldiers, spies, battles & sieges from the Peninsular & Waterloo campaingns.

THE FIRST DETECTIVE *by Edgar Allan Poe*—The Complete Auguste Dupin Stories—The Murders in the Rue Morgue, The Mystery of Marie Rogêt & The Purloined Letter.

THE COMPLETE DR NIKOLA—MAN OF MYSTERY: 1 *by Guy Boothby*—*A Bid for Fortune & Dr Nikola Returns*—Guy Boothby's Dr.Nikola adventures continue to fascinate readers and enthusiasts of crime and mystery fiction because—in the manner of Raffles, the gentleman cracksman—here is character far removed from the uncompromising goodness of Holmes and Watson or the uncompromising evil of Professor Moriarty.

THE COMPLETE DR NIKOLA—MAN OF MYSTERY: 2 *by Guy Boothby*—*The Lust of Hate, Dr Nikola's Experiment & Farewell, Nikola*—Guy Boothby's Dr.Nikola adventures continue to fascinate readers and enthusiasts of crime and mystery fiction because—in the manner of Raffles, the gentleman cracksman—here is character far removed from the uncompromising goodness of Holmes and Watson or the uncompromising evil of Professor Moriarty.

THE CASEBOOKS OF MR J. G. REEDER: BOOK 1 *by Edgar Wallace*—*Room 13, The Mind of Mr J. G. Reeder* and *Terror Keep*—Edgar Wallace's sleuth—whose territory is the London of the 1920s—is an unlikely figure, more bank clerk than detective in appearance, ever wearing his square topped bowler, frock coat, cravat and muffler, Mr Reeder is usually inseparable from his umbrella.

THE CASEBOOKS OF MR J. G. REEDER: BOOK 2 *by Edgar Wallace*—*Red Aces, Mr J. G. Reeder Returns, The Guv'nor* and *The Man Who Passed*—Edgar Wallace's sleuth—whose territory is the London of the 1920s—is an unlikely figure, more bank clerk than detective in appearance, ever wearing his square topped bowler, frock coat, cravat and muffler, Mr Reeder is usually inseparable from his umbrella.

THE COMPLETE FOUR JUST MEN: VOLUME 1 *by Edgar Wallace*—*The Four Just Men, The Council of Justice & The Just Men of Cordova*—disillusioned with a world where the wicked and the abusers of power perpetually go unpunished, the Just Men set about to rectify matters according to their own standards, and retribution is dispensed on swift and deadly wings.

ALSO FROM LEONAUR

AVAILABLE IN SOFTCOVER OR HARDCOVER WITH DUST JACKET

THE COMPLETE FOUR JUST MEN: VOLUME 2 *by Edgar Wallace—The Law of the Four Just Men & The Three Just Men*—disillusioned with a world where the wicked and the abusers of power perpetually go unpunished, the Just Men set about to rectify matters according to their own standards, and retribution is dispensed on swift and deadly wings.

THE COMPLETE RAFFLES: 1 *by E. W. Hornung—The Amateur Cracksman & The Black Mask*—By turns urbane gentleman about town and accomplished cricketer, life is just too ordinary for Raffles and that sets him on a series of adventures that have long been treasured as a real antidote to the 'white knights' who are the usual heroes of the crime fiction of this period.

THE COMPLETE RAFFLES: 2 *by E. W. Hornung—A Thief in the Night & Mr Justice Raffles*—By turns urbane gentleman about town and accomplished cricketer, life is just too ordinary for Raffles and that sets him on a series of adventures that have long been treasured as a real antidote to the 'white knights' who are the usual heroes of the crime fiction of this period.

THE COLLECTED SUPERNATURAL AND WEIRD FICTION OF WILKIE COLLINS: VOLUME 1 *by Wilkie Collins*—Contains one novel 'The Haunted Hotel', one novella 'Mad Monkton', three novelettes 'Mr Percy and the Prophet', 'The Biter Bit' and 'The Dead Alive' and eight short stories to chill the blood.

THE COLLECTED SUPERNATURAL AND WEIRD FICTION OF WILKIE COLLINS: VOLUME 2 *by Wilkie Collins*—Contains one novel 'The Two Destinies', three novellas 'The Frozen deep', 'Sister Rose' and 'The Yellow Mask' and two short stories to chill the blood.

THE COLLECTED SUPERNATURAL AND WEIRD FICTION OF WILKIE COLLINS: VOLUME 3 *by Wilkie Collins*—Contains one novel 'Dead Secret,' two novelettes 'Mrs Zant and the Ghost' and 'The Nun's Story of Gabriel's Marriage' and five short stories to chill the blood.

FUNNY BONES *selected by Dorothy Scarborough*—An Anthology of Humorous Ghost Stories.

MONTEZUMA'S CASTLE AND OTHER WEIRD TALES *by Charles B. Cory*—Cory has written a superb collection of eighteen ghostly and weird stories to chill and thrill the avid enthusiast of supernatural fiction.

SUPERNATURAL BUCHAN *by John Buchan*—Stories of Ancient Spirits, Uncanny Places & Strange Creatures.

LEONAUR

ALSO FROM LEONAUR
AVAILABLE IN SOFTCOVER OR HARDCOVER WITH DUST JACKET

MR MUKERJI'S GHOSTS *by S. Mukerji*—Supernatural tales from the British Raj period by India's Ghost story collector.

KIPLINGS GHOSTS *by Rudyard Kipling*—Twelve stories of Ghosts, Hauntings, Curses, Werewolves & Magic.